Praise for

LYNNE HUGO

"*The Unspoken Years* is one of the most intense
coming-of-age novels that I have ever read, but it rings true
and the author has a graceful writing style that makes this
harrowing tale flow smoothly."
—Curled Up with a Good Book, *curledup.com*

"Skillfully constructed and impressively written...
a near-poetic quality."
—Betsy Willsford, *Miami Herald,* on *Swimming Lessons*
(coauthored with Anna Tuttle Villegas)

"A superb tale about the empowerment these women
find… Engrossing and thoroughly enjoyable."
—Toni Hyde, *Booklist,* on *Swimming Lessons*

"I suspect that every woman who reads it will find something of an
'of course, I understand.'"
—Carole Philipps, *Cincinnati Post,* on *Swimming Lessons*

"Bittersweet and rewarding."
—*Publishers Weekly* on *Swimming Lessons*

"Beautiful in its use of language and unsettling in its observations,
this story was the worthy recipient of the River Teeth Literary
Nonfiction Book Prize."
—*Library Journal* on
*Where the Trail Grows Faint:
A Year in the Life of a Therapy Dog Team*

Author Note

Last Rights and *The Unspoken Years* are two novels about the source of our deepest wounds and our most tender joys: family. Ironically, even in the midst of our families, we sometimes feel lost and alone, but most of us keep trying to find our emotional way home. We try to make it work. How *much* connection, how *much* involvement, how *much* control do we require? How much can we tolerate? How deep, after all, are these bonds? This is the stuff of the human drama we all live. In this collection, one book deals with too much connection between family members, and one with not enough.

The Unspoken Years deals with the universal struggle of young people to establish autonomy. It's much more difficult when a parent is mentally ill, as millions of children and teenagers know. In this story of a deeply troubled mother-daughter relationship, the daughter, Ruth, must come to terms with her disturbed mother's inability to let her go, as she is torn between her mother's demands and the love she finds with Evan.

Last Rights, on the other hand, looks at a father and a daughter who are literally strangers. Lexie experiences her father as no more than a shadowy notion, and feels the anger of abandonment. Lexie and her father, Alex, are brought face-to-face against both their wills after a tragedy, and Alex discovers that a teenager's revenge can be fiery and relentless. Where is the point of no return, no reconciliation? Or is redemption always possible?

I'm very interested in your thoughts about these questions. They're the ones with which I grapple in every book I write. Your stories are mine, and I hope mine are yours.

Lynne Hugo

www.lynnehugo.com

LYNNE HUGO

Last Rights

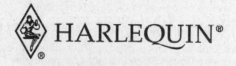
HARLEQUIN®

TORONTO • NEW YORK • LONDON
AMSTERDAM • PARIS • SYDNEY • HAMBURG
STOCKHOLM • ATHENS • TOKYO • MILAN • MADRID
PRAGUE • WARSAW • BUDAPEST • AUCKLAND

Recycling programs
for this product may
not exist in your area.

ISBN-13: 978-0-373-23074-7

LAST RIGHTS
Copyright © 2009 by Harlequin Books S.A.

The publisher acknowledges the copyright holder of the individual works
as follows:

LAST RIGHTS
Copyright © 2009 by Lynne Hugo.

THE UNSPOKEN YEARS
Copyright © 2006 by Lynne Hugo.

This edition published by arrangement with Harlequin Books S.A.

® and TM are trademarks of the publisher. Trademarks indicated with
® are registered in the United States Patent and Trademark Office,
the Canadian Trade Marks Office and in other countries.

www.eHarlequin.com

Printed in U.S.A.

CONTENTS

LAST RIGHTS

Acknowledgments
Len Endress, fire chief of Oxford, Ohio, was generous with
time and explanations. Anna Tuttle Villegas served as first
reader; her perceptive suggestions were invaluable.
Tara Gavin edits with insight and precision.
Her hand improves a book. My warm gratitude,
always, to Susan Schulman.

Dedication
For the men in my family who love their children well:
Alan, Dad, Bob, David and my brothers-in-law,
and for the men in the next generation, who will.

1987

one

"WHAT DID CHRISTINE ever see in him?"

"Those eyes. It's always a man's eyes get to a woman if she's gonna fall hard, and big brown eyes like that, she's thinking she sees the good earth instead of a pile of crap on top of it."

"Black Irish," Cora muttered.

"Sure I remember," Jolene said on beat, as if Cora hadn't interrupted. "I stood behind you at their wedding. What're you going to do about him?"

"Nothing."

"Do you think he might hear about Christine?"

"I can't worry about that," Cora said, but then she went on, because worry was already eating at her mind like a mouse working on drywall making a hole big enough for his whole body to slip in and do its dirty work. "You know well as I do," she said, "I wouldn't trust him to get that child across a road safely, could of been a road that hadn't seen a car in ten years, wouldn't make a bit of difference. I'll do whatever I have to. Christine might've loved him, but young as she was, even she figured out to let him go."

"Just not soon enough," Jolene said, but there was no criticism in her voice, just a worn cotton blanket of understanding.

Cora had been rocking off and on through the calling hours, not that the chair was a rocker, but she'd rocked her large body as if it were. She'd rocked her babies through whatever small and large pains had seized them for so long it was natural to her, even if her arms were empty now. Everyone except Jolene had left, even Christine's surviving child. Lexie was waiting at Cora's, kept company by the small throng of school friends, until whenever Jolene brought Cora back home. Cora wasn't ready, but the fifteen-year-old had had all she could take.

The arthritis in Cora's back, hips, knees and feet complained. She felt every one of her sixty-three years and then some. First her one son stillborn, then the death of Lexie's twin, then Marvin taken by a heart attack. Now cunning old death had swooped down and stolen Christine while Cora was spending all her time trying to beat back its black wings from hovering over Rebecca, her other daughter, whose left breast had been cut off not six months ago.

"I don't see how I can go on anymore," she said softly to Jolene, a handful of tissue in her knobby right hand. Glasses, framed in neutral plastic, lay on Cora's thighs. She needed them on to talk, something no one particularly believed, but it was true, so they'd been off and on all day between private crying and turning to greet people politely.

"I know, honey. I know," said Jo, whose only child had been killed by a land mine on the Ho Chi Minh trail. She hesitated a minute, not from uncertainty, but for the sake of timing. Her head, dyed a deep brunette, was an inch and a half of Cora's, though they both faced Christine. "But you've got to think about what Christine wanted. She named you guardian. Lexie needs you."

"I won't fail her," Cora said. "I just don't see how, right now. It just feels like I can't… She needs me to be strong."

Cora closed her eyes against new tears. "Oh, Jo, this would kill Marvin. He loved her so much. He wasn't much for telling them, you know how he was, but he loved the girls so much."

"And you," Jolene said. "Talk to him tonight. He'll help you through."

"He's a better listener now than when he was alive. Doesn't interrupt so much," Cora said.

Jo persisted. "Sometimes I feel Paul when I talk to him. I just get a feeling. Not always, but…" She was quiet, letting Cora absorb the thought before she changed the subject. "You going to bury Christine by Marvin and the babies, right?"

"There's a place for me, too. I bought another one."

"You can't be using it anytime soon," Jolene cautioned.

"He was handsome, Alex was. Stringy but handsome." Cora wasn't finished on the subject of Christine's ex-husband. "No way around that much. Give the devil his due. He was like a mosquito on Christine—got her itching and then she was scratching, and the next thing she knew, she was out to here." She pantomimed a swollen stomach. "Course they thought it would keep him out of the war...."

Cora took off her glasses again, to wipe her eyes, reddened all around the pale blue irises. She knew she was rambling, but Jolene had been her friend for forty-five years, and if Cora hadn't kept talking, she would have climbed into that box, squeezed herself next to Christine and pulled the lid down over them both. Instead, she was going to have to pick up her cane, walk out and shut the door behind her.

"I know, honey. Sometimes it happens that way. Christine managed to keep Lexie from that mess, though, and look at how she loved that girl. She would've gone through it all over again to keep her. In spite of what she lost, don't you think?"

"And she was a good mother, too."

"The best. She learned from the best." Jolene's dark head nodded. The roots of her hair were grayish white; she needed a touch-up. It's not possible to schedule hair coloring to coincide with unexpected funerals, she'd decided that morning while she tried to blur the line of her side part. She needed another permanent, too, but there hadn't been a minute of time or space to make herself presentable.

"I don't know about that," Cora said, and Jolene sensed that Cora had been reviewing her relationship with her daughter. "I tried. I always tried."

Her voice dropped to a near whisper even though they were alone with a dead person surrounded by cold and the silence of a small town closed up for the night. "I'm thinking about raising a teenager. It's been a long time, Jo. Things are different. I always thought Christine told me most everything where Lexie was concerned, but there's a lot she didn't want me to fret over. I'll have to now, won't I? No choice. You know what Lexie said to me in the first hour after Christine was gone? She said, 'I won't have to go live with Alexander the Goddamn Great, will I?' and I just told her no, I was her guardian. But I never heard a word like that from Christine. Do you suppose Lexie picked that up from Marvin before he died? And she doesn't know the whole story, not as far as I know, anyway. I don't know why Christine kept it from her."

"Thought it would upset her, I guess. The kids all talk like that to each other, with the swearing. She's just scared."

"Well, of course. But she *needs* her mother," Cora said and left silence after to demonstrate the sucked-in yawn of emptiness where Lexie's mother had been. "I feel like I'm in a terrible, terrible mistake, and some giant hand is going to reach down and make things right again any minute. Like a bug, caught in a spiderweb and I'm not even the kind of bug the spider can eat, and a human being comes along and says, oops, this was an accident, and cares enough to get me out and let me go on my way. This can't be happening."

"I know what you mean, like it's too big to take in, and it can't happen. It's wrong."

Cora ducked her face into her cupped hands and let her shoulders heave. Jolene inched forward on her chair so she could rotate her legs toward Cora. She reached behind her friend's hands and extracted the glasses from her face. After she set them in her own lap, she took Cora in her arms and the women rocked awhile together while Cora sobbed. "It's so wrong, it's so wrong. I don't mean to be sacrilegious, but what kind of God would do this? What kind of God takes away a girl's mother and a mother's daughter, a good person like Christine? Thirty-five years old." Cora pulled back a little so she could see Jolene's face, half of it lit by the glow from the light behind the casket, the tops of wrinkles highlighted. Jo's eyes were mostly pupil, black-looking in the low light.

"I don't know."

"You think that's bad to say?"

"No. I've said it myself. I didn't take the least comfort from the church when Paul died, that's for sure. Just over time, I accepted it better, that I'd never know the reason, not while I'm alive, anyway. What reason would we ever think was good enough, anyway?"

"So where is she? I mean, it just doesn't seem possible that everything that was in her mind and heart and soul can be wiped out. I know I can't see it, but it's got to be somewhere. Lexie wants to put all kinds of things in the casket with her, you know, pictures and the like." As she spoke, Cora stood up. Jolene picked up the cane Cora had propped against the back of the chair and extended it, but Cora waved it away and leaned against the side of the coffin, right alongside her daughter's face. Jolene took a step down toward Christine's waist to give Cora space, but stayed next to her.

"That's all right. The pictures and all. That doesn't mean you have to do it, too."

"I know. I want to know where she is, that's all."

"Try talking to her, sometimes it works. Try talking to her, then be real quiet and wait to hear her inside you. It's not like a voice, it's just like you know something, like she's answered you."

Cora stroked her child's face and put her fingers in Christine's hair the way she always had when Christine was little. "They put too much hair spray on her. Christine didn't like hair spray. Even her hair doesn't feel like her now," she said. "She had good hair. Thick. I got to like it short—once I was used to it."

"Yes," Jolene said. "She had good hair." She put her arm around Cora's waist, lightly, but enough that Cora could feel her living flesh to living flesh.

"I need to get home to Lexie. Can you take me now?" Cora whispered, picking up her cane from where it rested against the back of Jolene's chair. As a girl, Cora had been tall, broad-shouldered, and in spite of her arthritis and the stoop in her back, she was still bigger and heavier than Jolene. It took both Jolene and the cane to support Cora when she stepped away from the casket and the first minute toward the door, but the farther they got, the more Jolene could feel Cora plant each foot toward where she had to get herself.

two

NOBODY CAME TO GET me at school when it first happened. I was sitting there in Civics and my mom was having an aneurysm and I didn't know. School was just getting out when my grandmother came to pick me up. I didn't think anything about it, because sometimes she came when Mom couldn't. All Grandma said was that Mom was in the hospital. I thought it was a breathing problem because then Grandma said she'd stopped breathing. We were at a funeral just last month, my first, because Mom's cousin's husband got shot. When we came home, she showed me where her life insurance was and said there was enough to support me and get me through college. Almost like she knew something was going to happen, only the next morning she was in such a good mood, teasing me, and not even really tired or having a hard time getting up so I never even thought about it anymore. I didn't know I was supposed to worry. Now I'm an expert on funerals, and I hate them. It doesn't look like my Mom in that coffin, but Grandma says it definitely is.

We had to wait for Jill's bus at my grandmother's house before we could even leave for the hospital, so we couldn't even go to the first hospital where they took her, which is pretty close. By then, though, they took her in a helicopter to another hospital in Indianapolis where they have more equipment, and that's where me and my grandma and my cousin went. Aunt Rebecca was having chemo, that's why Grandma had to wait to get Jill, too, but I couldn't believe I had to wait for my cousin while my Mom was in Indianapolis maybe dying. I was so scared she might be dying and it turned out she was. They were still working on Mom when we got there, we went running in through the emergency room. Mom had left work feeling bad. On the way home she stopped and called Sharon at the office. Either Mom or Sharon, we're not sure yet who, called 911 then, and Sharon took off to where Mom's car was. It's a red Dodge Spirit, I don't know what will happen to it now. When Sharon got there, an ambulance and the police were already there and Mom was unconscious.

At the hospital, they worked on her until after eight, shocking her and doing whatever with their machines. Later, they only let us see her once, when they were moving her to another room because they decided to put her on the life-support machines to see if maybe she'd start breathing on her own. Then they let us be with her until they turned the machines off. She was all swollen and bruised on her chest and down her arms. She didn't look like herself at all. It was like something on TV that makes you say, "Oh, those poor people." I think they must have hurt her, but the doctor said no, she wasn't conscious when they were banging on her. But then they said she could still hear me maybe, and I might want to tell her goodbye. So if she could hear, how could it make sense she didn't feel them hurt her? I told her I loved her and I lay beside her with my head on her chest and my arms around her. They made me get down from the bed, but let Mom hold my hand. When they turned the machines off, I could feel her hand get stiff but then it moved so I didn't believe them that she was dead. A nurse told me it was just Mom's muscle, that it happens.

In the hospital the first time I saw her, I was there with my head on her crying and crying and saying, "Not my mommy, not my mommy." I didn't care what anybody thought. I'm a little embarrassed now, but I'll never see those people again. I hope I don't. I think they hurt my Mom.

She didn't look like herself in the coffin, either. I had to put her in a long-sleeved dress, her blue one with the lace collar, not the green silk blouse and skirt she really liked, because her arms were bruised from the IVs. She would have been mad at me for letting them do her hair flat like that; she hated for her hair to be flat, but they didn't put too much makeup on her, which was good. She used to be so pretty. If I frost my hair, I think I might look more like her. I brought her own lipstick to the man because they put an ugly color on her, and I made him change it to her own, but she still wasn't my Mom anymore. Mr. Smith at the funeral home asked if we wanted a picture of her in her coffin, he said it was an included service. Grandma said no, but later I went over by myself and told him I did. In case I don't believe it's really happened. I'll get it soon, I guess. Grandma wouldn't like my saying yes, but it's an included service so it won't cost extra. I put some pictures in with her, too, so she won't forget who I am.

I have her ring on, the opal she always wore that was on her in the coffin. Mr. Smith asked if I wanted it and the little pearl earrings she had on. I said yes to the ring, but no to the earrings because she used to say she felt naked without earrings. And I have the Bible she was holding in the coffin. I have the clothes she was wearing when they took her to the hospital. Her navy blazer is okay, but they cut everything else off her. It's strange because they didn't give me the legs of her panty hose, just the panty part; you can see how they cut the legs off because they were going to try to put a tube up her leg to get to her heart and put a balloon there to open it up. It didn't work. I think she'd still be alive now if they didn't turn off the machines, and that would be better. Even if she couldn't answer me, I just want her to be alive. I could still talk to her. Before they turned them off, some priest came in and asked me would my mother want last rights. Grandma told him no, like she was mad.

The TV screen had a straight green line across it that just went on and on and then they turned that off, too.

SHE HAD DIARIES THAT started back in high school when she was going with her ex-husband who ran away because of the war in Vietnam. I can't really call him my father. I said the word *goddamn* to my grandmother about him, but she didn't slap me. My Grandpa called him that. And some poems. She wrote one about how birds are like spirits that was published in a book with other people's poems. It was pretty, the way every verse had "take me in your beak, put me on your back, raise me on your wing." We put it on the memory card and had it read at the funeral, too. That bothered Jill a lot, I don't know why. She might have cried more than I did, which I thought would hurt Mom, but Grandma said I'm shell-shocked. I hardly cried at all. Jill snuck outside with Emily and smoked a cigarette while the people who weren't driving to the cemetery came up and talked to me and Rebecca and Grandma. I smelled it when they came back even though Jill had gum. She better be more careful. There'll be another death in the family real quick if Aunt Rebecca finds out, but Jill says who cares? Because not smoking doesn't keep you from getting cancer. She proves it by her mother never smoked. I can see her point. Nothing you do keeps bad from happening.

I looked at Mom's diaries a little bit, but I couldn't read them because it made me feel like I had to talk to her. I didn't tell her I loved her or hug her. Now I feel so bad and when Tim says bad things about his mother, I tell him to stop and to talk nice to her. It made me mad when other people started looking at her diaries, people who don't have any rights. I made them stop. They're closed in a box now in Mom's old closet at Grandma's, and Grandma said they're mine.

three

CORA'S HOME WAS the two-story frame farmhouse in which she'd been raised, once white, but painted light gray now, with black shutters. The front door, tucked behind the wraparound porch, was still a red echo of the old barn; that much had never changed. She and Marvin had moved back from Darrville when Christine was a baby, even before Cora's mother needed any help to keep the house. The land and outbuildings from the original farm had long been sold off. The house was short on bathroom space as old houses are, but had plenty of room for Lexie—who'd spent the night there close to once a week since she was a baby anyway, and more often in the summer. It made sense that she'd be awkward as company during the comings and goings around the funeral, but a few days later it seemed she ought to be settling in. Instead, Lexie was stiff and distant, crying when she thought Cora couldn't hear her over the noise of the running tub water. She took a lot of baths.

"It's like she doesn't remember Christine was my daughter... I mean, she keeps to herself so much it's like she thinks I don't understand, or I don't have my own crying to do. When I try to hug her, well...and she was always so affectionate with me," Cora said to Jolene over coffee at Cora's kitchen table a week after Christine was buried. Her cup sloshed over, clattering in the saucer as she set it down.

Jolene reached over and patted Cora's left hand, where her wedding ring was a pinstripe of worn gold. Last night's dinner dishes jutted at odd angles from the sink and the chipped yellow counter had remnants of food on it, neither in the least like Cora. The old linoleum floor could use a good sweeping, too, although it had been in place so long that some of the darkened areas were like that from age, not dirt. Like liver spots, Jo thought, just like my liver spots. "Well, be patient," she said. "Has Jill been around?"

"Some. But she doesn't stay long, so I wonder is Lexie shutting herself off from her, too? Maybe it's because Rebecca is feeling poorly though, and wants to leave. I don't really see, because Lexie and Jill disappear into…oh, that's the other thing. She won't use Christine's old room anymore. She wants it left as it is, you know, and she wants to use Rebecca's old room or my sewing room as her bedroom, set it up like the one she had at their house. What do you make of that?" Cora's cloud of hair drooped over one side of her forehead, tired-looking, a step in front of unkempt.

"Maybe she's trying to make it like it was, you know, like she is really still just a guest."

"Could be, but you know she never was a guest here."

"It's all changed now, though. She's got to be feeling that. When's she going back to school?"

"Maybe tomorrow. Not so many kids calling here as the first two or three days."

"They don't know what to say after I'm sorry, no more than anyone does."

"I guess." Cora heaved herself out of the dinette chair and said, "You keep me company and maybe I'll get these dishes done. Seems like I don't have the heart to do much of anything."

"I'll do better than that. You wash those, I'll sweep the floor, then we'll dry 'em and put 'em up."

"You've got your own work to do."

"Come on, now. This here is Jo. I'm going to throw in a load of laundry just to get it started," she said, opening the door to the basement and picking up the basket of dirty clothes and towels that sat on the floor next to it. "I'll be right back." Jolene clicked on the basement light and went downstairs without waiting for an answer. She knew when to overlook an objection.

Cora stood at the kitchen sink and stared out the window into her backyard. The bird feeder near the lilac bushes was empty and so was the suet holder. Wouldn't Christine have a fit about that? It was because of her there were four bird feeders and two birdhouses on the property. When she and Lexie lived in an apartment, Chris kept giving them to Cora and Marvin for Christmas, or Mother's Day or Father's Day and then fuss at them if they didn't keep each one crammed with a different kind of seed. "They're to attract different birds," she'd explained when she brought the platform feeder. "Doves like this kind." (Would that be morning doves or mourning doves, Cora wondered as she looked at the empty wooden structure, and resolved to look it up even though she knew she wouldn't bother.)

To bring hummingbirds in summer, Christine had hung baskets of hot-pink petunias from a sunny spot on the front porch right next to a hanging feeder for red sugar water. Cora favored dahlias herself, and every summer had their bright round faces all along the front walk that linked the long gravel driveway and the front porch. Once Chris had her house, new bird feeders went to her own yard. "There's something to be grateful for," Cora had said to Marvin. "I can hardly walk outside without a bird pooping on my head."

Had Christine had a premonition? Cora's mind turned to wrestling that particular demon. Why were her files so orderly, everything so clearly labeled? Her will, her life insurance, her financial records. She'd been to a funeral in October, a distant cousin whose husband was murdered by her enraged former spouse, or some such trashy story fit for a talk show which Cora had decided to skip knowing about. Danny would have been about the same age as Chris. Maybe his dying had put the idea in her head.

Lexie appeared in the kitchen door. Smudges dark enough to look dirty were beneath her eyes, and her shoulder-length hair was scraggly, even greasy. As though she suddenly noticed that herself, Lexie used the fingers of one hand like a rake to pile it toward one side of her head. The girl did look some like her father, thanks to that near-black hair, but by some genetic gift she had her mother's light eyes, more blue than Cora's which had too much gray. Snow White, Christine used to call her daughter, but she was named Alexis—after her father, Alexander. Lexie's lips had a deep upper bow like Christine's, too, the top fuller than the lower, ever so slightly out of proportion. (Christine had learned how make the bottom one look bigger by some lip-pencil trick she'd learned at a make-over. Who would teach that to Lexie now?) A shallow widow's peak echoed her upper lip.

"Hi, Grandma," Lexie said. "I'm getting myself a piece of toast. Is that okay?"

"Honey, you don't have to ask. You never asked before. This is your home, always has been. How about an egg, maybe a little bacon with that toast? You know, we still have all this food. The refrigerator is stuffed. I need to be making some room. Can you help me out?"

"No, thank you," Lexie said in her polite voice. Her steps were almost noiseless. She wore white socks, gray sweatpants and a shapeless gray sweatshirt.

Cora watched, propping herself against the sink while Lexie toasted a piece of bread. She couldn't think of a thing to say that sounded halfway normal. From the basement, the washing machine hiccuped and began filling. Jolene's heavy steps began a slow ascent, though not slow in comparison to what Cora's speed would have been.

"Jolene, honey. Just Jolene," Cora said, responding to the anxious question on Lexie's face. "You weren't scared were you?"

"No," Lexie said, but Cora didn't find her credible. "Do you mind if I take this upstairs?" Lexie said, skimming the toast with Cora's applebutter. "I'll be sure to bring the plate down."

"Of course not," Cora said, though she'd always had a rule that food wasn't to leave the kitchen, and Lexie knew that as well as she did. "Here, let me give you some juice with that," she added, and rinsed out a little juice glass languishing in the sink.

This one's from yesterday morning, she thought, a guilty string twanging in her head.

"Thank you," Lexie said. Everything but the curtsy, Cora thought.

"You leaving?" Jolene said to Lexie from the top step. "Come sit and talk a minute."

"I'm…looking over my school work. Please excuse me."

"Well, sure, honey," Cora said hastily. After Lexie was through the living room to the stairs, she turned to Jolene and whispered, "See what I mean?"

"I do see," Jolene said. "I do see."

CORA'S MIND MUST HAVE been running alongside a track parallel to Lexie's. Before Jolene left, Cora had said, "Look at this splinter I've got in my finger," extending her forefinger for Jolene's inspection. "There's nothing much to see, but to touch anything with it hurts like the devil. Could you get it out?"

"Sterilize a needle, wash your hands," Jolene said.

The flame had reached up and darkened the metal point. Jolene's silver-framed glasses slid down her nose as she settled herself back in the kitchen chair and angled Cora's hand toward the window light. "Hurt?" she asked.

"Yeah, but go on. See how red it's got? It's infected. I left it go too long."

"Doubtless. Not had anything else on your mind, either, have you?" Jolene was good at backhanded absolutions, and Cora relied on them.

"Not much," Cora said. "No more than I can bear without being in the ground myself." Tears welled in her eyes and she willed them back down. "But I can't figure out what to do about Lexie, about being her guardian, I mean. She's scared Alex is going to show up and claim her." Cora's head shook as she spoke, as if her body were saying no, no, no.

"This hurt?" Jolene asked.

Cora winced but shook her head. "I don't care if it hurts. Just clean it out."

Jolene had broken the skin at the center of the reddened tip of Cora's forefinger, and now squeezed it between her thumbs. Yellow-white pus oozed out. "Lotta junk in here," she said. "I need to get alcohol on it. Got some?"

"In the medicine cabinet," Cora said, and lumbered up to get it out of the downstairs bathroom.

When Cora came back, a couple of minutes later, she was using her cane—something she didn't ordinarily do in the house. She handed the plastic bottle to Jolene and sat back down, finger extended all the while Jolene saturated a cotton ball and recapped the alcohol.

"I was thinking how this puts me in mind of Alex, the splinter I mean," Cora said. "It hurts even though you can't see it. Even when you get the pus out, it's still there ready to get infected again. Only thing to do is get the whole splinter out, no matter how hard it is to do."

"So what's in your mind?" Jolene asked, knowing she'd not heard the end.

"I don't exactly know," Cora said. "I've just got to hope something comes to me."

Then, within an hour of Jolene's leaving, Lexie padded into the kitchen where Cora was sitting at the table staring out of the window. "Grandma, can I talk to you?"

Cora thought about how hard it was going to be to get Lexie's socks white. She could see the heel and under the ball when Lexie sat down and crossed one leg over the other knee, gray and stubborn as winter rain, the white under the arch a last patch of snow. "Of course, honey. You can always talk to me" was all she said, though. Lexie could just throw out all the socks and buy new ones for all she cared, or for all the laundry that was getting done these days, anyway.

"I was wondering. Could you, like, could you like…adopt me?"

"Well, honey, your mother made me your guardian. That's like the same thing."

"But what if Alex shows up? I mean, if you'd adopted me, then he couldn't take me away from you. I'd feel a lot better."

Cora's inclination was to reassure Lexie, with *He's not going to show up after all these years, honey,* and *How could he even know anything's happened to your mother?* She bit back some of what came to her own mind: *He didn't want you then, he's not going to want you now,* and *Alex doesn't want anything that might cost him.* She had to swallow some bile to do it, but Cora had standards and there were some things she just wasn't going to say to any child about her parent no matter if he *was* a bottom feeder like Marvin always called him. *A goddamn bottom feeder,* Marvin said, and Cora had shushed him for his language.

"We can look into it, honey. There's a lot to think about. I need to get your mother's social security. We might lose that if I adopt you."

"Mom had life insurance, she told me there was money to raise me after Danny's funeral." Lexie's face was reddening from the neck up. Cora couldn't tell if it was anger or embarrassment.

"We just have to take it a little at a time, okay? You know that. I've been loving you since the day you were born, and I want you right here with me. I'm not going to let anything bad happen to you." Immediately, Cora wished she could call the last words back to her, like errant but trained puppies.

"It already has," Lexie shot as she got up and let her footsteps be heavy to underscore her leaving the room. "So how're you gonna stop the next thing?"

When she said that, the fear-mouse that had been eating its way through the wall of Cora's mind swallowed and saw daylight.

THREE DAYS LATER, Cora was driving around and around the dissolute blocks of downtown Richmont, looking for the lawyer's office. Brenda Dunlap was a partner with the man who'd handled Marvin's estate, the original attorney who'd drawn up both their wills after Cora's mother deeded the house to them ten years ago, before she died. Given a choice of the three lawyers who had the small office now, Cora picked the only woman. "I'm thinking a man might in his heart feel sorry for Alex," she'd confided to Jolene. "And the man doesn't deserve a speck of feeling."

The traffic befuddled her, though Richmont was only a smallish run-down city grown like a patch of weeds left unmowed for years in the middle of tended farmland. The county courthouse sagged at the top of steep stairs two blocks away, and Cora used the parking lot marked for court business only. Early Sun was a good deal smaller, but not a suburb by any means. The nearest of those would be the ones outside of Indianapolis, an hour and a half's drive. No, Early Sun wasn't even incorporated, just an area east of Richmont with no real town of its own except a blinking yellow light, the boarded up Old Time Holiness Church, Randy's Live Bait Shop and Niki's, a weedy gas station selling cigarettes, candy bars, pop and milk in that order of importance. Early Sun's children went to school in Darrville, to the south, due to the vagaries of how districts are drawn, no kind of logic to it. Darrville had a real town, with a grocery store, post office, a video rental place, Baptist, Methodist and Catholic churches and talk about a Kmart coming. Where Cora lived, the houses were old and two-story with middle-drooping porches, listing shutters and long distances between driveways where the cut-off brown stubble of corn stalks in the winter fields between neighbors looked like the unshaven cheek of God.

"I really don't know how to start," Cora said, taking a tissue from her purse to clutch in her nervous right hand, after the receptionist had shown her—ten minutes late—into the law office. She was breathless from exertion or nerves, or both. "We're not the kind of people who have much call for a lawyer, Miss Dunlap. Is it Miss or Mrs.?"

"I use Ms., but call me Brenda. What's on your mind today?" Brenda was a small sweet-faced woman wearing wire-rimmed glasses. Her hair was lightly streaked with gray, but one side was tucked behind her ear the way Lexie's teenage friends wore theirs. *I wonder if she's over twenty-one,* Cora thought, and worried that Brenda wasn't tall or strong enough to take on even a half-runner bean like Alex. Maybe she should have taken one of the men after all.

Brenda listened patiently to Cora's explanation, interrupting two or three times to ask a brief question. She took notes on yellow lined paper, which Cora was glad to see. At least she was paying attention. When Cora stopped, Brenda kept looking at her pad for a minute, then cleared her throat.

"The problem, Mrs. Laster, on the issue of adopting your granddaughter isn't the social security. It's that for you to do it, Alexis's father's parental rights have to be formally terminated by the court, or he has to give permission for the adoption." Brenda didn't even look up until she'd almost finished.

"Well, then, we'll just tell the court to terminate his rights, is that what you called it? He's never had any." Perhaps Brenda didn't entirely understand. Maybe Cora had left out some crucial detail, like the center of a thousand-piece jigsaw puzzle.

"No, ma'am. It doesn't work that way. He has rights. Courts nowadays are very cognizant…uh, aware of…fathers' rights." Brenda had suddenly thought to use a simpler word than *cognizant*. She tucked a straight strand of hair back behind one ear. Then that too seemed out of place, and she wanted to give up. Her own husband hadn't paid his child support for two and a half years, but the court wouldn't suspend his visiting rights. She felt his garlicky breath laughing in her face when he picked up their son.

"I don't understand. You mean he'd have to know?"

"Yes, ma'am, he'd have to know. It's a calculated risk. Your granddaughter is only three years from turning eighteen, and her father hasn't been heard from for…what—" Brenda consulted her notes, then continued "—fifteen years. Maybe you should consider letting sleeping dogs lie. And I don't use the word *dog* lightly."

"Lexie, that's what we call Alexis, she's afraid. She feels she can't have any peace of mind, you know, and I confess I think about it, too."

"But you say there wasn't any actual legal finding that terminated his parental rights?" Brenda sighed and began to go back over the facts. "If his rights weren't terminated by the court, and he's the legal father, it's not good."

"Not so far as I know."

"Did your daughter leave any files, any papers you can go through to check? Records?" Surrounding Brenda were file cabinets and shelves filled with the documentation that wins cases word by inked-in word. The essential trail of whole lives can fit into manila folders, and Brenda had won a lot more cases with thick files than with thin ones, although no matter how thick the file she compiled on her ex-husband, it was never enough.

"I have her will that names me guardian, like I said, and it's witnessed, and her life insurance that goes to Lexie. There's some other stuff, letters and her diaries." Cora was wedged between the arms of a too-narrow chair, her hips and thighs bulging out beneath them, refusing the suggested confinement.

"How far back do the diaries go?"

"There's a lot of them. I haven't looked. It seemed like I didn't have the right, you know, that's personal. My other daughter, Rebecca, she's the one who got them out. I told her to put them all in a box, along with Christine's letters, and give them to Lexie."

"Perhaps you could go through everything and see if there isn't some legal paper you might have overlooked. Or anything we might use in court…against the father, I mean."

"I'll talk to her about the…risk. If she still wants me to adopt her, will you do it for us?"

"It could get very ugly. It could also get expensive. Of course, we can go after back child support," Brenda said, warming to that subject. But then she flipped to the other side. "I have to warn you, this kind of thing usually *does* get ugly, and after it gets ugly, there's still a good chance you'll lose and it'll all have been for nothing."

"I don't want his money. Just Christine's social security for Lexie. My husband's pension isn't a lot, and I just have that and my own social security to raise her. But would you try anyway? If Lexie wants to, I mean. I've got to be able to tell her one way or another. Myself, I don't think Alex is going to do anything that might cost him, any way you look at it. He wasn't the most industrious."

"If you ask me to represent you, I'll give it my best."

There was a metal girder under Brenda's voice when she answered that made Cora feel better about not having a man lawyer. Still, she hoped Brenda had enough actual muscle to help her out of the chair she was sure she was stuck in.

"As long as I don't have to see him," Lexie said that night at dinner, pushing Cora's meat loaf from one side of her plate to the other. She picked at a cooked carrot. "I don't ever want to see him, but I want you to adopt me." Cora wondered what Lexie knew, but she didn't want to provoke questions on the subject of her father. She sighed, her head starting to ache again. Had Christine told Lexie something bad, that Lexie was so vehement?

"I hate him," Lexie said, as if in confirmation.

Four

GRANDMA TALKED to a lawyer named Brenda. She has to have my father's permission to adopt me. That is so stupid. The lawyer says it might be best to just let it go, because she'd have to publish some notice to try to find him. Grandma says maybe some cousins still live in Richmont and would see it. Maybe they're all dead, though. Maybe he is, too. I'm not counting on it, nothing else has turned out that good.

I want Grandma to adopt me, but I think she doesn't want to lose the social security money. It will be expensive to raise me. Mom wants me to go to college. A real estate person already looked at my house 'cause of Aunt Rebecca nosing in, wanting Grandma to sell it right away, and Mom's car, too. I think she's afraid that if Grandma runs out of money she won't have enough to make loans to *her*. I should just say 'enough to *give* her,' because Mom said Rebecca doesn't pay Grandma back. Mom got disgusted with her because Mom saved up for everything she bought us.

We only just got our house a year ago and I love it. We got new furniture and everything. It's small, but we each have a bedroom and there's a fence around the yard. Grandma's house feels more like it's not mine than it did when Mom and I lived in our own house. Back then, I'd just come in and help myself. I could just make peanut butter and jelly, or take cookies and milk. Now it seems rude. I don't want to eat too much because

Grandma has to pay for all of it. I know there's insurance, but Grandma says she's going to save that for college.

I went back to school on Monday. All the kids stared at me and then pretended they weren't, like I'm a freak and they have to be polite to or they'll get detention. I think maybe Tim wants to break up. He's really sweet to me, but maybe he just thinks he has to be because everybody would think he was lowlife pond scum if he broke up with me right after my mother died. He kept trying to give me half of his lunch on Monday because Grandma didn't know I bring my lunch and didn't make me one. I didn't say anything because she feels bad all the time already. I didn't take any of Tim's lunch. First of all, I hate baloney, and second, I can't stand for people to do stuff because they feel sorry for me. Now I buy my lunch and don't eat what I don't like. Which is most of it. Mom used to pack me little containers of chocolate pudding.

I wish Jill went to my school. She sort of understands because Mom was her aunt, but still, it's different. It wouldn't kill me if Aunt Rebecca died. I felt all right with Emily at first, but a red Dodge came into the parking lot after school and Emily and I were waiting outside like we always do, because her mom drives us to school and my mom picks us up. I thought it was my mom and Emily turned and said, *I thought that was your mom,* after I'd already thought that. Then I cried. She thought I was crying because of what she said, and she said she was sorry so many times that then I didn't really feel okay with Emily any more. It took ten more minutes before Grandma came. I could tell that she'd been crying so I didn't say anything about the red Dodge.

I don't ride with Emily anymore in the morning. I have my grandmother take me to my old house before school every day, then I feel like it's normal and I'm going to school from my house. But this morning before we left, Aunt Rebecca called and said a line from *Gone with the Wind* like she and my mom always do. She told me I was going to be late for school if I didn't get going and then she said, "Horse, make tracks," and to put Grandma on the phone. She always did that, call too early in the morning and say a line from *Gone with the Wind* and tell me to get Mom. I read *Gone with the Wind* last year for my independent reading third quarter and Mrs. Rupel gave me credit for three books because it had so many pages. When Aunt Rebecca did that today, it was like my Mom was supposed to be there and I was supposed to get her to the phone, and then I couldn't. It was my fault, I felt like, and if I was better, I'd have made her want to live enough that she would have come back when they shocked her heart. Nothing is ever going to be normal again, no matter what house I go from.

I don't want to go to the cemetery because the whole heap of flowers on the ground is brown and dead now, even with how cold it's been. Grandma goes every day. There's a regular little family plot there now. Grandpa, his and Grandma's stillborn boy, and my twin sister that Mom's buried with. And Mom. I'm afraid Grandma will slip on the ice and hit her head and then what'll happen to me? I feel like Prissy when she was flipping out and crying, "Miss Scarlett, I don't know nothin' 'bout birthin' no babies." I don't know what's going to happen to me and I want *somebody* like Scarlett did. She didn't know anything, either. Actually, Scarlett really wanted her mother. Miss Ellen wasn't dead though, so Scarlett still had a mother.

My mom wanted me, I know that much. We used to fight, but I don't think she'd have died on purpose. My father, though, that's something different. Grandma says she wants me and the social security isn't the important thing. I hope that's true, cause I think I have to tell her yes, let the lawyer put that notice in the paper if she has to. Alexander's not going to show up, and if he did, why wouldn't he just sign the papers? He never wanted me before, he couldn't have, the way he just ran away when my mom and me needed him the most and never showed up again. Goddamn him.

I haven't opened the envelope from Mr. Smith yet. It came today. I got the mail, and I didn't show Grandma I had it since she'd told him no. I think the picture must be in it.

The word for me is *orphan*.

five

EXCEPT WITH JOLENE, Cora's voice rarely betrayed her. "She says she can't feel safe unless she's adopted, that he'll sign off anyway."

"Those two don't quite go together, do they?" Jolene said. They were in Jolene's kitchen, only a half mile out of Cora's way back home after she took Lexie to school. Jolene examined the sludge in the bottom of her cup. "I mean, if he won't care and he'll just sign off, then what's she got to worry about? Why doesn't she feel safe?"

"I don't know. Brenda says let sleeping dogs lie. I can see it that way myself. But if I don't try to adopt her, she'll think I'm just stuck with her, that I don't really want her." Cora sighed and shook her head. Her coffee cup was half-full in front of her, getting cold, next to a blueberry muffin. Jolene noticed and got up to get the pot. Like Cora's, her kitchen had been there a long time. White curtains framed snowy branches outside the window over the sink. Last night's snow had been hardly more than a dusting, but because the day was cloudy and windless, it remained on the trees, light and temporary as wishes.

"I'm warming up your coffee, and I'll be upset if you don't eat that muffin. Keep your strength up."

"It all done drained away," Cora said, and imitated the drain suck of an emptying bathtub.

"Are you thinking what I am, that she's maybe a little curious about Alex? Wants to get her own take on him? Watch him deny her again, maybe… She only knows about him running off, right?"

"Oh. I hadn't thought of it that way. I don't think so. She doesn't want anything to do with him."

"Hmm" was all Jolene said. After a minute she spoke into the silence that was comfortable as old clothes. "She's putting a lot of energy into locking a door no one's knocked on for years and years. Hmm?"

"SO YOU'RE SURE. You're willing to take the risk?" Cora had tapped on Lexie's door a little after nine at night. She'd asked Lexie not to close it at first, but then she saw it made Lexie feel she didn't trust her. Actually it was Cora whom Cora didn't trust—didn't trust herself to know what a teenager was thinking or feeling or doing. Having Lexie where she could see her gave Cora a chance to study the clues. Now she sat on the end of Lexie's bed in light that was too dim not to ruin Lexie's eyesight.

Lexie closed the notebook she was writing in. "I'm sure, Grandma. I know it'll cost something. Please take it out of the college money Mom left. I know there's enough."

Cora sighed for all the sweet certainty of youth, that a fifteen-year-old child could think she knows what kind of money it will take to get her through college, or even to college for that matter. "Money has nothing to do with this, honey. Please believe me. You are more important than any money, whether it be coming money or going money. You know I've never been of a mind to think that way. I want to make sure you know you're taking a chance here. See, it's like you're locking a door that nobody's knocked on for years, but to lock it you have to make a lot of noise and that may wake somebody up to come knock." Cora thought that was the gist of what Jolene had said.

"You don't understand." The statement was flat, resigned, and Cora felt as if she had to defend herself or the conclusion would stand and become a barrier between them, invisible but impenetrable as Plexiglas.

"I think I do, honey, and I want to adopt you. I have to give the argument against it because if something comes of this we'll

have to deal with it together, and I don't want you to be unprepared, or to not be thinking we couldn't end up with a plateful.
There's…a lot to it. Sometimes it's best not to be dredging up
pond sludge."

"I know. I'd rather take the chance," Lexie said. Then she
looked at Cora and smiled at the same moment her blue eyes
filled up with tears. Cora heaved herself up awkwardly toward
the head of the bed and took Lexie in her arms. For once, the
girl relaxed into Cora's embrace, laying her head on Cora's
bosom and letting herself cry. Cora wrapped her hand in Lexie's
thick dark hair, the smell of it so like her Christine's that she let
herself cry a little with Christine's daughter. Lexie's ribs felt
frail, birdlike beneath her other hand. But right away, with the
first, smallest shake of Cora's shoulders, Lexie straightened and
composed herself.

"There's nothing wrong with our crying a little bit together,"
Cora said, sensing what had happened. "Sometimes it's better
than crying alone all the time."

"I'm okay," Lexie said.

Cora knew she wasn't, but the moment had passed. *I mustn't
cry around her,* she reminded herself. Cora looked around the
room that had been Rebecca's. It was unrecognizable to her
except for the placement of windows, closet and door. The pink
dust ruffle and curtains, and white chenille bedspread had quite
vanished. Tim, Lexie's boyfriend, had used his father's pickup
truck to help Lexie move her room from Christine's to Cora's
house: posters of dolphins, whales and panda bears, the colored
beads that hung in strands between upper and lower windowsills
in place of curtains, the stuffed animals, the bulletin board, the
emerald-green-and-black zigzag quilt and pillows, even the
nightstand and the lamps from her old room, shrouded with
emerald green cloth over the lampshades to produce an eerie
light. It certainly wasn't Cora's taste, and the mauve carpet, laid
during Rebecca's early teen reign, didn't exactly complement the
decor.

"How about we go get ourselves a bedtime snack?" Cora said.

Lexie swallowed irritation. Her grandmother was always

trying to force-feed her, as if cookies were giant Valium tablets to be washed down with chocolate milk to mellow her out. "No thanks. I'm really not hungry."

"You sure didn't eat much dinner, honey."

"I had a big snack after school." It was a lie, but her grandmother had been at the grocery store and wouldn't know.

"Oh, good. Well, goodnight, dear. Sleep tight and don't let the bedbugs bite."

Lexie shuddered. She couldn't stand all the cheerful little admonitions. "Okay," she said. "You too."

Cora made her way out of Lexie's room and closed the door softly behind her. She stood in the upstairs hallway leaning heavily against the banister, something she and Marvin had always told the children not to do. Then she went the wrong way down the hall and opened the door to Christine's old room, little changed since she moved out to marry Alexander O'Gara. Cora had stored Christine's personal papers and books in the closet, not having the heart to read anything except the legal documents she had to. Her jewelry was back in her old jewelry box, her makeup, which Cora couldn't bring herself to throw out, was in the top drawer, and some of her best clothing—items that Lexie might want someday, a few good sweaters and the like, were folded into the dresser drawers with a sachet of Christine's lilac perfume.

Christine's old bedspread, a print of lavender and white lilacs, was in place over the pillow that had always been hers and sheets she'd actually slept in. Though the room was chilly, Cora turned on the little lamp on the maple night table next to the bed and sank onto the bed to think. She caught sight of herself in the mirror over the bureau: how old she looked, how deep the lines around her eyes and mouth. She pushed her glasses back up on her nose. Christine was always telling her to get them tightened. She did, when she went to the eye doctor, but they loosened up again right away. Nothing ever stayed the way it belonged.

Life is an endless circle of doing what you thought you'd already finished over and over. Shopping, dishes, laundry,

weeding, now even raising children. Nothing stays finished until
you die, and then you can't enjoy what you finally got done. She
was just sitting on the bed thinking thoughts like those when,
on an intake of breath she felt Christine. Smelled her, rather:
lilac, and then she remembered the sachet in with the sweaters.
Surprised it was still strong enough to penetrate even the thin
winter air, Cora gave way to nostalgia, and got up again to get
one of Christine's sweaters to wear for the scent and feel of her
living daughter.

She opened the drawer and gasped out loud. On top of the
loopy fisherman sweater, next to the sachet, was a picture of
Christine in her coffin. Shock first, then a wave of anger washed
over Cora, like the breakers she'd seen in Florida. A color close-
up showed Chris's eyes closed beneath the width of her forehead
and arched, full brown brows. Her short, frosted hair was
arranged more flatly than was Chris's way, with too many bangs
pulled down. The small, straight nose was completely itself, but
the mouth—lips quite closed over her good, even teeth—looked
puffy. Well, the whole face looked puffy, yet somehow drawn,
when Cora really examined it. Still, there was a nearly translucent quality to the image that made it otherworldly.

Lexie put it there, she realized, which meant that weasel un-
dertaker, Ogle Smith, hadn't accepted the *no thank you* she'd
given him and had approached Lexie. She turned away from the
picture and pulled Chris's black cardigan out of the drawer and
slid her arms into it, though it was too small. All of Christine's
clothes would be way too small for her, but not for Lexie, though
she still had a little growing to do for them to be a fit—even if
teenagers did wear shirts the size of trash bags.

She backed up to the bed and sat again, rocking herself as she
had in the funeral home, holding the casket picture and talking
silently to Chris after another crying spell. *I don't know what to
do. I don't know how to raise her. She won't talk to me.*

One thing at a time. Let the picture be. She needs her mother.
Cora heard it clearly, and understood it to be Christine, not that
she could say she recognized the voice. There was no accompa-
nying vision, and nothing further came to her, though she sat in

the room breathing the faintly scented air, not pondering what she'd heard, but absorbing it and waiting in the silence. A half-hour later, when it was conceivable to sleep without fear of dreaming, she replaced the sweater and the picture, closed the dresser drawer and left the room. That night for the first time since Christine had died, Cora did not wake until morning, not even for the two trips to the bathroom she usually absolutely had to make.

"So NOW WHAT?" Cora said to Brenda, recapping the pen she'd used to sign the petition to adopt. She stared at Brenda's various diplomas, framed on the wall behind the oversize desk, and hoped again the woman knew what she was doing. The office held few clues to the lawyer's notions: it was sparse, without plants or personal objects or even pictures that anyone could see.

"I'll be sending a notice to Mr. O'Gara's last known address, which I understand was the apartment he and your daughter shared, by registered mail, and also publishing our intent in the paper and two legal journals. I suspect the letter will be returned with no forwarding address. Our best hope is, I guess, for no response at all. After six months, the court would go ahead and approve your petition. Or, of course, he can contact us and agree, though, that does sort of open a can of worms for your granddaughter, yes?"

"Yes," Cora murmured, because she thought it was true, not because Lexie would so much as acknowledge the possibility.

Outside, a slushy snow had started up again, and Cora tracked it through the dirty window using her peripheral vision. She didn't like driving in snow, even this, this kind that plushed the road and liquefied traffic dirt almost simultaneously.

"You and Alexis will have to appear before the judge, well, at the first court date I can get you, probably next week sometime. Actually, it's six months from that date, your appearance, when the judge can approve the petition. It's just a formality, nothing to be concerned about in the least."

"All right." Cora fiddled with the buttons on her old blue

cardigan as she looked at the lawyer seated primly behind the mahogany desk, randomly marred. Brenda looked the part: tailored brown wool suit, cream-colored silk blouse, a thin gold chain with some sort of charm on the end. "I was wondering, if you don't mind my asking, do you have any children?"

"Yes," Brenda said. "I have a son…I'm a single parent," and didn't offer any more. "My turn," she went on. "Of course, you don't have to tell me, but I'd like to know what happened to your daughter."

"An aneurysm burst," Cora said simply, "and then they couldn't get her heart going." She tried to hold Brenda's eyes, but felt her own begin to tear and looked back out the framed rectangle of gray sky to get them in check.

Brenda's brows went up and her uncolored lips parted in surprise. "There was no…warning?"

Cora shook her head. "Nothing. Far as anyone knew she was in perfect health."

"And this situation with her ex-husband?" Even before the question was fully formed, Brenda felt the change in Cora. The older woman sat farther back in her chair and took a minute to check for the whereabouts of her cane. She took off her glasses and wiped her eyes, after fumbling through her purse for a crumpled tissue, though the quick tears of the previous moment had already retreated.

"I don't even know all of it myself," Cora hedged. "Christine didn't like people fussing or worrying over her, including me, maybe especially me. I took care of Lexie when she asked me to, and listened when she had something to say, but she didn't want me upset. She said as much when we talked about it."

"Do you know how she arrived at the current situation? I mean, legally, she should have been receiving child support all these years, and I was thinking you might want to ask for back support and offer relief from that or a future child support order in return for his agreement to the adoption. It gives you some bargaining room."

"No, I don't want money for Lexie, that'd be like buying and selling her."

"I can assure you that's not how the court would see it." Brenda's tone was a hair over the line into defensiveness.

Cora leaned forward. "It's how Lexie would see it," she said, vehemently. "No, we'll just hope he doesn't slither out from under his rock."

"Really, Mrs. Laster, just hear me out. If you let me ask for back support, then you can always drop that request. Can you see that if we publish a request for a back support order along with the fact that if he's not located in the next six months, Lexie will be adopted—he's less likely to answer the summons?"

Cora slumped against the back of her chair.

"Do you understand? It's that…"

Cora rubbed her forehead and then shaded her eyes with a drooping salute, as if she were being blinded. "I understand what you're saying. It's trying to make him think he's got a lot to lose."

"Right."

"He's already lost everything that counts. He's just too dumb to know it. But do you understand me? I…don't…want…his… money." She emphasized the separate life of each word. "I just want him to sign the paper if he's got to have anything to do with this at all. Can't you just lay low, put the notice in print too small to read? I don't think he'll come forward."

"Then let me see what I can do," Brenda said, not resisting a slight shoulder shrug and headshake.

"I guess that's what I'm paying you for. Are we done for today?"

"Yes, ma'am. Try not to worry."

"Worry is my middle name these days, but thank you anyway."

Without getting up as was her habit, Brenda watched Cora steady herself after she hauled herself up from the chair to make her slow way to the office door in a three-beat clumping gait.

Brenda picked up the one framed picture on her desk from where it nestled between her and some upright reference books. Her son had been just short of his third birthday when it was taken four months ago, needing a haircut, but his eyes still bright and penetrating from beneath his dark-blond bangs.

Brenda consulted her Rolodex and picked up her phone. "Hi, Dixie, it's Brenda, I need Joe, please," she said a moment later, then fiddled with a pencil, doodling little circles with jagged lines intersecting them on the yellow pad in front of her while she waited.

"Hey, Bren, what's up?" a baritone voice came on the line.

"I need to publish for a father," she said, making another doodle. In a perfect world, Alexis's father *would* see the notice of intent. In admirable legal maneuvering, Brenda would extract back child support and then trade off his signature on the adoption papers for a termination of all parental rights and obligations. Cora and Alexis would have what they wanted, and a lump of money that could be planted like a seed smack in the fertile earth of Alexis's future. "There isn't a reason in the world why this asshole should get off scot-free."

six

I DID IT. I OPENED the envelope from Mr. Smith and I was right, it was the picture. Mom doesn't look like herself, but she doesn't look like anybody, either. When I first saw it, I cried a long time because I hoped it would be like she was just asleep, but no, it doesn't look like that. And then I started to get scared. What if Grandma sees it? She might get really mad at me. We're not as close as we used to be. She says no to things I want to do, and she never did that before. Everything in my life seems to be no. No your mother isn't coming back, no you can't keep the house you and your mother lived in, no you can't stay home from school, no whatever. I want to say yes, I can too have my mother's picture even if she is dead in her casket, I don't care. But I wouldn't dare say that to Grandma. So I hid it in my mother's room in the drawer with her sweaters.

Grandma won't go in Mom's room, she goes to the cemetery instead, but I know she comes in my room when I'm not here because sometimes there'll be clean clothes on my dresser or my bed will be made. She just says, oh, Lexie, your sheets needed to be washed or makes some other excuse, but I know she's trying to find out things about me. Grandma's good, but she's on my nerves always trying to hug and pet on me, and asking me questions. Aunt Rebecca says I can't talk back or Grandma could get stressed out and... She didn't finish her sentence, but I yelled DIE, real loud, because I knew she meant it would be my fault. Then Aunt Rebecca sighed and shook her head like I just belong in the fruit-and-nuts department at the store.

I don't care if I am crazy. Sometimes if Grandma's at the grocery or bank, I go into Mom's room. I smell her sweaters and look at the picture. If I'd been a better daughter maybe she'd have lived. I tell her I'm sorry sometimes. I think about saying prayers, but nothing comes to me. I don't know what to ask for, anyway. Even God isn't going to bring my mother back, no matter how good I am now or how nice I say please. Sometimes I get so mad I want to kill something. Maybe Alex, my so-called father. I'd sort of like to know what he looks like, so if I saw him on the street I could spit on his shoes. All he cared about was himself and running away so he wouldn't have to go to the stupid war even after my sister died.

Tim has dark hair and dark eyes and braces. I hope he doesn't look like Alex. I don't see why my mother had to go and name me Alexis. I want to change my name. When I go to college, I'll go by my middle name, or have a new name completely. I don't see how anyone there would find out since I don't plan on taking my grandmother with me. Maybe I could be named Tina Laster, after my sister and my mom before she married Alex O'Gara. Or maybe I could be a whole different person, one with a regular mother at home. I'd like that.

I hope me and Tim stay together forever, but I'm afraid he feels sorry for me and I hate that. Last week he put his hand up my shirt and started to feel me up. First I told him no and he stopped, and I thought he stopped because he felt sorry for me so I told him he could go ahead and do it. Then he said no, he didn't want to upset me. So I don't know what to do. I wish I could talk to my mom, but I wouldn't tell her that anyway. That'd be a ten on her Hindenburg Scale, that's what she called it. I never asked her what a Hindenburg Scale is, and now I can't.

I'm getting to where I can hardly stand Aunt Rebecca. I don't care how sick she is. All she cares about is get the house sold, get the car sold. —Mom, I'll help you pack up Christine's stuff—she says all sweet. She took some things from our house, too, some lamps and some of Mom's furniture and clothes. She couldn't wait to get her hands on stuff, all the while pretending that she was just helping me and Grandma. Oh, right, big help. Grandma would just be a total wreck if she had to figure out what to do with Mom's radar detector. It sure was big of Rebecca to take it off her hands. I don't get it. I don't get what use it is to have a family. They ditch you, they spy on you, they steal from you, they die.

It's cold and wet outside. I don't think this winter is ever going to end.

seven

NOT AN HOUR AGO, Rebecca, who bore a striking resemblance to Marvin's side of the family—dark-blond hair, hazel eyes and tendency to a scarring adolescent acne that always left its mark—had stared at her mother trying to digest what she'd heard.

"Don't you know you'll lose the social security money?" she said, outraged. Sometimes she thought her mother might not be crazy, but she'd do until crazy came.

"The lawyer thinks we might be able to get around it," Cora answered, trying not to be defensive. "But I don't care. She's not right, I can tell, and this is something she thinks will make her feel safer. She's really scared."

Rebecca tried to keep her voice calm. "How're you going to take on raising her, Mom, without help? I'll do what I can, you know that, but…" She looked down then, faintly gesturing toward her chest where a prosthesis filled out one side of her bra, a little higher than her remaining breast. Her face was puffy, a bit mushroom-like, as Christine's had been the night she died, from all the drugs. She'd picked up weight, too much, defying the conventional notion about the skeletal chemo patient.

"Don't you worry. This will come out all right," Cora said confidently. She had always believed a positive attitude made all the difference, and she was just getting around to reminding herself of that as the shock of Christine's death wore off, and relentless reality set in like the dregs of winter in her cup. She had to cope, that was all. She had to make herself cope, for Lexie. It was the only gift she could still give.

Now, though, Rebecca was sorting through the boxes of knickknacks and collection of teacups from Christine's house to decide who should get what, when the doorbell rang. Several brown cardboard boxes sat on the dining-room table. Since Rebecca was sitting on the rug laying out piles, Cora went to the front door slowly, making her way down the hall where family pictures hung three-quarters of the way, like an interrupted story. A uniformed man wearing a hat and star-shaped badge stood on the porch. Cora judged him to be thirty at most, and instinctively looked past him to the driveway. A blue-and-white patrol car idled there, Pender County Sheriff blazed in gold print across the side.

"What on earth?" she said, opening the storm door.

"I have a summons for Cora Laster, and one for Alexis O'Gara," he said, his face and voice a practiced neutral.

"A what?" Cora said, chilled by quick fear and the cold that hit her face and bare arms through the open storm door.

"A summons, ma'am. Are you Cora or Alexis?"

"I'm Cora Laster. Wait. She's a child."

"I wouldn't know about that, ma'am. I just deliver these. Please sign at the line marked with the X. It's just to show that you received it. Is Alexis O'Gara here?"

"I told you, she's a child, she's in school."

"Would you be her parent or guardian?"

"Yes."

"Then her summons goes to you anyway."

"I don't want these…what's it for?"

"I don't know, ma'am. But you don't have a choice. A summons means you have to appear."

Cora hesitated longer, biting her lip. The sheriff extended a clipboard toward her, and she saw he wasn't going to leave without her signing his paper and taking the folded ones he pushed at her again.

She signed her name with the black pen he handed her. The sheriff tipped his hat and said, "You have a good day now, ma'am," as Cora shut the door. She leaned against the wall to steady herself.

"Who is it, Mom?" Rebecca called in from the dining-room floor. Then, again, "Mom? Who is it?" When Cora didn't answer, Rebecca came down the hall quickly. She was wearing baggy black slacks and what looked to be a maternity shirt. Her hair hung unwashed around her shoulders. For a moment, as she came through the darkness of the hall, she appeared ghostly to Cora, as if there were no help for her, for any of them.

"A...summons. It was a sheriff."

"A summons to what?"

"Some kind of court. I...have to read it."

Rebecca snatched the papers from Cora's hand. "Oh, my God. This says Alexis O'Gara."

"Let me see one of them," Cora said, and extended her hand. Still reading, Rebecca handed the other summons to Cora.

"In the matter of Alexander O'Gara versus Cora Laster, regarding custody of the minor child Alexis O'Gara, you are commanded to appear in the Court of Domestic Relations of Pender County on March 30, 1993, at one o'clock."

"What does that mean?" Cora said.

"It means Alex is suing for custody of Lexie." Rebecca felt a small triumph, and she didn't quite keep it out of her voice: *See? I told you.*

"He can't do that. Christine left her to me. I'm her guardian."

"You'd better be putting a call into that lawyer of yours."

"Don't say anything to Lexie. Let me talk to her. I'll fight this. Christine's will is clear as glass." Cora's heart was beating in her ears, fast, hard, scared. She knew enough to know that Alexander O'Gara had no business with his daughter.

BRENDA DUNLAP HAD BEEN in court when Cora placed her distress call and had gone home from there, not even calling in to pick up messages. She knew about Alex's suit, but thought the summons couldn't go out for another day. "Dammit to hell," she muttered the next morning when she rifled through the sheaf of little white phone message slips the secretary had left under the paperweight on her desk. They had fallen one at a time, like petals plucked from a daisy, until she got to the last two, both from Cora Laster asking about the summons she'd received. Those she held, shaking her head in frustration. "Susan," she called through her open office door. "Would you hold my calls a while? I've got to do damage control." Then she sat down, took a drink of her coffee, opened the window a crack because the heat—coming from old forced-air registers—made her mouth too dry, and dialed Cora's number.

"Mrs. Laster? This is Brenda Dunlap returning your call." She smoothed the sleeve of her gray suit with her other hand, wedging the phone between her ear and her shoulder, letting the awkward position cause a little pain. "Well, it seems we have a problem… Yes, ma'am, I do know. I'm so sorry I didn't call you in time."

THE COURTHOUSE WAS nearly a hundred years old. Parts of it had been renovated but even those showed almost thirty years of wear. A high, columned building, its main outside doors opened onto the second floor. Cora had had to stop twice to catch her breath before she and Lexie reached the top. "This puts me in mind of a bad dream," she panted once, when she stopped and propped herself between the railing and her cane just to breathe. "Like when you're trying to wake up and it's like you're trying to climb out of it. Ever had that happen?"

The truth was that, since her mother's death, Lexie had had exactly that happen a number of times. But she'd not give her grandmother the satisfaction of having something in common with her. "No," she answered, and drew her chin back and raised her eyebrows slightly, an expression to suggest Cora was perhaps just a tad insane.

They'd had an argument that morning, and its residue hung on like a frightened skunk's passing. Lexie had tried on three separate outfits. When she asked Cora to iron a fourth one, Cora's patience evaporated, and her tone had a serrated edge when she said, "I've done all the ironing I'm about to do. What's going on here? I thought you never wanted to lay eyes on this bottom feeder."

"How can you say that? I hate him. I just don't want to look like a dork in public. You could at least help me. It's not like I have any decent clothes anymore," Lexie said, her voice too loud to be respectful in Cora's opinion.

"If you don't have any decent clothes, how come my credit card is over four hundred dollars and there's all these rags lying around that you want ironed?"

It was the first time the tension between them had separated, like grease from pan drippings, and Cora had recognized a chance to skim off the bad and make a little gravy. "Honey, we've got no call to be at each other. We're in this together. We've got to help each other through. It's you and me, kid," she'd said, her tone light and kind at once as she opened her arms and stepped toward Lexie.

But Lexie only tolerated the hug. Her grandmother was way off the mark. Her only interest in her father was to make him eat shit and die when he saw what he'd run off and left when she was hardly born and her twin hardly dead.

Now, though, entering the building, the notion of seeing her father had hollowed out the center of her indignation, leaving space for a strange, guilty fear. She held the heavy door for her grandmother and followed her in, shielding herself behind Cora's large, cane-wielding body widened by the flare of a gray cloth coat. Lexie let Cora lead the way, even knowing Cora had as little idea as she where Hearing Room 204 might be. Lexie walked behind Cora at just enough distance to make it indistinguishable whether the two were together or not. Her father would recognize her grandmother, though certainly not her, she knew. She kept her eyes down.

Cora looked around the wide hallway that served as a lobby. Wooden benches full of people edged the walls. Most were in blue jeans and baseball caps, a few more formally dressed. Now and then, a man in a dark suit with a muted tie, good haircut and shined shoes, or a woman in a business suit, understated jewelry and mid-height heels walked purposefully down the center of the floor where millions of footsteps had worn a track into the tile. Cora peered through the bottom of her glasses at the numbers printed on plaques one side of each closed door.

Brenda Dunlap appeared then, through a door farther down the hall and gestured. "There you are," she said when they approached. "I'm glad you're early. Would you like to wait in an attorney-client room? It would be more private." She glanced around at the people seated on the benches, and Cora understood Alex might be one of them.

"Please," Cora said.

Cora and Lexie followed Brenda's fitted gray suit down the hall, Cora trying to use peripheral vision to look for Alex, and Lexie studying the floor.

"This is supposed to be only for attorney-client consultations," Brenda said, opening a door into a narrow hallway with several more doors on each side, "but, well, sometimes it can be difficult to have to look at someone in the hallway while you wait. I'll come get you when they call us."

"What are you going to say?" Cora asked.

"We'll demonstrate that Mr. O'Gara effectively abandoned Alexis as an infant, and *try* to demonstrate that prior to abandoning her, he wasn't a fit parent." Brenda glanced at Cora to see if her oblique reference to the lack of the full story had been received, but Cora's expression didn't change from terrified determination. "We'll enter Christine's will and the appointment of a guardian into evidence—of course, the guardianship was already taken care of, you remember, at the same time we handled the will—anyway, we'll ask the court to terminate his parental rights. That'll clear the way for the adoption to proceed. Alexis, do you have any questions?"

"Will I have to say anything?" The girl was pale, Brenda noted, her eyes an unusual light blue with long black eyelashes beneath heavy brows. Maybe it was just the thin light from the small, high window, but Alexis looked almost ephemeral. *I hope she's got some backbone,* Brenda thought, wondering how thoroughly she should warn her clients about the possibilities of loss. Today was only a pre-trial hearing, unless some agreement was reached.

"Not today," she said, noticing Lexie deflate a little as she registered the answer. "The judge might ask you some questions himself sometime, but not the other attorney. Not this time…this is what's called a pre-trial. Today, you won't even come in. The other attorney issued a subpoena, but I'll get that quashed. It's improper with a minor in a custody issue, unless the judge wants to talk to her himself. It's just harassment, and not something the judge will put up with."

"I have to come back?" Lexie interrupted, looking panicky.

"It could happen," Brenda answered. "Anything could happen. Try not to worry. We'll handle it." She wished the hearty confidence that propped up her voice and smile were real. But she'd advised Cora at first to let it alone, so her conscience was nearly clear.

LEXIE AND CORA WAITED over an hour for the case to be called. Brenda had left them alone to fidget and worry, make small, flat conversations and then lapse into silence. Then Brenda came back. She smiled without it ever reaching her eyes and said, "Cora? We're ready. Lexie, you can stay here. You're not to appear today."

The hearing room was nothing like what Cora had expected, her private vision having been shaped by the movies where robed judges presided from raised mahogany benches and a uniformed bailiff intoned "All rise" when the judge entered from a private door behind his bench. Instead, it was an un-adorned, high-ceilinged room, windowless, a nondescript beige. Three large, marred conference tables took up most of the space, two of them arranged side by side—with several feet of space left between them—facing the third which was centered, and about ten feet away. A tape recorder lay on the single desk, a cassette tape alongside it. The two tables each had four chairs lined up on one side, to face the person who would sit at the single chair behind the other table.

"This is the court?" Cora whispered to Brenda.

"This is the court. That's Reardon Greevy, Alex's attorney," she added, nodding toward a tall, good-looking man who'd come in seconds after they had. "I haven't been on any cases against him, he's an out-of-towner. Brett says he's good, though.

He has a reputation, perfectly willing to play dirty. We'll see. We've got a decent draw with the judge—not exactly Mr. Personality, but he's usually fair."

"Brett?"

"Brett Fuller, one of my partners."

"Where's Alex?" asked Cora.

"He's here, I imagine."

Brenda set a brown leather briefcase on the table and opened it. She pulled out a long manila file and as she turned its pages one at a time, Cora studied her. How young Brenda's hands looked, nails short and manicured with clear polish. No rings. A simple, leather-strap watch. But the skin was unwrinkled, almost like Lexie's hands. Cora snuck a look at Brenda's face, not more than a foot from her own, in bent profile. No lipstick, but a little eye makeup behind her glasses. A small face with small, regular features. Cora wondered how she could have trusted Lexie's future to someone who probably dyed the gray streaks into her hair to make her look old enough to practice law.

Lately, Cora's own glimpses into any mirror had been almost startling. Her eyes and cheeks and chin all had heavier pouches than she thought should be there. Often she hardly recognized herself, the discrepancy between the young woman she was in her head and the old one whose face and hands looked more and more like those of Cora's mother, dead twenty-one years. Errant hairs jutted from her chin; she plucked them with a vengeance, remembering how her mother hadn't.

How had all this happened? As she waited next to her attorney, Cora felt bewildered that she could be sitting in a courtroom trying to retain custody of her dead daughter's daughter. She'd never been in court for so much as a traffic ticket. She and Marvin had planned their lives. They'd made decisions. Some of the decisions had stood, oak-like in their apparent permanence, while others seem to have been the laughingstock of fate. We have control of our lives, all right, she thought. Some anyway. The trick is you never know when you have it and when you don't. You have to assume you're in charge of at least your own life, and as often as not, something else entirely takes over and you find yourself in a funeral parlor or a courtroom or someplace else you had no intention to be.

Cora didn't even notice at first when her former son-in-law slid into a seat next to his attorney on the far side from her. She was mapless in the forest of her thoughts.

THAT NIGHT, CORA lay on her side in the dark beside Lexie, on Lexie's bed where the girl faced Cora fully for the first time since Christine died. Though her arms were bent at the elbow, the pull of Cora's arms around her back pressing her hands like flowers against her chest, her head nested of its own accord between Cora's breasts, and if she moved at all, it was to draw closer to her grandmother for the visceral sense of her protection. Cora used her free arm to rub Lexie's back. "Shh, shh, it will be all right, we'll beat it, shh, honey, it will be all right. I'm here," Cora whispered. As unforeseen and as unbelievable as the spring tornado that had ripped the roof from their house five years before Marvin died, a gavel had fallen after a judge consulted a manila file and declared that Alex O'Gara was the legal father of Alexis Marie O'Gara and that, as such, custody of the minor child would automatically revert to him due to the death of the custodial parent, Christine Laster O'Gara.

"Objection, Your Honor." Brenda had been on her feet. "This is a pre-trial. We intend to show that Mr. O'Gara is not a fit par…"

"Save your objection for trial, Counsel. You are, of course, free to refer this to social services for investigation, but in this court, we don't terminate a man's parental rights without there being proof of unfitness." The judge's eyes were close-set, Cora saw. He was a man she would have disliked just meeting him in line at the grocery.

"If it please the Court, the minor child has had no contact with Mr. O'Gara for fifteen years. As is noted in the brief, Mrs. Laster was named guardian in the mother's will…"

"Save it, Counselor. That provision is null and void unless Mr. O'Gara is shown to be presently incompetent. Are you prepared to offer such proof today?"

"Your Honor, it was our understanding that…"

"I'll take that as a no. Do you wish to file any motions on behalf of Mrs. Laster at this time?" The judge interrupted without even looking up.

"I certainly do, Your Honor."

Brenda had filed a motion for a stay of execution. Of course, the court had just called it a temporary order that Alexis remain with Cora until social services could conduct an investigation regarding her best interest in the matter of permanent custody. It was Lexie who had called it a stay of execution when Brenda explained to her what had happened.

Cora and Lexie had walked out together, reeling, and ridden home in silence for an entirely new reason.

Now Cora listened and comforted and soothed, not even trying, yet, to review in her mind all Brenda had told her. She circled with her palm, letting her fingers define the separate, delicate muscles that crisscrossed Lexie's back, and the ladder of her ribs. How fragile it all is, she thought, how losable, and how much suffering comes with the loss, and still, we love like this, this unbearably much.

eight

I HATE HIM. I HATE him more than Hitler, geometry, Frank Vallus The Biggest Jerk in the School, a whole summer at Camp Tree-branch, and clarinet lessons. Take Grandma's lima beans, her disgusting meat loaf, her fried rubber-chicken steak, and her fisheyes vanilla tapioca pudding, and roll it all into a giant burrito and I'd rather eat that than have anything to do with my father. The only thing I hate more than him is my mom being dead. I hate my mom being dead the most of anything I've ever hated in my life. Sometimes I used to tell her that I hated her when we'd have a fight and I was mad. I never really hated her, but I told her I did, and now there's nothing I can do about it.

I saw him at court. He didn't see me, he's too stupid to know where to look, but I saw his skinny ass. He looks like a piece of rope. I wish he'd make a noose out of himself and tighten it real good around his own neck. I mainly saw his back and what he looks like sideways when he was walking out with his lawyer. Our lawyer had us wait until he left, but the door was part open and I stood behind it and looked out the crack. He's got dark hair like me (note: buy bleach). It's short, and he's got real white skin, I think, but his cheeks were blackish looking. Probably he forgot to shave. His shoulders are kind of hunched, and he's pretty short. Not like a dwarf, but I don't think he's a lot taller than Mom was. She was taller than me, I remember that much. He had on a jacket that was too big, I mean, his fingers barely hung out, and a tie that was so long it could have got caught in his fly.

When I think about it, I start crying again. That judge is such an idiot. Grandma told me what he said. Maybe it was like on TV and Alex paid him off. How else could he do this? It's my life. He didn't even ask me what I wanted.

When the lawyer said what happened, all I could do was cry. Last night Grandma lay on my bed with me, but I didn't mind. I think she was crying, too. I don't want to leave my grandma. She says we'll fight in court, and she thinks we can win, but I don't trust anything anymore. Who would have thought Mom would die? You can't believe anything will work out right, that's just stupid, anyone can see that most of the time everything's all wrong. Stuff is backward, not the way it should be at all, like God has dyslexia or gets high by making people suffer. Or maybe He's just so involved with *important* things like poking black holes in the universe that He just doesn't notice what's actually going on. Anyway, what's His point, if He has one at all?

I don't even think there is a God anyway. I've got to figure out what to do.

In World History, the teacher wrote Beware the Ides of March on the blackboard and went on about Julius Caesar and Cassius and Brutus and all that. Caesar thought he was so great and then, bam, they got him back. Tiffany said they were evil and wanted his power, but I thought old Jules deserved it. I don't care if I'm evil. I went into Mom's room tonight while Grandma talked on the phone. She yells at me for talking to Tim too much, then she spends an hour talking to Rebecca or Jolene or someone. I know she was talking about me because she was whispering. Like I'm stupid or something. I don't care. I went into Mom's room and just sat there for a while. I put on one of her sweaters and looked at the picture. It sounds stupid, but I started talking to it, because it made me feel better. I told her everything, what happened at court, and about Alex and even about Rebecca stealing her stuff. I don't know if that last part would upset her, but it just came out so now she knows anyway, and I guess there's nothing I can do about it. The weird thing is that after I cried, I talked to her and then I cried a little more and then I said—What should I do, Mom? It's not like I expected her to answer or something, but it was almost like I heard her voice saying *I'll help you.* I looked at her picture, but it wasn't changed at all. It was freezing in there because Grandma turned the heat off, but I sat on her bed and tried to figure out how she was going to help me, but I didn't know. Then for some reason, I decided to look at her stuff in the closet. It took me maybe twenty minutes just to get all her note-books out and figure out how they should go. I looked at the first page of every one and put them in order from the dates. She crossed a lot of stuff out, and she kind of wrote messy, like me. I'm going to read them. Grandma probably doesn't want me to, but I'm not going to tell her. In the first place, I don't want to upset her. And in the second place, she thinks the lawyer can help us, but like I said, I have no faith because things just don't turn out the way they should. Unless you *make* them, somehow.

Beware the Ides of March, Alex. I'm going to get you. One way or another, I'll get you back.

1972

nine

THE FIRST TIME Christine Laster laid eyes on Alexander O'Gara, they didn't much linger there. In the first place, he was too short. She liked bigger guys, more like Bobby Miller whose pale hair and blue eyes were at the top of a body that looked tall and mountain-solid to her. Alex was built like the afterthought of a litter of puppies, runty and meatless. His black hair stood out, and his dramatically fringed tobacco eyes, but his skin was sallow. "That's his father's side," Christine's father told her in what was, for him, a lengthy speech. "Black Irish. Except his father had high color in his cheeks, you know. I remember Michael from school. Didn't he pass on a while back? Heart attack or something? Graduated a year ahead of your mother and me, I think. Maybe two. Trouble. He was trouble. Likely as not the son is, too. Not the best stock."

That's how it was in Darrville, the town next to Early Sun on Highway 40, and the only place to go anyway, since all the schools were there. Everybody into everybody else's business. A teenage girl couldn't sneeze without some school chum of her mother handing her a tissue and telling her she'd best get to bed early to ward off that cold. Gossip was handed out like the straws that came with fountain sodas at the drugstore counter. Even as the town had grown, with the Redpath farm implement building, the expansion of Washington Supply Company, and the new Thriftway, it wasn't an area that exactly imported citizens. Kids grew up, married each other early, had kids that grew up to have kids faster than the old people died, and thus Darrville grew. Early Sun seemed, in contrast, stagnant, even shrinking, like one of its ponds in a dry high summer.

This time, though, Christine had actually asked her daddy if he knew the O'Gara bunch. Alex had been looking at her blatantly, suggestively, rolling his eyes from her head down to her chest, and after laying them there long enough to make her squirm, palpable as a warm hand, let them rove on down to her hips and the length of her bare legs. He'd been around, she guessed, as long as she had, but she'd taken no notice of him until lately, when he'd taken notice of her, though he never spoke. That, as much as anything, made him irresistible.

When Alex finally asked her out maybe two weeks later, Christine was intrigued enough to lie her way out of a date with Bobby himself despite her father's oblique advice. What intrigued her most was that she was attracted to him in spite of the fact he wasn't her type. He had a strange, startling laugh— like a clogged tuba—not that he laughed often. Something about his manner, alternately high-strung and lazily insolent made him seem like the apple dangling from the end of a high thin branch, the one she had to have.

They began dating, though only Christine called it that. She knew exactly what her parents would think of him. Once a month or so, Alex would casually drop that he'd be at Red Dog—a pizza place in Darrville with pinball games and a pool table in the basement—that night, and maybe he'd see her there. Christine would tell Marvin and Cora that she and Summer Milliner or Jessie Bolander were going to meet at the mall and then she'd spend the evening watching Alex shoot pool with his friends. He'd lean over, a cigarette stuck impossibly on the edge of his narrow bottom lip, while he lined up the stick and balls. One night after he won, he kissed her hard on the mouth, his hand low on her hips, and she felt his tongue graze her lips. She'd been taken by surprise, and he'd covered her closed mouth with his open one.

It went on like that, furtive, like a bud opening in the secret night of Christine's mind, for the last month of the school year, all summer, and right on through into senior year. Cora had a sense of Christine sliding out of her cupped hands like so much water going to waste. Her grades went down, though under Cora's pressure she applied to the Indiana University branch at Richmont, where someone could go all the way to a two-year degree. She was accepted. "What are your plans?" Cora would ask when her daughter went out, but Christine didn't tell her anything anymore, only shrugged.

"I don't know. Hang out. See people." Her hands, beautiful as if they'd been sculptured with their oval nails and narrow wrists, fluttered like nervous birds around her long, straight brown hair. By then, Alex was calling the house.

"Kin I tawk to Chris," he'd mumble, a statement instead of the polite question ending with *please* that Cora had been taught and taught her children. But Christine didn't talk about seeing Alex; didn't even mention who'd called unless her mother asked her directly. Jolene had given Christine a blank book diary for Christmas, and Cora thought about looking for writing in it, but when she halfheartedly began searching in Christine's dresser drawers, she felt soiled and resolutely closed the drawer and then the door to Christine's room.

Cora drew the line finally when Christine admitted she was meeting Alex at the McDonald's in Darrville one Friday night in April. She'd first said she and Jessie were going out, but Cora had become suspicious and pressed when Christine frantically insisted *she* had to drive, though Jessie had her own car and could always pick Christine up. Marvin had Cora's car up on blocks, and Christine wasn't allowed to take her father's truck.

"This doesn't sound like he has much respect for you," Cora fussed, even though she was trying not to drive her older daughter right into the boy's arms by openly disapproving. "Wouldn't a decent young man have the good manners to come get you properly? And come in to meet your parents? You know we have rules. No meeting him anywhere. If he wants to see you, we'll have to meet him first."

By then, Christine was mired in the layers of the desire and confusion a woman of any age is apt to name love. Alex, masterful at holding himself just out of reach, was persuaded to pick Christine up and shamble in to meet Cora and Marvin. "Hey," he said, jerking his head to shift the hanging black forelock out of his eyes.

"How do you do?" Cora said, nodding her brown bob politely while Marvin stuck out his hand for Alex to shake. Alex blinked and removed his hand from his pocket when he got what he was supposed to do.

"I can't stand those sideburns," Cora said to Marvin after Christine and Alex were gone in Alex's dented Mustang. "He looks like a hood. And where do you suppose he learned his manners? Dungarees for a date…and his shirt wasn't even tucked in. Did you see how he looked at her? It looked like… well, it looked indecent. That…*thing* of hair in his eyes, too."

Marvin, whose early-grayed hair had begun to thin five years ago—which hardly seemed fair since his own father had died with a thatch of thick white hair edging the same hairline he'd had since boyhood—grunted, which Cora took as reluctant agreement. That worried her as much as her own assessment.

Normally Marvin didn't have the patience to just sit and rock on the porch, even on a soft spring evening when the apple trees were in bloom, but that night activity seemed leached out of him. He and Cora sat silently, watching night rise off the grass toward the melon sky while they sipped the lemonade Cora had mixed. Cora didn't know Marvin had lingered in the kitchen to spike his with the rum Cora kept in the cabinet for her yellow bundt cake recipe, or she would have worried even more. A talker by nature, she usually put her worries into words. The lines around Marvin's eyes were deeper, like the dry creek beds ready for Cora's tears.

When Christine came in, forty-eight minutes late for her eleven-thirty curfew, Marvin took over. "You'll not go out with him again," he said. In Marvin's house, as in that of his father, a man's word was final.

"You can't pick my friends," Chris cried hotly. "You can't stop me. I'm almost eighteen years old."

"While you're living under my roof, you'll do as I say."

Christine faltered. Her chin quivered. "This is totally unfair. In the first place, I told you, my watch is slow. See?" She jabbed her wrist in the direction of Marvin's face, but he didn't lower his eyes toward it by an iota. Under the overhead light in the kitchen, her makeup looked smeary, especially around her lips, swollen and blurry. "I've been late for curfew before. You don't even ground me if I'm late when I'm out with my friends. You just hate Alex. What did he ever do to you? You don't even know him."

But the discussion was over. Marvin's forefinger aimed at Christine's chest. "I said, you'll not go out with him again." He turned his back and headed for his bedroom, leaving Cora with their daughter's ragged rage. With Cora, Christine reverted to defiance.

"You and Dad can't tell me who to like."

"Honey, we're just worried about you."

"Why? I didn't do anything."

"Alex doesn't seem like…the right…type. We never know what you're doing…and you were forty-five minutes late."

"Thirty minutes! And I told you what happened."

"More than that."

"You're treating me like a baby. I'm the one who's going out with him, not you. I know what I'm doing. You can't tell me who to love."

It was the last sentence that set off clanging alarms in Cora's head.

"Honey, you're too young. You hardly know this boy." Cora's forehead wrinkled into parallel pleats, and her voice rose, a frenzied pitch in certain words.

Christine had let too much out, but she wasn't going to back down from her mother. She tried to blunt the effect of what she'd said while defending her right to say it, but it came out like a mess of tangled fishing lines. "It's none of your business…it's not like I'm going to marry him or something," she shouted between Cora's pleadings, which soon turned to commands.

When Christine shouted, "It's not like I'm going to marry him or something," for the third time, Cora paid attention.

"Well, of course not," she said. "I know that. He's about to get drafted, for heaven's sake."

"He is not," Christine yelled.

"What is he, 4F?" It was the only reason any boy from Early Sun or Darrville didn't go into the military those days, except for the few who went all the way to Bloomington and actually lived in a dormitory on the main campus of Indiana University, or the one every other year who was an eldest son, needed to run a farm for a widowed mother. The war wasn't a daily topic in homes where there were only daughters, but in those with sons, it was a topic both obsessive and feverish. Enrollment at the two-building Richmont branch of the university had definitely risen, but most boys and their families just accepted their fate, wearing a sash of patriotism on their graduation robes. Darrville High School had taken to announcing what service branch the boys were entering as they were handed their diplomas. Their fathers, Second World War veterans to a man, applauded mightily while mothers dabbed their eyes with lace-edged hankies.

"No, he is not 4F!" Christine shrieked.

"Well, honey, maybe you and Alex have been too busy making kissy face to notice, but there's a war on and America's in it." Cora didn't resort to sarcasm often, and she regretted the tone immediately. It always inflamed Christine and boomeranged right back at her. It didn't even occur to her that Alex might be college-bound. A look at him plus his two or three words had weeded that possibility right out of Cora's mind.

"He's not going!"

"Well, of course, he might not get ordered to Vietnam right away, but…"

"No! He's not going at all."

"What do you mean?"

"It's none of your business." Christine's eyes teared and her lips showed their fight not to form a sob. Seeing that, Cora took a step toward her daughter, opening her arms in an invitation, but Christine grabbed her purse off the kitchen table and ran into the hallway. Cora heard her take the steps upstairs in a rapid, hard beat. She stood in place, finally lowering her arms and deciding not to pursue her daughter. At the sink, she sprinkled scouring powder on the white porcelain. Scuff marks from the cast-iron frypan came off with elbow grease, Cora's mother's solution to every blot, but the abrasive sound was too much like an echo, and she cried a little.

CORA ENTERED HER own bedroom on the defensive. Marvin couldn't stand it when Cora argued with one of the girls. He said she lowered herself to their level, and whenever he said it, Cora felt like a chastised child herself, which made her doubly angry. "I know. Don't get started on me," she said, preempting him and knowing she sounded like Christine. Cora knew he'd heard the shouting, but most likely he'd not been able to pick out the words. He usually couldn't, or didn't bother to try.

Marvin shook his head back and forth, disgustedly. He was stretched out on their olive-green chenille bedspread with his clothes and shoes still on, which he knew drove Cora right up the wall because it left little fuzzy pills on his pants and shirt that Cora had to pick off by hand before they went into the wash. His hands were between his head and the pillow, his jutting elbows casting shadows on the greenish-yellow wall behind him. Cora wished—as she did nearly every night—that she could have guessed how sickly that paint color would look by lamplight. Wasn't that always the way? she thought. You think you know exactly how something will turn out, and then, when you get it, the let-down has the weight of an elephant's foot. Worse, Marvin hadn't liked the color to begin with, and she'd told him all his taste was in his mouth.

She began undressing, then, suddenly self-conscious under her husband's expressionless stare, Cora took her nightgown across the hall into the bathroom and finished changing there. When she climbed into bed, she just said, "Goodnight," and curled into her sleep position, so Marvin would get the hint. After a while he sighed, got up, and put on his pajamas. He sighed again when he turned out the light, but it wasn't long before Cora heard the ripple of soft snoring as Marvin relaxed into the first wave of a sea of dreamless sleep while Cora's large bones lay on a hard raft above it trying to puzzle out what her daughter had said.

In her room, Christine was propped on two pillows, huddled as if the night were cold. "I'm going to marry Alexander O'Gara," she wrote in her diary. "I'm the only one who knows how good he is, and I can save him. And he loves me, too. I know it."

ten

"WHERE'VE YOU BEEN?" Cora said to Christine one afternoon in June. Christine's hair was rumpled, and grass clippings clung to the back of her white blouse when she came home from school at five-thirty, even later than her new habit. It was the day before graduation, six weeks since Marvin had forbidden Christine to see Alex.

"Library." Christine's voice was layered, evasion over defiance.

"Christine…"

"Don't call me that."

"I'm sorry. Chris. You're still a…good girl…aren't you? I mean, you wouldn't…" Even as she despised her own anxious wheedling, Cora could see by the way her daughter drew a curtain just behind her eyes that she probably wasn't a good girl anymore, and wasn't likely to discuss it with her mother even if she were.

"What's that supposed to mean?" Christine picked a leaf off the side of her print skirt and flicked it on the linoleum, but furtively. She didn't know the grass clippings on her back had given her up.

Cora hesitated. She was making meat loaf, mixing ground beef by hand with egg and white bread because it made for a better texture. The long, low sun of late afternoon was a downhill creek of light running into the window over the sink, which Cora had raised all the way for the softness of the air. She pulled her hands from the pink mixture in the glass bowl and washed them with soap and water. Used to be the feel of mixing meat loaf made her squeamish, but she'd adjusted over the years. There'd been a lot to adjust to, a lot to ignore, and Cora had refined the art. Some things, though, couldn't go unremarked, no matter how hard. While she dried her hands on her apron, she tried to look at her daughter squarely. "I mean," she said, "I have a feeling you may be seeing that boy against your father's wishes. And...I'm finding myself wondering if you're letting him... touch you?"

Christine snickered. Something in the sneering, dismissive tone and the gesture that accompanied it snapped a bass string deep inside Cora. On blind swift impulse, her hand—still half-wet—flew like a part of her with a separate mind into a stinging slap on Christine's cheek. Immediately, Christine covered the spot with her own hand. "I hate you," she shouted, her eyes tearing from the burning place on her face and the humiliation.

"You can hate me if you want, but you'll answer me...or your father," Cora said, furious even while she recoiled from what she'd done; she'd never struck either of the girls except small padded smacks on a diapered bottom when they were toddlers exploring the limits of danger. Marvin had, not all that often, but when they needed to be brought back into line, always with just his hand and always on the rear. It took a lot to push him to it, but it was that rather than a lot of words, which was Cora's way. Even Rebecca was really too big for it, now.

"I'm not telling you anything," Christine said, turning her back and walking into the hall in a defiant, separate way.

Cora sank into one of the kitchen chairs, hard and straight-backed wood with just a little cushioning on the seat. She ran her hands through her hair, wiped her eyes on the edge of her green print apron, and waited for Marvin to come home.

The meat loaf, mixed, rested in the bowl. Peeled, knife-ready carrots lay bright on the counter, and potatoes to be mashed cooled in the pot for a good half hour while Cora fought her own mind about what was happening to her family. Here poor Jolene had to worry about Paul in a war zone. Shouldn't a woman with just two daughters have nothing to worry about? Could Christine be doing it with that boy? There really wasn't a shred of evidence, just that look on Christine's face and the cold feeling that had settled like winter fog over Cora when she'd asked straight out. Marvin wouldn't have it; Cora knew that much. He'd send her away.

"WHAT DO YOU THINK?" Cora asked Jolene a few days later. "I can't keep her locked up—that's how Marvin would have it if he knew—but I can see her life circling the drain. And she's thinkin' that spinning in her head is love." She drew out the last word mocking it in a way to make Jolene chuckle, but Cora's face was serious. It was past time for Jolene to go so each could start cooking supper in her own kitchen, but they kept rocking on Cora's porch, sipping the melted ice cubes from their iced teas as though there were something of substance in their glasses that kept them there.

"Did she say that?" The breeze lifted Jolene's hair as she spoke and Cora noticed more gray around her friend's temples. Her own hair was already salt-and-pepper, but then her mother had grayed early. Having children: that's what did it to you.

"In a roundabout way. Said we couldn't tell her who to love. And then, you know, when she came in she looked mussed up and smeared, like she'd been, well, what they call making out."

"You don't think…"

"I don't know. I pray not. But this is tearing us up. She hardly speaks to Marvin or me. Rebecca, she just ignores Rebecca, but with us, it's like she…it's like we're people to hate."

"Well, you know what they say about hate being so close to love. Maybe you're taking it too serious."

Cora paused, considering, then shook her head in rhythm with her slow rocking. The sun was low enough now that she squinted when the chair took her forward into the rays, and Jolene saw the narrow folds around Cora's eyes. Jolene herself had stopped rocking and held her chair on the back tip of the rockers to keep her face shaded by the porch overhang. She was like that, naturally practical, while Cora led with her heart and immediately played the hand she was dealt without thinking how to change the cards.

"I don't think so," Cora said. "I know what you mean, but this

has a different feel. It doesn't feel like one of hers or Rebecca's
tantrums, when they say they hate you, but you know you just
have to hold firm and let them come around on their own. It's
more like she's planting herself in cement over this. Nothing's
going to move her."

"Then maybe you've got to think this out different. Maybe
it's backfiring to say she can't see him."

"I tried to be careful about that, not drive her to him, you
know? But it didn't work. She went there anyway."

"Sure, but that's not what I'm getting at," Jolene said. "Maybe
you've got to let her see him so she won't be driven away from
you. Let this thing run its course, but keep her close to you."

"Oh, but what if she…?"

"Yeah, she may. No gettin' around that one."

The two women sat a few more minutes in silence. Then
Cora reached across the space between their chairs and squeezed
Jolene's hand. "I know you got to be thinking about Paul every
minute," she said. "This is silly compared to what's on your
mind. I hope you…"

Jolene interrupted. "It's a help," she said. "Keeps my mind
off it."

Cora smiled then. When her face relaxed, she looked younger
and unmarked, like the sky between birds, and Jolene smiled
back.

CORA MIGHT HAVE BEEN impulsive with her own reactions but
she planned her husband's carefully. It was easier for her to see
what would work when it wasn't a mirror she was looking into.
Without ever telling Marvin about the grass clippings that Christine had somehow gotten on her back while in the library, Cora
began to work on Marvin. "Maybe we're not being quite fair,"
she'd say quietly. "You know, his father's dead. Maybe he just
hasn't had a good man show him how to act." Later, when they
were talking about something else, she slipped in, "Well, she *is*
eighteen. She'd best decide that for herself. Lots of young people
on their own at eighteen. She's got a summer job, it's her money
she's spending."

"Time for her to be paying a little room and board then if she's so damn independent," Marvin muttered and went back to his newspaper. But eventually he came around. Cora had a mountain of chips saved up for when she needed to get her husband to change his mind. Neither she nor Marvin spoke of it when she pushed a pile in front of him; they were cashed silently and without rancor on either of their parts.

That summer, Alex came around more and more, it seemed, and started to make himself quite at home. Too much at home for Cora's comfort, though she bit back whatever wanted to come out of her mouth about it because Christine had warmed back up to her parents, as Jolene had predicted. The girl had a job bagging groceries at the Thriftway, but—though Alex claimed he was working in his uncle's bait shop in Darrville— Cora noticed his work hours never seemed to conflict with Christine's, no matter how many times she had to trade shifts to accommodate a regular clerk.

"Alex must have gotten his induction notice by now," Cora said to Marvin. "We just have to hold out."

Marvin took off his glasses and rubbed his eyes. It bothered Cora to see him sink his face into his hand and rest it there a minute. His eyebrows bushed out above his forefinger like caterpillars crossing a branch.

"Absence makes the heart…" Marvin trailed out, his tone like a warning.

"Think about it, honey. She's going over to Richmont. She'll meet some other boys. He doesn't seem much like a letter-writing type, does he?"

"I doubt he can spell that many words," Marvin, whose own spelling left a good deal to phonetics and chance, said.

Mom and Dad will think we're getting married because of the war, Christine had written in her diary a week earlier. "They've forgotten all about love. It's true Alex doesn't want to hurt anyone but that includes me. He said so."

"IT HAS NOTHING TO do with the war," Christine shouted. "You don't know anything, you just assume." She and Cora and

Marvin were in the living room and the television was off, which meant the conduct of very serious business. Beyond the picture window, sullen clouds were teething on the treetops, making it darker than it should have been at seven-thirty. The three-way light, turned to the brightest wattage because Marvin had been reading the paper, threw bad-tempered shadows on the green tweed chair where Marvin sat facing his daughter, stiff on the matching couch. Cora sat in the rocking chair she'd had since she was pregnant with Christine. On the end table next to her rested Christine's framed graduation picture and the two Hummel figurines Cora's mother had given her to start a collection. Since Edna's death, though, nobody had remembered to give her any more. In the picture, Christine's hair was backlit; she wore the black drape all the senior girls did, and Cora's faux pearls. The picture was always a punch to Cora's solar plexus; Christine was stunning, her fine features composed and adult-looking, but studio lights adjusted to make her eyes wide, theatrically starred, dancing toward a future only she could see.

Marvin's face was fierce, the tenor of his voice deepening with anger while Christine's got higher. He'd run his hand over the top of his head, somehow mussing it so some thin strands poked the air in a wild aura. Cora didn't want to look at him, didn't want to see the narrowed eyes and the angry furrows, but Christine faced him squarely. Cora reached over to try to calm her daughter, but Christine batted her mother's hand off her thigh, which only fueled Marvin more. Since the day when her own frustration had flared into the slap, Cora had been a little frightened of all of them. Sometimes everything seemed normal enough, but when Christine and Alex were there the house had a tinderbox feel Cora hoped she was imagining.

"There's no way I'll sign for this, period," Marvin shouted. "And don't let me ever see you treat your mother that way. Ever."

"Marvin, it's okay…" Cora tried, but Christine interrupted.

"See how much you know? Nothing. I don't need your permission to get married in Tennessee. I'm eighteen. We'll go there."

"You'll not leave this house."

There was no way anything good was going to come of this. Cora would have been just as upset as Marvin, except one of them had to stay cool enough to think. Sometimes it seemed like a luxury to her, Marvin's role, wide and roomy enough to explode in. Still, she'd stunned herself when she slapped Christine. It was much more like Marvin than herself, and it left her feeling uneasy rather than liberated.

"Christine, Chris I mean, honey, we don't want you running off to get married. It should be the happiest day of your life. We're just worried because you're so young. We'd like you to…"

"Wait. You want me to wait and *we* don't want to wait. I don't see what there is to talk about," Christine said, only slightly mollified by Cora's tone.

"Actually, *I* want Alex to get hit by a truck," Marvin said. "A very big truck."

"He doesn't mean that, honey."

"Oh, I certainly do," Marvin said, but he heard Cora's tone and pulled his own down a notch.

"Wouldn't it be a good idea to wait until Alex is out of the army? I mean you two can write and see each other when he's on leave. Did he get his induction notice yet?" Cora asked.

"No…yes, we just don't want to wait."

"Is it no or yes? Seems simple enough," Marvin said.

"Rebecca, this is none of your business. Get out!" Christine yelled angrily. She'd seen or sensed the movement of her sister on the top step of the stairs, out of sight, to eavesdrop. Christine had done it herself a hundred times. Complete silence answered, and Christine knew Rebecca was edging back onto the top landing to tiptoe to her room as if she'd not been there. "I'm not stupid, you little twerp. I know where you are."

"That's enough." Marvin leaned forward as if to rise and strike his daughter.

"I'm not afraid of you, Daddy. I don't care if you hit me." Christine's eyes—as blue as Cora's own, though Marvin's brown should have dominated—were almost black in the low light.

"Nobody's doing any hitting here," Cora said. "Let's stay on the subject. What is Alex's situation with the military?"

"I'm not telling you anything," Christine said, standing up.

"He's using you," Marvin said. "He won't get away with it."

"Oh, yes, he will," Christine said in a deadly voice as she walked out of the room, thinking she was saying Alex would marry her.

Cora sat a minute, dazed, recognizing the insane courage her daughter had borrowed from the notion of love. She saw, too, that she and Marvin were not going to win. Time was, she herself would have walked through fire to be with Marvin, though it wasn't until long after they married she realized she did love him after all.

"They think they know everything," Christine wrote that night.

eleven

THE WEDDING, SET for August 31, had gotten completely out of hand as far as Marvin was concerned. He'd agreed to something simple, but every day it seemed there was one more "little thing" that Cora agreed with Christine would add a nice touch. Not carnations or daisies or chrysanthemums in the bridal bouquet, but roses. And trailing ivy, just a little extra. Not red gelatin salad on the buffet in the church fellowship hall, but fresh fruit cups. Not even workaday Indiana cantaloupes in the damn fruit cups, either, but blueberries (in season) and strawberries (definitely not), because Christine loved berries.

"I'll make them," Cora said, shaming him. "That way they won't cost that much more. And there's really no reason I can't bake the hams myself. Jolene offered to serve at the buffet, so that'll save." On and on and on. He was begrudging every bit of it, they both knew. "You don't want her running off and eloping, and us not even be there, do you?" Cora kept pleading, but Marvin caught the glinting blade edging her voice. "We can't drive her off. This is her *wedding,* after all."

"No, we'll just *pay* her off," he muttered, but when Cora asked what he meant by *that* he just shook his head. "I'm taking all the overtime they offer," he said instead. "What else do you want?"

There was tension between Christine and Marvin when he walked her down the aisle of the Darrville Methodist Church. He'd flat refused to wear a tuxedo, on grounds of unnecessary cost, he said, but really because he thought it would make him look as if he approved. (It had been Cora who signed the consent for a minor to marry, though Marvin knew full well it had to be done.) Even without the monkey suit, sweat beaded on his forehead, and he felt his shirt getting soggy under his gray suit coat while he and Christine watched Rebecca do the hesitation step to Here Comes the Bride three-quarters of the way down the aisle, until the pressure of Christine's arm against his got his feet moving. In the front row, Cora's chin was quivering above the lace collar of a new dusty-rose dress. He could actually see the tiny movements and the starting tears as he and Christine approached the front of the church, and Marvin fought down nausea born of nerves and frustration to look strong for his wife. In his peripheral vision, he saw Alex, but avoided eye contact. The little he saw didn't help. Alex looked self-important as high noon, silently declaring himself the winner.

"Who gives this woman to be married to this man?" The reverend, whose name Marvin never could remember, looked at him. He felt rather than saw Christine turn her white-veiled head to look at him to make sure he gave the right answer.

"Her mother and I do," he answered as he'd been coached at the rehearsal, the words catching on the hump of his Adam's apple, buttoned flat in a shirt that was too small around the neck. Christine exhaled and a little smile made its way to the front.

"This is my wedding day," Christine had written in her diary at seven that morning. "I will never be the same again."

"SHE'S LIKE A STRANGER," Cora said to Jolene, who'd been in the pew behind her and Marvin during the ceremony and had stayed at her elbow during the reception except when it was time to serve the buffet. "I feel like I don't even know her. I knocked myself stupid with this wedding, she knows that, and you'd think it would count for something, but she just shuts me out. For *him.* I think he can't stand for her to have anything to do with us. He told her we were trying to poison her mind against him." Cora had been ruminating on it for weeks while she and Jolene

made table decorations and altered Rebecca's mauve maid of
honor dress as well as Christine's gown, which was too tight
around the middle a quick three and a half weeks after it was
bought.

"She'll be back," Jolene said. "She'll be back."

"I don't know. From your lips to God's ears. I *feel* like I've
lost her. Everything's a secret anymore. Except what ought to
be..." Cora, with her head, gestured toward Christine, dancing
to some kind of rock-music record with Alex. "Are people
talking?"

"Not that I've heard. You know, she looks beautiful. That
neckline shows off her face just right."

Cora softened and smiled a small acknowledgment. "Yes,"
she said. "You're particularly nice not to use the word *glowing*,"
she whispered. Then, in a normal tone, added, "I just want her
to be happy, you know."

"Hush," Jolene said. "I know that and she does, too. And look
how good our room looks." Accordion-foldout wedding bells
hung from the stark ceiling, white on white like Christine's
gown and veil, though Cora and Jolene had tried to soften the
edginess with white crepe paper, artfully draped. The table decorations had been labored over, silk ivy and little pink silk
flowers along with white candles, and silver glitter scattered
beneath the centerpieces on the church's linens. Every now and
then the glitter winked like so many eyes in the candlelight.
Outside, the sun was hardly beginning to set, but daylight was
apparent only through the glass doors so the effect still worked
just as Cora and Jolene planned.

Twenty feet away, near the doors, Marvin and Jolene's stocky
husband stood off to one side of the fellowship hall, surveying
the scene. Each held a glass of beer. "What's the matter with
him?" Bob said. "Not religious, is he? What?" He nodded
toward Alex who at that moment lit a cigarette, took a long drag,
and then pinched it between his thumb and first two fingers
pointing the ashy tip behind him. "Looks like a punk," he added.
His face twitched with a small gesture of disgust, though he tried
to hide it by keeping his face turned toward Alex instead of

Marvin. Bob was a kind man, usually tolerant enough to wait for people to show their hands directly to him, but the war ignited him like a flare. His son put it on the line every day while others trumped up ailments and excuses, pulling them out of their sleeves like so many cards.

"He *is* a punk," Marvin said. "Don't know what's the matter with him, but it's not religion. He's no CO, even though I think he'd like to try that one on the Board. Someone must have tipped him that Samuels sees right through that CO crap. If you're not a Quaker or 4F, you're 1A. I'd like to have a talk with his father, only the SOB is six feet under, drank himself to death most likely. Thing that eats me is how all this 'let's get married' stuff heats up after he gets his lottery number, and Christine don't notice a connection. Thinks they're in love." He spread the last word over three sarcastic seconds.

"Not the way we did things, huh?" Bob was getting a hold on himself, folding anger inside his cotton affability. His plaid sports coat had been contributing to his sense of suffocation, and he'd just shucked it.

"Not exactly. I dunno if it would bother me so much if I thought he really felt for her."

"No sign of it?"

"Not to my eyes. Christine maybe has Cora a little bamboozled. I can't tell 'cause there's been so much commotion about… all this." Marvin gestured with his arm to indicate the spectrum of a wedding reception.

"Room looks good," Bob said.

"Yeah. That's Cora and Jolene's doing. Nice of Jo to help her so much."

Bob chuckled and took a drink of his beer. "Somethin' to be said for having a son. Guess you got yourself one now, too, though." He mock-punched Marvin's upper arm. Marvin, however, didn't smile at the joke.

"It's not just the draft, though I can see where that'd be more than enough for *you*. What really bothers me is that he's… unformed, not that he knows it. Maybe he could be a man. I don't know. I don't know what his intentions are, not that good intentions prevent bad results. You know…?" Marvin trailed off in embarrassment. "Nothin' good gonna come out of this one, I'm afraid," he said.

THAT NIGHT, ALEX AND Christine stayed in the bridal suite of the Lewellen Hotel in Richmont, a wedding gift from Bob and Jolene. It wasn't a suite, really, just a big room on the fifth floor. The bathroom had an oversize tub though, and a walk-in closet and a coffeemaker. Although neither of them drank coffee, it made Christine feel grown-up to be in a room where someone thought she did. She was dying for someone to call her Mrs. O'Gara. A bud of hope that Alex would carry her over the threshold hadn't bloomed, but then she thought maybe he was saving it for tomorrow when they moved into their own apartment.

Alex switched on the television set and flopped on the double bed. "Cool," he said. "Dodgers and Reds, bottom of the fifth… thought I was gonna miss the whole thing."

"Honey," Christine said, trying out the married-sounding endearment, "we're not watching TV tonight, are we? I mean, it's our…"

"Nag, nag, nag," Alex said, but she could see he was teasing. "Is this what it's going to be like, now that you got the ball and chain locked on?"

"Well, I just thought we could have supper downstairs while we're still all dressed up, and then…" Christine tried flirtatious wheedling, obviously coy, but it worked on Alex.

"I'm still stuffed," he interrupted. "Let me just see the end of this. We'll get that nice supper you want and then…I'll show you what's the point of being married."

Christine sighed and sank into an upholstered chair, smoothing the skirt of her pink going-away outfit beneath her. A corsage of pink roses and baby's breath was pinned above her heart and she left it there, patiently folding her hands to wait for her husband. Maybe he'd be hungry when the game was over and her late-supper-in-the-dining-room idea would be lovely. She had an idea of what men were like, and considered it her place to learn to give in, even though it infuriated her when her mother gave her father his way.

While she was washing her hair that morning, the thought had come to her—what if they're right? Her parents had made no secret of their disapproval, staining Christine's daydreams like grape juice on a tablecloth. She'd drawn determination out of the necessity that she not weaken under their pressure. But this morning Cora had smiled and given her a hug when she'd come down for breakfast and chirped her pleasure that it was a pretty day after all.

What have I done? Christine had asked silently, letting the shower pound on her upturned face. Then, she'd reassured herself—if it doesn't work out, I can get a divorce. But that thought clanged an alarm in her mind. If I'm thinking about a divorce on my wedding day… No. This is what I want. This is just nerves. He is much better than they see. I'm not wrong about him.

She'd rinsed her hair with deliberate attention and busied herself with setting it on rollers, and doing her nails in a pale-pink frost while the dryer hose anchored her in one place, rushing an ocean in her ears, an ocean to drown words that might have held hands and pulled one another to shore.

When she stood in the back of the church and saw that Alex and the minister were in place, she wanted to feel something other than floaty and disembodied. *This is the happiest day of my life,* she told herself, and then the notion that the happiest day of her life was already half gone made her feel sick. The piece of life women dream over like the slice of wedding cake young girls put under their pillows: it was almost over for her. Christine watched Rebecca's slender hips sway like a metronome as she got farther away and away down the aisle, and she felt something like envy. When her father didn't step up to the line to begin their slow march to Christine's new life, she knew the fight wasn't over after all, and the pressure she applied to his arm brought her back around to her insistent joy. But then again, when the minister asked, "Who gives this woman to be married to this man," she had a last thought that her father might put an end to it. She turned her head, cumbersome beneath the gauzy veil, to say, "All right, you win, stop the wedding now," but her father did not look back at her.

"Her mother and I do," he said, and his voice sounded broken and too loud. She decided again that she was happy.

"This was the happiest day of my life," she wrote that night after Alex was asleep. "I didn't even think about the baby today. It was just for Alex and me, perfect and romantic. At dinner in the dining room, he thanked me for believing in him."

THEY HAD A TINY efficiency apartment in Darrville, a second floor walk-up above a storefront law office, from which Christine could walk to work at Thriftway. She'd only signed up for one class her first semester at the Richmont branch of Indiana University because she didn't know how she'd get there if Alex wasn't home. She could tell he wasn't all that keen on sitting home himself while she took his car to school and she certainly didn't want to ask her parents. Alex had promised to get a job and was out all day every day looking, but hadn't found anything he wanted to do yet. "Do you think I want to bag groceries?" she'd challenged him once. "Do you think I *like* it?"

Alex had acted chastened, put his head down and said, "No. Okay."

"Okay *what?*"

"Okay, get me an application. From the store. I was just trying to do like guys are supposed to, y'know? Make something of myself for you. Do better." His shoulders went up and down in a resigned shrug.

Christine had jumped in. "Oh, honey, I know. It's okay. We're getting by. I do want you to have a chance to make it." And when she said it, it was what she really felt, even though the next day when she came home and found Alex watching *Truth or Consequences* on television, she'd been angry again. Yellowed venetian blinds sliced daylight through their apartment like an onion, but she couldn't pay for curtains as well as rent, groceries and gas out of her check even with her ten-cent-an-hour merit raise. Sometimes she even thought she smelled the onion, and her eyes stung. If the blinds could have been raised, it might have helped, but they were broken—like the deadbolt lock and the handle off the medicine cabinet. An orange-and-brown flowered couch from the Goodwill store looked terrible on the braided rag rug, too, not cozy as she'd hoped, and sterling silver chafing dishes and candlesticks were plain silly set on the too-small slab of counter alongside the chipped porcelain sink.

"What's for dinner?" Alex asked nightly, and before the end of September she was sick of answering tuna casserole or baloney sandwiches. Every now and then, Cora would slip Christine a twenty; she tried to put a little aside for extras like candles or a picture for the wall, but it usually went to replenishing supplies like sugar and toilet paper and noodles.

He says he wants me to be proud of him, and I don't want to take away his pride, but sometimes I just wish he'd get any old job. What's going to happen when I have to stop working? I can't say anything, because he already says I nag him, but the only reason I can still wear my black pants is that I don't button them underneath my apron at work. I'm so tired all the time, I know it's a drag for him. I don't have anything in common with my friends anymore, or even with Alex, since he's not the one throwing up or dragging himself off the couch to go bag stupid groceries. Their lives are mostly the same as when we were in high school—their mothers even still do their laundry and cook dinner for them—except I'm the one who does it for Alex. But I know I'm doing the right thing and I love Alex so much. All this is so hard on him, too.

Christine hid the notebook under her sweaters, tucked in cardboard boxes in the back of the closet that had no pole to hang anything on.

twelve

"LOOK, BOY, THAT'S the way it is, signed and sealed by the Commander In Chief in this here Executive Order. It's the amended Military Selective Service act of 1971. Look it up yourself. Been no paternity deferments for months, see, so it don't matter if you do have kids. Your draft board already done tol' you, you is *goin'*."

Alex sat on the other side of a uniformed man's desk in a closet-sized room with puke-green paint peeling from the ceiling and upper walls. Sgt. H. Jackson, his breastplate said. The dark-skinned Negro cackled like a hardwood fire at Alex's rage. He leaned back in his swivel chair and slowly lit a cigarette and exhaled languidly.

Alex's induction notice lay face-up on the desk between them, a crinkled piece of paper swathed in dirty window light.

"Man, you can't do this. I got the birth certificates right here. You can't do this." Alex was shouting at this man lording it over him.

"What choo complainin' 'bout? You *got* thirty days." Then, narrowing his eyes and leaning forward, Sergeant Jackson, who'd had nothing to do with the induction notice, who, indeed, had been posted in Maryland until the day before yesterday, decided to take the credit. He exaggerated his speech into caricature Southern black again, the way he liked to tweak the redneck white boys. "Jes' watch me do it. You think you ain't gonna take no orders from no black muther, huh, boy? Think again, because you *is,* boy, you is. I picked you out the pile myself."

Trapped. Like a damn animal, Alex thought. The rusty muffler that hung too low beneath his car banged on the street when his right front tire careened in and out of an unfilled pothole. The sound and thump were a sudden jar, and then he heard the airy roar that told him a hole had opened in the pipe. *"Goddamn,"* he shouted, hunkered over the steering wheel and then he was crying and bearing down on the accelerator in rage. He rocked back and forth on the hinge of his elbows, as if trying to shake some sense into the steering wheel. He felt as he had on his wedding day when he saw Christine approach on her father's arm, a beautiful specter displacing the air he was trying to breathe.

He'd been paralyzed for months and months, terrified at the notion of little men in black pajamas shooting at him while fire rained from the sky. He'd been the worst hunter in his family, the butt of his uncle's jokes about his terrible aim and squeamishness. Never once had he bagged his own deer, and the time he'd shot a squirrel, he'd thrown up in the bushes when his father made him skin it. "Considering jungle law," they'd laughed, "it's a damn good thing for Alex here the squirrels ain't got themselves no guns, or he'd be one dead boy." The first year he had his own permit, the year before his father died, his uncle and his father drew straws to see which one of them would get to use it. They carried pints of Wild Turkey inside their hunting vests, and pulled them out for long, deep swigs. Alex had reddened when the game warden congratulated him by saying, "Now you're a man."

It was bizarre: mocked and punished by his father for his failures as an O'Gara, Christine's father hated him most for being an O'Gara. Alex got that much.

The whole business with Chris had seemed his salvation at first. She made him feel something good. More than the sex, too. Something was soft. Once they were married and the baby came he'd be exempt. It should have worked. The baby part terrified him, but Chris said he didn't have to be anything like his own father, that she'd teach him. The whole thing should have worked. Even though from the beginning there were glitches, the exemption was worth whatever he had to put up with. Chris had bitched at him for months until he'd got a job, but he had, after all, hadn't he? He'd hoped he could find something that would show her father he'd been wrong. Being a stock boy at the hardware store wasn't his idea of a good time, but it was better than the army.

He'd nearly fainted when Chris's water broke, and she began pacing and gasping the length of the living room. It was almost a month too early, and when he tried to call Cora she wasn't home. He'd not wanted to be in the labor room, but a nurse pushed him and said, "Hold her hand, be sweet to her." Chris was covered in a clammy sweat. Then, suddenly, there was a frantic jostle of activity and she was wheeled into the delivery room. He stood outside until he heard her wailing, and then he had to leave. It was like he had been accidentally cast in the wrong part in the wrong play; he had no idea what his lines were supposed to be or how to act them, overcome with a surreal sense of impossibility. His life was always someplace he couldn't catch up to.

That same aura of unreality he'd known on the hunts, at his wedding and for weeks after the unpredicted birth of twins, overcame him again as he careened his car away from the draft board office toward the apartment where Chris was surrounded by diapers and bibs and spit-up cloths while at least one of the girls was always crying. Cora, of course, practically lived there, and her disdain for him was palpable. She shooed him aside when he was near one of the babies. He was afraid of himself. His hands were too big. Certainly they were too clumsy, too jumpy, too O'Gara.

In late winter's dirty midafternoon glare now, he pulled his car to the curb in front of the apartment. He was supposed to be at work, but he was too shaky to go. Maybe he shouldn't even tell Chris. Maybe he should just take off for Canada. No, he'd have to get some of his stuff. Maybe Chris could get some money from her parents and she and the babies go with him.

They were a family, even if Cora didn't see that. Fear rose like flood water and he sloshed and waded against the current. Soon it would rise to his chest and then cover his mouth and nose while his eyes watched him drown.

Alex turned the ignition off and sat in the car while the chill outside dissipated the small heat that had circulated. His feet were leaden and his hands immobile. He couldn't leave with nothing, but he couldn't stay; he couldn't tell Chris, but he needed her help. Perfectly split like an apple through his core, he sat and trembled.

A sharp rap on the driver's-side window startled him conscious. The early darkness had almost fully overtaken daylight though part of the horizon was vivid above a remaining slice of great red sun. Alex jumped, his heart pounding too fast, unevenly, against the wall of his chest as though answering the knock on the glass. Chris's face gathered shape and gradations of light in front of him when he turned.

"What the hell are you doing?" she shouted, trying to open the car door. It was locked. Her face looked too white. Long strands of brown hair had pulled loose from the rubber band in back. Maybe she hadn't even combed it today. Maybe she hadn't washed it in three or four days. She wore no coat. The top of her jeans still wouldn't button.

Alex shook his head no.

"What do you mean, no? Open the door. Come in. What's wrong? I left the babies alone, I've got to get back to them. You got the formula, didn't you? Come in, I need help. What's the matter?" She rattled off questions he didn't answer. She must have seen him from the window.

Somehow, Alex made his body move. He'd just go upstairs and tell her before he left, he thought. She could come when he'd got them a place. The babies, too. They'd be bigger then, not so flimsy. The slam of the car door behind him made him think of a gunshot.

Upstairs, in the apartment, Alexis and Tina were screaming in the one crib, swaddled tightly as Cora had taught Chris and tried to show him, at opposite ends of the mattress. Formula and baby powder and dirty diapers mingled into one choking scent. The bulb in the lamp was still burned out, so Chris had put on the harsh overhead light.

"Here, walk around with them," Chris said, thrusting first one baby and then the other into each of his arms in turn. "They're hungry. I'll put water in their bottles and go get the stuff." She wasn't even bothering to blow up at him, though she'd obviously figured out that he'd forgotten to buy the formula. That must have been why she was looking out of the window for him. The din was too great. Alex's head hurt, but he moved his feet and tried to jiggle his arms a little to soothe the babies. When they weren't crying they were sweet and fragile as little rosebuds and he felt something tender that made him want to cry. But their crying—this raw need and demand—terrified him.

Chris slapped two bottles on the scratched coffee table. "I'll be right back," she said.

"Wait, I'll go," Alex managed to say.

"No. It's your turn to listen to them scream. You're the one who had the car and forgot the formula." She pulled on an old jacket and took Alex's keys off the table. "I can't take it any more. I've got to get out of here for a few minutes. But don't worry. I won't do you like you did me. I'll show up with the milk." The apartment door banged behind her. She hadn't even remembered to ask what had happened at the draft board.

Awkwardly, Alex laid one of the babies down. He'd not been alone with them before and wasn't sure which one he put on the couch and which he was holding. Cora and Chris said they were easy to tell apart by their faces, but Alex had to rely on what they were wearing after Chris told him each time which was which and then he'd call them by whatever color they were wearing. Now one was in a yellow terrycloth sleeper and the other in a pink one. They were old enough that their navy eyes made tears when they cried, and both their faces were wet with tears and mucus. Alex tried to jiggle the arm cradling the enraged pink baby while pushing a nipple toward the yellow one on the couch with his freed-up hand. "Come on, take it," he said. "Good baby, good girl."

The yellow baby rooted and clamped her mouth hard on the nipple, dragging deeply. A moment later she spat it out in a violent burst of coughing. When she tried to take a lung full of air to scream, a terrible noise came out of her, a gurgling, choking sound. Alex put the other baby, who was red-faced with rage and wailing ceaselessly on the couch next to her sister, and picked up the choking one. "Quit it! Please stop!" He shouted, without realizing he was shouting until his own voice was louder than the screaming.

The baby needed air. Alex hit her on the back and held her up so he could see her face, now like a bruised peach, darkening toward purple. "Oh, my God," he moaned, and shook her. "Stop!" he shouted. "Help! Please! Somebody help!" Alex's ears roared with blood. "Breathe. Goddamn, somebody help me. Please!" He ran to the apartment door and threw it open. "Help!" He tried to make her breathe, but her head only flopped forward and then back, like an untended puppet. "Help!" Alex shouted. "Please!" The frantic cries of the other baby drew him back inside—he knew not to leave her alone—and the draft from the hallway or his spinning movements or the unfair chaos of the world banged the door shut as if on cue.

He and his yellow baby daughter shook together. No one came to help. The pink twin screamed on until her screaming mixed with her father's, and her father's screaming and shaking mixed with the noise of the street, and her mother came home with the milk.

Thirteen

CHRISTINE DROPPED THE BAG she was carrying before she reached the top of the stairs. The howling from the apartment was tormented, and she thought her husband and babies were burning to death. The door was locked and she banged on it, adding her own cries to the din, until she finally took the time to separate the right key and get it open. She threw too much of her weight onto the door—a shoulder, as her hand turned the knob—and fell blindly into the glare of the light inside like a rock into water.

Alex held Tina at arm's length, his hands like a hinge at her middle while her legs swung. Her head was loose, back against her neck and Christine sucked in the breath to yell, "Hold her head!" when Alex shook her and her head flopped forward.

"Breathe," he sobbed, "Come on, you're all right, good baby, it's just water, breathe, *please* breathe," and his sobbing was hoarse, an agony. Christine screamed then and after a paralyzed second, bolted to get one hand behind the baby's furry black head, the other beneath Alex's, on the baby's bottom, and drew her daughter toward her own chest. For a moment, it looked as though Alex might not let go, but then he did, though an inchoate stream of begging came from him. The other baby lay on her back on the couch, arms and legs flailing, her face blotchy red, shiny with tears and her screams like a high descant over Alex's.

Christine dropped to her knees and put Tina on the floor. "Call an ambulance," she shouted. "Go, go—call for help." She frantically tried to remember anything she'd seen on television about mouth-to-mouth and awkwardly tried to cover the baby's mouth and nose with her mouth. Then she pulled back, to pry a thumb into Tina's mouth, to open it, and tried again, long brown hair draping around their heads. Alex stood rooted to the rug. Christine came up for air and saw that the sense of motion she'd had was from her other daughter. "Put her on the floor and go call!" She could feel a cold draft from the open apartment door. "Go, go, go," she screamed. "See if there's anyone downstairs, or the pay phone!" The lawyer downstairs just locked up and left a sign on the door when he had to be in court during the afternoons. He could only afford a morning secretary so far.

Alex looked wildly around himself, found the baby on the couch but couldn't bring himself to touch her. "Keys," he sobbed. That was the image Chris would have of him later, his hands clawing air, his whole being out of control, eyes like wild marbles, desperate and despairing at once.

Christine fished in her coat pocket and threw them, an overhand motion while she gulped air and tried to cover the baby's mouth with her own again. They bounced off Alex's chest and clattered onto the floor where the rag rug stopped and cold linoleum started. Chris's head was back down over Tina's and she didn't grasp what happened next. Alex hesitated perhaps two seconds.

"I gotta go…sorry…*sorry,*" he rasped, the words squeezing themselves out as if Alex were being choked by enormous invisible hands. She felt rather than saw Alex bend to pick up the keys. Then the floor shook a little beneath her knees with the pounding of Alex's steps running for the door.

Chris scrambled on her knees over to Alexis, moved her onto the floor, all the while screaming *"Tina, Tina, Tina,"* and then threw herself back to the still bundle. She was not about to give up. If she gave up she'd have to think about what had happened, she'd have to ask how it happened. She labored on, leaving Tina for only a couple of seconds; once to run to the dinette table for the pacifier she'd left lying there and again to snatch cotton blankets to shield both her babies from the draft. As she ran back to Alexis, whose shrieks had subsided until she realized there was no milk in the nipple her mother had thrust into her mouth, Christine partially closed the apartment door to reduce the cold, yet still signal the emergency people to get right in. Other than that, she remained huddled over Tina, reaching to pat Alexis briefly, but puffing air ineptly into Tina's tiny mouth and nose. Tears ran down her face; she wiped them off with her coat sleeve and kept breathing.

She had no idea how long it was until the wail of a siren sounded far away, mixing with Alexis's cries. Alexis was hiccuping and sucking in long shuddering breaths while she wound herself up to scream again. Christine ran to the window to check for the flashing lights. A police car pulled up in front of the apartment while the ambulance was still a half-block away. Chris opened the window and yelled, "It's my baby, up here, my baby," and two officers slammed white cruiser doors scanning the building for the apartment entrance. "Around the side," she sobbed, a thin streak of hysteria mixing into the sob. "My baby!"

Seconds later, heavy steps pounded up the stairs and the apartment door was bounced violently against its backstop. The first police officer ran to the wrong baby, the crying one.

"No," Christine screamed. "There!"

The officer bent over Tina. "Blue baby," he shouted to the one behind him. "Blue baby!" The second officer ran across the room to shout out of the open apartment window down to the street, where the ambulance siren blared and the sound of slamming doors repeated. "Oxygen! Blue baby!"

Christine felt as if she were hovering over the scene like a ghost, watching first one man in blue, then another, then two more in orange jumpsuits cluster around Tina while she dissolved, knees buckling toward Alexis's ragged wails. Outside the open door the grocery bag with its four cans of formula had been kicked aside by one of the medics. Christine tried to tell someone to get it for her, for the crying baby, but she could not shape a single word.

THE CLANGING AND screaming had stopped, at least immediately around Christine, as she sat, boneless, protected by an invisible force field of shock. A nurse had taken Alexis off somewhere and was giving her a bottle. "Your mother is on her way." The nurse spoke just above a whisper and patted her hand.

"Can you tell us what happened?" A man in a lab coat stood in front of Chris, but she shook her head numbly.

"She's in shock," someone explained to Cora, who flew in the emergency room door wearing no coat and the soft-soled slippers she padded around in.

"What happened?" Cora said, enfolding Christine in her arms, but speaking to the nurse. Her heart thudded up against Christine over and over.

"I'm so sorry for your loss," the nurse, who wasn't too young and had bottle-blond hair, said quietly. "We think the baby choked first, and then—" she motioned with her head to indicate Christine "—she tried too hard to get her breathing. She must have panicked. But the baby's color indicates she'd stopped breathing before she died."

Christine took in what the nurse said to her mother, and for the first time the idea began to take shape in her mind that Alex wasn't on his way to the hospital or waiting at their apartment for her to bring their daughters home.

The death certificate indicated accidental choking. It wasn't that the doctor didn't know the baby had been shaken; he did. He also knew that the baby had first choked, and he knew what panic does to a mother's hands, especially a new, young, utterly inexperienced mother. He also knew that the dead baby had a twin sister who needed her mother, especially since there was no father in evidence. He was a compassionate man who talked gently to Christine about emergency procedures for choking, and about the delicacy of a baby's spine, the potential effects of jarring, and he was absolutely confident he had done the right thing when he went home that night and kissed his own toddler girl who squirmed to escape her father's too-tight embrace.

Much later—when Alexis was asleep in a carriage next to Christine's bed in her parents' house and Christine, still silent, was staring at the ceiling in the numb darkness—she remembered about the induction notice and considered that Alex might be gone for good.

Fourteen

THE CASKET WAS TINY and white with white satin lining, like a jewel box. Christine could have held it in her two arms and wanted to. Given Alex's disappearance and the hushed questions flying around rooms like trapped birds, she had only felt up to a graveside service.

At the cemetery, Cora had been holding Alexis, but when Marvin wouldn't let Christine pick up the coffin—made her get off her knees from the cold dirt—she'd taken Alexis back and clung to her. The sky was a pewter ladle about to spill, though the wind wasn't as bad as it had been when they'd first gotten out of the car and it had cut through them as if it intended to wound. Still-bare old trees arched over them.

The last time she'd held Tina was at the hospital. She'd sat, Cora at her side until she asked her mother to leave her alone a few minutes, stroking Tina's cheek and curling the little fingers around the perch of her own forefinger. Then a chaplain had come in and asked if the baby had been baptized, and if she wanted last rites.

"No," Christine whispered, transfixed with guilt, and there was something in her hesitant refusal that made the priest press on, though gently.

"Are you Catholic?" the priest asked.

"Not…really. Could…would you baptize her? It's not too late, is it?"

The priest hesitated, then said, "No, of course not," and produced a white cloth and a silver vial of water he said was holy. Cora managed to hold her tongue about a Catholic baptism; anything Christine wanted was all right by her.

Cora's own grief hadn't taken its black shape yet, though there'd not yet been a day of either baby's life that Cora hadn't fed or diapered or rocked her. She was consumed by the yawning emptiness she felt in her daughter, desperate to alleviate it, yearning to mother her own suffering child.

"My baby." Christine broke into sobs just once when the minister said "Suffer the little children to come unto me. Theirs is the kingdom," leaning with Alexis against Cora, who braced herself with one foot wide and behind the other, planted in the slushy gray remains of the last snow to absorb her daughter's weight. When Christine said *my baby,* Cora's heart twisted in her chest and she looked at the stone marker over her stillborn son. Alexis waved a mittened hand aimlessly and let out a random sound. Marvin stood erect and separate, moving only to swipe his raw, bare hand beneath his nose, runny because of his tears. Jolene and Bob were planted, solemn and staunch as oak trees behind them, and minding Rebecca. A couple of cousins and Marvin's sister had wanted to come, but Cora knew that Christine couldn't handle any more, and had asked them not to. Jolene and Bob were there for Cora and Marvin, of course, but even more because their son, Paul, had died in South Vietnam in November. They and Christine lived in a foreign, isolated place now, one inhabited by people who have lost children and can only bear each other's company, for whom they reserve anything they might be able to truly say.

It would be a couple of months before the stone could be set. Cora and Marvin had quietly paid for it, the casket and the cemetery plot by their stillborn boy's grave, without particularly discussing that part of it with Christine, who had recently enough been living with her parents that she didn't automatically recognize such matters didn't take care of themselves. At the end of the service, the casket was left discreetly beside the covered hole and Cora pressed Christine, who was wearing Cora's too-large gray wool coat since her high-school jacket seemed inappropriate, toward their car.

"No, I have to stay. I can't just leave her," Christine said.

"Honey, you have to. It's over now, it's time to go home." Cora looked at Marvin for support. He stepped closer.

"Time to go," he said, without his usual sternness.

"No, I can't." Christine's eyes filled again. Alexis squirmed and whimpered, a pink cloud with a fringe of black down sticking out of the front of her knit cap.

Jolene came up behind Cora. "Let her stay," she said. "You and Marvin take the baby and Bob back to your house. I'll be here and bring Christine whenever she feels ready." Jolene, in the black she'd worn to Paul's funeral, still had grief's rings around her eyes.

"I should be with…" Cora began.

"No. That's good. You take Alexis, Mom," Christine interrupted and it was the most she'd said since she'd left the hospital two and a half days ago. The little cluster was inching uncertainly toward the drive where they'd left their cars to walk to the gravesite, in the same cemetery where Cora's parents were buried, but not near them.

Cora felt this was all wrong, that she needed to take care of Christine, but the baby was thrust into her arms.

"Take care of her for me," Christine said, and it chilled Cora, as if Christine weren't coming back, but Jolene nodded and answered for her. "She will, you know that. You go on, now," she added to Cora.

When the family and minister had left, Jolene said, simply, "Now where do you need to be? We could sit there and watch over her, if that's close enough." She pointed to a large grave two plots away, one that had a flat ledge on which the marker itself stood. "That would let us sit and not be on the wet ground."

"All right."

Jolene put her arm around Christine's back and walked her the fifteen feet. After they were sitting, thigh to thigh on the narrow edge, knees up and coats pulled around their ankles, Jolene knew not to say anything. She kept her arm around Christine's back, that was all.

Christine cried a while, Jolene handing her tissues when

Christine's breath was so jagged it seemed she couldn't get air, and then just sat and looked over at the casket. A cemetery truck pulled up, but Jolene waved the two men away back into the chill daylight of the road. Then she went back to the silent place, deep and wide, where she and Christine mourned.

"I have to go to Alexis," Christine said, finally. She had been shivering and her lips were chapped and colorless. Her long brown hair lay limp and resigned on her shoulders.

"All right, dear," was all Jolene said. They picked their way across muddy, partly melted tracks to Jolene's car, numb-footed, soul-seared after the gaping wounds through which their lives had bled out and disappeared.

BACK AT CORA'S HOUSE, Christine kicked off her wet shoes and headed straight upstairs to where Alexis slept in the carriage in Christine's room, the one that had just cooled from her leaving. She picked the baby up, violating every mother's rule about not waking a sleeping baby, and held her close to her chest. Then she went downstairs to the living room, to the rocking chair Marvin had refinished, and nestled Alexis face-down on her chest to sleep in her mother's arms. She fit the hollow of her cheek over the curve of the baby's head, and breathed in her powdery, living scent.

Later, when one of her arms had gone to sleep, Christine called for Cora to help her. "Take Lexie for me," she said, "my arm's gone dead." From that time on, Alexis was Lexie, and even Marvin only had to be corrected once, privately, by Cora. Everyone took to it with unnamed relief.

Although it was never actually discussed and decided, Christine stayed on at her parents' house. Cora or Marvin made regular trips to the apartment to pick up needed clothing or baby supplies until it became apparent that more had been moved to their house than remained in the apartment, and Marvin talked to the lawyer downstairs about breaking the lease without penalty, given the circumstances. Christine moved in a daze, and although Cora wanted to talk with her about Alex—about getting a divorce, really—Christine seemed incapable of any decision, even whether to start Lexie on strained peas or carrots first, so Cora didn't broach the subject.

In July, when Lexie was five months and had her second tooth, a belly laugh, and it was evident her eyes were going to stay quite blue, Christine answered the phone one afternoon while Cora was in the basement folding laundry.

"Chris? It's me…I'm…so sorry."

"You know there's a warrant out on you?"

"The baby?" Alex's voice was a hoarse choke.

"The draft."

"Oh. I knew that." There was a long pause. "I didn't mean to…" he began, but Christine cut him off. She looked out the kitchen window.

"I know you didn't. Anyway, they think I was with her. Are you in…"

"Toronto." The phone crackled as if to confirm the distance.

"I figured."

"Do you wanna come?"

Christine hesitated. The phone cord was taut as she pulled on it with her free hand. "You have no idea," she hissed. "How can you ask me that? There's a baby here, remember? There were two of them. How do you think I'm surviving? How did you know where to call me? It's not like you even tried. Did you even know Tina was gone?" She was surprised to hear the sudden rage her answer was rooted in, exposed tentacles wrapped around her soul.

"I knew," he said. "I called Jake."

"For money, I guess."

"To find out."

Christine thought she could imagine him—in dirty blue jeans and T-shirt, a couple of days unshaven, skinny, long-haired and broke. "So why now? Are you thinking I'll send you money or what?"

"No," he said. "I just…look, I just wanted to say how sorry… God, Chris, I didn't mean for it to turn out like this."

"Well, it did, didn't it?" She wanted him to feel bad. No, she wanted him to suffer, and knew, even as she was wanting it, that she'd gone so far alone he might never join her. "Never mind. Just…don't call me again. For all I know the phone is tapped."

Christine swung around abruptly, her hair a swirling brown trail following her head, and hung up the phone. She walked over to the back door and looked out of the screen. A light-gray dove, no mate in sight, waddled on the grass pecking here and there, and Christine whispered to it, "Tina, Tina, my sweet Tina." The dove's wings ruffled out then, and it disappeared in the elm tree, blending like an oversized leaf.

Christine thought she heard Lexie, a small sound in the house, and turned to go check. Cora was standing on the top basement step, the door ajar. Christine had no idea how long she'd been there, what she might have heard. In a rush of words then, Christine said, "I've been thinking, I'd like to put a bird feeder outside. Do you think Dad would care?"

Cora looked at her hard. "I think that'd be fine," she said. "I don't see why not."

DAYS BUMPED UNEVENLY as rocks for the first long year, then pebbles for months more before beginning to sift more evenly, like dust, into a routine that was familiar if not happy. Cora kept Lexie while Christine bagged groceries, took classes at the Richmont branch of Indiana University. Marvin paid the bills while Christine banked her checks, whatever she didn't spend on diapers and books, for the day when she and Lexie could be in their own place. She decided to become an X-ray technician because she could do it in two more years if she could carry four classes each term, and it seemed like she'd be able to get a job almost anytime, anywhere. Sometimes she thought Lexie might be confused about who was her mother, and Christine—though at first she'd given over the job with relief—realized she had to give Lexie a clear answer about that. "I'm her mother," she said one evening to Cora when Cora told her that it was past when Lexie should have been in bed. "I need time with her. She can sleep when I'm not here."

Cora noted the resolution in Christine's voice.

Fifteen

IT WAS LEXIE, REALLY, who started Christine back into keeping a journal. Lexie, with her delicious fat little legs seeming to lengthen daily while her hair grew into skimpy dark ponytails that thickened and sprouted bows, and her mouthful of even square teeth, shaping around words, then sentences, then paragraphs. Sometimes Christine wrote about Tina, the unsettling sense she had occasionally that Lexie was looking for her, too, in the same ache of regret and memory. Lexie grew and spilled things and crayoned on walls while Tina remained a six-week-old fragility. It became hard for Christine to imagine them as twins, Lexie was so different now from the only way her sister had shape in their mother's mind.

She'd begun by recording the facts: "twenty-three pounds, four teeth, scrunching herself up onto her knees," first copying the notes Cora had taken for her at each doctor's appointment into the notebook she'd started after the girls were born, though those days had been so frantic that what she'd scribbled was hardly intelligible. Then she had to include the little stories of how and where she'd taken her first steps, spoken her first words, parroted the alphabet at eighteen months. She needed to describe how Lexie's eyebrows had seemed to just appear overnight in neat arches as dark as her hair, and how her eyes were the startling light blue of the sky at nine in the morning.

When she was having one of her bad days, she wrote about it. She didn't want to talk to Cora about Alex or Tina. Alex was

a sore spot with everyone, though in different ways, and Christine still worried that her mother might have notions if she'd
overheard Christine's end of the conversation the one time
Alex had called. Maybe Christine had forgiven Alex—some
days she thought she had, or could—but there was no question
that her parents never would. She hoped all they thought was
that he'd run to Canada because of the draft, which was the
community's common (and correct) deduction. Whenever
Christine watched the war news on television, she thought of
Alex. She couldn't see him in Vietnam any better than he'd
seen himself, though her father insisted that *it would have
made a man out of a scared boy, that's what war does,* and
Christine wrote it again in her journal on days she hated Alex
with a fierceness that spread like liquid into every cranny of
her mind. Alexander the Goddamn Great, she called him, including Marvin's expletive. For the most part, though, life
went on without explicit reference to the world beyond Early
Sun and the university branch at Richmont, with forays into
Darrville for groceries and hardware, and without reference to
those outside the circle of family.

Of course Christine thought about Alex. Day in and day out
she took care of his remaining daughter, and whether she wanted
to or not, saw small mirrors of Alex all the time. Memory and
conjecture, fact and fantasy went into her notebooks. She wrote
poems for Lexie, too, recopying them in ink scrupulously
centered on their own pages. Some she showed to Cora, who
said they were wonderful, and asked how she'd been able to
rhyme so perfectly, and not just simple words.

When peace came—at least on paper—to Southeast Asia,
Christine thought Alex might come back. Lexie was still in
diapers, and Christine actually wrote "Maybe it isn't too late."
Then, of course, she realized the peace made no difference at
all; Alex would be arrested and tried and sent to jail if he did
come back. Marvin even checked it out, to reassure himself that
Alexander the Goddamn Great would still have to pay his dues.

"Don't be ridiculous," Cora said. "The dues he owes would
take a hundred men working the rest of their lives to pay off."

"I'll be satisfied to see the son-of-a-bitch rot in jail," Marvin answered, his coffee cup clattering in its saucer. It was Christine's late night at school, Rebecca was at a soccer game, and they were finishing supper as best they could with Lexie flinging squashed peas at them from her high chair. "And pay a major hunk of child support. How long do they have to be separated for her to get a divorce on grounds of desertion?"

"She's already past that. It was a year," Cora reminded him.

"So has she done anything?" Marvin always consulted Cora to find out what was going on, even though usually someone had already told him. Having Cora just saved him having to remember anything. He raised his chin to look at her through his glasses, which had slid down his nose again.

Cora sighed deeply and put some little pieces of chicken, most of which would land on the kitchen floor, onto Lexie's tray. "Nothing that I know of."

"Did you change your hair?" Marvin noticed it was longer, or something.

"I parted it on the side to cover the gray on top."

"Now who's being ridiculous? You're not gray."

"Says the bald man," Cora laughed. "Forty-nine. Did you ever think you'd be feeding a baby at forty-nine?"

"I'm not," Marvin pointed out in his factual way. "And I'm not bald, either," he said, running his hand over the thin mix of brown and gray retreating from his forehead.

"You're right about not feeding her, anyway. I'd think you'd be ashamed."

"The person who should be ashamed is..."

"Leave it alone, will you? Christine isn't after revenge."

"Well, a little revenge would be good for my soul, I believe."

"Your soul's not the point here. And it wouldn't, anyway."

"You be the Christian charity lady if you want. I'm not that good." The words were all Marvin, but Cora heard beyond them to the respect he was giving her in his way.

She smiled, her eyes leaving her granddaughter only long enough to lock onto his and say, "You're a good man. A good man," she repeated softly to Lexie when she turned back to her with a spoonful of applesauce, which Lexie promptly blew into a waterfall ending in a pool of giggles when Cora jumped back.

WHEN LEXIE WAS JUST over three, Christine graduated from her program in medical technology. It took her an extra summer and semester because of her job at Thriftway, and because the rubber band attaching her to Lexie would stretch only so far and long, then Christine simply had to spend extra time with her. It bothered Cora to see Christine's life so closed that she never went out, only worked, went to school and hurried home to Lexie.

Chris got a job as an X-ray technician in an orthopedic surgeon's office in Richmont; she'd done well in her clinical placement, the X-rays she took almost never needed to be repeated, and she had a kind touch with the patients. To Cora, her daughter looked the same as always: when she was home, her long hair down and without any makeup, she could have passed for sixteen. When she began working, though, her hair up in a French twist, lipstick filling in her thin mouth, and her dark brows balanced by enough eye makeup to bring out the blue of her eyes: well, she was a lovely woman, and Cora couldn't imagine that no one asked her out. She surmised Christine was turning down invitations. "You know I don't mind if you go out at night, don't you, dear? You could even put Lexie to bed yourself and then go out. You must have some friends you'd like to spend some time with." Cora said it more than once.

"I'm just fine, Mom," she'd get as an answer, which told her nothing at all.

Although it had been implicitly presumed Christine would move out on her own when she could afford to, no one mentioned it when she got her job. Although the daily commute to Richmont took up way too much time, there was a certain security, maybe for all of them, that came with being together. Rebecca had graduated and gone to Bloomington to the University where she lived in a dormitory, and perhaps Cora clung to Christine and Lexie more than she would have were Rebecca still there. Besides, inertia is a powerful force; they had a life, such as it was, a life. And when Marvin had his first heart attack, a mild one that put them all on notice, Cora felt much more secure with Christine there, even though she immediately signed up for a CPR class herself, afraid Marvin's heart would go haywire again when Chris was at work. Marvin was walking outside for ten minutes at a time within two weeks, back to work within two months, though the doctor wouldn't sign for him to return to full duty, which included climbing utility poles. "You're fifty-two years old, the doctor said to him. "Pushing fifty-three. Lighten up. Let the young ones do it."

"Got a family to support?" Marvin asked, buttoning his flannel shirt back up.

"Sure."

"So do I," Marvin said, as if his point were made, proven and underlined.

That evening, when Lexie climbed into Marvin's lap in the battered wingback chair in the living room where he read the evening paper, Christine told her to stop squirming on Grandpa. Marvin hugged the little girl and said, "Let her be. I'm fine, and I don't want anyone fussing over me." His face still lacked color, and his hair seemed translucent to Christine, his body almost ephemeral after the weight he'd lost.

"I'm glad you're home, Grandpa. I missed you," Lexie said into his neck. He tickled her and she squealed and wiggled more loudly than she would have if her mother hadn't just told her not to and been overridden by her grandfather. "Look, I made this heart for you, 'cause yours got hurt." She bounced onto the floor and ran to the coffee table. Her dark pigtails had yellow bows on them and they swung back and forth. A small, deft hand snatched up a colored cutout heart and ran it back to Marvin. "A new one. Don't mess it up, all right?"

"Yes, ma'am. I'll keep it safe. I love you, baby," he said, and it actually scared Chris to hear him say it.

WHEN PRESIDENT CARTER signed the Amnesty Proclamation the next year, it occurred to Christine that Alex might come back to Indiana. The square, tawny-green fields of soy, corn and wheat, the enormous stands of trees here and there, the narrow back roads around Early Sun and Darrville were, after all, his home. He was a stranger to her now, though; she'd been granted a divorce on grounds of desertion and although the circle of her life was small, it was closed and complete. She was getting by and Lexie was thriving.

Lexie began kindergarten. Cora went to Jolene's for coffee and company.

"Still nothing," Cora said, sitting at Jolene's kitchen table while Jolene took a sheet of scones out of the oven. Jolene's kitchen had been redone in avocado green that year, even the stove and refrigerator, and Cora never could decide if she liked it or not. "I guess it's going to be all right after all. She doesn't mention him, so maybe she's not even thinking about it."

"I wouldn't bet on that one," Jolene said, putting a green place mat and one of her old blue plates in front of Cora. "My dishes don't match anything anymore. I'm watching for a sale at Sears."

"I shouldn't eat this, you know. I'm trying to avoid the blimp look for the upcoming social season." As she spoke, Cora smiled broadly and bit off a piece of scone. Her glasses slid down as she tried to see over them to look at her friend. "Umm, raisins. Can I take one of these to Christine? She loves them. Did I tell you she gave Marvin another bird feeder for his birthday? Actually, this one's some platform type. I think the birds might put her in mind of the baby, you know, not that she talks about it. But she started with the bird thing after Tina. Anyway, she had him put it next to the lilac bush."

"Good thing Marvin tolerates birds."

"Of course, I'd like her to stay right where she is," Cora said out of the blue, as if Jolene had asked if Christine was ever going to move out, which she hadn't. "What would she do with Lexie afternoons, anyway? I worry about her, you know? It just seems like she's too old for her years. Everything revolves around Lexie. Don't you think she should have some kind of a social life?"

Jolene shrugged. "I've been thinking the same thing about

you, actually. Lexie's still at an age where most mothers would make their life around her. It's you doin' it that worries me. Besides, it takes something out of you forever to lose a child, I can tell you that much."

When she and Marvin were in bed that night, Cora whispered, "Maybe you and I should go away for a weekend sometime…get away by ourselves."

"Hmm." Cora couldn't tell whether it was a question or an agreement. A moment later Marvin's breathing had downshifted into the faint snore that meant sleep had overtaken him. She lay on her back thinking about what Jolene had said, about what it might be she'd like to do if her time were her own. Nothing came to her. The sheets she'd dried on the clothesline outside were crisp and smelled of early-autumn sun and air and she tried to remember what it was she'd loved as a young woman.

Two bedrooms away, Christine's light still threw an amber circle around her bedside table and one side of the book she was writing in. "Of course it's too late," she wrote. "It's probably been too late since the day he left. Get on with it, Christine."

SHE DIDN'T TELL HER parents she was looking for a place of her own until she'd found it and signed the lease. A clean, two-bedroom apartment on the first floor of the new three-story apartment complex, it was in Darrville—which meant she still had a half-hour drive to and from work, but lived close enough to her parents for Cora to take care of Lexie after school. When she told Cora, she put it as a fait accompli so her mother couldn't talk her out of it.

"But where will Lexie play?" Cora fussed. "It's all concrete over there."

"She can ride the bus here, Mom, after school. I checked on it. Then I'll pick her up after work and take her home."

"But *this* is her home, and yours."

Christine looked around the living room, where Lexie had dumped a wooden puzzle on the carpet, and left a box of crayons open on the chair. Lexie's small-toothed grin and high pigtails with crimson bows shone at her from the end table across the room. "It's not fair to you and Dad. Lexie's not your responsibility, she's mine. I'm through school, I've got a job, it's time for me to get going. I can't stay here forever. I wasn't ready before, but now I am."

"But, honey…"

Christine leaned toward the other cushion of the couch where Cora sat, picked up her mother's hand and held it between her two smaller ones. Her body was more slender than Cora's had ever been, as delicately boned and quietly colored as one of the wrens at the feeders. Lexie would be built like her mother, Cora thought, and pushed aside the notion that her granddaughter's stature had anything to do with Alex.

"Mom, try to understand. The longer I wait the harder it will be. Can't you see that? I have to stop waiting around. Everything seemed so unfinished, even after the divorce. It just seems like this is what I have to do to finish. I'm not explaining it very well…"

"No, I do understand. It's right. Whatever will let you put it…him…behind you, and maybe find someone else, I'm for it." It was much easier for Cora to say that than to give voice to the shadowy part of herself that once in a while thought of not raising children anymore.

Christine smiled and gave an exaggerated sigh. "Thanks," she said simply. "Now what furniture can I have?"

HOUSEKEEPING SCALED TO HERSELF and Lexie involved more than she'd anticipated. Christine bought beds, a couch, and a kitchen table and chairs, and furnished the rest sparsely with pieces her parents gave or loaned her. She made a bookcase out of boards and cinder blocks for the living room, and painted it blue in a shade to match her couch. On the wall above the couch, she hung a print of hawks crossing an enormous sky.

She taught herself to macramé from a library book with detailed pictures, and made two hangers for the plants she started from her mother's cuttings—only ivy and philodendron, but they took root, delighting her with their willingness. Magazines

and coasters appeared on the coffee table; plant by knickknack, the sterile white-walled rooms took on the aura of a home. And when Jeff Tricca, another med tech graduate stopped by Dr. Simcoe's office to say hi and to ask her out for the third time, she didn't say no. In fact, she had her hair cut a couple of inches and tried it in a flip. She filed and polished her nails before the date, and bought Crystal Mauve lipstick, a livelier shade.

sixteen

"LIFE GOES ON," Cora said. She and Marvin and Jolene and Bob were playing canasta at a card table set up in the living room. "We couldn't do this here very well when Lexie was running around, I admit."

"I know you miss her," Jolene said.

"I do, but what's important is that we all get on with it. You know Chris's seen that Jeff Tricca several times, and she even got a babysitter for Lexie that weekend he and I had the flu." She gestured at Marvin with her head.

"I still say that was food poisoning," Marvin grumbled, looking disgusted with the cards he held, or the dinner that had preceded the illness, Cora couldn't tell which.

"That is so insulting, Marvin Laster. There was nothing in that dinner that could have been spoiled. Do you think I'm not careful?"

They were adjusting. There was a little more bickering than they'd had the attention for when Christine and Lexie were there, but they were adjusting. They'd gone to the movies several times, and Marvin had gone to the grocery store with Cora once, just to keep her company on a Saturday morning. Cora was fixing recipes that Lexie wouldn't eat, and Marvin could leave a screwdriver on the kitchen table without someone having a conniption because it wasn't safe for Lexie.

MARVIN WASN'T EVEN home when Alex showed up. It was Cora who answered the front door, expecting the mailman with something too large for the mailbox.

"Oh," was all she could get out.

"Chris here?" Alex said, just as casual as daylight, as if he'd been there yesterday. In the driveway, a blue pickup truck sagged with age.

Alex had changed, but not in a way that had improved him any, as far as Cora could see. The ordinary magic of his handsome face was obscured by black shoulder-length hair falling from a middle part and a pack of cigarettes plumped the pocket of his plaid flannel shirt. The denim jacket he wore over it couldn't have begun to keep him warm, even in the January thaw that had begun the last week. Only his eyes—deep brown, lash-scalloped—were the same.

"No," Cora began, casting for what she should say or do.

"Where is she?"

"I...don't know." An obvious lie.

"Where is she?"

Cora, panicked, started to shut the door.

Alex stuck his foot in the way. He was wearing heavy, battered boots, and when Cora looked down, she recognized they were steel-toed, like Marvin's work boots. The weight of the door wasn't going to bother Alex a bit.

"You get out of here before I call the police," she said, frightened and enraged.

"I'm askin' you where my wife is. And my little girl. Please."

"She's not your wife."

"Look, I just wanna talk to her. What d'ya mean, she's not my wife?"

"What I said. You'll have to leave. I'll call the police..." she repeated through the inches he was keeping the door open.

"Call 'em. I'm not breakin' the law. Please. I just wanna talk to Chris."

"And I'm telling you, she doesn't want anything to do with you." Cora thought of how far Christine had come, how hard she'd worked, how she'd finally settled into some kind of peace with the past. "Trust me—nobody wants you here."

Alex used the side of his wrist and arm to push against the door Cora had wedged against his foot. "I got a right to see my daughter. She here? That why you won't let me in?"

Cora snapped a little, like a runner bean, not loudly, but raggedly around the center string. She heard the little pop inside. "You have no rights here," she said angrily. Her heart was pounding in her ears. "How dare you come around here talking about rights? You had your last rights a long time ago when you did what you did."

"What're you talking about? It was an accident."

"It was an accident that you ran off and left?" Cora was incredulous. "An accident?"

The two stood, each suddenly confused, staring at each other for long seconds. Cora was the one who put it together quickly enough, the echo of a phone conversation overheard soon after Tina had died clicking into place in a way that let her know she was right. She sucked in a breath and skipped over what she'd not known for sure like a flat stone skimming water. "You hear me, and hear me good. We'll get the law after you for what you did. Christine'll testify. Only thing saved you until now was being gone. Get yourself gone again, and we won't put you in jail for murder."

Alex was stunned, she could see it. The aggressive insistence slid off his face and he looked smaller. "Please, Mrs. Laster. Can't you give me a chance?"

"I'm giving you a chance. I'm giving you thirty seconds to be off this property. Then I'm going to get Marvin's gun and shoot you and say you trespassed and threatened me. And then Christine will go to the police with the whole story. Now get out, and don't ever come back. Not ever." Cora had never spoken to anyone like this; she hardly knew the words belonged to her.

Alex withdrew his boot from the door and took a step backward. "Tell Christine I'm sorry for everything. I'm sorry." Then he turned and left. The truck coughed several times in the driveway, and she was afraid he wasn't going to be able to get it going, but he did and gunned it through its intention to quit again. She watched his wheels kick up the cinders on the road from the last snow, standing and listening until she couldn't hear the sound from the giving-up muffler any longer. Then Cora shut and locked the front door.

By the time Lexie's school bus let her off after her half-day of kindergarten, the roar that reverberated through Cora's head and chest was subsiding. She hugged the girl long and hard before helping her out of her snowsuit, and then hugged her again. She had already decided there was no need to tell anyone what had happened. Maybe she had managed to take care of it. Christine didn't need to deal with this, and neither did Marvin. Cora's heart was stronger than his.

CHRISTINE BROUGHT JEFF Tricca to dinner at her parents' house twice, and dated him for a good three months. When she started to try some activities that included Lexie, though, the six-year-old was whiney and difficult and refused an ice-cream cone Jeff bought her right after she'd begged her mother for one. It wasn't another month before Christine broke it off, after an outing to the movies was disastrous, Lexie making Christine take her to the ladies' room seven times during the movie, and overturning the bucket of popcorn in Jeff's lap.

"I can't see it, Mom," she said over the phone. "Lexie hates him. Or she hates sharing me, or whatever. But if it's not going to work with Lexie, there's no point in my seeing him at all, because she's got to come first."

"How about just dating him so you have something for yourself, you know? Just don't include Lexie. You know we'll keep her."

"Jeff wants to get serious, Mom. It's not going to work."

Next, Christine dated a pharmaceutical company representative. Briefly. He was divorced with two children, and not particularly interested in picking up another one. Then there was Ron Meier with whom Christine went so far as to have lusty sex and genuine friendship, but Christine could see he tolerated Lexie because she had an early bedtime. It was always something. Cora said as much to Christine one evening.

"It's okay, Mom, don't worry. I'm fine by myself. Please

don't think I have to get married again. I used to really want to be married, you know, and maybe have more children, but maybe I don't anymore. It's not just them, the guys—I don't have much trust in men, and that causes problems, too. This is delicious—of course, I was completely famished. Did Lex eat it? Sometimes she's picky about onions."

Cora had already given Lexie supper and saved a plate in the oven for Christine, who'd stayed late at work. Lexie and Marvin were playing checkers in the living room, so Cora and Christine were alone in the kitchen while Christine forked pork chops, potatoes and onions into her mouth. She'd been keeping her voice chipper, but her face had the tired pallor of her white uniform. Christine O'Gara, her nametag said, and Cora wondered for the thousandth time why she'd kept the O'Gara name.

"I picked out the onions for her. I just worry about you. It's not still…you don't still think about…Alex, do you?" The subject had been taboo for so long it was difficult to say his name. The three of them had, by unspoken consensus, avoided the subject of what had come between them and what had brought them back together.

Christine started to shake her head. Hair fell across her cheek and a few strands stuck on her lips. She'd had her unremarkable brown color highlighted, and it flattered her. She swiped at her face, missing a couple of times, then got it out of her mouth. "I'm going to cut my hair short, I really am." Then she paused, and went back to Cora's question, but this time she didn't start with no. She thought a minute. "Maybe. I don't think so. I was such a kid, you know? I still can't believe he never came back. I know you and Dad never could see what I did in him but he, well, he couldn't hurt *animals*, Mom, and I think you and I scared him some about the babies. He *wanted* to be good. At least once, he did. I can't believe I was so wrong. I hope you and Dad don't say anything about him to Lexie."

"I don't. And I don't think your father does. But you're going to have to soon enough. You always made excuses for him." Cora abruptly stood and started to clear the table. The overhead light

threw shadows into the hollows of her eyes and the wrinkles around them. Her mouth, thin like Christine's, was pursed, and for a moment her daughter saw her clearly, differently.

"Mom and Dad still hate him, and they only know half the story," Christine wrote that night. "I told Mom I couldn't believe he hadn't come back or called me or something after the amnesty, but I guess he hasn't got a use for me now. Still, I wonder if we'd have made it—there were a hundred strikes against us, that's for sure. And I do wonder what happened to him, and what to tell Lexie. So far, she hasn't asked much, I guess because I'm all she's ever known, but I don't expect that'll last forever. I guess nothing does."

1988

seventeen

LEXIE'S EYES BURNED. She'd stayed up four nights in a row, first checking dates and putting her mother's notebooks and journals in chronological order, and then reading them to piece together oblique references. Sometimes Christine hadn't written exactly what she meant, although other times she had exercised no caution at all, as if she'd been in an undertow of anguish.

Each night, Lexie had made a show of saying she was tired from schoolwork and going to bed early. Cora wouldn't go to bed until Lexie had, not wanting to leave her granddaughter alone with shadowy memories, and not wanting to be alone with her own.

When Lexie could hear her grandmother settle into a light snore like a distant, idling motor, she crept across the hall to her mother's old room and shut the door behind her. She put on one of Christine's sweaters, inhaling the faint scent of her mother—the late-March nights were still cold in the unheated room—covered herself with the blanket folded at the foot of the bed, and picked up where she'd left off. At first, she'd read hurriedly, skimming even, but when she realized that sometimes an entry pointed ahead or back or even at someone, she went back and read slowly, deliberately, as if it were a school assignment and she'd have to explain what the author meant. Except for the parts in which her mother had written about Lexie, upset with or disappointed in or angry at or worrying about her: the guilt of those passages was too much, and she sped up to a skim.

Each night, Lexie propped the picture of Christine in her coffin against the bedside lamp on the table to her left while, leaning back into her mother's pillow, she sat on her mother's bed reading her mother's words. The second night, she sneaked a candle out of Cora's hutch and lit it beside the picture like a small shrine. "I need to get you a flower, too. You protected him, didn't you? But you thought he'd come back," she whispered to the picture.

Lexie reread whole notebooks the fourth night. "You kept him out of it because you didn't know he was going to run away. That's it, isn't it? And then it was too late to get revenge. It's not too late for me, though. I'll do it for you, Mom. You said you'd help me, and now I know." Saying it, she felt better, as if she had a purpose, a direction, a reason. And a way to make it up to her mother for the times she'd hurt her, maybe for all the people who'd hurt her. Beside, there was no way the judge was going to make her live with a baby-killer.

"GRANDMA, CAN WE TALK about something?"

Cora nearly swallowed her teeth. Lexie spent most of her time shrinking from talk with Cora, ducking from room to room as if she were in a great hurry, and claiming fatigue at an absurdly early hour, though Cora was grateful to be able to retire early herself.

"Of course, honey. What is it? Come, sit by me." Cora was in her bedroom folding laundry on her bed. A large, framed picture of Christine was on her dresser next to one of Rebecca taken when she'd graduated from the University.

"How did Tina die?"

"Well, she, uh, choked on something. What did your Mom tell you?"

"That she choked."

"Well, then, that was right."

"Who was with her?"

"Your mother said *she* was." Cora set aside the pieces that needed ironing and turned slightly, toward the pile of clean towels. She lifted the first, a brief curtain between her and Lexie.

But Lexie saw through it. "Do *you* think so?"

"Why, honey?"

"Because it wasn't my Mom. It was Alex, and Mom protected him."

"Goodness. What makes you think that?" Cora, having reached and used the same conclusion herself nine-and-a-half years earlier but never once worded it, was shocked to have it thrown up against the wall like spaghetti to see whether it would stick. She stopped folding towels and sank onto the bedspread next to Lexie.

"I've read Mom's diaries." Lexie's tone was defensive, and her light eyes looked ethereal in the fading afternoon light. "You told me they were mine."

Cora was taken aback. "Of course they're yours. I just thought you'd wait, until you were older. Does it actually say that in a diary? About Alex, I mean. Did Rebecca…?"

"She didn't get to read much—remember, I freaked when people were touching Mom's stuff?"

"Yes," Cora recalled the scene. "I remember. Does it say that in her diary?" she repeated. She wanted to question the girl about when she'd read this—Cora knew the diaries were boxed up in the closet in Christine's room—but she thought better of it.

"Not exactly. But you can figure it out. She says something about how it was her fault, 'cause she knew better than to shake a baby that was coughing, but she had to get formula, and she was going to lose her mind if she didn't get out for a few minutes. Something like that. It's like she wrote it, but not exactly."

Cora wondered whether she should tell Lexie that Alex had come back when she was six and she herself had run him off— that she'd picked up the same idea and used it like a loaded gun.

"Did I look like Tina, Grandma?"

"Exactly, honey."

"It could have been me."

"I guess that's true." Cora sighed, sticking out her lower lip so the exhalation would be directed upward and raise the hair on her forehead like a bird ruffling its feathers. "I guess that's true."

"Grandma, we have to do something. I mean, we can tell the judge, can't we?"

"I brought it up to the lawyer, already."

"You knew? Did Mom tell you? Why didn't you get him for it? Is that why Grandpa called him Alexander the Goddamn Great?"

"Lexie, I don't want you using that language. Grandpa was wrong to say that, but it was because of the war. See, Grandpa was drafted in the Second World War, you knew that, right? And he thought Alex was wrong not to serve his country in Vietnam."

Lexie didn't know one war from another. "But you knew? About Tina?"

"No, honey. I might have guessed once, but remember, the doctor said accidental choking. Your mother's the only one who could have said otherwise."

"But how can you stand it? I mean, it's not right, he just can leave Mom, and…"

"I *can't* stand it, honey, but I don't have a choice, do I?" Cora answered it simply, in the same way she'd admonished herself after the first glimmer of plausibility.

"Well, I do. I can tell the judge."

"We can talk to the lawyer about it. I did already, but…she's the one who told me the person who could have testified about it was your mother." Cora tried to pick her way through a mine-field of possible words, to find the ones that wouldn't detonate.

"You asked her?" Lexie was outraged. The light in the room was waning, but Cora could still see the anger on her face.

"Well, I can't prove anything, of course."

"Why didn't you tell me?"

"That was your mother's place, not mine."

Lexie stood up, sputtering, her hands in the air. "I think it's my business. I'm the one they want to send to live with a murderer." Cora could see Lexie's back reflected in the mirror over her dresser, behind Lexie, and even from that angle the small-boned girl seemed to loom fiercely over Cora.

"I don't think it was like that, Lex."

"How do you know?"

Cora shook her head and shrugged slightly. She felt every minute of her age. She put her head down into one wrinkled hand for a moment, then looked back up at her granddaughter. "I really don't know," she said. "And I did hate him, I admit that. It's not like I'm not fighting for you, Lex." A slightly apologetic tone shaded the last. Cora reached out and turned on her bedside lamp. "Look how late it's getting. I need to go start us some supper." She used the edge of the table to pull herself stiffly to her feet on the second try. "Hand me my cane, will you? This dampness—"

"I want to talk to the lawyer myself," Lexie said, not stirring toward the cane propped against Cora's nightstand. She couldn't believe Cora could possibly have explained it adequately or the lawyer would already have put a stop to all this.

"Well, you know, there's that investigation by social services. They're coming next week, Brenda said."

"And I want to talk to whoever that is." Lexie was going into a stubborn mode, reminiscent of Christine at the same age. Before she'd died, Chris confided to Cora that Lexie was getting cheeky and defiant, that they fought, but Cora hadn't seen it herself.

"I imagine we can."

"I'm doing it. My mother will help me." Now Lexie's hands were on her hips, and Cora saw how the blade of defiance might cut. And what did she mean by *my mother will help me?* It was unnerving.

"All right. Will you come give me a hand with supper?"

"I'm not hungry right now."

"Please, honey, you've got to eat."

"No. I've got to get him for what he did."

THE SOCIAL WORKER CAME to do a home investigation on Tuesday of the next week. Cora, who'd known of the appointment since the previous Thursday, had scoured every inch of the house. Jolene had come over to help her wash, iron and rehang the curtains. There wasn't enough time to get the drapes cleaned, but windows were washed and a toothbrush used on the grouting in the bathrooms. For once, Cora insisted that every bit of clothing be picked up and put away in Lexie's room and made her take down the rock-star poster on which the singer's hips were thrust forward and he wore an earring. She herself removed the green cloth Lexie had draped over the lampshade that made the light eerie as a séance.

Cora baked fresh gingerbread and had a pot of coffee all set up to drip fifteen minutes before the appointment. Lexie picked out what Cora should wear as meticulously as if she were a designer—a white blouse and black skirt with stockings and her good black shoes, not the slacks and sneakers she usually wore. "And no apron, Grandma. These earrings."

"We'll take a tray into the living room, I thought," Cora said. "And use the good china, don't you think?"

Lexie, whom she'd picked up from school an hour early, had changed into a green plaid skirt and green sweater. Cora could tell she was nervous and tried to hide her own nerves, frayed to the breaking point.

"I'm going to tell her," Lexie said. "Did you clean the bathroom mirror?"

"No, would you take care of that?" said Cora, who had, indeed, spit-polished the bathroom mirror and every other glass surface, as well as the wooden and plastic ones. "I guess I should wish this person came every week, huh?"

"This isn't something to joke about."

"No, honey, I'm sorry. I guess not.

At five after three the doorbell rang. A woman who looked barely older than Lexie stood on the porch. She wore a trench coat and carried a briefcase. Brown hair waved past her shoulders. "Mrs. Laster?" she said. "I'm Heather Guard and I'm here for the home investigation regarding your granddaughter."

"The report's in," Brenda told Cora two weeks later.

Cora twisted the phone cord around one hand and leaned against the wall for support. "What does it say?"

"Well, she'd checked the death records and found that Tina died of accidental choking, so she gave no credence to what Lexie told her."

"But Lexie showed her Christine's journal. It does sort of say…"

"*Sort of* are the operative words there. Apparently, she discussed it with Alex and he stuck to his story. Says he wants a relationship with his daughter, and I guess he's got a decent job and a place with a room for her."

Cora closed her eyes and swayed slightly. She'd just returned from taking Lexie to school and had been heating up some coffee for herself when the phone rang. She pulled out a kitchen chair and sat down to take in the rest of the news. "So, we lost?"

"Well, not technically. We don't lose until the judge rules, but I have to tell you, it's very rare that a judge would go against the findings of social service, especially when he's already disposed toward the natural parent."

"Do we go back to court?"

"Unless we settle, and just agree that Lexie goes."

"No, we can't do that."

"I can argue for visitation for you," Brenda said.

"Yes…definitely. But I…we want to keep fighting this."

"I don't want to run your bill up, Mrs. Laster. It may be a losing issue."

"Just keep fighting."

"Well, then, we'll want a hearing date and we'll call witnesses. Of course, Mr. O'Gara will call the investigator."

"She…did she have something bad to say about me, about Lexie being here?"

"No. She just raises the issue of your age."

Cora straightened her shoulders as much as she was able. She'd gone without her cane when the investigator came, trying to make herself look more spry, and had Lexie put a little lipstick and blush on her so she'd look younger. Not enough, apparently, though now that she thought about it, Lexie had used a dollop of mascara, too. "It's not a problem," she said.

"I know, Mrs. Laster, and I'm sorry. See, from their point of view, it's…"

"But they don't know him." Cora was clenching the phone. The arthritis in her hand hurt.

"I know. I know. We'll do the best we can, all right? I'll file a motion for a full hearing. We can get that much, at least. Lexie can ask to speak for herself, too. Often the court will consider the expressed preference of a child over twelve."

"There's no question about what she wants."

"I know that. I do know that."

Cora asked Brenda to call her as soon as she knew the hearing date. Outside her back door, the air had softened and a pale chartreuse halo was emerging around the naked branches. The undergrowth around the edges of the yard was leafing out. And Christine's birds: the early returnees were already evident in the early mornings when their chirping preceded dawn and penetrated Cora's sleep. The damn black grackles had taken over the feeders for the past month, chasing off the cardinals. The dark underbelly of spring.

Without really deciding to, Cora made her way upstairs and down the hall to Christine's old room. She opened the door, and went to the bureau where she knew Lexie kept Christine's picture. She took it out, the last picture ever taken of her daughter, and sank onto the bed. "What can I do?" she whispered. She felt her eyes fill and put her head down into her hands.

Green Jell-O. The thought came to her and Cora decided she was losing her grip if she couldn't even pray without her mind wandering to some ridiculous unrelated notion. It made her feel like a well gone dry, and more than a little hopeless.

eighteen

THE INVESTIGATOR LADY didn't believe me, even though when I talked to her she said she did. She had already talked to Alex, and he snowed her. He's such a liar. She said she'd talk to him again, about what happened to Tina, and how he dumped Mom and me, and how nobody ever heard from him again. If that isn't showing you're guilty, I don't know what is. But obviously he just lied some more and gave her this crap about how he wants me and never had a chance. He probably wants to kill me like he did Tina. She doesn't decide anyway, the judge does, and Brenda the lawyer says I can talk to him probably. She's going to tell him I want to.

Aunt Rebecca and Jill came over for dinner tonight. Rebecca was a complete idiot, blabbering about how maybe she could talk to Alex and see if he's sincere. I think Grandma wanted Rebecca here to help her calm me down when she told me about the report, but Rebecca told Grandma, "It *is* a lot for you to have a teenager." I know she wants me gone. Jill and I came upstairs right after dinner. I'm not as close to Jill as I used to be, but she understood how I felt about what her mother said, and she told me she was sorry her mother is a moron. I wish my hair were blond like Jill's, even if her face does look like an apple. Sometimes I hope Rebecca's cancer comes back. Why couldn't God have the sister die who already had something wrong with her instead of my mother? When Rebecca and Jill are here it just makes me miss Mom more anyway, not feel "family support" (gag) like Grandma says they mean it to. I try not to think about it.

And Grandma made pork chops again, with potatoes and carrots and green Jell-O. That made me feel awful, because Grandma never makes Jell-O and I think she must have made it so I'd feel close to Mom. Like everything else, it worked the opposite. And green was her favorite. She used to put a frozen strawberry on top, with whipped cream out of a can, but Grandma must not have had any. Besides, I've told her I want to be a vegetarian. She says that's not good for me. Sure. Me eating pork chops is good for pigs or something.

We're supposed to go to court again, and Grandma told me I could probably talk to the judge if I wanted to, but we could just not fight it anymore if I didn't want to. She said she didn't want to put me through it unless I was sure I was strong enough. Like I'm some fragile flower in a greenhouse and she's worried about taking me outside. Well, Grandma, outside is where I live now, and I'm still alive. That was when I got so mad, and Rebecca said maybe Jill should show me upstairs, like I was a little kid being sent to her room. What does that mean, *show me upstairs?* I live here. I'm the one who can show someone the upstairs, not Jill. That made me mad at Rebecca, too, and I said something about her under my breath, but I don't think she heard me. Jill *was* nice about her mother having cotton balls for brains. But I don't get how Grandma can even say that to me. I'm not going to Alex's, case closed. She knows that, and she says she wants me. I guess it's possible that she doesn't really. A lot of things are possible that I never thought could be.

I think Tim wants to break up with me. We fight all the time and he blames it on me. He says I'm moody, which I'm not. Grandma says I'm too demanding, that men don't like being tied by apron strings. She says I shouldn't fuss when he wants to do something with other guys, but I'm afraid they'll talk him into going out with another girl. I'm so lonely. Nobody else's mother is dead, or if she is it was a long, long time ago and they don't remember. I hardly talk to Emily anymore. I used to think she was so pretty, but her hair looks awful because it sticks up behind her stupid headband from ratting it. She made friends with Tara Rusco who is a cheerleader, and Emily thinks she can be popular if she rats her hair and hangs out with cheerleaders. She'll never be a cheerleader because when she jumps her boobs flop up and down even with a bra on. Everybody can see it. They're like watermelons. Jill called me last night and asked me if I wanted to go to the movies on Saturday. I told her I would. I don't care what we see. She can pick.

I've gotten really far behind in Spanish. I don't get what the teacher is saying, because she's started talking only in Spanish, no English. My mind used to wander around the room when she explained things in English, but now it actually leaves the building. My grades have gone down, and Grandma is worried it will count against us in court. If she'd told me sooner, I'd have tried harder.

Grandma tries to act like she's not nervous about court, but I know she is. I'm only worried about the judge giving me a chance. He has to, I know it.

After Grandma went to bed tonight, I came into Mom's room. I got the picture out and the candle, which I lit. First I laid one of Mom's scarves around them on the dresser, the blue one she liked because it brought out her eyes, but then I had another idea. I got my old teddy bear that Mom said she bought me after Tina died so I wouldn't be lonesome in the crib and set him on the dresser like a guard. Then I put Mom's scarf on him, the candle next to it, and I propped her picture against his foot. Then I put her pearls around his neck. Grandma said I could wear them tomorrow. I don't know why she had to tell me that, they're supposed to be mine now, anyway, not that I've worn them yet. Then I sprayed a little lilac cologne, and it smelled the way Mom used to. It was making me feel better and I just said, "I wonder what else?" sort of out loud, but really just like you do when you're talking to yourself and in my mind somebody said, *The birds. Feed the birds.*

Why would I think about that now?

nineteen

ON COURT DAY, THE WAY Lexie carried her head put Cora in mind of an Egyptian queen, at least the picture-book profiles she'd seen. On the drive, Lexie had responded in monosyllables to Cora's chatter, containing herself in a separate, elegant vase, while Cora spilled worries and thoughts all over both of them. Cora was a talkative woman living with an adolescent girl who wanted to be left alone—unless, of course, *she* didn't. Cora had hoped that uniting against Alex would bring her and Lexie as close as they'd been before Christine died, that Lexie would confide in her as she had when she was small and their lives had been a braided hearth rug all laid out, every strand showing.

It appeared it was not to be. Whatever the reason, the only time Lexie had really let her close was the night they'd lain in the dark and briefly cried together. Cora remembered the way Lexie's shoulder blades felt: each like the bones of a bird's folded wing.

But it was daylight now, and Lexie's back and shoulders were high and straight and she touched nothing as they made their way up the courthouse stairs. Cora, the hump of her back weighing on her wide hips, held the chilly wrought-iron rail with one hand and leaned on her cane with the other.

Brenda spotted them before their eyes had adjusted to the dim wattage of the lobby hall. "Upstairs," she said apologetically. "Another flight. We're in a full hearing room. It's just a formality."

The wooden steps each dipped in the middle from the weight

of thousands of grievances. Cora was breathing heavily by the time they reached the landing and stopped to rest a moment. She patted the front of her hair back into place and took a tissue from her pocket to wipe her forehead, where a cool sheen of exertion had appeared. At least they'd dressed right, she thought. Or, more accurately, Lexie had dressed them right; for Cora, a navy pantsuit and shoes with a white shell top and a print silk scarf of Christine's artfully tied, and more makeup. "To make you look...healthy," she'd said. For herself, she'd gone with a gray skirt and a white dressy blouse, and, "to make me look older," stockings and low-heeled black pumps that had been Christine's and were a size too big. Not an outfit Lexie would normally consider, but she had an eye for visual effects. Cora made no comment about the eye makeup Lexie wore, nor that she'd put her hair in a bun, which did make her look older, though certainly not as if she were on the edge of turning eighteen and an unnecessary subject for the court to be taking up at all, which was Lexie's hope.

The hearing room Brenda led them to was daunting. There was, this time, an actual raised bench with an American flag flanking one side and a witness chair on the other. Before the bench were two wooden tables with chairs facing the judge's spot and a polished brass rail. Behind the rail, rows of chairs were empty. In spite of the high windows, the room was dark and imposing.

"Are there going to be other people here?" Lexie asked. "Who are those chairs for?" She'd not imagined an audience, though now that she thought of it, of course courtrooms on TV shows were always packed.

"I don't anticipate the other side will be calling witnesses, no. It's just that full hearings are held in a courtroom like this because, well, sometimes custody hearings turn into a circus." ·

"What?" Cora said, uneasy.

"Oh, one side calls in a neighbor who swears he saw the child's father kicking their German shepherd, and then his lawyer calls in the mailman who swears it was actually the child's mother doing the kicking only it wasn't kicking, she was having sexual relations with the dog and both of them seemed to be enjoying it. You get used to stuff like that."

Cora muffled a small shock at the reference while a smile flickered on Lexie's face, exactly the reaction Brenda hoped to elicit from the girl.

"Is Alex going to say something bad about me?"

"Nobody in their right mind has anything bad to say about you, Mrs. Laster, but we'll see. Basically, what we're up against is the investigator's report. It doesn't find him certifiably evil or permanently demented, which is pretty much what it takes to terminate parental rights." Brenda had to try once more to prepare them. Nothing in this case had gone the way she'd planned. Even this morning, she'd stuck a fingernail through her last pair of stockings and had had to rush into her standby tan suit and stop at the drugstore for another pair on her way to the courthouse, which had left her feeling thrown together and short on time to review her preparation.

A tall, tanned man walked into the courtroom and deposited his black leather briefcase on the table. He had an aquiline nose, gray-streaked hair with a deep wave, and groomed fingernails that had been buffed like a prize antique car. "Good day, Ms. Dunlap," he said, and Cora thought she detected a fingerprint of sarcasm on the *Ms.*, enough to confirm the instant dislike she'd taken to him.

"Hello, Reardon," Brenda answered, and Cora wondered if maybe she'd one-upped him, using his first name. "Good to see you again. Excuse me a moment." She turned her back to him and drew Cora and Lexie toward her, to one of the tables. "That's Alex's lawyer. I met him last week. Naturally, he asked us to drop our opposition to Alex having custody. That's routine."

"Did you tell him to get Alex to drop it?" Lexie said hotly, her small stature somehow underscored by the width and breath of her emotion.

"Of course."

Just then, a uniformed man entered from a different door, scanned the room, and disappeared again.

"The bailiff," Brenda said. "We're still a little early, and it doesn't appear that Alex is here, but neither is the social service investigator."

"Speak of the devil," Cora said and Brenda and Lexie followed her eyes.

Alex was inside the room and hesitating, looking at Cora and Lexie and then at his lawyer. He wore the same dark suit and Lexie noted again it was too big. He needed somebody with a brain to take him shopping.

Alex's attorney gestured to him when it was clear Alex was considering approaching Lexie and Cora. They could see him waver, but Lexie made a show of turning her back directly to him and then Alex did walk to the spot Reardon was indicating with a scowl and a pointing index finger.

At the same moment, the investigator, Heather Guard, blew into the room with a fan of folders in one hand and anxiety on her face, while the bailiff entered from the door behind the bench, and said, "All rise. The Court of Domestic Relations of Highland County is now in session, the Honorable Thomas R. Donnelly presiding. All who have business before this court come now and be heard."

The robed judge, a late-middle-aged man with a ledge of unruly gray eyebrow, struck the gavel.

"Is the attorney for the plaintiff ready to proceed?"

"We are, Your Honor."

"The attorney for the defense?"

"Yes, Your Honor, and may I remind you there is a counter-motion before this court?"

"Unnecessary. The court is aware of the case. Attorney for the plaintiff, call your witness."

"Heather Guard, social service department."

"The court calls Heather Guard to the stand," repeated the bailiff.

The young woman carried a manila file with her and was sworn in. Her hair reminded Cora of Christine's before Christine cut hers, it was that good and strong and thick. The memory made uncried tears quarrel to get out of where she stored them while the young woman affirmed she would tell the truth, the whole truth and nothing but the truth, so help her God.

"God help us all," Cora thought. "Help us."

BRENDA WAS PERSISTENT, you had to give her that much. "So, then, Ms. Guard, to make sure I'm clear on what you're saying, it's that Lexie wishes to be with her grandmother, has what *she* believes to be reason to think her father was responsible for the death of her infant twin sister, and has no relationship—and has *had* none—with Alex O'Gara since she was six weeks old, yet you feel that placement with Mr. O'Gara is appropriate."

"I'll object to that," Reardon said.

"Your Honor, in light of the best-interests standard, I suggest that the child's—the young woman's—state of mind is relevant."

"I'll let that one in, but Ms. Dunlap, no additional hearsay will be entertained regarding the deceased twin."

Heather Guard cleared her throat and tossed her hair out of her face with the help of a hand. "Actually, what I *said* was that Mr. O'Gara is not inappropriate in light of the fact that he is claiming her, has the ability to provide for her, and has no record that would suggest that he would be abusive or neglectful."

Brenda sighed. She expected it was pretty much a done deal, and wondered how much of it was her fault. She could have advised Cora more strongly not to pursue it at all. Of course, they'd all thought he'd sign off. She should have expected the unexpected instead. Still, she had to press on. Cora had to see that she'd done all she could.

"Would you specify to the court exactly what Alexis told you about her relationship with her grandmother?"

"Objection. Asked and answered."

"Sustained."

"All right, then, Ms. Guard, if Mr. O'Gara *were* responsible for the death of Alexis's twin, would you consider him an appropriate custodial parent?"

"Objection. Speculative and relates to facts not in evidence."

"Sustained."

"All right, then, Ms. Guard. Would it be accurate in general to say that a trusting relationship is in the best interest of adolescents?"

"Yes."

"And have you reached a conclusion as to whether Alexis O'Gara has a trusting relationship with her grandmother, Mrs. Laster?"

"Yes. She does."

"And would it be accurate to say that such a relationship exists with Mr. O'Gara?"

"No."

"Thank you, Ms. Guard. Your Honor, this completes my cross examination."

"You are dismissed, Ms. Guard. Counsel, is there additional evidence at this time?" The judge's eyebrows were a forbidding single line across an expressionless brow.

"I would like to move that the court allow an independent psychological evaluation of all parties by a fully credentialed and licensed professional," Brenda said. This would be a considerable expense for Cora, she knew, but worth a shot. The social service department worker was in her early twenties; Brenda doubted that her Bachelor's degree was framed yet. The judge couldn't have missed that himself. The department didn't pay enough to keep the best, the ones who studied nights for a graduate degree, got the experience to hone their education and instincts, and then left to work in the private sector. Probably Heather Guard would turn out to be one of those, but the bud hadn't had time to open.

"Objection, Your Honor. Another evaluation process isn't necessary." Alex's attorney would have objected even if they thought a second evaluation would come out in Alex's favor. That way if the judge did order it, Cora would be the one to pay.

The judge wiped his mouth with his hand. "I'm inclined to grant that motion provided the expense is borne by your client, since the case was assigned to social services already."

"May I have a moment to confer with my client?" Brenda asked. She tucked her hair behind her ear and adjusted her glasses, knowing what was coming and trying to figure a way to cushion it. Sometimes her clients seemed like lambs to her.

Faith in the system dies hard in the hard-working and law-abiding, she'd found, and it hurt her freshly each time it happened. She often wished she could explain, if not apologize.

"Be brief, please."

Brenda sat, leaning forward and reaching to Lexie so the women formed as close to a semi-circle as they could at the table. It occurred to all of them, though there was neither reason nor time to speak of it then and they didn't—they were three women against three men.

"We're going to lose," Brenda said quietly. "I can get him to order another evaluation and Alex will be forced to participate, but it will be expensive because we'd go for an expert, a psychologist. The judge might allow us to wait for the next evaluation results to come in before granting final custody to your father, Lexie. What do you want to do?"

"Isn't the judge going to ask me how I feel?"

"It seems his opinion is that your feelings were included in the social service report."

"I want to talk for myself," Lexie said loudly, pointedly, and stared at the judge.

"I can ask for that," Brenda said. "What about another evaluation, Mrs. Laster?"

"Could it come out different?" Cora was picking at a hangnail, wanting to get hold of it and pull until it tore and bled and the smarting of air on the small wound would be something reliable.

"I think a lot depends on how much weight an evaluator puts on Lexie's preferences. Maybe we can get psychological testing…show that Lexie's mental health will be impaired. The social service worker obviously felt that since Lexie doesn't know Alex, her extreme negative feelings aren't founded on…well, aren't founded."

"I want him to let me talk," Lexie repeated. A couple of strands of dark hair had fallen from her bun and lay against her neck emphasizing its pale fragility to Cora.

"I'll pay the money," Cora said.

Brenda stood up. "Your Honor, if it please the court, Alexis O'Gara would like to speak."

"Opposing counsel will have the right to cross if she's sworn in," the judge cautioned.

"We're aware, Your Honor."

The judge paused a moment. "I'm inclined to allow you to have your say, young lady, but you may remain in your seat and address me."

"Objection, Your Honor," Reardon Greevy was on his feet. It was the first time his smooth surface had the smallest ripple.

"Overruled," the judge said, and Brenda was suddenly optimistic. The judge wasn't going to let Alex's attorney have a shot at the girl. Maybe he was looking for a reason to rule for Cora.

"Alexis, you may talk now," he said.

"I want to stay with my grandmother," she started, her voice scraping over sudden nerves. She cleared her throat. "I want her to adopt me. I mean, my mother had a good reason for wanting me with her, and I know her and I want to stay with her. He killed my sister, and he left my mother and me and ran away. If you make me live with him, I'll run away."

"I don't appreciate threats, young lady. Do you know your father?"

"No," Lexie said, not recognizing a rhetorical question, but Brenda saw immediately where the judge was going.

"You've formed an opinion without any direct basis, you see. I'd like to take your preference into consideration, in addition to your mother's stated desire that your grandmother be your guardian, but the law is clear. In the event of the death of a custodial parent, custody reverts to the non-custodial parent barring clear evidence that he or she would be inadequate. Your father's parental rights were never terminated." He spoke quietly and patiently, his swath of eyebrows slightly raised to ask if she understood.

"You don't understand, I can't..." Lexie started.

"I've heard you, and indeed, I do understand your desires. I simply cannot base a ruling on them."

Cora was looking down at her folded hands, breathing as hard as if she'd already been crying over failing Christine.

"I am ready to issue a ruling. The court finds that Alexander

O'Gara is entitled to custody of Alexis Michelle O'Gara and therefore, the petition to terminate parental rights and proceed toward adoption is denied. However, in light of Mrs. Laster having been named guardian and the expressed feelings of the minor Alexis O'Gara, the question of permanent custody is deferred for six months during which time Alexis shall make her primary residence with Mr. O'Gara. Mrs. Laster shall have visitation on alternate weekends and one night weekly, according to Schedule B. A final hearing is set for November 30 at ten o'clock. Mrs. Laster, you have forty-eight hours to relinquish your granddaughter and your visitation will begin not this coming weekend, but the next. Is that clear? On the motion for an independent evaluation, the motion is granted with the understanding that the evaluator be approved by the court, the cost borne by Mrs. Laster, and that she initiate the action, which she may choose not to. Clear?"

Cora nodded numbly, thinking he was addressing her.

"Thank you, Your Honor," Brenda said.

"Court is adjourned." There was a gavel bang and Brenda felt rather than actually saw Cora flinch.

"All rise," the bailiff intoned, and they all did except Lexie who sat stunned, fever-spots of color rising on her cheeks which were otherwise translucent as empty glass. Even her eyes looked glazed, as if she couldn't absorb what had happened. Brenda slipped behind Cora and stood a half step behind and between Cora, who'd struggled to her feet when instructed to rise, and Lexie, who hadn't moved at all. She put her left arm around Cora's back and her right on Lexie's shoulder.

"You can sit back down," Brenda said to Cora. "Take a minute." Then she squatted, keeping a hand of comfort on them both while Cora sat, a reconfiguration of the earlier semi-circle.

"Do you understand what he said?" she asked Lexie.

"He says I have to go to Alex?" The girl had that much, but Brenda realized she probably didn't grasp the whole ruling any more than one can take in a whole horizon at once.

"Yes. But he's going to reconsider in six months. I think he's sympathetic, but doesn't have grounds to terminate parental rights. See, that's very hard to do. But we can get another eval-uation and in six months nobody can say you don't even know him. Then, I think, since you'll also be over sixteen at that point, right? That the judge might not let your grandmother adopt you, but give residential custody to her and visitation to your father. With older kids, too, visitation isn't enforced by the court."

"What're you going to do? I'm not going. They can't make me."

"This is so wrong," Cora inserted.

Brenda sighed and moved one bent leg to adjust her balance. "There's nothing we can do. You've got forty-eight hours, then you've got to go."

Brenda felt someone approach and she looked behind Cora. Alex stood perhaps five feet away. "I'd like to speak to my daughter," he said to Brenda. His voice was different from what she'd expected, deeper. Brenda couldn't tell whether there might be a shade of apology to his tone or he was warming up to a con-frontation, but Lexie shook her head violently anyway.

"Maybe not right now," Brenda said.

Cora turned and looked at Alex. "Haven't you done enough? Do you have to take this away, too?"

"I have a right…" he began, and now he was reddening.

"Don't you dare talk to me about rights. Don't you dare." Cora was like a large, gentle animal who'd discovered her anger. "I'll fight you until one of us is dead," she said, her voice rocking as if her Christine were in her arms and she had one chance to save her.

twenty

WHAT DID I DO WRONG? First I get a psycho-killer-draft-dodger father, then God makes my mother die and the goddamn court won't pay any attention to her will and says I have to live with him. I felt like my mother was going to help me, and it sort of made me believe in heaven, like she could watch over me and not let bad things happen anymore, but that's obviously not true. When I talked to her before court, I thought I heard her say, *feed the birds* and I didn't do it. Would she be mad at me for not rushing out to buy birdseed and let me end up with Alexander the Goddamn Great? Grandma says there's nothing we can do about it, I have to go. I told her I was going to run away and she said that was a bad idea because she was going to get some psychologist to talk to us all and say I should live with her, and then it would only be six months and I'd be back. Sometimes I think she doesn't have all her tires on the road. I'm not staying there for six months. I'm not staying there for six days or six minutes either.

Grandma says I'll have to change schools. How is that fair? Why should I have to change schools? Why shouldn't he have to move? My life is his fault.

So now I got sunflower seeds at the grocery store and put some in each feeder, but Grandma said they're supposed to get different kinds. I don't see why it has to be so complicated. I don't even know why I did it. Grandma is doing all my laundry and folding my clothes. I told her to quit it, I want my clothes to stay here, but she said I have to take enough.

Last night I stayed in my Mom's room a long time. I put everything out and lit the candle and tried to pray to Mom. Maybe she couldn't hear me before. Or maybe she was mad because I didn't feed her birds, or maybe there's not any such thing as heaven, or God, either. I just thought I could try again. I told her about everything except cheating on my Spanish test, which didn't count because I failed it anyway. I asked her to ask God to strike Alex with lightning or maybe let a big truck run over him. I really don't care how he dies, unless if I get a choice, then I'd make it really slow and painful. But really, I just want him to die and leave me alone.

Tomorrow. I can't believe it's happening tomorrow. Last night, it felt like my Mom said *you'll get him,* and then I thought maybe she means *get even* with him. Maybe I could get even with him for her and for Tina. And for Grandma. And me.

I don't know what I'm going to do when I can't come in Mom's room. Now I can make it smell like her, and I can put on clothes of hers, and I can sort of talk to her. But I don't know when she listens. Maybe sometimes not at all, because she's off doing something else. Jill said she'd prayed to her a couple of times about passing Geometry. Maybe she was listening to Jill when her own daughter needed her. I asked Jill to quit, except then she said, "Well, I also sort of asked her to help my Mom get well because there might be more cancer," and I couldn't ask her not to do that anymore, even if Aunt Rebecca is a witch. I wish I knew how this works but there's nobody to ask.

twenty-one

ALEX LIT ANOTHER CAMEL. Even though Greevy had assured him it was a no-brainer that he'd win, he wasn't prepared to, and wasn't entirely sure he wanted to. It wasn't something he could know, one way or the other, his last experience with a child having seared him like a red-glowing iron brand. What he'd really wanted was to, well, see her, and talk about Chris. Unthinkable, her being dead. He'd imagined enough about his own dying, but as much as he still thought about Chris, her death had never shadowed his mind.

Reardon Greevy had explained it was all or nothing. He'd have to sign to give up his rights, or he could claim them, in which case custody would go to him as a surviving natural parent who wasn't in prison or an insane asylum.

"Her family wishes I was," he'd told the lawyer.

"And would they be right?"

"No. Might be. No."

"Well, it doesn't matter anyway. It just helps to know what mud they're going to throw up on our windshield. Since you haven't been committed or convicted, it's a no-brainer."

"I don't want to cause any…I sort of wanted to…talk to her, let her know I…"

Greevy cut him off. "Well, there's a restraining order, you remember. All she wants from you is your John Hancock."

"My…?"

"Signature." Reardon Greevy had given a falsely apologetic

smile, though the gesture that would have come naturally would have been to roll his eyes. "Sounds like you'd better think this over. Maybe you really don't want to have your daughter." Alex detected a thorn of contempt in what he'd said. He knew the man looked down on him. He was so tired of being looked down on, so sick and tired of it. Pictures of what must be the lawyer's children were framed in thick sterling and pewter on the bookcase and his desk. He either had an awful lot of kids or just kept adding new pictures next to old ones as they grew up.

"It's not that." Alex coughed, and cleared his throat again.

"Well, what is it? It is, ah, your responsibility, after all." Alex could feel the man's impatience. Reardon shifted his long legs as if to signal his mounting contempt. "You have rights," he added, "but maybe you're not the sort to claim them. I take on clients who want to win."

And then, of course, he had won. Wearing his buddy Dink's suit, since Al was an even bigger guy than Dink, with a shirt and tie he'd bought at Value City, Alex had won.

HE HAD A TRAILER. It had been his mother's, and when she'd died four and a half years ago, it had passed to him along with enough money to have it moved to a park closer to the factory where he installed locks on replacement windows. Then he'd been fired from that job for drinking, but had gotten another one, close enough, as a worker ant on the loading-dock side of another colony. He took his smoke breaks, threw his money in for burgers when one of the men made the lunch run, went home and watched television. He'd gotten used to hating it, waited until he got home to drink most nights, and it wasn't so bad as actual dying. "No second chances," his father used to say. "No second chances around here for little assholes," after a ham-sized hand had stung his cheek, or his back, or wherever it had happened to fall. He was small for his age, always, taking after his mother's side, though he had his father's Black-Irish coloring. His father hated small men, and children, as best Alex could tell. He'd hooked up with a waitress whose second husband had been shot and ran around with her before he died.

Alex always liked those nights best, the ones when the old man hadn't come home.

"No second chances," Alex said aloud as he looked around the bedroom and picked up two full ashtrays, dumping the contents into a paper bag and went on to collect the cans and food wrappers that had accumulated just since the social service investigator had been there to interview him. What had he done? He'd tried for some kind of a second chance when he had every reason to know better.

He'd told Reardon Greevy that he'd go get Alexis at Cora's, but the word had come back through the attorneys at a hundred an hour, which made three five-minute phone calls cost him twenty-five dollars. (He wanted to, but didn't ask why hearing the word *no* from Cora's lawyer had to take five minutes.) He'd have rather picked her up because he didn't know whether he was supposed to invite Cora in. In fact, he didn't want her even to see the trailer park. He'd as soon do the driving himself, about an hour each way.

His bedroom would have to be hers, now, he guessed. The social service investigator mentioned it would be best if her report mentioned that he did have a separate bedroom for Alexis. The woman had seemed so young, but she must have been three or four years older than he'd been when the twins were born. He still thought of them that way, the twins, inseparable in his mind. Maybe he'd flirted a little with Ms. Guard, who'd told him to call her Heather. Maybe he'd overstated wanting his daughter; maybe he'd lied just a little, but only about how he hadn't had any idea where she was all those years, or about how he'd tried to find Christine when he'd come back, how Mrs. Laster wouldn't tell him and waved a shotgun around. Maybe Heather had seen him as a little heroic, resisting the war that her generation had learned was all wrong, and a little tragic in the loss of his family.

What were teenage girls like anyway? he wondered. The last one he'd been around was Christine, and nothing he'd done with her seemed like useful experience. Nor did having been a fugitive in Toronto, always spooked, picking up day jobs and night girls, rootless as a stone and with as much feeling. There were gatherings and networks of Americans who'd fled like him, but he found they talked about Daniel Berrigan and Bill Coffin and books he'd never heard of. He tried to read one that was pressed on him, but found it full of long words and it didn't seem to have a story to it at all.

The guys at work who talked about teenage daughters did it with exasperation and sometimes fury. "Jesus," said Dink, the one whose daughter Jennie had five earrings in one ear and three in the other, something that kept Dink in constant fear that she was dabbling around the edge of a satanic cult. "Why else would anyone dye her hair orange and blue and punch holes where God never did?"

Alex ventured to tell Big Al, who was too sluggish to have a temper, that his daughter was coming to live with him, making it apparent but unspoken that he'd receive advice without offense. Big Al said, "Well, the first thing is that about half the time they're in the monthly thing. The way you know is that they don't talk to you, they're pissed off, act like you're dumb as cement, and cry and carry on if you say squat. If you was married, you'd recognize it."

"Half the time?" That didn't sound right to Alex.

"Yeah. And the other half is when they're bad to be around."

CORA WAS TO HAVE Lexie at Alex's by five o'clock. At four minutes to five, a station wagon inched its way like a pained turtle over the speed bump and paused at each of the three trailers before his. The car pulled up at an angle—Alex's parking space was filled with his pickup—and idled.

Nothing happened. Alex was sidelong to the bedroom window, angling himself so as not to be seen. There were blinds on the window, ones his mother had put up, which were down but open. He made the double bed that took all but a couple of feet of floor space around it while watching for some movement. Finally, the passenger door opened and Alexis's dark head appeared. The door slammed like a heart against the wall of his chest, and she stood there, staring at the trailer. The driver's-side door opened then and Cora pulled herself out, her cane like a feeler on the asphalt first, even though the afternoon sun was scarcely down and Alex thought she must certainly be able to see perfectly well.

He stepped back, toward the door, waited for a knock. And waited some more, each second elongated like a late shadow.

Finally, he sidled to the window and looked again. Alexis was dressed entirely in black, long pants and a long-sleeved shirt in spite of the spring warmth. She'd pulled her hair straight back in a relentless bun of some sort, and her lipstick was blackish purple. She and Cora stood in front of the car, talking, perhaps arguing. Alexis gestured, looked agitated, shook her head no. Cora, her back to the window from which Alex watched, put her hand alongside Alexis's cheek and caressed it, and then the girl, his daughter, the phantom featureless in his mind all these years, stepped forward and laid her head on her grandmother's chest, and put her arms around that expanse of back, linking her hands. Alex studied his daughter's face looking for Christine, but saw only a stranger.

When he couldn't bear it any longer, he went through the small living room flicking on the television as he passed it, hoping to make the situation appear casual. He'd rehearsed what to say, but it had fled his mind, which had dried up. His stomach lurched and flopped like a landed fish as he opened the metal door and stepped out onto the stoop.

"Hi," he finally managed to get out.

Alexis stared at him with the open, unyielding eye of a creature newly dead. He involuntarily took a step backward, bumped his heel on the step and looked down.

"Hello, Alex," Cora said, carefully polite. She straightened her green-and-blue print blouse over the top of her slacks to give herself something to do with her hand, seeing that Alex was considering sticking his out to shake. "This is Alexis, but she likes to be called…"

"I go by Detta," Lexie said. Cora looked at her.

"Detta?" Alex said.

"That's what they call me."

"Okay. Detta. You wanna come in?"

"No."

"Um…" Alex stalled.

"Her things are in the car," Cora said, peeling her eyes off the granddaughter on whom they'd been stuck since she'd said her name was Detta.

"I'll get 'em," Alex said, and they let him struggle back and forth from the car to the door three times.

"Do you…uh, want to come in?" Alex said to Cora.

"Yes, she does," Detta said.

"Just for a minute," Cora said.

The two followed him through the trailer door into the dim living room where the furniture was a worn brown tweed. "Your room's back there, through that door, uh, Detta," Alex said. Detta looked around the living room and rolled her eyes. "The bathroom's there." Pointing. "I made space for you. And I got you some towels."

"I brought my own," she said coldly. "Are there locks on the doors?" she said, and somehow her voice managed to make it a challenge rather than a question.

"I…guess."

"Fine. I'll be using them."

"Would you want to sit?" Alex said to Cora.

"She's coming back there with me," Detta said, dragging a duffel bag toward the door Alex had pointed out. Quarters were tight with three people standing in the living room—the trailer was only a single-wide—and Alex had to step back for her to get past him. Although she drew herself in tightly, as if in revulsion at his nearness, it was the closest Alex had been to her in over fifteen years, and he saw that her skin was pale and clear, eyes as light blue as Christine's but bordered with black lashes. He couldn't see if her teeth were good; her mouth was like a straight line drawn above her chin in heavy crayon.

"Maybe she'll be more comfortable if I do," Cora said. "If you don't mind."

"Okay. Yeah, sure," he said, feeling like a monster. He sat on the edge of the stuffed chair while they went in the bedroom, considered getting himself a beer and thought better of it.

A few minutes later Cora emerged alone. "She's making the bed," she said.

"It's already made," he protested, knowing he'd just done it, an afterthought that hadn't involved changing the sheets.

"She wanted to bring her own sheets. Have you made arrangements with the high school?"

"Uh, no."

"What?" Cora's eyebrows shot up when she became flustered. "Where's she going to school? There's a copy of her birth certificate and her transcript in here." She drew a white envelope out of the large tan purse hanging from the wrist that leaned on her cane.

"I, um, I'll find out."

"Look, Alex. This isn't a game. This isn't Mr. Alexander the Great just getting what he wants. You did this. It's the worst thing you could have done to this girl. Did you even think about her? It wasn't enough just to ruin my daughter's life. It's done now, you won, and God help you. She has to go to school, be registered. She's got to have some help adjusting. Did you even think about her changing schools the last month? Did you ever think about anyone but your sorry self?" Cora was shaking. She wasn't one to lose control of herself and now she had, however quietly. "Is this about the money? You can have the money, damn you, just let me have her," she hissed, the watery sheen on her eyes obscured by her glasses.

Alex blinked and coughed. "What money?" he said.

"Damn you," she said, making it evident that she thought he was playing dumb.

"Lex…Detta! Detta, honey, I need to go on now," she called. "I'll be here to get you on Wednesday, and we'll go out to eat, okay, honey?" Cora called to the bedroom. Before Lexie came out, Cora turned back to Alex. "You get her in school. Tomorrow."

"I gotta go to…"

"You don't go anywhere until that child is in school. Hear me?"

Alex put his head down. He hadn't the slightest advantage,

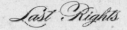

especially with conviction's blaze on her side and him already asking himself what the hell he was doing and how could he ever fix anything. "Okay," he said. "Okay."

twenty-two

I CAN'T BELIEVE I'M stuck here with this freak who smokes like a bad engine and stares at me. Grandma left yesterday and I don't even see her again until Wednesday night. I didn't speak to him last night. He kept knocking on the door to my room, if you can call it that, it's really a closet, but I didn't answer him. This morning he knocked again and said, "It's time to get up, we got to find about school for you," which I figure he should have thought of a while back, but I was actually relieved that I'll get to go to school. God only knows what he does all day. Probably goes around looking for women to ruin their lives. I wonder why it was Tina and not me.

I was already up when he knocked, because I'm used to getting up so early and I wanted to sneak into the bathroom. I had to use it so bad since last night, but I didn't want to. It's real small, and he's got a roll-on deodorant, which is disgusting because it gets all over the hair under a guy's arms. He's got a brand of toothpaste I never heard of and I was glad Grandma said I could bring my Pepsodent, which is what Mom always bought, the one with fluoride, which I had to remind Grandma about. Then I had to get in Alex's truck, which reeks and has garbage on the seat and floors, like crumpled-up cigarette packages and McDonald's wrappers. He picked a bunch up and threw it behind his seat. I was going to ask him where there was a McDonald's, but I didn't want to talk to him. But then I didn't have to, which was cool, because he drove into one and asked me what I wanted to eat. I was starving, but I just stared at him and looked away. He asked me again, but I still didn't answer, so he went in the drive-through and got coffee. I was hoping it was close enough that I could walk to it because I got the money Grandma gave me. So he drinks his coffee, and I'm just looking out my window and not saying a word. I hate it here. It's ugly. The houses look all beat up, real old and jammed together. In the town, it looks like people are mostly black, but at the trailer park, I saw white people so I don't really know.

The school is a dump. It's got some kind of wire on the windows and it's three stories high. Alex walked in with me and we went to the office. It was kind of funny because the lady asked him a whole bunch of questions about me and he didn't know the answers, except he told her that my name was Alexis Michelle O'Gara, but I went by Detta. That's right, Alex. That's Detta as in *Vendetta*. Vendetta Christina, you jerk. Not that you'd know, but I'm a whole new person here. Lexie's at Grandma's and Detta moved here. At first I wasn't going to tell her any of the other answers, but then she said I couldn't go to school there if they didn't know any information.

I want my old life, I want to be Lexie and have my mother back. I want to at least go to Grandma's, but she said I couldn't unless Alex wanted me to, because it wasn't her weekend. I decided I'd make him want me to go. How long would it take to make him want me never ever to come back? Only Alex knows, but Vendetta Christina will figure it out. She's the one who will take care of Lexie. I can see no one else is going to.

twenty-three

ALEX SHOOK HIS HEAD. Big Al and Dink, both hiding shit-eating grins like polyester shirts underneath their sturdy wool concern, had asked how it was going. Machinery noise, the breath of the factory, expanded like heat around them. Alex held up his hand. "Quit," he said. "I'm in no mood."

"Oh, Daddy's in no mood…" Dink, out of punching range, mocked him, but his languid, Southern-edged baritone held out an invitation that only an initiate would have recognized. "What'd she say?"

"Nothin'." Alex was way late, his arrival coinciding with the first smoke break of the day. Big Al and Dink were drinking coffee out of paper cups, flicking ashes on the cement floor of the loading dock, where they held their shape until disturbed, like small long-dead flowers. They sat on brown metal folding chairs that Dink's wife had pronounced too ugly to keep. Instead of dropping them off at the Goodwill as she'd told him to, he'd brought them to the dock and told her he'd lost the receipt.

Big Al repositioned his cap, briefly flashing a well-receded hairline, prematurely so to be sure. With the cap on, he looked ten years younger. Alex figured he wore it right through showers and sex. Big Al pulled the brim lower. "Nothin'? So what're you complainin' about? I'd kill to hear nothin'."

"Yeah, well, I mean like *nothin'*. Nothin', man. It don't matter what I say, how nice I say it. She ain't talkin' to me."

He tapped a cigarette on the outside of its box to pack the tobacco before he lit it.

"Oh, she's just mad at you." This was Dink's observation from long experience with his wife.

"No shit, genius," Big Al said, rocking the chair onto its back legs.

"But see, I didn't do nothin'. How can she be mad at me when nothing happened? Tried to get her somethin' to eat, she won't even say what she'll eat...makes no sense, it's not like we had a fight or I told her no about something. Last night, I knocked on her door a couple times and asked what she wanted. I heard her movin' around in there, but she wouldn't say a word. This morning, I catch her when she comes out to use the bathroom, and I tell her I'll take her to school again. What's wrong with that? How can she be mad at me?"

Big Al was at least trying to suppress laughter, but Dink just hooted. "Oh, man, you think they need a reason to be mad at you? She's a woman-child ain't she? Don't need no reason, not now, not never."

Alex shook his head impatiently. He wasn't close to either of these men once you scratched the top layer of skin or borrowed a suit once, but they were the best he had. He talked as they did— which they'd taken on in the military—with cadences part black, part hillbilly, part redneck—just from being around them, but they hadn't really taken him in and he knew it. It was either that they had families, or disdained that he hadn't been to 'Nam, as they called it, or worse, "in country," which made him an unwelcome foreigner. That war seemed to have made blood brothers of every guy who'd been there, as if they'd all been in one battalion together and constructed an invisible, impenetrable force field between those who'd been there, those who hadn't.

Big Al said, "She's mad about all of it, you getting her especially. It don't have to be somethin' just happened."

"Well, she can't stay mad about that forever."

This time even Big Al hooted. "Hoo-ee," he chortled. "He's a father for sure. Got the tire tracks over his face to prove it."

SHE REALLY COULDN'T STAY mad forever, could she? That night, after the second day of school, Lexie had locked the bedroom door and didn't answer or emerge when Alex knocked after work. "I fried up some meat," he said. "It's not too bad. Or you can fix something else. I can give you money to get something if you want." Between each offer, he paused, leaving room for hope to rise like a roll for the chicken-fried steak, now cold, hardening in its white grease in the pan.

But silence came back at him.

He tried again later. "Hey, wanna watch some TV?" he said to the blank face of the door. Then he realized she probably had homework and that he probably shouldn't be inviting her not to do her homework. "When your work's done, I mean," he tacked on, trying to sound like a parent. On the other hand, she'd like him more if he didn't get down on her.

It must have been thinking about the schoolwork that fired the sudden realization that made his eye twitch. How had she gotten back from school? He'd flat forgotten that he took her there himself this morning. And yesterday morning. It was just so disconcerting to have her look at him—through him—the way she did. It took him five minutes to get back to Lexie's door. "Hey, um, you got back from school okay. Um, how did…do you…" He didn't even know how to say it. Shit, she didn't even have the trailer key. He just wasn't used to reckoning in another person.

Fifteen minutes later, he thought, *What if…*

No way, he answered himself, but the logic of it, Lexie's lack of a key—not that Alex always locked the trailer door—was plain beating him down. And he'd not heard the bed creak the way it did when someone sat or lay on it, the sound a cross between a squeal and a moan as if the bed itself remembered beginnings and ends of life. Maybe it did, for all he knew. He'd bought it used. Last night, he knew the girl had been at least on the bed, if not in it.

"Alexis…Detta, Detta! Are you in there?" He banged at the door much harder than before, with a force he didn't think anyone could sleep through. He went to the kitchen and got a screwdriver. "Look, I'm comin' in, Detta. You better answer me." He began working on the hinges, continuing to call, his voice tacking back and forth between certainty she was there and certainty that she wasn't, until the door was off and he saw the room, empty as the cavity of his chest, all the air sucked out of it.

"Jesus, Mary and Joseph," Cora said. "No, of course she's not here. Did you bring her here? How would she have gotten here?"

Alex gripped the phone, hating the call he'd placed as much as any in his life. "I thought she might have called you to come get her," he said, trying to smooth his voice out. He fumbled for a cigarette, cramming the phone between his shoulder and neck to get one out of the pack, then wildly grabbing for it when the receiver slipped loose and banged on his chest and knee on its way to the floor.

"Alex? You there? What happened?"

"I dropped the phone," he said, standing in the tight space the phone cord allotted him between the kitchen and living room. He was too jumpy to sit.

"Did you call the police?"

"No, I called you first, I should have, I guess, I will."

"How'd she get home from school?" Cora persisted. Alex could tell she expected him to know the answer.

"I'm...I dunno."

"What do you mean?"

"I, um, forgot to ask."

"Was she *in* school?" Cora's pitch was rising toward panic.

Alex was relieved to get a question that he had the right answer to. "Yes, took her there myself."

"So how was she supposed to get home?" Cora dropped back to asking simple, one-step questions. "I mean, what did you tell her?"

"I don't...I didn't..."

"What do you mean? She would have had the sense to ask you if you didn't tell her."

"She never asked."

Alex was just as glad he couldn't see Cora's face, though it was flashing in his mind, a mask mutating through confusion, incredulity and rage.

"How did you think she was getting home?" Cora was using the tone a sensible person takes with an escaped lunatic who has precious information that must be carefully pried loose.

Alex, pacing, caught the phone cord on his belt, then caught his lit cigarette on the cord. A splay of burning embers cascaded down his hand toward the floor. "Shit," he exclaimed.

"What?"

"I dunno."

Cora's impatient sigh made a whooshing sound in his ear. "You don't know what you said, or you don't know how she was getting home."

"How she was getting home."

"Was she in school yesterday?"

"Yes, sure she was. Took her myself, just like today, on the way to work. I was late." He tacked on the business about being late thinking Cora would think that was good.

"Well, how did she get home yesterday?" It was hard for Cora to term Alex's trailer *home* to Lexie, but for clarity and simplicity she did it.

"I…dunno." Then, again, trying to remove the defensiveness that red-circled the way he'd said it, "I dunno."

"Could she still be there, at school?"

It hadn't occurred to Alex. "I dunno," he said. "Should I…"

"For God's sake, get over there. If she's not there, just stop and call the police. Then you call me, hear? I'll have Jo come stay by my phone and I'll drive over there."

Alex very nearly said, 'Yes, ma'am.' He cut the ma'am off abruptly, as if it were an admission. "Okay."

BY THE TIME HE gunned up to the school, it was through a languid twilight, though he saw, relieved, a bunch of little kids still outside playing kick the can on a side street, so it must not be too late for kids to be out. And it wasn't cold, either, just seasonable for late April. Alexis—*Detta,* he had to get used to that—was sitting on the steps. Two books were next to her, a

third in her lap. When she looked up and saw the truck, she looked back down, almost as if she wasn't going to move so much as a toe. Alex had no idea what he should do if she didn't come to the truck, but she shut the book in an elaborate embroidery of slow motion, laid it on top of the others, picked them all up and stood. She adjusted the books in a front carry, covering her chest, which, of course, contained her heart. Then she began to move toward where he waited, looking into his lap, trying to quiet the thudding inside him.

twenty-four

I HATE HIM SO MUCH.

He takes me to school and leaves me there, never says a word about how I'm supposed to get back to his horrible little tin can. I figured he was going to pick me up since he took me, so the first day I waited outside on the school steps and watched a Cub Scout troop play baseball on the field, if you can call that mess of ruts and mud a field. At least it was sunny, but I felt like I was in some kind of prison camp because of the metal fences. The steps up to the school are high, though, and I figured I could see trouble coming if it did, so I really wasn't too scared. At four-thirty, the principal came out, on her way home I guess, and asked me what I was doing there. So I told her. Then she says it's not an area I should sit around in by myself once the Cub Scouts are gone which will be any minute, so she's going to drive me home. What was I supposed to tell her, no? So I get in her car, and of course, she asks me where, and I don't know how to get to the trailer park, so she goes back into the school and looks up the address and drives me there.

"Talk to your dad," she says. "But you can take the bus, you know. Come into the office tomorrow, and I'll look up exactly where your bus stop would be, most likely at the entrance to the court."

She's a nice lady, older than Mom, not as old as Grandma, and she colors her hair brown. I know because her roots show, but only a little bit. Her teeth are sort of buck and at first you just keep looking at her face trying to see her teeth, because they're funny, but then she smiles and you forget to check out her teeth when you have that chance.

So we get to the trailer court and have to drive around because I can't even remember exactly what the outside of Alex's place looks like, actually, they all look pretty much alike, but I finally figured it out. I was so embarrassed. He's not there, of course, which I was glad of, and I don't have a key, but I didn't have to tell the principal that because the door was unlocked. She got out of the car and said she'd like to talk to him, but since he wasn't there, she just checked to make sure nobody was in there and told me to lock the door. "Talk to your father," she says, like I'd ever do that, and then she gives me a hug. I was so surprised I just stood there like a tree, but I wanted to hug her back and then it was too late.

I was pretty hungry, even though I had lunch money from Grandma and ate at school, so I took some bread and some lunch meat stuff out of the refrigerator and put it in my room. Then I quick went to the bathroom and washed up and went into the room and locked the door. Alex showed up at maybe five-thirty, but I was already locked in, so I was glad. He banged on the door a couple of times, but I didn't care. I guess he went to school and I wasn't there, and I hope he shit his pants.

So yesterday, I come out in the morning to use the bathroom and he's all dressed and says, "I'll take you to school." So I think, *okay.* He drives through McDonald's like he did the first day, and I didn't speak to him, and he just gets coffee again. I was going to go in to the principal's office and find out about the bus, but then I just felt stupid because I wouldn't know anybody on the bus, anyway, and what if I didn't know where to get off, and they'd all think I was in Special Ed. I decided I'd just wait for him, and get a ride that way. There's only like five more weeks of school; I can do anything for five weeks.

So I sit there, and I sit there, and the stone steps make my butt cold, and I read my lit assignment, which is a bunch of completely retarded poems, and I look at the geometry, but you need to do it with a compass and I left mine at Grandma's, and I just wait like some idiot. He's probably getting even with me for freaking him out by not being there when he came to pick me up yesterday, but he could have told me when he was coming at least. So today, I sit there and my stomach is growling and my butt is sore and cold and I'm thinking I'll start walking and find a pay phone and call Grandma collect, that's all I can think to do because I don't even know where Alex works, not that I'd call him. Anyway, he must have gone home from work anyway, and just left me here for revenge for yesterday. I wouldn't call him there and beg, that's just what he wanted. He finally shows up at something after seven o'clock. I don't talk to him, but I try to make him wither up and die with my eyes. Tim used to say a person could make his eyes into laser death rays, and I tried, but it didn't work, not that I really thought it would.

On the way back to the trailer, he drives through McDonald's and he buys two Big Macs, a nine-piece Chicken Nuggets, large fries, two milk shakes, a soda, and some of those chocolate chip cookies. This costs him like fourteen dollars. Then he takes one of the Big Macs and one of the milk shakes out of the bag and puts the bag on the seat next to me. I could smell the fries and I was starving. He says, "Look, there must be something in that bag you like, take whatever you want, it's all for you." He eats the Big Mac while he drives. The milk shakes is between his legs and I'm thinking *Good, I hope it freezes his balls off.*

We got to the trailer when it was almost dark. I left the bag on the seat of the truck, went in and peed which I'd had to do since school got out, but there was no place to go since it was closed. Then I just went in and locked the door and tried to pray to my Mom, but I don't think she's there anymore.

twenty-five

ALEX STUMBLED ON HOW to get Detta to speak to him. By the end of the third day, when that morning she'd successfully held out through his saying, "I'll be by the school at four o'clock to pick you up. That early enough?" and he hadn't seen her eat anything at all, he tried, "Do you wanna go spend the weekend at your grandmother's?"

Detta had stared at him for maybe ten seconds and then said, "Yes." That's all. Just yes. But Alex went in and told Dink and Big Al, with a powdering of triumph in his voice. They mocked him, snorting into their coffee.

"Yep, Daddy, you done good. She jus' be fallin' all over her daddy now." Even Alex knew that she'd only spoken to him so she could get out of there.

It was no fun calling Cora for the third time that week. All he'd told her when he called the second time, to say he'd found Detta at school, was that they'd…"gotten our signals crossed."

"Can I talk to her?" Cora had asked anxiously.

"Uh, she's in the bathroom," he'd lied, afraid Detta would refuse to respond to him if he called her to the phone, and Cora would know.

"Well, is she all right?"

"Yeah. I bought her dinner and all," he'd said, again neglecting the rest.

"Will you let her call me if she wants to talk to me? She can reverse the charges."

"No need," he'd said gruffly.

Now, Alex was wrapping the phone cord around his hand like cold rubbery spaghetti—and in his own house again—keeping his voice low. "Cora? I, uh, this is Alex O'Gara." Stupid. Of course she'd know who Alex is. Probably had paid to get his name put on God's curse list at some church. "Uh, could, uh, well, I thought maybe Detta could come see you this weekend. If that's okay."

Cora didn't let on if she knew anything was amiss. "Of course it's okay. I miss her something fierce. Shall I come get her?"

The notion of not seeing Detta's you're-a-dead-man stare suddenly relieved Alex. "She might like it fine if you pick her up from school."

"I can do that."

"Four o'clock," Alex said. "You know where? Over the other side of town, on Southwest Ninth. Just stay on forty-three, turn left on Central and go to the first light. Big brick place."

"Tell her I'll be there," Cora said.

"Okay," he said, and hung up without either of them saying goodbye.

HE LEFT HER OFF at school, once again having driven through McDonald's, offered her breakfast and bought only coffee when she turned her head and stared out the passenger-side window. He could see her reflection in that faint mirror, washed out, her mouth set like already-hardened cement. She sure had his father's coloring, even with Christine's eyes like stones under pale-blue water in the window reflection. He didn't think of his own coloring, nor take in the fringe of black lashes and honed chin that were his own. He remembered Chris as bird-like, quick, small movements. He'd not seen it in Detta, but then, how much had he seen her after all? She was fragile-looking, the way Chris had been, bony shoulder blades like useless wings.

She got out of the car sullenly, leaving the door swung open so he'd have to lean across the seat and grasp after it to pull it closed. "Remember your grandmother's picking you up after school," he called, thinking it sounded normal. She didn't even glance in his direction.

As he drove to work, though, he shook his head. Once, he banged the steering wheel. He reached down and turned the radio off, then back on.

"Ooh, ho, ho, she's getting to Daddy good," Dink taunted on their break. "Hey, bud, cat got your tongue?"

Big Al said it. "Ain't the cat got his tongue. It's the little mouse." He followed it with a barrel-belly laugh and tossed an empty carton at Alex, who batted it against the wall.

Talking to women had never been Alex's strong suit.

CORA'S FACE WAS LOW, cradled between her two hands. Her shoulders raised and fell, though not with sobs, but rather deep, dry sighs, as if her chest were between stones and each breath the labor to hold them apart. Alex's was the second call of the day. The first had been from Rebecca.

"Mom," she'd said. "I don't want you to worry."

When she heard that, Cora knew right away she might as well go ahead and open the door because worry was about to move right into her guest room.

"I won't. What is it, honey?"

"Now promise me, you won't."

"Becca, honey, I'm a tough old bird, you know that. What's the matter?" As she spoke, Cora moved from standing at the kitchen wall phone to one of the kitchen chairs, lowering herself into it with the help of the kitchen table. Her cane was propped up against the wall by the back door. It was chilly for the thirtieth of April, downright cold her bones said, though they'd come to complain during hot weather as well as cold, as well as rainy.

"There's another spot, Mom. But they're going to hit it with radiation. I don't have to go on chemo unless the radiation doesn't get rid of it all the way, but it looks like, I mean the doctor thinks radiation might be enough."

"Where?"

"Around my pelvis. The right side, where it's been hurting. You know, I told you."

Cora tried to steady herself, not to betray the rush of panic that made her hands tingle. This meant it had spread, another place entirely in Rebecca's body. Where else was it hiding, an evil secret spreading corruption? "Well, all right then. I guess we've been there before, haven't we? We left it behind us, now we'll leave it again. So we just need the map out, right?"

Rebecca laughed. "That's funny, the way you said that. They're going to tattoo a map on my skin, so that they don't have to find the place to radiate each time. It's little lines and points and markers."

"When does this start?"

"Monday morning. I'd…like it if you'd come with me. If you're busy, I can…"

"No, of course I'll go with you."

"Then I have to go five days a week for four weeks."

"Honey, I'll be there. Do you want me to drive?"

"How about I drive down, we can take my car at least the first day, and you drive home?"

The hospital was in Indianapolis, close to an hour one way. Cora hated that drive; there wasn't a dust of good memory associated with it, and the traffic made her nervous. She didn't entirely trust her own reflexes anymore, though she was sure she could still pass any driver's test.

"Maybe sometimes could we take your car? I don't know if mine'll hold up," Becca said.

"You bet." Cora made a mental note to ask Jolene's Bob to look her car over. He'd done it every couple of months, and changed the oil for her since Marvin died. "So you'll be here… when?"

"Eight-thirty. The radiation is at ten—well, on Monday, actually they'll just mark me, so I guess that means the radiation itself will go into the fifth week."

Cora didn't let herself think about driving to Indianapolis daily for a month. She wouldn't have refused under any circumstances when one of her children needed her. She'd never know how she'd failed the stillborn boy, but it was in her that had she done something differently, she could have saved him.

She'd gone upstairs to wash her face, get a hold on herself and was in the bathroom drying her hands when the phone rang again. Alex wanted to know if Lexie—Detta he'd called her—could spend the weekend with her, and then he hadn't let her talk on the phone. The court had said Cora could call once each week between visits, and Cora hadn't used the call yet. Now she wouldn't even have to: she just had to pick Lexie up at the school at four o'clock. And get her mind off Rebecca until Monday.

After Alex's call, Cora really tried to straighten up the house and put in a load of laundry, but she never made it farther than her bedroom. In the middle of emptying her own hamper, she was overcome with heaviness and had to lie down. Now, here she was, an hour later, flat on the still-unmade bed with her shoes on, her hands over her face, trying to remember how to breathe.

JOLENE CAME OVER AS soon as Cora called, not even changing out of her house shoes into decent ones. She and Cora had an unspoken pact—they didn't say, "I need to talk," unless there was some unliftable new load, and when one of them said it, the other was there within minutes. Altogether, the words hadn't passed between them more than the fingers on a hand and a half all these years. Cora had said it this morning.

Cora didn't even protest when Jo pointed at a chair in the kitchen. "I'll tend to the coffee," she said, and then turned her back for a minute to make it easier for Cora to get started.

"It's Rebecca," she said. The next sentence was a boulder to move, something she had to gather herself for. "Another spot…the pelvis. Radiation starts Monday…no, they tattoo the spot on Monday, then radiation Tuesday. For a month, five days a week."

Jo finished measuring the coffee, turned it on, and then walked around the table and stood next to Cora's chair. She pulled Cora's head with its wispy gray clouds to her own chest and stroked it like a mother would. Cora set her glasses on the table, covered her face with her hands and sobbed. "I can't bear to lose another child, Jo. I don't think I can bear it."

"If that's what happens, you'll find the strength."

"I just don't know if I can believe that again." Cora's back heaved a while under Jo's hand. Then she went on. "I used to think I was a good person. Not a saint, just a good person. And I'm no Catholic like my mother, you know how she always thought that if you were good, God wouldn't make you suffer."

Jo murmured assent. "I remember."

"I never thought that myself. I always accepted it was part of life. But this is different. My children...dying...dying one at a time in front of my eyes. How can there be God and goodness at all, and be no mercy? If I believe in God and goodness, then I have to believe I'm not good, because there's no forgiveness or mercy for me."

Jo didn't argue. "You have to get through life is all," Jo said softly into Cora's hair. "We get all these visions of...victories and miracles and...joy...and those happen sometimes, but mainly, we get through." She smoothed a wayward strand into a curl and stroked it between her thumb and forefinger. "People just limp through not knowing anything, and the limping is the only way I know to do. You've done the best you could, Cora, the best you could and a lot of the time *better*." She leaned back and pushed Cora's shoulders up just enough so Cora would look her in the face. "Listen to me—if that's not good enough, then nothing is and nothing ever will be, so we might as well let it go, and just carry on. It's not something that's going to make sense to us, either one. Not in this lifetime." Then she relaxed her grip and let Cora sink back against her to finish crying.

Cora finally pulled back. "I need some tissue," she said. "Here I am soaking you."

"Hush," Jo said, and went to the hallway bathroom, coming back with a wad of toilet paper. Recognizing that the first moment had passed, she got them each a cup of coffee.

"I saw this coming," Cora went on, after she'd blown her nose and put milk in her coffee. "That's the thing. I knew it. All winter, Becca kept reminding me of the birds at the feeders on the worst days—all fluffed up, in layers, you know, and that big hair—and the way she was eating, like the woodpecker—he was such a glutton for the suet. But it was all puff, you know, just blown up for insulation. Since the weather changed and she doesn't wear the big sweaters and jackets, you can see it—you can see she's started to waste. I didn't say anything…she keeps such hope. And Jill—what about Jilly?"

"Her dad'll have her."

"I know, but a girl needs a mother."

"She'll have you."

"Not if this kills me, and I'm thinking it might. I'm not even there for Lexie now. I wonder if Christine blames me."

Jolene knew when not to dignify nonsense by answering it, and Cora knew what her silence said.

"And Alex called, after Rebecca, before I called you. I'm to pick Lexie up at school at four today."

"Not for good?" Her eyebrows went up over her glasses.

Cora shook her head no. "Nothing's that easy, is it now? He said he thought she might like to spend the weekend with me. My poor Lexie. You know, the other night, Alex and she got their signals crossed, he said, and he didn't get her at school till…must have been close to seven."

Jolene shook her head in sympathy. "Life is too small sometimes, and then it's too big," she said. She looked down and saw she'd buttoned her shirt wrong in her haste to come. She sighed. The buttons were small and her fingers stiff.

Cora caught her drift. "Of course I want her. For her own self and my Christine."

"Stay strong," Jo warned.

"I'll manage," Cora said. "That lawyer filed for another hearing, you know, with the evaluations and all."

"You got a plate full of liver and onions," Jo said. Cora used to fix liver and onions once a month for Marvin, who loved the dish, although it made Cora gag. Those nights she'd have scrambled eggs or canned soup. She was a woman who'd been brought up to please her husband.

"Hospitals and courtrooms," Cora agreed.

"WHERE WERE YOU?" Lexie said as she climbed into the station wagon, her voice tangy but careful not to sound too sassy. She'd been standing out in the driveway in front of a school building that looked antiquated to Cora, and it had disconcerting metal fences.

"It's only five to four, honey. Are you all right?"

"School got out at two forty-five."

"What? Alex told me to come at four. Are you all right?" Cora set the car in Park, and leaned across the seat to gather the girl in by the shoulders. Lexie stiffened at her first touch, but then gave way and bent toward her grandmother. Cora sensed, rather than saw, that tears swamped Lexie's eyes. "Honey, honey…it's all right. We'll get through. He didn't hurt you somehow, did he? I mean, did he…?"

Cora wasn't even sure herself exactly what she was asking, and it was too many questions anyway. *Don't ask questions,* Cora chided herself as Lexie predictably straightened, wiping her eyes as she looked out the passenger window.

"He's just…mean. Could we stop and get something to eat?"

"Of course, just tell me where. Have you been getting enough to eat?"

Lexie shrugged. Her hair, again pulled straight into that severe bun, looked dirty to Cora, a carelessness Cora hadn't seen except briefly when Christine died. She was dressed all in black, too, just as she'd been when Cora brought her to Alex's. They might even be the same clothes, Cora thought, yet knowing Lexie, it seemed quite impossible. "There's a McDonald's back over toward the trailer court, but I'd rather wait until we're out of this…place." She spoke with disgust, as if she wanted to say *sewer* instead of *place.* "Grandma, I had to use the money you gave me."

Cora looked at her, then back at the road. "That's okay, honey. That's what I gave it to you for. Did you get yourself something?"

"I used it for lunches at school, and they made me buy two workbooks and I needed a loose-leaf binder for one of the classes. It's so stupid to make me buy stuff when there's only five weeks left."

Cora was quiet a minute, negotiating through the turns that would take her to the state route. Once she was on it, she said, "Honey, don't you worry about the money, that's not it. I just want to know, wouldn't Alex buy you what you needed? And give you lunch money?" Cora was infuriated.

"He didn't."

"Did he refuse? What did he say?"

"Nothing."

It was Cora's nature to press, but she hesitated then, the way a dog will point and wait unmoving. Talking with Lexie was tricky as seeding clouds: sometimes Cora hit just the right time, just the right spot and she'd get torrents. Other times she could fly back and forth with her load of help and hope—doing nothing different than before—and failure would be so complete, it would seem Cora had personally created and extended the drought down on the ground below.

Cora opted for a couple of minutes of silence and then waited to get through a stop sign and back up to speed so that Lexie wouldn't think she'd have to make eye contact. "So, what did you have for lunch today?"

"Not much. The food is really bad. It was tacos today, and...Jell-O."

Cora couldn't bring herself to ask if it was green Jell-O. She was going to ask Lexie what had happened the other night, when Alex had called, but while she was waiting for enough time to elapse before floating another question, Rebecca came back into Cora's mind and stayed there, just in front of Lexie and Alex.

AFTER CORA BOUGHT Lexie the hamburger and milk she wanted while worrying it would spoil Lexie's dinner, they drove in silence on the road to Early Sun. When they went through Darr-ville, Lexie asked Cora to stop at the Washington Supply Company, and then asked for money.

"What do you need, honey? I've got to grocery shop tomorrow. You can just add it to the list. Maybe you'd help me." It was hard for Cora to walk around the grocery store, even using the cart like a walker for support.

"Um, just a little thing, please. I'll earn it doing work at home tomorrow." She sounded embarrassed.

Cora rifled through her purse, which had become disorganized with receipts, notes, and various random items she'd stuck in, thinking them necessary at the moment. The Supply Company stocked most everything that wasn't in the Rexall or the Thriftway—and some that were. It sprawled right up to the curb of the narrow parking lot, where some lawn-care equipment they were pushing (along with hanging flower baskets) had been arranged on either side of the entrance. Anyone could have walked off with the display items, but no one ever did.

"Will five dollars be enough?" Cora knew perfectly well she wasn't going to get five dollars' worth of help out of Lexie, but Marvin wasn't there to ride herd on her indulgences. She could just hear the fit he'd throw if he knew Alex would get the social security money for Lexie, while Cora was the one passing out money like potato chips.

"I think so."

"Here's seven."

Lexie had come out of the Supply Company five minutes later with two bags that looked heavy. When she put them on the floor of the backseat, Cora glanced over her shoulder furtively, while Lexie was closing that door and moving to open the front one. It looked as if all she'd bought was three kinds of bird seed and those suet and seed cakes that are really supposed to be for winter.

twenty-six

I DON'T THINK TIM wants us to be together forever anymore. I called him as soon as I got to Grandma's, but he said he couldn't come over because he was already doing something. He didn't say what. He did come over yesterday, but not until night. He could have spent all day with me. He said it was because his mother made him do spring yard work and he didn't know I was coming home. I said—neither did I, stupid, and he shrugged his shoulders. I let him feel under my bra when Grandma fell asleep in front of the television. Maybe I should let him do more. Now I have to go back to Alexander the Goddamn Great and it's too late. I feel like maybe Tim's sitting by someone else at lunch every day and just thinking about her.

It's like nobody has a clue, like I'm over there in some other world that no one else has ever seen but they think it doesn't sound so bad. Grandma started talking about Rebecca right in the middle of me telling her about school. I was going to tell her I didn't speak to Alex the whole time, but she got off on Rebecca and I don't think she really cared. And she's the one who asked me.

After Tim left, I went in Mom's room. I lit the candle and put the cologne on me. I had to take her sweater off—I was getting sweaty and I didn't want to make it smell gross. I looked at her picture and talked to her. I think the picture is fading. I remember it clearer than it looks now. I started to cry, and then it was like in my mind something said, *It's only a little harder to see me now,* but that doesn't make any sense. It makes me mad, like she could come back but she won't, and it's my fault because I ought to be able to see her. I don't know if I believe in angels or anything like that. I thought I could figure that stuff one way or another when I was old. Grandma says she believes, but I don't believe her. She sounds like she doesn't know any more than I do. She said birds don't need suet in the summer. Then last night she just happens to mention that last year Mom had already put up the hummingbird feeders by now. I'm probably doing everything all wrong, and that's why I can't see Mom.

Jill came over today. Aunt Rebecca has to have radiation, but that doesn't hurt, she even said that, so I don't get what is such a big deal. Grandma says I ought to be able to understand what Jill is going through, but that's stupid because her mother is alive. She even drove Jill over, so okay, I mean, how is Jill like me at all? I suppose they think my mother is driving a Cadillac around heaven. Even if she is, I'm not riding in it. Jill says Rebecca may lose all her hair, and if she does then she's going to shave her head to help her Mom feel better about being bald. I swear she's saying this stuff to make me feel bad. Like I wouldn't have shaved my head for my Mom, except they forget I didn't get a chance. Like I should have known when I was sitting in Civics that my Mom was dying instead of talking to Rosa and Gareth and writing a note to Tim. Jill is being all nice to Rebecca now. Sure. But she used to say she hated her when I said I hated my mom.

twenty-seven

"WHAT THE HELL DO hummingbirds eat?" Alex said to Dink and Big Al. He was careful to have already struck his lighter so he could be lighting a cigarette the minute the words were out and have something other than either one of them to look at. It had taken him until their second break on Tuesday to ask.

"What?" Big Al was just taking his own pack out of the rolled short sleeve of his T-shirt and stopped to stare.

"Say what?" Dink said at the same time.

"What do hummingbirds eat?"

"How the hell should I know? You wanna date one or something?" Dink said, while Big Al laughed, appreciative.

"You'd probably fit right in…" Big Al said, leering, pausing on the last words to signal that he was being lewd.

"No, serious, you know what they eat?"

"Bugs 'n shit, I suppose. I dunno," Dink said. His mustache bobbed in concert with his shrug.

"Prob'ly. Who cares?" said Big Al. The baseball cap came off and was resettled on his head, pulled farther down. A reddened track around his forehead that continued like a road on changing terrain was briefly visible, sweat above and below it. The dock was hot as July this afternoon.

Alex considered whether to answer. "Detta asked me, only thing she's said to me ever." He stretched the bottom of his shirt over his hand and, hiking it halfway up his back, used it to wipe his face.

"Detta? What the hell kind of name is that? Who's Detta?"

"Alexis, y'know, my girl. She goes by Detta. I told you that."

"Nah, didn't know that," Al and Dink backed each other up on the point.

"Why's she want to know that?"

"Dunno."

"So she's talkin' to you now?"

"Just asked me that much, is all."

Big Al and Dink both shook their heads, and no one returned to the subject of hummingbirds, mysterious as women and possibly as aggravating.

ALEX CHECKED OFF THE cartons on the tracking sheet fastened to his clipboard. He'd never really thought those guys would know about the birds, but he didn't know who else to ask. Damn Cora would've known, he guessed, but Detta must've already asked and Cora came up shooting blanks.

He'd driven out to Cora's on Sunday night to get the girl, pretty much wishing he wasn't. It was damn hard to swallow how she'd just wither him with her eyes then stare out the truck window. He'd give her back to Cora, maybe, except if he did, his lawyer said he could get slapped for a truckload of back support, which he didn't have, and for sure he'd have to pay up till she was eighteen. The lawyer told him Cora was still trying to get custody away from him, but not to worry, he'd win unless he came off like a complete lunatic in the psychological evaluation. Maybe that'd happen. Sometimes it just came into his mind that maybe he was crazy. He'd think about his life, and he'd think, *Yeah, I'm crazy.*

It was Sunday night that Detta had spoken to him that one time and he'd been chewing on it ever since, one more sign he was nuts. He figured that Cora had fed her up good, so he wouldn't worry about that part until tomorrow morning at least. But he had nothing to say, and she wouldn't answer him if he asked her anything.

"D'ja have a good visit with your grandmother?" which he'd said in an elaborately casual manner, had been answered with the death stare. So had "Pretty good weather, huh?" So Alex had gone silent himself, a familiar place for him, except he found himself thinking about the dead baby and wondering if she'd have looked like Detta and if she'd have talked to him.

They were almost to the trailer when it had happened. Detta didn't look at him, but she'd said it. It was right after he'd said, never expecting an answer, "I don't guess you're hungry. You must eat like a bird," to which there was the expected silence for a good two minutes.

"What do hummingbirds eat?" she'd said, not looking at him, but in a strong enough voice—though without a shave of feeling in it—so he knew he heard her right.

Of course he had no idea. And she'd taken him so by surprise that all he'd done was stammer, "I—I—dunno."

DINK APPROACHED THE subject of Detta while Big Al was in the can for a while on Thursday morning, thanks to his having eaten four cream-filled chocolate-frosted donuts. Alex had bought a half-dozen donuts before he dropped Detta off at school thinking she'd take a couple by now, but no such luck. Tuesday night she'd broken down and eaten some of the meat he fried, though she'd done it without a word and put it between two pieces of white bread, blank and sullen as her face, and taken it to her room. Even though he heard the lock turn—loud as if she'd found a way to amplify it—he'd thought she might be coming around. But then Wednesday night he never even saw her, only heard her the one time she slipped into the bathroom, and wouldn't even glance at the donuts on Thursday morning. "You're bustin' my balls," he'd said to her as he started the truck again and saw immediately that he'd given something away. A little involuntary smile flickered before she turned it off.

"I take it she's still bustin' your balls," Dink said. Alex did a double take at the echo.

"Man, I just said that to her. Wouldn't even look at the donuts."

"I was thinkin', the only time my kids didn't hate my guts was when they wanted to get their license. She sixteen yet?"

"Yeah, couple months ago."

"Got a license?"

"Nah."

"Well, then. There you go."

"Where do I go?"

"Man, you got bricks for brains? Ask her if she wants to learn to drive."

"Then she'll want a car."

"Of course, you asshole. Welcome to fatherhood. That's all you're good for, cash and a car. But she'll have to talk to you."

Alex thought it was possible, but not likely, that Dink was setting him up. "Thanks. Maybe I'll do that."

"You try it," Dink said. "Works every time. Don't work a long time, but works a while."

THAT EVENING, ALEX planned out how to ask Detta if she wanted to get her license. He prepared a little speech as he drove home from the plant. Detta had been taking the bus home from school now, and she'd taken the key he left in the kitchen on top of a piece of paper with Detta printed on it, so maybe things were better. A little bit anyway.

She didn't answer his knock at her door, but he was used to that. "Detta," he called. "Detta. Listen up. I got something to say. I was thinkin' and rememberin', when I was your age how me and my friends, and…Christine…all of us was dyin' for our license. I was thinkin' I could maybe teach you how to drive so you could get yours. See that way, you could maybe have a car and, you know, then you could go see Cora when you want to, and you could drive to school. I mean, you make any friends? Maybe if you got a car, they'd like to go someplace with you…ya know?"

All in all, he'd thought it went pretty well. He thought Dink was right, that she had to want her license; she was a kid, wasn't she? So she didn't answer him. That was all right. She was sitting on her bed thinking what to say back to him, to tell him she was sorry and that she wanted for him to teach her to drive.

He drank a beer, called for a pizza, dozed on the couch for maybe twenty minutes, then woke with a start and laid out the money to give the pizza boy. He was catching on. Maybe he wouldn't give her back to Cora after all.

When the knock came, he called out, "Detta, I got a pizza," and opened the screen door. The pizza boy, acne-plagued and gangly, held out the box and said something, but Alex didn't hear. He stared over the boy's shoulder at a girl who looked like Detta, just coming out of a door four trailers down from his, where the lane curved and the trailers alongside it staggered away from his like uneven teeth. "You come on back any time, you hear?" floated after her on the still air, called in a lilting, accented alto. He caught the motion of a shadow shutting the door as his daughter came down the three steps and onto the ground between them. Dark-skinned foreigners lived where she'd been.

In Toronto, there'd been a black woman, Negro they were called then, big, with firm mounds of flesh that circled impossibly far in front and behind her, as if she were made with four basketballs just under her skin. Olivia was her name, and she'd said it "Oh-livia," which wasn't what came naturally to Alex's tongue at all.

twenty-eight

ALREADY THEY WERE on their way for the fourth time that week. "I'm tired of this trip," Rebecca murmured as she slid into the passenger seat of her mother's car on Thursday at eight in the morning, "And I can't be, you know?"

Cora reached over the armrest to pat Rebecca's hand, keeping her own counsel for a moment. She herself was exhausted; three and a half more weeks of the daily trips to Indianapolis were unfathomable, a murky lake in which she couldn't see her own reflection. But she rarely knew exactly what to say to Rebecca anymore. It was as if her daughter were undergoing some sort of sea change or dreaming in a new language since this diagnosis: Rebecca had decided that if she had enough faith, the radiation would serve as God's healing eye cast upon her in reward. That was, at least, the best Cora understood the notion.

But Cora didn't believe it. Not for a minute. Still, she knew the oncologist had encouraged Rebecca to visualize healthy cells multiplying, cancerous ones shriveling up and vanishing, and she knew better than to mess with whatever helped someone get through suffering, so when Rebecca started in on God's miracles, Cora held her tongue. It did make the trip more lonely, not to be able to say, "If I lose you, too, it will kill me, Becca. And I know I can't go ahead and just die with you because of Lexie, Christine leaving her to my care the way she did." Sometimes she wondered if Rebecca had concluded that God had somehow taken her dead baby brother and grown sister for lack of faith. It was all beyond her figuring. She was unspeakably weary, and weary of looking in lightless places for answers.

Then Rebecca chinned herself right back up, peering over the bar and saying, "But it's a beautiful day, isn't it? And not too hot. We're lucky we get to see everything that's starting to bloom, how the scenery changes from day to day. That's the kind of thing people usually forget to notice, then all at once the dogwood is out, or all at once it's gone. Are the lilies of the valley on the side of the porch opening yet?"

"I'm not sure, honey, I haven't looked." Cora was grateful she could give a factual answer and didn't have to comment on how lucky they were. If Rebecca had continued to sound disheartened, Cora was perfectly capable of thinking and saying exactly what had just come out of Rebecca's mouth, but in the face of Rebecca's relentless cheerfulness all week, Cora had been all too able to hear the counterargument in her mind, like an invisible saboteur. Cora noticed Rebecca hadn't brought the thermos of green tea (noted for boosting the immune system, she'd said, used medicinally in China) and hulled strawberries or little bag of organic raisins and peanuts for them to snack on, and she put it on her mental list of things to be sure to do herself tomorrow.

In fact, it *was* a beautiful day, the sort that smells like line-dried wash and makes whatever you have to do inside seem dark and pointless. Cora would have liked to have been setting out bedding plants. Bob had turned the soil over for her. Cora knew that Jolene sent him, out of her heart's memory that Christine had done it every year since Cora's arthritis started insisting she use a cane. Bob had spaded, cut the clumps, mixed in peat to loosen it along with handfuls of fertilizer, little white pellets that said, *I will make you live* to sickly seedlings. Cora hoped she didn't seem ungrateful, since no plants were in yet. Maybe when Lexie came, she and Jill would pitch in and they could do it all in an afternoon. Of course, Bob had offered, but Cora had refused, and not out of politeness. She had a little gardening stool she sat on to plant and weed, and she *wanted* to. And she could still manage it if one of the girls helped her. Jolene said Cora just craved a patch of normal life to cultivate.

They were passing the Old Time Holiness Church outside of Darrville when Rebecca floated a memory of Christine like a petal on light, dancing above what Cora most feared. She did it just as if she had no idea of the abyss below it, the erratic nature of the breeze.

"Chrissy's grave needs something more, I think."

Cora shot her a look but Rebecca's eyes were casual on the dark, rich field where soy faintly greened through in long, mounded lines. Here and there were graceful curves, like wave marks on sand.

"What do you mean?"

"It's too bare. I was thinking I might put a flowerpot on each side."

"Lexie wanted me to take her there yesterday. It's the first time she's been since the funeral. She wanted to put a bird feeder there. She had a suet holder, you know? I had to tell her suet's a winter thing."

"Do you…I mean, do you think Christine knew she was going to die?"

Cora felt herself closing up, like a moss rose sensing evening. "I think she was just a very organized person, you know, that all her affairs were always in order."

"No, I mean that day, when it happened. Do you think she was conscious, that she knew that something was happening right then?" Some of Rebecca's hair had fallen out of the tortoiseshell clip she had used to fasten it at the nape of her neck, and she let it screen her face.

"I don't know. I hope not," Cora said quietly.

"Because if she did, you know, she would have had time to pray, and then…"

Don't go there, Cora thought. *Please, Becca, don't go that way because I can't go with you.* "I think aneurysms happen in an instant."

Rebecca spoke as if her mother hadn't said a word, right on the next exhalation. "And of course, if we had known, we could have prayed for her."

Cora said softly, "Becca, don't put that on me. I can't bear it." Cora was wearing a blue, long-sleeved button-down shirt, and she used the sleeve of her right arm to wipe her face where small tears had begun to gather in the corners of her eyes and a sheen of sweat felt like a hot flash starting up. She'd not had a hot flash in close to fifteen years.

"I'm not putting anything on you, Mom. We're talking about Christine."

"And whether anything might have saved her," Cora pointed out. She did not want to be having this conversation, especially now, when there was plenty of time before they even were on the fringe of Indianapolis where traffic would pick up and she could claim the need to concentrate. "I don't believe anything could."

"Nothing but God, you mean."

Cora hesitated. She wasn't one to say less than what she thought, but if God was fixing to heal Rebecca in return for her faith, then it wasn't going to be Cora and her nasty basket of despair to get in the way. But what was choking Cora was how Rebecca was wanting her mother to be on Becca's side, not Christine's, as if they could roll their faiths together like a ball of yarn and the bigger and more colorful it grew, the bigger and prettier the protective afghan God would knit them. That same God who had already cast Christine aside, as good a person as Christine was. *Choose up, Mom,* Becca was saying whether she meant to or not. And not for the first time. Becca and Christine had been vicious rivals when they were little: *Who do you love most,* they demanded, one way or another. Cora couldn't think like Becca, but Christine couldn't be hurt by anything Cora said and Becca could. "Anything but God," Cora repeated dutifully, not misspeaking on purpose.

ON THE WAY HOME, Rebecca's fatigue was palpable as warm water in a tub and she thought about slipping below its surface. "Mom..." she said, after the air had been cotton-quiet for perhaps a quarter of an hour.

"Yes, honey," Cora answered, her eyes on the road after a fluttery anxious look.

"Don't, Mom. I'm all right. Quit looking at me like that. I just want to ask you, will you, I mean, if something happens to me, will you take Jill?"

Cora felt a wire pull taut inside and then she was the brown and gray bird balanced on it. "Don't talk like that. And why, anyway? She has her father."

"He's a man. He couldn't handle it and she, well, she needs a mother. Girls do."

"You never thought you needed a mother when you were her age."

"Yeah, well, you were busy fussing about Christine and Alex." Rebecca tried to keep the wounding point of the knife toward the ground, for safety, as her mother had taught her, but Cora was injured anyway.

"Becca…" she began, then sighed and shook her head a little to clear it and to shake off the impulse to defend herself. A headache hazed the edges of her vision to reddish brown, like the insides of her eyelids, like she could close her eyes and leave them be and scarcely notice the difference except for the relief of it.

"I'm sorry. I'm not myself," Rebecca said, sensing she'd not hear the simple yes she wanted. John would automatically get custody anyway. That much was clear to the whole world now if it hadn't been before Alex showed up. And it was best, even if John was as about as sensitive to a woman's needs as a dog to a squirrel's. That had been her real reason for divorcing him. His one infidelity had provided a reason other people would understand, and she'd latched on to it with gratitude. But he was a good father in his bumbling way, and Jill knew he loved her.

As Becca had told her mother, she wasn't herself today. At least she wasn't the new Rebecca; her careful cheer faltered toward irritation as she tired and the sheen on her optimism tarnished. She called it *optimism* when she couldn't muster it and *faith* when she could. Maybe she could distract God with a change in terminology and He wouldn't notice. She hoped as much.

twenty-nine

I HATE HIM AND NOW I know he's crazy, too. After we lost in court, Grandma told me to try to wait to pass judgment until after I got to know him because people change sometimes, but obviously my so-called father hasn't. I have to talk to some doctor before we go back to court and I'm going to say that Alex is definitely dangerous and nuts. He showed his true self today. I think he's a psychopath. I saw a show about one on TV and he was skinny and smoked like Alex.

I was walking to the trailer after school and Ramon, he's in my study hall but he sits on the other side and we never said a word to each other, pulled over to the side of the road and drove real slow. He called out something like—Hey, chiclet, want a ride? and he scared me because he smiled and his teeth were real big and white, and it made me think of the wolf in Little Red Riding Hood. I called back—Get lost, juicy fruit, and just walked faster. He stopped the car and I thought maybe he was mad so I quick cut into the alley between Third and Fourth Streets. Then he gunned the car and followed me, driving real slow and I knew I'd made a mistake because there were buildings on both sides of me and he was behind me. I started to run and I felt like a complete fool. I couldn't go faster than a car, especially because I was wearing my sandals since I didn't have gym today, but what else should I have done? Then he just stopped the car behind me in the alley and I heard the door slam and he was running after me. He yelled something, but I didn't even try to hear it. I thought okay, this is it, I'm going to get raped and then he's going to kill me because I know who he is, but I kept running because if I can get to the end of the alley then he can't get me because there's another street and there's probably cars on it. My heart was pounding so hard it made my ears sound like a tin roof and I thought maybe I'd have an aneurysm and die like Mom.

When I got through the alley, right at the end, he caught up to me. I figured he probably couldn't rape me right there on the street and maybe someone would see if he was trying to drag me off, so I just barely got on the sidewalk and stopped. I had to anyway, I was so out of breath. Maybe Mom was like that, she couldn't breathe and her heart hurt and she was more scared than a bird trapped in a basement, like what happened in our old house.

—Why'd you call me a fruit? That's what Ramon said and he shouted it, really mad. He had an accent, from somewhere, maybe Mexico. I'd never heard him talk before.

—Because you called me a chiclet.

—I ain't no fruit, don't you call me fruit.

—I called you a juicy fruit, you jerk, I said. I wasn't so scared now, I was mad because he chased me.

—I ain't no fruit.

—*Juicy fruit.* And I'm no chiclet.

Then he said—*Chica,* I called you *girl.* I was just trying to ask if you wanted a ride. You're from over in the trailer park, right? I live there, I seen you in your daddy's truck.

—He's not my daddy.

—Okay, your brother, your boyfriend, who cares?

—Why'd you call me that?

—Cause I don't know your name, I called you *girl.*

Then I really felt like an idiot. How was I supposed to know? I stood there looking stupid for another minute or so, and then I just said,—Oh. So I started to walk away, and he said,—So, you want a ride?

Well, it was probably stupid in a way, but my heart was too

fast and hard and I thought, I don't want to make him mad again, and I don't know why but I felt bad, too. So I was scared but I felt like maybe I'd been mean, and I didn't know what to do so I said okay.

Then we started back to his car, which is big and used to be blue or something, but it's got a bunch of holes in the fenders, not too big, but there's rust around the holes and all on the silver parts. The paint is peeling in some places. It's a sorry mess is what it is, like Mom used to call my room, only my room was perfect compared to this.

Right then at the other end of the alley, a police car turns in. It drove up to where Ramon's car was blocking the alley, and Ramon said,—Oh man. The police car's light was flashing all of a sudden, like Ramon's car wasn't already stopped, and the cop says over a megaphone, like he couldn't have just gotten out of the car and talked like a normal person,—Step away from the car and put your hands up.

I just froze because I didn't know who he was talking to. I thought it couldn't really be Ramon, or me, but I couldn't see anybody else. I was scared to move, and I didn't put my hands up, but it didn't matter because the policeman went over to Ramon. He had his hand on his gun, but he didn't pull it out. He made Ramon stand with his hands on the brick building and he searched him. For no reason except his car was in the alley. Then he came over to me and he said—Are you having a problem with him, Miss?

I said no. Then the policeman said—Who's your friend?

I have no idea why I answered, it just popped out of my mouth without planning it, even though I was scared of Ramon, now I was scared of the cop and I just said—Ramon.

Find yourself better friends, the policeman said. He had acne scars on his face, like it had been real bad, sort of like Aunt Rebecca's. That's one gene I'm happy I didn't get. Then he said—What's your name?

—Alexis O'Gara. I was going to make one up, but my ID is in my backpack and I thought I could get in trouble for lying to him if he was arresting us. Not that he had any right to, but since when do rights matter? I was looking at his shoes then, and they were scuffed, not shiny black like I thought uniform shoes are supposed to be. There was mica in the gravel in the alley and it glinted like it was worth something, and there were pieces of a green bottle, too.

—Where do you live?

—Over…in Early Sun. (Partly true.)

—With your parents?

—My parents are dead. I live with my grandmother. (Not too true.)

—Phone number?

—We don't have a phone, I said. I never looked at him.

The policeman looked disgusted and I was really scared. Then I said—Ramon is supposed to take me to my grandmother's. I was thinking, I've done it now, because I'm carrying two books, and any moron would figure out I'd been at school, but I guess this policeman isn't just any moron, he's bigger than most, and he said—You'd better watch who your friends are, miss.

The scared part of me won over the mad part and I wanted him to go away.

—Okay, I said, and I didn't even know what I was saying okay to, but I just thought maybe he'd go away.

—Don't let me see you again, he said to Ramon, and when he got into the police car, he spat on the ground before he shut the door and backed it up out of the alley. Ramon was still standing with his hands on the brick building.

—Thanks, Ramon said to me, I didn't know why.—Go on, get in.

I got in the car and he did, too, and he started driving down the alley, to the street I'd run to, away from the way the policeman went.—Bastard, Ramon said, and it sounded like *he* was spitting then, and I looked at him, working up to scared all over again, but then he said,—*Cops,* like he was tasting rotten bananas, and I knew he didn't mean me. Then I thought about why didn't I just tell the policeman Ramon had chased me? I still don't know why I didn't, except I thought Ramon was trying to be nice, just offering me a ride home, and it was my fault for flipping out. I've never been around men much since Grandpa died, and what I know of them has been all bad news except for Tim and sometimes I wonder about him, so I automatically don't trust them.

So anyway, Ramon and I got to the trailer court without saying anything more. I looked at him a couple of times, when I thought he wouldn't notice. His skin is sort of light, sort of dark, and he's got big eyes. His nose isn't like a black person's, more thin, like a white person's. and his hair is black and wavy like cooked noodles, not frizzy. He's real good-looking, even though I've never seen someone that looks like him, and I knew he had big white straight teeth like tiny piano keys. I tried to figure out why I thought he was Mexican, and it's because in school one of the stupid stories that goes with our grammar lessons in Spanish had a boy named Ramon. People who speak Spanish come from Mexico, so that's where I got the idea.

But then, when we were driving in the trailer court when we got to the second speed bump, Ramon said—My house is real close. You want to go there?

—No thanks, I said.—But thanks for the ride.

He must have figured out what I was thinking.—Somebody's home, he said —My mother, she's there. And then I thought, I'm insulting him, he's just trying to be nice, and I wasn't sure what to do so I just said—Okay. I'd already spent the whole afternoon not knowing what to do, like being in the Twilight Zone with no one to ask for directions. That's what Mom used to call being confused, the Twilight Zone.

He passed Alex's trailer and went around a curve, but then parked next to a trailer just three or four down. I guess I've never seen his car; I wouldn't have forgotten it because it's not a sight you'd forget unless you got really lucky, which obviously has never happened to me. Besides, Grandpa had a big one like it before he died. Ramon's trailer has these hanging baskets of pink flowers by each door, and what I really noticed was two bird feeders hanging from a pole stuck in the grass past the bedroom end. And there's a glass one with what looks like cherry Kool-Aid in it.

—What's in the bird feeders?

Ramon shrugged.—I dunno, he said. You can ask if you want, she'll tell you.

—What kind of car is this? I asked then, figuring he'd know the answer to that and trying to be polite.

He grinned.—It's a Pontiac. I'm fixin' it.

He isn't making much progress.—It's nice, I said.—Is it yours?

—It's mine, he said, and I could see he loved it.—This here's my freedom. He patted the dashboard, which is this faded grayish-blue with a couple of cracks in it like a sun-dried raisin or something, and I knew I didn't have one tiny bit of freedom, not really, unless you count not speaking to Alex. No one can make me do that. I shouted back at him tonight when he freaked out, but I wish I hadn't. I wish I'd just never said a word to him.

Why would Alex flip out and throw a fit when he didn't have the smallest reason? He doesn't even know those people, Ramon's mother told me she didn't know him. I bet she never killed a single baby. She told me that hummingbirds eat nectar in flowers or sugar water, but if you give them the sugar water, you have to color it red. Who is Alex to go nuts about my coming out of their trailer? A psychopath, that's who he is. I do not understand how people act. I don't understand anything at all.

"NOW SHE'S HANGIN'" with trash," Alex said to Dink and Big Al, dark-faced with outrage and incredulity. They'd each arrived at the plant, not a minute's lapse total between them, just before the whistle. The men had, over time, become masters of split-second timing, careful not to donate minutes to the company. Alex slammed his locker door. "Jesus H. Christ."

Big Al and Dink suppressed grins. Big Al pulled off his cap and briefly fanned his face with it. It was so obvious Alex would be the target of all jokes that he could afford to give a glimpse of the giant curve of his baldness. "Whew. Daddy's hot."

"You would be, too. I caught her in a trash-trailer, boy there and all. Lives down a couple spaces. Weird, some sort of voodoo, I heard. Brown and black folks in there, you know? And this boy, he thinks he's a stud, walks like he's cool. Like them...y'know." Alex almost imperceptibly jerked his head toward the maintenance department, where most of the blacks worked. Not that the white guys made much more, but they didn't have to mix.

"You caught her doin' it?" Big Al was impressed, the juicy milk-mustache of a grin finally wiped off his mouth.

"I don't know if she did or not. Saw her comin' out, thought she was in her room the whole time she'd snuck out and been over there. Said she was talkin' to his *mother*."

"Oh, man," Dink said, his brows drawn together. Then, behind Alex's back, he mugged to Big Al, waggling his hips—

which made the keys hanging from a loop on his jeans clang softly. When Alex turned to look, Dink rearranged his face into appropriate sympathy for a father's worst nightmare.

The day was already muggy, which deepened Alex's sense of oppression. He wiped the sleeve of his T-shirt across his forehead, though no moisture had beaded there yet. The whistle cut the air, colliding with his bones. Nearby, the drone and clang of machinery started up after first inspection.

"What'd you do?" Big Al had to shout to be heard. He'd pushed his cap back enough so his view of Alex's face wasn't shadowed.

"Man, I lost it," Alex said, but Big Al couldn't hear him.

"What?"

This time Alex shouted. "Nothin' yet."

That wasn't true. He'd told the truth the first time. Before Detta had even crossed the handkerchief yard of the trailer next to his he'd gone apoplectic.

"What the hell?" he'd sputtered, his voice banging on outrage like a broken tailpipe. "You got no business anywhere but here." He'd pointed to the trailer with one hand and lunged to grab her shoulder with the other as she approached, but Detta had jerked back to make him miss. Alex felt himself being watched from the trailer Detta had come from, which embarrassed and incensed him. He'd looked like a fool when his daughter—all in black again like some kind of ghoul—sidestepped him so easily. He moved to get between Detta and the spectator, a Negro woman looking at them from behind a screen door, her face a faint reshaping of the darkness behind her. "Goddammit," he spat, not so much at Detta as in her direction.

It was too late, of course. Not only had the woman seen him, he'd blown it with Detta. When he'd first shouted, he'd seen the look on her face—genuine surprise—before she closed it behind a blank mask. She kept walking toward the trailer, so his effort to position himself to keep the black woman from catching his face and words ended up with Detta effectively keeping her back to him by simply continuing toward the trailer. He'd expected her to stop, to hear out his explosion, the way he'd always had to with his father, but she just brushed by with an expression that was partly bored and partly designed to suggest she'd just stepped in dog do. He was left gesticulating on the asphalt, sputtering fury. "Hey. Get back here," he yelled into her wake. The screen door slapped shut.

Alex couldn't rein back the impulse to glance over his shoulder at the other trailer. The woman's face retreated as she withdrew. She'd seen him puny and impotent. He headed into his trailer, slamming the inner door and hoping the woman heard it. "Detta! Detta!" he ordered, but he was shouting at the closed door of her room. Locked, of course, when he tried the handle; he'd slammed back to the kitchen for his screwdriver to take the door off the hinges again, but as quickly as he got back with the tool in his fist, his will was leaking out, dissipating into air reverberating with failure. He went back into the living room and just stood, looking out of the window. From this angle, he couldn't see the door of the trailer where Detta had been, only the bedroom end of it. One light was on, the blinds drawn.

OLIVIA HAD HAD those kind of blinds when he lived with her. Everybody in Toronto did it seemed, the same grayish color, though it wasn't the trailer woman's blinds that brought Olivia back. It was the mounds of her body, audacious and dignified at once—that, and the rich matte brown of her skin and deep, musical intonations of her voice like a memory of an exotic country following Detta off the stoop.

Olivia lived on Ottawa Street when he met her, though later she moved over to the west side of the city and he'd gone with her. Then, although they never discussed the fact, he'd simply spent the night more and more often until he didn't remember the last time he hadn't. His trappings were showing up in her medicine cabinet and closet until one day there was nothing left at Jimbo and McConn's apartment where he'd been camping on the couch, though he still saw them at the trucking company where they all worked. Jimbo and McConn were draft dodgers, too; an anti-war honcho owned the company.

Olivia was Haitian, it turned out, mistaken by Alex and everyone else for an American Negro until she opened her mouth. Every now and then a *n'est-ce pas?* or *s'il vous plait* surfaced, woven into her conversation like a yarn of a different color that shaded the whole fabric. He'd told himself a thousand times she wasn't Negro, that it was all right, but then he'd hear her sing in the kitchen or the bathroom, and she sounded so black he'd think what his father would say and feel sick. Olivia had a thing for candles, too, and some religious mumbo-jumbo that he tried, but couldn't connect to his chopped-off Catholic roots, even when he remembered the mass in Latin.

Olivia. Olivia. Oh-livia. "What're you doing in Canada, anyway?" Alex asked the first time he spent the night, but she shook her head.

"Too much *tristesse,*" she said, "*ce n'est pas* a story *bon* to the ears."

Alex hadn't pressed. It wasn't in his nature. He was glad to find a woman who didn't want to talk. He couldn't describe the color of her skin—not black coffee, but not coffee with cream either. Best not to dwell on it, anyway, he thought as he stroked her, honey-soft and startling to his eyes against the white sheets. Her body was nothing like Chris's which was thin, a little jutty with elbows and knees. Olivia was flower gone to fruit, round-breasted, with a rump good to squeeze. At first he avoided her coarse black hair, but after a while, even that, even her hair, he touched.

Olivia was better to be with than Christine, not just because of the sex, lustier for Olivia's lack of guilt, but because of the other opposites: she didn't always want him to talk to her, didn't expect him to be there all the time or stay out of the bars. It was like his just showing up was all right and enough. He knew Olivia was afraid at night, and wondered if that was why she put up with him. He didn't like the thought, but didn't know what to do with it, and so put it away on a back shelf of his mind.

Days slid into weeks. The summer passed, cooler than at home, and autumn came a month sooner. Alex stopped worrying that uniformed men would appear and drag him away. He didn't know whether Olivia was less afraid, but she didn't have bad dreams as often. That much he could tell. The trees emptied before November, and Toronto hunkered down for winter. The twins came to mind in February when their birthdate twanged like a sudden sprain in his mind, and he thought about calling Chris, but remembered her warning about the phone maybe being tapped. After that, his helplessness convinced him to leave it alone, let well enough alone, and he didn't notice Chris's birthday until it was nearly two weeks past. Let well enough alone.

And he did. For a long time he left it all alone. Chris, the babies, his father and mother, the whole of Indiana and his so-called life there—he put all of them away. Alex and Olivia lived in the here and now, not the there and then, each for private reasons, each with private scars.

So why did his life have to run on ahead and leave him lost again? "I want to have it," Olivia said, stretching her hand across crumbs on the chipped kitchen table where they sat. A window was behind her, but not so much as a postage stamp of sky in it; the next house, subdivided into apartments like theirs, was so close Alex could've spat through an open window into a sink over there. There must have been a sunset, though. The siding of the other house was gilt to blood orange as the last of the day sank between the world's cracks.

He knew he was supposed to say, "I want to have it, too." The words wouldn't come. It wasn't that he thought he could go back to be with Christine and the baby. Too late for that. Unlike most of his friends, he hadn't sneaked over the border for a rendezvous, and certainly no one had come to see him. If anyone had, they'd have come with an arrest warrant—and probably a death sentence stapled right to it. He most likely would have just stayed on with Olivia without planning to and without planning not to, the way a whole, all-right life can just happen in the present tense if you're lucky. Except for this. He knew about babies, about their screaming, peeing, shitting, spitting, about their choking, about how they died.

When he'd been on the run, he'd thought the movie in his

head and the shakes inside, like the pink baby's jerky choking, would be with him until he killed himself. He'd fumbled when he called the operator from the pay phone outside the Rexall, sobbing into it for an ambulance, and then stood, trembling and glued to the sidewalk while first a police car then an ambulance had screeched by him. He knew the baby was Tina from hearing Chris's *Tina Tina Tina Tina* as his feet had threatened to knot, stumbling down the apartment stairs to the street, to his car.

After the ambulance passed him, huddled miserable, unnecessary, useless as a broken pool cue under the Rexall sign, he got into his car and went east, into Ohio, just because it was the nearest state border. He sped, but he couldn't clear the movie from his head. It came to him that it was Tina who'd had the angriest diaper rash because Chris had said that if all else failed, he could undress them and compare their rear ends to tell them apart. Alex remembered her word, *angriest*. She'd said he'd know that if he changed more diapers. Something else to hate himself for.

He had to stop at three convenience stores in southern Ohio before he found one with a map that included Canada. He routed himself north then, found I-71 to Cleveland until he could let the New York State Thruway hurl him through Erie, chain-smoking and working on a six-pack of Coke. He wanted the humming road to overcome the soundtrack of Chris's word and the crying babies, then *Tina, Tina, Tina, Tina*—and it finally did, but the last scene kept playing, a translucent skim in front of on-rushing highway signs when his eyes were open, and as real as living it when he pulled into a rest area for gas and sleep.

Outside of Buffalo a sign veered him left, to the Peace Bridge, to Canada. He had fifty-two dollars and seventeen cents, fifty-one of it because he hadn't paid the utility bill the way he was supposed to before he went to the army place. The folded bill was in his pants pocket with the money. He was ready for the Canadian Customs agent. "I'm just headed to Ridgeway—" he said without blinking or looking away, which his dad used to say showed a fat liar for what he was "—to see a friend." He'd picked the town name off the map, well short of Toronto. "Nah, nothin' coming in but me and my Coke." True enough. "I'll be back home tomorrow." Definitely not.

Even after questions asked in the third Toronto bar led him to Jimbo, and Jimbo led him to his boss, even after he got a couch and corner at Jimbo and McConn's place, even with a job to learn, he'd see it and flinch—close his eyes and try to bat the memory away. Alcohol helped some. So did weed. Then Olivia.

But now, another baby? A colored baby? The image of his father, rage-reddened, spitting on the sidewalk where a Negro's path had collided with his own, came to him like the cringe when he thought of his father's rough board of a hand.

Alex felt like a nest of ferrets were fighting it out in the burlap sack of his mind. He couldn't think of a thing to do but drown them all. The next day, after Olivia had gone to her job in a nursing home, he'd put most of his things in four pillow-cases and left. It was one thing he knew how to do. He didn't take Olivia's foil-wrapped savings from its hiding place in the freezer; he even left some of his own money on the table in her cramped yellow kitchen, enough for her to get it taken care of if she changed her mind. He was going to leave a note, but then, since he couldn't get it beyond "Dear Olivia," crumpled it into his pants pocket and abandoned the thought. It was easy to hitch a freight toward Vancouver. There was a lot of work in fisheries, he'd heard, and he'd never seen the ocean. The first hundred miles, though, his stomach was sick and his heart thudded like a bird throwing itself against a window, the way they do, again and again and again, as if they're intent on doing themselves in.

ALEX HAD AWAKENED slowly that morning, his head pounding without mercy, to the small liquid sounds of Detta in the bathroom. He opened, then quickly closed his eyes again, trying to remember what had happened. He'd slept in his clothes; his shoes were on his feet. He elbowed and pulled himself to a sitting position, making slits of his eyelids against the light flooding in the open blinds. His foot hit a beer can and then, when he tried to put it down in another spot, several more. Detta appeared, all in black again, wearing some sort of brownish-purple lipstick. Her face otherwise was colorless. She'd lined her eyes with something heavy and black, like a death mask, which went right along with the death stare he'd nearly grown used to.

Normally, he'd take her to school, but she walked by him—pausing just long enough to stare at the cans littering the floor. Cotton-mouthed, he tried to stand to go after her, but his feet had tangled with the debris and he'd been too slow. She was two trailers down by the time he made it to his own door. Then it was obvious she was heading to the same trailer she'd been at the night before. Someone answered her knock, and while he stood there, struck stupid again by her nerve, the boy came out and joined Detta. They'd gotten in his rusty blue boat of a jalopy and taken off.

"So what're you gonna do?" Big Al said, keeping his eyes off Alex's face.

"Got no idea," Alex said, morose. His head still ached. "I lost it, y'know? I mean, hanging with them. What's she think she's doing?"

"So ya lost it," Big Al said. "Didn't hit her, did'ja?"

"Nah." The question surprised Alex, because it made him feel like Big Al could read his mind. He'd wanted to hit Detta and wondered if he would have, given a decent chance.

Big Al nodded approvingly. "So you're all right. I mean, with that court thing."

"Jesus." Alex had been too woolly-headed to think about the psychological evaluation coming up. He settled his cigarettes back into the roll of his short sleeve, which had started to come down, wishing it were break time. "Jesus God. I gotta see this shrink doctor, then I gotta go again and bring Detta."

"That doctor gonna talk to your mother-in-law, too?"

"Yeah. She's gotta go, and then Detta's gotta go with her. I gotta get time off. Shit."

"Hey, as long as you don't hit 'em, you're okay. Don't beat yourself up," Al said, the voice of experience. He mock-punched

Alex on the arm. "If ya think ya fucked up, y'know, it don't hurt to say I'm sorry. Women eat up that shit."

Alex couldn't imagine those words in his own mouth. Besides, Detta had no business over there. None.

"Yeah," he said, tired.

"Nah, ya don't wanna do that," Dink said, coming in on the tail of Al's advice. Al pulled his cap lower and with his thumb and forefinger flattened out his mustache, his gestures of restraint. Dink was shaking his head no.

"Ya don't want 'em to know when they're bustin' your balls," he said. "Just lets 'em know they got their aim right. That's what they like about it." He tossed his clipboard onto a shelf and popped open a can of soda, which was against the rules unless they were on a break.

"It ain't time," Alex said, ignoring Dink's wisdom for the moment and pointedly looking at his watch. No point in attracting a write-up from the foreman.

"You gotta be the one to say when it's time," Dink said. "Sometimes you just gotta say when." He took a deep swallow and offered the can to Alex.

"Hey," Big Al said, ruining the drama of Dink's moment because Alex looked away from the proffered can to Big Al, who was holding up a forefinger indicating he'd just remembered something. "I forgot to tell ya. I asked my girl Anna—she's a whiz with books—to look it up. The encyclopedia says hummingbirds eat sugar water, that's what she says. You're supposed t'color it red. You can tell that to your girl."

Detta was already locked in her room when Alex got home, late because he'd stayed to clock in some overtime against the time off he needed for the appointments. At least he assumed her door was locked. He didn't try it. No point doing that unless he was up for feeling like a fool again. That, or taking the door off the hinges, and he wasn't sure about that with the court thing coming up. He just knocked and waited, the whorls of the fake wood door, inches from his face, making him faintly dizzy. His stomach was still off from last night. "Detta?"

An exaggerated sigh from the other side. "What?"

He felt like an idiot talking to the door. It made him mad, but he said what he had to say anyway. "Hummingbirds eat sugar water. You color it red."

"I *know*." Disdainful. And *she* was the one who'd asked *him*.

She didn't answer when he said he'd heated up a frozen lasagna, and she didn't come out. Before he turned out the light, at nine-thirty—though it felt like two in the morning, the evening that dead, long, silent—he tried one more time. "We got that evaluation thing on Monday. You gotta see the doctor with me, y'know."

"*I know*." Her voice was as disgusted as his father's had ever been.

thirty-one

RAMON GAVE ME RIDES to school yesterday and today. He said —Just show up in the morning, and you can go with me. I'm going to ask Grandma for some money to give him for gas.

While he was berserk, Alexander the Goddamn Great shouted —*I forbid you to go over there.* There it was, big as a half-dollar on the road where someone lost it: he's a lunatic. So, in the morning I just walked past him and all his nasty beer cans on the floor, and kept walking to Ramon's house. I wish I had my camera, so I could prove he's a crazy drunk, but it's at Grandma's with my real life. I'll bring it back with me next time.

Ramon's not Mexican like I thought, and he's not a regular black person. His family is Afro-Cuban, and he said his mother had escaped. I was embarrassed to ask what she'd escaped, whether it was a psychopath. They used to live in Miami, but then his mother knew some people up here and they made it this far, but now she wants to go back to Little Havana. I don't know why, or how she knew she'd run far enough or too far.

His mom is Rosa. She told me how pretty my blue eyes are, but hers are prettier. Ramon's are like chocolates in a box, but Rosa's are like tobacco. So's her skin, and when she talks it sounds like a cross between a clarinet and a flute, and her voice and skin all flow in the same color, like a song. I never thought I'd miss band, but I do. Ramon introduced us the first day he gave me a ride home, and said my name was Alexis. I said—

My name's Detta. Ramon looked at me funny, but I could tell he wasn't going to tell his mother about the police. She said hi, real nice, and told Ramon to fix us something to eat.—Sit to visit me a minute, she said, and she sort of patted the kitchen table, so I sat. Their trailer was fixed up with bright colors, crowded like Alex's, but friendly-crowded, like a party instead of a funeral. There were yellow curtains up, and a woven cloth of all colors tucked in around the couch. Lots of pictures were up, and there was a sort of altar in one corner, covered with a cloth, with different heights of candles and pictures propped on it. I tried not to look like I was being nosy. Ramon got us sodas and opened a bag of pretzels. I was starving, but I tried not to take too many.

—So you're new? She said, and I told her yes, the court made me live with my father.

—We are new also. Your parents, they have divorced?

—No, well, they were, but my mom died.

Then she looked so sad for me, and she put her hand over mine, and said,—That's a terrible thing. My mother was lost early, too.

I don't know why but I told her about Mom and Grandma and Aunt Rebecca and Jilly. And that's when I asked her about the bird feeders, what she put in them and how she knew. She showed me in a little book she said I could borrow (but it was in Spanish) to learn the different birds if I wanted to, and that's when she told me about her hummingbird feeder.

—Perhaps you feel your mother's spirit in a bird, she said. Where I come from, we have Santeria, and we talk to our dead. But the spirit in a bird, well, not so much that. That's just my thought.

I liked how she talked, strong like Mom. And she was so pretty, I felt stupid in the clothes I was wearing and for making myself look like Darth Vader.

—My mother was fast, like that hummingbird, I said. I mean, the way she moved. And she was little and then, too...I talk to her, I said, even though Ramon was there and I was afraid he'd tell someone at school.—Don't tell, I told him. He just shook his head no, like he wouldn't.

—And that calls her spirit to you, child. Feel no shame about that.

—Sometimes I think I can hear her. I whispered that, because I was afraid she'd think I was crazy saying I could hear a dead person talk to me, but she said —*That's good, that's good,* like it wasn't insane at all.—You are listening to the great soul of life which is you and her and all that is seen and unseen. You are joined to life, child.

—She told me to get my father, I said.

—Get him? Like have him for you?

—No, like get revenge.

—But get means…

—Oh, it's something we say, *get him,* like stomp him. It's just something people here say.

Rosa looked at me funny.—Sometimes it's hard to know the wishes of a spirit, Detta-chica. One way or another, you get your father, I think. When she called me Detta-chica I could feel Ramon wanting me to look at him so he could say *told you* with his face, but I didn't.

—Oh, that's for sure. I hate him, I said.

Rosa closed her eyes for a couple seconds and I thought I made her not like me, but then she opened them, all soft and amber and glowy and said,—You will work it out. She got up then and took a couple of steps and before I knew what was happening she gave me a hug and already backed off.—Ask your mama to help you, she said then.

—I will. I am, I told her.

—And she will, too. When Rosa said that, she looked like an angel because the sun was coming in the window behind her and made a halo on her right then. I don't think there's such a thing as angels, but Rosa looked like the pictures they used to show in Sunday School when Grandma took me a long time ago, when I was little, when Mom hadn't died, when I thought things were different.

When I left that first day, she told me to come back anytime. She even called it after me, so I know Alexander the Goddamn Great heard it. I want to and I will, I don't care what my so-called father says.

—WHY'D YOU TELL US your name is Detta? You said Al-ex-is to the cop, Ramon said, exaggerating the syllables like his tongue got stuck between them. I'd gone over the morning after I met Rosa to get a ride to school from Ramon.

—It's a nickname.

—For Al-ex-is? he said, like *yeah, sure, right, that makes sense.*

—No.

I didn't want to tell him more, not right then. I'm putting all my energy into making Alex lose in court and I didn't know if I could trust him to help me. Maybe. I'll see. In spite of what Rosa said about how Mom is with me, I've got to rely on myself, think of what to do to convince this doctor. I have to make Alex show himself for what he is. I'll make him get himself.

thirty-two

BECCA'S CALL DIDN'T surprise Cora. It was as if her daughters vied for her full time and attention, even if one of them had to do it from her grave. Becca needed Cora to come stay at her house for a while, "…a few days, until I'm strong enough to get around again," and it was also Cora's weekend to get Lexie from Alex. Not only that, the appointment with the psychologist for Cora and Lexie together was to be Saturday morning. Cora had already gone once by herself. But there was no doubt Becca was desperately sick, scarcely able to stand unassisted; she'd been started on some new pain drug along with the radiation, which they'd had to cancel until Monday. The old feeling of being put to a test she was destined to fail flipped back to life in Cora's stomach.

She was trying—as she always did—not to say *no* to anybody. Becca wasn't happy that she'd have to rely on Jill Saturday morning—and Lexie wasn't happy about spending the weekend with Becca and Jill rather than in her room at Cora's, but at least everybody was getting something she wanted. Except perhaps Cora, but then what she usually wanted most was to keep them happy, so maybe this arrangement qualified.

Now it seemed the whole compromise was about to collapse like a house of twigs *gone with the wind,* as Christine would have said. Cora's car wouldn't start at nearly two on Friday afternoon when she should have been already on the road in order to get Lexie at school at two-thirty. It was hot, the car having gathered up and stored the sun's midday heat. Cora impatiently rolled down her window as sweat popped out on the forehead she'd actually powdered, for once, after her shower. She was sticky in her sweater—she'd not gotten around to getting light-weight clothing out of storage yet—but wedged in the seat, she was too bulky to pull it off.

The engine coughed and Cora kept pressure on the key, but then it was grinding with a high harsh refusal that made her startle back afraid even to try the key again. She pounded the steering wheel with her fists once, and then put her head against the top of it, wanting to bang it, or just sob and quit. Finally, she looked at the distance to the house and sighed, opening the car door with her left hand while her right dragged her cane out behind her.

She'd counted on Jolene being home, or Bob, but after seven rings, Cora knew neither of them was. She looked at her watch, felt panicky. She reached information for the phone number of Lexie's school, and called. "Please tell my granddaughter to take the school bus to her…father's house," she said to the secretary who answered. "I'll get there if I can. She should call me, though. Will you be sure she gets this message before school gets out?"

"I'll do my best, ma'am. It's Alexis O'Gara, you said. That right?"

"Yes. But you might have her listed as Detta O'Gara. It's… um…her nickname."

A commotion sounded in the background on the school side of the connection. "That's not the bell now, is it?"

"I'm afraid so, ma'am. Early dismissal for an assembly."

"Will you still be able to…"

"If my student aides can spot her in the assembly, she'll get the message. That's all I can do."

Cora started to reiterate the problem, as if by explaining it adequately she could ensure the right result. A sense of futility came over her, and she ended by asking the secretary to please be sure to have Alexis call her if she got the message. Then she pulled out a kitchen chair and sat down heavily. She rocked slightly, chanting *calm down, calm down* like a mantra. She was not a woman with an excessive need for control, never had been, but lately her life seemed like a closet with coats, pans, gift wrap and screwdrivers all jumbled together, and she couldn't stand it.

She knew where Alex worked. She could get the number from information and call him. Really, there was no other choice, at least not until Jolene came home.

His voice, low and reedy, came on the line after three transfers, scarcely audible over machinery noise, but distinctly suspicious.

"Hello?"

"Alex?"

"Who's this?"

"Cora. I'm sorry to bother you at work, but it's something of an emergency." Cora had been raised to politeness, just as she was to church teachings. The politeness had been less beaten down, although it had been Alex who'd most sorely tried it. "My car is broken. I can't get to the school—I called, but there's an assembly and they may not get a message to Lex…Detta. I'm worried about her standing outside the school waiting and nobody coming."

A long hesitation. "Can't Rebecca get her?"

Cora didn't want to tell Alex anything. Maybe it could be used against her in court that her children died off prematurely. Cora instinctively shook her head and remonstrated herself for having such a thought; Becca wasn't going to die.

"She…can't. Lex…Detta and I are supposed to spend the weekend there, um, helping out. For me to help out, I mean. Becca is…not feeling well."

"Okay."

"Okay, what?"

"I'll bring her to Rebecca's. Detta knows where, right?"

"Yes, of course. Would you do that?"

"Just said I would."

"Well, thank you. Thank you very much. Uh, I can't let her know, I mean, in the message I tried to get to her, I told her to take the bus to your house and I'd try to get there. But I don't know if she'll get the message."

"Okay."

Cora hated to ask again. "Okay…what?"

"I'll clock out. Probably have to come back here, so can't bring her till tonight."

Alex was word-stingy, or maybe hard-up for them, Cora thought. Her polar opposite.

"That's very nice of you. I'm sorry to put you to the trouble."

"Okay."

Cora hung up, relieved and confused. Now all she had to do was call Becca, and wait for Jolene to come home. Jo would take her to Becca's and she could use Becca's car to get to the appointment tomorrow. She guessed she'd have her car towed into Darrville. If things were starting to go wrong with it, though, she'd have to think about getting another. She had to have *something* she could rely on.

Tears came. She covered her face with her hands and her shoulders heaved. "Christine, oh, my Chrissy, Chrissy. I'm doing my best, but I don't know if I can do this. Oh, Chrissy, Chrissy, my Chrissy." Her nose ran and her hands were wet, and just to go to the bathroom for a tissue was too far.

SATURDAY MORNING, CORA could tell Lexie was trying to shake off apprehension and the sour mood she'd been in from Alex's having picked her up instead of Cora. ("Ramon would've brought me," she'd complained to Cora after Alex dropped her off at Becca's. "Who's Ramon? Cora had asked immediately, but didn't pursue it when Lexie said, "Just a guy who lives where Alexander the…does." Cora, of course, knew the part of the moniker Lexie was omitting in the three-beat pause she left after the name. Lexie was testing her, she guessed, and she wouldn't bite.)

In Rebecca's rattly green Dodge, scarcely in better health than Rebecca herself, Cora tried to reassure Lexie as they headed back to Cora's so Lexie could dress them both for their interviews.

"Honey, Dr. Vallade is very nice. My appointment was fine, even though I was a nervous wreck before I went. She's going to talk to you by yourself, then talk to us together."

"What do we have to talk about?"

"She said nothing special. She just wants to see how we communicate, you know, how we get along together. *Our relationship,* she said. I don't know what she'll ask you when you're in there alone, but just answer honestly. Tell her how you feel. Don't hold back, but, you know…"

"Be polite and show that I'm a lady," Lexie inserted, her tone skimming the surface of sassy like a mosquito on a pond, not exactly landing there. Her hair was falling out of the high ponytail she'd worn to bed, and sleep sticks were in the corners of her eyes. She tipped her head against the back of the seat and closed them. "Don't worry," she said a minute later. "It's Alex that has to worry."

Cora started to ask what Lexie meant by that, but then thought better of it. She was too tired to take on a conversation the end point of which she didn't know in advance. Rebecca had been awake from pain, up a lot in the night, and Cora had been up with her from three o'clock on. Finally, she climbed into Rebecca's double bed with her and stroked down Becca's forehead over her eyes, barely grazing the lashes, until she felt her daughter release into sleep. Then she'd not dared move from her—Rebecca was lying on one of Cora's arms—and had stayed on the bed as the night gave way to soft gray, infused with yellow and blue as first light reached a tangle of clothing, then a hung picture.

Then Lexie had, at six thirty, come in to get her, and Cora had been immobile, her arm so numb, then so pain-streaked that Lexie had had to go wake Jill up, and it required both of them to get Cora off the bed. Becca slept through the whispers, Cora's muffled gasps and the girls' extraction of Cora's arm, which made the current crippling stiffness and exhaustion worthwhile.

"What did she ask you?" Lexie said a minute later as they were crossing the town line.

"You know me. She just asked what was going on, or something vague like that, and I told her about your mother…and you and me, and it was a half hour before she got to ask another question."

"You told her about *him,* didn't you? About what he did?"

"Yes, honey, but it's important you tell her what you want her to know yourself."

In fact, Cora had abided by Brenda's instructions and not emphasized Alex's shortcomings. "That can backfire," the lawyer had said. "A psychological evaluator wants to know about you, not what you think of him. All that stuff—about Tina, I mean—will come out…better from your granddaughter than from you, in case Dr. Vallade decides it's fantasy."

That had outraged Cora. "Fantasy!" Her voice had cracked over the word. "He basically admitted it to me. I told you about that."

"Yes. And I believe it. But I'm trying to tell you how to play it with the evaluator."

The use of the words *play it* had troubled Cora, but nonetheless, she'd worn the exact outfit Lexie had dictated, had had Jolene billow her hair into something youthful with a curling iron, worn makeup, gone way early so there'd be no risk of being out of breath—and told the truth. Without emphasizing Alex, what he'd done, what he hadn't done. There'd been questions about her background, her marriage, her children. She'd cried when she'd told the doctor about Christine's death, hadn't brought up Rebecca's illness—so it wouldn't seem she had too much on her plate to provide proper supervision for a teenager—and otherwise stuck to the truth.

DR. VALLADE LET Alexis choose whether to come in alone first or with her grandmother. Lexie hesitated, then said, "I'll go myself."

"We'll be about an hour, Mrs. Laster, maybe longer, until we're ready for you to join us," the doctor said as Lexie got up to follow her out of the waiting room. "You're welcome to leave and come back, if that's most convenient, or wait here. Whatever you like…"

Cora pegged the doctor as fortyish. Wide-set, broad-lidded green eyes and high cheekbones. Petite—which always made Cora feel like a horse—and a cap of short dark hair, thick, wavy, expensively cut. Blue slacks, white knit top, red earrings and a red scarf artfully around her neck today: Lexie would like that touch. She'd tried to get Cora to wear a scarf to hide the lines in her neck, but it gave Cora a choking sensation, so Lexie had reluctantly substituted a necklace. Dr. Vallade had three children, Cora had surmised from the pictures on the desk, and Cora hoped it would help in some nebulous way, that the doctor would empathize with a mother's loss.

"I'll wait here, if you don't mind," Cora answered, trying to sound chipper and energetic. "I brought a book." She'd also left her cane in the car, quite on purpose, steadying herself on Lexie's arm until they got to the office door.

"That'll be just fine," the doctor said. "We'll see you in a bit."

Cora settled in the padded chair—she'd had to wedge her hips between the armrests—and thought about how she should practice to make sure she could get out of the chair without help, with reasonable grace, in case the doctor was observing when she had to do it. The room was neutral, with horizontal blinds on the windows, beige walls and carpet, Monet water-lily prints framed on two walls, and an enormous peace lily in one corner. Violins argued then settled it on a hidden radio. Cora had, as she said, brought a book, but she never got it out of her purse. And she didn't practice getting out of the chair. Sleep slipped over her like a gown.

"YOU WERE SNORING, Grandma. Your mouth was open. Oh, my God. What if she'd seen you? You looked about a hundred years old," Lexie said when they were safely in the hallway outside the doctor's office suite.

Cora had seen the upset on Lexie's face when she'd been dragged back to consciousness by Lexie's frantic whispers and shoulder jostling. It hadn't even been like wakening, really. Truth be told it was more like reluctantly swimming up from the bottom of a midnight pond, that dark, that deep, that still. Lexie's face had emerged from the moon after Cora broke the surface, trying to remember how to breathe and where she was. She'd stalled for time by having Lexie go ask Dr. Vallade where the bathroom was, and say her grandmother would like to use it before she and Lexie had their joint session. Fortunately, Lexie came back alone, and helped Cora haul herself out of the chair. As she was about to enter the bathroom, Lexie hissed, "Don't wash your face, it'll take your makeup off." So Cora cupped her palms for cold water but only to freshen her mouth. She folded and wet a paper towel and laid its coolness on the back of her neck for a minute before turning it over and sponging off the front. She used the toilet, checked herself in the mirror, fluffing the back of her hair where it had been flattened out, and removed the evidence of sleep from the corners of her eyes.

Lexie was waiting right outside the door. She gave Cora a critical once-over. "Okay," she said quietly. "You look fine. Are you awake?"

Cora nodded.

"Just follow my lead." And Lexie smiled then, the sort of heartening smile a mother gives her child, and the backwardness of who was taking care of whom broke Cora's heart nearly as much as anything else ever had. It was a spur that made Cora will herself to stand upright, forget anything and everything else, and show Lexie that she still had something of a mother in Cora.

They answered questions about Christine, about her rules, expectations, communication and how Lexie saw her grandmother's ways as compared to her mother's. Cora suppressed a double take when Lexie explained, "My mother was strict, but she wasn't unfair. I thought her rules made sense even when I didn't like them. Grandma has the same rules Mom did." When Dr. Vallade asked how they were coping with the death, with death itself, Lexie said, "Grandma and I have talked a lot about Mom's death. I think I'm doing better because of that," and Cora worked to keep her astonishment invisible. From what reserves the girl had pulled such an on-target performance, Cora had no idea, but she was fairly sure *performance* was the operative

word. Lexie even looked the part: nicely conservative in an un-
adorned cornflower-blue dress––not too short—stockings, flats,
light makeup befitting a sixteen-year-old, no jewelry except a
locket Christine had given her. She'd worn her hair down,
demurely curled under, as if she had an eerie instinct for what
an adult would think the perfect sixteen-year-old should look
and sound like. Still, Cora saw it: even when Lexie wasn't trying
to look older, the adolescent juts and angles were softening.
Lexie wouldn't be hers much longer however things turned out.

"What issues are there between you two that aren't so easy
to work out?" Dr. Vallade asked, an array of framed diplomas
from Michigan schools behind her.

"I wish Lexie would talk with me more than she does, I mean.
I worry that too much stays inside her," Cora had said quietly.

"Grandma, I want to, except now it's too hard, I mean, I'm
not with you very much and it just doesn't feel right on the
phone."

"What about on your side, Lexie?"

"I think Grandma should let me go to parties without calling to
check if the parents will be home. I mean I think she should
have…"

Dr. Vallade drummed her fingers lightly in punctuation. They
tapered to blunt, unpolished nails. She wore a fat silver wedding
band with a delicate-looking engagement ring perched over it,
like they were never intended to match but she could make
anything work. "That's something a lot of good parents do,
Lexie. Mrs. Laster, what are your feelings about this?"

Cora hesitated. It had never once happened; Lexie hadn't asked
to go to any parties when she'd been with Cora. "I, um, didn't
know this was a problem for Lexie. I always said I'd do that
because even good kids, and I know Lexie's a good girl, can get
into situations they can't handle." Cora warmed to the subject, as
she could be counted on to do almost any. A talker, Marvin had
always called her. "With drinking and smoking and marijuana so
common, I don't know how young people can be expected to fend
it all off without some adult help. Especially for a girl, well, I just
don't think it's safe to go someplace without adult supervision."

"But, Grandma, Tim would watch out for me. I mean, do you think he'd let some guy touch me?" Lexie interjected.

"Honey, that's not a job for your boyfriend. You shouldn't be in a situation where it could happen anyway."

"Sounds like you have a good handle on safety issues, Mrs. Laster," Dr. Vallade said, and her approval was clear and warm as amber. "Lexie has raised some disturbing issues regarding her father," she went on. "She says you're aware of them."

"Yes."

"Would you be willing to schedule another appointment to give me the background information you have?"

"Yes, I can do that." Cora felt a click of recognition, like dentures sliding exactly into place. It was as Brenda had said. Information had come from Lexie, and now Cora was being asked to corroborate. *It makes a much stronger impression on the evaluator that way,* she'd said. If Dr. Vallade was dismissing what Lexie told her, she wouldn't be asking for more, Cora surmised.

Even before they were out the door and Lexie started in on her again about having fallen asleep in the waiting room, Cora was trying to decide how she felt. On the one hand, she thought they'd both made a good impression. The issue of her age hadn't even come up, the only question and answer they'd both feared and rehearsed. On the other—what, exactly, was going on with Lexie? It was as if the girl were captain of a boat, and Cora along for the ride, hanging on to a rail in the stern, woolly-headed and slightly seasick.

"What did you say to her?" Cora interrupted Lexie's complaint. "No, that's not what I'm worried about. You told her you'd talked to me about your mother, and you…"

"Don't worry about that," Lexie interrupted. "I know what I'm doing."

Cora braced herself against the hallway wall, the fatigue of the previous night and the strain of the interview making her breath break like surf. "Honey, this is too hard. Would you run to the car and get my cane? I'll wait here."

"Grandma, lean on me. I can get you there as well as your

cane. Better." Lexie looked small to Cora, as if she were caught in some warp between child and woman. But right then, she looked like Christine, too, the color of her eyes heightened by the blue dress. The set of her head was Christine's, the unspeakable stubbornness, the will. Christine had used those very qualities to ruin her own life and then to rebuild it.

Against her better judgment, Cora put her hand on Lexie's shoulder, but Lexie slid in next to her so that Cora's arm went around the girl's shoulders, and she took on more of her grandmother's weight.

BACK AT BECCA'S, Cora hoped for a nap. She'd made lunch in the kitchen for the girls, sat on Becca's bed while Becca stirred and restirred a bowl of chicken broth, and then waited for Becca to slide back through her thrashing-sleep stage to her deeper, molasses-breath one. Today, Becca had finally upped her own pain medication, as the oncologist had said she could. A clump of ashy hair was strewn on the pillow, and Cora picked it up and stuck it in her pocket, angry at helplessness. She arranged the sheet over Becca's shoulder, and picked up the dish with one hand and her cane with the other. The fatigue of the lost sleep and the exertion of the morning were overcoming her.

She'd hardly made it to the kitchen when the phone rang and she pushed herself into high gear to get to it before it rang again and disturbed Becca.

"Cora?"

"Yes, hold, let me pull myself a chair over." Cora panted. She set the phone down on the table, ran a glass of water and lowered herself into a chair. "It went okay," she said when she picked up the receiver again, anticipating the reason for Jo's call. Sunlight streamed into the kitchen, early June dropping July hints when it should have been remembering May instead. Cora swiped at her forehead with a crumpled tissue she pulled from her bra. She tucked it back in and blew at the hair that had flopped back down onto her forehead.

"You sound out of breath. You all right?"

"Tired is all. Becca had a bad night."

A murmur of understanding in Jolene's voice, raspy, though she hadn't smoked in twenty-five years. "So it went just okay?"

"Nothing bad. I don't know what Lexie is pulling, exactly. She was too good—you know?—when we were in there together. Said we'd spent all kinds of time talking about Christine dying and the like."

Jolene knew the truth. Cora could imagine her considering this piece of information, her eyes closed, weighing its potential for harm or good. "Who knows. A psychologist would probably rather hear that than that she shuts herself up in her dead mother's old bedroom and looks at a picture of her in her coffin."

"You don't think it can backfire?"

"Did you contradict her?"

"No...not really."

"I wouldn't worry about it, then. Did Lexie like her?"

"You know, I never thought to ask. Didn't take one of her instant dislikes, at least."

"That's a good thing, then. Do you need to get back to something now, or have you got a minute?"

"Becca's asleep and the girls are...actually, I'm not sure where they are, but the house is quiet. I was just going to nap a bit."

"You do that, then."

"No, it's all right. Hearing you is a tonic. What were you going to say?"

"Nothing to upset you. Just a curiosity." Jolene hesitated and Cora felt a small foreboding, a hangnail on her consciousness. She tangled her fingers in the phone cord and felt slightly claustrophobic; Becca's kitchen was cramped, papered in a harvest-gold gingham that made Cora dizzy if she looked at it straight on.

"What is it?"

"I sent Bob up to your house this morning to see if he couldn't fix your car."

"Oh, Jo, you didn't need to do that. They're coming to tow it in this afternoon—I called yesterday, but it was too close to closing time and they said they'd come out this afternoon."

"I know, but I thought we could save the money." Jo did that, said *we* about saving money, when, of course, it was Cora's money stretched to squealing. "Anyway, you need to call and cancel the tow, because the car is fixed."

"Bless that Bob." It would help not to have a repair bill, with all the psychological evaluation expense to be paid.

"Honey, it wasn't Bob."

"What? I tried and tried and it wouldn't start no matter what I did."

"Bob found a note on your door when he was going in to get the spare car keys." Cora and Jo had always had keys to each other's houses. Jo paused and took a breath.

"From who? What does it say?"

"Something like, I hope you don't mind, I took a look at your car and it was easy to fix, so I did it. It's just signed Alex."

"God almighty," Cora exhaled. "I don't know what to say. Do you think it's right? I mean, what he said...could he have been messing with the car? Do you think he would?"

"Bob had that thought, but he got the keys and tested it out, and the car's working fine."

"But...the keys..."

"I know. Bob said the house was locked up tight and nothing disturbed. He found another way to start it, or he figured out what was wrong by looking, maybe. I don't know. Bob didn't know because it wasn't broken anymore. He did look under the hood."

"What do you think, Jo?"

"I think for now you just say thank you, and keep putting one foot in front of the other."

thirty-three

SO. GRANDMA'S appointments with the shrink are finished. I was glad I went with her first because I'm thinking I have to scale back the plan for when I go with Alexander the Goddamn Great. The doctor isn't as smart as Grandma thinks she is but she's not as dumb as I hoped she'd be. I was going to wear the black stuff and not talk at all, but now I think it's better to work on Alex.

Why'd he go and fix Grandma's car? Grandma couldn't figure it out, but I think maybe he's nervous about talking to the shrink because he knows he's a psychopath. He's hoping Grandma will call it off in gratitude or something. Fat chance. She promised.

The car thing did give me an idea. The doctor has this sign in her office that says twenty-four hours notice is required to cancel an appointment. If Alex cancels our appointment on less than twenty-four hours notice, it'll start her off annoyed with him for sure. It's time to find out how good a friend Ramon wants to be.

thirty-four

A DIRTY LIGHTBULB of sun was trying to burn through the haze of the day. Cora's mind fragmented into tasks: did Rebecca need a pill just now? Air out the cream-colored summer comforter on the clothesline while Rebecca was in the tub, but hurry back to sit on the side to help Rebecca wash herself. Get Jill from cheerleading practice. Think of something Becca would eat and Jill at least endure for supper.

Becca's strength was still down, and Cora hadn't been able to go home at the end of the weekend. "I'll get there, Mom," she'd said. "Dr. Simcoe said to hold on and see if I can't tolerate the new drug because the trials have been pretty good. It's brand-new, y'know." Radiation had been suspended for the week, which would have been a relief if Cora could have been at home the days they weren't making the drive. She needed to catch up on her own housework, gather a thought or two in a coherent order and rest. Now, though, it was already Wednesday and she was in the middle of chopping celery for a tuna salad, when she realized with a start that she'd not heard from Lexie about her appointment to see Dr. Vallade with Alex on Monday. It was only noon, though and Lexie couldn't possibly be home before around three, so all she could do was berate herself for letting Christine down. She wrote herself a note so she'd not forget to call later on, after the laundry was folded and the dusting done.

She had spoken to Alex on Sunday when she used her own car to take Lexie back to him. "Thank you very much for repairing my car," she'd said in a formal tone. "I'd like to pay for your time and, of course, whatever part it needed."

"That's okay," he answered, gaunt-looking in the twilight.

"What do I owe you?" Cora persisted. Lexie was glowering at Alex. Amazing that laser-thing she does with her eyes doesn't melt him into the concrete, Cora thought.

"Nothing. It's okay. Hardly took a minute."

Cora had started to protest again, but decided to just be gracious. "Well, thank you very…" she'd begun and then Lexie cut her off.

"Thank you very much to stay off our property in the future. It's called trespassing. Whatever you're trying to pull, it's not going to work." Then she'd stalked between Cora and Alex and gone into the trailer without saying goodbye to Cora. A screen door—Alex must have just put it up—had slapped the door frame two times then sputtered against it two or three more before it was still.

Cora was embarrassed even while part of her admired the gumption.

"I'd better get going…" she offered weakly. Slant rays of late sun came over Alex's shoulder at her, and she put up a hand to shield her eyes and, incidentally, her discomfort. "I'm sure she didn't mean to be rude."

Alex had shrugged. His skin looked pasty to Cora, and his pants looked like they were failing in their effort to find hips or a rear to rest on. They rode low, no swagger in the body underneath, a uniform for defeat.

Cora hadn't missed any news. The appointment was actually going on right when it startled its way into her memory. And she'd rightly read Alex as losing stamina even before his troubles had shifted into high gear. First, he'd had to cancel the Monday appointment with the court psychologist because his truck wouldn't start. It had scarcely taken a glance to see what caused the problem: the distributor cap was gone, stolen sometime during the night, obviously, since the truck had worked fine just ten hours earlier. He'd discovered it long after Detta had ridden off with that boy just as cocky as you please, never glancing over her shoulder, just getting in his wreck of a car and slamming the door. What bothered Alex the most: he saw Detta smile—no it was more, it was a laugh—at something the boy said. Alex had never once seen her smile until that moment. She had pretty teeth, like Christine, at least based on that flash from a distance.

It wasn't that he couldn't fix the damn thing, or didn't have enough money to get a new cap; it was that there was no way he could hitch into town, get a new cap at the Napa Auto Parts, get back and fix it in time for the appointment. He'd thought to call to cancel, and was informed by some crisp-as-celery secretary that he'd be charged for the time even though Mrs. Laster was responsible for the other costs of the evaluation.

"I took off work," he protested. "Can we make it later today? I could fix the truck and get there this afternoon."

"I'm sorry, sir, but the doctor has no other openings today. We'll have to reschedule. She can see you Friday at ten. How's that?"

Terrible. He'd have to ask off twice in the same week, and then he still had to go back by himself so that would make a third time. The foreman wasn't going to take it well. He might even stick him on third shift, which made a mess of his days and nights. And Dink and Big Al wouldn't be there. Just the thought of meeting new men made him feel like he'd eaten too much chili.

"Anything on Saturday or at night?" he asked, as if office hours might have changed in the last two weeks.

"The doctor is in Monday through Friday between the hours of eight and four." Snap. Chopped celery.

"All right," Alex sighed. "Friday at ten. Is this the one I'm supposed to bring my girl to?"

"That will be fine," she'd said and Alex guessed that was a clear answer.

Monday morning, though, turned out to be about the high point of his week.

On Wednesday, Detta went on to school so she wouldn't miss

her first two classes. He was pleased and surprised to see she didn't wear her death ghoul outfit, not that he'd told her what to wear, which would have absolutely ensured the black ensemble. Even he had caught on that much. But on her own, Detta wore blue jeans and a T-shirt, which he supposed was acceptable. Alex was supposed to pick her up in front of the school at nine-thirty for the appointment. He showered and shaved and started to get dressed. He pulled on a new pair of khaki pants, because Big Al said they would go okay with Dink's sports coat, the lightweight navy blazer Dink's wife made him wear to church. But when he yanked on the zipper, it wouldn't budge, off its tracks at the very bottom and not about to go back on. He didn't think it had been that way at the store, but then he hadn't tried them on, so maybe it had. He thought maybe he could just keep the sports coat buttoned and wear them anyway, but then both the buttons were missing from Dink's coat. Both of them! He couldn't believe his eyes. Why would Dink loan him a coat with the buttons gone? So now he was down to clean jeans and the dress shirt he'd bought for court.

How could he have missed that his last pair of decent jeans had a hole in the knee? How could he have missed the stain (coffee?) on the front of the new-for-court shirt? He didn't even remember that he'd had coffee that day, though he must have, nervous as he'd been. And why hadn't the stain come out in the laundry? He *had* washed it.

He ended up in the jeans with the hole in one knee and a clean T-shirt, the one with the least writing on it. He guessed it would have to be all right. That's what Detta was wearing, and Christine had probably taught her about stuff like that.

He noticed something like a smile playing around Detta's lips when he picked her up, right on time even though he'd been pretty rattled trying to figure out what to do about the clothes.

IT ALL WOULD HAVE passed over him like a summer storm if the distributor cap, the *replacement* cap, hadn't been gone on Friday, when the doctor had agreed to see him right at eight, so he could still get in most of a day's work. He was spiffed up in the khakis and the sports coat—Big Al had asked his daughter Anna, the oldest, who was taking home economics at the junior high school—if she'd sew buttons on the coat and see if her teacher knew how to work with the zipper. He'd have asked Patsy, his wife, except Patsy didn't approve of Alex keeping a young girl from her grandmother. "A girl needs a woman to mother her, not a mutant beerhead."

All dressed up and the truck won't start. It was like a bad dream replaying.

And it came together in his head, suddenly it seemed, although the parts must have been brewing on some back burner in his mind because it came whole when it came. The picture of Detta getting in that boy's car not fifteen minutes before, laughter on her lips, and the mirth on the boy's face as he drove off had burned an after image in his mind.

Alex popped the hood, swung out of the truck to the asphalt, and took a look at the innards. Sure enough. Only this time he knew who the vandal or vandals were.

Back in high school, one of Alex's gym teachers had tried to talk him into trying out for the basketball team in spite of his height because he was so quick. That fast, he was across the tiny areas that passed for yards belonging to the three trailers, ducking clotheslines and skirting several lawn chairs and a cement goose, and banging on the door of Ramon's trailer.

Rosa answered. She started a smile, but it disappeared into a furrow when Alex began shouting.

"Your boy messed with my truck! I want him to stay away from Detta. I don't want her over here or him over t'my place. Not ever!"

"What?" Rosa's eyebrows arched over the question. Her chin went up. "What are you saying? Ramon hasn't been to your place."

"Well, he damn well was last night. Second time this week my distributor cap's gone."

"What makes you think Ramon did this?" She stepped out on the stoop and cushioned the door, closing by spring action, from slamming. It made him angry that she could be in a pink bathrobe and he could be dressed like he was going to an office, and she was the one who looked dignified. She didn't raise her voice, either.

To show her, he raised his even more. "I know, all right? I know. You keep him off my property and my girl."

"You're having problems with Detta." It wasn't a question, but it didn't sound like an accusation either.

"That's my business."

"Seems like you here shouting and carrying on makes it mine, as well."

Was she making fun of him? He'd never been able to tell with Olivia, though she always denied she was.

"Well it ain't. I told you, just…"

Rosa interrupted. "I'm Rosa, Ramon's mother. Detta says you are Alex. How do you do?" He could hear the formal construction of an English as a Second Language class in Adult Education held in Santa Maria parish in Miami, though Alex didn't know that. He thought she was doing it to make him look stupid. His speech always fell apart when he was exercised.

And now he felt like chewing one of her damn bird feeders to the ground. "I ain't here for tea. Look…"

"Have you thought Detta may have done this?"

"Messed up a truck? What does a girl know about messing up a truck? You're crazy."

"Well, perhaps you guess her less than she is."

Alex was losing the upper hand. He felt small and stupid and despairing. He took a step back down, to leave, which made matters worse since Rosa was now over a head taller than he. "I don't want her here, or in your boy's car. All right? I'll take her to school myself." Of course, Alex couldn't do that without being late to work. Cutting off his nose to spite his face had long been a specialty of his. She could just take the bus was all. Take the damn bus.

"Mr.…Alex, if I may. Your Detta is confused and afraid and crying for her mother. And she's upset about her aunt's cancer. Be patient. Give her a chance."

"She's the one won't give me a chance!" It revved him up again when Rosa said that.

"There's always a second chance with children. They are forgiving."

"Not this one," he said, angry. "You don't know. Just keep your boy away, hear?" He turned and left, striding the small distance without looking back though her eyes were heavy as bowling balls on his back.

Her aunt's cancer?

thirty-five

CORA HAD HARDLY BEEN home in a week. It was worth it, though—worth the mess of her yard, worth the undusted furniture in her parlor and the empty refrigerator in her kitchen—because in strands thin as each single day, Becca had picked up strength like a ball of gathering yarn. This morning, she'd polished off a soft-boiled egg and toast, combed her hair, dressed in elastic-waist khaki shorts and a Nike T-shirt and folded a load of towels before exhaustion took her hand and unraveled her back to the bed for a nap. "If you need to get home, Mom," she'd said over lunch, "I think I'll be all right this afternoon. Maybe you could come back tonight? Just in case Jill needs help."

"…In case Jill needs help" was code for "in case I pass out, begin vomiting uncontrollably, hemorrhage or experience any of the other horrors that might precede my decline into death." Becca was vehement about not wanting Jill to witness a "medical emergency," which was the furthest she'd specify the range of contingencies about which she'd been warned. Rather, she talked around it all, skirting the gaping black hole of what could happen, and using phrases like "empower my body to heal through the power of the Lord" to rehearse her plans. Cora didn't see that Becca's body was empowered to do much except suffer, nor that Lexie had been helped one bit by being safely in school during her mother's "medical emergency," but there'd be no good in pointing out even the latter to Becca. Not that doing good seemed to make the smallest difference; whatever good she'd tried to do for her children, well, what, really, had ever come of it? She hadn't even kept the majority of them alive, surely a minimum standard.

Still, there was an upbeat today, which was that Cora and Becca both felt comfortable with Cora leaving—as long as she went back to Becca's to sleep. On the way home, Cora stopped at the Thriftway and picked up groceries, not too much produce, though, because who knew how long she'd be home? On the other hand, school would let out for the summer on Thursday, and Cora was to have extra visitation with Lexie during vacations, so maybe she'd have to stay home more since Lexie had such an aversion to being at Becca's. The same old dilemma: *choose!*

As she drove home, a sulky sky lurked over the trees, and the late spring land—already opened and reclosed in neat furrows and in lush ornamental bloom—managed to look dreary and doomed. She'd hoped to call the Miller's teenage son Mark to catch up on the yard work—he was saving for a car—but the rain was going to beat her home. She sighed, but wouldn't let herself cry because it would use up too much energy and make her nose runny the rest of the day.

When her wheels first crunched onto the gravel of her own driveway, she didn't notice, and then when she did, it was only the sense of something different. Then she began to pick out details. The rest of the marigolds and dahlias and impatiens were planted where Bob had spaded and hoed their beds, rescued from where Cora had abandoned the flats, partway under the porch for shade. Really, she'd let the job go too long already. Why on earth had she clung to having the gardens?

Now, though, the plants—leggy and pale—were drooping onto the ground as new transplants will do, edging the walk from porch to driveway and under Christine's bird feeders. The lawn was shorn and the woodpile restacked like Lincoln Logs, the winter's sprawl of chips and detritus raked up and gone. The weeds that had grown up alongside the house had been neatly whacked. *Bob,* Cora thought immediately, but then realized, no, it couldn't have been Bob, he and Jolene had left yesterday to visit his sister in Detroit.

So who, then? And why?

thirty-six

IT WAS REALLY HIS OWN fault when you get right down to it. Alexander the Goddamn Great went too far this time. This morning he told me to take the bus to school, that I couldn't go with Ramon anymore. Like he's some big dude or something, he announces who I can't be friends with. I just stared at him like he was an escaped lunatic, which I think he is anyway, and then I say —well, since you don't approve, maybe I'll just marry Ramon. So he gets in my face. Right in his puny fake kitchen, he points his finger at me and says —You stay away from him and from that trailer. That's final.

—That's final? I yelled at him. —So *you* say. Maybe I'll just have Ramon's baby before I marry him. It made me really mad because I started crying then, and I was mad that I was crying.— Or, maybe I'll just have twins and you can kill them both. Get it right this time!

Then he swung his hand back like he was going to slap me.— Go ahead, hit me. I dare you to hit me. I was really screaming and I grabbed the frypan off the stove to hit him back with if he did. I forgot he'd cooked bacon in it, which I knew because the whole tin-box house reeked from it, and the grease flew all over. It wasn't that hot, but it got on him and me both, plus on the floor and the walls and stuff. I don't know what he was going to do, he started coming at me, but he slipped on the grease and crashed on his butt. It sounds funny and when it happened, I wanted to laugh in his face, but I was too mad, and then when I saw his face I was too scared. His eyes were like black ink and he had red spots on his face. He looked worse than Mom in her coffin with those spots of rouge on her face.

Then he got up—well, he slipped again, but he grabbed the refrigerator handle and got up. He grabbed his keys and banged open the door so hard it broke the doorstop and bounced back on him before he got to the screen. I heard him peel out, the idiot, he went to work like that with little bacon bits and grease all over his T shirt, nasty as Grandma's spinach salad.

I went to the coat closet where he keeps his clothes. I just had to do something after he left. I was so furious I *had* to do something, so I got all his clothes and dumped them in a heap on the kitchen floor in the grease. I don't know what made me get the clothes, it was just the first thing I thought of. Then that wasn't enough, it didn't look bad enough, so I picked up the frypan and dripped the grease that was still in it—there wasn't much as I recall—over the top. And it really did make me feel better.

Then I got my backpack and went over to Ramon's.

When I knocked, Rosa came to the door. She was nice and all, but she didn't open it the way she always does, and Ramon didn't come right on out through the kitchen.—Detta, did your father tell you he said you can't ride with Ramon anymore?

I didn't know he'd gone over there. It made me mad all over again, and embarrassed too.—I don't care, I said.

—But we can't go against him. He could get the law after Ramon. I'm sorry, Detta.

I saw Ramon, just like a moving shadow, really, his face a little light spot on the dark inside. She was standing there in a white terrycloth bathrobe that made her skin look really dark and pretty, telling me they're not my friends anymore, all because of Alexander the Goddamn Great. Then Rosa said —Detta, honey, you're a good girl. I'll try to talk to your father after he's calm. He thinks Ramon bothered his truck. You and Ramon stay apart for now.

I wanted to scream at her like I screamed at Alex. "Ramon didn't bother his truck, I did, I did, I did. And I'm glad. I'll bother

it again. Please! Ramon is my only friend. Don't take him away from me."

But it was Ramon showed me *how* to bother the truck, and I thought Rosa might figure that out or make Ramon tell her the truth, so I left it alone. He'd showed me on his own car, he never went near Alex's damn truck, but I didn't want him to get in trouble so I just backed down off their steps with nothing left for Alex to take away from me.

When I went back to the trailer, what I did wasn't exactly what I meant to do. I don't know exactly what I meant to do. Well, I did mean for him to lose, too, I admit that. But not everything. Just his clothes.

When I picked up the book of matches—always lying by the stove because the pilot light doesn't work right—when the match scraped like a fingernail file and lit on the first try like *yes!* and I dropped it on the pile, I only meant for him to lose his clothes. That's the thing, though—I never know quite what will lead to what, leaping from my fingers to spread out of control.

thirty-seven

NOBODY EVEN CALLED Alex until after ten in the morning, and then, for God's sake, what the twangy female voice on the phone said was that Alexis O'Gara was unhurt and he needed to pick her up at the police station. Alex thought he'd misunderstood over the machinery din in the shop. He and Big Al had been checking off invoice items for one of the trucks when the supervisor gestured to him to pick up the phone.

"The police station?" he said, confused.

"Do you know where it is?"

"What'd she do?"

"Oh, my. I'm sorry, sir. I must have wires crossed. I thought you'd been called, I must have misunderstood your daughter. There's been a fire, but don't worry, she's unhurt. Paramedics examined her at the scene. She refused to go to the hospital."

"A fire?" Alex's head felt clogged, cotton-tongued. Big Al heard Alex say it and stopped what he was doing, waiting for the next slice of information.

"I'm sorry. I really don't know the details, I'm just the dispatcher. Officer Eshbaugh asked me to follow up on the girl."

"Where? A fire at school?"

"No, sir. I believe, uh, where you live. I don't know how you weren't notified to come, but…" She trailed off, waiting for him to jump in and say, "I'm on my way," but he was stunned into paralysis and couldn't string that many words into a strand. Big

Al pushed his cap back on his forehead as if it might help him eavesdrop more efficiently. But the look on his face was concern. "You need to come get her," the woman continued, "and I'm sure you'll want to start insurance claims for your property. Really, I'm very sorry to tell you like this."

"Yeah, uh, okay."

After he'd hung up, Alex stood in place, bewildered. The bacon grease on his shirt was oily and moist, and some had gone on his jeans and work boots, too. The smell of it was ripe and strong. Dink and Big Al had had a field day with it, and Alex's obvious agitation had only fueled them more.

"Fire. At my trailer," Alex got out to Big Al, who immediately adjusted his hat higher on his forehead, tilting the brim up.

"Jesus," he murmured and pulled his cap back down. Blue Devils, it said, in gold on bright blue. He claimed it referred to his in-laws. "Lose much?"

"Don't know."

"How'd it start?"

"Don't know. Detta's at the police station."

"Jesus. Hurt?"

"They said no."

"She was there?"

"I guess."

"Hey, man, you better get going. Don't clock out. I'll take care of Hicks." Hicks was their shift foreman, a redheaded giant in plaid who'd already made vaguely threatening comments about the number of times Alex had clocked in late, out early or missed work altogether.

Alex stood in place, staring at the wall phone he'd just hung up as if it were going to tell him more.

"Man, go!" Big Al said, and nudged Alex's elbow. "Wait. I got a clean shirt in my locker. You can switch."

It infuriated Alex that Al had had a shirt all morning and hadn't offered it.

"No," he muttered, shaking his head.

DETTA WAS SORT OF huddled in a chair, but when she caught sight of him she switched to a defiant posture.

"You okay?" Alex said.

No answer, just the smallest look that said, "Obviously I'm okay, stupid, I'm sitting right in front of you."

"What happened?" Alex demanded.

"How should I know?" Her voice was almost gone, just a raspy shell around a whisper.

"They said you were there. You okay?"

She didn't soften a bit. "I was cooking breakfast. It caught fire, not that you have a fire extinguisher. Isn't that a law or something?"

She'd never cooked anything before, he knew that much.

"What's wrong with your voice?"

A shrug.

"You been checked over?" His own voice was picking up volume and intensity.

She reacted to it and conceded a nod. "Just from the smoke 'n stuff…heat."

"Doctor say that?"

Her eye roll this time. "Paramedic."

"You gotta do something for it?"

A head shake.

"How bad is it?"

"Breakfast?"

"Goddammit. How much damage to the trailer?"

She swallowed and started to rub her throat, but took her hand away. "Whole thing."

"The whole thing?" Right about then, Alex noticed that the stink of smoke was overcoming the bacon smell on him. Detta's hair was disheveled, and there were some streaks on her face. "Did you try to put it out?"

"Yes, I tried to put it out." Mincing, being crappy to him for no reason, even with her voice like that.

"What were you cooking, for God's sake?"

A barely perceptible hesitation. "Bacon."

She was lying. He'd used up the last of the bacon that morning. He made no comment.

"The cops want to talk to you," she said, her voice failing by the time a uniform rounded a corner and approached them, a clipboard under his arm.

"You Alexander O'Gara?"

"Yeah."

"Alexis here has identified the original source as a cooking fire." The officer would have been a handsome man were it not for his teeth. They were crooked and stained and spoiled his face entirely. "I'm real sorry, sir. We gotta do a police report for your insurance."

Was it a law that you had to have insurance or was that just cars? Alex had let it lapse, the year after his mother died. He thought it best not to mention that. "Yeah, okay," he said.

The policeman pointed out some light blue squares Alex was to sign. "This oughta be fire-department stuff," he sighed, "but it came to us because at first they thought it might be arson." He shrugged. "Anyway, at least we can close it out so the claim won't drag. You'll want to contact your insurance company right away."

"Yeah, okay." Alex ran his hand over the top of his head. This stuff wasn't registering. He wished he'd taken Big Al's shirt.

"Looks like when Alexis here tried to get the pan out of the kitchen because of the flames, what with the heat 'n smoke 'n fire comin' up into her face, she tripped. Spilled it, fire and all, onto a pile of clothes you left on the floor." He shook his head. "Nuthin' hotter or faster than a grease fire."

He hadn't left clothes on the kitchen floor. Used to, in the bedroom when it had been his, but not anymore, and for sure not in the kitchen. Something else to set his head spinning. Detta was studying her hands in her lap, rolled up like two balls of yarn.

"There's still a couple men on the scene, prob'ly. Making sure the embers are dead. It'll be real hot next day or two. You won't be able to pick through stuff yet. 'Fraid there's not much left. Red Cross'll help. Want the number?"

"Yeah, okay," Alex said, which seemed to be the only words his mouth would form.

"Lookit, I'm sorry nobody called sooner. Guess somebody

misunderstood you, miss, about how he'd been called." The last was aimed in Detta's direction, but she didn't look up.

"Okay. Yeah. Thanks," Alex got out, adding a word to the repertoire as he accepted the carbon copy of the police report.

LATER, HE WASN'T SURE when he'd gotten it, that Detta had started the fire on purpose. The first lie, about the bacon, had only confused him. The business about clothes being on the kitchen floor had thrown him off because maybe the police meant the living-room floor. Not that he remembered what he'd left where. It seemed to him that it just came to him whole cloth when he glanced at her after they left the police station, and he saw the defiant set of her head, the mask of her face.

"You did it." When he said it, they were in his truck. He kept both hands on the wheel, his eyes on the road, and it wasn't a question.

"You're crazy," she rasped. There was a ring of fear around her then, like one of the rings around whatever planet it was that had rings. "Where are you going?"

In fact, Alex had no idea. He was just driving. "To the trailer," he said, his voice wooden, as the obvious thought of where to go finally emerged.

"Well, let me out." Detta didn't want to be anywhere around him when he saw the wreckage.

"What?"

"Just let me out. I don't wanna go there."

"Too bad," he said, and kept driving.

HE HADN'T KNOWN what to expect. The shell of the trailer was still standing, though the roof had collapsed into it. Waves of melted aluminum scalloped down from the top of the walls. A fireman, his gear shucked into the neighbor's parking area, was hosing embers through a broken window over whatever remained of the brown couch, while another was sitting up in the truck chugging from a bottle of water. An incongruous sun, cheery and peaceful, sparkled on the stream from the nozzle.

A huge dark circle was apparent under each arm of the

working fireman's denim shirt. He was wiping his forehead when Alex and Detta drove up, ducking his head like a bird to rub it against the upper part of his sleeve. The tree next to the kitchen side of the trailer was charred, the leaves looking like late fall instead of late spring, scarce, curled-up brown scraps. The trunk was white, like some foreign species. The trailers on both sides of his had smoky stains on them. What grass had been between was dead as concrete.

"You the owner?" he said, when Alex got out of the truck. Detta stayed put.

"Yeah."

"Pretty well gone," the fireman said. He looked around fifty to Alex, once he got close enough to see, but he was built like a young man, a weight lifter at that. Next to him, Alex was scrawny and he hated that. A loser all the way around. "Did what we could, but it's not a big place and it went up fast," the fireman said. "These places always do. You can't go in yet," he added, apologetic.

"Yeah." Did he know any other words anymore?

"That your daughter?" he said, pointing to the truck with a jerk of his head because his hands were busy with the hose.

Alex hesitated, weighing the idea. He could always say he'd misunderstood the question if it came up later, if it had some importance. He was dead broke now. Let them go after child support. Who cared? "Nah. I'm just keeping her for her grandmother."

After they left the trailer, without telling Detta what he was doing, he called Cora from the pay phone outside the Rite Aid pharmacy a half-mile away. He didn't slam the door this time. Detta sneaked a peek at him but couldn't tell anything from his face.

"It's Alex," he said without a greeting. Behind him, Detta was stony-faced, still in the truck. In spite of the heat, she'd kept her window rolled up, so her profile was hazy, a sun glare igniting the back of her head to his eyes.

"Oh, yes. Hello, Alex." He could hear the wariness in Cora's voice. She always sounded like that to him, like he'd once pulled a gun on her or something.

"Been a fire at my place. I need to bring Detta back to you."
He turned his back to the truck, not that Detta seemed to be
looking at him. He stuck a finger in his free ear to block out the
traffic noise beyond the parking lot.

"Oh, my god. Is she all right?"

"Yeah."

"Well, of course, bring her. Right away. I mean, now is fine.
I'm here. What happened?"

He was going to do it, tell Cora what her precious granddaughter had done. At the moment, he couldn't have said why
he didn't. Certainly not because he wasn't sure.

"Just an accident. Look, I'm in a pay phone…on the way."

"Oh, yes. Of course, all right." Polite as always, that was
Cora. And she hadn't even asked if he was all right, not that he'd
really expect her to. So why did it grate on him so?

Alex grunted a syllable that could have been "Bye." He hung
the receiver in its cradle, but didn't turn around right away. He
studied, without concentrating, the parts of the pay phone worn
to a dull ready-to-be-retired patina by thousands of hands and
coins and extremes of weather, while he considered whether to
call N. Reardon Greevy, his snotty pin-striped lawyer. He pulled
the attorney's card from where it was tucked behind his driver's
license in his wallet and felt in his pocket for change. Four
pennies, a dime and a nickel. He was damned if he was going to
ask Detta for money. He turned and walked back to his truck
where the girl sat exactly as she'd been when he got out, that
rigid.

Neither of them spoke a word the whole way to Cora's.
Within five minutes, of course, Detta figured out where he was
taking her. Was he imagining a smug aura around her silence?
Was that exhalation a little sigh of triumph?

thirty-eight

I WAS SURE HE WAS going to tell Grandma I did it, even though he doesn't have one bit of proof, but he didn't. Well, actually, he couldn't when we got there, strictly speaking, because she wasn't there, but he didn't call her up later to tell, either. Probably he forgot due to brain damage.

Grandma had left a note on the door saying Rebecca fell in the bathtub and she had to rush over there to help Jill. Well, that's right, I guess she should do that, since Jill is such a namby pamby spoiled little ditzbrain. Grandma certainly couldn't tell her no, I have to stay home for Lexie's sake on account of she was almost killed in a fire (for all she knows I was almost killed) and her psycho-drunk father is bringing her here within the next hour. No, of course not.

So I'm stuck with Alexander the Goddamn Great standing on the back porch, too damn close to my mother's bird feeder, looking right at me and saying—What's the deal with Rebecca?

—None of your beeswax, I whispered. Not too original, but it was all I could come up with.

— I hear she's got cancer. That right?

—Where'd you get that idea? We didn't want him to know so he couldn't use it against us in court.—You spying on us?

He sort of snorted, like he was saying I wouldn't waste my time.—Never mind that, is what he said.—How bad is it?

—She's fine! I shrieked. The effect was sort of ruined because my voice cracked big time. I went back to a whisper, which is

what the paramedic told me to stick to. Well, he really said try
not to use it at all and drink a lot of fluids.—She's completely
fine. Didn't you ever slip in a bathtub? Does that mean you've
got cancer and are going to die?

   —She's dying?

   —No! didn't you hear me? I said she does *not* have cancer
and she's not going to die. Are you deaf? That many words made
my throat hurt again, so I just shut up and gave him death rays
again.

   By then it was late afternoon and I hadn't had anything to eat
all day. My stomach let out this enormous growl. Alex cracked
up. I don't think I've ever heard him laugh before. First it made
me mad because I was already mad over how he was going on
with lies about Rebecca. Well, it was true but he didn't know it
so that made it lies. Then I didn't appreciate him laughing at me.
But his laugh was *so* weird, sort of like a goose honking, and
he sounded *so* stupid that I laughed. For a minute we were both
laughing, but then my face got all wet and I guess I was crying
because Grandma wasn't there and I was hungry and because
the fire got so big so fast.

   At first it didn't seem like the fire was even going to catch. I
must have dropped the match where there wasn't any grease. I
stood up and tucked in the cover of the matchbook so I could
light another one. I was madder than any fire, that's what I
thought. But before I could do it, Whoosh! Flash! and the whole
pile blew up into flames. He was finally going to lose something,
not that the clothes he wears are actually worth anything.

   I got to be happy for all of two seconds. Then, black smoke
was coming down from the ceiling. My eyes stung and watered,
and it was just like if you open the oven door and put your face
in to see if cookies are done, that hot, only all over, and when I
tried to get a breath, the coughing started. I knew I had to get
the fire out before it spread. I filled up a glass with water—even
left it running so I could just keep filling it and throwing water
until it was out. But it was just like I had thrown a glassful of
flames; the fire splattered, just splattered like I had no idea a fire
could, and then it was on a wall and over on the doorway into

the living room and the smell—plastic melting? I don't know
what it was except the worst smell that won't let you stop
coughing enough even to get a breath in to cough back out—
and the fire that was like something alive: those two things were
everything and everywhere.

I tried again with another glassful, but the same thing
happened. It made no sense, but I was afraid to keep trying, and
the truth is, I couldn't anyway. For a minute I couldn't even
figure out where the door was. My eyes wouldn't stay open
because the smoke was so thick and stinging. I got turned around
and was headed the wrong way, and when I felt around for the
door and it wasn't there, I thought *This is it, I'm going to die,
I'll see my mother if she really is anywhere.* I started to panic,
but then I saw the living-room window and I realized I was
backward. My face and hair and clothes were sopped with
sweat; I felt it running down my back and legs. I remembered
that thing about *get down on the floor* because the smoke goes
up, and I found the door. I don't know why I thought of bunching
up my T-shirt between my hand and the doorknob, but even
through the cloth, it burned. Maybe my mother gave me the idea.

I got outside and I tried to scream, but a croak came out. I
pounded on the Rockwell's trailer door, but no one came. Then
I just ran to Ramon's, even though it was farther, because I
don't know any of the other people.

At first, I thought Rosa wouldn't even come, wouldn't open
the door because of Alexander the Goddamn Great telling her
not to. I saw a movement behind the curtain, and Ramon's car
was still there, so I *knew* they were there and I pounded and
pounded. I think I was crying. Finally, Rosa opened it. I could
see on her face she was going to say, no, we have to do what your
father says, but then her eyes got big and I looked over my
shoulder. Two windows were shooting fire. "Did you call
firemen?" I heard her say. As soon as I started shaking my head,
she ran back in shouting, "Ramon! Detta...*fuego!*" I was
standing there on the bottom step outside the screen door with
no idea what to do.

Then Ramon came to the door, and his eyes got like Rosa's

when he looked over my head, past me. He almost knocked me over, running out. He got the hose Rosa uses for her flowers, but it was nowhere near long enough even when he stretched it all the way out. He unscrewed it from the house and dragged it like the world's longest tail over to the Rockwell's trailer, next to Alex's. He used their spigot and turned the water on. I was grabbing at him, trying to stop him, trying to tell him what happened when I threw the water on, but my voice wouldn't work. By then, Rosa was there, still in her bathrobe, and she grabbed me away from Ramon while she was shouting Spanish to him. She pulled me back, way back from the fire and shouted, *"Movate!"* to Ramon again while she waved her arm. He backed up, farther from the fire, and used his thumb over part of the hose to make it spray into one window. I was trying to tell Rosa what happened, about the glass of water I mean, but I was shaking and she just put one arm around me and used the other hand to pull my head down onto her chest, just like mom used to. Just like my Mom, and then I cried harder and I couldn't stand up, so she squatted down next to me and held me that way.

The water didn't make things any worse this time, anyway. There was no way that fire could get worse by then. Some other people came, and a man tried to help Ramon until we heard the sirens and Ramon dropped the hose and ran out toward the road to show them the way.

ALEX PUT OUT HIS hand like he was going to touch me, but I took a step backward and used the bottom of my T-shirt, which was already filthy, to wipe my face. The shirt was still damp. There wasn't a mirror in the bathroom at the police station so I never saw how dirty my face was, and of course Alex never said anything.

—You got a key? he said then, real gruff.—Can you get in and get you something to eat?

—Of course I've got a key, I whispered.—I *live* here. He is so dense.

—Well, use it, he said. So I got it out of my backpack and went in. I didn't invite him, but he followed me through the door and looked around. The kitchen was a mess, not like Grandma at all except for a while after Mom died. But there were a bunch of dirty dishes around the sink, not even soaking in it like she sometimes did them. The floor was sticky, and the garbage hadn't been emptied.

Alex looked in the refrigerator, bold as you please, like he had a right to which he didn't. There was a gallon jug of milk with a slosh or two in the bottom, some margarine, dill pickles, two eggs and a lot of salad dressings in the shelves on the door. Wilty lettuce was browning on the bottom shelf, and two puny apples. She always keeps them even when they're mushy. As usual, Grandma had a box of Esther Price soft-center chocolates in there, too. Don't try to get between Grandma and her chocolates, Mom used to say. When I was little, she'd give me a pack of M&M's when she took me over, so I wouldn't bug Grandma for her candy. I haven't thought of those M&M's in a long time, and suddenly they were in my mind and I wanted to cry again.

Not that I would in a million years around him. He sort of blew out a sigh and shut the refrigerator door.—I'll be back in a while, he said.—You get cleaned up and then do these here dishes.

—Don't tell me what to do. I kept breaking my own rule about not talking to him but it just popped out.—And don't come back.

—Do it, he said, just like I hadn't said a word, and just walked out the kitchen, and across the porch. I watched out the kitchen window while he took his skinny butt across the yard and got into his truck.

Then I had what Grandma calls a dilemma. I knew it would make Grandma happy if I did the dishes, but Alex had told me to, which meant that doing those damn dishes was the very last, the very, very last thing I could even consider doing or he'd get the idea that he could boss me around. I still had to set him straight about Ramon and Rosa. I went up to the bathroom to pee and wash my face and think. That part had been my own idea before he said anything. The mirror pretty much freaked me out, I was such a mess, and I knew Grandma would get upset if she came home and saw me, so I washed my face—which did have soot stuff in places I'd missed—changed my shirt, combed my hair and brushed my teeth. I did that, brush my teeth, just because it would feel good and for some reason I thought the toothpaste would make me less hungry. I put the T-shirt I'd had on into a bag and stuck it under some soap wrappers and used tissues in the wastebasket because once I'd washed my face and brushed my teeth, I realized it reeked and I didn't want Grandma to *see* it, either. But then I realized *I* reeked, and I got rid of the rest of my clothes and took a shower. I left my hair wet—it felt good like that anyway, and my stomach was complaining again.

I headed downstairs, back to the kitchen to call Tim, which meant I had to pass all the pictures of Grandma's dead relatives on the wall along the stairs. Most of the time they don't bother me, but today they did. Grandma's mother and father and a slew of aunts and uncles and people I never even knew were all smiley once, like it would never end. I thought maybe Tim could come get me and we could get something to eat in town, and when I wasn't so hungry I'd figure out what to do next. There was no answer at his house, which in some ways was for the best because I'm probably not even his girlfriend anymore, not the way I used to be. Big deal, it's long distance to Alex's. His mother would let him call, at least sometimes. I wish I hadn't let him feel me up. Or maybe it's the opposite and I should have let him feel whatever he wanted of me. Maybe I should have let him get to third base or even home and he would have stayed my boyfriend.

But then I thought: Who wants a boyfriend? Look how my mother's boyfriend turned out, we all know that story.

I stood there in the kitchen and looked around. The rest of the house hadn't looked that good, either. Grandma's bed wasn't made, which is a mortal sin to her, and stuff wasn't picked up. It was like she'd left in a hurry long time ago and dust had settled on top of whatever was wherever. I made her bed real quick. Then I thought, wait, I *can* do the dishes because I was the first in the door, I saw them and I thought of how bad they needed to be cleaned up, so it was my idea, not his.

I didn't want to examine that too close, so I just marked that thought done and ran water in the sink. After the dishes were finished, there'd be a clean saucepan and I could open a can of soup.

Which I did. Split pea with ham, the chunky kind, and I ate it right out of the pot, which Grandma says is disgusting, but I don't care. Then I washed the pot again.

I heard a car out in the driveway.—Grandma! I said out loud, but then out the living-room window I saw no, it was Alex. He pulled up in front of the path to the kitchen door, turned the damn truck off like he meant to stay, got out and went around to the back. He pulled two brown bags out of the truck bed and carried one in each arm up to the back door like they were twin babies or something. He's carrying grocery bags and I'm thinking about twin babies. I really, really hope his weirdness isn't coming off on me.

He opened the door and walked right into the kitchen, set the bags on the kitchen table and went back out. I thought he was leaving, but then there he was right back again with two more bags.—Help me unload this stuff, he said. I just stared at him. What was Alexander the Goddamn Great doing bringing groceries into my grandmother's house?

He looked at me.—I *said*, help me with this stuff. I don't know where things go. He looked around.—Good, you got the dishes cleared up. You look better, too. He was completely ignoring that I didn't answer him.—I'll put stuff into the refrigerator and freezer. You put the rest away. He was back on that like a broken record.

I walked out of the room, down the hall and into the living room where I sat in Grandpa's old chair and tried to think. He shouldn't be in our house, I thought. I could hear the brown bags giving up the food and the refrigerator door opened and closed about six times. So did the freezer door, which closes with a shorter higher wump. I know that because I can always tell whether Grandma is after Esther Price chocolates or ice cream when she can't sleep and goes downstairs real late.

A minute later, he was standing in the hall outside the living room as if there was an invisible fence keeping him out of the room. Which I was glad of.—I'm leaving now, he said.—I gotta look for another place. You stay here.

—Another trailer? One of my ears was clogged up and it made my voice sound like I was choking again.

—I guess. If I can find a furnished one. He sort of shrugged, like it was already impossible. He looked raggedy, sort of like a bum, because he hadn't shaved and his cheeks and chin had black shadows like mine did before I washed. The front of his hair had separated from the main part, too, and slopped over onto his forehead.

—I'm not going in a trailer. It's a firetrap. I'll tell the judge there wasn't a smoke detector.

—Look…I was…glad you were okay even though you.…

I didn't want him to say what he thought I did, so I just interrupted.—Sure you were.

I was ignoring the fact that I started it on the grounds that I didn't mean for the whole thing to burn, but that's just what happened so it wasn't my fault. It's not like some of my stuff didn't burn up, too. Fortunately, I keep my good stuff at Grandma's. All I ever took there was the least I could get by on until I came back here. I turned my back on him and stared out the window hoping Grandma would drive up. A moment later, he clunked down the hall, the kitchen door opened and shut and then his tires crunched the driveway gravel. He was leaving. Again. It's his specialty, leaving.

I went upstairs to Mom's old room then. I could watch for Grandma from there. I got the picture out of the drawer and propped it on the dresser. Then I set out the candles and I was going to light them, but suddenly I was afraid I might drop the match and start another fire. I got sort of shaky thinking about it, and I wrapped Mom's turquoise sweater around my shoulders even though the room was hot from it being closed up all the time, especially now, with the weather turned summery. Hot like after a fire, but I was cold. I didn't even talk to Mom. I'd thought she'd like it, the fire, because of getting even with him, but then when I could tell her about it—I didn't. I felt a little ashamed, which was dumb because I'm sure she hated him. I heard her voice then, strong in my head, but the words didn't make any sense. *A bird in the hand…?* Is worth two in the bush, she used to say, but what did she mean? And there was no more, nothing else. She could at least have explained it. I stayed still, but once she's gone she never comes back.

Finally, I went back down to the kitchen. A bunch of cans and boxes were on the table. He'd put away the refrigerator stuff and left the rest out. Well, I stood like a stupid statue for a few minutes and then I just started putting it all away. It was my idea, though.

Even though I knew perfectly well it wasn't going to happen, I went outside and filled the big platform feeder with sunflower seeds after the kitchen was all straight. I used up all there was left from before Mom died, out of the big bag that was in the garage. Grandma always fussed about field mice going after it, but Mom said that was one seed she could buy cheap if she bought the really big bag. I wanted never to use them up because it makes it seem longer that she's been dead if they're gone. You can't use sunflower seeds in some of the other feeders. I knew that much, but I remember Mom saying the mourning doves like to eat off a flat place, and the doves like these. You wouldn't think they'd be so picky with free food, but hey, they are. There were tiny husk things, like empty shells, on the ground all around the feeder, with little tufts of grass poking up through them here and there. I sat down under the feeder with my back against the hard metal pole and waited for Grandma. I kept my right hand out so a bird could get in it, even though I knew perfectly well there was no way.

thirty-nine

"I'M DONE WITH IT," Alex announced to Big Al. He slammed his locker shut after depositing the convenience-store tuna sandwich—halves neatly side by side in a slanty clear plastic container—he'd bought on the way in.

"Done with which?" Big Al said, squinting. He'd driven right into the rising sun on his way to work—it was like that every morning from early summer until the time change in October—and was still squinting in the factory dimness. Adjusting the brim of his cap made no difference but he did it anyway. Alex looked bad to him, hollowed-out and, come to think of it, unshaven and sort of dirty. "Where you stayin'?" he thought to ask. Dink had gone out for a smoke before starting time and sometimes Alex would tell Al something if Dink weren't around to mock him.

"I got a place," Alex mumbled.

"Where?"

It was no good if Big Al was going to corner him, so Alex answered the first question. "Done with the Daddy routine."

As if he knew there was more to it, Al asked, "What'd she do?" Still Alex didn't tell Al that Detta had started the fire. Not that he could prove it anyway, but he knew. What he didn't know was why he was keeping it to himself.

"I dunno. Haven't seen her since I took her to Cora's." Alex had spent the day after the fire looking for a trailer and, when he gave up on finding one furnished, had been thinking about a furnished apartment. The fire department had given him a number for emergency services and for the Red Cross but he hadn't called either one. What were they going to do? He didn't have insurance, it was that simple. What he had was the cash he'd been carrying when the fire happened, which happened to be about a hundred eighty of his last paycheck. The rest of everything plain burned up. He'd just sleep in his truck until he got a paycheck on Friday and then he'd have deposit money. He'd spent a good part of the money in his wallet on groceries for Cora's place, but hell, if Rebecca had cancer, well, Jesus God, how much more trouble could rain on Cora?

There was a one-room efficiency—not much more than a motel room—over on M Street, and he supposed he could take that for a month and see if he could stand it. He'd come to work today so as not to lose more pay, and what else could he do, anyway?

"So why you saying you're done with it?" Al checked his watch; three minutes until they had to be at their stations.

It had come to him, was the truth. Alex just woke up—stiff from lying across bucket seats with the gear shift in his back—knowing he couldn't hack it anymore. He knew it when he went to McDonald's and got two Egg McMuffins and a large coffee, and he knew it when he washed his face in the restroom there, combing his hair with his fingers and wishing he'd bought a toothbrush before he came to get breakfast. Detta had fought a war of attrition before the big boom, and she'd flat-out won.

"Ah, y'know," he said vaguely. "She's better off."

"What if they go after back child support and all?"

Alex honked as he did when something unexpected struck him funny and he didn't remember to suppress audible laughter. "Oh good. Let 'em. In fact, I think they oughta go after all my property, too."

In spite of himself, Big Al chuckled. He meant to ask again where Alex was staying but the warning whistle blew. He hiked his jeans up and hurried out of the locker area to get the stack of invoices detailing the stock they were to pull and load.

LATER, AT MORNING-BREAK time, Alex and Big Al sat with Dink who wasn't particularly surprised at Alex's decision to defect on fatherhood. "Only thing you got to worry about's the truck," he said. "There's ways to hide anything else y'got."

"That there's voice of experience," Al explained, bobbing the bill of his cap toward Dink.

Dink, who was known for being able to dish it out but not take it, immediately got defensive. "Hell, the bitch would've taken my Jockeys if I'd listed 'em as property. You got no idea…"

Al ignored him and aimed at Alex. "I thought you was doin' okay. Takes a while with kids."

"Yeah, so says Daddy of the Year," Dink came back at him. "Second world title, right after Bald Man of the Decade." He ran his hand through his own lush hair, as thick on top as on the sides, even if it was graying early. "Jeez, I need a haircut again."

Al tipped back on the back chair legs. "Some people got nothin' to be proud of except somethin' they had no part in bringing about. Pathetic if you ask me."

"Speaking of parts, is mine straight?" Dink tipped his head down and pointed to the side.

Al ignored him and turned to Alex, who'd stayed out of it. "Man, I'll tell you one thing. You best be callin' your mother-in-law and makin' arrangements. I wouldn't just let it go. Y'know…that legal stuff. Right now, you got the responsibility."

"*Ex*. My *ex*-mother-in-law."

"Yeah. Your ex-mother-in-law. You told her this?"

Alex took a long drag on his cigarette. "Trust me, the two of 'em will be thrilled never to hear from me."

Big Al leaned forward. "No, man. *You* trust *me*. That ain't the way the law works. You call. No need to be adding some police knocking at your door to your pile of trouble."

Dink hooted, and Alex let out a half honk before he shut it out. "Like he's got a door left to knock at…" Dink laughed, and the cavernous loading dock reverberated with it.

But Big Al's advice was usually sound, and that was especially true when Dink disagreed with it. Alex decided that trouble with the court would be a real pisser after he was the one who started this whole mess by suing for custody. Why *had* he done that? All he remembered now was the business about back child support, but must've been there was more to it. Some fantasy about another chance. As if there were such a churchy thing as redemption. Of course, his father had been right all along. He could feel the old man reaching out of the grave to slap him upside the head for being stupid.

After work, he waved off Big Al's invitation to come home to supper with him. "Patsy's a hell of a cook," Big Al said. "Why not? You got a date or sumpthin'?"

"Got...stuff I gotta do."

"Tomorrow, then? She said today or tomorrow is okay."

Alex didn't have a ready rebuff. "Yeah," he squirmed. "Sure... uh, thanks." He hated being the object of pity. He'd met Al's wife at a company picnic. She'd sized him up through eyes narrowed beneath a puffball of teased bangs, and though she'd been perfectly polite, Alex knew she'd seen right through to the worst of him. A supper in her house would be just dandy if he wanted to confirm his identity as a total loser.

As he drove to Dave's Speedway Eat 'n' Gas Stop to fill his truck, he remembered there was a pay phone on the side, by the restrooms. He dreaded it, but he might as well get it behind him. He didn't know what to say.

It was too much to have hoped they wouldn't be home. He cleared his throat. "Ah...Cora? This is...uh, Alex."

There was a hesitation before she said, polite as ever, "Yes, Alex. Did you want to talk to Lex...Detta?"

"No, that's okay. I just called to say, uh, I hope it's okay for you to keep her."

Another hesitation, this one on a surprised intake of breath. "Well, of course. *Of course.* Uh...do you know for how long? Are you still looking for a new place?"

"No." He meant no, he didn't know for how long. Forever was what he had in mind.

"So you found one?" Cora said, puzzled.

Alex twisted the silver phone cord with his left hand, then shifted the phone to his other ear. Stalling.

"Not yet."

"Where are you staying?"

"A friend."

"Maybe you could give me that phone number? I mean, since you have custody, there are things I can't sign for, in an emergency, you know."

"Uh, he…there's no phone there. You can get me at work." Any idiot knew that wasn't enough.

He could almost hear Cora trying to figure out what to say. "Well, um, maybe a neighbor's then? I don't mean to press you, Alex. I've just…well, I'm aware that medical emergencies don't always punch a time clock. I just want to be responsible about her."

He finally got it out. "Look, okay, you're right. I'm no kind of father. I'll call you again. You just keep her, all right?" And he replaced the receiver in its hook with less than a slam, but more force than was required to break the connection.

FOR HER PART, Cora was left standing at the stove where she'd been frying up chicken parts for supper when the phone rang, holding the receiver in her hand and staring at it. She put it back up to her ear, unbelieving, but indeed, Alex had hung up. She made her way—carefully, without her cane which was propped in the doorway to the hall—to the wall where she hung it back up and returned to the meat crackling toward golden in cooking oil. Even then, she just stood a moment, considering.

Outside the window, mourning doves were at the platform feeder and an enormous blue jay at the other. Cora hadn't seen a hummingbird yet, even though there was lots of red and pink in the bedding plants. Christine would want the hummingbirds to have their sugar water, like Christine had wanted Lexie to be with her. Cora sighed. Sometimes it was so hard to know into the secret heart of things, what lay on the other side of obvious.

"Lexie!" She threw her voice upward, toward the second

floor where Lexie was listening to an Aerosmith tape instead of
setting the table as she was supposed to.

"Lexie!" Louder. "Come on down here."

A succession of heavy thuds descending the stairs. How could
such a small, lightweight Snow White girl sound like the
Seventh Army in her stocking feet? Cora had been wondering
on that one since before Christine died. "I said I'd set it! I don't
see why I can't do it later, as long as it's done before supper,
why does it matter when I do it?" Lexie's voice was a long
whine.

Cora ignored the complaint. "That was Alex."

"I hope you hung up on him. No way I'm going to another
stinking firetrap."

"So you've said. No, I didn't hang up on him. He hung up on
me."

That got her, Cora saw. Lexie's eyes, a startling clarity of
blue in the light from the kitchen window, widened. "What?
What happened?"

"He called to say you could stay here, honey."

"For good?"

"He didn't exactly say. But he did say something like, 'you
were right, I'm no kind of father,' and he wouldn't give me a
phone number where he's staying."

Lexie ignited. Her ponytail bobbed as her body jerked—
almost as if she'd been shot, Cora observed, the same bullet-jolt
that made her flat refuse ever to go again after Marvin had taken
her squirrel-hunting the first season they were married, his idea
of a romantic way to spend time together. "I knew he never
wanted me," Lexie shrieked. "I hate him so much. He never
never wanted me." She stomped out, down the hall and back
upstairs.

Cora was so taken aback she turned off the gas under the
chicken even though the meat would absorb too much grease.
What was that about? How was she to understand if it meant
something at all, what under the sun it might mean?

Forty

I REALLY THINK GOD hates me. When I screamed and prayed about the fire, the way it jumped up the dishtowel hanging on the stove and the ugly shit-tan curtain at the kitchen window, did He help me? I tried to get water on it, but it was too fast and too smoky and it took too long to fill the glass with water each time. And nobody was home in the next trailer, and not the next one after that, and when I went to Ramon's 'cause it was practically as close as the third one, Rosa didn't come to the door right away. I don't think she was even going to let me in! So in that way, it was Alex's fault. And why was the fire department so slow? I don't care if they are volunteers, they have molasses instead of blood in them. By the time I even heard sirens, we could see fire in the living room, and it was in the bedroom already by the time they got to the hydrant.

Of course, when I told Grandma what I thought about God, she said—On the other hand, maybe He saved your life. Well, that's garbage, because he didn't save my mother's life, and personally, I don't think He's going to much bother with Rebecca's either.— And what about the stillborn baby you're always bringing up, Grandma? I wanted to say that, but I didn't. I didn't want to make her think God hates her, too, even though I think He does.

And now this: She gets up this morning, goes off to see Becca, goes off to see Jolene, comes home and trips on the stairs. I didn't even hear her fall, but there she was lying on the floor and yelling for me. Like a banshee, which is what she always says about me, how I don't have to yell like a banshee.

Of course it took me like ten minutes just to get her into a sitting position.—My knee! She was moaning and grabbing it.—I'll call an ambulance, I yelled and got up to go for the phone, but that made her fall back (I forgot I was sort of holding her up) and she yelled—No, no ambulance. I don't want one. At this point we were yelling at each other not so much like we're mad, but like we both need hearing aids (which I swear she does, anyway) and she started to cry. Then I started to cry, and she grabbed my hand and then my shoulder, and she tried to get up and couldn't. So then I was down on the floor with her and we were holding onto each other and crying.—Get me some aspirin, she finally said.—And some tissues.

So I propped her up by helping her swing her butt around and putting a sofa cushion between her and the stairs. She was right there underneath the swirly wood of the end of the banister, in her beat-up navy-blue pants and a shirt so old it's gray except for where she spilled coffee on it this morning, and there it's tan. Her eyes were all red and her hair was like thunder and she looks so old and so pathetic to say nothing of so fat, I had no idea what I was going to do. All those dead relatives were grinning at her from over her head and it gave me the chills. I brought her the tissue and the aspirin, but of course, I didn't think about water, so then I had to go get that. She blew her nose and stuck the tissue in her sleeve, which I think is the most disgusting thing Grandma does other than take her teeth out, and it sort of shook me out of being upset about the dead relatives hovering over her. I love her, though. I love her a lot. I need to say that right now.

—Can you get up? I said. Knowing the answer perfectly well.

—Let's try, she said.—Get my cane. So I got her cane from where it was propped in the kitchen. The wood floors are slippery. When I wear just socks I can slide half the hallway. She had shoes on, though—the old-lady ones that look like brown lace-up tires—so I'm not sure why she fell.

She held on to the cane, completely awkward because the handle is too high or it's on such a slant that it's useless, and I got to one side of her and wedged my hand under her armpit and lifted. Completely hopeless. She didn't get a quarter of an inch off the floor, so help me.

—This isn't working, she said.

(Duh, I thought to myself.)—I'll call Becca, I said.

—Becca? She can hardly lift a glass, let alone me.

—Okay, well maybe Mr. Dudley? That's our one neighbor, a farmer.

—Honey, he'll be in the field 'til after dark. He's cultivating the soy. And Pamela works at the Washington Supply.

—Jolene and Bob. I'll call Jolene and Bob! Why didn't I think of that first?

—Okay, she sighed.—That'll work.

Well, of course, Jolene was sweet as pie to me, and she and Bob broke land speed records getting to our house. I was thinking okay, now I'm out of the woods, Jolene'll take over and I've practically never been so happy to see anyone come barging right in without knocking.

It took the three of us to get her up because she couldn't help and couldn't put any weight on the one leg. Grandma was gasping and grunting and broken out in a sweat by the time Bob and Jolene, one on each side of her, got her to the couch in the living room.

Jolene's glasses slid to the end of her nose and she couldn't push them back up because it took both her arms to keep Grandma steady. Then Jolene sent me to get a cold washcloth, and she washed Grandma's face and neck. I should have thought of that. Grandma said it felt good.

Jolene said—We need to take you to the hospital, and I'm thinking, thank God the voice of reason, it's so obvious, but Grandma freaked out.—No, no, no, she said.—I can't, Jo, I just can't. And damn if Jolene doesn't sit on the couch next to Grandma and just look at her hard and sigh and say—Okay, love, I know. I know. But don't you think you need an X-ray?

—It's not broken, Grandma said.—I twisted it bad, but, you know, this is the knee I had the trouble with a couple of years ago.

—I don't remember that, I said.

—Well, honey, you were young, and you don't remember. Becca came and stayed with me, Grandma said to me like I'm six. All she missed was patting me on the head. I still think she's making it up.

—Okay, then, do you care if I see if Dr. Hess will stop by on his way home? He goes right by here. Jolene's persistent, I'll give her that.

—Oh, I hate to bother him. Grandma's not much for backing down either. She looked pale, though, and didn't even shove back the hair flopped on her forehead, which is about the same gray as her skin.

Jolene leaned forward. She was wearing a skirt with no stockings and she has the most enormous veins in her legs I've ever seen. They're almost as dark as her hair, which is definitely dyed. But she's really nice.—Well, you've got to be checked. Bob and I can get you to our car.

Well, you could tell that idea tired Grandma out just thinking about it.—Okay, she says.—Dr. Hess, if he will.

—He will, Jo said. Dr. Hess was one of the doctors that Mom used to go to. She had a crush on him because he's a drop-dead dreamboat. He's a good doctor. Maybe if he'd been there she wouldn't be so dead now.

JOLENE WAS RIGHT. Dr. Hess did stop in on his way home. Grandma was right, too, of course, which she wasn't slow to point out.—I told you it was a sprain, she said maybe a hundred times. Dr. Hess wrapped the knee—swollen like a giant grapefruit now—with a tan bandage (the tan made me think about Alex and his ugly trailer which I didn't want to do) and told her to stay off it completely for a couple of days and then use crutches. He gave her a prescription for pain medicine, which Grandma insisted she wouldn't use, and said to put ice packs on it for a day or two, anyway.

—Lexie, you leave me to talk with Jolene alone now, Grandma said after the doctor left. Bob was already settled in front of the television with some baseball game on. The whole afternoon is gone. It made me mad that Grandma sent me out of the room like some little kid, but I didn't have any choice.

Jolene stayed with Grandma a long time before she came into the kitchen where I was just sitting and staring into space.—We've got to be on our way, honey. I never even got my stockings on! Bob and I were getting ready to go away when you called. We'll be back on Tuesday. Will you be okay, dear? Your Grandma said there's plenty of food in the house.

Tuesday! Today was only Thursday. I thought Jolene would even stay overnight for Grandma and here she wasn't even going to be in the same town.—I guess, I said.

—I'd stay, dear, but we're to be at the Cleveland Clinic tomorrow morning for tests on Bob's heart. We really have to go. We have reservations up there tonight. She looked at her watch like I'd figure out how long it would take them to get there or something. How could I say *no! Don't go! I don't know how to cook, I don't know how to take care of her.*—I'll be okay, is what I said. Not too graciously, maybe, but I said it.

Jolene looked around. The breakfast and lunch dishes were all over the place.—It's easiest to get meals if you start with a clean kitchen, she said. I wanted to shoot her between the eyes right then, even though I like her.

And then Bob and Jolene leave and I start to catch on to what I should have figured out ages ago, that God hates me.

THE NIGHT WAS REALLY bad. I hadn't thought about Grandma getting to the bathroom. We had to use her cane and a straight-back chair as a cane for her other hand and it took almost a half-hour to get her down the hall and in. I had to pick up the chair and move it a couple of inches at a time. It wasn't pretty. Then Grandma wouldn't drink anything no matter how thirsty she got, which meant she wouldn't eat the canned vegetable soup I made her because then she'd have to go.—I need crutches, she said a jillion times.—Maybe I could manage on crutches. But she was all sweaty again from the hurting. Stuff was piling up around the blue couch—a towel, the melty plastic bags of ice, Grandma's glasses and cane and tissues, a couple of plates, the tall glass, smudgy with fingerprints, the pillows off her bed in mismatched pillowcases, one with yellow flowers, the other plain pink.

—Can I call Becca? I said when I brought her a piece of toast. Grandma was watching *Wheel of Fortune* and trying to make herself do the puzzles instead of think about her knee. She was pretty bad at them.

—Honey, Becca can't drive and she'll just worry herself to death and feel terrible.

—Well, what am I supposed to do? I didn't mean to sound peeved, but I was exhausted and I'd thought Grandma would be taking care of me after the fire, not the other way around. It was like she'd forgotten all about it now. I suppose that's selfish of me. Being scared was wearing off, though.

—I don't know, honey. We'll just have to make do.

So Grandma slept right there in her clothes, right on the blue couch. Or didn't sleep, I don't know. I kept waking up and the TV was always on. I was afraid to go to bed, but she said I should and she could yell loud enough to get me up if she had to.

This morning, though, it was the same. She said she was going to go in her pants if she didn't get to the bathroom and we had to do it the same way again, with the chair and all. Then Grandma was trying to tell me how to make oatmeal and I burned it and then I started thinking about the fire because of the smell and I got really upset. Then Grandma got upset because she hurt so much and aspirin didn't help and because I was upset.

I didn't do it when I first thought of it because everything bad in my life is his fault. How could I even think of calling Alex? After what he did to my sister—who would be right here now to help me with Grandma if he hadn't killed her—and how he went off and left Mom and me, he's the last person on the earth I'd want to call. But the idea didn't go away. I thought about how he brought the groceries. Then I thought *but he'll get the wrong idea, and it'll be like I want him around.* And I don't. Want him around, I mean. And what about my vendetta for Mom and Tina?

Well, then I thought Tina is probably sitting in Mom's lap right now, and I'm here by myself with neither of them to help me. That made me mad. I couldn't figure it out anymore, and there wasn't anything else I could think of to do. I didn't ask Grandma, I just went upstairs saying I needed to change my shirt. I got his phone number off the list she keeps by the phone next to her bed and I called the place Alex works and asked if he could come to the phone. It took a long time, but he did. There was a lot of noise in the background, like a hundred cars revving.

—Hello? He sounded like he thought the phone might blow up in his ear, real paranoid.

Of course, then I froze and didn't know what to say.—It's me, Detta. Alexis. Grandma fell and can't walk and she needs crutches and she needs a prescription from the drugstore and I don't have anybody else to call. Jolene and Bob are gone. Becca does have cancer, she's real sick. (I felt like I should say I'm sorry for lying, but I didn't say it.)

—Did your grandmother tell you t'call me?

—No. She doesn't know.

He didn't say anything at all for a minute, just the sound of machines was coming over the phone.—Okay.

—Okay what? I said. I said the *what?* too loud and I was afraid Grandma might have heard me, but I was starting to panic.

—Okay I'll get you the stuff.

—Um, when?

—Well, can it wait 'til I get off work?

I sat down on Grandma's chenille bedspread and looked at the picture of Mom on her dresser, which was next to the one of Grandpa. It felt like the walls were moving toward me, all four of them, an inch or two at a time and pretty soon they'd squeeze me to death. I picked at the little white tufts and tried to say it.—Um, not really.

—Okay.

I wanted to scream. I really did, but I didn't dare get him mad and make him want to say no.—Um, okay *what?*

—I'll clock out, he said, his voice tinny against the machines and through the wires.

My face got hot then, but I made myself get *thank you* out of my mouth. I hated that I had to, but it was only right.

Before I went downstairs, I went into Mom's room and shut the door. Like Grandma could possibly get up the stairs! I just wanted to look at the picture and smell Mom's sweaters, even though they don't really smell like her anymore, which I can hardly stand. Everything I had left of her gets taken away bit by bit. I told her I was sorry for calling Alex, but I didn't know what else to do and I had to take care of Grandma. She'd wanted that, didn't she? I looked out her window and there was a cardinal all blood-red and cocky, and then I saw the female, sort of quiet brown except for her red beak and belly, and I thought I heard my mother: *Build a nest.*

forty-one

BY THE TIME JOLENE and Bob were back from the Cleveland Clinic, Alex had been coming every day and then some. Friday, he'd been there within an hour of Lexie's call. He'd picked up the prescription, had it filled at the pharmacy and found out that the only place to get crutches was from the Mauntel-Meier Regional Hospital, over in Adria. The Early Sun Pharmacy usually carried them, but the Darrville High School track team had had an unfortunate season, especially the last meet when five of the hurdlers had done the two-hundred-meter hurdles after getting completely stoned on pot, back in the woods behind the track while the girls' running events were going on. There wasn't a set of crutches left in stock. So he'd trucked over to Adria and brought them back to Cora. He'd also stopped at CiCi's Chicken Wings 'N' Things and bought a bucket of fried chicken, a half-dozen biscuits and cole slaw, which Lexie had always hated, even though Cora's recipe was widely thought to be the best—and best-kept secret—around.

When he brought all that in, along with the crutches and prescription, Cora had thanked him warmly. Like they weren't all enemies, Lexie noted to herself sourly, even though she'd been the one who called him.

"Alex, stay and eat with us," Cora said after she'd washed down two of the pills with the water Lexie brought.

"That's okay," he said. "I'm all right. Anything else you need? Before I…"

"Well, if you're not busy, I'd like to try to stand with these crutches. I'm just too big for Lexie," Cora interrupted. She shot a look at Lexie "—ah, Detta, to catch."

"Okay," Alex said.

"But I think I'd best have something to eat first, since I just took those pills. I, you know, sometimes medicine will make you dizzy. Detta, you go get us some plates, please, and napkins. And three forks. Don't forget some honey for the biscuits." Cora looked around herself, ensconced on the couch, as if there'd be some cue on the area rug or the end table or in her lap. "Oh, knives. You'd better just use a tray, honey," she called after Lexie's petulant back. "I'd really appreciate it if you'd stay," Cora said to Alex quietly.

He'd shifted his weight from one steel-toed boot to the other and made a gesture that was somewhere between a shrug and a nod. Still not likely to win the Mr. Personality title, Cora thought, but smiled and repeated, "I appreciate it. And I appreciate what you've already done to help."

"'S okay," Alex said, and looked to each side of himself. Cora realized what concerned him and pointed.

"How about if you pull up that chair?" she said, indicating a straight-backed wooden one over beside the window. "And maybe, if you wouldn't mind, you could pull that coffee table…there." Pointing, her index finger was mottled, knobby with arthritis. "Then Detta can sit next to me." Cora stopped then, out of breath from the exertion of talking over pain. Alex, who'd been moving pieces as Cora pointed, brushed off the seat of his jeans and sat as Cora's waving hand directed him. The bucket of chicken was on the coffee table, between them now, where Alex had first deposited it. The two of them were just waiting for Lexie.

Misery was his first, middle and last name. Alex squirmed a bit and cleared his throat. "Sorry…um…about…Christine." The sentence seemed to take forever to clear his lips and Cora waited, as if it were visible, floating toward her on the air. Lexie's entrance dissipated the last of it just as she cleared her throat to respond.

Lexie looked at them suspiciously. "Here's the stuff," she said, glancing around and taking in the rearrangement. She set a big tray next to the bucket.

Cora pushed for cheer. "Well, thank you, sweetie. Goodness, are you as hungry as I am? Fix me a plate, will you, dear? Let's dig in."

Lexie handed Alex a paper plate before she began to fill one for Cora.

"Thanks," he said.

The supper was awkward. Cora, who was never out of words, kept casting for something to say. Every topic seemed loaded. Alex and Lexie were, of course, not the slightest help and finally Cora stifled a sigh and joined their silence, let the scraping of forks and the small clink of bones dropped on plates pass as companionable.

Afterward, Alex and Lexie carried the messy remains to the kitchen. They returned and Alex braced himself to hoist Cora to her one good foot and wedge the crutches under her arms.

She couldn't get the hang of it. "I'm not very coordinated," she said.

"You're trying to do it in three steps instead of two," Lexie said.

"No, it's that you got to take your weight with your hands, there, not under your arms. It's making you too low," Alex corrected. He wiped his hands on his white T-shirt and put his hands on Cora's upper arms. "See, don't hang yourself on the crutches—they shouldn't be wedged under your armpits. You'll get all sore anyway if they are." He demonstrated then, flapping one hand under his arm to show that there should be space there.

"Oh, I see, yes, that's much better," Cora said. Lexie hastened to pull down Cora's old blue blouse pulled up by the crutches. "If I can get to the bathroom, I'd like to wash up. I think Lexie and I will be okay now."

Exactly as Cora said the words, she'd wobbled and started to pitch backward. Alex leapt forward and caught her, easing a fall back onto the couch which was still just behind her. Across the room, Christine's solemn-faced high-school graduation picture watched the scene from the piano top. She'd been trying to look older, which broke Cora's heart then and still did. Alex had kept his eyes averted from the portrait after his scan of the room had included it; he knew exactly why she'd been trying to look older, even remembered the day she'd had the proofs taken, how she'd coyly said, "Lots of girls use their graduation pictures when they get engaged."

Cora yelped in pain and then quickly covered it with a forced laugh. "Goodness, I lost my balance," she gasped out. "You go on ahead, Alex. I imagine you've got things to do. Lexie and I will be okay. I'll just wait a minute and get up again. I don't want to keep you."

Lexie stood, dumbstruck and terrified. "Wait. I couldn't have caught you then."

"Oh, don't worry, honey. I won't fall again. Just got to get my sea legs." Cora struggled as she spoke to edge her rear toward the edge of the couch for leverage to get on her feet again. It looked pathetic and utterly ineffectual.

Lexie had turned to Alex, a little ragged edge of panic in her voice. "Can you stay? I mean, I'm afraid." A lock of dark hair had worked loose from her ponytail and hung alongside her face. She swiped at it, but it fell right back down.

"Okay," Alex said, his two-syllable vocabulary for requests.

"Well, if you think it's necessary, honey," Cora said, pushing it a smidge further, "but I'm sure we could…"

"'S okay," Alex said. "You wanna get up now?"

Cora nodded, and Alex took her crutches, handed them to Lexie, and hoisted Cora up by grasping her upper arms and lifting as he took a half step backward. The effect was effortless this time since Alex had already taken measure of her and how much pull to exert. Alex supported Cora on one side, a crutch on the other, all the way down the hall to the bathroom near the kitchen. "I'll stay outside here," he said, "you call if you need help. It won't bother me none."

"Lexie can come in with me, maybe," Cora said, blowing the cloud of damp gray hair back off her forehead, sweaty with exertion. She was hanging on to the knob of the bathroom door, which released the crutch from beneath her arm. It clattered to the hardwood.

"See, Grandma?" Lexie had said, leaving what her grand- mother was supposed to see unspoken.

After that, it hadn't been discussed again. But Alex had been there until late Friday evening, and had showed up Saturday morning before eight with fast-food bacon, egg and cheese biscuits, and hash browns in cardboard holders for all of them. He made a pot of coffee, while Lexie poured three glasses of orange juice. During the day, he mowed the lawn while Lexie did the laundry, though Alex had to show her how to run the machines first. Later, Alex vacuumed the downstairs after Cora mentioned, embarrassed and apologetic, that the dust bunnies seemed to be running a derby of some sort. "I used to keep the house meticulously," she said, shaking her head. "Lately, though, I've sure gotten behind. Becca hasn't been well."

"I know," Alex said, and when Cora looked at him quizzically, he added, "Detta said."

"Oh," Cora said.

"Where's the vacuum cleaner?" Alex said.

"Oh, goodness, I didn't mean for you…"

"I don't care," Alex said. "I can do it easy."

After he'd found it and plugged it in and started to vacuum, he turned to Cora. "I used to sit on that same couch there while you did this."

"Oh, don't I know. I used to ram it into your feet."

Alex snorted, trying to hold back a laugh, but the honk came anyway. "Never did think that was an accident," he said.

Cora laughed. "Oh, no. Well, one part was an accident."

"Yeah?"

"Never quite managed to cut you off at the knees." Alex honked then, and Cora laughed with him, as much at that ridicu- lous sound as at the memory.

JOLENE CALLED TUESDAY. She'd called twice over the weekend, but Cora couldn't talk freely either time, and all Jo got was "Oh, we're managing. Pain's better thanks to the pills. Yes, Lexie's a big help and Alex is here, too." This time, however, Alex—who'd called in sick at work for the second day in a row—had gone to get more milk, and Lexie was out in the kitchen washing up the lunch dishes.

Cora kept her voice close to a whisper. "No. Not yet. It's going pretty well. I heard them laugh in the kitchen before. They were sort of arguing about whether Alex could cook, but it was more teasing, you know? I'm okay, honest. I'm not about to have either one of them wash me, so pretty soon I'll need you for that. I'm ripe enough now that we don't need any bug repellent, that's for sure. I don't see how I can get any worse by holding off until tomorrow. I'm going to mention the room tonight, so we'll see."

Jolene had said, "Good going. Okay, then, I'll just keep things up at Becca's and tend to her. Don't worry, now, she understands this just fine. I think Christine would want it this way if she knew, too."

And then Cora teared up for just a minute. "Oh, God, I pray you're right. I ask her, you know, in my mind, when I pray, I ask her. I haven't heard *stop* yet."

"Well, maybe she's waiting to see how it works. Like us."

"Maybe so," Cora said. "Maybe so."

"Nothing wrong with your hearing. You're a wise woman, Cora Lee Laster. You trust yourself, hear?"

"Oh, Jo. I'm just trying to do the right thing by her and Lexie both. I'm trying to think about what she wanted before she gave up on what she wanted, you know? She saw something good in him. I'm thinkin' she could have been right all along. And I don't think I'm going to keel over today, but some mornings I feel Mr. Death just laying on my chest, you know? About to force himself on me. Maybe that's 'cause of Becca, I don't know, but Jo, I feel it. And I feel like he's going to kiss me with his old sour breath before Lexie is grown and what then? What then? I can't be sure Becca will..." She couldn't finish the sentence.

She didn't have to. "I know" came Jolene's voice through the earpiece. "I know."

"ALEX," CORA BEGAN. "Are you still staying with that friend, or did you sign a lease on that new place you found already?"

Alex looked confused momentarily, then his face cleared. "Yeah. Um, no, I'm just stayin' with a guy from work. Didn't get over t' the place to sign yet."

They were at the kitchen table, where Alex had set out the pork chops with roasted potatoes and onions he'd made while Cora sat and directed him. Lexie had paid minimal attention to this, the second how-to-make-this-good-and-easy-recipe session Cora had run in as many nights. It was close to six, so the light outside the kitchen had softened toward twilight, but Cora had already mentioned how much she'd like to get outside on the porch to take some fresh air if Alex would help her navigate the one step down after supper.

"Well, I'm not surprised." Of course she wasn't surprised. She'd figured out that Alex wasn't staying anywhere, based on the frequency of his clothing changes and the fact that she'd actually seen him through a window using an outdoor faucet to wash his face and hands before he came into the house on two mornings. She thought he must be sleeping in his truck, nearby at that. The amount of driving implicit in what he'd said were his temporary living arrangements was virtually impossible. "When would you have had time? You've been here so much. But I was wondering if you'd even consider this—for a little while, I mean until I'm back on my feet, wouldn't it be easier if you just stayed here?" In her peripheral vision, Cora saw Lexie—at the refrigerator getting herself a glass of milk—whip her head around in surprise. Cora carefully gave no indication she'd seen the movement, but tried to surreptitiously take in the expression on her granddaughter's face. It was less than abject horror, and Lexie didn't say anything, which Cora took as license to proceed. "I mean, you're driving back and forth so much, before work, after work, back to your friend's…well, just the gas, let alone all that time, it just seems like it would make sense. I don't know if you're paying your friend, but of course, you wouldn't pay anything here. I could even…"

"No, ma'am. Nothing like that. Okay."

"Okay? You mean you'll stay?"

"Yeah, I can do that. Want some potatoes?" Alex wiped his mouth on the paper napkin balled up in one hand and passed the potatoes without waiting for an answer. Anything to change the subject and avoid looking at Lexie, who, he imagined, might be having a fit behind his back. She set her milk on the table then, though, and didn't say anything. What he'd said was true enough in a way, the part about not having had time. But he'd also been informed that he not only had to pay the first month's rent and a security deposit, but the last month's rent as well. At the same time, he'd had to pay N. Reardon Greevy again, who was less than ecstatic with the new turn in the road down which his client was steering a battered pickup truck littered with fast-food wrappers.

forty-two

OF COURSE HE DIDN'T have to talk to Cora about it. As his lawyer
kept pointing out, he was the one with custody; he was the one
with all four aces; he was the one in charge. Alex talked to her
anyway, without puzzling for long about why because the *why*
was simple: nothing he'd done with Detta had been even as good
an experience as the root canal he'd had on his upper right
incisor, and Cora would probably have some decent advice.

He waited until Detta had gone to a movie with Jill one airless
evening. He knew, in fact, exactly where she was since he was the
one who'd driven her to the theater and would pick her up. Jolene
was staying with Becca while Jill was gone. It seemed Jolene had
spent an awful lot of time with Becca, but he guessed she was
filling in for Cora while Cora was laid up. Jolene was family to
Cora and families did that sort of thing. Not that he'd know from
his own experience, but he'd had glimpses from the outside.

Sometimes when Jolene called, Cora seemed to lower her
voice—even whisper—which convinced Alex they were talking
about him. But he'd made his bed now, literally, upstairs in the
yellow guest room with the crooked shade and creaky closet
door, both of which he could fix, and the complete lack of cross-
ventilation, which he couldn't. If Cora was talking about him,
well, what could he do? This whole thing had been Cora's idea,
he reminded himself. It wasn't like he'd asked for a place to stay.

He waited until Cora finished watching a show on television

before he came into the living room and cleared his throat. "I wanted to get your opinion…about something," he began, and shifted his weight from one foot to the other.

Cora sensed his discomfort. "Well, sit down," she said heartily. "It'd be nice to be useful for something." She used the remote control to reduce the volume of the television. Alex could see a toilet-bowl cleaner commercial on the muted screen and hoped it wasn't an omen.

He came deeper into the room and sat in the wing chair. Christine's picture watched him from across the room, but it didn't bother him hardly at all anymore. There was something to be said for getting used to a situation. "I've been thinking about maybe teaching Detta to drive. When I'm at work, you two wouldn't be stuck here, then, like if you had to get to the doc…"

Cora interrupted. "I think that's a wonderful idea. Becca wanted to teach her, you know, sort of for Christine, but that hasn't…and things have been so hectic I haven't done anything about it myself."

"I'll see if she wants to, then," Alex said. A small smile flickered across the lower half of his face though he reabsorbed it as quickly as possible. "Might be better not to teach her with my truck…startin' off with the shift and all." It was a question, of course, but he hated to put it that way since it seemed to make a negative response more possible.

"Would you like to use my car?" Cora jumped in on cue. She looked shiny, the way the lamplight crossed her face, hot, as if light had weight. Almost at the same time, Alex realized the room was stultifying. The window was open, but the curtain hung as limp as the damp hair flopped on Cora's forehead.

"Might be a good idea," he said. "After she gets the hang of it, I can put her in the truck and get her onto the gears and clutch and all."

"Yes, that's a good thing to know. Of course, when I learned to drive, the gearshift was up by the steering wheel. But then, it wasn't too hard to go from that to a floor shift when the style changed. Now I like my automatic, though Marvin never approved of them."

"I remember," Alex said. And he did. "Mr. Laster called mine a wimpmobile. After that, I pretty much stuck to standard transmissions. That was later, though. I just always thought of it when I was lookin' to buy something."

"No. Really?" It amazed and rather touched Cora that Marvin might have had the smallest influence on Alex, an unexpected flower blooming from between cracks in cement.

"Really." Alex's nails had grease edging them. Marvin's hands had been rough but clean. The memory, here in Cora's living room—which looked much as it had seventeen years ago—made Alex ball his own into fists.

"Well, that would please him."

"It'd be the first time I ever did, then."

Cora paused. Fair was fair. "I imagine you're right, Alex. Marvin was hardheaded sometimes." She paused, and considered how to put it. "People change," she said pointedly. "Poor Marvin didn't have a chance to, but I like to think he might have come around to some things."

Alex thought he got her drift, but didn't want to push it, in case. "Yeah. People change." There was a moment of silence, then, though it wasn't as uneasy as Alex had come to expect. He sighed, a little puff of air, a sound that could have accompanied a nod of agreement.

"You okay?" Cora asked, misinterpreting.

Alex was puzzled, but then went with what came to him. "Yeah. Hot in here."

"I try not to think about it," Cora said. She used the tissue she had tucked between the cushion and the side of the chair to wipe her forehead. She'd put on an old housedress that morning which made her look exactly like her own mother. In fact, that dress had *been* her mother's; she'd worn one daily even after it became acceptable for a woman to wear slacks. Cora had pulled the dress off her closet shelf that morning just for the thought of having some air on her legs. The short sleeves were a bit tight about her upper arms, but when she was alone she could spread her legs a little and flap the skirt to cool herself off. Being plunked in a chair almost every waking hour was not only really old, it was really hot. July looked to be stifling, too, at least if the Farmer's Almanac could be trusted. Marvin had sworn by it, even after it had completely missed mentioning the Blizzard of '78, when the drifts had trapped them inside for days.

"Be right back," Alex said. He clomped down the hall, still in his work boots, got the big fan from where it was, still aimed at the empty kitchen table, and carried it back to the living room. "Shoulda thought of this before…sorry," he said as he plugged it in and aimed it at Cora. He adjusted the control to High. "That too much?"

"Nothing would be too much," Cora said. "Thank you very much. That was nice. Marvin would turn in his grave if he could hear me—sorry, Marvin—" she interjected into her own sentence, rolling her eyes to the starry heaven she imagined outside "—but do you think I could ever air-condition this house? I mean, could it even be done?"

Alex considered. "Sure. You got forced air heating, so the ductwork is there. I got me some friends at the plant know some about it. Want me t' ask how much it would be?" He itched for a cigarette, but knew better.

"That would be wonderful. I couldn't afford it right now, I don't think, but maybe…" Cora was alluding to the legal bills she'd amassed, along with the cost of the psychological evaluations, though she knew Alex wouldn't infer it and she didn't want him to. Guilt induction wasn't her intention, certainly not now.

Another pause. "Guess I'd better get…"

Cora cut him off before he could say *going*. "Oh, why don't you stay here and watch this with me? The fan'll keep us cool and you don't have to get Lexie for another hour, do you?"

So Alex stayed. Once, the slapstick got to both of them at the same time and then Alex's honk was like a quick French horn mixed into the throaty clarinet of Cora's laugh.

THE LESSON WASN'T going that badly, Alex assured himself. Not as bad as Dink had predicted, anyway. No body damage to Cora's car nor any buildings; no dead or maimed pedestrians.

It was ten o'clock on Sunday morning. Alex had figured the churchgoers were in their pews and traffic would be light until at least eleven. He doubted he'd be able to take more than an hour, anyway.

Once she'd gotten the feel of gas pedal and brake and the lurching stops and starts didn't threaten to put him in a neck brace, Alex tried to teach Lexie how to back up, but she steadfastly refused even to try Reverse. "Forward is my friend," she intoned, staring at the road as if hypnotized, her hands riveted to the wheel at precisely ten and two. She was wearing Christine's opal ring, Alex noticed—not that he hadn't noticed it on her before, but somehow the death-grip she had on the wheel accentuated how much her hands looked like her mother's. Alex wouldn't have even guessed he remembered what Chris's hands had looked like, but there he was, recognizing them with a kick to the gut of longing and nostalgia.

Cora had watched them leave, keeping herself hidden behind the swag of her kitchen curtain. Lexie had been flushed, spots of color on her cheeks. She'd wanted this for a long time, Cora knew, but she also knew that it was killing Lexie to accept even what she wanted so badly from Alex. ("Can't *you* teach me, Grandma? You can get in the car, and that's all we need." But Cora held out, saying it wasn't safe because she wouldn't be able to intervene if Lexie had a problem, not laid up the way she was. *Laid out,* she'd almost said.)

Cora had taken Alex aside and coached him on how to handle Lexie. "Girls are different," she'd told him. "Every little thing she does right, be sure to praise her. If she messes up, say 'That's okay, you can do it.'" Alex had looked at her like she'd sprouted a blue mustache, but said "okay," his all-purpose answer. Cora had seen Lexie shoot Alex a furtive look, then approach the driver's side with her chin jutted out exactly like Christine used to stick hers. God help them both, Cora had thought, and had shaken her head.

"But I still think it's the best thing, don't you?" she'd said to Jolene on the phone once she got away from the window and to the phone. "They've got to get to know each other. I think it's too easy for them to avoid each other when I'm around. Not that Alex is a fountain of conversation around me, but there's not the same tension as between him and Lexie," Cora said, pouring herself another cup of coffee. "You'd think I'd be the one to hold the grudge," she added, musing aloud. "I mean, there's a lot more history."

"That's for sure," Jolene said from her end. "How're you holding up? Enjoying those crutches, are you?" Teasing.

"Oh, Jo, don't be making me feel guilty," Cora said. She glanced at the crutches, splayed against the hallway wall beyond the kitchen door. "It's you I'm worrying about. You and Becca. I hope I won't be punished for taking this time away from her."

"You're doing a good thing, Cora Lee," Jolene said, her voice strong and sure of herself. "This takes a big heart, a good heart. I won't believe in a God who won't give you the time to make up. I just won't. Becca's no weaker."

"Maybe I'll be able to ask Alex to bring me over later."

"I'm sure she'd like to see you."

"I'll see what they say about the lesson, you know, when they get back."

"If one of them hasn't killed the other one."

"Right you are. If they're both alive."

AT THAT MOMENT, they were both alive. Alex and Lexie were, in fact, approaching a four-way stop and Alex was trying to explain how Lexie was to know when it was her turn to proceed. Fortunately or unfortunately, there were no other cars in sight, so the discussion was entirely hypothetical.

"Doesn't matter," Lexie muttered. Her hair was up in a high ponytail that swung in punctuation. "I don't consider this a necessary stop sign. There's never any traffic here. Never will be unless those horses stampede." She inclined her head toward Rob Price's small herd, munching on leftover late-June lushness. One dapple-gray mare had her head stuck between the flimsy wire fence strands to get at the thick green between her and the road, as if the pickings were skimpy in the field—which they weren't.

Alex, who was quite capable of such a thought himself, as well as of running an obviously unnecessary stop sign, was horrified. "Oh, yeah. Great. Excuse me, Officer, but I didn't stop because I don't consider that a necessary stop sign. And by the way, I don't consider that a necessary ticket you're writing." He stuck his elbow out the window and resisted the urge to reach into his T-shirt pocket for a cigarette. At Cora's suggestion, he wasn't smoking in front of Lexie. "Listen, Dets, it don't work that way. Stop, hear me? Even when it's a stupid sign."

Lexie obliged by applying too much brake and nearly sending Alex through the windshield. "You can call me Lexie," she said, something she had to get out of the way because she didn't know what else to do about being called "Dets" in front of her grandmother. Cora eyed her accusingly when Alex said it, too.

"Why'd you say you went by Detta?" he said. It had dawned on him weeks ago that, in fact, she didn't.

Lexie shrugged, though the answer was wanting out, tap dancing on her tongue.

"So you're both alive," Cora said when they came in. "How'd it go? You ready to get your license...Dets?"

"Yeah," Lexie said in some new mix of hopeful defiance. But Cora noticed that Lexie wasn't talking to her when she said it, but shot the syllable in Alex's direction.

Cora looked at Alex, who was sweating, but maybe that was just from the heat. Lexie looked a bit damp, too, her bangs—newly cut thanks to the ten-dollar bill Alex had handed her when Cora said no, she really couldn't advance any more allowance—sticking to her pale forehead. Just a smatter of freckles had popped out across her nose and upper cheeks from the few hours she'd spent in the sun. No sunburn, let alone the light tan she could muster with concentrated work; she and Jill hadn't logged any time at the Knights of Columbus swimming pool since they had no transportation there except on the weekends.

"*Lexie* is *not* ready to get her license," Alex said, so Cora knew that at least one thing extra had been accomplished. Two down. Good enough.

"Having trouble with…" Cora said, aiming it to Alex, who'd opened the freezer and was loading a glass with ice.

"I am *not* having trouble. I drive fine," Lexie injected, insulted, and flounced toward the bathroom. Midday flooded the kitchen, heating it.

"You care if I finish off this tea?" Alex said, holding up the pitcher he'd pulled from the refrigerator.

"Not at all. I've got another pitcher of sun-tea started," Cora gestured toward the back porch where the sun was particularly intense in the mornings, then brought herself up short and went on quickly to distract Alex. "So really, how'd it go?"

But Alex had caught it. "How you get it out there?" he said, eyeing the crutches propped against the kitchen table where Cora sat.

Cora decided to chance the lie, since Lexie was still in the bathroom. "Lexie…before you left. What about her driving?"

Alex dropped the tea-on-the-porch question. He glanced to make sure Lexie couldn't hear him. "Not that bad, if you don't mind whiplash and think you can always find a way to go forward since Reverse is 'an unnecessary gear.' And certain stop signs are unnecessary, too, of course." He used the index and third fingers of both hands to draw quotation marks in the air around the word *unnecessary.*

"HEY, LEX," ALEX said maybe ten days later. "Get it in your head. I'm not signing for you to get your license until you can change a tire and use jumper cables. That's for emergencies. And you've gotta know how to change your oil, too." They were in Cora's yard after Alex got home from work. The afternoon was sliding toward twilight while Alex was demonstrating the use of a jack and lug wrench and Lexie was giving him her bored inattention. A hummingbird hovered at the red sugar-water feeder between two baskets of bright-pink impatiens, all hanging from the porch roof.

"Oh, my God, of course. Changing my oil would be the first thing I'd need to do in an emergency." Lexie seemed to have inherited Chris's gift for sarcasm. "But could you refresh my memory on exactly why?" She'd been to the pool over the weekend and her shoulders were still sunburned. Cora had reminded Alex to remind Lexie to wear sunscreen, an admonition to which she'd obviously paid little attention. The bridge of her nose was pink and her lips were peeling, too.

"Okay. The rest is for emergencies, though."

"If it's so important, how come the license bureau doesn't put it on the test?"

Alex didn't even bother to try to come up with an answer. He just busied himself jacking up Cora's car. Then he realized, this was sort of missing the point. He stepped aside and pointed to it. "Go on now. You do it. Just pump up and down, like I was doing."

"You just don't want me to get my…"

Alex interrupted. "Have you got fruitcake for brains? You think I'm spending every night driving around with you because I like the scenery?" In fact, it had nothing to do with liking the scenery; it had to do with liking the time with his daughter. She was starting to open up a little, just like Big Al had said happened when a teenager is past the initial stages of having to think about every single move behind the wheel and they're just logging practice time. Alex had already decided he was going to make her learn how to drive a stick shift, too, just because, well, she might need to drive that kind of car in an emergency.

Already she'd told him about how she'd been in Civics while her mother was dying and how she still didn't like the cemetery and felt closer to Christine when she was feeding the birds. She had a picture of Christine in her coffin that Cora didn't know about; that had sort of slipped out when Lexie was talking about how the cemetery seemed too cold and far away, but Christine's room upstairs and the bird feeders were where she could talk to her. She'd shut up for the rest of the drive after she said that much, as if she regretted it. Alex hadn't known what to say, so he'd shut up, too.

"Well, I'd think you'd be in a hurry for me to get my license then. It's not my fault you have to drive around with me. I could pass the test now and you know it."

It was quite true, not that he was going to admit that to her. "I dunno. And it don't mean you're ready to handle an emergency," he said. "Now look, you've got the car jacked up, right? So…"

But Lexie wasn't to be deterred. "So since when are you so big on emergencies?" she said, a dangerous edge to her voice.

Alex, who always used to be caught off guard by what anyone said, actually thought he knew what was coming. He set the lug wrench on the gravel of the driveway and went from forward-leaning kneel to one that rested his rear back onto his upturned heels. "Since I used to be really, really useless in one," he said matter-of-factly. "And I feel real bad about it. I'm sorry."

Lexie dug in. He wasn't going to get off now, not just like that, with some stupid simple little "I'm sorry." She seemed to gather herself in, consider and decide to strike. "You killed my sister," she said, her voice scraping the jagged rocks of an adult bitterness. "I know what happened."

That one did take Alex by surprise. He didn't think Christine had told anyone. Did Cora know, too? "Yes," he said simply, finally. "It was an accident, but yes, it was my fault. There's no way to make it right. Hell, there's no way. Nothing'll ever be right no matter what I do." He forced himself to look Lexie in the eye, but when he managed the contact she turned her head to break it. Alex felt tears but refused them the room they wanted so he wouldn't seem to be asking her to feel sorry for him. "I'm sorry. I messed up about your mother and your sister. And you. I'm sorry. It was me. It was my fault." By my fault. *By my fault. By my most grievous fault,* he'd been taught to say in the confession of sin, the closed fist of his right hand knocking against his left chest with each repetition. That came before the absolution from the priest during the masses of his boyhood. He couldn't remember the last time he'd been to mass.

Lexie's head was rigid. She sat on the ground in denim shorts and a red tank top, an emergent woman who, he saw, had no more inclination to forgive him than the women lined up in his mind wearing their shrouds of condemnation. Cora's kindness had given him a delusional hope. No matter. He'd already done what he could to make it right for Cora.

"Well…I, uh, I guess I can show you about the tire another time. If you ever want to know," he said with a shrug he didn't feel. His feet and knees had stiffened and one foot was asleep; he knew he looked ridiculous trying to get up, using the handle on the car door for leverage. When he straightened up, he bent over to pick up the tools and headed toward the porch. He'd get the car off the jack after she went in.

From behind him on the ground, Lexie's voice barely reached him. "I burned up your trailer."

He stopped and turned around but didn't walk back to her. "I know," he said, from that distance.

He saw from her quick look up from the ground that he'd surprised her. The hair she'd let fall to curtain her face swung away then, back against her cheek. She still sat on the ground, Indian-style, dwarfed by Cora's car behind her, in a three-quarter profile until, with that quarter turn of her head, she met his eyes.

She looked down again. "I didn't mean for the whole thing to burn down. That part was an accident."

"I know," Alex said. Then he did walk over to her. When she didn't look up, he touched the top of her head. The touch was soft and brief, the curve of his hand shaping itself over the curve of her head, the way to palm a baby's head.

Forty-three

NEITHER ALEX NOR LEXIE was in the house when Brenda Dunlap phoned. "I have news," she said. "You're not going to believe this."

Cora had had too much practice getting unbelievable news. She sat down, lodging her body between the chair and the kitchen table for support. "Oh, dear God," she said. "You got the psychologist's report. Is it bad?"

"Not bad in the sense that there's a single negative word in it about you."

"But..."

"But she says that even though Alexis has a close and bonded relationship with you and there's no evidence she does with her father...that he's not psychotic or incompetent or unwilling and therefore there aren't psychological grounds on which to terminate his parental rights. She does say she thinks Alexis would be *happier* with you...but..."

Cora exhaled. The phone cord was taut and her wrist felt, suddenly, too weak and tired to hold the receiver. She needed to get off, to think about how she'd tried to prepare all of them for this. "I knew this could happen. I thank you for trying..."

Brenda interrupted. "Hold up, Mrs. Laster. There's more."

"More?"

"Alex has dropped the suit."

"What?"

"He's dropping the custody action. You'll remain the guardian and if you want to proceed with an adoption, he'll sign over his rights so that you can."

"What?"

"Yes, ma'am. You heard me right." On her end, Brenda smiled. Sometimes she'd take a gift-wrapped win for a client and just breath out *thank you* without worrying about who or what she was trying to thank.

OH, MY CHRISSIE, my Chrissie. Did you bring this about? Maybe Alex always was what you saw in him, the boy you loved. If he was, honey, I'm so sorry I missed it, I'm sorry your daddy missed it. Of course, I guess you and Daddy can work that out between you, can't you. I'm so sorry. Or is this part of it, are you changing him? Or changing us all?

Cora closed her eyes and tried to feel her daughter's presence in the bedroom that had been hers, as she was sometimes quite sure she did when she had the patience to wait for it. When it didn't come, she shook her head and talked on as much to herself as to Christine. The distant sound was that of the lawn mower out in back; Alex was mowing, but he had Lexie out there, too, weeding out the stalks of tall grassy weeds that had grown in the shrubbery nestled against the foundation—a task Lexie found particularly pointless. "I'll explain why it needs to be done," he'd said, "as soon as you climb down from your high horse." When Lexie stood, hands on hips, waiting, he'd finally conceded, "I don't know exactly why, and I don't care. Your grandpa always kept it that way and that's the way it's gonna be. You wanna go to Kim McBride's party tonight, then you get that done." Lexie had given him her most disgusted sigh, tried to stare him down and failed. Her father had given the stare right back to her, started the mower up and pushed off walking in the path of green fragrance the rotary blade created.

Ten minutes before the phone had rung, Cora had been watching the two of them through the kitchen window, thrown wide open more for the thought of air than the fact. Once she'd hung up, keeping her hand on the phone a long moment after it was cradled in the hook, she thought of flagging Lexie and

Alex, motioning them to come in so she could tell them the news. Then she realized: of course Alex knew. He'd done this some time ago without telling anyone but his lawyer from what Brenda said. Cora would have to think through what to say to him, and let it be his to tell Lexie.

Upstairs it was, if anything, a little cooler rather than hotter. Alex, bless him, had discovered and fixed the attic fan which Cora hadn't even remembered existed and had no idea how many years it had been broken. He had a friend named Dink coming over to see about the cheapest way to do air-conditioning, too, though Cora was hesitant. Even now it was hard to do what she knew would give Marvin fits.

I didn't want to let Lexie get sullied by life, you know. Cora shook her head again and gave a small shrug as if to say "how could I have been so stupid?" *As if I could back up time somehow and have her be what she might have been if you hadn't died. When you're little and your parents say you can do or be whatever you want if you just put your mind to it, all that faith we try to give them. That life is good and fair and it's up to them to make what they will of it. I used to love your face shining up, yours and Becca's, too—before you knew that some mistakes can't be reversed and before you failed big-time at anything. Before you understood about lies or misery or sickness and dying.* Cora closed her eyes, trying to invoke an image of Christine, how she would nod her head in understanding. *So I tried to keep her from her father. I thought it was what you wanted, I thought it was the right thing to do. And then it all blew up, and he ended up with her so then fighting him seemed the right thing to do.*

Cora's hands were nested together in her lap, though she didn't think of herself as praying. *Then I was trying to make it work with him, for her sake, make it better with him. I was getting somewhere, too, wasn't I? He's teaching her to drive and how to change a tire and change her own oil. Except now the court or you or God or your daddy up there putting up a stink— Someone or something has given her back to me. What am I supposed to do now?*

After minutes had passed, long minutes of listening to her heart count out its ponderous cadence, she got up and went to the closet. She'd not read Christine's diaries, though she knew Lexie had. Some days while Lexie had been at school or with Alex, Cora *had* holed up in Christine's room—though she couldn't bear the picture Lexie had hidden in the top bureau drawer—and tried to capture some living trace of her daughter: will, spirit, yearning, faith, love.

Now Cora took out Christine's last volumes and began to look for directions.

1983

forty-four

HERE'S WHAT IT IS. I saw potential in him. I knew he was a jerk a lot of the time, and of course there was the sex thing, but that wasn't why I wanted him so much when I was in high school and it certainly wasn't why I married him. Mom and Dad thought that was because I was pregnant and that I got pregnant so Alex could stay out of the war. After Tina died and he took off, I pretty much saw it that way myself, but in the past couple of years, now that Lexie is a teenager herself, I remember it more the way it was, the way we were. I loved him, and he loved me. I was the hope in his life. Really, I just wore myself better than he did; the only real difference between us was that I knew I'd be okay, that I could do what I had to do and that I was a good person that other people could count on.

Alex had a good soul. The problem was that he didn't know it himself. He didn't have the words. Nobody ever held up a mirror to him and said, "Look, you can do this. You're a good person." I liked it that I could see what other people couldn't. I saw inside him sometimes when he didn't know I was looking. I saw how he touched the babies when they were sleeping; I know he could have been a good father. I hope he's forgiven himself and I hope life has given him another chance.

1988

Forty-five

FALL HAD COME LATE, which meant the impatiens had grown leggy but they'd bloomed right alongside the marigolds and dahlias and the flame-shaped red salvia until an unseasonable—unreasonable, Cora said—freezing rain actually encased the blooms in clear ice. Cora wanted life, including God and the weather, to be reasonable. Jolene reminded her how rarely they were.

"But look. Sometimes it's not reasonable but it's better than reason. You and I have to remember that," she said.

"Last year when it turned cold, I still had Christine," Cora pointed out, one of the non sequiturs she and Jolene routinely lobbed each other, confident of the return.

"I know. And there's nothing more unreasonable than that."

"Unless it's Paul being gone, that whole pointless war," Cora said. They were in Cora's kitchen warming their hands around cups of coffee. Jolene had stopped in on her way home from her blood-pressure check. Cora had heated a Sara Lee coffeecake she'd had squirreled away in the freezer, and they were cutting themselves tiny slices. Many tiny slices.

"Or Rebecca…she does look better, doesn't she, though? So how do we know what's the unreasonable part? That she got this cancer or that it's in remission?" Jolene set the knife away from herself, where it would be harder to reach.

"Remission for the time being. It's not her first remission. Everything's just for the time being," Cora said, looking at her hands and then up, at Jolene. She could see herself faintly reflected in Jo's glasses. "For the time being, it's working out. I'm hoping she lives to see Jill graduate from high school." She sipped her coffee.

"From your lips to God's ears," Jo said, their favorite endorsement. "Give me just a half a thin slice more, will you?"

Cora obliged without breaking her thought. "And I'm hoping Alex and Lexie stay here until she's out of high school. That's only two more years."

"She's got the best of both worlds now, that's another good thing," Jolene murmured.

"Sure, except that her mother's still dead, which was the very worst of a world that's gone forever."

Jolene leaned across the table and took Cora's free hand into one of hers, the easy bridge of women who love each other. "It's always that way, honey. It's always that way. Anything's for the time being. Time and being's what we have. And sometimes another chance."

"My Christine didn't get another chance."

"No. And neither did Paul. But you and I have. And maybe Becca will. And Lexie. And how about Alex?"

Cora looked out the window. She'd taken down the old curtains and replaced them with just a white valance so that from anywhere in the kitchen there was always a view of the bird-feeding station Alex had made for Lexie. They'd hung several kinds of feeders from a black metal contraption that looked like four shepherd's crooks of different heights nestled back to back, with hooks extending north, south, east and west. A purple martin house was atop a high metal pole farther out in the yard. "Time flies," Cora said out loud. In her mind she heard Christine's voice, as clearly as she ever had: *Like a bird...* "I wish there was more of it. Time, I mean," Cora said feeling tears start behind her eyes even as a small, close-lipped smile reached her face because right then she felt her daughter's life much as she had in the first secret quickening, as if so many years hadn't been lost.

"Me, too," Jo said, seeing the small battle on her friend's face, the little muscle that jumped just below her cheekbone, the rue and tenderness in the eyes that opened after a few seconds during which Jo knew Cora was seeing Christine. She put her hand lightly over Cora's and stroked along a ropy vein. "But sometimes we manage to stretch it out."

Forty-six

I ASKED GRANDMA if she believes there's such a thing as angels. They're getting pretty popular lately. Jill believes in angels for sure; she's collecting little china ones and she's got them all named and lined up on her windowsill where they've got a direct shot to heaven. She thinks they have something to do with Becca being alive. What I really wanted to ask Grandma was if she believes in God, but I knew she'd never say *no I don't,* even if she thought God was a made-up bunch of hooey, which is what she said about my reason for not getting the dishes done. About angels, she finally said she didn't know what she believes anymore. There was a time she did, then she didn't, and now she plain doesn't know. She said she's sure some real people turn out to be angels in their actual life.—Like Jolene, she said.— And like your mother. Then she waited and said, real quietly.— Maybe like your father, Lexie. It's so strange how things turn out. You sure couldn't have predicted, could you?

She wasn't really asking a question, but I'll answer it anyway. No, I couldn't have predicted, even though he still makes me blind furious when he won't let me out past eleven with the car. It's Grandma's car, even, so when she says it's up to your father, I get mad at her, too. You'd think it would make *her* mad to have him say what I can do with her car, but no, it doesn't faze her a bit. And at dinner, it's questions, questions, questions. How'd you do on that Algebra test, Lexie? When's that English paper due, Lexie? What do you think about the hostage crisis, Lexie? Did you make that dentist appointment, Lexie? Sometimes I feel like my neck's going to break from whipping my head back between questions from the two of them while I'm trying to concentrate on avoiding whatever mushy vegetable on my plate is the grossest.

Tim and I broke up because I found a note from Jennifer in his history book. It was signed Love and had x's and o's underneath her name and she used a dorky little heart sign to dot the *i*. It also stank—I mean really—because she sprayed perfume on the paper. Then he got mad back at me because I frosted my hair, and he said it was because I wanted to flirt with other guys. I don't care, because now I like Matt Demos but I think the real reason Tim started liking Jennifer instead of me is because my father practically made him fill out a questionnaire every time he came to pick me up. I tried to get him to quit, but he said,— I know what's on *his* mind, and told Tim,—I'm dusting her for fingerprints when she gets home, you get my drift? I swear he leaves Matt alone because Matt says Yes, sir, and No, sir, and We'll be home on time, sir, Thank you, sir. Just Sirs him up and down like Alex is wood and Matt is a brushful of wet paint.— You don't have to do that, call him sir all the time, I told Matt, but he said,—hey, fathers like that crap.

I thought he was right, too. Until my father says to him, real slow,—You know, Matthew, I've got your number, and I can use it to count backward anytime. You get my drift…sir? Like a hiccup Matt says,—Yes, sir. And looks startled and scared at the same time. He was pathetic.

I swear my only hope for ever getting married is to elope with a stranger while my father is in the shower.

I still talk to my mother. Something happened yesterday, on the one-year anniversary of the day she died, and I didn't have time to think about asking her and waiting to see if I felt an answer. Grandma was upstairs putting on warmer clothes, and I was just getting my jacket and gloves out of the closet when Alex asked if he could go to the cemetery with Grandma and me. It was just like a reflex when I said *no*. Then I realized he was sort of dressed up, in khaki pants and his blue plaid shirt he knows I like because sometimes if he's gone to work before I leave for school, I sort of borrow it to wear to school over my light blue tank top. (It's way too cold to wear that by itself now, but the shirt looks really good over it and Matt says it makes my eyes look like sky.)

Alex didn't get mad, though, he just said okay, real quietly. Then he took his wallet out of his back pocket and picked a ten-dollar bill out of it,—Well, on your way, would you get some extra flowers to take her from me? He knew Grandma and I were going to stop at Flowers by Frederick; we did on her birthday and holidays and sometimes for no reason.

I didn't know what to do. I just stood there in the kitchen like a big dummy, with all the dishes dumped helter-skelter in the sink—I was supposed to do them, but I hadn't yet. My face got hot and I tried a couple of different words but I quit because anything I said was just going to make it worse. Then he said —It's okay, Lexie. I understand. But could I give her some flowers? Please.

And just stood there like he was waiting for my judgment, whether I'd take the money or just cut off his arm and be done with it. He was holding out that money, his hand jittering a little, and waiting for me to decide.

I know it's not just my story. It's my mother's and my father's and Tina's. Grandma's, Becca's and Jill's, too, I guess. And we could throw in Jolene. But him standing there, holding out that ten dollars made me feel like it was all my story and I had to decide whether to let it end and how to let it end. And if it should start over and how it should start over. I know he's sorry, and all he wants is a chance to do what he can to make it right. Well, some things you can never make right. But then there's what you can do, and you've got to do that much. And sometimes it's enough.

So I took the money out of his hand and I said,—Yes, I will. What do you want me to get her?

I thought he'd say, "Whatever you want." But he didn't. He said,—Get one pink rose and one yellow one. And one of those little cards for flowers that says thank you. That's all. She'll know.

I looked at his face then and it was new-shaved, and his cheeks had spots of color I'd never seen before, like he'd scraped them. His eyes were too shiny, they wanted to water. I don't know what came over me, but I just took one step and put my arms around him. It was the first time. I could hear his heart, fast and hard. He hugged me back and put his cheek on the top of my head.

—It's all right, Dad, I said.

THE UNSPOKEN YEARS

For Jan, my sister, with love

I imagine us seeing
everything from another place—the top
of one of the pale dunes
or the deep and nameless
fields of the sea...
Looking out for sorrow,
slowing down for happiness,
making all the right turns...
—Mary Oliver,
"Coming Home"

Acknowledgments

Special thanks to Susan Schulman, my good-listener agent, and
Tara Gavin, whose work editing this book I genuinely appreciate.

The Mind Alive, mentioned in this novel, is by
Harry A. Overstreet and Bonaro W. Overstreet.

Alan, Brooke, David and Ciera deCourcy are consistent and
steadfast in their support of my work. My love and gratitude to
each of them, every day.

PROLOGUE

THE BLUE PITCHER I MADE SO many years ago isn't my most perfect piece but it's precious to me. I wasn't new to the pottery wheel when I made it, only to the notion of feeling what shape the clay will sing itself into when my hands listen and guide rather than fight it. (Like my life, which had finally begun taking its own shape at the time.)

As I pick it up now from the hutch near the window that overlooks the bay, I remember the pleasure I took feeling it emerge like a new baby. I shaped a graceful handle, with a place for curling fingers, heel of hand and thumb to fit naturally; and the glaze fired exactly true: the shade of the ocean when it is pure sapphire, perhaps on a day when ashes are being released at its edge. I'd imagined it as a cream pitcher, a special gift, but it came out too generously sized, so I kept it myself, as a reliquary for my childhood's dried tears.

I *did* make the cream pitcher, though. I've always loved cream, especially the old-fashioned kind you can't find anymore. For a little while when I was a child, we used to have a milkman bring whole milk that had to be shaken up to mix the cream in with the skim because it wasn't homogenized. Or you could save the cream by pouring it off the top, like my mother did for her coffee and cereal. I took it as a sign that something fine and good could be saved, although I lost hope many times that such a natural law might apply to me. My brother and I were born to guilt, and we took it on like a mantle. Of course we were innocents. In her own way, perhaps our mother was, too, although that's more difficult to see.

I had to wait weeks longer until a lump of clay finally bloomed into the cream pitcher I'd hoped to make. I knew, the way you know something you have already lived, weather in your bones, that it was right. That one I glazed in a joyous array of ascending, blending color: gold and green for the sand and the marsh grass of the solid earth at the bottom, tones of aquamarine for the moving bay and ocean, to a lighter and lighter blue of opening sky. And it has endured, intact and beautiful, on the table in the center of our home.

This isn't a story I thought I'd ever be willing or ready to tell. My mind's eye has retained a run-down glamour image from childhood: me, running off alone with only a brown bag lunch and babysitting money in search of my father by hitchhiking the country to look for men I resembled. Once I could have set out that way, without baggage, running to him for rescue. (Not that I knew him nor he me, but I idolized the idea of him.) Now, this story is my baggage and to know me, he would have to know what he left me to, and what I did to survive. But the cream pitcher on the table is brim-full; I have had enough very good years that I can bear to seek him out and let come what comes.

And whether I find him or not, this story is part of the heritage I think my children will have a right to know. I hope I do not sound self-justifying as I tell it. I realize there are those who would say I am guilty of murder, and those who would say I am not. There are a few who would say my mother tried to kill me more surely than herself. I've told it without flinching, this story of all that has remained silent but unforgotten where I left it, in the blue pitcher of memory and dried tears.

I

SHE WAS ALWAYS CRAZY. Looking back, I see no doubt about it. It was a deceptive craziness, though, sometimes luminous and joyful. Even when it was, my brother and I knew it was important not to relax. If one of us let down our vigilance, a bottomless pit could open right beneath our feet, eclipsing the ground we'd been foolish enough to trust, and the sickening freefall would begin again.

We blamed ourselves, of course. Mother blamed us, too. In a way, that was best, because we could all be saved if Roger and I only perfected ourselves, and I used to believe that was possible—until the summer after eighth grade, when she went for weeks without speaking to me. I had no idea what I'd done or how to fix it, and bang, one afternoon while I was lying on my bed, this thought came: *it's not me*. Instead of being relieved, I cried a long time, letting the tap of water against our mildewed shower curtain obscure the sound. I was ill-equipped to deal with the insight, which didn't last anyway. Maybe Mother smelled my doubt of her; she had an uncanny sense of when she'd gone too far, although I can see now she took full advantage of the vast and open space we gave her, the miles and miles before she reached our edge.

But there was this, too: she had the most wonderful laugh, rich and tinkly at the same time.

My mother had an undisguised preference for male over female, inexplicable considering the relationships she'd had with men. She both worshipped and loathed the memory of her father, who'd died before Roger and I were born, and implied grossly preferential treatment of her brother, Jacob, to whom she hadn't spoken in a good fifteen years. It was all an enigma to me until she and I made a journey to Seattle to see her dying mother. Neither Roger nor I had never so much as met our grandmother before then. Mother had told us the distance from Massachusetts to Seattle was too great for visiting, but we also knew that when Grandmother called, Mother would often end up banging down the phone or pretending to have been disconnected.

My brother and I speculated that we were the children of different fathers. Our discussions on the subject were rare and secretive because Mother gave us to understand that she was a Virgin. Any question that didn't use that tenet as a given would bring quick punishment. As a reward for her purity and devotion, God gave Mother the Truth. It was a serious mistake to disagree with Him through Her. She had elevated her non-male status by having had adequate brains to become the Bride of Christ, as she put it, a position she evidenced by wearing a solitaire pearl on her wedding ring finger. Since He only needed one Bride, the lowliness of my gender was unredeemed.

One time it was better to be a girl, but I couldn't enjoy it. Mother had taken us on an impromptu camping trip, as she did at least once every summer. Each time she found us a new place to trespass; we never went where it was legal to camp, because, she explained, those places had already been discovered and ruined, or, more likely, they hadn't been the best places to begin with or rich people would have already bought them up. Every year we collected treasures from our trip and after we got home we'd make a collage. "Look! A whelk and it's not broken!" one of us would call out as we walked a heads-down souvenir search. "From an eagle!" we'd pronounce a feather fallen from an ordinary gull, and she'd proclaim, "It's a keeper and so are you." Of course, she also regularly threatened to return us to the Goodwill store, where she claimed to have found us at a clearance sale, but she loved us. I know she did.

Even now, after all, I remind myself of that. And she had the most wonderful laugh.

All in all, I hated camping, but I pretended to like it because it was God's Great Outdoors and it would have added another flaw to the list she kept on me if I didn't like laying my bony body down on God's Great Hard-As-Rocks Rocks and hearing Mother remind us of the Rock of Ages on which we should rest our lives. We didn't have a tent or anything. Three thin sleeping bags, a couple of dented pots, paper plates, ancient utensils stolen from various diners, matches and a red plaid plastic table-cloth constituted our equipment. Mother said a tent would spoil the view of God's Great Starry Heavens. To myself, I added that it would also spoil the feast enjoyed by God's Great Mosquito Plague, but I would never have been dumb enough to say it out loud. The thought was a grimy smudge of rebellion on my soul, and I was amazed she didn't notice and purify me again.

This particular trip involved a drive of two hours south into Rhode Island, to the oceanfront estates of Newport. She figured that by parking on a kind of no-man's-land on the obscure boundary between two huge properties, we could unobtrusively carry our gear onto the enormous cliffs and climb down, out of sight from the main houses, onto lower rocks where cozy sandy nests were revealed between them when the tide withdrew. Now it seems absurd to even contemplate, but I guess security systems weren't so nearly perfect in 1969.

I was too nervous to enjoy the scenery. There was a catch to the plans Mother made. If some disaster befell us, such as being arrested, she'd be furious because, she'd say, she had been testing our good sense by inserting a flaw into the plan. By not finding it, we would have proven again that her lessons had gone unlearned, she had Cast Pearls Among Swine. On the other hand, questioning the wisdom of a scheme was to certify Lack Of Faith, a major sin and stupid to boot; we knew that much.

We set up camp just as she'd imagined, on a huge fairly flat rock above a tiny spit of sand, below the cliffs and the manicured lawns and formal gardens that spread from elegant verandas toward the sea. Finding driftwood was the first task she set us to, and not a simple one. There isn't a lot of vegetation on those cliffs, and she was not happy with the skimpy pile we amassed. At some point we must have satisfied her, and she began working to get a fire started. We had to remember to praise the results profusely or we'd have displayed Lack Of Appreciation, another major sin. The wood fought back; there wasn't enough kindling and nothing we'd found was adequately dry. Roger might have contributed to the green wood problem by sneaking onto a lawn and uprooting a small tree. He sometimes did things like that when we were desperate, and I didn't say anything. We helped each other out that much, at least. Mother finally got a small blaze started, pale-appearing against the brilliant blue sky, and I breathed again. It was only late afternoon, too early for supper.

"We'll take a treasure walk." She tended to announce her decisions. "Watch your step."

We set out, climbing from one level of rocks to another when necessary, along the jagged shore guarding the back of Newport's spectacular mansions.

"Children," she exclaimed, her face animated and ecstatic, "You see? God's riches are ours. We don't need money." (Thank goodness we're not tainted with filthy lucre, observed a dangerous whisper in my mind.) But then Mother began to sing, *"Amazing grace! how sweet the sound that saved a wretch like me! I once was lost, but now am found, was blind but now I see."* Her fine, strong contralto wove itself into the noise of waves stunned by their meeting with cliffs and, as always, I was immediately reconverted to every word she had ever spoken. Her face was sun-gilt, and what she said about being the Bride of Christ had to be true, I was positive, or no way would God let her be so beautiful. She put her arm around me and hugged me to her, and I thought I would die then and there of pure happiness.

And all the signs were good, that was the thing. When we were in front of one estate, two big, short-haired dogs came charging out at us, barking ferociously, and I thought we'd done it, we'd failed another test. But Mother waved cheerily at the man who came out after the dogs. "Yoo hoo, how are you this beautiful day," she called, just as though we belonged there, and kept right on going. The man waved back and whistled for the dogs who went to him reluctantly, whining their disappointment at being denied fresh kill.

We went on a little farther, and the three of us sat on the rocks of a small promontory, a melon sun spilling color over the edge of our world and sea. My goose-bumped skin smoothed out, and Mother said my hair was a glorious titian. A great peacefulness settled over us, each with our arms wrapped around our knees, and time slowed for our gratitude the way it does when you're by the water, your dry soul soaking up its magnitude and kindness. Mother rubbed my back and I wriggled into the crook of her arm and put my head in the hollow between her shoulder and cushy chest. We were all mostly quiet, but every now and then, something would pop into her mind and she'd say it and laugh, full and real and utterly joyous. She had the most wonderful laugh. I know I've said that, but it's still true. Even when we had no idea what she was talking about, her laugh would make us laugh with her.

It grew chilly as the sun continued to sink, and Mother said we needed to get back to camp. Roger and I hurried along, eager not to let anything interrupt the good feeling. When we reached the small campsite where we'd built the fireplace, a circle of stones in the middle of the flat rock by which we'd left our bedrolls and cooking equipment, Mother's face changed. Neither Roger nor I caught it quickly enough, and neither of us, even when we did see the change, knew what had gone wrong. Mother pointed angrily at the area and shouted, "How could you have let this happen?"

Roger and I looked at each other anxiously after each of us had taken a quick inventory. Nothing appeared to be missing. Mother realized we didn't see what she wanted us to and it infuriated her. "There! There!" she shouted, pointing at what had been the fire, now quite dead of neglect. We scurried to pacify her.

"I'll work on another one, Mother," I said, and started to gather up the couple of remaining kindling pieces, while Roger went over to the site and began stirring the ashes with a stick to see if any were live, but it was too late. We had to be reminded how dangerous happiness is.

Mother charged over and pushed Roger to the side. He had been squatting and her rough shove upset his balance; he landed on an elbow and hip. She yelled, then, "It's a man's job to keep the fire going." This was news to both Roger and me, but he knew better than to argue and I knew better than to draw her in my direction. It wouldn't have diminished Roger's punishment, only convinced her that her efforts were wasted on both of us and her rage and sorrow would lengthen like our shadows. I slunk backward toward the shadow of an overhanging rock, my back to the ocean, watching, and not wanting to.

Mother grabbed the stick Roger had used to poke the ashes and told him to let his pants down. At thirteen, though he hadn't a trace of beard of his high-colored fleshy cheeks, Roger was already man-size, of a hefty rectangular build. Still, he obeyed the humiliating order. His underwear gaped open and I could see a thin gathering of dark pubic hairs. I'd wondered if he had it yet. I was nearly twelve and had some, but the health teacher had said boys got theirs later. I could hear Roger apologizing, saying he understood and it wouldn't happen again, but Mother layered her sorrowful look over her steely one and said he'd have to be taught so he'd never forget again that a man is to tend the fire and provide for women. She reached over and yanked his shorts down, pointed at the rock he was to lean against and raised her other arm, holding the stick.

I lost count of how many times it came down. Behind her the sun was melting into the horizon and it looked as though she was pulling a great red fire down from the sky. Her arm was silhouetted in a slow black curving upward, until, after a momentary pause at the top of the arc, it blurred as it fell, a sickening sound splitting the air before the green stick cracked on his pale flesh, leaving another streak of the bloody sunset there. *When we've been dead ten thousand years, bright shining as the sun,* was the last verse she'd sung, *we've no less days...than when we first begun,* and I thought this time he might die but her killing him still wouldn't stop. When it was over and Roger was alive, I wanted to be happy that I was a girl, but I wasn't. Maybe I was jealous in spite of what she'd done to him because, when it was over, she pulled Roger into her arms and held him while he cried, loving and comforting him, and telling him it was all because he had to be a man, a man, a man

ROGER HEALED UP, WE always did, though normal walking was usually hard for a week or so, and we had to make up stories to our gym teachers so we wouldn't have to put on shorts. He had to earn his way back into grace, and I had to agree with Mother about how badly Roger had let her—us—down. Perhaps it sounds cowardly, the business of not standing up for each other, but until we were well into our teens, both of us kept trying to tilt the map of the world we held until it fit the puzzle Mother presented. We convinced ourselves it *did* fit, even if we had to lop off a country here, an ocean there to cram it into place. Later, we really did know better, but by then, we knew something more important: she had to have one of us to hang on to. When Roger defended something I'd said, even though it was to shore her up, she couldn't stand it. She simply couldn't stand it.

2

LATER, ROGER AND I AGREED IT was after Newport that the abyss began to spread, or maybe it was just our awareness of it. Not that we talked about it. The night was interminable after the campfire died, and the ocean exhaled a choking fog to overtake the flat rock on which we did not sleep. At least I didn't. I knew the flame on his buttocks and thighs, the nauseous sweat on his forehead in the clammy air, while movement and stillness were separate agonies. I went over and over what had happened trying to make it come out right, and finally told myself that it must be God Testing My Faith, as He often did Mother's. But I couldn't quite believe it in my core where it counted. The *it's not me, it's not us* refrain I'd heard and silenced earlier started up again, as though the long bow of a cello were parting the darkest waters.

But life proceeded largely unchanged for the next couple of years, except for Mother's vagaries, to which we were long accustomed. We stayed in one place longer than usual, and I thought maybe God was getting forgetful and had neglected to give Mother her usual instructions that it was time to move. So much the better for us. I hoped He'd never get His memory back. Roger took Driver's Education at school the semester before he turned sixteen and took his test three days after his birthday, irritated that he had to wait so long. Mother had repeatedly warned him he'd not be using *her* car, but we knew how soon there'd be a bad day when she'd want an errand run, how fast she'd command his foot to the gas pedal then. Mother was a flute teacher whose students came to our house right after school until seven at night. He knew she'd send him to get food, especially on the days when she'd stayed in bed until ten minutes before the first student arrived. Sometimes more than a week would go by with her barely rousable. We'd dig through her purse for change to get cafeteria lunches while she subsisted on canned food until it ran out and hunger flogged her to the grocery.

"Ruthie, want to go out to eat with me?" Roger asked me late one afternoon. We were, as usual, exiled to the kitchen while Alana Seeley, face jolted with freckles and buck teeth, hailed Schubert's poor Maria to her most miserable death yet. Mother's students were frequently untroubled by much talent, but Roger's imitation of Alana included sucking in his lower jaw when he got on his hands and knees to act like a dog howling at the moon. "Just us," he said.

"Without Mother?" It was unthinkable.

"We'll go at five. She's got Jason McAlister at five-thirty."

"Will we walk, or…?" We were a good two miles outside of town then, in a little house we rented from a real estate company. Darrville itself was a town like a sprung trap, where most of the houses were old and close together, with porches that sagged in the middle.

"She'll let me use it," he answered confidently. He was right, too. He asked when Alana left, and Mother did let him use the car. She even told him it was a nice idea in her sugar voice, the one that melted right into my kettle of jealousy. And it made me nervous. I told myself to have faith.

But the nervousness persisted through the burger, French fries and Coke I ordered at the diner. The beaten-up vinyl seats in the booth were cushy, the grill was giving off wonderful smells over by the counter where a few men in blue work uniforms lingered over coffee and the place was tacky and homey at once, with awful pictures above the booths. A jukebox played five songs for fifty cents. Mother, a rigid purist, detested rock and roll, so I was usually late learning the hits. I tried to keep up without her knowing; Mother's interpretations of God's secret messages to her had affected me. I didn't see why—if He spoke to her by putting Spam on sale—He couldn't speak to me by the songs He let me hear most often. On the way to the diner, I'd shushed Roger so I could hear Rod Stewart rasp about looking for a reason to believe, the meaning of which had bothered me for some time. Mother said faith was all about not asking for a reason. Not from her, not from God.

I was free to say whatever I wanted after we ordered, but nothing surfaced through my edginess. Roger didn't notice my fidgeting. He had something else entirely on his mind.

"Mrs. Klimm called me in today during study hall," he said, unwrapping a straw. Mrs. Klimm was the guidance counselor for the junior class.

"What did you do?" It wasn't like Roger to get in trouble in school.

"Nothing, it was nothing like that. She wanted to talk to me about my plans."

"Like your schedule?"

"Ruthie, like college."

"College?" I was sounding dumb, I knew, but dread coated my tongue with the stuff from the bottom of a murky lake. One of the men at the counter got up to leave and winked at me as he walked to the cash register. *Bob* was embroidered on a white patch above his shirt pocket. Maybe my father was a man named Bob. Maybe he winked because he was friendly and nice, and maybe the daughters of men named Bob heard them say, *I'm here, honey, don't be afraid.*

I studied a French fry as I twirled it in salted ketchup. "Do you think our father, or, well, *my* father, might be named Bob? That would be a good name…. Maybe someday he'll…"

He wasn't going to take the bait. It was amazing how square he could make his jaw when he was determined to ignore something. "She thinks I could get into engineering."

"Who?" Somebody had put a quarter into the jukebox and was picking out their songs.

"Mrs. Klimm. Me." He rolled his eyes then and exaggerated his enunciation for the benefit of the mentally handicapped. "*Mrs. Klimm* thinks *I* could get into engineering. There's a scholarship. More than one, actually."

"What about…?"

"I don't know. I'd have to go away, it's inevitable, Ruthie."

Inevitable? The O'Jays were wailing out "Back Stabbers," which had just made it to number ten this month. I tried to shut it out, make it that God was sending a message to someone at the counter or at another booth. "No…" I began. "No…she…"

Roger knew exactly where I was going with it. "Don't worry about it, yet," he said then, backing out of the minefield he'd planted like he was certified Vietcong. "Give me that ketchup, will you?" He hardly skipped a beat, turned casual as daylight. "I hope you're doing better in Spanish than I did. How's old lady Mortina? Nothing put me to sleep faster than that whiny voice conjugating verbs."

Don't worry about it yet, he said. As though that were possible. His leaving would begin the unraveling of the world like a ball of blue yarn. I knew that much.

Roger wouldn't say any more on that subject, and I didn't want to talk about anything else, so neither of us said much on the ride home. I'd abruptly switched the radio off, not particularly wanting to hear what God had to say at the moment. It might be "Alone Again (Naturally)," and then what would I do? Dusk had been overtaken by night while we ate, and the road was little trafficked. People were home already, in their normal surroundings and normal families, laughing or complaining and telling each other what had happened during their day. Roger reached over and patted my hand once, almost like a father, and tears pushed behind my eyes. When he pulled Mother's claptrap Rambler into our driveway, he cut the engine, pulled me over to him and held me while I cried.

"Don't go." My voice was froggy and my nose running like a little kid's.

"Ruthie."

"Rog, don't go."

"Well, maybe when Mother moves again, you and she could just move near the university, wherever I get in and get money, that is."

"It's not the same, I can't…be enough, you know."

"Yeah. I know." It came out as a sigh. He paused a long time, tightening then relaxing his arm around my shoulder. "You know, you're really getting pretty, Ruthie."

"Oh, yeah, Rog. Of course. Lots of guys are really hankering for bone bags with orange hair. What're you saying that for, anyway?"

"No, I mean it. Your hair isn't orange, in the first place, and it's real thick. You've got nice eyes, like green and gold at the same time, and good skin, and when you get older, and, you know, put on a little weight… Look, you're going to be a lot prettier than Mother. Her face is more pointy." This last was heresy, a complete break from gospel. After another pause, he went on. "And you're really smart. You could do anything. You should be thinking about what you're going to do."

I got the drift, and was not about to make it easy for him. He knew as well as I what was possible and what wasn't. "Well, I can tell you this much. I'm not pretty. And I'm not smart enough to take care of her without you."

We sat in the car a long time. I could feel how Roger was squarely in the middle, with me pulling on him from one side and the beguiling idea of his own life pulling from the other. Roger just wanted to be normal. Part of me knew I wasn't being fair; I had a few friends at school, I knew how different their lives were. More than once I'd longed for a meal of meat loaf and mashed potatoes and a platter of sliced tomatoes set out by a regular mother wearing an apron and nagging me about homework, but it was a part of me guilt still readily squelched.

We sat that way a while longer, my head resting on his chest, until a small movement at the window, a minuscule change in the light around the car, perhaps, attracted my attention. Mother was standing at the window, holding the curtain aside and staring at the car. Instinctively I straightened and pulled away from Roger.

"We'd better get in," I said.

Roger sighed as he pulled the keys out of the ignition. "Wouldn't you think one of them—either one, who cares?—could have stuck around?" When he shut the car door on his side, he didn't try to muffle the sound it made as I did mine, and the noise made me flinch though I couldn't have said why.

"I still think Bob might have been nice…" I whispered to his shadowy form next to me on the path where grass and dirt stuttered from the driveway to our back stoop.

"I think he's a jerk. Or they're both jerks," he shot back before we were in the small range of light from the house.

"So, did you two have a good time?" Mother asked when we got in the kitchen door. She held herself at a distance, her tone like fried ice cream, melty and warm on the surface and frozen in the center. "I guess you didn't even think of me."

"No, Mother, we did. I mean, we really missed you. A lot. We were talking about how lucky we are, and…" Roger babbled less than I, but tried to help weave a coherent cloth that would cover us. Mother took the carry-out bag Roger handed her and tossed it on top of the garbage. Some of the French fries spilled, their odor full and rich in the kitchen. She loved French fries.

"I'm not hungry," she said and went into her room, not slamming the door but closing it definitively so the click would resound where she wanted it to, in the lightless caverns of our fear. Although it was only seven-thirty, Roger and I took turns in the bathroom getting ready for bed without speaking another word. By eight o'clock, the house was dark and each of us in our bed, doing our homework with the least possible motion and light.

I fidgeted through my Spanish and algebra but couldn't even begin to concentrate enough to read the lit assignment. My eyes felt gritty with worry. Finally I just turned off the small amber circle of light from the lamp by the daybed and tried to sleep.

It seemed hours that I lay there. The tension of the house that had earlier linked us room to room now seemed to have drawn itself into one place and coiled around me like a snake. Mother hadn't come out of her room, but it had been so long now it seemed she wouldn't, that she must have gone to sleep. Occasionally I observed—without allowing myself to *think* it—that an episode had to have been planned. How else would it be that she'd already gone to the bathroom, or I'd notice dirty dishes on her nightstand the next morning?

I got up and crept to Roger's room. His light was off, but he must have sensed movement near his open door because I heard his breathing change. I tiptoed barefoot to his bed and he lifted the covers back with one arm. I'd not done this for a long time. While we were in elementary school, we'd rented a tiny two-story house for a while. Mother said the stairs bothered her knees and often slept in the parlor to avoid going up to bed. She'd be there in the morning when we left, and still there in the same clothes waiting for her first student when we got home from school. That year, when things were particularly bad, I'd sneak into Roger's bed and sleep next to him for the comfort of it.

I hadn't done it for a long time, but when Rog lifted the covers, I slid next to him and lay with my head in the hollow between his arm and shoulder and his arm around me. I put one of my arms across his chest and pulled myself close to him.

"Don't go," I whispered into his ear, maybe an inch from my mouth. "Please, Rog." I began crying again, stifling it so as to remain as soundless as possible. I pressed as close to him as I could as though to attach him to me for the permanent alleviation of loneliness. Little did I know then that such a thing is not among the blessings available, no matter what anyone says.

Roger answered with a pressure as he moved his thumb on my upper arm and whispered an accompaniment to each thumb stroke, "It's okay, it's okay, it's okay." But I needed much more.

"Will you stay home?"

"Yes, Ruthie, yes. It's okay, I'll stay." As the thumb stroke refrain became that specific, I started to relax. Finally, we were both quiet.

"You know, we can just stay together. We could, like, you know, get married and take care of her together." I wasn't in the least bit serious, not about the getting married part, anyway. The part that was serious was that there was no way out.

He knew what I meant. His voice was teasing, but I knew he knew what I meant. "Yeah, okay, great idea. We can…"

There was a slam and a click and the overhead light flooded the room. Mother stood in the doorway, her eyes and hair wild, her nightgown voluminous as though she could call down wind and storm at will. "Filthy children," she shouted. "Filthy, filthy, filthy." Instantly she had crossed the room and jerked me from the bed onto the floor. She kicked me and pointed to the door. "Get out of this room and don't let me ever catch you here again." I tried to scramble to my feet, but she kicked me again, and I toppled over. "Get out," she screamed, and even as I tried to get up and out, she drew her foot back another time, and I knew this could go on forever.

3

I STILL LOOKED TO FIND A REASON to believe. And I clung to Roger's promise, though after that night we rarely dared be alone or talk between ourselves. As the school year progressed, Roger stayed out more, but he still did his part with Mother, and I trusted him.

Roger and I had become less cheerful about all the moving Mother insisted on as we'd lurched further into our teens. God routinely wanted us to "strip down," remain undistracted by material things, and Mother's version of moving involved abandoning much of our property. The consistent exceptions were six cardboard boxes of hers, always carted place to place. They contained our heritage, she said, and that we'd understand someday. Maybe she'd really kept the found treasure collages we'd thought had been left behind in one move or another, or, Roger's theory, they contained our fathers' bones. Roger and I often knew nothing about a move until one morning, Mother would announce that we should bring everything home from school because we'd be moving that night.

Before the beginning of Roger's senior year, The Word came down again and we moved over the Massachusetts line into rural northern Connecticut. Mother found us the bottom floor of an old house divided into two apartments by the elderly couple who owned it, and doubtless, needed the income. (Mother confided to people she met that she'd graciously taken in Mr. and Mrs. Jensen. I could read the confused expressions of the neighbors; Malone was a small town and Mr. and Mrs. Jensen had been in that house for most of their fifty-two married years.) The place had a certain run-down charm, with bay windows and front and back porches. The Jensens had old, white-painted rockers on the front porch, which was theirs to use, while we had the much tinier back porch. We occasionally sat out there in descending order on the steps, Mother above Roger, Roger above me, when August nights settled like a sticky quilt.

The inside floors—except for the chipped kitchen linoleum on which languished long-outdated appliances—were scuffed hardwood, which could have been spectacular if sanded and re-finished, but Mother set down gray-blue rag rugs from Goodwill, which was also the source of our motley furniture collections. The main problem with the apartment was that none of the rooms downstairs had been intended as bedrooms, so we had neither privacy nor closet space. Mother had the frontmost area of the house, and her things went into a small, freestanding wardrobe in the room which also held her dresser and double bed. Roger and I slept on open-out couches in what had once been connected sitting rooms partially divided by open archways, but he and I might as well have slept on separate planets. Our clothes were kept neatly folded and stuffed behind our respective sleeping places. The only regular doors were on the bathroom, where a claw-foot bathtub stood on a carpet remnant aged to colorless-ness and curled back as though recoiling from the drafty corners, and a swinging door Mother kept propped open into the kitchen. Mother's room had a pocket door between it and the area where I slept. No need for secrets in our family, she said. There was no escaping one another. We were God's *found*.

MOTHER HAD BEEN DEPRESSED for several weeks and life was hard. We were growing frightened; our jockeying to cheer her was either ineffectual or unaccountably worsening her mood day by day. I threw myself into being quietly helpful with whatever she roused herself to do, and the evening she decided to examine her life, as she put it, I was there to help. I was accustomed to spending weekend nights at home. Mother felt lonely and sad about how she'd been cheated out of a normal girlhood if I went out, and anyway, I was afraid of boys other than my brother, having been vigorously warned about their lack of awareness of the sacred spiritual nature of marital intimacy. Roger, who fit himself with friends more easily than I, was at the football game.

I couldn't believe it when she took most of the oft-moved boxes that held our heritage from the hinged window seat beneath the bay windows. They were taped shut and even Roger had never had the nerve to snoop. He was going to be really ticked if I found out something about my father while he was at a football game.

She pulled the heavy tape off the boxes, the larger ones, and began opening them randomly. For the first time, I saw what they held: old clothes. Item by item, she took out each musty piece and told its story, ruminating about how awful she'd felt in one dress or another, *like a fat hag,* she said. "And I wasn't, then," she whispered, face quivering. I gleaned that she believed no one had told her she was beautiful and because of that, she'd missed the knowledge herself. She held dresses against her bodice and cried for the young woman who had missed her own loveliness. Tears rolled off her chin onto the tailored V necks tucked between the great padded shoulders of the forties. Things softened a bit when she got into the fifties' printed shirtwaists with full skirts, and she wondered aloud if a few of these dresses weren't still wearable. I'd worried she might come to that, doubting that any would fit her—she was overweight by a good sixty pounds. These wide-skirted dresses held more hope than any of the earlier, sleeker fashions, and I cast about for the one that looked largest. At the same time, she pulled out a long-sleeved, full-skirted chocolate-brown jersey dress with a strip of fluffy white fur all around the low-cut neckline.

This is the truth: even as I recognized that by normal standards she was overweight, I saw my mother as beautiful. Her body was, to me, in the way of a Botticelli painting, classically, truly beautiful. My own very thin, small-boned frame was compared unfavorably to hers by both of us; I was not "womanly," which, roughly translated, meant I had negligible breasts. When she said she was too heavy, it was my job to disagree with her, and in a strange way, I was able to do this honestly, to tell her she was beautiful, I mean. She had short brown naturally wavy hair, unmarred complexion, blue eyes, straight white teeth and a voracious bosom, the inaccessibility of which, she claimed, put men into straitjackets of frustration. I glossed over her pinched nose and the way her chin led her face. Long after the last time I saw her, when I was grown and had gained a little weight, I began to like greenish eyes and the distinction of my red-soaked hair, but she was the standard of perfection then.

This particular dress was horrible—the fur around the neckline a scant step above clownish—but this was the one she chose to try on. Stripping to her bra and underpants, she wrestled the material over her head and pulled the skirt over her substantial rear. The jersey clung to the rolls of flesh that obscured her waist, and the fur, resting midway down her cleavage looked absurdly out-of-place on a grown woman. She slipped on a pair of brown heels and looked at herself in the full-length mirror. I braced myself, but something that would have been bizarre had it not been so welcome happened then: my mother smiled.

"Well, maybe the old girl still has a little something left," she said coquettishly twirling in front of the mirror, then looking back over her shoulder at me. Although Mother liked to test us, she'd been much too down for this to be a trick, and I quickly shifted into gear.

"Mother, you look stunning. You are so beautiful," I said.

"Do I really look okay?"

"Not okay, Mother, beautiful, just beautiful."

She began to walk like a model on a runway, back and forth from the full-length mirror in her bedroom into the living room and back to the mirror, where she would turn and examine herself again. Her face was lit by God's lamp behind her eyes, and shoulders consciously back, she moved with an artful glide. I pushed on, sensing what she wanted.

"I don't see how you could ever have missed that you were beautiful. You simply have to see it for yourself once and for all."

"Yes, I guess I shouldn't have needed people to tell me, should I?" This was a crucial spot. Now I know: I should have told her it wasn't her fault, that her parents and the people around her had been cruelly insensitive, but she'd have to believe it now and recognize that she was still as beautiful as she had ever been. I missed the turn.

"No, you shouldn't have needed people to tell you. I wish you'd looked in the mirror and seen how wrong they were."

At first she liked that approach, affecting a childlike manner, wanting to be scolded for failing to recognize the inevitable link between Love and her own loveliness. Led on by my success, I continued in the same vein. Within ten minutes, a magical transformation had occurred. My mother had risen from the dead to laugh, smooth her hands over her breasts and hips and say the old girl's still got it, and I was the witness God put there to say that not only did she have it, but she wasn't old.

Then the phone rang, and Mother picked it up. I panicked when she sank into a chair, the lilt in her voice fading, and I realized it was Grandmother. I must have gone into overdrive, scowling, continuing to gesture and mouth the word *beautiful* to remind her that she'd wrongfully let people such as Grandmother cloud her vision.

At first it worked. She smiled and nodded at me and straightened in the chair. I should have stopped then, but I didn't. A moment later, she thrust her arm at me, an angry, dismissive gesture, and shifted in the chair, swinging her back to my face.

Right then, Roger came in. I hadn't even heard the car that left him off, nor sensed the deepening evening beyond our kitchen door. I could see him trying to read the situation, but it was much too complex. Mother slammed down the phone.

"I'm sorry, Mother, I just wanted you to remember…" was as far as I got.

"She's berating me for something that wasn't my fault," she shouted to Roger.

"No, I was telling her she shouldn't have listened to…." Desperately I tried to fill Roger in, which further enraged her.

"Listen to you, *twisting the Truth*. You're just like everybody else, aren't you? Leave me alone," she screamed, tears streaming, and went into the kitchen.

I started to follow her, but Roger signaled me not to. I slunk back into the living room unbelieving the turn things had taken, hoping against all experience that I could still redeem the fleeting joy.

I heard her voice, agitated, and then the teakettle's keening wail over it. I guessed Roger was making her a cup of cocoa, trying to settle her down. Outcast, I lit one of Mother's votive candles, folded myself into a ragged Salvation Army chair and prayed. I prayed wildly and unreasonably, begging to cash in any chips I'd accumulated with God, that in a moment they'd come to get me, smiling, saying everything was all right.

I had begun pacing to the jerky cadence of Mother's voice and the occasional soothing overtones of Roger's soft baritone. When I couldn't endure anymore, I crept to the kitchen door, which Roger had swung shut behind me, and felt its slight give as I put my ear against it.

"But Ruthie was just trying," he was saying, "to help you realize..." He was interrupted by a long screech, chilling, a woman's scream beyond rage to something otherworldly, an unidentifiable animal sound. I heard Mother's heavy footsteps and jerked back a second before she crashed through the door, the teakettle in her hand. It trailed a hissing stream as she flung it at my head in the same instant Roger tried to grab her arm from behind. His lunge, and grip—though she tore loose easily— skewed her aim, and the kettle shattered the window behind me before it fell to the floor, spewing steaming water. The hand that had held the kettle continued the trajectory of its arc and Mother swung her body around after it, slamming Roger in the face with her wrist and hand.

She screamed and, clutching her wrist, kicked Roger in the groin. He doubled onto the floor, gasping and gagging. She turned then and spat at me, deliberately, as though in slow-motion. Time instantly leaped up again, frenetic and out of control. She pushed past me and out the back door, snatching her car keys from their hook on the kitchen wall. Only a moment later, I heard her tires spinning on the loose gravel of our driveway, then, out on the road, the accelerating roar of the engine gunning down the night. She did not come back until the next afternoon, but she did come back. She always did until the time she didn't, but there was a lot of sky left to fall before then.

4

AFTER THAT, WHO COULD BLAME HIM for breaking his promise? Who except I, that is. Of course, Roger went. Mr. VanFrank, the guidance counselor for the senior class in our new school, had picked up right where Mrs. Klimm had left off, starting after Roger with his bewitching encouragement as soon as our transcripts arrived. I think Mrs. Klimm might have even called him, or maybe she sent a letter. Why else would he have come to talk to Mother, who smiled and nodded and agreed, and then disappeared for two days?

Buoyed by his first success, Mr. VanFrank came back with a financial aid form, filled it out for Mother by asking her questions and put it in front of her to sign. Because it came to seem inevitable, and because Mr. VanFrank cagily praised her for having done such a fine job preparing Roger for college and the lucrative employment opportunities that would follow, Mother slowly came around. It was just an unfortunate coincidence that the University of Colorado, which had the country's only program in some esoteric combination of geology and engineering *and* a phenomenal grant package for Roger, was some eighteen hundred miles away. By the time his graduation was at hand and everything was settled, Mother had established that the brilliant notion of Roger's higher education had been hers, and that she had insisted he apply, overcoming his objections to leaving home. When Mr. VanFrank was at the door to leave after visiting Mother to get the financial aid application filled out, he had turned and pointed his index finger at me.

"Keep those grades up," he said, and winked. "You're next."

"When cows fly," Mother had said to the door closed behind him, and shut herself in her room with a furious door-slam, a sound to splinter hope into equal shards of envy and resentment.

THOSE SHARDS WERE POKING sharply out of my heart when Roger left for the long drive across two-thirds of the country. Mr. VanFrank had talked to a car dealer who was in the Lion's Club with him, and the money Roger had saved working the grill and fryer at the diner during his senior year was miraculously enough for a car that had been used as a repair loaner for five years. Its rivets were bulging; he'd crammed in everything he could, knowing Mother would abandon anything he left behind if we moved. The car reminded me of the Oakies moving west in *The Grapes of Wrath*. Roger hugged me close to him but the shards jutted right through my skin, and I pulled away.

"I'm sorry, Ruthie," he whispered, glancing sidelong to gauge Mother's range of earshot. "I swear I'll come back, we'll stay together. You can call me."

"Yeah, during the many hours when I can speak freely, I'll call you."

"Pay phone?" he whispered.

"With all my spare money."

"I'll send you money…" he said, and with that he was commandeered by Mother who was issuing her final instructions with tears and a cobra's embrace. And then he was gone.

SEVERAL GRIM DAYS PASSED with Mother alternately banging throughout the house and setting objects down in a way to let me know she wanted to shatter them, and sliding, ghostlike, silent and sad, from bed to bathroom and back. Those days she had me call her students' parents to tell them she was sick and cancel their lessons.

One morning in the fourth week of August she came into the kitchen and asked when school started.

"The day after Labor Day," I replied, the same day school has started every year since kindergarten in every school I've ever been in, but I'd never have said the second part.

"Really? Good. Then we have time to get away on a little vacation." She sounded cheerful. I would have climbed into the car without clothes or questions had she told me to, but she went on to fill me in. "Lorna Mack said that her brother-in-law is painting their house in Truro, that's on Cape Cod, you know, and her husband can't stand him, doesn't get along with him at all, that's why they came home early. The house is empty, because the brother-in-law lives in Provincetown. He's just painting the outside, I guess. Anyway, she said we could use the house for a few days if we wanted." Lorna Mack was the parent of Mother's best student, Hannah, the one with actual talent, and Mother *had* brought her a good distance in the year we'd been there.

"That sounds wonderful, Mother." I would have said that no matter what I felt, but, as it happened, I was absolutely sincere.

THE LANDSCAPE OF THE CAPE seized me right after we crossed the Sagamore Bridge. But when we reached the lower Cape, past Eastham where the National Seashore started, its grip on me intensified to one that would never let go. Truro was like a place I'd lived in and loved throughout a whole previous life, a startle of recognition and old yearning suddenly satisfied. I didn't know why, and even after all these years of returning, I still don't entirely. It has to do with hills covered with beach plums and scrubby vegetation, half-down dune fences and sudden glimpses of ocean when you round a corner and there is sun glinting off the sapphire water and sea oats flexing their backs like dancers in the breeze. A certain quality of light, shining and purely crystalline, makes everything—even people—shimmer. Painters say it's because the Cape is a narrow peninsula and any light, even that of a dark day, is repeatedly reflected by the water on three sides, like a visible echo, but it seems more than that. There, it's as though everything lights from inside itself with an ongoing joy, unquenchable no matter what else happens. It's why I went there when I'd lost everything, and it's where Mother lives now, at least to me, and at least the part of her that taught me—in a backward way, yes, but taught me nonetheless—to hope for another day and take love where I could find it.

The Mack house was nothing like the little shingled cottages that dot the Cape. It had been Lorna's family's year-round home when she was growing up. A porch wrapped around three sides of the two-story house, weather-beaten from generations of overlooking the ocean from the top of enormous dune-cliffs. A ladder rested against the house, and on the ground were drop-cloths and two paint pans with rollers alongside. We could see the line where the house was crisply white, almost but not quite matched by the oblongs where shutters had protected the last paint job. Several scrub pines and wild beach grass completed the yard, if you could call it that. We'd parked back on the narrow strip of asphalt that wound off Route 6 over the tops of the Truro hills, and made our way to the house on a wooden walkway. Steep wooden steps led down to the beach. I couldn't even see another house, that's how isolated it was, but in a thrilling, not a frightening way. Gulls rode the thermals over-head, only occasionally bothering to flap their wings as they cawed to one another.

I wanted to go down to the beach, where I could hear surf breathing hard, but Mother said we had to get settled first. I lugged in what we'd brought while she inspected and noted what the Macks had left, like salt and pepper and cooking oil. Whitecaps sliced the ocean here and there to the horizon as I made my trips between house and car. The breeze smelled like clean laundry, crisp and dry and fresh.

We'd not been there long when a man appeared on the porch and knocked on the screen door. Mother's voice turned sharp. "You stay put," she hissed at me, heading for the door through a long hall from the kitchen. "Yes, may I help you?" she said to the man who stood at the door in jeans and a plaid flannel shirt.

"I'm Ben Chance, it's spelled like 'chance,' but you say Chaunce, Lorna's brother-in-law. She called Marilyn to say that you'd be up for a while. I didn't want to startle you by working around outside without introducing myself."

"I'm Elizabeth Ruth Kenley, and the girl in the kitchen is my daughter, Ruth Elizabeth," she said, opening the door and stepping onto the porch. My chest tightened. Mother always introduced me that way, as though I were herself backward. The screen door banged shut like a slap.

"I hope you'll have a nice stay. The phone has been disconnected for the season, I hope Lorna told you that, but you let me know if you need directions or anything else. Do you know where Day's Market is, over on 6A? The only supermarket nearby is in Provincetown, a good nine miles one way, so if you just need a few little things, you're best off running to Day's." Mr. Chance was medium height and build, with nothing to distinguish him: a clean-shaven face, sandy brown hair and regular, if somewhat rough-hewn features. But he had a smile that made you think you'd died and gone to heaven, there was that much plain goodness in it. In spite of what Mother had said, I was edging my way down the hall.

She glanced inside. "Well, here she is now. Come on out, Ruth, and meet Mr. Chance."

"Oh, call me Ben."

"Thanks, and you call me Elizabeth. Ruth, this is Mr. Chance," she said, taking care with the pronunciation.

He extended his hand and took mine in a gentle grip. "Ben," he repeated, looking at me. "Hi, Ruth. How do you like the place?"

"I love it."

"Well, I'm sure glad to hear that. You two have a good time. I'll try not to get in your way."

"Ben, would you like something to drink?" Mother said. I couldn't imagine what she'd do if he said yes. Cooking oil was the only liquid in the house as far as I'd seen.

"No, thanks, I've just had lunch and I've got a thermos in the truck, anyway. I'll just be getting back to work."

"Well, thanks so much for coming by. We'll see you again real soon," she said, and it seemed she waggled her rear as she came back in, but I could have been wrong.

THE NEXT WEEK WAS IDYLLIC. Mother's mood was sunny as the beach where I read two novels and got a slight tan for the first time in my life. I didn't even mind the extra freckles that popped out on my dead-fair complexion. I began to think I could survive without Roger. Ben's truck pulled up behind our car by nine o'clock each morning and when I was at the house to use the bathroom or for a cold drink, I could hear him whistling "Daisy, Daisy, Give Me Your Answer, Do" through the screened windows. The air was September-like, as it often is on the Cape at the tail of August, but sometimes it would heat up in midafternoon. Those days, Ben would peel denim or flannel and paint in his cotton T-shirt, grousing good-naturedly to me or Mother about the heat and how he couldn't believe Marilyn's father had gone and painted the good cedar shakes that would have weathered to their own dun gray, "like everyone else's house." He'd grouse about his three kids, too, saying they drove him nuts. But he showed us their school pictures, lined up in plastic sleeves in his wallet, and you could tell he wasn't really mad. That was the thing about him, he was never really mad.

I guess Mother noticed that, too. Or maybe that's what I liked and she liked something completely different. Either way, each day she left me on the beach earlier, saying she'd had enough sun, and when I finally came up to the house, she'd be outside in a dress, leaning against the house and talking to Ben as he painted. She'd laugh, toss her head and clink the ice in the tall glass of tea, where a translucent slice of lemon straddled the rim, as though she could hold the sun anywhere she wanted. She was beautiful, she really was. The day before we were supposed to leave, she'd asked Ben if it was okay if we stayed on, since the weather had been so perfect and I still had time before school started.

"No problem. It's nice to have someone to talk to," he said, and Mother beamed. Ben still had one side of the house, the porch and all the shutters to go.

I can't say what happened next, the ninth day we were there. Mother left the beach at one-thirty, saying, "You stay as long as you want, sweetie." At about three, I climbed the steps to the house to use the bathroom, but I saw Mother and Ben sitting close to one another on the porch, Mother in a spaghetti-strap print dress that was the blue of her eyes and her favorite. Two glasses of tea were set to one side of them and Mother leaned toward Ben. I thought she'd be embarrassed if she knew he could see down the front of her dress, the way she was sitting. They were intent on their conversation as I took the first couple of steps toward them. Mother seemed to be holding her head at a funny angle and at the same moment I thought *she's going to kiss him,* I thought *no, she'd never.* But I stopped. The air felt charged and I was afraid. I backed up and turned back to the beach. It's embarrassing to confess this, but after I waited another half hour, I still couldn't get up the courage to go to the house and I finally went in the ocean up to my waist and relieved myself in that freezing water. Warmth spread around my thighs, welcome and shameful. The towel I'd been lying on was sandy when I wrapped it around my waist and sat on the beach just staring at the breaking surf, listening to it inhale, exhale, inhale, exhale. I couldn't read for worrying about when it would be okay to go back to the house and get into something warmer and more comfortable than a bathing suit and a damp, gritty towel.

Dusk was coming on when I knew it would seem suspicious if I didn't go on up. Gulls were resting on the sand, some with heads tucked under wings. You could just tell by the feel and color of the air that it was time.

The house looked deserted. Ben's truck was gone. Quietly I opened the screen door into the kitchen. Nothing was out for supper, although that in itself wasn't unusual. I couldn't attach the foreboding I felt to anything; it just free-floated around me and I was too afraid to call her name. I began going as quietly as I could from room to room. When I found no one there, I looked up the staircase to the second floor and called softly.

"Mother? Mother? Can I come up?"

There was no sound. I sat against a half-dozen throw pillows on a tweed couch that edged a braided rug, and tucked my legs under me. A big wooden coffee table, covered with magazines and coasters, squatted in the center. The living room was homey, with remnants of good furniture left over from when Lorna and Marilyn Mack's father had been the best plumber on the outer Cape interspersed with tag sale fill-ins bought since the house had become the Mack daughters' vacation home. An upscale Goodwill with goodwill to spare, like Ben. Overstuffed chairs reached out in invitation. Big clam shells and smaller scallops and whelks—even a starfish—lay scattered on end tables. Books, board games and jigsaw puzzles waited in stacks in the living room, shelved for a rainy day. Seascapes and sailing ships that looked to have been painted by a member of the family, an amateur with fair talent, hung on the walls. There was a fireplace, too, with some driftwood on one side of the hearth. It was the kind of room I most wanted to belong in, a room for sinking into cozy familiarity, but as evening began to close against the windows, I sat still, caging wild anxiety within my ribs, and waited.

I WOKE, STIFF AND FREEZING, IN THE same position in early dawn light. It took minutes to unbend my legs, minutes more before they would hold my weight. I shifted the still-damp towel from around my waist to my shoulders, over the top of my bathing suit. I looked out the window, which, of course, I should have done the previous night. Gulls roiled the sky, gray, with no notion of sunrise. Our car, the top of which would have been visible from the living room window, was gone. Still, even knowing that much, I crept up the stairs and called "Mother?" softly several times before I dared go to the bathroom and get into jeans and a sweatshirt. I came back downstairs into the kitchen to make myself a cup of tea while I tried to figure out what to do.

Several hours passed. I puttered around the house, looking for any task that might need doing. The last thing I wanted was for her to come home and find me idle. Every dish was washed, the bathroom scrubbed, the house swept and straight. Nothing seemed to warm me: not the clothes, not the tea, not the work, and finally, everything else done, I dared a hot shower. I washed my hair, standing too long under the hot spray, sudsing it twice before I let the force of the water rinse it. I cried a little, then, but not much. I needed to keep a hold on myself, I knew that much. Afterward, I folded and hung the towels I used and cleaned the bathroom again just to be sure I'd left no annoying trace.

For lack of something else to do, I set my hair on the rollers I'd stuck in my suitcase but not used in ten days. For a moment, I tried to find myself in the mirror, mirror. A jittery, spotted girl, her eyes yellow and face spectral in the strange light was there: not exactly reassuring. I put on a little rouge and lipstick, and encouraged by looking better, added a trace of eyeliner. I just wanted to look like a person, that's all it was.

I was at such unraveled ends, and so frightened that I moved constantly in an effort to distract myself. I refolded everything in my suitcase and straightened the linen closet in which the Macks had odd towels and sheets stuffed in irregular folds. When my hair was dry, I brushed it out, and went downstairs again.

Then I just sat. It must have been another hour before I heard a motor outside, and hurried to the window. It was Ben's truck.

"Hey, Ruthie. You look mighty pretty," he said when I went out onto the back porch. He was carrying a paint can in each hand, a sheet of plastic tarp rolled under one arm. Every evening, he cleaned up the paint supplies, and every morning toted them back to the house from his pickup. "I hope your Mom won't mind if I keep on working. I'll do the shutters and stay out of the way."

"Sure," I answered, completely baffled. Since the first day, he'd never *asked* about working. Why would he? It was *their* house.

"I'm...sorry, Ruthie," he said.

"Huh?"

"Look, I mean, can I talk to her a minute?"

"Mother? She's not here."

Ben looked confused. "She run to the store?"

"No. Well, I mean I don't know...where she is."

"When did she leave?"

"I guess she was gone last night when I came up from the beach."

"God," he exclaimed. "Why didn't you call me?" Then he

slapped himself lightly on the cheek. "No phone, stupid," he muttered. "Are you okay?"

"I'm fine." This conversation was not comfortable for me. Had I made Mother look bad? There could have been six working phone lines into that house and I wouldn't have called him or anyone else. Except Roger, but I didn't have a phone number for him yet, so that was a moot point.

"Can I…do anything to help?"

"No, thanks."

"Well, Ruth, I mean, is this *like* her, leaving you alone like this?" He was hesitant, stammering a little. Embarrassed.

"I'm fine. Thanks, though," I said, turning back toward the door.

"Look, I'm not going to just leave you by yourself."

"I'm really fine. Thanks, Ben," I said and went inside.

I stayed inside, pacing from room to room. Reading was impossible and I couldn't find anything to do. *Maybe this is the time she won't come back:* as it happened it wasn't, but the thought was surely in my mind.

Perhaps another hour passed. The truth was, I simply couldn't take it any longer. His niceness just got to me. I needed it, so what came after was my fault.

I went outside to find Ben. Shielding my light-stunned eyes with my hand also let me avoid looking at him. "I was thinking…maybe I could… Could I help you paint?"

Ben looked startled. "Of course, you can. That would be fine. Come on here, let me get you set up. You take this shutter. I've got an extra tarp over there. You grab it, spread it out." He demonstrated and I copied. "Good. Make your brushstrokes go like mine, sideways, okay?" He went on, explaining minutia that I didn't need explained, but his voice was soothing, as though everything here were normal.

We worked on like that the rest of the morning. Usually Ben went home for lunch, and today followed suit. Around noon he said, "Marilyn'll be looking for me about now. Come on, we'll get something in you, too." He gestured with his head toward the truck and put a lid on his paint can.

"Thanks, but I'm not hungry," I lied. What if Mother came home and found me gone?

"Nope, like I tell the kids, don't even bother to argue. You're coming!"

He didn't live far, as he'd said. He lived in a modest little Cape house, less than five minutes away. I hung back a little as he went in the side door. He reached back and gently took me by the shoulder, pushing me in front of him.

"This is Ruth Kenley, Elizabeth's daughter, who I told you about. Her mother's off shopping, and Ruth's been good enough to help me with the shutters."

Marilyn was a sweet-faced tiny woman who wore glasses. One side of her dun hair was tucked behind an ear. Her kitchen had wooden cabinets and yellow curtains and smelled like chicken. Ever since that day I've loved a kitchen with yellow curtains. "Wonderful!" she said. "I would have been happy to have your mother, too. Come, sit down. I've got some soup on, and the kids will want peanut butter and jelly. How about you, honey?"

I felt as though the power of speech were gone. "Anything. Thank you very much for having me." My voice sounded dry and whispery.

A sunbleached, sneakered boy of about seven tore into the room. "Daddy! Mark said I couldn't touch his Tonka truck! But you said share!" He was indignant.

"Where are your manners?" Marilyn admonished. "Matt, this is Ruth."

He reined himself to courtesy and looked at me. "Hi." He got it out, and wheeled back to Ben.

"Hi, Matt," I said, but he was paying no attention.

"What about the trucks?"

"Hey, buddy, I just walked in the door. My stomach thinks my throat's been cut. Let me get some food and we'll talk to your brother before I go back to work."

The lunch passed quickly. I had the peanut butter and jelly, not because I liked it, but because it was what I thought would be the least trouble. Ben attended to the Tonka crisis. Jenny, his daughter, wanted to show him a painting. Marilyn laughed and said, "It's like this all the time, they keep us hopping. Actually, this is mild—there's another one, Claire. She's at the beach with a friend today."

We drove back to the house and worked on the shutters. Ben started to replace some of the dry ones on the front of the house, where he'd also finished painting, because, he said, the place might as well look good even if we were the only ones looking at it. Then he laughed at himself.

The afternoon was settling. I could feel the change in the light, how it was mellowing. Ben had talked to me all afternoon, telling me stories about his family, and when he was a boy, and why he and Marilyn had settled on the Cape, after all. Throughout the hours, I had been torn between a guilty happiness—deciding my father's name might be Ben rather than Bob—and a deep unease. Where was she? What was wrong? What would happen? Ben began his cleanup ritual.

"Well, sweetheart, I'm sure not going to leave you here," he said finally. "We'll put a note for your mother on the front door to let her know you're at our house." I knew perfectly well how Mother would take such a thing.

"Really, I'm fine here."

"Ruth, I feel…responsible. There was a misunderstanding, and your mother's feelings may have been hurt. And, even if that weren't so, I'd not knowingly leave anyone's child by herself at night."

At that I simply couldn't help it. I had no warning from within, but I couldn't have held on anyway. Tears started out of my eyes.

"Honey, I'm sorry," Ben said, and put his arms around me. I lay my head on his chest, and I do believe I would have sobbed there forever had I had a chance to start, but that was the moment Mother chose to drive up.

"I SEE NOW, MR. *CHAUNCE*, I SEE everything with total clarity." She mocked the pronunciation of his name. "It was my *daughter* you wanted." Even the car had sounded enraged as she slammed it to a gravel stop. She crossed the walkway in yesterday's blue sundress looking terrible—haggard and distraught.

I watched Ben absorb her words and recoil. "Oh, my God, Elizabeth, no."

She didn't let him or me get any further. "Excuse me, but I've seen for myself." Turning to me, she said icily, "Get inside."

"Mother—"

"*Now.*"

She was furious, and it was my fault. I never should have made her look bad by accepting the care of an outsider. Worse, I had wanted it, I had sunk into his arms like a rock into the ocean.

"Please," I began desperately. For a moment I thought there was hope. She glanced at me dismissively, but then it was as though something had occurred to her, and she turned to me fully and stared. She studied my face, and I thought she was going to listen. But revulsion crossed her features; she'd seen something and hated it.

"It was you, too, wasn't it?" she said softly, only it wasn't a question. "It didn't take long."

I stood there, confused as tangled thread, unable to follow her line. I knew I'd been wrong to lean into Ben's comfort, but it seemed she was onto something else entirely. I had no idea what that was.

"What…I don't know, I'm sorry Mother," I was stammering.

Ben tried to intervene. "Look, Elizabeth, I'm not sure what you're getting after here, but—"

"What I'm getting after? What *I'm* getting after? It was *you,* mister. It was what *you* were after all along."

Ben appeared dumbfounded. He was trying to have a reasonable conversation with her, to straighten something out, but he didn't know her.

"I'll thank you to get out of here this minute," she shot. "If you come around before we're gone, I'll make a police report."

Ben shook his head and started to say something. She took a step toward him, her eyes dangerous as an animal about to attack. Ben extended his hand, spoke quietly, "Ruth, come with me."

She exploded. "She'll not step one foot with you, or any other man, no matter what she paints herself up to be. I'll deal with my daughter. Get out."

Ben was looking for my eyes, I could feel his on my face the way people look at something caged, something that can't hide. I wouldn't look at him. Mother would have seen me, and it would have made everything worse. "Please, it's fine. We'll be fine. It's best you just go," I said to the ground, terrified that he'd say something like "call me if you need help," or something equally kind and disastrous.

He didn't. I felt his eyes on the top of my head before he turned and walked away. I wanted to call "thank you, thank you so much, I'm sorry, I'm very sorry," after him, but of course I didn't.

He didn't even pick up his equipment, just quietly turned and walked to his truck. Mother waited until the motor started and Ben made the U turn that would take him inland toward Route 6.

Then she turned to me. I opened my mouth to begin an apology. She raised her hand and I braced myself for a flame of pain and humiliation on one cheek, but it did not come. Instead she put her palm upright in a stop sign, which I took to mean I mustn't speak. She turned and went into the house. Within a few minutes, she was throwing our belongings onto the back porch, and I knew vacation was over.

5

AFTER WE GOT BACK FROM TRURO, I began my junior year. I was on the young side of my class and didn't turn sixteen until October. Mother made me wait until second semester to even take Driver's Ed at school. I think she felt that after Roger got his license, he kept right on rolling and had ended up most of a continent away. In my secret heart, I knew this theory wasn't all that off base.

Indeed, Roger's absence left a frayed hole in the fabric of our existence. It seemed to me, too, that after we got back from Cape Cod, Mother had less to say about God. It might sound strange, but secretly tired as I had grown of how she usually insisted the most mundane events of life had a cosmic spiritual significance, the change frightened me. I couldn't imagine Mother without that dimension to define and hold her together, and when she changed ketchup brands without reporting that God had led her to the store brand instead of Heinz, I actually found myself suggesting that perhaps it was His will. She shrugged, and I realized then that whatever is familiar is what we try to save, however strange or painful.

Am I making us out to be worse off than we were? I remind myself of how utterly I loved her, and how an approving smile, to say nothing of her laugh, was enough to live on for days. I know others felt her charisma—she never had trouble recruiting new students no matter where we moved—and by that I reassure myself: what I saw in her was real. I remember the early days, how her enthusiasm was like perfect, dry kindling for a winter fire, how her laughter warmed like a lit hearth. Expeditions to find used clothes and furniture were adventures; she could find life and beauty ordinary people had overlooked and thrown out. She'd warned me the world didn't know or understand her; how could I know my heart's doubts were anything but proof that I, too, was merely ordinary? That I, like outsiders, couldn't see the Truth? Even as late as that fall, there was a string of October days clear and perfect as blue beads. One Sunday, we raked all the leaves for the Jensens just to have a reason to be outside. It was Mother, not I, who jumped in the pile and came up giggling, her hair spilling bright maple leaves. It was Mother who shouted, "Jump!" to me, clambering out of the way and shaping the pile of rustle back into a mound so I'd get the full effect. So how could the teacher who was supposed to discuss math, but instead told Mother how I was too old for my age: how could she have known what she was talking about? It was Mother who jumped in the leaves first. It was Mother, not I, who'd gotten us a half gallon of fresh-pressed cider and powdered sugar doughnuts and started us hooting with laughter at our bizarre white lips. You see? There were very sweet times, too. In the end they weren't enough, but they were real.

GRANDMOTHER HAD BEEN calling with increasing frequency since we got back from the Cape at about the same time Mother seemed to be abandoning God (or vice versa: who knew?). She was disdainful of *Jesus Christ, Superstar* when it came to the little Malone movies. I'd thought she'd want to see it, but I was definitely wrong. She said the music was profane and disgusting when I borrowed the album from a girl at school.

I mentioned it to Roger when he came home for Christmas, but he, too, was unable to discern what was going on. His visit brightened Mother for a week before his arrival, but shortly after he arrived, she began to anticipate his departure and began a descent back into gloom. I could tell Roger agonized with his own guilt, yet I never felt him truly waver about returning. I was angry and impressed in equal measure.

Roger returned to Colorado on January 2, and the winter of my failure to compensate for his absence slushed and lurched into a late spring. One day, I came home from school to find Mother in a frenzy of clothes, shoes and toiletries.

"We're going to Seattle," she announced. "Get packing."

"Seattle?" I parroted dumbly, putting down my books.

"Your grandmother has to have help. She's sick."

This was treacherous ground. "Oh?" I was cautious.

"Is that all you can say? Don't you care?"

"Of course I do. I'm sorry." I was quick to add the automatic apology.

"Well, move it. We need to go tomorrow. It'll take a good four days. You can help drive."

"What about school?" I was supposed to take the Scholastic Aptitude Test in a week and a half.

"You can make it up."

Another curve in the road. I'd not told her that I, too, wanted to go away to college, or that Mr. VanFrank was in there pushing me just as he had Roger. I stood in her bedroom like a tongue-tied four-year-old, fidgeting and twisting, and the little I finally got out was the closest to rebellion I'd yet come.

"I need to take my test." I couldn't look at her. When I checked my feet, the penny in one loafer was brighter than the other.

"What test?" she demanded, her face a cross between surprise and anger. I'd paid the fees out of babysitting money, and hadn't found a way to even tell her I'd registered.

"My college test."

"How can you be so self-centered? How? How?" she bore down on me. Then I saw there were tears in her eyes, and guilt claimed me again.

THE NEXT MORNING, I DIDN'T even call the school, although it was dawning on me that I'd probably not finish the year. Mother made mention of returning—if we were no longer needed then in Seattle—via Boulder and helping Roger get ready to come home. It was just mid-April and his semester ended May 15. My finals would be the last week of May, but I couldn't imagine being prepared to take them even if we were back.

It took us until almost noon to pull out of town in Mother's turquoise Rambler, her at the wheel and the small car almost groaning in dread. Mother had grossly overpacked, distractedly including all manner of objects for which she imagined we might develop a need. It seemed that we'd never return and I wondered if that was her intent, that we'd just abandon everything, leave the bills unpaid again and start over, but I knew it couldn't be: although she'd brought her flute, she'd left behind our heritage, reboxed and in the window seat.

Through the afternoon, we pushed across upstate New York and across the northernmost tip of Pennsylvania on I-90. *"I once was lost, but now am found, was blind, but now I see,"* Mother sang. We slept in the car that first night just after crossing into Ohio, finally pulling into a rest stop, where we washed in the ladies' room sink and bought snacks from a vending machine before cramping our bodies into the front (me) and the back (Mother) to sleep. I'd begun to realize that there would be no relief in the landscape, which was dreary and industrial, no school day for respite. I would be with Mother every minute, always, always *found*. I prayed, but Roger did not appear, nor, it seemed would God show up in any other form.

By the time we were approaching Chicago the next day, Mother had begun to talk a little. "Cancer," she said at one rest stop. Later, while I was driving, she added, "in both lungs, and metastasized," as though it were a sequitur, which it wasn't, and as though I knew what metastasized meant.

"Oh," I tried the cautious response again and got by with it this time. Perhaps it sounds inhuman of me, but remember, I didn't know my grandmother, and Mother's references to her were usually bitter, with a terrible, unfinished edge.

"Well, who knows what to believe. It's not as though she hasn't…" Her sentence trailed off suggestively. "We'll see," she finished, and fell silent. We spent the second night in a rest stop nearly indistinguishable from that of the previous evening, several hours west of Chicago. I was losing track of what state we were in at any given time, and was confused late the next day to see a sign announcing the number of miles to Sioux Falls, when Mother roused me, cottonmouthed and dazed, to take another turn driving, this time into a slanting glare of sun. We were no longer in Wisconsin, where I'd last paid attention, but nearly halfway across Minnesota. It made sense, though: I was stiff, and my eyes gritty, stinging with fatigue and worry. When Mother drove, the speedometer crept to over eighty on a fairly regular basis. I felt safer during my turns at the wheel, though the enormity of the trucks that would sometimes flank me on two sides made me clench the wheel, my hands cramping toward paralysis.

"For God's sake, Ruth, get in the left lane if the trucks bother you. Then they'll only be on one side of you. Pass him, will you? I'd like to arrive there before the end of the century," she said more than once. If I let up on the speed too much—though I never dared drive as fast as she—she'd instinctively wake and instruct me to step on it, so I didn't dare get in the right lane where I'd have been more comfortable; I'd never driven on a freeway until two days earlier.

It was late afternoon the next day before we left I-90 for the first time, at Kadoka, east of the Badlands. Certainly it wasn't for sightseeing, although all day I'd been catching signs for astonishments like Badlands Petrified Forest, Black Hills this and Black Hills that, to say nothing of the town of Deadwood, which a billboard informed me has one street on the narrow floor of Deadwood Gulch while the town clings to the steep sides of the canyon. I wanted to see the *dogtooth spar* in Sitting Bull Crystal Cavern and Beautiful Rushmore Cave, but Mother had decided we would get a motel room, so we could shower and get a better rest. The hum and grind and relentlessness of the drive was, I believe, getting to her. We'd been stopping as little as possible, watching money closely, but we got to that point between exhaustion and giddiness and she let go of her single-mindedness.

For a while another dimension had entered the monotony, too. When I was driving, I got to pick the radio station. At first, I left it on the classical station to please her, but as we both became glazed by life in the car, I'd put it on a popular station while she slept and noticed she didn't change it as soon as she opened her eyes. "Tie a Yellow Ribbon Round the Ole Oak Tree" was hop-scotching to the top of the hit parade so, of course, it seemed Tony Orlando and Dawn were bopping ahead of us across the country toward some fanciful welcome. How soft was the tie that binds when it was yellow ribbon; how we kept time with our bodies, how even my hands let go the death grip on the steering wheel to tap out the beat. My mother singing and snapping her fingers to rock 'n' roll? Is it any wonder I thought we'd crossed more than state borders?

We went into town in search of an inexpensive room, fol-lowing what Mother thought was the route noted on a highway sign we'd seen, but apparently, she took a wrong turn. We found ourselves on a road that seemed headed out of town; the houses were suddenly spaced much more widely, and whole fields between them appeared vacant. Spring was greening the ground and underbrush, but the trees had only just begun to bud. Still, the afternoon was close to hot, in the unstable manner of late April.

Suddenly Mother slowed the car to a crawl. Ahead of us, in the middle of the road a small girl was hunched over the body of an animal. Mother pulled the car to the shoulder and got out. I followed.

"Are you all right?" she asked the child.

The little girl looked torn between running away and staying with a muskrat lying open-eyed and breathing across the dotted yellow line.

"Don't be afraid," Mother said, her voice low and kind. "We only stopped to see what was wrong. I know you're probably not supposed to talk to strangers, and that's good, but we won't hurt you. What's happened?" She leaned over to look at the animal. The little girl, who looked perhaps seven or eight, shifted enormous brown eyes back down to the muskrat, whose dark, dull fur visibly rose and fell in rapid but steady breathing.

"She's hurt, but she's just resting. She'll be fine. See? Her eyes are open and all," the little girl said, eagerness winning over fear. She had on denim overalls, a red plaid blouse underneath.

Indeed, the muskrat's eyes *were* open, though they didn't appear to be seeing anything. I could have been wrong, though. What did I know about animal injuries? But the little girl was positive. She knew.

Mother reached toward the animal, which made no reactive flicker.

"Honey, I know it looks as though she's just resting, but see, she's hurt badly. She's bleeding inside where you can't see it. She's not going to get well."

"Yes, she will. See, she's breathing and everything."

"What's your name, dear?"

"Gayla."

"Well, Gayla, this little muskrat is hurt too badly to live. The thing is, she may be in a lot of pain. If we try to move her out of the road, she's likely to bite us, because she's wild, you know? The best thing we could do for her is to let her die quickly, so she won't suffer or be afraid."

"No, she'll get well." Gayla's skin was so white it was translucent, with a smattering of light freckles over her nose. Her hair was a deep brunette, cropped short. Tears started in her eyes. I would have left it at that, maybe tried to work some cardboard under the animal, pull it to the side of the road, so that Gayla—I surmised she had no intention of leaving—would be safe, and go on. Maybe I would have asked for her phone number and stopped at a phone booth to try to call Gayla's mother. But, then, maybe Gayla was in front of her own home. I don't know what I would have done. But I wouldn't have done what Mother did next. Not that I'm saying she was wrong. I don't know about that. I just know I didn't have the strength to swim upstream against what someone else wanted and needed with her most earnest being. Not then, anyway.

But Mother did. She always said that when you do God's will, He gives you the strength. But how do you *know?* How do you know what's right when choices glisten with separate certainties? I was a long way from getting it: in the end, you really *don't* know, and tough luck, you have to decide anyway.

She climbed into our car and backed up onto the pavement. From behind the windshield, her face looked eerie and distant, the glare of a low sun bouncing off the glass. I saw her motion me *out of the way,* and I took Gayla's hand and pulled her to the side of the road with me. It was Gayla's face I was watching as Mother gathered speed and aimed the driver's side tires straight for the muskrat. "No," Gayla screamed, and again, just as the car hit the animal. "No."

Years later, while I sat in a sidewalk café in Paris drinking café au lait, a man stepped off the curb ten feet in front of me and was struck by a speeding taxi. I recognized the sound of the impact from my memory of Mother running over the muskrat. A crunch overlaid with something like a muffled thud: sickened, I heard it over and over in my mind and to this day, I can call it up. I tried to get Gayla to turn her back, but she wouldn't.

Mother backed up, over the body again, and parked back where we'd first pulled over. Gayla's face was a frozen, horrified mask leaking tears.

"Get the newspaper I bought this morning out of the backseat," she ordered me.

I saw her bend over Gayla, who shrunk from her wordlessly. Then Mother squatted by the muskrat (no longer breathing, but still open-eyed) and waited until I brought her the paper from the rubble of the backseat. By pulling the animal's tail, she eased its body onto the paper, then pulled the paper to the side of the road. A small pool of blood soaked into the paper and left a trail partway to the side of the road. Still Gayla said nothing. I wanted to take the little girl in my arms, caress her hair and tell her that it really was okay, that Mother was right: sometimes what seems unspeakably cruel is a kindness. But the truth is, I didn't know it for sure myself. I just didn't know.

In spite of that, when we drove away a few minutes later I put my hand on Mother's arm and said, "I know that was hard, but you did the right thing." I confess I said it to align myself with her, in spite of my doubts. What did I know of all that was to come, and how I would help her the next time? I flinch when it plays in my memory, and wonder if deaths are connected like paper dolls in a line, joined hand to hand.

She turned her head to look at me, tears hovering over the edge of her bottom lids, and said, "You have no idea what you're talking about," and hardly spoke for the remainder of that night. Certainly there was no more singing. Much later, in the spotty noise and darkness of the motel room we finally found, I lay next to Mother on the sprung mattress of a cheap double bed and thought about the mistrust on Gayla's face, and how we'd left her there crouched over the muskrat's body in the scrubby roadside weeds. I wanted to say something to the little girl, something that if she could just believe it, true or not, would help her live. I had no idea what those words would be.

NEITHER MOTHER NOR I spoke of Gayla and the muskrat again. The next day was consumed with cutting a hypotenuse across the northeastern tip of Wyoming and climbing Montana, west by northwest, always clinging to I-90 like a divining rod. We stopped for the night in the upraised finger of northern Idaho. Another rest stop, this one dim and deserted, with stale crackers in the vending machines, dirty toilets and an empty paper towel dispenser. I was afraid to sleep, but, of course, fatigue claimed me. The enormous dome of sky that had opened up in South Dakota and expanded as we progressed was thick with a clarity of stars, but the air felt thin and piercingly cold. In the front, with my body split again by the ridges of the bucket seats, I huddled under my jacket and fashioned a haphazard pillow out of my hands—as much to keep them warm as to cushion my head.

The next day, Mother seemed unrested. I drove more and more of the time. Once into Washington, she drew into herself, while I imagined versions and versions of where we were going, of the sick woman who was my grandmother, of what I was to do.

"Maybe…I'd, um, like to hear more about the…family," I said. The topic was, as I've said, a minefield Roger and I had learned to tiptoe around. Maybe sheer tiredness made me daring, or maybe it was the sensation of power it gave me to be the driver.

Mother said more than she usually did, but it wasn't terribly enlightening. "She made us lose Daddy," she said. "What he did was wrong, but she could've kept him." She shook her head, off in some other world. "I did what I could, but by then, *that witch*...it was too late."

Yes, of course I wanted to know what witch she was talking about, and of course I wondered if she'd noticed that Roger and I didn't have daddies, and whose fault was that exactly? But surely by now it's clear how dangerous it would have been to verbalize criticism, direct or indirect. Besides, I wanted information, not to set her off.

"I can imagine how much you missed him," I said, not a smidge of irony in my voice. "So...um...when did he leave?"

In my peripheral vision I saw pastel blue shoulders shrug and her arm, sleeved in the same color, reach for the knob to turn the radio concerto louder, though she'd told me to turn it down not ten minutes earlier. It was her *I don't want to talk about it* shrug, not one that said, I don't remember.

I knew she did remember, and a lot. By midafternoon, when we reached the outskirts of Seattle, Mother took back the wheel. She seemed to know how to get around, although she would occasionally mutter that something had been changed, and then she'd pull to the curb. Finally, irritated, she bought a street map at a gas station. She began reacting to places we passed with fragmented words of anger. She detoured a couple of miles to glimpse her high school, chanting, "God, God," like a mantra as it came into view. She told a few stories: a boy had tried to put his hand down the waist of her skirt, a teacher had not believed something she'd said and other similar miseries, the beginnings of the vast misunderstanding between Elizabeth Ruth Kenley and the world.

IT WAS TO FIND THIS PLACE THAT she'd needed the map, I realized. The nursing home was less than homey. A stench of stale urine competed with antiseptic and won, while the furniture in the reception area looked exhausted, with darkened spots on the backs of vinyl easy chairs where heavy heads had pressed for hours. Mother asked for Sarah McNeil and it was the first I knew that Grandmother's name was different from ours. Uneasy, I held back as Mother followed the directions, leading with her chin and bosom: down the hall, through the swinging doors, then turn left and room 423 is second to last on the left. She turned and motioned me to catch up to her. Ubiquitous television sets, tuned to game shows in patient rooms and nursing stations alike, all spewed garish laughter intermittently. Here and there in the hallway, walkers waited as though someone had abandoned them midstep. I glanced into one room and momentarily stood still in shock and fear: a white-clad worker was changing a man's diapers in the bed nearest the door, and I saw his penis, a small dead thing sideways against a bony thigh, the first time I'd seen a man. He looked still young, and terribly, terribly sick, with a shock of black hair against the white pillowcase.

As we turned the last corner, Mother's low-heeled shoes clicked a faltering beat on the linoleum tile. She slowed, but breathed heavily, as though she'd been running. I felt sorry for her then, even frightened and unnerved as I was. She stood a moment outside room 423, then squared her shoulders. She reached for my hand and I gave it to her. The pressure of her grip cut my ring into the fingers on either side of it. She stepped through the open door ahead of me. "Mother?" she said. "I've come."

6

WE'D FALLEN INTO A CERTAIN rhythm by the third day, eating a carry-out dinner in front of the television before going to bed in my grandmother's efficiency apartment, then sleeping late and picking up a Dunkin' Donuts and coffee breakfast just before ten on the way to the nursing home. The pattern of the days was the only trace of predictability. You couldn't have told anything else by me.

On the walls around the bed were framed place mats of the state capitol building, state bird and state flower. While we were in her room, I studied them, trying to keep from staring at the tiny woman cocooned in sheets on the bed. Her jaundiced face was deeply wrinkled, almost pitted, like a dry peach stone, that small and shriveled. She didn't look like someone to be hated, let alone feared, but I could feel the tension in Mother, the way she perceptibly drew into herself. It was as though she were bracing herself with a corset of distrust, so rigidly did she carry herself across the threshold of Grandmother's room each day. To me, it made little sense; it didn't seem that being in each other's presence brought either of them comfort, but Mother was determined to see something out. Whatever it was.

To make matters worse, Grandmother took to me, and I to her. The only thing that made it a little easier was the frequency with which she fell asleep midsentence. After a while, I noticed that it often happened when Mother would enter the room, or seem to take note of what Grandmother was saying to me. She would nod off then, and I was grateful. Although I craved the praise and admiration Grandmother gave me, I felt a quick guilt, as well as disloyalty, when I thought Mother might overhear. (It might have occurred to someone else that Grandmother had figured how to put a splinter or two in my confidence in Mother's side of the story, or worse, that she knew how to plain get to her daughter. All I can say is that at the time, it seemed sincere to me and given what was to come, I'd rather remember it that way.)

Mother had begun complaining after the first night that she couldn't sleep, and had waylaid Grandmother's doctor to ask for some sleeping pills. He pulled a prescription pad from his lab coat pocket.

"Don't drink any alcohol with these, and don't overuse them," he cautioned as he scrawled.

"I don't drink." Mother was huffy, but what she said was true.

The protocol for Grandmother included morphine at certain intervals. Her pain generally began to increase in intensity a good hour and a half before she was due for a dose, and I found it almost unbearable to watch her writhe and twist the sheets. I held her hand when Mother wouldn't because, she said, a flute teacher's living is in her hands. I guessed I could see her point. When the pain started to come back, but before it was at its worse, Grandmother would talk. (The mercy of morphine would knock her out for a while. Anyway, by the time it came, she was exhausted from the wait.)

"Jacob was here two weeks ago, you know," Grandmother said one morning. "Such a good son. He stayed quite a while. Said he'd be back the end of this month." I hoped he'd come while we were there. I was getting quite an education, even if I still didn't know what part of it to believe.

"Really…" Mother said, not with a question mark, but a period at the end of the second syllable.

"I don't understand why you blame him," Grandmother said.

"Really," Mother said and glanced at me. "Would you like me to read another *Reader's Digest* article to you?"

THAT AFTERNOON, I WAS ALONE with Grandmother while Mother went in search of new magazines. "What's wrong between you and my mother?" It was a daring attempt for me.

"Not forgiven for her father," Grandmother answered. Her sentences were often diminished to a phrase or clause, sometimes only a verb or a noun, depending where she was on the morphine continuum.

When Mother came back, as though picking up where she and I had left off, Grandmother said to Mother, "I forgave you, you know." This was Grandmother at her most lucid.

"What do you mean, you forgave me? None of it would have been necessary if you'd done your job." Mother picked up the thread effortlessly, as if this were the only conversation possible.

Grandmother did not respond, only shifted her arms uncomfortably and muttered, "Tired. Too tired."

"Don't give me that. You just don't like what I'm saying. He wouldn't have run with her if you'd kept him home. You nagged and you cried and you locked your bedroom."

"Did my best."

"You did not. At least I tried. You wouldn't do anything, Jake wouldn't do anything. Someone had to try."

"Not right. Worst sin."

"I just wanted him to stay with us. How were we going to live?"

"We lived."

"And look at what we got, and what she got. And once she had the baby, he forgot Jake and I even existed."

Grandmother's pain was increasing, then. She was gasping between words. "Just want peace. You, me, peace. Let me go. Tired."

"Well, I'm tired, too, Mother." With that, my mother shook her head and stood so abruptly that I lurched to catch her chair as it began to topple backward on two spindly legs. "I don't need your help," she shot at me, and left the room.

I had no idea what to do. My head was awash with trying to decipher the conversation. I wanted to take Grandmother's hand, but knew that if Mother returned and caught me like that, I'd be one of the Betrayers, again. Sooner or later, she always said, everyone betrayed her.

I had to, though. Take her hand, and ask again, keeping my voice down and an ear tuned to any approaching footfalls. "Please. Please tell me what happened. What are you and Mother talking about?" I hesitated and then added, "I won't...tell her you told me."

She didn't open her eyes, but I knew she could hear me. There was tension in her hand, and her lips moved—as if she were starting to say something then hesitating.

"She...got...in bed—" a groan, then, with a slight shake of her head "—with her father..."

That was all she said. Even though I said, "What? What does that mean?" my grandmother seemed to fall asleep then. What could I do? You can hardly shake a dying woman and demand she explain what she's told you. Did she mean literally? Why would my mother have done that? I had no idea. None.

Even more confused, I slipped as quietly as I could to the other side of the room, where there was an empty, unmade bed and sat in one of the chairs intended for a second patient's visitors. I sat and listened to my grandmother making little moans as she exhaled into a sleep without rest.

"LET ME GO," BECAME Grandmother's theme. We tried every way we could to make her comfortable, but nothing helped.

"What do you want me to do," Mother came close to snapping at her several times.

"Sorry. Peace."

"What are you talking about? What do you want me to do?" Mother would say, but wouldn't touch Grandmother other than to lift her head to press a glass against her lips. I'd take her hand when I could, and say, "It's okay, Grandmother, it's okay," but I dared not say, "I love you," or anything close to what I thought I should say. What I *wanted* to say.

We stayed later than usual that day, because we'd come in later. The night before, Mother had again shifted and tossed for a long time before she'd dozed off. She'd slept until nearly eleven in the morning; I'd not dared wake her. The second shift nurses and aides came on duty at four o'clock. Nora, who took care of Grandmother regularly, came in and said to Mother, "I'm surprised she's still with us. Try to let her know it's all right to go…sometimes they hang on and on, waiting for…permission. You know?"

But Mother was not about to give permission for anything as best I could tell. "Love you," Grandmother breathed rather than spoke the words to her daughter. I heard her myself, twice, that evening alone. The first time, my mother didn't answer at all. The second time, she said, "Don't try to talk. Save your strength."

"I can't take this," Mother said to me that night in the car. She began crying and used both fists to pound the steering wheel at the first red light. "It's not fair. I can't take it. We're going to have to go."

"Now?" I was incredulous.

"I don't know," she answered, something I'd almost never heard my mother say.

But we didn't go. The next day, Mother went into Grandmother's room with a grim look and a set to her shoulders that I recognized. "Love you. Let me go," Grandmother started right away.

"How about some applesauce?" Mother answered.

"No, no, no. Please."

"Okay. I'll read to you then," said Mother, deliberately misunderstanding, I thought. "Here. How about 'My Most Unforgettable Character'?" Grandmother moaned. Not long after that, even sleep did not seem a respite. She moved her head from side to side and gasped. When she woke, it was as though it were a waking sleep and she was still dreaming. "Filth," she said once. Later she looked straight at Mother and said, "Whore." Mother flinched.

"You have no idea what you're talking about. You never did," Mother retorted angrily, but it was obvious nothing was registering in Grandmother. Mother's face was a deadly pale, with gray smears beneath her eyes and her cheeks hollowing moment by moment. A brilliant sunlight was being sliced like an onion by the venetian blinds and my eyes stung with fatigue and worry as if the air were filled with the acrid odor. The bed next to Grandmother's was still empty, a small mercy.

Mother picked up her purse, a huge, needlepoint affair that reminded me of a carpetbag. "Shut the door," she said. I knew better than to hesitate. Mother took her purse over to the small dresser and set it on the top. An oval mirror was mounted over the bureau, in which Grandmother's underwear and a sparse collection of toiletries were stored. Light green walls made the striped light in the room illuminate us in an eerie way as though we were suspended underwater, lingering briefly just below the surface before our descent to the bottom.

She stared a moment into the mirror. Her mouth was set in an absolutely straight line; I remember noticing that the way you notice odd details in a dream. Is it possible to communicate the aura of unreality that overtook the room? I was caught upside down in an undertow, disoriented, unbelieving and terrified until I relinquished myself and drew a full measure of water into my lungs. That is all I can say for myself: I have no other excuse.

Mother reached into her purse and drew out the bottle of Seconal that Grandmother's doctor had prescribed to help Mother sleep. I remember the capsules were bright blue. "You'll help me, won't you?" she said, and I looked around, because she didn't seem to be talking to me. Her voice was low, soft and suggestive, not one she'd used with me, though I'd occasionally heard her speak to Roger that way. But, of course, Roger wasn't there. I was.

"What do you want me to do?"

By then, Mother had crossed the room and gotten Grandmother's water glass from her bedside stand. She brought it over and sat on the empty bed, the pill bottle still in one hand. With something near a giggle, she said, "Quick, empty these," and began opening the capsules and pouring the powdery white contents into the glass, which she held between her knees.

I was slow to comply and this time she looked not at, but right through me and said, "Come on, help me."

All the pills together made perhaps a quarter-inch deep reservoir of powder in the glass. Mother got up and poured several inches of water into the glass. Of course, the powder floated. Without seeming to particularly watch or listen for an approaching nurse, Mother sat down and began to stir the water with a straw, in trancelike rhythmic circles. Slowly the powder turned translucent and seemed to disappear. I comforted myself with that, though I couldn't have been fooled because I hurriedly collected the empty pill bottle, slid it into my pocket and went over to take the other chair by Grandmother's bed. Then we sat and waited.

While we waited there in the light, already sliced, which had begun to dapple as a tree outside filtered it even before it reached the blinds, Mother did not speak except once. "Don't think you can stop me," she said, features hardened to a grim mask. I thought she must be speaking to me because a wave of "no, no, no" had begun to rise in my chest. But she wasn't. She was staring right at her own mother's face. Still, the tone was enough to keep me still and make me prop Grandmother's head when she woke and drank through the straw her daughter held to her lips.

AFTERWARD, MOTHER SEEMED in no hurry, even when Nora poked her head in the door and asked if Mrs. McNeil needed anything. Mother didn't answer. "No, thanks, we're fine," I said. My voice must have revealed my turmoil, but Nora mistook it and crossed to me. Her thighs sandpapered each other between noiseless nurse's-shoe steps. She put an arm around my shoulder.

"You okay?" she said gently.

"Yes." Tears came to my eyes. Nothing undid me quicker than kindness.

"It's so hard, I know, the waiting. Has she been awake since her last shot?"

"Not yet," I lied.

"Just as well," said Nora. "Just call me if there's anything I can do. Dr. Henderson left new orders this morning so we can give her a shot every three hours instead of four. That may help. You can never tell about these things." She picked up Grandmother's wrist to take her pulse. "Slow," she mouthed to me. Mother sat like a zombie through this conversation. I saw Nora look twice at Mother, but then she just sympathetically patted Mother's shoulder on her way out of the room.

Part of me was in a panic, and part of me took charge. I took the glass into the bathroom and washed it repeatedly with soap. After I dried it, I brought it back into the bed area, set it on the stand and poured an inch of water into it, as though it were what she'd left in the glass. I unwrapped a new straw and set it in the glass. The straw Mother had used to stir, I folded over and over and put into the pill bottle in my pocket.

That done, I sat back down, thinking to wait until Mother was ready to leave. But there was too much churning in me. My grandmother lay there, her breathing slow and labored, a slight rattle to the shallow exhalation, and I knew I couldn't pull it off if she died while we were still there. I'd crack in Nora's misguided sympathy, a fault line of guilt spreading rampantly across me. I touched Mother's shoulder and said, "It's four-thirty, Mother, we should leave," as if the time were relevant.

"Don't think you can stop me," Mother said hoarsely to her mother, and, to my amazement, got up to leave.

"Get some rest," Nora said as we passed her in the hall. "Try not to worry. We'll call you if there's any change."

"Thank you so much," I answered, but, of course, Nora had no idea what I was really thanking her for, how she had put her arm around me like I was a good person, worthy of her care.

"The old bitch," Mother said to the dashboard as I guided her into the passenger side of the car, but then she was silent as I drove us back to Grandmother's apartment. I didn't even stop to get a carry-out supper. We'd been there for perhaps an hour, barely moving, neither of us speaking, when the phone rang. The head nurse said simply that Mrs. McNeil had died quietly, without waking again after we left, and she was so sorry for our loss.

7

I'D BEGUN TO BE TERRIFIED. MOTHER didn't seem to be coming out of her stupor the evening Grandmother died. I heated some canned soup and fixed her dry toast—exhausting the groceries we'd laid in—and then helped her undress and get into bed. She spoke almost not at all and when she did, it made little sense. "It'll work," she said once, and I realized she could have been thinking of almost anything. I was much less sure.

I slept little that night, trying to figure out what had to be done. I needn't have bothered; in the morning, Mother's old self appeared. "We've got a lot to do," she announced. "We need to call Roger and get over to the nursing home to get her things. I guess they'll arrange cremation…we need to see about that."

"Do you need to call Uncle Jake?" I asked tentatively, not really sure, even, what I was supposed to call him.

"He can rot in hell," she snapped. "The only thing he's going to get is the bills forwarded to him. What use has he ever been to me?" It wasn't a question I could begin to answer.

IN FACT, IT *HAD* WORKED, or seemed to have at the time. The nursing home did arrange cremation, and must have called Jake, too, because Mrs. Short, the administrator, said that Mother had been "cleared" to receive Grandmother's ashes. "Like it's some privilege" was her response, muttered in an aside to me. Later,

she told me, "What I want is to be free of her once and for all."
Still, when Mrs. Short held out the cardboard box, double-tied
with white cotton string, she accepted it.

Mother went through the apartment, taking virtually nothing.
"What would I want to remember? Let Jake deal with it," she
said, and left the keys in the building manager's mailbox. "I want
to get out of here before he shows up."

And then we were on the road again, headed south. On top
of the jumbled heap of our bags and what Mother had taken from
Grandmother's apartment loomed the cardboard box. Mother
occasionally addressed an angry remark to it, but other than that,
she showed no consternation.

"What are we going to do with…it?" I asked her.

"Find a suitable final resting place," she answered.

"Are we taking…her…home with us?"

"Not if the sky opened up and rained gold coins. I intend to
be free of her forever."

This kind of owned hostility was a new side of my mother.
Of course, she'd always had a lion's share of anger, but it
pounced at its target from its stance on God's righteous will,
rather than from anything Mother thought or didn't like or didn't
want. I was frightened as she drove on, not knowing exactly
where we were headed next, or why. Ironically I remembered
thinking it was like driving headlong over a cliff.

I DIDN'T HAVE TO WAIT long. The second day on the road, Mother
said, "Roger's semester is over on the fifteenth. We'll get there
the fourteenth and help him close everything up. Then we can
drive on home in tandem, save on motel rooms and the like."
This was the first thing she had said in a long time that sounded
like a good idea to me. I felt like someone who'd been in an
earthquake, unable to trust the ground, sensing tremors and
faults everywhere. Would I tell him what we had done? The
question hung and thrashed in my mind but didn't diminish my
need for him. Surely he'd find a way to understand. He knew
her.

"That's more than a week away. What will we do until then?"

"It's not like we can't arrive early," she said, irritably. "But I've always wanted to see the Grand Canyon. Seems stupid that someone who grew up in the west has never seen the Grand Canyon. Well, my mother was terrified of heights, so of course, we never went. Just like we couldn't go up in the mountains. She said the idea of looking down made her think she'd lose her mind and jump. Didn't it, Mother?" This last was addressed over her shoulder to the cardboard box—which seemed larger than it had the day before, but doubtless, that was my imagination. "So, let's go take ourselves a look."

"That will be wonderful," I said, an answer programmed by old, robot enthusiasm for any plan of Mother's. I was taking as few chances as possible.

"I ABSOLUTELY DO NOT see how you can sleep your way through this spectacular country," Mother said. "You've never seen it before, who knows when you will again, and you waste the opportunity." She was right. I'd slept most of the day, whenever it wasn't my turn to drive. I'd slept as though I were fevered or drugged, a thick, dreamless sleep through Washington and on south, into Oregon. As much as I wanted to go down 101, which traced the curves of the ocean coast with a lover's finger, when Mother put us on the inland route 5, I hadn't even bothered to mourn. The dream of sightseeing I'd had on the way west seemed just that: the dream of a child. Other images pressed themselves against my eyes, like blue capsules, a clear glass, the iridescent wings of the sunlit fly that had bumped and buzzed its way across the window while I sat on the empty bed. I could not believe what my mother had done, what I had *helped* her do. And an unthinkable thought had passed through the darkness of my mind like a shooting Dakota star barely glimpsed. For just an instant, I could imagine Mother in a nursing home, myself stirring a skim of white powder into the translucence of water.

Did she sense it? A moment later she reached across the seat and patted my thigh. "Well, I know you're tired. Come on, lay your head on my lap." When I did, she stroked my hair a while, driving with one hand as she lulled me back to sleep.

"IT HAS OCCURRED TO ME that my father may come to me, now that she's gone." Mother made this cryptic statement shortly after she announced that we would treat ourselves to a motel room in Riddle, still a way north of the California border, that night, worn-out as we both were. "And now that we're out of her house…."

I braced myself, and thought about Roger. Hang on until we get to Roger, I told myself. He'll know what to do. Mother left the highway and drove into the town, ignoring a cheap Mom and Pop motel on the outskirts. The nondescript town plunked apropos of nothing in southern Oregon, was old and run-down. A main street of two-story buildings was the only show, with nothing higher except a decrepit three-floor hotel. Mother pulled up in front of its brick exterior as though she'd known exactly where she was headed, and said, "You keep the car running while I see if there's room."

While I sat in the car, a parade of hot rods passed. I could hear them before I could see anything except their headlights darkening the late twilight in contrast. Teenagers were crammed into souped-up cars, roaring their engines as they laughed and shouted through open windows. I could see some of them raising beer bottles to their lips. As each drew abreast of me, I felt music throbbing from the car. A few couples rode motorcycles, boys driving, and dark, loose-haired girls with crimson nail polish circling their arms around the boys' waists. The wind of the ride lifted the girls' hair and the fabric of their blouses like the dark-tipped wings of the gulls at the Cape. One threw back her head in the exhilaration of flight as they passed me tethered, motionless, alone.

"There's room. Come on, get your bag. There's parking in the back." Mother had almost broken into a trot coming down the hotel steps, her face animated with exertion or pleasure as she passed beneath a painted Rooms To Let sign above the porch. "This is what it'd take, an old place like this, a place with history. My father worked around Medford for a while…I sort of remember the name Riddle, because it was…funny."

Of course, I did as I was told. I always did, until the time I didn't. But, as I've said, there was a lot of sky to fall before then.

THE ROOM LOOKED LIKE THE building, which looked like the center of town: a throwback. A double bed, covered with a thready chenille spread was in the center, a wooden rocker and a battered floor lamp on the side near the single window and a dresser against the far wall. Faded floral wallpaper peeled up from the baseboards in several places. A communal bathroom was down the hall and around one corner. It gave me the creeps.

Mother seemed delighted with the room, pronouncing it perfect. She turned on the one lamp and began rooting through her suitcase. "You'd better go get ready for bed," she said. "If you think you're going to sleep in this bed with me, you'll take a bath."

I had no idea how one goes about getting ready for bed in an old hotel with shared bathrooms. Surely one doesn't walk through the hall in a nightgown? I decided I'd bathe and put on clean underwear beneath the clothes I'd worn all day, just to get back to our room. I picked up the clear plastic bag containing my toiletries, a towel and clean underpants, and quietly left for the bathroom. The bag embarrassed me, much too intimate to dangle from my clenched fist in the public hallway, as were the towel and underwear. But I didn't know what else to do. Mother, busy with her suitcase, seemed to be nearly in another world, behind a door at which I dared not knock.

Luck was with me. I didn't see anyone in the hall and I began to relax just a little. It was a large, old-fashioned bathroom. The shower I'd imagined wasn't there. Rather, an enormous claw-foot tub was in one corner. There was a sink, its pipes exposed beneath, and a small oval mirror hung above. The toilet lid and seat were up.

If I'd had any sense at all, I'd have washed my face and hands, used the toilet and gone back to our room and lied through freshly brushed teeth that I'd bathed. But I stood in the center of the bathroom, skinny and dumb as a scarecrow, fiddling with a lock that turned in each direction, but which, from the inside, never seemed to secure the door. I opened it halfway and tried the lock various ways until, from the outside, the handle wouldn't turn. Then, I shut it and replicated the number of counterclockwise turns that had locked it. Hesitantly I took off my clothes. The tub looked grayish, and I wondered what I was supposed to do to clean it after use. Then it occurred to me to wonder when it had been last cleaned. Still, I adjusted the water to comfortably hot, and knelt to bend double and put my head under the faucet to wash my hair. My shampoo acted like bubble bath as the water rose, and when my hair was rinsed and the water nearly to the top, I lay back and breathed. How long may one stay in a shared bathroom, I wondered. Where was there another in case someone else needed a bathroom?

There was a knock at the door, and I timidly called, "I'll be out soon," quickly beginning to scramble to a stand, even though I'd been obsessive about trying and retrying the lock. I must have confused myself about the lock operation, and I must not have called out loudly enough, because suddenly the door opened and a man was in the room less than five feet from me. His eyes swept my naked body midway in the act of standing, and he hesitated a split second before addressing my chest. "Excuse me, miss," he said, taking a step backward as I panicked and floundered for the towel I'd left on the toilet seat. My heart thudded uncontrollably. When he shut the door, I could see his afterimage on its painted wood, like an apparition burning into my mind.

"WHAT DID HE LOOK LIKE?" my mother demanded.

"I'm not sure, I was so scared. He had brown hair, sort of curly."

"My God. God, God, God. I think that was my father, looking for me."

"I…I'm…I don't know, I'm not sure."

"What did you do," she demanded. "Did you say anything?"

"I was scared. I may have screamed a little, and I tried to get a towel."

"You little fool. If you've done anything to startle my father away, I'll never forgive you."

"I didn't mean…" This is the truth: it hadn't for a minute

occurred to me that my dead grandfather had somehow opened a locked bathroom door and accidentally appeared to me instead of my mother.

"You never mean anything, but you still do it, don't you?" She meant cause problems. Mother picked up a towel into which she'd folded some other things, and her bag of soap, toothbrush, toothpaste, and the like and headed for the bathroom. I didn't notice that she had also taken the separate little bag that contained her makeup.

While she was gone, I hurriedly locked the door behind her, changed into my nightgown and unlocked the door so as not to annoy her when she returned; the big metal key that fit into the old-fashioned keyhole beneath our doorknob lay on the dresser where she had set it down. In perhaps forty-five minutes she was back, perfumed and nightgown-clad, with her hair freshly brushed and makeup on. One shoulder of the gown was pulled down to rest against her upper arm as though casually. While she was gone, I had sat in the rocking chair and tried to pray, but words stuck and sank half-formed, as though my spirit had filled with quicksand.

"He didn't come," she said flatly. "We're going to turn the lights out now and wait for him. Don't you dare make a sound. Get into bed."

I did, of course, and she climbed in next to me but sat up against a pillow expectantly. I made my body as small as possible and tried not to move or breathe in an audible way. An enormous tension loomed like another being in the room. Mother had not drawn the shade, and a streetlight just below us threw an arc of light through the window she'd left partly open. Outside on the street, the hot rods still roared and honked their way up and back, and in my mind I heard the carefree laughter. Next to me, with eight inches of deliberate space between our bodies, my mother glittered away from me. Her face was lean and bright as a full moon, revealing everything and nothing at once as she waited.

8

I WOKE COLD AND STIFF ON THE FLOOR of our hotel room in Riddle. I had no memory of getting out of the bed, but realized I must have taken my pillow and lain on the area rug to avoid provoking Mother by moving about. At least that's what I told her—and doubtless myself—when she asked, but I suspect nothing could have been more uncomfortable than being in that bed with her while she awaited the ghost.

Mother was grim. "You scared him off. First it was her, now it's you, too. Damn you both," she said.

I began an answer in spite of the danger of protest; if she really got started categorizing me with Grandmother, I didn't know what she might do. Maybe she could get more of those blue capsules.

But she held up a hand to silence me. "I don't want to hear it," she said flatly. "I know you didn't mean to scream. That's not the point. He sensed your Lack of Faith, that's why he couldn't enter this room." Her voice capitalized the condemning words.

"I'm sorry, Mother."

She did not answer, only looked wounded and withdrawn and went on about folding her nightgown back into her suitcase.

"I'm not hungry," she said. "If you want something, go on and get it yourself, and come back when you're satisfied." I was, indeed, starving because we'd had only apples from the car the night before, but I knew from the way she'd phrased it that if I ate, it would be evidence that I wasn't upset about how I'd prevented her reunion with her father.

"No, thank you. I'm not hungry this morning. But maybe it would be better if I run and get you something light."

"No." Her voice was flat. Then she didn't let me carry her suitcase for her as I usually did, and I knew there would be no softening for at least a while.

MOTHER WOULDN'T LET me drive, and I didn't dare escape into even a pretend sleep. She needed to see that I was suffering for what I'd done. And, in fact, I was, but not necessarily for the reason she wanted me to suffer.

We drove steadily south in California, stopping for a quick lunch and to stretch our legs. We wouldn't even turn east until we got a little below Bakersfield, almost another day's drive after we got to Sacramento. Mother announced that she had decided against a motel for the night; we could save some money, and then have more leeway when we got to the Grand Canyon. She pressed on. Finally she asked me to drive, and from then on we took two-hour stints. I was beginning to realize the magnitude of our side trip to the Grand Canyon before heading back northeast to Boulder; it was hundreds and hundreds of miles out of the way. Donny Osmond crooned "The Twelfth of Never," like a foretelling as the distance on the map translated into stiff hours, a slick of oily grit on my face and a ferocious mix of anxiety and boredom. I didn't protest. If Mother said something, I responded with automatic deference, as I had well learned. But, when we lapsed into silence and my mind turned on itself, the word came to me: *murderer.* Grandmother's remains were in the nondescript cardboard box on the shelf above the backseat of our car, like an accusation.

We stopped, an hour beyond Sacramento, in early evening. We used the bathroom in the diner in a small town where we stopped for tuna sandwiches, and then she drove around in the darkness looking for a parking lot that was unlikely to be patrolled, yet lit enough to be safe. During the day, there'd been only the slightest thaw when she spoke to ask me to drive.

We were in a light commercial district, I remember that much, because it seemed we'd passed small houses, stores, a gas station and an elementary school all within a couple of blocks. Suddenly Mother slammed on the brakes and our tires screeched at the same time I was thrown forward against the dash and then beneath it on the floor, where my body stuck in a tangle of arms and legs. Something thudded within the car and Mother yelped in shock or pain. A loud squeal of tires seemed to come from another car, and I thought we were doomed, that we were about to be hit. Our car fishtailed into the start of a skid, but then as quickly, I felt a sudden acceleration and our car lurched forward without an impact. Mother drove on. Gasping, I struggled to get up off the car floor where I'd been wedged.

"Are you all right? What happened?" I stumbled over the words, frantically scanning out the windows. Behind us, a white sedan was turned sideways on the road, eerily lit by a streetlight just overhead, but it didn't appear to have hit anything. Slowly the driver righted it and proceeded to drive, but much more slowly than we. The car diminished and then we turned a corner and it was gone.

"Something hit my head, but I'm okay." She sounded too calm.

"What happened?"

"That'll teach the bastard a lesson."

"Huh?" I must have sounded like a cartoon character, dumb and expendable.

"He was right on my tail. It's dangerous and he was driving me crazy. I showed him."

I sat in silence, trying to absorb what she'd said. I wasn't sure exactly what had saved me from going headfirst through the windshield, other than the slumped angle my body happened to be in at that moment.

"Some damn thing hit me in the head," she complained. "Look back there and see what's not secure."

I looked. Things were jumbled around some, but I couldn't discern what could have flown up to hit Mother. Then I noticed: the box of ashes was not on the shelf above the backseat. When I twisted my body and neck to see the floor of the backseat, I spotted it behind the driver's seat, one corner smashed, little ripples circling the dent in the cardboard.

"Things look okay," I said, and turned to face the windshield.

We drove on. Still dazed by the logic of what she'd done to "teach" a dangerous driver, I tried to quell something near outrage which came and went like a whale breaching into moonlight, remaining quiet and pretending sleep as soon as Mother found a place she deemed suitable to park for the night. I had this to ponder: when we stopped and she claimed the backseat to sleep on, Mother had seen the box where it had landed, and figured out that it had been Grandmother who had, literally, slapped her upside the head.

"Damn her. Even dead, she finds a way to hurt me. This has got to stop."

IN THE MORNING, I woke with an all-over ache that radiated from my right shoulder. After a quick and meager breakfast of juice and toast at a diner, we were on the road again. The terrain had changed from the lush, moist new green of Oregon and northern California as we'd traveled south. Beyond Sacramento, it increasingly dried and reddened, and more and more buildings popped up pastel stucco with tile roofs, until, by Bakersfield, it seemed that was all anyone had ever thought of.

We turned east there, toward Barstow, edging the Mojave Desert. It was unusually hot for May, someone said to me in a gas station restroom, seeing me soak the scratchy brown paper towel in tepid water and run it around my face and neck. It evaporated instantly. Sweatless, I baked, my lips cracking, chapped from repeated licking until my tongue couldn't summon saliva. By the time we picked up Route 40, my head was cottony, coherent thought gone, the last moisture sucked from the seabeds of my eyes. Cactus and brush were random as life in the distance, isolated and empty as I. Once, when Mother shook me to take the wheel, I pretended to be in such a deep sleep that I didn't feel her. My head lolled of its own accord. I have no idea where we stopped that night, only that for a while, I welcomed being cold. Mother was disgusted with me. She'd loved the desert, saying it did her arthritis good, and she grew chatty as the moving sand smothered whatever words I'd ever known.

Looking back, I think it might have been best had my mind never returned to itself. But that night, I slept dreamlessly and long and adapted better the next day. We went steadily east until turning sharply north, where the Grand Canyon waited to diminish and swallow whatever we'd brought. The air, still utterly dry, was cooler. Humphrey's Peak beckoned like a respite, but I did not mention it. Between Flagstaff and the Canyon, the earth undulated like a red sea. Junipers and desert shrubs were already anchored into the sunset.

We arrived before dark, but made no attempt to see the Canyon. A small, cheap, one-story motel with parking right outside each door, fourteen or fifteen miles from the south rim, provided a hot shower in which I lingered as long as I dared. I was coming to. Mother had a preoccupied, charged air about her. She emerged from the steamy bathroom with a towel around her and playfully flicked her wet hand in my direction. I noticed the flesh of her bare arms, more dimpled, and how her breasts almost folded an extra layer between them and where the towel pulled taut across them. I was sure I'd lost weight since we left home. Sometimes it was hard to believe I was hers, our bodies were so different. I thought of a thin, red-haired man and wondered if he freckled in the sun, if he had green eyes, if he was smart, if he was sane. My birth certificate said unknown in the blank for name of father, which Mother had once explained by saying she had written Holy Spirit but it had been changed by hospital personnel.

"Well, I've decided," she said.

"Decided what?"

"You'll just have to see," she said. "But it's exactly right." The words were innocuous, but I felt danger in her improved spirits. Normally I wouldn't have looked such a gift horse in the mouth. I was changing.

The aura was present again in the morning, and there was a kind of foreboding, a tightness in my chest, which I tried to mask.

"I can't wait to see the Canyon," I tried cheerily. "Are we getting breakfast first, or shall we go right there?"

"I think we'll go look around first. I want to find the best spot. The highest spot."

"I hope we have a nice clear day. I didn't think to pick up a paper last night. What's it supposed to be like?"

"We'll have to see," she answered. So far so good, I thought. Maybe I can pull this off.

We repacked the Rambler, as we did every morning, though daily the jumble seemed less manageable. It wasn't that we were buying things. We weren't. It was that it became more and more laborious to manage the "tight ship" that Mother generally insisted on, with everything arranged just so in the trunk and backseat. We had a cooler, a couple of thermoses, pillows, blankets, shoes, rubbers (her absolute requirement for wet weather), some books, suitcases, a jacket each for cool weather and other seeming necessities for a trip of indeterminate length, across the country and back. Even Mother was growing tired of trying to keep order. I noticed this morning that the jigsaw puzzle of the trunk was off, as though someone had done it in the dark and forced pieces where they didn't really fit. Like my life with her, I thought, a jigsaw puzzle done in the dark, and then I glimpsed how close to chaos we really were.

WE PAID THE ADMISSION, about which Mother complained, and headed for Mather Point. There the Canyon took me by surprise, as the forest shuddered and gave way to the abyss, from which emanated a vast and lonely silence. An enormous hole in the ground. I never did adjust, then, to really seeing it: the subtlety of the strata in the rock, the variations and harmonies in the colors, how early and late light raise and move unspeakable scarlet, rust, magenta, violet, blue. Years later I went back and discovered *royal purple.* I hadn't wanted to go back, I admit, but I'd finally learned not to give up on a place—or a person—when the inevitable disappointment waved a handkerchief and called yoo-hoo at me, like a garrulous neighbor always stopping by. But the reason I wasn't stirred by that first sight was more than my character flaw of easily drained hope. What I saw were scrubby junipers growing out of rock, dwarfed, pathetic and clinging, while ravens rode thermals, their wings unmoving as death, watching for what they might scavenge. The desolation repelled and mirrored me.

WE WENT ON TO THE PARK headquarters, where I gathered literature, thinking we were going to explore the Canyon area, then to Bright Angel Lodge, where the terrace was crammed with cameras attached to faces. There, Mother was impatient, not even looking at the Canyon. *I* wanted to take the mule trip to the bottom, and risked a mention, but Mother brushed it away like a gnat. Finally she said, "Wait here a minute." She approached a uniformed employee, who gestured briefly in each direction. "Come on," was all she said when she returned and briskly set off in the direction of our car.

Now, it seems inevitable and obvious. How could it have taken me so long to catch on? Even after she unlocked the car and took the box of Grandmother's ashes into her short-nailed hands, I didn't see it coming. "Come on," she barked again and, of course, I did. She set out to the west, where there seemed to be the lesser concentration of people. I was wearing penny loafers, and she her regular beat-up brown shoes with a one-inch stacked heel. We both could have changed into shoes much better suited for the mile walk on which she led me. The number of people thinned out as we went, and then there were stretches in which we'd actually see no one. She kept going until there were neither people nor guardrail. Nausea stirred my stomach when I looked down so I tried not to, but Mother seemed elated.

"This is it," she announced. "Right here, right now, I declare myself free." With that, she began fumbling with the string around the box, which put up a brief fight and then let go. She opened the box and stared into it as she said, "It's over, Mother. Dad and I are both free of you forever now." With that, she looked at me. "Come closer. Help me, here. Stand back a little and hang on to me." She extended her hand, which I grasped, and leaned, perhaps a foot over the edge, holding the box with her other hand. "Free," she shouted, and turned the box over, not all at once, but slowly, so that the grayish powder and uneven pieces of matter formed a river on the air. If she'd just done it, I think it would have worked, but she had to milk the height of her revenge. A raven floated up, out in front of us like a herald of the shifting upcurrent, and Grandmother's ashy body rose, suddenly and silently flying into Mother's face and then mine. Her scream mixed in a spasm of coughing, as I tried to jerk her back from the edge. For a moment her weight pulled like something determined to kill us both, and my scream mixed into hers. I planted my feet, deciding in an instant that if I couldn't keep her from falling, I would have to fall, too. I wasn't going to let go. There was just long enough for that split-second test which I either passed or failed according to how you see it, and then I fell back onto the trail and she fell on top of me, both of us choking on the ashes we'd breathed, the remains of history in and all over ourselves.

9

MOTHER STRUGGLED TO RIGHT herself from her position—like an overturned bug—on top of me. It was another of those situations in which I had no idea what response from me was expected. Her face was red, and I thought I glimpsed fury, but then her face seemed to contort toward a smile, and I thought she was casting for how she could declare herself the winner. I tried to get up quickly once her weight was off me, and I gasped, "Are you all right?" The drama continued to play across her features. Unsuccessfully I fought to suppress a spasm of coughing. My hands flew to my mouth to hide the impulse to wipe my tongue with my fingers. Ashes were on my sleeves and, chalky, on my eyelashes like snow. A shudder went through me and I wanted desperately to brush myself off, but I had no idea how Mother would receive that action. I swallowed, and tasting the residue in my mouth, gagged. It was the best thing I could have done.

"Lean over," Mother instructed me. "Come here, I'll hold you. Just get it all out over the edge." She coughed herself, then, and brushed her hands against one another. She took my arm and pulled me closer to the edge.

"I'm okay," I managed to get out, not daring to fight her grip, but unable to approach the precipice, even though there were some rocks that formed a low natural ledge between it and me.

"Don't you trust me? Come on, hang your head over and get rid of it."

Of course, what finally made me throw up was revulsion and terror, more than the ashes. Not that many were in my mouth and nose, just enough to know that they would be inside me forever. She held on to my shirt to anchor me, and blinded with dizziness and horror, I retched over the precipice a couple of times. It was enough.

"I guess we showed her. She'll not hurt us again," Mother concluded, holding my chin in her grip and cleaning my mouth with a handkerchief moistened with her spit. And then it was over. Indicating that I was to follow, she marched back toward Bright Angel, the thrust of her bosom and chin leading us both.

As far as Mother was concerned, the Grand Canyon had suited its purpose and it was time for us to push on toward Boulder, toward Roger. The lifelong desire she'd mentioned to see the Canyon disappeared. She had worked the irony right out of what had happened, and was in a good mood which I wanted to appreciate but couldn't. I'd begun to accumulate the guilt that sticks to you if you just stay alive long enough, without even killing someone, the guilt of what you do to live.

With the new baggage inside me and the residue of vomit still in my mouth, within the hour we were on the road. My head felt stuffed with cotton, that fuzziness and unreality, and I must have moved on autopilot when we stopped. Mother drove that whole day, while during each leg of the trip, from stop to stop, I lapsed into a sleep that felt drugged. Perhaps it was the heat again—it seemed to collect and magnify itself in the car— perhaps not. I barely noticed the steady progression east into New Mexico, and I barely cared. When I glimpsed it, the land felt vast and dusty, offering no place to hide except within myself, and that's where I went with no desire to return.

I think she'd been pressing to make Albuquerque, but stopped well short of it. Once, she asked me to drive, but the words came to me as though from a great underwater distance and I couldn't rouse myself to respond. She didn't ask again. It was after eight at night when she pulled into another rest area and parked off in a corner. I'd not eaten that day, but even my stomach seemed stuffed and muffled.

"Have an apple," she commanded, thrusting one at me.

"If you don't mind, I'd rather…"

"I said, eat the apple." She anticipated the refusal that had, indeed, been on my tongue.

I took it and bit. The apple had lolled about the backseat with several others for days. The inside was mushy, with a slight vinegar taste, like hardening cider in large brown spots. I have no idea how I kept it down.

"There, you feel better now, don't you?" she said later, after I'd thrown out the bare core.

"I do, thanks," I answered. How could she be so wrong? It was a moment of crystalline clarity. The Ruth inside me who was discreet, separate, unknowable to her, didn't *have* to work to bring what I felt into sync with what she wanted me to feel. With a whole different sense of privacy, I locked the stall of the bathroom door when we went inside to wash up.

The next day, I tried to hang on to that sense that I could *want* to be separate, that my power lay in my separateness, but by noon it was slipping away. Mother was trying to engage me, I could tell, with cheer and a solicitousness about how I was feeling, and I was unable to resist.

"Look, we're really coming into mountains," she said that afternoon, when we'd finally swung north onto Route 25, toward the Colorado border. There were fewer adobes already, although most signs were still in Spanish as well as English, and Indian artifacts dominated at little roadside stores when we left the highway. I longed for some turquoise earrings, but all of them were for pierced ears, something my mother considered an inarguable sign that a woman was a tramp, so they were out of the question. Timbered ranges rose, inviting and cool-looking on the horizon. Perhaps it was that, and that I knew we were drawing closer to Roger with each hour, but by the end of the day, I was more my familiar self and, at least outwardly, back to trying to keep her happy. I must have thought that all of us would slip with a satisfying click into our roles, that Roger would help me, and our family would lurch on as before, as God intended.

"Tonight, we'll call Roger and tell him we'll be there late tomorrow. Won't it be wonderful to all be together again?" It was as if she'd read my mind and the sense of separateness I'd discovered the previous day eroded a little more.

"Yes, Mother, it will be wonderful."

OF COURSE, WE WERE much later than we'd said we'd be. Mother was infamous for grossly unrealistic estimates of travel times. I knew that Roger knew that, but I also knew that he'd been standing at the curb at least a half hour before Mother had said we'd arrive. That was what we did, part of going the second, third, fourth mile. We knew what Mother expected. Still, I felt guilty as soon as I saw him, wanting him to know that I'd had no part in making us so late. It was beyond dusk, darkness rising skyward off the ground, and a deepening chill gathering. Roger stood without fidgeting, his square body massive and steady, bare armed, a grin spreading across his features as he made out our faces behind the bug-smeared windshield.

He had the good sense to hug Mother first. I watched him, inwardly marveling at how sincere his joy appeared. Eyes closed, he wrapped her in his arms and leaned back, lifting her off her feet. I saw that he'd let his dark sideburns grow much longer, and wondered if Mother would say anything right away.

"Put me down, young man," she giggled. Rog laughed in response but held her another minute before he let go.

"Get over here, Ruthie, it's your turn to get squeezed to death," he said, still laughing and turning his wide arms to me. When he pulled me to him, I hugged him like a drowning person. All that had happened, all he didn't know, everything I'd done and not done, the extent of my aloneness coalesced in the strength of my grip on him. I think I intended never to let go.

"Hey, hey. I'm the one supposed to squeeze you to death. Down, girl," he gasped.

I let go and stepped back, looking at the pavement. Tears had started in my eyes; too much feeling was in the moment, more than I could stand. I wished I could tease him, say something to lighten myself, but at the same time, it was all much too serious for that, and I opted to just be silent. He looked at me for a clue, but I couldn't give him one.

"I got you a room pretty near campus," he said, our old way of taking each other off the hook. "Let's head over there and I'll unload your stuff. I want to show you around the school, too. Tomorrow, maybe. It'll be too dark tonight."

"Are you all packed up?" Mother asked.

"Not exactly. I've been taking finals, you know. One more to go, Calculus, tomorrow afternoon."

"Good. Then we ought to be able to take off the day after tomorrow, first thing? I'm so tired of being on the road."

Roger didn't answer her, just smiled and said, "I can imagine. How did...things go?" He meant, of course, grandmother's arrangements, but Mother answered brightly, misinterpreting the question or pretending to.

"I so wish you'd been at the Grand Canyon with us. It was simply spectacular, wasn't it, Ruthie? Just so beautiful. We loved it. You know, of course, I've always wanted to go there."

"I know. Great, I'm glad you had a good time."

This must be the twilight zone, I thought. A good time? Our grandmother was dead and I knew the cause of death, or one of them, anyway. I needed to talk with Roger alone, though I had no idea how I'd manage it. Since Mother and I left home, the only contact I'd had with him had been the briefest of impersonal conversations while she stood a foot away, impatient for the receiver. He didn't know what we'd done at the nursing home; he didn't know what Grandmother said to me; he didn't know about the ashes flying over Grand Canyon.

We all crammed ourselves into the Rambler's front seat and Roger drove us to the motel, a ramshackle one-story spread that looked out of place near the University buildings. "You two settle in. I'll leave you alone a bit, and we can go get something to eat in an hour or so. How does that sound?"

"No," Mother said, too sharply, I thought. "I haven't seen you since Christmas. You stay right here. Ruth and I will just wash up and we can go get something now. Maybe we should get carry-out anyway, and bring it back here. That way we can have some privacy."

We did it Mother's way. Roger just shrugged and said, "Sure," and within five minutes, Mother and I had washed our faces in cold water, combed our disheveled hair and were back in the car headed for a Chinese carry-out. Each of us knew exactly what the others would order: Moo Goo Gai Pan for Mother, Beef with Peapods for me, and Moo Shoo Pork for Roger.

Except Roger ordered Chicken Almond Ding.

"No, I already ordered a chicken dish," Mother objected. "You get pork, remember, and we all share."

"Nah, if you don't mind, I really like this almond ding-a-ling," he said very lightly, cheerfully. He was dancing on shards of glass. Mother drilled him with her eyes, her features sharpened beyond even their natural look by a harsh light that cast shadows into every inclination. She let it pass.

"Don't you eat in the dorm?" she asked.

"Not all the time, I'd starve to death. We come here a lot." I was stung by his casual use of "we," a pronoun that didn't include me. He had friends, I surmised, seized by jealousy and pride.

Cartons in hand, we drove the five minutes back to the motel and spread ourselves on one of the beds. Something felt out of kilter, but I told myself it was everything that had happened, that it would be all right, I had Roger now to help me.

He went back to his dorm, to study he said, and Mother and I fell into exhausted sleeps. I woke before the end of a dream in which I was imploring Roger to help me, and he did. The next morning, Roger called, but couldn't have breakfast or lunch with us: Calculus was critical for the engineering program and he had to get an A. "Never mind," Mother said to me. "We'll have the whole summer. He's going to have to transfer, anyway. This is ridiculous. We've tried it, but it's just too far away. He can get just as good a grant closer to home. For heaven's sake, he can look into another kind of engineering for that matter."

I certainly wasn't going to argue with her. I'd tried, and obviously failed to be enough for her. As ashamed as I was of that, I needed him. So, that night when he came after his Calculus final, I was on her side. She waited until we were at the diner next door to the motel to bring it up, alluding to it when Roger said he had to pick up more boxes to store his books in over the summer.

"I think you should just bring them on home," she said resolutely, buttering a roll.

"No need. The maintenance people will move anything I want to my new dorm over the summer as long as I have boxes closed securely and labeled. They're really good about that." He hadn't shaved and had on a denim shirt. Mother always said denim was hippie cloth.

"But what if you don't come back?" She bit into the bread and licked a crumb from her lower lip. The tip of her tongue looked narrow and pointy, like her face, at odds with her cushy body. The light in the diner, overhead and fluorescent, threw the same planes and hollows I'd seen the previous night into relief. I stared at my meat loaf and mashed potatoes; I didn't want to see her like that and, knowing what was coming, I didn't want to look at Roger, next to me in the vinyl booth. I played with the pool of muddy gravy sunken into the potatoes.

"Ruth, eat your dinner," she barked into the silence, then stared across at Roger, waiting.

"No danger." Was he deliberately misunderstanding her? He actually laughed. "I might have blown my A in Calculus, but my average is plenty good enough."

Mother inhaled, waited an extra beat, and breathed out, "I want you to stay home. There's no reason you can't commute to U Conn. I'm sure they have engineering, even if it's not a hoity-toity program," on the serrated blade of her sarcasm. I felt Roger look at me, but I kept my eyes down, as though not to intrude on a private conversation.

"I like this program," he said evenly. I wondered whether he'd repeat the whole explanation about geological engineering he'd repeatedly offered when he was a senior and just making applications. He didn't, though. Maybe he was tired and willing to just cut to the chase, unimaginable in our previous life.

"You can like another program. Or you can not go to school at all. It's your choice." It was an order.

"You're right. It's my choice, and I'm going to stay in this program."

At that, Mother stared at him, a long moment, her eyes glittering, flinty and teary together in a combination I couldn't bear. She wiped her mouth with her napkin, placed it on the seat beside her, picked up her purse and slid out of the booth. Her lips were a straight single grimness, a horizontal line on vertical rock. She turned her back and walked out.

Roger and I just sat, stupid and uncertain. I tried to decide whether I was supposed to follow her, and began to push against him to let me out when I decided I should, but I'd hesitated and the moment was lost. I didn't even see the car, because a curtain had been drawn to block the glare of the setting sun, but when I heard tires squeal, I knew she was gone.

AFTER A MOMENT OF standing on the diner floor, I took a few steps toward the door, then stopped and just looked at the door in confusion. Rog got up behind me and I felt his hand take my arm and guide me back to the booth. I slumped where Mother had been sitting, the seat still holding the heat of her body. I pushed the scraps of her salmon croquettes aside; she'd be extra angry, I noted idly, because they were a favorite of hers and she hadn't quite finished them. One more thing I'd need to remember to worry about. Rog slid back in where he'd been and slid my dinner into the spot I'd just pushed hers out of.

"Eat it, Ruthie, you're too thin. I'm sorry, I don't want this to cause problems for you," he said. "It's what I worry about most." Concern wrinkled between his heavy, near-black eyebrows. They'd always been darker than his hair. It was almost the only thing that felt familiar about him.

"I'm really not hungry anymore. What are we going to do?"

"We're going to finish eating, walk back to the motel, get an extra key at the front desk and wait for her to come back."

"What if…"

"Come on, Ruthie. She'll come back. She doesn't have much choice, you know."

"What's she going to do?"

"Not now. Let's finish eating and get back. I can see just looking at you how tired you are." And he returned to his French fries, chicken, cole slaw, with a steady knife and fork.

"There's a lot I have to tell you. I don't even know where to start. Grandmother was…I mean she was different from what Mother said, and Mother…got these blue pills from the doctor and put them in water, and then ashes…Grand Canyon." I was making hopeless stabs at the story, exhausted and completely distracted by the newest problem. I started to cry. Roger reached across the table and covered my hand, which fit entirely beneath his big one. There was hair on his knuckles I thought was new.

"Come on, Ruthie. It'll be okay." He took the napkin off his lap and handed it to me. "Don't cry. Let's go, now. It'll be okay." Of course, he didn't know how terrible things had been, but it was as though he couldn't remember how terrible things could be. Why else would he keep saying *it will be okay*, when nothing in our experience pointed that way?

"You have to help me, Roger, you have to come back and help me. I can't handle it alone, she's….not right, I mean, she needs us." I said it as we were walking across the parking lot toward the motel. Roger put his arm around me and rubbed my arm. When we reached the highway, along which we had to walk a short distance, he switched me to the inside to put himself between oncoming traffic and me. I noticed and took a little heart.

"You know I'll do what I can." The answer didn't satisfy me. I wanted words chiseled in concrete, explicit and unbreakable, but we were nearly at the entrance to the front desk. I waited outside, while Rog went in. He returned with a key.

"She won't like that we got a key. Maybe we should just sit outside the door."

"It's okay, honey." He spoke like he was my father. I so wanted to believe him, but not one iota of my life told me it was possible. Still, we went into the room. Roger turned on the lights and began moving bags and suitcases off the beds.

"I have to talk to you, I have to tell you what's gone on. Please," I tried again.

"Okay. Speak."

I sank onto one of the beds and faced him, sitting across from me on the other. I have no idea how long I talked, interrupted only by brief questions from him, when I spilled ahead too quickly. He reacted only once, lowering his face into his cupped palms when I told him about Grandmother sipping the blue capsule water. When I got to the ashes, how they'd flown up into my face and into my nose and mouth at Grand Canyon, he moved over to the bed I was sitting on and put his arm around me. My head, weighted with the unbearable visions, sank like a stone onto his shoulder. "I'm sorry," he said. "I'm so sorry."

At least he knew, now. He knew why he had to come home. "My nose is running all over your shirt. Let me get some Kleenex," I said.

"We might as well try to get some sleep," Roger responded, and stood to kick off his shoes. "Let me use a towel, will you?"

"Don't you think we should..."

"She'll come back when she comes back," he answered, his voice tired. We each washed with few more words, and Roger pulled off his sweatshirt and jeans and climbed into one of the beds in boxer shorts and T-shirt. I used the bathroom to change into a nightgown and got into the other bed. A moment later, he reached up and switched off the light.

I lay in the dark unable to let go of all I'd told him. I read the digital clock on the radio across the room, 11:57, and realized how long Mother had been gone. I felt tears start all over again. I got up to go to the bathroom, too worried to even just lie still and sink into grief. When I came back, I went to Roger's bed. "Move over," I said, in our old proprietary way.

I'd wanted him to extend his arm so I could lie on my side and rest my cheek in the hollow between his shoulder and chest the way I used to when we were children and I could siphon comfort from his body into mine. I just sat on his bed, though, in the imperceptible space he'd made, waiting for him to catch on, actually move over and invite me the rest of the way. He never did.

"I had a dream the other night. It was so strange, strong, you know? And you were in it," I said. Maybe I could make him understand how badly I needed him.

"Yeah?"

"Remember when we lived in Roseton, and those times when she would lie in bed or on the couch for days?"

"How could I forget?"

"Okay, remember that time she lay down on the couch and the frame cracked?" I felt him nod yes. "She got so mad she sort of came to and dragged it out into the backyard and just left it there. Remember it was that red flowered thing?" He nodded again. His body felt tense and I thought I was bringing back bad memories, but I wanted to tell him. "I dreamed about that couch, out in the rain. It was half floating, half sinking, because it had been raining for days and days. It looked like an empty rowboat. I dreamed it was night and I was out in that yard, and the rowboat, which was the couch, couldn't go anywhere. Then in the dream, I saw these beautiful, polished wooden oars, like they'd been handmade. I thought maybe you'd made them in woodshop…remember when you took that when you were a freshman? Anyway, the darkness was all watery, sort of, but these oars were just gleaming through it, like the moon was on them. In the dream, I'd see them but then I'd lose where they were exactly, the yard was all overgrown and filled with water, too, but then you came, and I begged you to help me find them, and you did. Do you think you can tell the future in dreams?"

Two things happened almost at once then. Roger sort of jerked up to a sitting position as he answered, like he was brimming with anger, "Take woodworking yourself, goddammit, Ruth, learn to use tools. Make yourself some goddamn oars." As he rose, my perch on the edge of his bed was dislodged, and I frantically tried to untangle my legs in a graceless clutching effort to break my fall.

IO

TWELVE HOURS LATER MOTHER and I were on the road, alone again, she furious, I dazed and terrified in equal measure. She had returned to the motel room where Roger and I lay, each awake but rigid and unspeaking on separate beds, at a little after three in the morning. I had tried to talk to him a couple of times; my mouth opened noiselessly as though the words were floating out there to be caught and instruct my tongue.

But it remained dumb. For the first time, an unbridgable chasm had split the earth we shared. Anything I could have said felt unpredictable in its effect, and so, in the end I said nothing. Neither did he.

In the car, I tried to trace the thread back to its spool, but, of course, there was no telling if Roger had decided he would refuse to come home for the summer before we ever got there. I searched the previous day and a half for the echo of his exact words, but most had dissipated and distorted into the killing fog of what had transpired between us. This much I could remember, all of it after the fact: Mother outside the door, fumbling to fit the key in the lock, and me flying across the room to open it for her. She had barely glanced at me, but directed herself to Roger.

"We'll leave after it's light. I assume your things are ready to be picked up."

He was already sitting upright, his both feet on the floor. His fists were closed and I saw a muscle jump in his cheek. Against my own heart, that moment I felt sorry for him, although I had no idea what he was about to say.

"I won't be going."

"Excuse me?" Acid.

"I'm sorry, I'm…not going. I'm staying here. I can work in the department—Dr. Chase told me months ago—as an undergraduate assistant. I can pick up an extra course, and I can manage it if I work in a restaurant, too." He picked up speed as he spoke, as though gathering strength from momentum.

"No." It was flat, unambiguous and nonnegotiable, a line to which neither of us had ever touched our toes. And certainly never crossed.

His eyes briefly pleaded. "I hope you can understand…."

"No," she interrupted. "You heard me. No. I will not hear another word on the subject."

He braced himself; I saw it, he physically, viscerally, braced himself and I understood why.

"Mother, I'm sorry, I've made up my mind. I need to stay here."

Something shifted. Mother seemed stunned, while the whole scene waved as though atoms were breaking up and rearranging themselves forever. She didn't know what to do. Her mouth opened once and shut, as mine must have been doing in the dark just a short while before, and then I felt sorry for her. I had no power to discern what was best for Roger, best for Mother, best for myself. All I could do was react to the moment in front of me, laden with history as it collided headlong with an unthinkable future.

She whirled and picked her purse up, as though to leave again. Then she must have thought better of it. Where would she go, unless she were to leave me here with Roger? She had already played the hand that used to work.

"Then get out. Get out now, God *damn* you," Mother said to him, her face flaming and deadly. She meant it, I could tell. She meant to call God's curse on him.

Roger held on to himself. "Okay," he said, very softly, and

stood, but he'd not yet taken a step toward the door when he turned in my direction and paused. "Ruthie, I'm…"

I was broken in perfect, congruent halves, like a peach with a split pit. I needed to connect with Roger however I could about what had happened between us, and here he was, speaking my name like an entreaty. At the same time, he was breaking every promise, refusing to help me, when he knew I was barely hanging on.

"You have nothing to say to your sister. And she has nothing to say to you. I said get out."

Maybe he would have changed his mind. But now Mother's only power lay in forcing what she'd put herself on the line to prevent. She instantly covered the several feet between them and roughly grabbed Roger's upper arm, simultaneously pushing and pulling him at the door. She flung it open and shoved him. When he hesitated, she shouted, "Get out, get *out*," and in an impossible gesture, raised her knee up and sideways in order to use the flat of her foot to kick at his rear. The last I saw before she slammed the door and fastened the safety chair were his eyes, white and round as a boy drowning. He looked exactly like he was drowning, about to go under for the last time. When we left the room, perhaps four hours later, after a fitful, exhausted collapse into dreamlessness, he was gone.

SHE WAS SPEAKING VERY LITTLE, and I couldn't read her. Both of us looked like death, I knew that. Deep circles ringed her eyes like carvings in wood that cast their own shadows. Her cheekbones did the same over the hollows in her cheeks, strangely gaunt over the extra flesh beneath her chin. I'd glanced at my reflection in the motel mirror when I'd washed before we left. My hair was dirty, stringy and dull around a face so pale as to make freckles leap out, three-dimensional in contrast. There was nothing to be done. I had used an old rubber band to secure my hair and looked away from the rest. My eyes and throat were scratchy, and I ached from tension or the onset of illness. I didn't know or care which.

I kept my head facing straight forward as we left Boulder. The

University buildings, and orderly, tended gardens appeared like a dream in my peripheral vision, then receded into the unknowability of Roger's life. Without a missed turn, Mother went north to pick up Route 80, then headed us east. As quickly as I got over the fact that I'd not had the campus tour Roger promised, that glimpse into the possibility of a separate life, I started longing for home, although I couldn't see how anything would be different if and when we ever made it there. I was grateful she didn't ask me to drive, though it was predictable. She was in control.

"Well. Are you hungry?" she said briskly, after perhaps a hundred miles of silence. It was a trick question; they always were. If I said "no," it could be interpreted as uncaring for her needs, being too upset by Roger when it was *her* place to be the upset one, or any variation of the theme. If I said "yes," then she could say that I must be utterly insensitive to what Roger had done to her if I could think about food. As I wrestled with which way to go, it never occurred to me to consult my stomach—to consider whether or not I was, in fact, *hungry*.

"Whenever you want to stop will be fine with me. I'm okay for now if you want to go farther, or you want me to drive."

"We'll stop, then. I never got dinner last night and I need to keep my strength." She had, of course, had dinner—most of what had been on her plate was gone before she left the diner.

"You must be starving. Of course, let's stop."

Two exits later, there were restaurant signs, and she slowed for the ramp. I was watching her closely, trying not to appear to, for a clue as to what frame she was putting around the previous night, but she gave none, except that she ordered a combination plate of pancakes, eggs and bacon and ate all of it. Roger's name was not spoken. I dabbled with tasteless scrambled eggs and toast.

"Will you eat that? You're much too thin. How are you ever going to get a boyfriend if you look like a board?"

More trick questions. I was too exhausted to sort through the ramifications of various answers, and just smiled weakly in her direction and took a forkful.

"We need to get on home as soon as we can now. You've got to get back to school."

"There's only another week, then finals. I don't see how I can take them...I...I've missed a lot."

"Well, then, I guess you'll just have to arrange makeups," she said. The conversation had the aura of unreality. Even though the subject matter was mundane, and welcome for being so, I couldn't change gear quickly enough.

"Mother, about Roger..."

"We're talking about you. If we push, we can get home in three days. You can go in Friday and talk with your teachers. I'll give you a note, of course. They'll have to excuse your absences."

"All right." I should have been relieved, but even relief was too heavy to pick up and feel. "All right," I repeated dumbly. She looked at me, then, and smiled.

"Finish up. I'm going to the bathroom." She got up from the table, which wobbled off of the matchbook someone had stuck under one leg. Her coffee sloshed in the saucer. "Damn," she said. As she picked up her purse, she gave me her penetrating look and a non sequitur, which I still knew how to insert in its place. "He'll learn," she said. "He'll learn."

INDEED, THREE DAYS LATER we were home, and Friday I did go in to school. Mr. VanFrank sighed and shook his graying head, when he read Mother's note about a family death and I thought he was angry with me.

"I'm sorry, my grandmother lives...lived in Seattle, and we had to..."

"It's not your fault," he said. "I understand how things are. Do you want to talk about it?" He took off his glasses and cleaned them elaborately before replacing them on a Roman nose. He'd grown a mustache since I last saw him, more brown than gray, so it didn't match his hair. I busied myself noticing such things while I waited for his question to dissipate in the air between us.

"I'd just like to arrange to take finals late, if I can, or make them up. Is there any way I can still be a senior in the fall?"

"We'll work it out—for you," he said, the *you* laden with emphasis. "We have to get teacher consent. If any of them won't agree, you'll have to go to summer school. Can you promise me you'll take those S.A.T.'s the first time they're offered, in September? I wanted you to take them as a junior for practice."

"I know. Yes, sir. I'll take them."

"Any thoughts yet about which colleges to apply to? Maybe you'd like to go out to Boulder with your brother?"

"I don't think that would work, sir. My mother would never go for that. She wants him to transfer back near here."

"Oh, dear. That's not good." He shook his head. "He needs to stay right where he is, an excellent program, and they've given him a first-rate financial package. Can you help out, maybe explain to your mother? Would you like me to call her?"

"I don't think that would be a good idea. Anyway, Roger said he's not coming back."

"Well, then, that *is* good. And next it's *your* turn. You keep those grades up and we'll find something just as good for you."

"I'll need to stay around here." Here we were, discussing my future, which I didn't believe I had, tiptoeing on the edge of Mother's long skirt, talking about her without talking about her. I was nervous and he sensed it, easing his gaze off me to adjust the volume on the classical music radio station he kept on all the time, and picked a dead leaf off a plant on his desk. Pictures of his children were framed on a bookcase in the tiny office, and there was a brightness to the room because of the travel posters he had put on the walls. "Florence," "Paris," "London," they proclaimed. He saw me taking them in.

"Would you like to go abroad? Someday, I mean," he asked.

"I'd love it," I said, an honest answer and, I thought, safe enough.

"Maybe you should look at places that offer a year abroad. It would be....good for you." Another meaningful, laden sentence. "Especially if you don't go far away to school."

I shifted in my seat. "That sounds great."

Mr. VanFrank gave me a long look, as though he knew I was putting him off, but let it pass. "Good," he said. "We'll keep that in mind. For now, I'll write you an admit slip. Have each teacher sign it, then get it back to me at the end of the day. I'll get a note out to each of them about makeup work and finals."

"Thanks, Mr. VanFrank. Really, thank you."

"Ruth, I have to say, I really think…you, well, your mother, but that's another issue. I think you could really benefit from some counseling. I can set something up…I'd just need your mother's permission, you know, because you're underage."

"Oh, no thank you, sir. I don't think…"

He forced me into eye contact. "Look, it would be a way to get her in. The doctor would say he had to talk with her about you, and then…" Mr. VanFrank didn't know how she'd react, but I sure did.

"Thank you. It wouldn't work, sir, but thank you."

He nodded and sighed. "We'll have to hold out for Europe, then," he said.

SOMEHOW, I PASSED. It took me most of the first month of summer vacation to get in all the makeup work, and when it was in, Mr. VanFrank met me at school four mornings in a row to take the finals, each of which was in a sealed manila envelope. My grades dropped, more B's than A's, and a C plus in trigonometry. I guess I should have expected they would, and it occurred to me Mr. VanFrank would think he'd misjudged me, that I wasn't as smart as Roger. I tried to shrug it off: *What does it matter? She'll never let me go, and I'll never do what Roger did.* I wasn't sure whether I'd want to; somedays I'd answer a hypothetical yes, but on others, loyalty overtook me like a poison gas. That's the way I see it now, anyway. Still, I got a job waitressing and the part of each paycheck I got to keep went into a savings account. Just in case.

We didn't hear from Roger for weeks. I wanted to write to him, but didn't even know where he was living for the summer, or if he was angry with me, as he'd seemed that last night. The hurt I'd felt was wiped away and returned on a regular basis, like a dusty residue on top of all my mental furniture. That night in

Boulder was unsalvageable, but murky as a long-sunken ship glimpsed from a great distance; I wasn't sure at all what had happened. Surely the bond between us transcended whatever bizarre glitch had occurred.

But there was this long silence. What could either of us say now? Indeed, what could Mother say? What would she say if he called? His name was rarely mentioned, and then only by her and in a matter-of-fact context such as, "Oh, that's just an old glove of Roger's. You can throw it out," a remark that could mean the "God damn you," she'd spit at him still held, or that things would return to normal. I agonized over nuances of interpretation.

The summer was cool and wet, which—along with having spent so much of June with schoolwork—made it seem almost no more than an idea I'd had when school started after Labor Day. I kept my word to Mr. VanFrank and took the S.A.T. exams the last Saturday of September. Coincidentally it was the day we heard from Roger.

"Your brother called," Mother said when I came home that afternoon. I'd let her think I was waitressing that day, afraid to stir her with a mention of college, so my first reaction was one of gratitude that she was distracted and wouldn't ask me how my tips had been.

"Oh. What did he say?"

"That he'd like to come home for Christmas." A certain smugness crept into her expression.

"What did you say?"

"The prodigal son returneth," she said cryptically. I wasn't sure if she was quoting herself or commenting. Afraid to ask, I just waited.

"I told him I'd been praying for him, that he'd be able to forgive himself for what he'd done."

"So he's coming?"

"I suggested he take a little more time to think it over, you know, to make sure he is *ready* to come home."

She was saving face, pretending that Roger was begging and she holding out to be sure he'd learned his lesson. For the first time, it occurred to me that Roger might win; she made no mention of his transferring. But this is just as much the truth: it did not occur to me that I could do the same.

MY S.A.T. SCORES CAME BACK, high. Mr. VanFrank called me into his office. A Beethoven piano sonata was playing, and there was a new poster, this one for Amsterdam, on the wall. He smoothed his mustache, grown into a little bush. "I don't think there's any need for you to retake these. Let's go with what you've got. Achievement tests are next. Meanwhile, what are your top three choices? Financial aid applications are going to need to go in with the admissions material, you know…will your Mother cooperate?"

"I don't know."

"I can play it the way I did with Roger, you know. How about I call her? Look, Ruth, I'm going to be honest with you. I'd like to see you get away from home."

"I don't know, sir. She may not take that very well."

That was a decided understatement. When Mr. VanFrank called and asked to see her, she let him come. Only this time she was prepared. She wouldn't fail on her own turf again. He was on the blue Goodwill chair, and she across from him on the maroon couch when she declared her mind.

"No, Mr. VanFrank. It's out of the question. Ruth may apply to schools in this area, provided she can earn enough to cover the expense. I'm not having another of my children so far away."

None of his arguments worked. He brought out brochures from a number of schools that had programs in Occupational Therapy, which I'd mentioned I might like. Really, I knew nothing about it, except that it didn't look too taxing. I was worn down.

"How about Columbia? It's a fine program. I think they'd be generous with their financial aid."

"Too far."

"Not really, Mrs. Kenley. She could take the train."

"No."

When I think back on it, the whole exchange was like a verbal chess match. I wasn't even a player. I knew about Columbia, and had told him I liked it, but little or nothing of the other schools he was touting. Finally I realized that each glossy brochure and catalog he brought out of his briefcase after Columbia was farther than New York City. He was smart.

Nothing shifted suddenly, I'm sure. When my awareness came into focus, Mother was leaning forward, her heavy breasts as precisely defined as an English teacher's dream words. She smiled and sat up straighter, crossing her legs and arranging her skirt around them.

"Well, I can see that these schools have fine programs, but Columbia appears to be the best to me."

"I'm still hoping that Ruth will take another look at Pennsylvania's program. Actually that's probably the overall best, given their internship opportunities," he said, meeting her eyes steadily. He handed her the catalog, which received a cursory thumbing from her.

"I'm sorry to be disagreeing with you," she said, only the edge of her voice blurred with coyness. "I just can't see it. The applications are expensive, you know. I think she should apply to Columbia early decision, and if she gets in, that will save the time and money that would go into other applications."

"Well, I hate to admit it, but I do see your point. Ruth, what do you think? Could you settle for Columbia?" He had played my mother the way she played her flute.

"I think so, if that's what Mother thinks is best."

And so it was settled. Before Roger came home for Christmas, bam, I'd applied and been accepted to Columbia, two and a half hours to Grand Central Station by the New York, New Haven and Pennsylvania Railroad, with one change of train in New Haven. With another bam, I was awash with ambivalence. Who would take care of Mother? Who would take care of *me*?

Ambivalence became as pervasive a theme for my senior year as *Thanks for the Memories* was for the senior prom, something else I had thought I wanted desperately. At least I'd wanted it desperately until I began talking to Suzanne Kline, who was in my Spanish IV class and who I'd begun sitting next to in the cafete-

ria at lunch at Mr. VanFrank's suggestion; she, too, was going to
Columbia. Suzanne was some thirty pounds overweight, which,
I thought, was her excuse for not being invited to the prom, but
as I got to know her, I was captivated by her confidence and rich,
loamy laugh, which she laid over my shallow attempts at conversation like topsoil, in which anything—any*one*—might grow.

"The hell with the stupid prom," she said. "Thanks for the
Memories? No, thanks. High school guys have all the desirabil-
ity of Howdy Doody and are just about as intelligent. I'd worry
about myself if one of them wanted to take me." This wasn't a
new light on an old problem—probably every gawky adolescent
girl switches it on and then back off—but the strange thing was
that I absolutely believed her. "Why don't you come over to my
house? We'll look at all the stuff Columbia has sent us, and have
a brownie orgy while we watch *Perry Mason*. I love that show.
You can spend the night if you want."

I was not very good at having friends; there had been too
much to hide. None had ever pursued me, either. Not that
Suzanne pursued me, but she steadily invited me. She had eyes
so dark brown they were nearly black and her hair was the same
color, short and naturally curly, unlike the long, ironed blond
hair that was the standard of beauty then. Suzanne didn't care
what the standard of beauty was, nor the standard of social
success and by inviting me to her house invited me not to care,
either. I was nearly ready for her.

"Okay." Then I warmed up, my emotions lagging behind
whatever I said, as always. "Yes, that sounds great." I hadn't
even asked Mother, who, it meant, would spend a weekend
night alone, for which I knew I'd pay. But right then, I was
feeling braver than anytime since I'd had Roger to lean on.
Maybe things would be all right. After all, Roger had come
home for Christmas and even if things were strained at first, he'd
survived, and Mother had taken him back, so to speak. In the
only brief privacy we'd had, no mention was made of what had
happened between us, but he took my hand and said *go for it*. I
knew exactly what he meant, and, I admit, what I was seeing
did encourage me to take heart. I didn't yet realize the cycles of

disaster and hope, how they climb on the backs of black and white horses and gallop in circles around you, only one in front of your eyes at a time no matter which way you turn.

Like most of my insights, the one I received from Suzanne, she of the hair so lustrous I took to brushing mine a hundred strokes a night, didn't last. Ronny Turley, a sophomore barely a quarter inch taller than I and cursed with an enormous mouthful of braces, asked me to the prom. Was I in the least bit interested in Ronny? Even though he didn't have acne, the particular plague of much of the male population in our school except for the haloed ones already going steady with cheerleaders, the answer was a resounding *no*. I had no idea why he asked me, either; we'd had no particular relationship other than that we sat at the same table in seventh period study hall. I didn't have enough sense or pride to grasp what he meant when he said, "A senior girl shouldn't miss her prom," a sweet but insulting sentiment coming from a sophomore boy.

"I'd love to, thanks," I said, and immediately was sorry. The demon ambivalence again: I should take this chance to be normal, I thought, but Suzanne had made our evening sound so cozy, a different kind of normal. For the first time, I began to realize that I was a sucker for men, not because I liked them so much, but because they always seemed to have what I didn't— themselves, and the freedom to leave. Maybe I thought if I glommed on to one, some of it would rub off on me.

Suzanne was nice about it, which made it all the worse. "Of course, I understand," she said. "You want to go to the prom, too, and that *was* your first choice...." Knowing that she really didn't made me envy her clarity.

"I guess," I said, and miserably banged my locker door shut. "It's not like I like Ronny or anything, though."

"Oh, God, I guess not," she said and let loose a cascade of mirth like a waterfall. It would be years before I had times of knowing my own mind, when what I truly wanted shone like mica out of rock. Even now, I batter myself with indecision, the constant practice of trying to please Mother still obscuring my will long after she's gone. Yet I can't blame this one on Mother:

I said yes to Ronny because I thought I *should,* I should want a real date before I graduated even if something else appealed to me more. It was that simple. And that miserable.

Mother took the notion of my going to the prom with surprising alacrity, and for the first time, it occurred to me maybe she had wanted to go to her prom, and that, with her recent de facto defeat with regard to Roger's school, she might be trying the tack of vicarious living. So much the better. I'd not yet lost the habit of hope for her. We went to the Goodwill store for a dress. "Look, this will fit you like a dream and it's only got this small tear in the bottom of the skirt. Looks like someone caught it in a car door. There's plenty of material—all it needs is to have the skirt removed, cut the tear out, reseam it and reattach it. I could do it myself if I had a machine." Much as I had dreaded the notion of a gown from Goodwill, this one was beautiful. Floor-length and full skirted, it was fashioned of a gauzy, off-white material. Tiny pleats and gathers puckered across the bodice, making me look much more shapely than I was. When I tried it on, the magical sweep of the skirt made me feel nearly beautiful. This is the truth: I loved that dress. Cinderella lives, I thought, in one of my more dramatic fantasies, and considered the possibility that even though I would be with Ronny, someone else might notice me. I began to be glad I was going.

But the night of the prom, the glow began to diminish before Ronny even knocked on the door, his mother waiting out in the car. When I slid the dress over my head, settled the skirt over my waist and hips and had Mother zip it up, the image in the mirror didn't match what I remembered at all. The skirt no longer had its graceful sweep, but was much narrower. A neighbor with a sewing machine had been kind enough to repair the tear by re-cutting and reattaching the skirt, just as Mother had said could be done. I hadn't realized how much the line and shape of the dress would be changed to something ordinary, or worse, drab. The light in Mother's bedroom made it look grayish instead of warm, and my hair seemed garish in contrast. At the last minute, I applied lipstick with a heavy hand and dotted some on each cheek, rubbing it in vigorously in the hope I'd appear less ghostly.

Trying to recapture the way I'd felt when I first put the dress on, I poufed the fabric out to the side and held it that way as I walked out to greet Ronny. Mother had let him in and was asking him questions that sounded coy and ridiculous to me, but he was responding like a trooper.

"You look beautiful," he said when he saw me, coached by his mother, I was sure. He handed me a corsage of white chrysanthemums, which, of course, was all wrong with the gown.

"Doesn't she, though! Goodness, these flowers are just lovely, aren't they, Ruth?" Mother chimed, pinning the corsage to my chest. "Come here, you two." I couldn't imagine what was coming. "Give me your hands." Each of us obediently extended a hand. She lowered her head. "Bless these children, oh, dear God. Light their path and instruct their hearts. Amen." I was dying, right there and then. What must Ronny think?

I wasn't to know. He spoke, covering our mutual fluster. "We'd better go—my mom is waiting in the car." Yet another humiliation. Here I was, a senior so pathetic that I was attending the prom with a sophomore whose mother was waiting in the car while my mother prayed over us. She completed the scene by etching a cross into the air as though she were the pope, as we headed for the door. I tried to regain some grace by holding my dress out to let it resemble its own royal memory.

"Leave your skirt alone, Ruth, you look like you're holding a hot air balloon under there," Mother called after me. "And have a good time, you two."

II

THAT WAS MY MOTHER'S LAST good year. Even at the time, when I was doing a verbal waltz with Mr. VanFrank and a jerky fox-trot with Ronny at that terrible prom, I had days, perhaps weeks, when my life approximated a normal one. Some part of me attributed it to Roger, as if he had intuitively divined not only what was best for him, but best for us all. And maybe he did. Even now, I really don't know what was ever best for anyone. All I know is that in our own way, we each did the best we could.

After I graduated, another summer without Roger rolled over Mother and me flattening us with its speed as it gathered momentum toward my departure. It seemed that every cent Mother let me keep out of my waitressing check went for college expenses, and college hadn't even started. I worked on a broader smile and more casual chitchat, hoping to increase my tips. But most of our customers at the coffee shop were regulars who'd come between eleven and one, wiping the sweat sheen from their foreheads and calling, "Just the regular, Ruthie, extra ice in the tea, huh?" and I'd know if that meant tuna or chicken salad on white or rye or wheat, or a burger with or without cheese and fries. The tips didn't vary more than the orders.

I was still in the habit of examining strange men, wondering if one of them looked or acted like my father. Local merchants in sports shirts who came in for an early or late lunch. Occasionally I'd get an attorney in a white shirt and silk tie, his damp jacket folded over his arm. Once in a while some school administrators came in a group, and it was strange to hear them laughing and talking about their children. One Tuesday in July, Mr. VanFrank appeared at the counter while I was wiping crumbs from a recently vacated pie and coffee order. He wore an open-necked knit shirt that nearly matched his eyes, and I realized, when he gave me a smile so large that dozens of little folds appeared around them, how glad I was to see him. How kind he had been to me, how thoroughly encouraging. What would it have been like to be his daughter?

"You'll let me know how it goes at Columbia?" he asked as he paid for his iced coffee to go.

"I promise."

"And don't let anything get in your way. You have a right to this…education, Ruth." He wanted to say something other than education.

I didn't know that I had any rights, but murmured an assent.

As if I thought I did, though, I made another try at asking about my father on the excuse of paperwork for Columbia. "Uh, Mother…I need to know, I mean this form has blanks about medical history. Um, I know what your parents died of…but, ah, is there any information about the…other side?"

She bore down on me with her eyes. "No," she said, in a tone daring me to ask more.

I took in another breath. "I'd like to know about him," I said.

"You were meant to be, that's enough," she answered. This time, though, she averted her eyes and left the kitchen. At the table, I wrote "not available" in half of the blanks, bottled rage leaking down my cheeks.

MOTHER WASN'T GOING to make it easy to go. After agreeing to Columbia with Mr. VanFrank, she'd had little to say about it, but I'd tried to do my part by mentioning it rarely and asking for nothing. The unraised topic was part of the ongoing illusion of my senior year, trailing like a vine across the summer. Of course, it couldn't go on forever. Some things had to be decided, like how

I'd get there. I didn't really want her to take me to school; I had an image of her blessing my roommate, or getting a bad feeling in the dorm and deciding I couldn't stay. On the other hand, how could I manage a trunk, a suitcase and a portable typewriter on the train?

"The traffic, Ruth. You made your bed, now lie in it. Don't think I'll be coming back and forth to get you."

Finally I called Suzanne. "Would it be possible for me to go with you and your parents? My mother's been quite sick." There was an obvious hesitation. I knew I was intruding, and that it would involve cramping them if they could fit me in at all.

"What do you need to bring?" she asked when she called back. "My parents don't think there's room. I have a trunk, how about you?"

"I only have a big suitcase and a typewriter. I'd really appreciate it," I continued on hastily, deciding on the spot to jettison the trunk and make do. It was still better than going on the train. I'd put my heaviest things in the suitcase and get a ride there, then come home the first weekend and bring back lighter weight clothing by train.

I'd not reckoned on Mother, puffy-eyed and pale, taking to her bed the morning they came to get me. She'd drawn the curtains and remained in her darkened room while I steeled myself, folding skirts and blouses over the heavy items I'd arranged on the bottom: an iron, an umbrella, shoes and the like. Before I was finished, I heard her in the bathroom. She passed me, holding a wet cloth to her head and using the wall to support herself.

"Mother! Here, let me help you."

"Leave me alone. You'll be gone in an hour and I'll have to manage, no matter what. You knew that when you made your decision."

She wouldn't kiss me goodbye when Suzanne knocked at the door, accompanied by her father, who carried my suitcase out and secured it to the car roof on a luggage rack I was afraid they'd rented. Her mother said, "We're so sorry your mother is sick. Is there anything we can do for her?" One thing I've learned: there are good people everywhere and the trick is not to ask too much of any one of them. Then you'll get by.

As we pulled out of the driveway, I saw Mother's bedroom curtain move. Her swollen face was like a wooden apparition there, marking my departure. I waved, but she was unmoving.

12

ALL THE WINDOWS WERE BARRED, even in the staff residence, which had been the old intake building before it was converted. I thought I had just taken movies with titles like *The Snake Pit* too seriously, but there they were: black, iron, at four-inch vertical intervals across the one window in the small grim room that would be mine for twelve weeks.

I'd arrived by bus, straight from my freshman year at Columbia for a summer internship in the hospital's Occupational Therapy department. Had Mr. VanFrank been clear that the summer internships were required for the first two years? Doubtless, he'd known it very well. I certainly hadn't grasped it, but then again, I don't suppose I would have wanted to.

I'd lurched and staggered through the year, going home to be with Mother almost every weekend, when I didn't study at all, but gave my time to her projects. My grades had been lower than ever in my life, and I felt as out of place with the other girls as I had in high school. Loneliness overtook me many times; my roommate, Mary, gave up on me quickly and joined a group that went out together regularly. After the first two weeks, they stopped inviting me.

And now, this: Mother, tight-lipped, saying, "I should have expected you'd do as your brother has," and knowing by that she meant *"you betrayer,"* as she withdrew behind the veils she lowered over her eyes to shut me out.

"I'll keep coming home weekends, Mother. I don't have to work weekends," I promised, even though now the trip involved a bus back into the city, then another to Grand Central, then the two trains. I took on the guilt of it when I told her how desperately I wanted to come home to be with her, but secretly I was glad I wouldn't be directly under her scrutiny all summer.

"What do you think you know about mentally ill people anyway?" she demanded another time.

Actually, I'd been reading a good deal, trying to match Mother's behavior against symptom lists in an abnormal psychology book, praying I wouldn't find a match, praying I would. I'd asked to be placed in a psychiatric facility. At the time, I believed that I wanted to learn something about my mother, to place her in the universe. In retrospect, I think that more than that, I wanted to be convinced that *I* was all right.

Anyway, they were supposed to train us. How hard could it be? That was how I looked at it then; now I see the story as an onion, growing layers around the pearly core where lodged the questions I didn't dare ask. I must have reassured myself by believing that sanity was like breathing, always on one side or the other of a dividing line, either inhaling or exhaling, breathing or not breathing, but never both at the same time.

"LOOK, IT'S NOT HARD. Lick your fingers, rub the thread between them and pull. See? That's a French knot," the instructor said to me with elaborate patience. The other four interns and I had a week to learn embroidery, copper tooling, ceramics, sand and clay sculpting, leather work and lesser crafts; we'd be expected to teach the patients *to express themselves* in these mediums. Someone looking through the barred window from the outside would doubtless have thought we were a group of patients, especially if he could glimpse the nervous effort of a slight, redheaded girl with too many freckles, who breathed as though the air in the stifling room were already used up. I made a pathetic wallet, a childlike embroidery sampler on which were displayed scraggly rows of uneven stitches, the names of which—other than French knot and chain—I have long since banished from memory, and a coiled clay pot that listed so badly it looked like the Tower of Pizza. Did I wonder about the mess of my French knots, falling apart as they did? Did I notice how the coiled clay pot might put someone in mind of a sleeping snake's impossible dream of rising? If so, I have no memory of it, and I was saved at the end of the week, by the copper tooling project. Although the design—a boat in full sail on stylized wind-whipped water—was traced, the piece (which I fashioned into a plaque by neatly nailing it to a pine square I sanded, stained and varnished) was the only craftwork I'd ever done that turned out well, and it encouraged me so much that I thought briefly about changing my major to Art.

Roger's birthday was the last weekend in June, and he was coming home for a week. Of course, I'd not seen him since the week we'd both spent with Mother over Christmas, which had been much like that of the previous year: only a little strained, but with no opportunity for us to talk freely. I think neither of us dared ripple the relatively smooth waters by trying to spend time together that didn't involve Mother. She had canceled her flute and clarinet students that week; it would have been natural for us to leave or at least talk quietly in the kitchen while sixth-graders agonized through scales and arpeggios, and it didn't seem like the lack of opportunity for Roger and me to talk was any accident. He was supportive of my being at Columbia; there'd been two brief notes in response to longer letters from me, but I missed the intimacy we'd had before that night in Boulder.

I had no birthday present for Roger. My funds were virtually nonexistent and would be until I got another check, small as it would be, the first of the next month. What I had was the plaque I'd made, which I dearly wanted to keep for my dorm room. When I first thought of giving it to Roger, I jealously rejected the idea, but it persistently reappeared as a shining solution. One of our mother's favorite aphorisms was "sail into the wind," meaning "meet challenges head-on," and it was one she used to pound Roger with repeatedly; he had tended to duck when he was small, not that he'd been doing much of that since he went away to college. Not only could I solve the gift problem, I figured to get points with Mother if I gave Roger something to remind him of her, and by the time I got home I'd decided.

After he opened a book from Mother, Roger wrapped his big hands around my present, clumsily working at the paper and fussy bow while I improvised a speech, none of it true, about how I'd made this for him thinking of what Mother always said. He loved it; I could tell the plaque touched and surprised him and for a moment I felt good about what I'd done. Mother turned very quiet, and our familiar uneasiness filled the room.

I touched her hand. "Are you okay, Mother?" I asked.

She slid her hand out from underneath mine, and avoiding my eyes, said, "Yes, of course" in a voice that was cool and remote.

As was often the case, I had no idea what I'd done, only that it was starting again, and this time she didn't want Roger involved, which meant he was in exceptionally good grace and that I would endure this alone.

Mother got up and began clearing the remains of the birthday celebration. Yellow crumbs and a few used candles slid from one of the plates. I reached to help her and she jerked back from me, her eyes fiery until she iced them over again. When she left the room, I whispered to Roger, a risk in itself.

"Do you know what happened?"

Roger shook his head, and reached to pat my shoulder. He pointed at the plaque and mouthed, "Thank you."

"Give me some time with her, will you?" I breathed.

He nodded. Then he shook his head the other way, a resigned motion. "Nothing's changed, I see. Give it up, Ruthie." I was terrified she'd hear his whisper.

"Did I do something wrong, Mother?" I asked her after Roger feigned fatigue and said he was going to shower and turn in.

"How could you do that to me?" she hissed, her eyes now wide with the wounding.

"Mother, I'm so sorry, I'm not sure what I did." I knew it would make it worse that I didn't know, underscoring my insensitivity, how all her teaching was wasted on the likes of me, as she'd predicted it would be.

Instantly she was furious. "You took what was special between Roger and me, you took it away from me, and you just had to show how clever you are, how you could make him something, you could give him something better than what I gave him." Even knowing the uselessness of it, I tried to defend myself, which enraged her more. "You just go back to that hospital where you wanted to work this summer, you just go on back there. If you don't even know how cruel that was, then you belong there."

In a terrible isolation, I took the train back the next morning, crossing the wavy heat of the city to the bus station for the trip across the Tappan Zee Bridge to Orangeburg, where the bus stopped at the main gate of the hospital.

"Ruthie, hi, I thought you weren't coming back until tomorrow," one of the other interns called as I was unlocking the door of my room. "Did you have a good time?"

"Great," I called back. "How about you?" Mother's rule: nothing was to be discussed with outsiders. Sandy looked like she was about to approach for a chat. I slipped into my room without waiting for her answer, letting the door click into place behind me. The close, colorless walls were still unadorned, the narrow bed made up with only white sheets and a small, flat pillow. I opened the single window next to the sink, its exposed pipes stuck into the wall like an afterthought, and looked out through the bars. I still prayed sometimes, and occasionally felt God, I thought, almost a visceral presence, a prickling of the scalp, a breeze from nowhere like a cobweb brushing my face. But that day, I felt nothing.

EACH OCCUPATIONAL THERAPY intern was assigned to two different wards for most of the summer, with brief rotations through the others for experience. There was the intake building, where hope lived with all new patients for up to thirty days and, in other buildings, the intermediate wards to which patients not discharged by the thirty-first day were sorted. There, if the TV

in the dayroom worked, Lucy and Desi would alternately shout
and sing, and June and Wally Cleaver reran a family no one
would have recognized even if the room were not dense with
smoke and Thorazine. By the time a patient was considered
chronic and moved to a back ward in a remote building, almost
everything was gone: all the bright, bizarre symptoms brought
to intake, the screams, the hands clutching sodden Kleenex, the
threats, even the occasional smiles were smothered into blank
faces, unroused by the mild activity associated with medication,
food and sponge baths. No one expected an intern to do anything
on a chronic ward, just "watch them," while the staff congre-
gated in the lounge and gossiped over Cokes.

I was assigned to an intermediate ward in the mornings and
to a back ward for afternoons. On the intermediate ward, time
or medication had softened symptoms, and we did things: we
worked in sand, pouring it from one container to another like
children, sculpting castles and faces by adding water. We
pounded nails into wood to make bric-a-brac shelves, we embroidered handkerchiefs while patients chatted about things that
seemed normal, everyday. Rachel, my supervisor, said, "Of
course. They're people, they have thoughts and feelings just like
you and me, and they're in a place that's safe for them, now."
As she spoke, I stared at the wedding ring on her hand, then at
the little stud earrings in her pierced ears and her blond hair,
arranged around them as predictably and consistently as
daybreak, and envied her safe life.

That night, as we picked at dissolute gray meat in the staff
dining room, I talked Sandy into piercing my ears. Two weeks
earlier, I'd seen a pair of stud earrings, tiny fourteen karat gold roses
that looked innocent and hopeful to me, and I bought them using
the remains of my first paycheck. Maybe I thought of wearing
pierced earrings as a talisman of the sort of a grown woman's life
spent with a kindly man, a father or protector, a man like the prince
girls were taught to dream of. I asked Sandy to do it because she
had not only pierced ears, but a solitaire diamond in a gold Tiffany
setting on her left hand. For all I knew these were connected, in a
secret world, closed to me, in which there was refuge.

Sandy and I brought two cups of ice from the staff dining room to numb my lobes. With great care I put tiny dots on each, to mark exactly where I wanted the holes. We removed the shade from the bedside lamp and brought the single straight-backed wooden chair to the side of it. Sandy threaded a large sewing needle with white thread and wedged a wine cork behind my ear. She lifted my hand and placed it on the cork. "Okay, Ruthie, hold this in place. Does your ear feel numb? I'll stick the needle through really fast. Once it's through, you don't feel it at all." I believed her. I thought she had probably had sex with her fiancé; she knew about these things. The thread was to stay in place only long enough to mark the tiny new hole, through which the posts of the earrings, soaking in clear alcohol, would slide painlessly.

I heard the cartilage of my ear lobe crackle. The needle was stuck in my flesh. I jerked my hand away; Sandy caught it, an edge of disguised panic in her voice as she said, "We can't stop now, it's stuck in halfway. What's the matter? Can you feel it?" I dumbly nodded my head, eyes watering from the stinging pain. Sandy's hands which had seemed steady and capable were birdlike, fluttering. Her diamond flashed once in the harsh light of the naked bulb, and then I kept my eyes closed.

LOIS WAS IN MY intermediate group. She was loud, buxom, bossy, and appeared supremely self-confident. One morning shortly after I first met the group, she asked me: "So what books did you have to read for your psychology classes?" I listed some; Lois had read them all. She asked if I'd read *The Mature Mind*. Without thinking, I responded. "I love that book—have you read *The Mind Alive* by the same authors? That one is really my favorite. They analyze the traits of people with good mental health."

"No, I've not read that one. Can I borrow it?" she asked. I was unprepared.

"Sure, I'll, uh, I'll look for it," I answered, studying my hands.

That weekend I went home again. I'd sensed on the phone that the cycle was rounding a turn. Not directly, not openly, but

Mother had begun to forgive me. I knew by the slight lessening of the tension on the ropes with which she held me. But as I walked from the train station toward our house, the signs were not good. The blacktop, melting and bubbling, stuck to my sandals, and dull heat seemed to rise up from around my feet, enveloping my head until it throbbed with my slowing heart.

"You're so lucky you're skinny and flat chested," Mother said to me, one of her devastating compliments. She pulled up her blouse and hefted a watermelon breast with one hand to show me the angry heat rash there, then lifted her cotton skirt and spread her legs revealing the same where her thighs chafed one against the other as she walked. I considered my response carefully.

"Yes," I said. She was speaking to me again, but I knew I was being tested. The afternoon was steamy and breathless. An ancient fan wheezed in the kitchen, turning its head hopelessly, surveying the faded, cracked linoleum, the chipped Formica of our kitchen table, three mismatched chairs. I'd hoped we might go out to the lake, but Mother wanted me to clean. As I vacuumed, she sat on the couch, perspiration rolling from her face. She ran her hand through the hair on her neck, lifting it from her skin while sticking out her lower lip to direct a long sigh upward, rippling the fringe of bangs limp against her forehead. For weeks, the patients on the wards had been sluggish in the same motionless heat, which was palpable and constant as an evil possessing all our minds and blurring boundaries. A fat psychiatrist had seemed to melt in group therapy, silent until he erupted in a rage at one of the patients who wouldn't answer him, overturning his chair as he tried to extricate his body to leave.

"Answer me!" Lois had demanded like his echo when I entered the O.T. room, after that session. "Did you bring the book?" I'd nervously felt the earring in an infected lobe, turning it to break the scab again.

"I'm sorry, Lois, I forgot it. I'll try to remember the next time I go home." The book wasn't at home; it was in my room in the staff residence building.

"I'll write you a reminder note, maybe you can keep it in your sticky little fist long enough to remember. I know it's a big thing for a busy person with a life like yourself," she'd said, her voice saturated with bitter sarcasm. She caught herself and added, "It's okay. I would really like to read it, though, if you'll loan it to me."

"Yes, of course, I'm sorry I forgot it," I'd answered.

"Dammit, Ruth, what the hell are you doing? You ran that thing right over the lamp cord. You'll start a fire, is that what you want, are you trying to kill me?"

"I'm sorry, Mother, I didn't realize…"

"You're sorry, you're sorry. You're dangerous. Pay attention, you hear me?" She struggled up from the couch and approached, jerking the wand from my hand when she reached me. She drew the metal wand back and hit me hard across both shins with it. Then she began to cry. Vacuuming furiously, in ragged motions across the carpet, she sobbed, "I'm so tired of having to do everything myself. I ask someone to do one thing and she can't do it right. You might as well go on and leave now, you're going to anyway. I'm so tired of it, I'm so tired of you," she finished, wheeling to face me, her face swollen and red with the heat and her tears. Right then, Mother noticed the earrings. "You cheap little tramp. You look like a whore who'd go chasing after anything in pants, a gigolo like…" Her voice clipped to silence. Instinctively I knew what she'd bitten off; she couldn't say "your father" and remain blameless. She raised her hand toward my face: I flinched and turned aside. With a guttural sound of rage and one step of pursuit, she grasped the earring and yanked down, ripping it from my ear in one heavy motion. I gasped in the sudden furious pain. I believe she meant to throw the earring out the open window, but her aim was high and it pinged against the glass like a pebble, bouncing onto the floor and skittering almost back to our feet, where it lay with its back clasp neatly still in place. Mother put one hand against each side of her head, her face screwed into an intense agony, and dropped to her knees. She swayed there for what seemed forever, her eyes tightly closed. "Jesus. Jesus. Jesus," she moaned, a curse, not a prayer. I stood helpless, afraid to touch my tattered ear, afraid to approach her, afraid to leave, tears all over the surface of my body, too small a world for that tide.

"OH, GOD, WHAT HAPPENED? Sandy's hand flew up to cover her mouth. I'd double-checked that my ear was covered by my hair before I went to Sandy's room Sunday evening to tell her I was back and catch up on the latest about Mark. It backfired. Sandy had looked at the heavy curls against my neck and said, "Aren't you roasting with your hair down? You should keep it off your ears anyway, until they're healed…how are they doing?" In the intimacy of girlfriends, a whole new experience for me, she'd just reached over and flipped my hair back over my shoulder to get a look at her handiwork.

I was reasonably ready for her. My first inclination had been to try to avoid Sandy until the ear healed, but I'd realized two things: it was going to take a long time, and I really didn't want to anyway. I was attracted to Sandy's openhearted friendship, by the way she sang "How Sweet It Is (To Be Loved By You)" to Mark's framed picture on her dresser, made room for me in the circle of her exquisitely normal life. Mother had predicted we'd be seduced by the world if we left home, and I'd persistently insisted that *I'd* not, at least. Even though I tried to keep it from her, even though I was ashamed, I was being drawn in. I thought I could have a life and keep my word, though. I still thought that.

"Oh, I know," I said. "Doesn't it look awful? I washed my hair at home and when I was brushing it out I forgot about my ears. You know, I'm not used to it. Anyway, there was a tangle, you know, and I yanked the brush through—it caught on my earring and ripped it right out."

Sandy moaned. She leaned in close to examine it, even took my shoulders and rotated me so it would be in better light. Then she looked me in the eyes. "It looks worse than that," she said. "Are you…"

Shamed, I tried not to avert my eyes. A flush began to rise as I cast for what to say. Then, bless her, Sandy dropped it. Maybe even that soon, she had an inkling.

MOST OF THE PATIENTS ON Building 3's chronic ward were elderly, "burned out schizophrenics," the nurses said, still hospitalized less because they were sick than because they had been there so long they had nowhere else to go. One had a niece who had written her a weekly letter for thirty-one years, two dollars allowance always in it, which Ella folded and refolded and tucked in the pocket of the faded print housedress she wore, struggling to tilt her body sideways in her wheelchair to expose the pocket on the side seam.

"Such a sweet girl, such a sweet girl," she crooned, patting my arm elbow to wrist in long strokes while I listened to stories about her mother's long tubercular dying while Ella was a girl, and the daughter she named after her mother who died, too, and said, "Oh, I just know your mother loves you so much, she's so happy to have a sweet girl like you." Some days I just said, "Yes," but some days I was too hungry for someone to call me a sweet girl and said, "Well, I don't know," so that Ella would wrinkle her forehead and say, "Oh, no, oh, no, she has to love a sweet girl like you" again, all the while stroking my arm with her pale, wrinkled hand. Sometimes she called me by her daughter's name, Therese.

"And what about your daddy?" she asked one day.

"I don't know what happened to him."

"Oh, oh, oh," she half sighed, half moaned in sympathy. "Oh, oh. My baby's daddy died a year after she did. By his own hand, if you know what I mean, dear. It was too much for him." She shook her head. "Just too much. My Therese. Sometimes, I think maybe it was best she did die, no daddy, you know, and just me then, a crazy old mother, when I get mixed up and I try to remember what happened first, you know? I can't remember what happened first."

My tears came up to meet hers. No daddy and a crazy mother, and no clue which happened first.

THE INTERMEDIATE PATIENTS had been doing an embroidery project. "That's not how you do a daisy," Lois had corrected me and taken over teaching the patient with whom I'd been working, dismissing me with a gesture of her hand. I moved across the room to sit with another patient, but she took up grilling me about my courses and books in a cultivated voice that carried across the room, her comments imbued with learning. She was, she said, currently interested in the experimental use of certain of the B vitamins in the treatment of schizophrenia. "By the way," she said, as though it were casual, but searching me, "did you remember to bring that book you said you'd loan me?" When Rachel came in toward the end of the session, Lois's face was blotched and tear-tracked. I'd said I had forgotten the book again, and Lois had begun to cry. "I don't have any other way to get it. I can't get any books I want like you can."

"You don't want to loan Lois your book, do you?" Rachel said after the patients had been dismissed to return to the ward. Her inflection was not questioning, but she spoke gently and privately. I felt a flush creep up my neck and face.

"No, it's okay, I just keep forgetting," I said. Rachel shook her head slightly and touched my hand. Just then, the Good Humor truck pulled up the driveway of the staff residence, sounding its bells and music for staff members who were off duty or on break.

"Come on," she said. "I'll buy you an ice cream and we'll talk." Some of the patients were crowded around the window looking at the truck through the bars that striped every view, and talking about Creamsicles and Popsicles and nutty cones. Lois's forehead was pressed against the upper glass. She pulled it away, still teary, leaving a smudge of oil there, as though she'd been anointed and was leaving that vague mark of her life.

"No, thanks, Rachel, really, I just forgot. I'll bring the book next time I go home."

That afternoon, perhaps because of the wilting heat, the Good Humor truck came back, slowly circling the narrow driveways between and around the buildings. Doubtless, the driver was looking for staff members, many of whom did run out to get themselves something, but it was torment to the patients—who had often no money and couldn't have gotten beyond the first locked door anyway if they had—to listen to the bells and be left to their longings. Sometimes the image of my mother as a patient here came to me and I'd shake my head to clear it.

Even on the third floor, where I sat with Ella, we could hear the ice-cream truck clearly. Ella struggled to reach her pocket and pressed a damp dollar like a fern into my hand.

"Won't you go get me an ice cream? Get one for yourself, too, and keep the change, dear, for your trouble. I'm so hot, I can just taste it, can't you? Wouldn't that be one nice thing?"

It was absolutely against the rules, but even now I can feel how much I wanted to please her, this old woman with tufts of sad, gray-white hair whose forehead and neck glistened with perspiration in the heat accumulated in the ward like a kingdom uncome, who stroked my arm and called me a sweet girl. "Wouldn't that be something nice?" she repeated.

I glanced at the door of the lounge, where the staff seemed catatonic themselves.

"I'll try, Ella. Don't tell where I went, though."

It was a long trip, unlocking and relocking doors and waiting for the rickety elevator that stopped at each floor on the trip down, the wide expanse of dead lawn to cross and return over, brittle brown grass crunching beneath each step as though even the memory of green had been killed. Before I was back inside the building, a watery little stream of cool vanilla had leaked from beneath its chocolate casing and reached my finger. I shifted the ice cream to my left hand and licked my right. As my tongue mopped it, the liquid was already warm. The elevator was crowded and on each floor white-clad staff listlessly and unhurriedly pushed the hold button as someone approached from a distance calling "Going up." On the fourth floor, three doors to unlock and relock behind me; through an open window I could hear the tinny song of the Good Humor truck pulling out and fading like *follow me away, follow me away,* to anyone who could, cutting out whenever the truck hit a bump, as though iron bars sliced the sound as it entered.

Ella wasn't where I had left her. As unobtrusively as possible, I checked among the patients staring blindly at steady static on the TV or slumped sideways, asleep in their wheelchairs in the dayroom, the bathroom and finally, the ward where narrow empty cots lined the walls. I found her there; she'd wheeled herself a laborious distance so as not to be caught with the ice cream. "Therese," she said, "Therese," as I walked toward her quickly, dread-filled, turning the stick to catch the rapid drips. I would have done anything to get that ice cream to her intact, but like dread's foretelling, it plopped off the stick onto the floor in front of her even as she reached for it, even as I tried to catch the sticky mess with my other hand. A blob of vanilla flecked with shards of chocolate coating spread on the worn tile between us. I sank on the bed and lifted the hem of my skirt to hide my face, and pressed it hard against my eyes. When I could open them to look at her, tears had reached the corners of Ella's cracked lips, wetting them to a shine, and she licked them. More ran down as she said, "It wasn't your fault, what happened, Therese, it wasn't your fault."

That night, as usual, I cleaned my infected earlobe with alcohol. As usual, too, when I replaced the bottle on my night-stand, I noticed the spine of *The Mind Alive* where it lay beneath a short stack of books and resolved again to take the book to Lois if morning came. Then, as I'd been doing all summer in order to sleep in the torpor, I soaked a towel in the coldest water the naked sink in the corner of my room would pipe and spread it across my pillow. Someone might have thought it was crazy, that pillow, as sodden as if the tears of a life might never dry; as if night after airless night any woman might lie alone on top of sheets, grieving for all she's lost or never had; as if any woman might try for the cool dream of ice cream in such a night, the tinny song in her mind repeating and repeating.

13

MORE THAN ANYTHING ELSE, I wanted a man. Or, more accurately, a man who would become a husband. I was a relentlessly serious young woman; all the dating stuff was just preliminary and an enormous waste of time if it wasn't aimed like an arrow at the altar. Every man—well, more accurately again, every boy—I met, I sized up and rejected on the grounds of his marriage potential, and by that summer, I already knew it was going to be tough. He would have to fit in with my family, difficult for anyone who lived on the right side of the boundary between rational and irrational, and loving me enough to even try could be equally problematic. Maybe part of what took me to Rockland was my cross-country trip with Mother the previous year. Perhaps it had begun to occur to me that a man with a certain type of experience could help me help her. I still thought that if she were happy, I could be, too.

I first saw Joshua in the staff cafeteria, winding overcooked spaghetti around his fork, and asked if he was saving the seat next to him for anyone, a ridiculous ploy since the cafeteria was nearly empty. We struck up a conversation and after that, I began timing meals to be able to set my tray next to his. Within a few days he was seeking me out if he'd been delayed or my timing had been off. It wasn't his looks that attracted me: only a little taller than my five-five, he had intensely curly hair, lackluster brown, and a short, sparse beard which got even thinner as it crawled up his cheeks to meet his sideburns. His eyes were an indistinguishable gray-blue, small and blinking at daylight like a nocturnal animal behind his glasses. He told me he'd been clean-shaven until he came to Rockland as a social worker, but thought he needed to look older than twenty-four because as "Discharge Planner," he had to deal with patients' families and community businesses. I had answered that a five-year-old would look old enough because as best I could see no patients were *ever* discharged, which elicited a pained look and a detailed explanation of why that was incorrect. I reined myself in to his earnest humorlessness. It was the *seriousness* of him that was important after all.

And, besides, there was that universal honey to draw me to him, deadly and irresistible. I'd seen him looking at me, and could tell that he found *me* attractive. Take a woman who's scared enough, and she'll *marry* a man she can't stand if it's plain he finds her desirable. But I didn't marry Joshua Levertov, in spite of the fact that he met the basic criteria. Mother saw to that long before the question could have formed on his tongue. It's just as well. He had feminine hands and blew his nose ostentatiously and often; he would have driven me insane. That's the truth, but on the other hand, if I had married him she would still be with me. I never would have really loved him, and wasn't that what finished it after all? Of course, I didn't know that then. I try not to recriminate anymore, to stop adding item after item to the list of all I didn't know.

"BUT DOESN'T IT SOUND like an enormous job to you?" Josh asked plaintively. "I mean, don't you wonder how one social worker could plan out lives for every patient within thirty days of discharge?"

"Yes, yes. Do tell. How does one superman handle it all?" I was still occasionally trying to be funny.

Wounded, he set down his fork and considered his answer. I swatted at a noisy black fly circling my tray, and realized I had gone too far. Not many people were in the huge dining hall because it was late, twilight already, and the sky darker than it should have been with incipient thunder.

"Josh, I'm sorry. I'm just hot and tired and sick of being hot and tired. Do you think it's going to rain?"

"You should want to know about this, Ruth. If you go into social work…"

"I'm not going into social work, though."

"It's better money than O.T., and there's a lot more intellectual challenge."

I was coming to agree with him about the intellectual challenge, at least here. Theory seemed dog-eared on a good day. I couldn't really see that I was doing anything but keep patients busy doing elementary school crafts for a little bit of the day so that the important work of mopping the dayroom floor and sanitizing the toilets could be accomplished. Still, I couldn't let him go unchallenged.

"What exactly do you know about occupational therapy?"

"Sand tables. Fingerpaints. Leather tooling."

I tried to act like a woman, after all. "Yep. That's about it," I said, squeezing out a smile like reluctant toothpaste. "So what would a social worker do with someone like Lois? Up on O. T., we let her pound sand. Literally."

"She's that big woman you've got on Intermediate? Loud and bossy? I only saw her a couple of times when they rotated me through for orientation." Josh had gone back to picking at the beef noodles on the heavy institutional plate which he'd lined up neatly with side dishes of canned beans and a lettuce salad. Sweat had plastered the edges of his hair to his forehead.

"That's the one." I was uncomfortable about Lois, and not only because of the book. She was so confident, so sure she knew The Truth on any subject. How could that not make me squirm in recognition?

"As I remember, Lois is a personality disorder, but I don't know what brought her in to begin with. Some manic depressive symptoms? I can't remember. A psychotic episode, maybe. Or a major depression." He used two slender fingers of each hand to put quotes around the diagnosis. "She's a tough cookie. Personally, my discharge plan would probably include setting her up for a date with Jimmy Hoffa. Buy her some cement shoes and suggest she meet him for a nice swim with the fishies." He laughed then, softening it. "Usually personality disorders aren't hospitalized for long unless they're suicidal," he said. "People like that are pretty destructive, especially with other people, but the thing is, the prognosis isn't very good."

"Why not?" I tried to remain casual. I couldn't eat, though, and pushed the plate to one side.

"Because therapy just doesn't usually work and neither do drugs. It's real hard to move them. And they're incredibly manipulative… So, anyway, when am I going to meet your family?" he said after a beat of silence, mollified by my having asked him about a patient. Josh reached across the sticky table and put his hand over mine. I *wanted* him to do that, but when he did I always chafed and would suddenly have to do something that required my hand be moved as soon as I decently could.

I wanted to probe for more about Lois. "Just finish what you're explaining. So what happens to someone like her?"

"Lois? I don't know. Sooner or later, someone will pronounce her cured and we'll turn her loose. How long has she been here?"

"I don't really know. Over thirty days, obviously, but I got the impression it was pretty long. I can ask Rachel, or look in her chart."

"Doesn't matter. Maybe she's been in and out. Sometimes their families try to get them back in when they can't take anymore." Josh laughed then, which bothered me as much as anything he'd ever done. "Anyway, back to us. When am I going to meet your family?" he asked, wiping his mouth on his napkin and then running the crumpled paper up and over his forehead. "Whew. Wouldn't you think the state would take pity and air-condition this place? At least for the staff? Maybe I can go with you this weekend?"

"Right now, it's really only my mother. My brother is at the University of Colorado, remember? But I wasn't planning to go home this weekend."

"Wow. Why not? This is the second weekend you've stayed here."

"I thought maybe you and I could do something special. And Sandy wanted me to come to her house for dinner one night, too. You know, her family's only a half hour from here, and she's got her mom's car this week." This was dishonest. I wasn't going home because after the earring incident, Mother had withdrawn again, back to the desolate place she'd visited so many times, and had cut only curt, thorny phrases when speech was unavoidable. I'd known that leaving before Sunday night would be damnable so I had stayed, enduring the punishment of her silence and tears. When I left, though, I had flat-out lied to her, saying that I'd been asked to work the next few weekends because the chronic ward was short staffed. "It's because of vacations," I'd earnestly assured her. I'd never done this before, lied strictly for myself, I mean.

She had looked right through me and made no response. Since returning, my insides had been raw and unfamiliar. I'd begun rereading *The Mind Alive,* trying and hoping—without wording it so—to distinguish Mother from Lois. It was always a guilty balm, too, to go to Sandy's, whose home reminded me of Suzanne's. Settled. A made life that might hold a person in place. Her own bedroom with mementos tacked up: swimming medals, play programs, pictures of laughing teenagers. Pink curtains that matched the dust ruffle and quilt on her bed. Cranberry throw rugs on polished hardwood. Feminine, white furniture. A dressing table with a white skirt, edged with eyelet. She teased her mother and father. And, of course, Sandy's engagement ring still flashed its reassurance to her like a personal word from God every morning and night. She knew what her life would be and it was a life she wanted. So when I saw her kiss Mark, I studied her face. She liked it. She was normal. Maybe I could be, too.

"Great," Josh responded. "What would you like to do? Dinner? A movie? Dinner and a movie?" This was good; he'd pay, for one thing, and these were normal things to do.

"Whatever you'd like best." I wanted him to like me. With a gesture of apology, I slid my hand from beneath his to revisit my cherry pie, which had a hard, uninspired machine-crimped crust. The filling had a perfumy aftertaste, terrible, hardly a passing resemblance to anything natural.

SATURDAY NIGHT WE HAD dinner at a highway steak house, inexpensive enough that we sat in vinyl booths at a table set with a plastic tablecloth. Still, a single candle burned in a Mateus wine bottle, its wax dripping green over and between the bumpy ridges left by red and blue forerunners, and a track of popular music played softly for background. I resolutely ignored "I'm Not in Love" and tried to think of "How Sweet It Is (To Be Loved By You)" as applying to Josh and me, even though it was Sandy and Mark's signature song. I was not uncomfortable. In fact, I was as comfortable as I'd been with anyone since Roger. Maybe I even realized it a little then: I was looking to replace my brother, too.

"So what do you plan to do in the future? Is glorious Rockland your career home?" I asked the loaded question lightly.

Josh's voice was earnest, his look direct at my face. "That depends on what happens between you and me."

I nodded stupidly, not sure if he meant what I thought he might, the possibility that we would become serious about each other. I looked at him closely, trying to decide if I was in love with him. Or could be, at least.

"I mean, if something were to develop..." he added. He'd worn a jacket and tie, not as great a sacrifice as it might have seemed if the restaurant weren't air-conditioned, but a sign, nonetheless. I'd worn one of Sandy's sundresses, too, a light green that she wanted me to keep because, she said, it brought out my eyes.

Another nod from me. "My mother," I began. "My mother... well, it's sort of unusual, she's raised me and my brother alone, and I owe her a lot. What I mean is, I need to take care of her."

His turn to nod. "Of course. That's the right thing to do." A good answer, I thought. He reached for my hand. "I really like being with you," he said.

I stroked his forefinger with my thumb and gave the rest of his hand a slight squeeze.

"Is the difference in our background a problem for you?" he asked.

To the contrary. The night before, I'd gone to Sandy's. Her father and brother and Mark had attached yarmulkes to their heads with bobbypins before her father had begun a ceremony of candles, prayer and wine. The ritual seemed richly incomprehensible to me, trustworthy, a down quilt into which I could sink and rest like a cared-for child. "No, I'd like to study Judaism," I said. "I mean, I think it's beautiful." That statement exhausted my total concept of his religious and cultural heritage, but the mystery of it contained the potential for answers.

He must have needed someone as badly as I. Why else would we be discussing such things when all we'd shared were cafeteria meals, lingering over iced tea and a walk back to the staff quarters building? We'd not so much as kissed. Not that I had any desire to kiss him, but I guessed I was willing if it would prevent his disappearance. He looked at me meaningfully, but what I got stuck on were squinty eyes and hairy lips that suddenly sickened me. It was too much too quickly, but I couldn't back away.

"DON'T YOU THINK HE'S good-looking?" I asked my mother when Josh excused himself to the bathroom before dinner.

"His beard is scraggly. I always liked the clean-shaven look," was all she said. The first meeting was not going well. I felt it, with the antennae I'd developed over the years with her, rather than knowing it in any rational way. She was being too polite, distantly warm. He was trying too hard. I was in the middle, wanting too much for it to work.

Later, when he put his hand on my leg as we sat next to each other on the sprung blue couch twice conquered by Mr. Van-Frank, she looked at me with bullet eyes until I shifted my weight and recrossed my legs in a way that caused him to move his hand.

"Your mother doesn't like me," Josh said as the bus jostled us from the city back out to Rockland. "What was so bad about what I said about Nixon?"

"Calling him Tricky Dick, maybe…" I didn't want to get into

it. Mother's politics were erratic if she gave a thought to the world. She'd loathed John Kennedy until he was dead and then she nearly burned down the house lighting candles for him, but I rarely had to concern myself with managing the wider world. The war in Vietnam had largely been a nonevent for us; since the draft didn't affect Roger, Mother was inclined to believe whatever the president of the moment said about it. "It's not that, Josh," I sighed. "It just takes her time. She doesn't take to people quickly."

"It's more than that. She just really doesn't like me. Why? Did she say anything to you?"

"Not really."

"He's all right, I guess," was what she'd said. "Someone should have taught him not to bang his teeth on his spoon when he eats soup." And, "I'm surprised that his hemming and hawing doesn't get on your nerves. I like a man who has a definite opinion."

"So what…synagogue? Do you attend?" she'd lobbed at him, setting him up.

"Well, I'm really eclectic in my religious tastes." He'd taken a swing and missed.

"I think it's important to honor one's own heritage," she'd served again.

"Yes, yes, indeed it is. I plan to join one just over in Spring Valley." He conceded early, having learned.

I surprised myself by seeing him a few more times after mother met him, but it petered out quickly. Maybe he got tired of my fending him off, my practice of chastely angling my face at just the right moment so his mouth fell off center, sort of partly on my lips and partly on my cheek. When his hand slid from my waist down to my hip and then began to creep around me like kudzu, I pulled back and said, "Josh, we really shouldn't," as though I, too, wanted that intimate touch.

What it came down to was that I really didn't think enough of Josh. Had I loved him even a little, the relentless chastity I claimed on moral grounds wouldn't have been so easy. That very chastity was why I could, in the end, give him up. He never had my body, and he certainly never had my soul; Mother still had that.

14

JUST LISTING THE WAYS IN WHICH my notions of marriage were wrong would make a chain of words that could be looped around the institution numerous times. And I didn't learn anything to correct them from my summer with Joshua. I was never able to overcome the small shudder that went through me when he mashed his lips hard against mine, or worse, tried to wedge his tongue into my clenched mouth, all of which just fueled my worry that I wasn't normal.

At Christmas, Mother, Roger and I spent better than a week then with our much-touted family traditions—carols on the record player, a motley crèche, tree ornaments we'd made in elementary school alongside too-bright, fragile store-bought ones, and Mother's invocation of heavy symbolism regarding various miracles she anticipated in our lives. It seemed an enormous amount of work to fabricate the wonder she expected in our eyes, part of the whole business of creating Christmas for her.

Roger and I had minimal time to talk directly. The day before he was to leave we instinctively colluded to have some. At least I believed it was our old mind-reading and cooperation, but maybe it was just what it seemed: a fortuitous accident. Mother wanted to exchange the sweater Roger had given her before he left so he could see her wear it, and was going to the dress store in town. Roger had already said if she wanted him to spend time with her after dinner, she'd have to let him get packed and organized in the afternoon. It was the Roger who had a mind and life of his own and who said and did what he wanted. Openly. When she came looking for me to go with her, I pretended to be asleep. She shook me lightly. "Come on with me for company. They might not have the same thing in my size, and then I'll have to choose something else."

"Mother, I'd better stay here. I've got a bad headache and my stomach doesn't feel so good." It was code for getting my period.

"All right, then. I guess I'll just go on by myself. You'd best take a nap so you'll feel better to take Roger to the airport with me tomorrow. I'll get the Midol."

"I'll be okay."

When I heard her car clear the driveway, I was up. Roger looked at me knowingly and continued to fold clean T-shirts and boxer shorts, laying them on the kitchen table in two tidy stacks. "Feeling better?" he smiled. It felt like old times when we'd shared small seditions.

"Yeah. I guess I am," I gave him his smile back, but kept my lips closed, afraid to risk the teeth of our recent history. I needed him. "Can we talk?"

"Sure. How're you holding up? I heard you were dating someone." Of course Mother would have told Roger.

"*Were* is correct. Past tense."

"She didn't like it, did she?"

"I don't know. It really wasn't her fault, I just…" I put on the kettle to make myself a cup of tea and so I wouldn't have to look at him. Outside the window, the sky tried to keep a heavy load of unfallen snow to itself, but flakes were starting to escape here and there.

He stopped folding. "Ruthie, you can't let this happen. Don't you see yet? She's sick."

"The guy…Josh…just didn't…it wouldn't have worked. I didn't like him all that much, anyway."

Well, the last was certainly true enough. I wasn't going to mention how the non-love affair died even before I went back to school. "Do you ever say no to your mother? About anything?" Josh had finally demanded, albeit mildly, when I told him—again—that I couldn't see him because Mother wanted me with her over the weekend. ("Of course I do," I'd answered. Liar.)

"The guy is beside the point. *She...is...sick.* As in *disturbed.*" Roger enunciated the words very slowly, as though trying to penetrate the fog around a mental defective, the same way the staff talked to Thorazine patients at the hospital.

"How do you know that?" I demanded. "Exactly who died and made you Dr. Freud?"

"Oh, for God's sake, Ruth. Grow up. She's a virgin? You worked at a mental hospital. You think it's just normal that she denies we even have a father? Or fathers? She's not a virgin, she's *crazy.* You and I both know she's plain crazy."

"I don't think that. She's just been hurt a lot." Now I could segue neatly to my subject. I quit rummaging for a tea bag so I could face him down. "We have to help her."

He shook his head and kept shaking it as he spoke. "Don't you get it? *We can't help her.* What you do isn't going to make any difference." The words were tumbleweed spinning in a vehement wind.

My voice went directly to indignant. "That's it? How about all your promises? How about me? Sometimes I can manage, but sometimes I can't anymore. She gets...bad."

"I *know* she gets bad. That's the whole point. You don't make her get bad and you can't get her over it." He was getting exasperated. Another T-shirt came up against his chest to be folded, but it surely wasn't a white flag.

"Roger. Rog. We said we would be together. How can you just *bail* on us now?" I was starting to cry, making little effort to fight it down. It used to bother him when I cried.

"This is *not* about that or anything else," a hoarse shout on the *not.* His ears flamed and the same red flushed his cheeks, and even his neck in the V between the open top buttons. "I'm not just jumping ship..."

"Yes, you are!" An answering shout, now furious tears running with the others.

"I'm not. I mean, I'll give what I can, I'll come home when I can, I'll do what I can, but there's no point. You don't see that. There's no point. You're not going to make anything different." His voice was sandpaper, angry.

"But I can prove that not everyone betrays her, not everyone is like that."

"And then?"

"I can make up for bad things that have happened to her. I can help."

"And then?"

He was infuriating me. He could say, "And then?" forever, obviously.

"How can you just give up on someone you love?" Those were my words, but really, I was pleading, not asking a question.

"It's called reality." Now he got softer, explaining life to his forty-watt bulb sister again.

"It is not reality. Reality is that she hurts and we can help."

"You just don't get it, Ruthie. You're my sister and I love you, but you just don't get it. You can't always help. That's the truth whether you want to see it or not. There's just no point in going down with her. Couldn't you talk to someone? At school? There are people to talk to, you know."

Shades of Mr. VanFrank. Only Roger was smart enough not to suggest Mother might even be tricked into getting any kind of help. So what would Roger's nifty see-a-psychologist-at-school idea accomplish? *I* didn't need therapy, for God's sake, I needed help with Mother. Why didn't Roger get it? "She's not going down. I won't let that happen," I said.

He shrugged. "Okay. So maybe she doesn't go down. She won't go up, either. And neither will you. I'm not saying people shouldn't do what they can, I'm just saying there's no point in drowning yourself in a futile effort to save someone who's been underwater for years."

"I see you take your religion seriously."

"Welcome to crucifixion, Ruthie." He held his hands straight out parallel to the floor in a mocking gesture, then suddenly withdrew them. "I'm sorry. I didn't mean that. All I mean is that I don't think there's anything we can do. I'm sorry."

I just stood there spilling tears, not even wiping them as I looked at Rog, square and massive in the late afternoon slanting sun, remembering how much I'd loved him, how much I'd believed in him. Now he was lost. As I remember it now, that's exactly the way I thought of it—*he* was lost and had been since the night in Denver when the good blood between us turned poison. Once I got hold of that, as I stood there arguing and crying, I began sliding back in time to where life had shone with a magnificent clarity. It's like if a partner resigns from a business you started together—and starts challenging its founding principles. Human defensiveness gets revved up so loud the noise drowns out whatever doubts might have been whispering their worries in your mind. And if the business was your whole life? Everything you believed in, sacrificed for, thought you required? Well, you'll ignore plain logic, plain common sense, plain-as-your-nose evidence that maybe he's right. Instead you make up reason to believe, gun that engine, pretend you don't hear what's in your own head.

Of course, I see it now: the noise just gets louder and louder, the doubts start shouting to be heard, and then comes the explosion.

That's not what I saw at the time, though. What I saw then was *he* was selfish, *she* was in need. She believed Jesus would save her; I believed *I* had to. So I went back to school at the last possible hour in January, a full week after Roger left, and resumed my practice of cutting at least half of Friday or Monday in order to get home to take care of her. Roger called every week; sometimes I spoke with him briefly, sometimes not. I did whatever Mother wanted. Usually it was chores, but sometimes she would ask me to see a movie or help her pick out a new purse. I'd get groceries, cook some food ahead, carefully labeling it on shelves in the refrigerator. "You're a good daughter. What would I do without you?" she said one evening, hugging me to her. It was enough. I *was* a good daughter. As the year progressed, I discovered her checkbook was in disarray and began balancing it each month. By the end of the school year, I was billing the parents of flute students whose parents had caught on to the fact that Mother had quit keeping track of her life.

15

DURING THE COURSE OF OUR summer internships, Sandy and I had decided to room together the next school year. My first year's roommate had made friends with other girls and was moving to a suite with them. There'd been no animosity between us; there'd been nothing, which was the whole problem. I was secretive, went home all the time and shunned college social life considering it frivolous, while Mary had joined and gone to freshman mixers. This left me with no real connection, no one with whom it was natural to say—or to say to me—"Let's room together next year." I'd ended up checking the "no preference" box on the housing form where it asked about roommate selection, and had been assigned to share a room with a transfer student, so the switch was an easy matter for me.

Sandy, on the other hand, had plenty of friends. Blue-eyed, naturally blond, with long, curly eyelashes, high color on fair skin and a small, straight nose, she was so model-pretty that it would have inspired resentment among other girls had she not been so unaffectedly outgoing. Instead, and utterly unlike me, she was sought after. What made us a perfect match as roommates was a purely practical issue. I was gone for three days of every week and she was masterful at sneaking Mark into the dorm before, during and after parietal hours—as they were called then. I didn't care that they used our room, I didn't even care if they pushed our narrow sagging beds next to one another and used the double bedsheets that had disappeared out of Sandy's mother's linen closet. It wasn't that Sandy particularly understood my situation with Mother. She was just an uncritical person, and didn't question me, as Mary had regularly, at least during the first month or two. Also, it was to Sandy's advantage, something she'd obviously figured out before she suggested we change roommates.

If it hadn't been for Sandy, our tiny room would have resembled a convent cell. "Home" was, according to Mother, strictly construed as referring to wherever she was, and for that reason, making a dorm room homelike was almost disloyal. It might have meant I intended to spend significant time there. Sandy, though, homemaker hormones flying like sparks off her engagement ring, set out to create a little haven for her and Mark. Cheerful print curtains complete with a valance and harmonizing green bedspreads, bookcases, plants, Monet prints—framed thanks to her father—on the walls, all appeared that first weekend we were back to school. Then a hot plate (strictly forbidden in the regulations) and a set of four matching mugs showed up on a special little table with a selection of teas, instant coffee and cocoa. Boxes of cookies were in the table's cupboard, but only when Sandy's mother didn't send homemade ones. A record player and albums were in a corner with our reading chairs and a pole light Sandy brought from their rec room at home. Her mother even "dropped by" (from New Jersey) with two huge floor pillows she'd "picked up on sale at Bloomies, because they'd look so cozy." When she left she hugged me before she hugged Sandy and said goodbye to her again, moisture glistening in the corners of her eyes. "Have a wonderful year, you two," she called as her high heels clicked down the hall. "Don't forget to call, honey," she added to Sandy.

All Sandy's efforts, aided by her parents and their cash, added to the nicest room on the floor, a prefeathered nest. On weeknight evenings, I loved the draw of Sandy and our cheery room on the other girls. They came to see her, I knew, but I got to sit in there and laugh and belong—when, that is, I didn't have to be in the library cramming to get my schoolwork done before Friday. It was like straddling two worlds: home, where I was carrying increasing responsibility for the most basic functioning, and school, light and lighthearted because of Sandy.

And Sandy's Mark. How sweet he was to me, probably in gratitude for my regular disappearance, but he never made me feel that was the reason. "Nice sweater, Ruth," he'd say on Friday, if he was there before I left. "Looks good on you." Or, "How's your stat class? Sandy sure hates it. You know, I can give you a hand with analysis of variance if you want. Sandy gets it now, but maybe not well enough to teach it to you." How could I not fall a little in love with a guy like that? He offered to fix me up with fraternity brothers, but I was always going home for the weekend. I'd largely abandoned my Prince Charming fantasies after Joshua, anyway.

By spring, I was a sisterly coconspirator with both of them and had let down my guard more than I ever had with anyone except Roger. A few times I had gone out for burgers or pizza with them on Friday evening before taking a late train home; they'd ride the subway to Grand Central with me so I wouldn't be alone and then turn around and go back uptown to Columbia, to their weekend. The three of us would sit over beer and discuss poverty or war or the war on poverty and then the conversation would segue without warning to what shade the bridesmaids should wear in their wedding and whether to have the napkins be a matching pink, or if, as Mark said, that would be plain effeminate. After an evening of that comfort, it was hard to leave, to get on the train and go home to Mother, never knowing if I'd be greeted with tears or rage or silence or, occasionally, a smile.

Because of that comfort, it didn't seem especially strange when, in April, Sandy whirled into our room one Wednesday evening and said, "Mark wants to talk to you," and gestured in the direction of the floor phone, down the hall.

"Huh? Me? Why?" I was already in pajamas, my hair on giant rollers, bent over a statistics problem from mathematics hell.

"You'll see. Go."

I scooted down the hall and picked up the receiver she'd left dangling.

"Mark? Hi, it's me. What do you need?" I'd guessed he wanted to check Sandy's size on something or other; he'd had me do that more than once already.

"Actually, you."

"Huh?"

"I need a favor. Will you do it?"

"Of course. Name it."

"I'm going to hold you to that. My brother Evan—he's the oldest—is looking for a job in the city. He's been at the University of Chicago for the past five and a half years, if you can fathom that, getting his doctorate and he's actually finished next month."

"In what?"

"Well, it's in the School of Business, something to do with marketing management. But he wants to teach at a university in the long run. Right now, he's looking to work in business for a few years to pick up practical experience."

"Is that like advertising?" I was stalling, afraid of what was coming.

"It's related. Anyway, he's coming for interviews next week, and I'd like for you to go out with him—and Sandy and me, of course."

"I'd really like to, Mark, but I'm going home for the weekend. I really have to." The automatic answer.

"Hah. I knew you'd say that. The thing is, he'll be here all next week. This is for interviews—that's when businesses operate, Monday through Friday."

I cast for an excuse, nervously repinning a hair roller while I held the receiver between my ear and shoulder. "Mark, I...I really don't think it's a good idea. First, I have a huge paper due in Theories of Personality, plus you know what's due in Statistics. Secondly, he must be what? Twenty-five? I'd feel stupid, what would he want with a twenty-year-old sophomore?"

"Twenty-seven. He's a slow learner, what can I say? Well, that, plus he was in the service. I'm telling you, he'd like you and you'd like him. He'd be good for you."

"What do you mean by that?" A little defensive, but I liked Mark so much that he could get by with a lot.

"I don't know, Ruthie, I just think we'd have a good time, and that would be that. No big thing. I just don't want him to feel like a third wheel with me and Sandy, but Mom and Dad want me to take him out on the town. I'd want to anyway."

I was thinking that the last kind of man I'd be interested in would be one in the field of business, especially advertising. That was nothing but professional lying.

"Come on, Ruth, please? You said you'd do a favor. You can pick the night, Monday through Thursday, if it's okay with Sandy. I'm clear. He's tall, almost as good-looking as me. Lighter hair, too bad for him. He's a nice guy, I swear."

As I glanced up the hall toward our room, Sandy stuck her head out of the door to see if I was still on the phone. "Yes," she called, when she saw I was. "You're saying yes."

I turned my back. "Yeah," I said to Mark. "And I'm sure he'd be just thrilled to spend an evening with a skinny undergrad with orange hair and freckles."

"Whoa. What's this garbage? You're pretty, Ruth. The only reason you don't have a social life is that you don't want one." His voice dropped its teasing tone and turned brotherly.

"I wasn't fishing for a compliment. Get your eyes checked. I'd really rather not do this. Couldn't you ask someone else? Nancy Bradford would jump at the chance."

He ignored the latter. "I could, but I don't want to. It would be easier for me with you, too, it's easier to talk with you. Nancy comes on like she's looking to get laid. Excuse me. You said you'd do a favor. For me. Please."

Back in the room, I flew at Sandy. "Did you tell Mark to ask me? You know how I feel about blind dates." The roller in my bangs came loose and bounced off my nose, which made her giggle.

"No, I didn't tell him to ask you, but it is a good idea. I've met Evan twice, the last two Hanukahs. He's a great guy. And he's good-looking. I'm serious. You'll have a good time. I'll be there, for heaven's sake, what's the big deal?"

I retrieved the roller from under Sandy's desk. "I don't know. It just is." It sounded lame, even to me.

She was rummaging through her top desk drawer, ruining its neat organization, which bothered me. "Look. Here's a picture of him." I took a snapshot from her extended hand.

"Which one?" There were perhaps ten people in the picture, Mark's extended family posed between a Christmas tree and a menorah, Sandy and Mark kneeling in the front, their arms draped over each other's shoulders and grinning.

"The tall one with glasses next to Mark's mother. You can see he looks something like Mark only lighter hair, sort of dirty blond. They both look like their mother—she's the one who's not Jewish. Did you know that if the mother is Jewish, the kids automatically are? If only the father is, then the kids aren't. It's because you always know who the mother is and you're not necessarily sure who the father is. Isn't that disgusting? Thanks to me, our kids will be kosher." Sandy rolled her eyes.

I studied the picture. Indeed, Evan did look like Mark, with the same broad cheekbones, roundness of chin and even-toothed smile. I'd noticed how Mark's nose was a little larger and his face a little more round than "handsome," strictly interpreted, would have allowed, yet everyone commented on how handsome he was. Evan was taller and looked to be a little narrower of build, but there was certainly a family resemblance. Only Evan *was* better looking.

"It's not about how he looks, Sandy. I'd like to think I have a little more depth than that. It's…"

"Never mind what it is. We're going. You told Mark you would. What night? I'm supposed to let him know tomorrow."

"Oh, God. I hate this. Monday. Let's get it over with."

"You can wear my black dress if you want. I can wear the red one."

"What? I thought this would be like a pizza night."

"Nope. The Russian Tea Room. Mark's parents are paying."

I DIDN'T MENTION ANYTHING about it to Mother that weekend. It was dry enough to turn the garden over to ready it for flowers, and that's what we did. We took turns with the spade, the other using the hoe to cut down the size of the clumps. The New England soil yielded its usual spring harvest of stones. How did new ones keep rising year after year? Piling them into the Jensens's ancient wheelbarrow and finding a place to dump them fell to me, but I didn't particularly mind. Mother loved flowers. Even in her worst years, she never missed planting annuals. Wherever we'd lived, it had been an issue between Mother and the landlord: could she plant some flowers, even if it was only a few in a puny square of concrete-edged dirt? The Jensens had a real yard, though, and thought Mother was doing them a favor. She'd had me dig up an area twice the size we'd ever had before. Caring for it was a chore, especially since she demanded that it be kept pristinely weedless. Sometimes, we'd work together for hours, though, and it was then that she'd be in her best humor and my love for her broke the surface again, perennial as the stone harvest.

When we could, we started flowers from seed. Usually Mother couldn't wait for July when they'd finally bloom, and we always ended up buying some bedding plants to go in the front of the green shoots. That, though, wouldn't be until mid-May, after the last silvery breath of frost had given up, even in Connecticut. New York and Jersey were a couple of weeks ahead of us. In April, if the ground wasn't too wet and no extended cold was forecast, we could get seeds in, and Sunday morning, Mother said impulsively, "Let's go ahead today and put in a couple of sections of seeds. I think they'll be all right. If it's too early, well, we won't have lost that much."

I poured us both another cup of coffee. "Sure. We can do that. Do you have what you want?"

"Not a one. I'll write a list and you run and get them. The A & P will have them out."

A half hour later, I was back with packets of marigolds, asters, pinks, sweet william and daisies. I had also picked up a packet of zinnias, not because they were on Mother's list, but because we'd never had them and I thought they looked so pretty from a distance, bright splotches tall enough to stand out.

The Jensens would enjoy them from upstairs, where they lived whole days in rockers by the window.

"Zinnias weren't on the list," she said sharply as she went through the bag.

"I know. I just like them. Can we stick them in the back?"

"I don't want them. I hate them. I've always hated them."

"Oh. Okay. I'm sorry." Possibly disappointment was evident in my voice. I hadn't meant it to be so.

She was quiet for a few minutes, sorting the seeds into the order in which they'd be planted. "Okay. You're doing so much work, I guess you should get to pick something that gets planted. I'll see if I can stand some zinnias."

"You don't have to, Mother. It's okay." I was cramming my feet back into my old sneakers, ready to go plant.

"No. We'll try these seeds. Maybe I've gotten over my aversion," she said. *See, Roger?* I thought. *You said I couldn't help her, but see? You're wrong. She's trying and she's getting better.*

"Why don't you like them?"

"A long, old story. Never mind."

AS IT HAPPENED, I STAYED at home that Sunday night. The weather had been soft and sunny again and we'd put all the seeds in. Monday, I caught an early train to New Haven, where I changed, as always, for Grand Central. I remember the rocking of the train, half-empty in midmorning, as it churned past the backyards of houses. Some housewives had already hung wet laundry in the April breeze on those clotheslines that look like the skeleton of an umbrella, and I distinctly remember thinking that those women had such wonderful lives. Why would I have thought that? I leaned the side of my head against the window, watching backyards and undersides of bridges as we passed through stations on the express run. I remember how my reflection looked in the window when I focused on it: half a face, a colorless transparency. On the unoccupied seat next to me was a bouquet of lilacs I'd cut from the Jensens's bush before I left, wrapping their woody stems with wet napkins, wax paper and a rubber band to take them to our room. The scent was heady, ripe, tart and sweet at once, utterly distinctive. I picked them up and buried my nose in them to feel myself real. A whiff of lilacs still immediately transports me to that train as it lulled me to the beginning of more than I could handle. More than any of us could handle.

EVAN, WHEN I MET HIM, was almost shy, which I mistook for being stuck up. I assumed he was assessing me, wondering what had possessed his brother to ask me to come, looking again and still finding me lacking. If it hadn't been to please Sandy and Mark, I never would have put myself out as I did, trying to sparkle a little, trying to be intelligent if not interesting. It was this simple: I didn't want to reflect badly on them.

"You look sensational," Mark had said to me when Sandy and I came down. I had on Sandy's slinky black dress and had stuffed my bra with Kleenex to fill it out.

"Excuse me, sir. Your eyes are supposed to be on me." Sandy laughed, grabbing his face with her hands and depositing a loud kiss on him.

"Oops. And so they are, I swear. But, Ruthie, you do scrub up good. Told you, Evan. Evan, this is Ruth Kenley. Ruth, this here rube is Evan."

"Nice to meet you," Evan and I had said almost simultaneously as I shook the hand he stuck out. The whole evening began that way, a difficult mixture of Sandy and Mark's intimacy and Evan's and my awkward formality.

We took a cab to the Russian Tea Room, again courtesy of Mark and Evan's parents and I remember thinking it was going to be one long disaster, this favor I was doing Mark. We ordered in stiff, polite voices and looked around, making predictable comments about the decor. There wasn't an identifiable time it began to switch. It was more like the tide at the Cape, going out and out until at some moment when you looked again it was coming in. I found myself laughing at something Evan said, and then something else, and something else, slowly realizing what a genuinely funny wit he had, feeding himself straight lines and then playing off them. I could tell he found my laughter gratifying, but I wasn't laughing to flatter him. I wanted him to go on and on.

The pink walls, dark woodwork, enormous arrangements of fresh spring flowers and candles, the whole aura of elegance, contrasted with our inelegant laughter in a way that made our table seem like a gathering of members of some esoteric underground, tightly bonded and set apart from all others. And I fit. Then, between dinner and dessert, I took a drink of water at a moment exactly inopportune, as Evan finished a story with a one-liner and I tried so hard not to spit the water out that it backed up and came out my nose. I was horrified and that so delighted Evan that he spit a little bit of wine onto the tablecloth trying to contain his own hilarity.

I'd never enjoyed myself with such abandon before. The earth spoke that night as though it were a giant pinball machine: *tilt,* it said.

16

WE STAYED OUT TOO LATE considering Evan had an interview at nine the next morning. Tuesday, he left a message while I was in class. Before I had a chance to respond, he'd left another. Pink message sheets fluttered from the bulletin board on Sandy's and my room door. Until now, they'd always been for Sandy.

"I had a great time last night," he said when I called him at Mark's fraternity. I smiled to myself and twisted the phone cord.

"So did I. How did your interview go?"

"Hard to judge, but pretty well, I think. I've got more education and less experience than they want, but who knows? I'll tell you about it, but I called to see if we could get something to eat tonight."

"With Sandy and Mark?"

"No. Mark's got some meeting tonight. Just us, no big deal, maybe pizza and beer if you want. I don't care."

"I would…" A short hesitation, which Evan interrupted.

"But?"

"Not really a but, just that I've got this statistics project due and if Sandy can't walk me through it, I'm dead."

"Hell, I'll walk you through it. I'm pretty good at that stuff."

"Oh, I'd feel bad, that wouldn't be much fun for you."

"No, I'd like to, really. Bring your stuff and if we can't do it over beer, we'll hit the lab. Have you got a decent calculator you can bring?"

"I can borrow Sandy's. I always do," I added with a laugh. I didn't notice how readily I was falling into step, it felt so natural. Of course, before I met him, I'd decided it couldn't go anywhere. There was the big age difference and even if there wasn't, what would I do with someone who wanted to devote his life to *business* of all things? I didn't even have to list Mother as a possible impediment, there were enough other ones.

"That'll work. So, where and when?" he asked.

"D'Amato's? It's real close, Mark can tell you how to—"

"Passed it last night, I know exactly where it is."

"Good. I'm finished with classes now, so anytime you say."

"Perfect. Now."

"Are you serious? It's only three-thirty."

"Sure I'm serious. Grab your stuff and let's go now."

"I've got a paper to do, too. It's only half written."

"No problem. I've got to be in early—another interview tomorrow, nine sharp, suit and tie, the whole shootin' match, ma'am," he said.

I took the time to brush my hair and put on some lipstick before I gathered my statistics material and Sandy's calculator, but that was all.

Evan and I saw each other twice more before he returned to Chicago, once when he brought me an analysis of variance he had redone because he was sure I had a mistake in it, and once for coffee and doughnuts when I had an hour free between morning classes and he had no interview until one in the afternoon. I was licking a dusting of powdered sugar off my fingers when he said he was sorry he was leaving, that he'd really enjoyed my company. I thought maybe he was being polite.

"And I've enjoyed yours. I wish you weren't going, too." It was easy to say. I didn't think about what it meant.

"Really? If one of these jobs pans out, I'll be back. I'd like to see you." He had a way of looking straight into my eyes, not hiding, not protecting himself. The coffee shop clinked and rattled with spoons and cups and orders, but I heard him clearly.

I was surprised by the flush of pleasure that came over me, and embarrassed, tried to cover by busying myself with my napkin. "I'd like that, too. Except, you know, I'll be going home for the summer."

He didn't say anything while the waitress refilled his coffee, and for a moment, I thought it was a done deal. "That's only up in Connecticut, though, right? We can handle that." He wore a white shirt and a green and gold tie that highlighted his coloring. Handsome? Yes. Good, sturdy hands, too.

"Well…it's a pain, though, a subway and two trains." In that moment, I felt wary, as though Mother were about to catch me with my hand in her purse stealing her hoarded currency of my time. And I couldn't imagine he'd want to make such a tedious trip anyway.

"Worth every minute, no doubt." He smiled. When we parted, he gave me a kiss on the cheek. "I'll see you," he called as I left, like he really intended it. When I turned around, he was still there, ready with a wave.

CLASSES ENDED EARLY IN MAY. Largely to quell Mother's distress over the notion of my being away another whole summer, I'd asked—and been granted permission—to do my summer field work in a nursing home only twenty minutes from home. I'd have to use Mother's car, which meant she'd be stuck at home during whatever shift I got, but she was willing. "A small sacrifice," she said, stroking my hand like the petal of one of her daylilies. I wasn't sure which one of us she thought was making the small sacrifice.

By the middle of May, I was back on the fold-out couch that had been my bed for longer than we'd ever stayed anywhere before. Mother had made room in her wardrobe for the uniforms the nursing home required me to wear, and my shorts and tops were folded next to my shoes behind the couch. Underwear went in a drawer in Mother's dresser. Toilet articles, fortunately, had a home in the bathroom medicine cabinet. Anything I didn't need on a day-to-day basis, as before, had to be in boxes in the part of the basement the Jensens had designated for our storage. Even though I was accustomed to living this way, and indeed, had for quite a while, the sheer lack of privacy had begun to get to me. Now I wonder why, especially after living with a college roommate, it should have bothered me. I, of all people, was accustomed to chicken coop living. Of course, at school, Sandy and I didn't grill each other on the contents of mail, and the phone was at least out in the hall, where anyone on her way to the bathroom would catch a snatch of your conversation, but no one acted as though eavesdropping were a constitutional right.

I mention the mail and the phone because Evan did write to me. I came home to find a letter from him already opened, its page and a half of masculine ink scrawl laid on the kitchen table as obvious as a newspaper on the kitchen table.

"That came today," Mother said, jerking her thumb disparagingly toward it. She was sitting at the other end of the table with a glass of iced tea. "Who is this Evan?" An accusation.

"Mark's older brother." A rare, stubborn weed sprouted in me. She'd get what she wanted, but I'd make her work for it.

"And Mark is?"

"I've mentioned Mark. You remember, Sandy's fiancé."

"So what's his older brother doing writing to you?"

"I'll have to read it to know that," I said, picking up the letter, knowing full well she'd already knew every word of it.

"Don't act smart."

"I didn't mean to. I *don't* know what's in it. I'll tell you as soon as I've read it."

"How do you know him?"

"I went out to eat with him and Mark and Sandy when he was in town."

"You never mentioned that."

"Didn't I?" Of course I hadn't. What would be the purpose of giving her something to worry about when there was nothing to it?

"No, you didn't."

"What does the letter say?" As though she didn't know.

"Just that he got one of the jobs he interviewed for and is moving to New York."

"Anything else?"

The letter said that he'd gotten my address and phone number from Sandy, that he hadn't thought to ask me for it when we'd last seen each other. He guessed he'd not realized how quickly the semester was ending and we'd be moved out of the dorm. "How about coming into the city for a weekend after I get there? I should arrive on or about June 20, because the job starts July 1, but I'll have to find an apartment and move in my orange crates first. Or, if you're working some weird shift, unlike the normal population—me, for instance—then I'll come out to see you after I'm settled, if that's okay," the letter asked. "I'm sort of hoping you can come here, though…I could use advice regarding curtains and the like. This is the first time I've had my own place. Roommates with taste have always taken care of decor because after consulting me, each of them was smart enough to ignore my input. I hope to hear from you. This address will be good until at least June 15. P. S. Every time I see a redhead, I think it's you." I didn't mention any of that.

"It just says that he'd like to get together after he moves to New York," I said, putting it down and heading to the cabinet for a glass so I'd have an excuse not to look at her.

"What for?"

"I guess just to get together."

"Where will he be living?" She was taking the circuitous route, not mentioning the obvious, that she'd read my letter. A game, a pointless game. If I brought it up, she'd ask why I would mind if she opened it. What, exactly, did I have to hide?

"I don't know." This response, which she knew was honest, slowed her down for a minute.

"Were you two seeing each other or something?"

"Hardly. He was just in the city for a few days on job interviews."

"Where is he from?"

"Mark's family is from upstate New York." I put ice cubes in a glass after discovering there were no clean ones in the cabinet and washing one that languished with other dirty dishes in the sink. I was grateful—more time with my back turned, more time to answer her questions without my face betraying me.

"So is that where he's moving from?"

"No, he's moving from Chicago."

"What was he doing in Chicago?" She was starting to sound impatient.

"Getting his doctorate."

"In what for heaven's sake?"

"Business management."

"Oh." The syllable was laden with disdain.

"He's a very nice person, Mother." Although I tried not to be, even as I spoke, I knew I was defensive.

"I'm sure."

I answered Evan's letter the next day while I was on my break at the nursing home. Still feeling marginally defiant, I gave the receptionist the change for a stamp, and stuck my note in her outgoing mail basket. Not that there was anything so personal in what I wrote. It was just that I wanted a tiny corner of privacy. At the time I didn't realize how my not having immediately uprooted that stubborn weed would get everything off to a bad start. I didn't know that something had started, that was the problem. Mother smelled it, though. She smelled it when I made her beg and still didn't really feed her information, and she confirmed her conclusion when I defended him. She made me pay for my five minutes of faux satisfaction, and, later, pay again and more.

IT MUST HAVE BEEN SHORTLY after he received my letter that Evan called from Chicago.

"That boy who wrote you called."

I bristled, but ignored the implicit insult in "boy." I hadn't mentioned that he was nearly twenty-eight to Mother, but she knew he had a doctorate, so he could hardly be in his teens.

"Evan?"

"Yes. That was the name he gave."

"When?"

"A couple of days ago. I just remembered."

"Did he leave a message?"

"Not really. Just said to call him, but I told him you were working."

Again, that strange new growth in me, the errant weed in Mother's cultivated garden. I just said, "Oh. Thanks," and made no further comment. That night, though, when she sent me to the store for her, I got three dollars in change, and called him from a pay phone at the gas station.

"Hello." His voice was deep, cheerful as I remembered, the hello a statement, not a question.

"Evan?"

"Speaking."

I was suddenly shy. "It's Ruth, you know, Sandy's roomma...."

"Ruth! I'm so glad you called!"

"I'm sorry. My mother forgot to tell me that you'd called until today."

"I'm just glad to hear from you. Thanks for your letter."

"Well, thanks for yours. How are you?"

"Drowning in a cardboard sea. You should get a load of this place."

"Packing?"

"Well, only if you count every book I've owned since junior high school."

"How was your graduation?"

"It was good. You know, Dad shook my hand vigorously and Mom cried. And cried. And cried. And..."

"Well, she's proud. With reason, I might add."

"You know, it was a little strange. I don't want to put you off or anything, I mean, I'm not pushing myself on you, I hope, but I wished you were there."

"Thank you," I said after hesitating an awkward fraction. "I would have liked to see you."

"Really?"

"Yes."

"Well, then, will you come into the city after I get there?"

"Evan, it might be hard. I don't usually get two days off in a row." Actually I'd only been working a week and had little idea of what flexibility I could call on. My supervisor had said to let her know if there were days I particularly needed off.

"Could you ask? I mean, if you want to."

"I haven't been there very long. I hate to start right off asking favors. Let me see how it goes, okay?"

"Okay. I could come up there, if that's better."

"No." I was hasty with that reply. "It's probably best if I come down. I'll try. I'd like to. I'd really like to." As the words came out, I realized I meant them.

"MOTHER, I WAS THINKING I'D go into the city next Wednesday. I'm off, you've got a full day of students and I could meet with my advisor and preregister for the fall. I got cut from two classes last year because they were full."

"You're going to see that boy, aren't you? What's going on, here, Ruth?"

"Nothing's going on, Mother, honestly. I'll probably see him, yes, but I do need to meet with Dr. Santivica. I should have done it before finals, but I just didn't. He's around, I know, because he's teaching a practicum seminar—the one I'll have to take next summer."

"Why didn't you just say, I want to go see my boyfriend?"

"He's not my boyfriend. I hardly know him. I'm the only person he knows except Mark and Sandy, that's all."

Three weeks had passed since Evan and I had talked. One more letter had arrived from him, but Mother didn't know that because I happened to get the mail that day. It had been a much longer letter, more personal, even a little rambling. He'd written that he normally felt like he could tackle anything and handle it, but that he was nervous about his job. "I'm finding myself pacing a lot, trying to figure out how to solve problems at work and I don't even know what the problems are, yet. It's not like me. It's strange, too, to think about moving and not knowing anyone (except you and Sandy and Mark, of course, and I feel especially blessed to have met you)." Blessed. That was the word he used.

I should, perhaps, have taken it as a sign that in spite of Mother's grumblings, I went on Wednesday. Not only did I go, but I took the 6:25 train to New Haven so that I'd get into the city before ten. Evan was standing on the platform craning his

neck to find me in the crowd. I'd have noticed him even if I
didn't know him, tall, nice-looking, crisp in a pressed, light-blue
shirt he'd left open at the neck.

"I thought it would be nice to meet you," he said, a little
sheepishly. I'd been supposed to head over to his apartment to
measure for curtains. "Um…to show you where the apartment
is." He grinned. There was nothing in the least complicated
about his address.

"That's so nice," I said quickly, not wanting him to feel
foolish. I wasn't accustomed to treatment like this. Of course it
affected me. How could it not? How could it not affect me that
he put his arm around me when we crossed Forty-second Street,
and a cabby blared his horn as he jammed on his brakes at the
last moment?

We walked to Evan's apartment in Murray Hill, the din of
midmorning traffic limiting our conversation. The last days of
June had been rainy, and that morning the air was sparkling,
rinsed, still cool from the recent downpours. Light danced
around us.

"Here we are. What do you think?" He was searching my face
for a reaction.

"Evan, it's wonderful." And it was, a beautiful old brownstone on Thirty-second Street near Third Avenue, with window
boxes of red geraniums and trailing vinca vine, a tree arching
over the entryway.

"Wait till you see the inside. Not that I know how, but *someone*
could do wonders with it." He grabbed my hand and took the
stairs two at a time, while I tried to hit them double-time to keep
up with him. "Sorry," he said when I stubbed my toe and stumbled
forward. "I guess I'm getting a little ahead of myself. You okay?"

"I'm fine, really. Show me."

Evan unlocked the door and stepped back. *"Me casa es su
casa,"* he said with a sweeping gesture. "I think that means
welcome to my castle. And I do mean welcome."

The main room was beautiful, with hardwood floors and
splendid light from a bay window overshadowing piled-up
boxes, drop cloths, and soaking brushes. Evan had painted the

walls a warm cream color. A flourishing philodendron spilled green from the windowsill toward the floor. "It's got a lot of potential, don't you think? I've got to put the rug down and get rid of these boxes so I can see what I need in the way of furniture beside the couch. Come see the kitchen and bedroom," he said, hardly giving me time to take in the first room. "The kitchen is a little…rustic, shall we say, but since I have to read a cookbook to heat a TV dinner successfully, what the heck."

The kitchen was tiny, windowless, obviously added when the original house had been divided into apartments. A garbage can was half-full with carry-out cartons, cardboard coffee cups and sandwich wrappers. Mismatched dishes were stacked on the small tan counter area. "Mom's discards," he said, gesturing at them. "What can I say? The price was right."

"Hey They're better than what we use at home," I said laughing. "Let's not get insulting here."

"I want to hear about your family. Does your mother have red hair?" he said.

"No. Brown."

"You must look like your dad, then."

I smiled and gave the slightest suggestion of a nod, which could have been interpreted as either assent or a shrug. I'd been asked the same question a thousand times and was practiced at ducking it, though I hated every reminder of the missing and the unspeakable, the mysteries of my coloring, my bird bones and scant flesh. It was easier for Roger, having at least some resemblance to Mother, with his brown wavy hair and heavy build. Only the squareness of his body and his thick, dark brows insisted they'd come from emphatic genes other than hers, although even he didn't have her jutting jaw.

"So…there's you and your mother and brother, right?"

"Not much to tell. My brother's at the University of Colorado. So let's see the bedroom. This place is incredible."

Evan led me farther down a hallway. His back looked broad, accentuated by the narrow corridor. "Actually I've got two more rooms." In the first, a single bed was set up on a frame, made up with sheets and a blue, patterned afghan.

"Did someone knit that?" I asked, pointing.

"My mother. We've all lost count of how many she's made. As soon as she meets you, she'll probably start on yours." He laughed and then added, "I'm serious! You know, it's a mother thing, a mutant gene or something. They're all the same, I guess."

"I can't believe how much work must have gone into that," I said, moved. "I just can't imagine."

Evan's study was more finished than the other rooms. He'd unpacked boxes of books into modular bookcases, and moved a reading chair and light to the side of a wooden desk above which he'd hung his diplomas. A deep brown area rug extended nearly to the walls. A few framed photographs rested on the top of one of the bookcases, and, on what would have been the outside wall had the apartment not been in a row house, was a seascape print. I crossed the room and picked up one of the pictures.

"This is your family?" I said, stating the obvious.

"That's us. Mark, me, Jon, Doug, Mom, Dad." He pointed as he spoke.

"A good-looking group," I said.

"With the notable exception of Jon and Mark and Doug," he said. "Otherwise, definitely."

"They look so nice."

"Jon and Mark and Doug? Nah."

"Quit it. Your parents. They look so nice."

"They are," he said, serious for a moment. "Great people. They've done a lot for me."

"Tell me about them."

"Sure. What do you want to know? And first, how about a cup of coffee and a doughnut double-rolled in powdered sugar?"

"You remembered!"

"Of course I remembered. All you have to do is make the coffee. Unless you don't care whether or not it's drinkable, in which case, I'll be happy to make it."

"Oh, come on," I said, pulling the electric percolator toward me. "Any eight-year-old can."

"Watch it, there," he interrupted. "I know ten- or eleven-year-olds who don't do it as well as I do."

"Incompetence will not work as an excuse," I said while I went ahead and made the coffee.

Evan pulled a plastic drop cloth off a small sofa in the living room and overturned an empty box to make a little table for our coffee cups and the bakery bag. "Good coffee," he said. "Thanks."

"Thank *you* for the doughnuts. I love this place. It's wonderful." I looked around, absorbing the comfortable feel of the room, the arc of light on the creamy wall and darker floor, the green of the plant. "That philodendron looks nice," I said. "This is a great room for plants. You should get some more."

"Mom again," he said. "She's the plant lady. She stuck that in the car when I picked up all the stuff I raided from our basement."

"My mother loves plants, too," I said, and immediately wished I hadn't, but Evan didn't ask anything.

"You were going to tell me about your family," I said.

"Okay. Well. Where to start? Good German stock on both sides. Dad's Jewish, Mom's not. I guess their parents were less than thrilled, but what can anyone say anymore? They've been married for thirty-seven years. When they get into arguments, of course, it's like a reenactment of the Second World War." He trailed off laughing as he shook his head.

"Do they fight much?"

"Oh, God, no, I didn't mean that. It's just funny when they do. I mean it's over stuff like having ham and whether kosher pickles taste better." He put his hands palms up as if making a balance scale to weigh this important matter. "None of it is in the least bit serious, except every once in a while I think maybe it's just a little bit what they really mean. You know? Just enough real difference to make it interesting and drive each other up the wall. Dad owns a dry-cleaning business. I can't tell you how much he wants me to come in with him and how much I don't want to. It's okay, though. Even though he can't understand why I'd want to teach business instead of run one, he accepts it. That's what I mean about them."

This view into the inner workings of a normal family drew me right in. "What about your mom?"

"See, she's the one who can understand wanting to teach. She was a first-grade teacher until she started having babies. Now she works in the business doing the accounts."

"I guess I can see where you get your head for business, with both of them in it."

"Actually, Mom pretty much hates it, even though she's sharp with numbers. She started doing it so they could put her on the payroll for work she could do whenever she could fit it in. I think she went in for being a professional mother. She's not much of a cook, though. Did Mark ever tell you about her matzo balls?"

"No." I was smiling already, watching Evan's eyes look into the distance as though he were watching a movie of his family. He'd taken off his glasses as if to see better.

"Dad would want matzo ball soup at Passover and, you know, some other times. His mother had always made it, sort of like other people have turkey at Christmas. Mom's were so bad that my brothers and I would fish them out and wrap them in our napkins, which got pretty soggy and disgusting, but we were boys, we were stupid, what did we care? After dinner, we'd go outside and go two on two with her matzo balls as weapons. They were small, but deadly. You'd think they'd get soft in soup, wouldn't you? Nope. Not Mom's. I think maybe a little cement was her secret ingredient. You know, if they were bad enough, Dad would quit asking for them. Only he never did. Still hasn't." He started laughing again, ahead of himself in the story. I loved how alive his eyes were, loved listening to him. I wasn't just deflecting the possibility of questions about my own past. "Anyway, one year genius Jon got the idea of having the fight on bikes, but Doug got Jon with one of Mom's masterpieces and Jon fell off the bike and broke his arm. Naturally we all told different stories about how it happened. I don't think Mom knows to this day what did." As Evan spoke, he'd now and then lapse into a particular rhythm of speech and I could hear his boyhood, vibrant and happy.

"Tell me more."

I'd done this before, peeped into people's lives like a voyeur, marveling and self-indulgently sad at once. Evan went on talking as I fed him questions and measured the windows. "Blinds," I said.

"Huh?"

"I think you'll want blinds on this window. Curtains, too, if you want, but right here in the front…"

"Yeah. You're right, good idea," he said.

"So go on. What did you do after Doug went to college?"

It was midafternoon when I looked at my watch. "Oh, my Lord. Evan, I've got to get up to school and try to see my advisor. He's probably already left for the day, his course is over at one." We were in the kitchen then, and I was arranging the cupboards.

"Good. Then you'll have to come back next week. How about we go get some curtains, or drapes or blinds or whatever you said I needed?"

"My mother will have a fit," I said, sticking the last two glasses onto the shelf we'd just lined.

He was startled. "Why? Why would she care? Ruthie?"

Good question. "Oh. It's hard to explain. She's just…" I'd noticed he'd called me Ruthie, his tone affectionate, and it distracted me from the thought of Mother's anger, just as Mother's anger distracted me from soaking in Evan's warmth. "She's a wonderful person, she's been through a lot and she depends on me. She…expects me to be there."

He seemed to accept that. "Well, look. Let's grab the subway up to Columbia, see if you can catch him in. Better yet, we'll call. There's a phone at the deli—mine isn't installed yet. We'll worry later about getting you back here."

I was relieved and grateful for how he'd eased it for me, yet knit into that blanket draped like his arm around me was a black thread. I was resenting my mother, her claim on me utterly indisputable and utterly disputable at the same time.

"I'LL HAVE TO GO BACK, MOTHER, either next week or the week after. Dr. Santivica wasn't available. It's my own fault. I should have called instead of assuming I could just see him after his

class." I'd rehearsed the lines on the train home. It was just as
well that I had had some transition time for pulling my thoughts
from the day with Evan, turning them back to Mother, bracing
myself for the storm that would surely break over my head.

She was lying on her bed in the dark, a heating pad on her
abdomen, a washcloth on her forehead. She'd barely acknowl-
edged my return and not commented on the late hour, only said
her time of the month was starting and she didn't feel well.

"You know, I could still have another child," she said in non-
response to my explanation. "I think about that, and then I look
at my body and think no, it's too late. But I've gotten to almost
like my time of the month, like one part that hasn't betrayed me
yet. Look, Ruthie. Look at this. Turn on the light." She removed
the washcloth from her forehead and propped herself on an
elbow. With her other hand, she ran her fingers through her hair,
lifting it from the roots like a fierce wind. The gesture contained
anger and despair. "Look at the gray. I can't even cover it up with
that stuff anymore." I'd had no idea she used anything on her
hair. "Look at these circles under my eyes, bags like an old lady.
My legs look like cottage cheese" She accompanied each
outburst with a separate gesture, insisting I look. "In the
mornings I hurt all over, like an old lady. Old. Old. Old. All
wrinkles. My hands look old. See? I don't know what it means,
what God wants of me. I look like everyone else. He doesn't tell
me anymore." The overhead light I'd reached to switch on at her
direction was garish. She looked much older than I'd seen
before, the puffy flesh beneath her eyes cast into bas-relief by
deep purplish curves beneath them. Tears had gathered as she
spoke and when she lowered her head to study her hand a second
time, they began running from each corner.

I was prepared for almost anything else. Sitting on the bed,
I took her head against my chest and held her, rocking her
slightly. "Mother. Mother. Everything will be all right. I promise
you. Everything will be all right. You're beautiful and you have
me. Nothing bad is going to happen. You'll know what God
wants you to do. You always do. Just be patient."

17

THE NEXT MORNING AT WORK, I used my break to write Evan a note. I wrote,

I had a wonderful time. Please understand that I really can't come back; my mother is having a hard time and needs me here. I'm sorry about not helping to put the blinds and curtains up, but I'm sure they'll look great. I hope you have a good summer, and that the job goes well. Fondly, Ruth.

I took an envelope from the receptionist's drawer, left her change for the stamp I took and dropped it in her outgoing mail basket. That was Thursday. The next Tuesday afternoon, Susan tracked me down in the activity room. "Ah ha! Even though it meant leaving the front desk uncovered and I'll probably get fired, it's all in the name of true love." She shook her long brown hair, ironed-straight down from its center part. "You have a letter and the return address seems to suggest a person of the masculine persuasion. Open it so I can hurry up and spread gossip." She laughed, extended a long envelope addressed to me in care of the nursing home, and headed for the swinging doors that put me so in mind of the ones at Grandmother's nursing home. I tried to blot out the memory, but the whoosh and thud of them was a daily echo of the last time we'd left her, still alive.

"It's not what you think, but thanks so much," I called after her.

"Anytime. I'm a sucker for romance," she called back. I knew she was; a movie magazine blaring about Luke and Laura—whoever they were—on some soap opera had been in the top desk drawer with the stamps.

I stuffed the letter in my uniform pocket and returned to the leather work group. Mrs. Hodgkins ducked her head and smiled at me, only her upper plate in today. "Oh, dearie, you go ahead and read the letter from your young man."

"Oh, Mrs. H, he's not my young man, he's just a friend."

"Well, you should have a young man, pretty as you are."

"Thanks," I muttered, embarrassed. Mrs. Hodgkins was one of the patients who regularly reached to touch my hair, fascinated by the color, or the thickness or both. I'd let it grow much longer than I'd worn it in high school, but fastened it in a ponytail or up with barrettes to keep it out of my way at work. When it fell over my shoulder, Mrs. Hodgkins and Mrs. Smith and sometimes old Mr. Angus would want to feel it and tell me whose hair it reminded them of, someone long lost to their touch.

"I bet he loves your hair and those pretty eyes. Green eyes. A little hazel. My Dennis had eyes almost that color," she said.

"Honestly, Mrs. Hodgkins. He's just a friend. I don't know if I'll even see him again."

"Tsk. Tsk." She shook her head. "A pretty girl like you."

"Let's see if we can get this wallet stitched up. Is it hurting your hands? We want to keep them moving." Just keep moving, I thought to myself. That's the key. Keep yourself moving.

BUT, OF COURSE, I DIDN'T. If I hadn't stopped and read the letter, if I hadn't sat in the car for a good twenty minutes, reading the letter, and smoothing it into the creases his big hands had made and then opening it and reading it yet again, what would have happened? So many turning points.

Love, Evan, he'd signed it. He knew it was quick, but he'd not felt this before and thought we might grow into something special. Wouldn't I reconsider? He didn't think he'd been wrong that I enjoyed being with him. He understood about my mother, we could work around that situation. He'd help me. "I'm not a complete novice at *not* doing what my parents wanted me to," he wrote. "The important thing is what *you* want." His underlinings were emphatic.

Writing back to him wasn't an unconsidered act. I thought I'd given up on old hopes, that I'd learned from my experience with Josh. How did I jump from that first distant note of refusal I'd sent Evan to almost immediately agreeing to go back? My only way of understanding it is that I had been drawn to the idea of Josh, not the man, while the pull I felt to Evan was visceral, beyond reason. His letter, with its appeal and its *Love, Evan,* was undeniable.

I intended a long letter of explanation about Mother, about Roger and the complex tapestry of us, and let it scare him off if it was going to, but after several tries while Mother slept that night, I gave up. It was too convoluted, too laden with the inexplicable. And, probably, too crazy. It would be easier to talk face-to-face, when I could see his eyes and sense his reactions. Finally, all I wrote was,

I know you're only off on weekends now that your job has started. I'm not scheduled for a Saturday off until July 23, but even so, I think it's best to tell my mother that I have a meeting with my advisor and because of that, it would have to be on a weekday, anyway. I'll come in to see you, if you still want me to, a week from Thursday. (I'm off Monday, too, but I'm not sure this will reach you in time for that.) I'll go ahead to school while you're at work and then come to your apartment at 5:00. If this isn't all right, could you call the nursing home? I can't get personal calls, but the receptionist will take a message.
Love, Ruth.

The closing said much more than the letter.

I'd not expected a response, but Evan had paid for special delivery. Susan waved the envelope triumphantly when I came in the door Tuesday afternoon for the second shift. "I had to sign for this one! I know, I know. He's just a friend. I believe you, really I do." Her nails were long and shapely, painted a dramatic red. She was loving this.

Can you make the same train as last time? I'll meet the 9:50 arrival from New Haven. I'm taking the day off. Thanks for the chance. Love, Evan. P.S. Don't worry if you miss a train. I'll wait.

It seemed we'd crossed some bridge. Evan hugged me on the platform at Grand Central, then kept an arm around me as we headed for the exit. "I'm just so glad you came," he said. His khaki pants had neat creases, his loafers were shined, his short-sleeved red polo shirt looked new. He'd gone to trouble to look nice, and I knew it was for me. And it was for him that I'd taken much more care than I would have if I were merely going to see my advisor. A Kelly-green sleeveless A-line dress Sandy had insisted I keep, perfectly simple, but it gave me a bustline with well-placed darts and the skirt widened just where it needed to, filling out my too-narrow hips. I knew my eyes looked wholly green when I wore it, not just vaguely so. I'd applied more makeup on the train, concealing freckles—Sandy's trick—and adding mascara, a smudge of shadow, more lipstick.

"Me, too," I answered. "You didn't need to take the day off work. I really do need to go up to school."

"I know," he said. "I'm going with you." He pulled away enough to look me up and down. "You look gorgeous. Gorgeous."

Right then and there, I wanted to say, "Wait, there's too much you don't know about me." But suddenly, as much as I thought I had to tell him, that much I didn't want to. I wanted to be just a normal woman with a normal man, a young woman who didn't carry contingencies and worries stuffed in a purse she couldn't put down. It was 1976, for God's sake. Women were supposed to be able to make decisions.

"Can we just pick up the subway and get up there now? Then we'd have the rest of the day clear."

"Dr. Santivica's in class until one o'clock. And I probably should get a late afternoon train back, the 3:44, or I could stretch it to the 4:03."

"Stretch it." He grinned. "Let's go over to my place then. No sense hanging around outside his office when we can be comfortable." We went out onto Lexington where the wind, already hot, assailed our faces.

"How's the job?" I asked.

"So far so good, I guess. Hard to tell. I keep getting introduced as Dr. Mairson to the administrative assistants and secretaries and they look at me like I have some fungus growing on my face. The senior staff seems to want to demonstrate how much more they know...oh, who cares? I'm glad you're here."

"I care. Tell me about it." We sounded like a couple, an intimacy in our tone, new and thrilling to me.

Evan squeezed me against him briefly and was silent a moment, considering his answer. "I really *don't* know," he said. "I feel like I have to win people over, like I'm not starting out on an even playing field. I think they resent my degree, you know. They assume I think I know everything about marketing. Which I don't, think I know everything, I mean." He shook his head and shrugged. "What's a body to do?" he said, mimicking an accent. "To quote my father, oy vey."

We talked continuously as we walked toward Murray Hill. The neighborhood felt familiar, welcome to my eyes, as though it were mine. The geraniums on Evan's building were fuller, and some ageratum among them that I hadn't noticed the last time was now in bloom, blue as Mother's eyes, but I didn't think of her just then. Or I pushed the thought of her from my mind.

"Oh, Evan! I can't believe this! How did you get so much done?" The main room of his apartment was cleared of boxes and paint accoutrements; an oriental-looking area rug was in place. The Wedgwood-blue sofa I'd previously seen, and a new, cream-colored easy chair were arranged on two sides of a coffee table, a floor lamp arching its neck over the chair and a matching ottoman off to one side. The philodendron poured its heart out over the windowsill and other house plants were interspersed with books, brass candlesticks and several mugs, paperweights and the like. Evan had put a Monet print, a Venetian water scene, on one wall. Light blue and green water glistened beneath pink windows shadowed in burgundy, perfectly braiding all the creamy hues of the room's rug and furniture. I felt foolish, believing he'd needed my help.

"I wanted to get the damn blinds up before you came," he said. "But you like the rest of it?"

"It's beautiful," I said. "Perfect."

"Maybe you could advise me on more stuff for the walls. They look bare to me. We could go to the Met and check out the prints."

"You definitely don't need my advice. You're much better at this than I am. I've never lived in a place this nice."

Evan looked at me intently. "I'd like your advice. I'd like to put up something you choose," he said. "And I haven't even started on the other rooms. Everything I know about setting up a kitchen could be scratched on the head of a pin and still leave room for an encyclopedia. If you hadn't put the dishes and glasses away, I'd probably have stashed them under the sink."

"I don't believe you. I think you can do anything." And I believed that. Then and there, I was seeing his capability and feeling very unsophisticated in comparison.

"For you I'd try," he said lightly. "I'd sure try."

We didn't talk about anything too serious that day. He had powdered sugar doughnuts for us and I made coffee. Later, he rode with me to Columbia, waited while I met with Dr. Santivica and then we took a bus to the Met where Evan insisted I pick out a print.

"You show me three or four that you like, and I'll tell you which of them I like best. That's all you're getting out of me," I answered. In the end, I chose another Monet, "Pourville," a deserted beach and water scene, edged by rough-enough land. "My favorite place in the world is the Cape," I told him, "and this one looks just a little like Truro. I have a good memory of it. Have you ever been there?"

"Tell me about it," he said.

"It's beautiful. The air is different, well, I guess it's the light, but the dunes and the ocean "

Evan interrupted. "I meant tell me your good memory."

I'd been thinking of how I loved the Cape from the moment we'd crossed Sagamore Bridge, the house on the dune cliff and Ben Chance. But then the end of the trip intruded in my mind, convoluted and impure, and no memory could be extended as a gift to Evan because each had its unspeakable aspect.

"I was," I lied. "I just meant how beautiful it is, that's the good memory."

"I'LL GET IT DRY MOUNTED and framed," Evan said. "Then next time you come we'll hang it together." We were back in his apartment briefly before I had to catch my train. "Ruthie, you haven't really said anything about what's going on, the business with your mother. Does she not want you to see me? The age difference?"

I shook my head. Even if I had all day left and did nothing but try to explain, how could I?

"Is it me? Maybe you didn't really want…"

"No. I promise you, it's not that. It's just so…hard…to explain. She's a wonderful person, but she…I don't exactly know myself. I'm not sure she's very stable. She's been through so much, I mean." I was stumbling, not completing any thought.

"Is your dad around?"

I felt my face flush, and looked down. "I don't know my father. I've never known my father. My mother…oh, God, Evan, look." I managed to look directly into his face for a moment. "My mother has always insisted she's a virgin. Do you see what I mean?" I looked back down, tears starting.

He lifted my chin with his hand, bent and kissed me gently on the cheek. Then he pulled me against him and just held me, one hand tangling itself into my hair while I cried.

"I'm sorry," I croaked. "I'm sorry. I don't usually fall apart like this."

"Shh. You have nothing to be sorry about. Nothing. You cry whenever you want to. It's okay."

"I've got to go," I said. "I can't miss that train."

"How can I contact you? Can I call?"

"That wouldn't be a good idea."

"I'll write the nursing home then, okay?"

"Yes, that's good."

"And you can write me back. Wait. I know. You call me. You call me collect, any night. Reverse the charges."

"My mother…"

"Do it from work. Do it from a phone booth. But, Ruthie, sooner or later…she's going to have to accept that it's your decision, right?"

I completely ignored the second part. "I'd have to pay you back—that's expensive."

"Don't be ridiculous."

"I have a job, too, you know."

"I don't care. Let me do this. Just call, please. Promise."

"I will. I don't know when, but I will."

MOTHER WAS DISTANT when I got home, even though, as I'd planned, it was well before dark. "So how did the meeting go? Was your advisor helpful?" I couldn't tell whether sarcasm edged her voice, or guilt affected what I heard.

"Yes. Dr. Santivica helped me preregister for a couple of classes that fill quickly. See, he signs a form that says I need a certain course during a certain semester to graduate on time and then I get priority registration."

"I see," she said, and then repeated, "Oh, yes. I see.

"And your friend…Evan, is that his name? He wouldn't have been registering, too…would he?"

"He's not a student, Mother. And, no, he wasn't registering. Look, here are my copies." I opened my purse and pulled out the student's copies of each course registration form.

"Oh, I don't need to see those. I believe you. Good God, Ruth." But I saw her glance at them and after that she softened.

"Let's go look at the garden," she suggested. "It's cool enough to pull a few weeds before dark."

The flowers were flourishing. They always did. Mother had

a way with flowers. They always leaped up like bright kites for her.

"Look at how pretty those zinnias are," I said. "I'm glad we put them in."

"I still hate them," Mother said. "But those do look nice." As dusk began to rise off the ground like mist, the zinnias seemed to hold their own illumination, the colors darker than in daylight, yet glowing. The stems and narrow slices of leaves receded, leaving the bright heads to appear unsupported and brave. They made me sad.

"Why don't you like them?" I asked again. This time she was in the mood to answer.

"My mother always planted a big bed of them because her birthday and mine are both in August, and zinnias are the August flower. One year after Dad…well, I went out and pulled out every one of them by the roots." She spilled a mirthless, bitter laugh that sounded more like choking.

"What did she do when you did that?" I asked, gentling my voice. Mother hadn't ever told stories about her girlhood. I wondered if I could keep her going.

"Nothing that helped the situation, I can tell you that much. But she never planted them again." She snapped her jaw shut and bent awkwardly at the waist to pull a few weeds. I squatted to help her, trying to keep my skirt out of the moist dirt border. "Oh for heaven's sake, Ruth, go in and change. I'll do this myself. I'm used to being alone."

FOUR DAYS PASSED BEFORE I was able to call Evan. I had figured out that when I worked second shift, the day supervisor's office would be empty during my dinner break, affording me both comparative privacy and a phone. It was also evening, when Evan would be at home. As I placed the collect call, I studied the framed school pictures of Mrs. Morrisson's son and daughter, and thought yes, I'd like to have children.

Evan didn't even let the operator finish her sentence. "Yes, I accept," he said, and then, "Ruthie! I'm so glad you called."

"I'm sorry about calling collect. I'm at work, and…"

"I *told* you to call collect. Call collect every *day*. How are you?"

"I'm okay. Work is…well, it's work. I hardly feel I keep the patients occupied, let alone doing therapy. It's a little disenchanting to work in a nursing home. It reminds me of my grandmother, and…well, it just does, and it makes me sad."

"Does she live near you?"

"No. She lived in Seattle. She died almost three years ago."

"I'm sorry. This is your mother's mother, I take it. Were you two close?"

"No. I wish we had been. Wait! Enough about me! Is the job getting better? More comfortable I mean? I've been thinking about you so much."

"I've been thinking about you, too. Yeah…I guess it's a little easier. The secretaries seem to be coming around, although the men seem pretty standoffish."

A wrench of jealousy twisted my insides a notch. "Are there any women executives?"

"Two. They're okay. They just don't fraternize much, period, so it doesn't seem like it has anything to do with me."

Good, I thought.

"Did you see the news last night?" he went on. "I was hoping you did, because a new study about the future of health related careers came out and the report was profiled on CBS. Occupational therapy was mentioned."

"No. What did it say?"

"Well, I was afraid you might have missed it, so I cut the write-up of it out of the *Times* this morning for you. Basically it said it looks like an expanding market because of more emphasis on rehabilitation, more insurance policies paying rehab costs in order to get workers back on the job more quickly. Some services that were previously excluded are more often being covered now. Anyway, I've got the article. But it's not going to do much good if you're deciding you don't like the field much."

"That was so sweet of you, Evan. Thank you."

"Hey, don't thank me. I'm interested. So, are you thinking

of changing? I couldn't tell from what you said about the nursing home?"

"Not really. Or not actively, I guess I should say. I don't think about it much, because I don't think I've really got a choice. I'd never get the money to start over—a lot of my classes wouldn't carry to another field."

"Ah." He muttered. "I hate the thought of you feeling stuck."

I laughed, to cover my seriousness. "I'm used to it."

But Evan heard what I really meant. "Well, you'll have to get unstuck," he said. "It's your life."

"Maybe. But I doubt it," I said, leavening my tone with teasing to cover what I knew. "You sound like my brother. Gosh. I'd better get going. My break is almost over and I didn't get anything to eat yet." I would have happily not eaten. I was worried about running up his bill. And about the direction the conversation was taking.

"Next time, grab something first and eat while we talk. Then we can talk longer. I want to see you soon, too. I miss you."

"I'd like that. I'll try to work something out. I just don't know… I miss you, too."

It was hard to say those words, dangerous, like a door cracked to a future. But then it was hard to hang up. I wanted to hold on to his voice, deep, confident, warm. Without his prompting me, I'd been trying to come up with a reason to go back into the city. I was thinking about him all the time, it seemed. I'd see his hands in my mind, the heavy gold ring he wore on his right hand from his undergraduate years. Big, older appearing than his face and body, his hands seemed to know how to do anything. More than once, I'd imagined them on me.

18

WEEKS OF SUMMER HUNG like the stifling humidity while I tried
to bring myself to tell Mother about Evan. I'd begun staying after
work whenever I had second shift, settling myself in the day supervisor's office to wait for the phone to ring, which it did
seconds after eleven, when the rates had gone down. Evan had
conceded that much to alleviate my worry about the size of the
bill we were running up. We were talking about ourselves, the
sides we hid from others; sometimes we even reached the
bedrock of what we usually hid from ourselves. When the
summer night was alive with stars, I'd open the window to the
left of the supervisor's desk and roll her chair in front of it so I
could lean on the sill and imagine myself next to him, somewhere, anywhere else. We two, alone in honeysuckle stillness
punctuated by peepers. I played it out in my mind, cradling the
phone.

Still, there was a fair amount I didn't reveal. I kept the worst
to myself, and, of course, how Grandmother had died. I avoided
talking about her when I could, but painting Mother sympathetically was crucial, I thought. Evan knew that she'd had some
"episodes," as I called them, and I even told him how she'd
seemed to worsen—deteriorate, I may have said—in the past
year, that I'd been writing the checks, billing her students'

parents for their lessons. How could I ever make it work if I didn't tell him that much?

Evan was fairly quiet about Mother, which I mistook as un-critical acceptance. What he was vocal about at first was Roger. I could picture him, glasses laid on the coffee table, leaning forward as he sat on the couch. He always leaned forward when he was intent.

"I don't get it, how he could just dump you with this. I can't believe he couldn't come back to relieve you during the summers."

If Evan had defended Roger, I believe it would have bothered me. Instead it was I who defended him.

"I think he just sees it differently. You know, it's like there's no halfway. You either give up your life and take care of her, or you go live your life and send postcards."

"Are you saying you'll give up yours?" He was incredulous. It was obvious to me, in the late amber of the supervisor's office, door closed to the two night nurses whose silent shoes might allow them close enough to hear me, that the very idea was insane to him.

I was careful. "No, I don't think so, not exactly. For a while I thought I'd have to—you know, he got the first chance, took it, and only one of us could. Now *he* wouldn't say that. He'd say I should do exactly what he's done, that neither of us, together or separately, can save her. That's almost an exact quote."

"Maybe it's true. But that doesn't answer what you think about you, your life. Do you get to have one whether it's true or not?"

"For a while I thought not. Now I feel like maybe…I can do both, have my own life and take care of her. No, actually that's not it. I guess I don't see those as different things…whatever life I have has to merge with hers. That's it. It's a question of whether I can add…my life to hers." It's hard to say. I held my breath for Evan's reaction, imagining him shaking his head back and forth at the other end of the phone, *no, no, no.*

"That's a tough one" was all he said at first. Then he went on. "If you get married, if anyone gets married, I think their first loyalty has to be to her…or his…husband or wife."

"But either or both can choose to take on the other's commitments, right?" How daintily we were talking around it now.

"Right...I guess that's right," he said. "Yes."

After we hung up that night, it was clear to me that I had some backtracking to do. I had to pretend to Mother that I wasn't already involved with Evan so that I could somehow get her approval to become so. I'd have to convince him I was my own woman, while fooling Mother into thinking I was still all hers.

I ASKED EVAN TO WRITE a formal little note of invitation to dinner with him, one that sounded as though we'd not been in contact, and mail it to our house. He agreed, though I could hear that he thought it was ridiculous. When I arrived home from work two days later, it was lying open on the table, rocking back and forth on its folded white spine in the breeze created by the movement of the screen door. I'd worked first shift, so the airless heat of the day was still present, the late afternoon sun glaring into the kitchen.

"There's mail for you," she said, gesturing sideways with chin and elbow.

I was careful not to look at her directly, but instead opened the refrigerator and took out the water I kept cold there.

"What is it?"

"It's from your friend...that Evan."

I poured water and stood near the sink while I drank it. Then I leaned over and used the faucet to splash some cold water on my face

"Okay. Whew, what a long, hot day. The Bicentennial fireworks are supposed to be spectacular, I heard it on the radio, but I hope it's not this hot. Oh, Mrs. Hodgkins finally finished that wallet. And guess what? They approved my purchasing a pottery wheel for the activity center. I never thought they would. I love clay. I wish I could do it myself. I loved throwing pots at Rockland. But at least this way, I'll get to help the residents make things. Some of them won't want to get their hands dirty, like Mrs. Sills, but I know some will love it. They like it when they have something to show, I think it helps them feel productive…maybe we could set up a display area…I wonder if we could sell anything, if they can make any really nice pieces, that is." I hoped I seemed to be musing aloud, my mind still at work.

"If they like you that much, maybe you don't even need to go back to school. Maybe they'll offer you a permanent job."

"Maybe they will." I washed my glass, hung up the car keys and, as I walked toward the kitchen door, pretended I happened to notice Evan's note. I picked it up and read.

"Oh, he wants me to go out to dinner with him," I said, tossing it back down. "I don't know. I've already been into the city twice this summer."

Mother seemed to relax, grow almost expansive. It was my having said, "Maybe they will," sounding cheerful and optimistic about a future at the nursing home for which I had neither desire nor intention. But wouldn't she just love it if I did?

"It *is* a long way," she agreed. "Of course, you might have a good time, though."

I'D BEEN BREATHING IN *please, God, please,* and holding my breath. "Mother, this is Evan Mairson. Evan, this is my mother, Elizabeth Ruth Kenley. I'm Ruth Elizabeth, you know," I added as though in a spontaneous aside to him. Mother beamed.

"Well, come in, Evan. It's nice to meet you. I must say, my Ruth had a lovely time when you took her out to dinner." She stepped back from the screen door and gestured him inside. I'd put on a dress, but she, as if to emphasize that the evening was nothing special to her, wore cotton slacks and a yellow sleeveless blouse, from which her upper arms spilled excess flesh.

But Evan had guessed exactly right as to how to dress for the occasion—navy blazer, tie, light blue oxford shirt, khaki trousers—without making it obvious. He looked respectful, respectable, reliable.

"I have so looked forward to meeting you, Mrs. Kenley. Ruth talks about you all the time. What a lovely place you have," he added, looking around. "I love the way it looks so warm and homey."

How did he know enough to say that? I felt a flush begin to

rise up my neck onto my cheeks as my gaze followed his. Had I told him "homey" was her word for it? How shabby it was, the threadbare blue sofa, the area rug with our traffic pattern across it obliterating a swatch of the maroon "oriental" pattern, the age-yellowed lampshades, mahogany-veneered end tables scratched and mismatched. Set on the mantel, of course, were Mother's cross and several votive candles, beneath a cheaply framed print of St. Francis of Assisi. Only the bay windows, with the covered window seats that held Roger's and my heritage, lent dignity to the room.

"Why thank you, Evan," she said, pleased. "I've always felt that way."

"Oh, yes, I do, too," I chimed in like a ninny. And unnecessarily. She was busy being charmed by Evan. He praised the baked chicken she'd made, the broccoli she'd overcooked, the minute rice. He let it slip that he didn't drink, which, of course, he did on occasion. He talked about his parents, how he felt family was the most important value in life. If I'd read a transcript of the conversation at dinner that night, I would have found it obvious, overkill, and been sure that my mother's eyes were narrowed with suspicion and distaste by seven-thirty. But I was there, I saw him reading her, responding to nuances, and getting it exactly right. I did not sense a trace of his mocking her, nor that he didn't genuinely like her.

By eight-thirty, I was relaxing into the sofa back as though it were Evan's arms, at ease for the first time in months. By nine, Evan and Mother were discussing how the tenor of the country had changed since King and Kennedy were assassinated, and she was nodding her approval of his opinion. She didn't seek mine, nor did I volunteer it. Evan fielded Mother's certainty that Carter would be the nominee, but Ford would beat him in November. They agreed the Viking I landing on Mars wasn't as important as the moon landing had been. They thought the Bicentennial had been disgustingly commercialized (but effectively marketed, Evan added). I sat next to Mother on the old blue couch, silently breathing out *thank you, thank you, thank you,* as Evan did the impossible: passed first muster. Part of me resented that he had to, part of me was simply, purely grateful that he was willing. Once during the evening I'd wondered if he'd done this before. Could he be this unerring with a girl's un-balanced mother just on good instincts? I decided I didn't care.

AFTER THAT FIRST DINNER, Evan came up two more times, on the tail of July and again in early August, when I had weekends off. Mother was much more tolerant if he came to be with us, *us* being the operative word, than when I went to be with him, which I did once in between those two weekends. She claimed she was afraid I'd catch that mystery disease the American Legionnaires were dying of, that it could spread city to city any old time. But the two days I spent with Evan in New York—having assured Mother that Columbia had overnight housing available for me in a dorm that remained open for summer students—changed me utterly, because I hadn't stayed at Columbia. I'd stayed with him.

As I'd grown comfortable with being kissed, to my own surprise, I wanted more. Evan's hands on my back seemed electrified, so visceral was my body's response, and when one strayed lower than my waist, I didn't want him to move it back up. (The first time he had held me to him tightly enough that his arms wrapped all the way around and ended almost on the sides of my breasts, I pushed closer to him. Mother had come out of the bathroom then, and we separated before she got into the living room; if she hadn't, I wonder if I might not have taken one of his hands and cupped it around a breast myself.) Twice, I'd felt him harden as he held me, and there was an ache between my legs then that I didn't recognize, couldn't name. But I wanted to feel it again, and wanted to feel his hardness push toward me.

Mother had, of course, been as adamant about sex as she was about God's other direct instructions to her. No Proper Young Woman Allows A Man To Touch Her. Men are to be Forgiven The Attempt, due to their Uncontrollable Hormones prior to Marriage. After Marriage, a Wife Accepts what a Man Must Do, to Fulfill Her Destiny. Virginity is a Holy State. Once sullied, a woman could never be a Bride of Christ, but she might be a lesser bride of a mortal man, do his laundry and bear his children.

What can I say? There I was, resonating like a plucked violin string because Evan's hand had brushed my rear when he reached to pick up my train case at Grand Central. There was moisture in my underwear, and longings of my body that seemed to focus themselves like a fine camera lens when I looked at Evan. How naive it sounds, now, unbelievable almost, yet this is the truth: even if I could have, I wouldn't have put words to the fiery desire awakening in me, how irresistible it was about to become. In Mother's words, I would have been a Cheap Little Hussy.

When I went to visit Evan after the first weekend he'd spent with Mother and me—Evan had slept at the nearest motel, two towns away—I went into his apartment more eager than anxious.

"Finally! You're all mine," he said, circling me with his arms, kissing the top of my head, and then, when I looked up at him, kissing me long and fully on the mouth. He took me to the couch, above which hung the print I'd picked out at the museum, newly matted and framed. It was the first time we'd been really alone since I'd come into the city in response to the first note he'd sent for Mother's benefit. We'd kissed then, but spent hours talking and laughing and plotting, before I had to catch the train home that night. Since that day, our conversations had continued regularly, still unknown to Mother as I continued to use the day supervisor's office where he called me ten minutes after my shift ended or during my dinner break. All this is to say that we'd not been simply marking time. Marriage had been mentioned, not in the sense of a Down On His Knees Proposal—the only kind Mother would have considered remotely proper, but in a more natural sense, as flower of what was taking root and greenly emerging between us.

I was supposed to stay at Columbia that night. I didn't. Standing next to his single bed, in one sweet, brief motion like a note in a dance, he took my nylon gown off, sliding it gently over my upraised arms. We held and caressed each other, and Evan took my breasts, then my rear in his big hands to which

I'd been attracted from the beginning. When I lay beside him with my head in the hollow of his shoulder, his chest was big enough that when I laid my arm across it, I could not reach the bed on the other side of him and I loved the sinewy height and breadth of him, the hard muscles that rested easy beneath his skin.

The ache between my legs intensified when Evan touched me there. "Ruthie, are you sure? Is this what you want?" I hesitated as Mother's voice, the image of her face came condemning then, and so, you see, I have to take responsibility. Even though it dried me up and blunted the edge of my desire, I made a choice. I chose Evan.

"I'm not…" on the Pill is what I was going to say, but Evan interrupted. He knew that. "I have a condom. Is this what you want, though, Ruthie? Are you sure?" He took my chin in his hand and lifted my face to make me look at him.

Maybe I was ready. Maybe I wasn't. I believed in waiting for marriage—and been positive I would. But here I was, the living moment eclipsing words, thought, belief, promises. Maybe I thought a man like Evan was losable, a man who had a condom and knew how to put it on. I wanted him, I wanted my own life. I wanted us. "Yes," I whispered because those wants were stronger than what else I wanted and I had to decide. "Yes."

He took my hand and we both guided him inside me. There was a searing, sudden pain, out of all proportion to what I'd understood might come, but I reminded myself I wanted this, I *chose* this, and pushed my own resistance back at him. When he finished and rolled over and off, to gather me in his arms, there was blood all around Evan's and my thighs. "My God, my God, I've hurt you, I never meant to hurt you," he said, propelled up from the bed. The sheet had a large stain, like a great amaryllis blooming beneath me.

EVAN'S PARENTS INVITED us for Labor Day weekend, and Mother agreed once she heard they had a separate guest room and bathroom and that Evan's parents assuredly would be present all weekend. Before then, though, Evan was to come up the second weekend of August, when I had Saturday and Sunday off.

Mother seemed to be more and more herself with Evan, but I do not mean that in the positive sense with which one usually uses those words. She was often either giggling, or leaning over deeply, revealing the long line of cleavage between the twin mountains of her breasts, or, just as embarrassing, speaking in sharp, contemptuous tones as she instructed me about whatever she wanted done. "Now, Ruth," she barked once, and I saw Evan's head jerk around in surprise, saw him suppress an instinct to intervene. Later, he tried to talk to me about her. "You need to stand up to her," he said later. "Or I may…"

"No!" I said immediately. "Absolutely not. I have to do this my way. Look, anyway, it's working, she's accepting *us*."

"While treating you like shit," he said, angry.

She preached her opinions, weighing them down with the Authority of God's Direct-To-Her Revelations, to make them unassailable. "Mark my words. Nothing good will come of this détente business with Russia. Jesus didn't compromise with unbelievers. He didn't call sin a difference of opinion. Coexistence isn't one of the options God offers the righteous." Occasionally she would seem confused or moodily silent, and even her pointy chin would go slack, sliding into the folds of her neck. Then the lines etched on either side of her mouth looked deep as the parentheses around a marionette's mouth, and sadness for her took my heart again. How could I not see her through his eyes (knowing, too, how much he wasn't seeing). Once she was sitting on the porch with her skirt hiked up because of the heat. She had her legs spread and I caught glimpses of her white cotton underpants. She stretched out her exposed legs and, thanks to the sunlight which threw the individual hairs into relief, I could see it had been months since she had shaved her legs. Evan either accidentally or on purpose had positioned himself so that he couldn't see how she'd arranged her skirt; I was often grateful to him for small acts of grace like that.

But I don't mean to imply that it was gratitude drawing me to him like metal to a magnet, though gratitude was certainly an ingredient, just as was my hunger to fill the vacuum Roger had left. The awakening of the sexual self is a powerful, powerful force, as is the illusion that one can merge with another person to escape a separate destiny. After the first night we made love, when I got up to clean away the blood in the bathroom, I noticed Evan's subtle cologne, the scent he always wore, emanating from me; I thought *yes, he is in me now, we are one.* The pull of Evan's body to mine was like an undertow that took away breath and control. Certainly it had that effect on me, and I believe I had the same effect on Evan. What I didn't see was how the wave pulled Mother in, too, how it ate away the sand on which she stood from beneath her feet.

I had the last Wednesday of August off. Evan borrowed his parents' car to come spend the evening with me and then take my belongings back to Sandy's and my room at Columbia. I was to return to the city on Friday, after my final shift at the nursing home.

Mother was still with the last of her students for the day when Evan arrived, at three-thirty in the afternoon. I flew out the back door and virtually threw myself at him before he even made it onto the porch.

"How did you get here so early?"

"Easy. I took the afternoon off."

"Evan! Won't that cause a problem with your boss?"

"Who cares? I have my priorities straight. Well, and part of my anatomy, too." He grinned, that warm, wide grin that went right through me and added, "But it just happens that I'm the one who worked last weekend on the storyboard for the new campaign. He gave me the afternoon off."

I gave him another hug and he pulled me in close, holding me against him for a long minute. "We have to walk outside or we're confined to the kitchen," I said. "Mother's still got a student."

"Okay by me," he said and, holding my hand, he headed for the road doing an imitation of a clumsy soft shoe and singing, *"Oh we ain't got a barrel of money, maybe we're ragged and funny, but we'll travel along, singing our song, side by side."*

"Oh, we don't know what's coming tomorrow. Maybe it's trouble and sorrow...." I could tell he was surprised I knew the words, let alone the old tune, but it was one Mother used to sing to Roger and me on our camping expeditions.

"But we'll travel along, singing our song, side by side." This last was a duet, the effect of which was spoiled by our compet-

ing to add dramatic vibrato to our voices and breaking into laughter before the last note.

"How do you know that?" he asked.

I thumbed toward the window from which a halting D major scale was being played with too much breath and several overblows. "She's a music teacher, silly. And every now and then, she used to sing something other than 'Amazing Grace' or the 'Alleluia Chorus'. Not often, I admit. How do *you* know it?"

"My dad sings all that old stuff around the house. Drives everyone nuts. If you give him a giant basket and put handles on both sides, he couldn't carry a tune in it."

We walked for fifteen minutes, but then headed back when the afternoon's accumulated heat got to us. Mother's student was still puffing away, so we stuck to the kitchen. Evan pulled out a chair and plunked himself down on it. Then he reached for my hand, and when I extended it, he pulled me onto his lap.

"I've missed you so much," I said, sniffing his neck to take in his cologne.

"Likewise, ma'am."

"It will be a lot easier in a couple of days, you know. At least we'll be in the same city."

"In the same room, in the same bed, too, as often as possible," he murmured, and kissed me.

I have no idea what Mother actually saw. I'd not heard her dismiss the student, nor the front door open and close. And I hadn't heard her normally heavy footsteps approach the kitchen. Had she heard the reference to the same bed? Did she see Evan's one hand welcomed beneath my shirt, the other curving itself around my rear where it met his thigh, while I alternately lifted my head to receive his kiss and replaced it on his shoulder? Nothing of that instant is clear to me except the burning flush that spread up my neck and face, the internal cringe as I sensed her presence and nearly jumped from his lap.

"What's the mat...?" he asked. Then he saw her, too. At the time, she didn't say a thing, but acted as though nothing had happened. Evan, too, acted as if nothing had happened, but because he didn't know what really had. I busied myself with getting a glass of water while Evan said, "Hi, Mrs. Kenley. It's good to see you. I hope my getting here early didn't disturb your teaching."

"Not at all," she said. To an outsider, she would have seemed fine. Long attuned to her, though, I felt the disturbance in the field and spent the evening trying to make up to her. But what Evan and I had let happen in the kitchen was the first mistake from which there would be no return.

THURSDAY, THE NEXT DAY, I arrived home tired from being up late with Evan the night before, then working the seven to three shift at the nursing home. Mother was waiting for me.

"Where's Carrie?" I asked. Mother should have been teaching.

"I didn't feel up to it today," she answered crisply, not at all like someone who was sick.

Privately I moaned. She had canceled a number of lessons lately, which meant her checkbook wouldn't have enough to cover the bills. I'd have to put in extra from my small check again. "I'm so sorry. Can I get you anything? Why don't you lie down, and I'll get you some dinner."

"No." Then I saw she was holding a leather belt in one hand, doubled, the way she used to hold it when she was getting ready to whip me. "Here. I want you to use this," she said extending it to me.

"What?" I had no idea what she meant. It had flashed through my mind she intended to whip me for what she'd seen the day before, in spite of the fact I was bearing down on twenty-one years old, but why was she handing me the belt?

"Don't act stupid. I want you to use this." With that, she picked up the dead weight of my right hand and forced the belt into it. Then she began to take off her shorts. In a moment she stood, flesh rolling above and below the elastic barriers of white underpants and bra, and turned her back to me.

"Wait. What? I don't know what you mean?" I was stammering and panicky.

She turned around to face me. Impatiently, angrily, she said,

"All right, if I have to spell it out. I've had some urges. Impure urges. This is what monks and nuns do to cleanse themselves."

I still didn't understand. She grew furious. "Beat me. You are to beat me. This is how I will be cleansed."

Horrified, I began backing up. "I can't do that, Mother."

"Oh. I see. All the years I've loved you enough to cleanse you, to give you what you needed to be good, and when I ask you to do the same for me, the answer is no? You *will* do it. I will not be made to live with unholiness or impurity. I will not be thinking about men or filth. Now do it," she ordered, and turned and bent, bracing herself against the old blue couch.

I stood as though paralyzed. "Please, I...no, you don't deserve it, I can't," I begged.

She stood and grabbed the belt from me, shouting, "You will do it, you will," flailing at me with the belt. "I will whip you until you obey me."

"Mother," I cried. "Mother, no." It did no good. She had completely lost control. The belt was landing hard across my back and thighs, where it lost momentum in the gathers of my uniform skirt. "Take it off." She was sobbing.

"All right. I'll do it." I was sobbing, too. She brought the belt down on me one more time, from close enough that it wrapped itself across my back, and around my chest, the very end snapping against my cheek. Then she thrust the belt at me again and turned to brace herself against the sofa.

"Do it," she screamed, as I hesitated. "Say this—you will not be impure. You will not be filthy."

"You will not be impure. You will not be filthy," I said, hitting her lightly with the belt, beginning to shudder as I did.

With a roar of rage, she turned, grabbed the belt and pushed me across the couch. "This is how you cleanse someone of filthy thoughts," she said, lashing with a force she'd pent-up forever. "This is how, this is how, this is how." With each repetition, the belt screamed down. She yanked the skirt of my uniform up to expose the flesh of my legs and thighs. "This is how, this is how." Finally I screamed, then Mother's scream mixed with mine and the belt's in a room empty of all but noise and fire. She threw the belt at me again. "Do it. Do it right. Say it. Say it right."

And I did. I said it and more. "You will not be impure." The belt rose and fell. Rose and fell to a feverish, furied shout in my mind. I believe it was only in my mind, but I think she must have heard. *You will tell me who my father is.* The belt rose and fell. *You will not drag me around place to place ever again.* Rose and fell. *You will not ever hit me, kick me, again.* Rose and fell. *You will not take away my chance for a life.* Rose and fell. *I hate you.* Rose and fell. Rose on *I hate…* and fell on *you.*

I STOPPED WHEN SHE screamed "Stop." Later, while she ran her tub, I controlled my trembling and used the cover of the open faucet to call Evan to say Mother was sick and I had to stay long enough to get her over the worst of it. "Don't catch what she has," he said.

"It's probably too late," I answered, my worst fear.

Three days later, Sunday night, I went back to school. In those three days, no mention was made by either of us of the unspeakable pain of walking, of putting on and taking off clothes. Filthy thoughts were not thought, and I went back to school carrying the marks of the chain Mother had created, the chain that bound me to my grandmother, and now to her, the same chain that had bound her to Grandmother even from three thousand miles away. For all I knew, it was the whole tie of generation to generation in our family, at least the women. The men seemed capable of escape, but not us. We were bound forever, not by blood, not even by sorrow. Guilt. Guilt pinned us like butterflies on the black velvet that passed for love.

"WHAT IS IT, RUTHIE, what's going on?" Evan pressed in his second call of the evening. Now that I was back in New York, he took advantage of being able to call whenever he wanted. I faced the institutional tan wall of the dorm hallway, slightly hunched, trying to keep my conversation private. I was barefoot, but wore slacks while everyone else was in shorts, yellow plums of bruises still on my legs.

"Nothing. I told you, nothing's wrong, except maybe I'm a little nervous about meeting your parents. I just want to have all this school stuff done so I can concentrate on being with you and getting to know them." I tried to relax, keep it convincingly casual.

I'd been ducking Evan since Sunday night. When he called, I'd tell him that Sandy and I were setting up our room, that I had to get my books, I had to check on my financial aid, whatever I could think of to put him off a few more days. I could lie to Sandy, tell her I'd gotten the mark on my face and neck when I was doing yardwork for Mother, that a tree branch had snapped back onto me. I could even lie to Evan to the extent that I could manufacture pressing tasks to keep us apart a few extra days, but I didn't want to look him in the face and lie about the bruise on mine, and I didn't want to risk his seeing the marks on my body. And the control I'd regained over my heartbeat, jumpy stomach, tremulous voice didn't feel solid to me yet. But

I look back and realize how much I'd already changed, that I never considered not seeing Evan. Perhaps I thought Mother really only took issue with sex, and certainly I could ensure that she never saw Evan and I so much as touch each other again until we'd been married for twenty-five years. Or perhaps, it was that ancient human bugaboo: convincing oneself that something is possible because one desperately wants it to be.

I FELT GUILTY ABOUT LIKING Evan's parents so much. His mother was welcoming, kind to me, and good-naturedly teasing Evan right off. His father, on the short side and balding, was more reserved, but bided his time and got a few licks in. Mrs. Mairson had set a beautiful, formal table with gold-edged china, sterling silver and Waterford crystal. I knew it was Waterford because she took a lot of ribbing about it, how she cared more for it than all of her sons put together.

"Damn right. And don't you forget it," she tossed back. "The Waterford is better looking and knows when to keep quiet. And it's…brighter than you all, too," she said sliding a candle to one side of the wineglass to heighten the effect. "Don't you let him get away with anything, honey," she said to me. "Keep him in his place." Evan wadded up his blue cloth napkin and threw it at her.

"What, no matzo balls tonight, Mom?" he prodded. "I've described their culinary splendor to Ruth. Actually, I'd wanted her to take a few back into New York, so she'd have bullets handy in case someone tried to mug her."

"Perhaps it would be better not to use them in that manner, anyway, Evan. I believe your Ruth is a sensitive sort, who would be troubled by killing someone, even in self-defense," his father said dryly. The remark seared through me.

We were circumspect at night, remaining in the family room with his parents during the evenings and sticking to separate rooms once we'd said good-night, but during the days, our time was quite our own. We went for walks in nearby woods, holding hands, sitting once on a fallen log to talk and hold each other. "This is the kind of family I want to have," I said to him. "No one afraid, no one unhappy."

"Ah, someone's always unhappy about something around here. The Jewish half, I guess. That's okay, though. It passes. But you're right, no one is afraid. Have you been…afraid with your mother or brother?"

"Afraid for my mother, yes."

"I thought maybe you meant afraid *of* her."

"That's not what I meant."

"That would make me crazy, you know? I can't stand the thought of you being frightened." He was looking directly at me. He knows I'm lying, I thought.

"I've never felt safer than with you." And that much was the absolute truth. Even with Roger, there had always been a little leftover fear, as though the little finger of danger still cast a shadow just behind him or to one side where he couldn't see it, but I could.

Sunday night, his dad barbecued chicken on a charcoal grill. We were on their patio, edged by lush late summer impatiens that ran up and down the major scale between red and white, hitting every tone and half tone. Enormous trees held hands over our heads while lit torches held back the early night. "Oh boy, are you in for a treat," Evan said. "Dad's original formula for the creation of fossils." That's how light the mood was, so at first, I didn't even catch on to what Evan was saying. Right after harassing Mr. Mairson about needing a hook and ladder company to extinguish the fire he was burning the chicken in, he said, casually, "I think you two ought to know that Ruth and I are making future plans. Nothing specific at the moment, but, well, now that you've met her, I just wanted to…well, I guess I just…well, now you know…" he trailed off in an uncharacteristic blush.

Mrs. Mairson's face lit and I recognized Evan's grin there. She shot her husband the told-you-so look of the long and well married, got up and came over to hug me, then Evan, then me again. "Nothing could make me happier, son. Nothing," she said to him over my shoulder. Mr. Mairson began to shake Evan's hand, then the hand that was on Evan's shoulder drew him into a bear hug. When Mr. Mairson turned to hug me, there were tears in his eyes.

"*Mazel tov. Mazel tov.* You make each other happy, you make us happy."

"Whoa, Dad. Don't use up all your *mazels* and *tovs* until I get a ring on her finger. We—well, I—just wanted you to know the direction things are going. Poor Ruthie didn't even know I was going to mention it." He turned to me. "I hope you didn't mind? It just sort of came out. These two are usually in on anything big I've got going."

My turn to blush. "I don't mind." And I didn't.

"Wait!" Mrs. Mairson exclaimed. "I think I've got…but it's not cold…" She hurried inside, a whoosh of long blue hostess dress behind her. In a moment, she came back, beaming, carrying a bottle of champagne. "I'm not trying to rush you two…" she said when Evan said she should save it for an official occasion. "We might not be with you, then, and…besides, this is to celebrate that you two have found each other."

Evan reached for the bottle. The cork popped like a shot.

That night, Evan's parents went to bed early, leaving us alone in the living room. I was admiring the room's unpretentious comfort and warmth. House plants, even one big enough to be considered a little tree, were set amid the soft colors, and family mementos along with books, magazines and pictures said, "This is a living room for *living*." I understood how he'd been able to do his apartment so beautifully, the same way Sandy had learned how to make our room best in the dorm. It had to do with what they'd absorbed by living with someone who had money, taste and wanted her home to be inviting and well-used. Evan and Sandy both lived in wealthy areas, at least compared to Malone and the other little towns we'd lived in; in Evan's hometown, there were newer, sprawling ranch houses on wooded acre-lots, but on the way through the village, we'd also passed elegant two-story houses impeccably maintained on manicured grounds with cushioned, white wicker porch furniture and croquet set up on the lawn.

I was musing about how much Evan seemed a combination of his parents, his height, fair coloring, features and expansiveness from his mother, his need for glasses, big hands, seriousness and intellectualism from his father, when he said, "I really was out of line saying anything without checking with you. I'm usually not like that. It felt really natural, having you here, and you fit so well with them. I can tell they like you."

"Really?"

"*Oy vey,* what's not to like? What's not to love?" he was mimicking his dad, then he turned serious. "I do love you, you know."

"I love you, too."

"For the rest of your life?"

"All of it." I was carried on a river of love for Evan and suddenly I was over the waterfall, letting go of what I should have worried about.

"I didn't plan this for tonight, but it feels right." Evan took both my hands, one enveloped in each of his. "Ruthie, will you marry me?"

"Yes. Yes, I'll marry you."

"So now it *is* official, right? This is it. We're engaged? You're sure, you're not too young, you really know this is what you want. I mean, *I'm* what you want…who you want? To marry."

"What *and* who. To marry. I know what I want, and it's you." Evan and I held each other's eyes for a moment, then each broke into a smile. He pulled on my hands to bring me closer, then put my arms around his own waist, and his around mine. "Come here," he said. "Come as close as you can. And stay."

We kissed, Evan caressing my head and wrapping his fingers with my hair. "I love you so much," I whispered. "It would scare me to love you so much, except that you make me feel so safe."

"You are safe with me." We were quiet for a minute. I was thinking about Mother, how to approach her when Evan said, "I bet Mom and Dad were giving up on me ever getting married. I am a bit…old…you know. And I do know that you're not, that we have to take your school into consideration. But I make enough to support us. We can get married before you graduate, if you're willing, and you can commute."

"Evan, it's going to take me some time to deal with Mother.

I have to think of her." Now, when everything I wanted was right in front of me—a man my mother actually liked, one I adored, one who tolerated her demands on me—was I going to risk it by insisting he see how sick she was? I still thought I had some control, that I could make it all work.

"I know, sweetheart. It's okay, I'll help you." It was the first time he'd used an endearment, and it was like he'd pushed a hidden button marked Core Meltdown. I hadn't known how hungry I was for that kind of verbal tenderness, but there I was, crying. I so wanted to believe I wasn't in this life alone, that someone can be fully with you. I wanted Evan to save me, with his strong hands, strong mind, strong love, and in return I would give myself over to him. It was still a while before I learned, the hard way as usual, that the best we can hope for is a companionship in our separate alonenesses.

I'D INTENDED TO LEAVE Friday after my last class, but Evan had virtually insisted on my staying at his apartment that night and going home Saturday morning. I hadn't yet told Mother about our engagement; I was certain it was best for me to do it alone and in person. Of course, I didn't tell Evan how unpredictable her reaction might be, or that I was unwilling to risk his seeing her at her worst. He thought it was rude, that he should be with me. "Really, you know, I should *ask* her, to be old-fashioned correct," he'd said. "At least for her blessing. But it seems silly, you know? We're adults, it's your decision after all."

I hadn't commented. My decision? As if I were unchained, free, unencumbered. As if the craziness, the pain, the sheer destructive force she'd unleashed first in herself, then in me right before I came back to school hadn't just double-locked the chain that bound me to her, made me complicit yet again. Blue capsules emptied into a sick woman's water weren't enough; no, she'd had to show me that in my depths I was no different than she, I was my mother's daughter after all. If I couldn't win her agreement, could I risk what she might reveal?

Evan finally accepted my going alone, but not on Friday.

"Nope. No can do. Can't go home to tell your mother without being with me first." Even over the phone, I could tell he'd made up his mind but I twirled a lock of hair, inspecting it for split ends, while I tried once more.

"Why, honey? I think it would be better if I spend as much time with her as I can…in case she thinks I'm still too young, or whatever." I was using the married-sounding endearments myself now.

"I have my reasons. You can catch the earliest train you want Saturday morning, but Friday night is mine. And one more thing…do you think you could wear that black dress of Sandy's?"

"The one I wore when we met?"

"That's the one."

"I'll ask her. What time do you want me to get there?"

"Nope again. I'm picking you up. Six o'clock sharp."

I laughed in resignation. "You drive a hard bargain, sir. I hope you'll be easier to manage when we're married."

"No chance of that."

"Well, I guess I'll just have to love you anyway."

"I'll try to endure. Good night, sweetheart." We hung up then, suppressed laughter bubbling through our voices.

AT SIX O'CLOCK, THE GIRL sitting bells in the lobby buzzed up to me. Evan was downstairs in a suit and tie, the same, I thought, he'd worn the night we met. He hailed a cab, a Friday night miracle, and directed the driver to the Russian Tea Room. When we arrived, he simply said, "I'm Evan Mairson" to the maître d' who smiled broadly, shook Evan's hand, and showed us to a table already set with a bottle of champagne on ice. The maître d' pulled out a chair for me.

"This seat for the beautiful lady," he said. Laid across my plate was a single red rose, resting on a fern and several sprigs of baby's breath in a cone of florist paper. A waiter hustled over with a narrow vase, which the maître d' set in the center of the table.

"Perhaps you would like to keep your flower fresh while you are here?" he smiled. "And may I add my best wishes."

"Oh, Evan. I can't believe this. Thank you." But there was more. When the maître d' removed the tissue in which the rose was wrapped, he uncovered a tiny white florist's envelope, which he handed to me. The rose bouquet was tied in a bow of white lace. The card had a wedding bell on it and said, *"For Ruth, With this ring…" comes all my love, today, tomorrow and always, Evan.* I looked up to see Evan draw his hand from his pocket.

"May I have your hand? Your left hand?" When I extended it, he separated my fourth finger and slid a solitaire diamond set in gold into place.

"Evan. I don't know what to say. I never expected…it's beautiful. How did you…?"

"Oh, that." He grinned, pleased with himself. "Easy. I had Sandy steal your high school ring from your jewelry box for me so I could have this one sized. It's back in place, safe and sound. Looks like a fit to me. So you like it?"

"Sandy knew? I love it. I love *you.*"

"Of course Sandy knew. Why else would she have been so decent about loaning you her dress again after you drooled all over it last time? I love you, Ruth. Count on it."

"At least it was water. Someone I know spit wine halfway across the room. I do. I will."

I'D MISSED THE FIRST two trains from Grand Central to New Haven. Evan and I had stayed out late, then stayed awake talking in bed after we made love in the amber light of two candles. Our lovemaking had already come a long way as my initial shyness dissipated slowly, like heavy smoke, and we grew into knowledge of each other's bodies. That magical night, riding excitement, courageous from the commitment we'd made, we were the most intimate we'd yet been, and neither of us wanted to relinquish consciousness to sleep. We shared a pillow and lay in each other's arms laying down layers of waking dreams. I loved him with unqualified first love—we always believe it will be the last, as well, though it only occasionally is—wholehearted, pure, the adoration we have for our truest hero before it is sullied by disappointment, by failure.

I should have been using train time to study my *Casebook of Occupational Therapy*, but, I suppose, like any twenty-year-old girl newly engaged, I studied my left hand instead, shifting its position by small degrees to see the diamond break the sunlight into tiny rainbows. I'd had to take a local, but I didn't mind so much because with a twenty-five minute wait in New Haven, I could connect with an express and still be in Malone by noon. When I arrived, I called Mother from the pay phone to come get me, but there was no answer. I sighed and shifted my bag, heavy with the books I'd intended to study on the train, to the other shoulder and began to walk. It wasn't far; we lived perhaps a mile from the small station, but there was no sidewalk. Walking on the uneven shoulder of the road—often unmowed and sometimes litter-strewn—was slow, and I was already later than I'd said I would be.

Just before I reached our gravel driveway, I slid the ring off my finger and put it beneath a handkerchief in the pocket of my denim skirt, which was deep. I patted it there, like a tangible prayer. I'd have to feel out how to tell her, to show her the ring, somehow involve her in the decision to accept Evan's proposal and ring, which, of course, I'd already done. But things always went much better when they were Mother's decisions. I hadn't lived with her for twenty years for nothing; she never did take surprises well.

Her car was there, which worried me. Either she'd just returned home or she wasn't answering the phone, a sure danger signal. The back door was locked, so I used my key.

"Mother? Mother, it's me. Where are you?" There was no answer. I went through the kitchen to the living room—not the room fixed up as a studio, where Roger used to sleep, but the one I slept in, the blue couch room—where I found her, disheveled-looking, sitting rigidly in the tattered stuffed chair. Her bare face was expressionless, and she didn't respond by so much as looking at me. Noon light speared through the silence of the bay window, backlighting Mother, making a halo of her hair and connecting her by dust motes in a direct line to the outside, to the sky, to God.

"Mother? Are you all right?"

Still no answer. "Mother! Are you sick?" I was alarmed. Even when I knelt next to her and used her head to block the sun from my eyes, her face looked gaunt, the clenched jaw emphasizing the hollows of her eyes and cheekbones. A button was missing from the chest of her faded blouse, some kind of a stain to the left above that. I knelt next to her and picked up the rough, short-nailed hand stiff in the cushion of her lap. She roughly jerked it away.

"Don't you touch me. What are you here for?"

"Mother, we talked yesterday. Remember?" Indeed we had talked on the phone five times in the two weeks since I'd returned to school, and she'd been cheerful enough. Nothing had ever been said about the scene before I'd gone back to college, but I'd been grateful enough for her alacrity that I'd not questioned it. As for me, as for what I'd done, I wasn't equipped to handle the implications. They could have shadowed, eclipsed, everything I had to believe to keep going. I treated them as I would any undetonated explosive device; I skirted them by a wide empty margin.

"No. I didn't talk to you," she said flatly.

It was impossible she didn't remember. "Honestly, Mother. I'm a little later than I said I'd be, and I'm sorr…"

"No. I talked to my daughter, not some stranger who sneaks around behind my back." Accusation and conviction clipped the consonants. I wore a new jersey top Mrs. Mairson had had delivered from Bloomingdale's yesterday because, she said, it matched my eyes and "I've always wanted a daughter to buy for." I'd worn traces of eyeliner, subtle green shadow and mascara Sandy had chosen when she helped me dress for the Russian Tea Room. Even my nails were longer, coated with a pale polish, and my hair was brushed out unrestrained, the way Evan loved it. How could I have been so stupid as to show up at home like this? As if she might have said I looked pretty?

"I haven't done anything behind your back." I don't believe I even flushed when this rolled out of my mouth, smooth as pudding. It was a marker of either how far I'd come or how low

I'd sunk. It wasn't the makeup at all, I thought suddenly, but the flush and scent of sex, as unwashable as a soul. Either that or it was the shouts of my mind, audible after all, as the belt in my hand had risen and fell.

"No? That isn't what your future mother-in-law had to say this morning." She kept her head turned away as if the sight of me sickened her.

"What?" I couldn't figure out what to deny quickly enough.

She snapped her head around to stare me down, blue ice-eyed. "Oh, yes. I suspect you know the one. She called to say how much they liked you, how delighted they were that you and her son were…how did she say it?…oh, yes…making plans, and what a wonderful match you are."

Panic began to flood me like a broken water main. Had Evan called his parents and told them he'd given me an engagement ring? Had that spurred his mother to call mine? I'd told them I lived in Malone, Connecticut, but surely if Evan had called his parents this morning, he would have told them I was on my way to tell my mother. We'd told *them* the morning after Evan proposed, but they knew *my* mother didn't know yet. Maybe because I was on a later train, the wires had somehow been crossed? My mind was wild, racing, frantic.

"Wait, Mother. What exactly did she say?" I angled for time. "I don't really know what's going on here."

She gave a snort of disgust or disbelief or both. "I told you what she said. Apparently you and Evan have plans you haven't bothered to discuss with your mother."

I had to risk it. Forcing myself to look at her, I said, "Mother, I think I know what happened. You know, I'd accepted the invitation to visit them before…uh, before I went back to school. Evan mentioned to his parents—remember, they didn't even know we were dating until a few weeks ago—in sort of a light-hearted way that there might be a future in this." I paused, as if figuring it out. "I think his mother must have caught that ball and run for a touchdown with it. I didn't want to embarrass Evan in front of his parents, but later I told him I'd have to discuss it with you, and that he might be getting too serious for me. She's very nice, Mother, but maybe a little overly enthusiastic." The die was cast.

"She did sound a little gushy. But she certainly gave the impression that you and Evan were, as she put it, making plans. And she wanted to know if I'd talked to you about it."

I frantically laid track even while the train was barreling down after me ready to derail. "Here's what I think it is. You know how Evan's a little older than I am and finished school and all that. I think they just want him to get married, so maybe she just sort of jumps at the smallest thing."

"I didn't really think you'd do that to me," she said, childlike now. Is a sick person always innocent in some defining way?

I kept my hand carefully away from my skirt, where the ring was setting fire to my pocket, and smiled as though it were a simple misunderstanding. "I'm so sorry she upset you. Of course, I had no idea what she was thinking. How about I make us some ice tea? What needs doing around here? I'm all yours."

"The garden is a mess." The tension had drained from her voice. She so wanted, needed it all not to be true.

"Well, I'll get you some tea and then I'll go see what I can do about it." I headed for the kitchen, trying to breathe normally, not reveal the shaking legs that felt like sticks too fragile to carry me. I got the tea, smiled at her and went outside to the garden, still trying to fill my lungs. Then, I saw how close I'd really come, and couldn't imagine what would have happened if I hadn't risked the lie. My mind reeled, darkened like a fading screen trying to black out the memory of what she'd done to me and I to her the last time I'd been home. Every zinnia, every single one, had been uprooted and tossed into a heap of chaos, the bright, full blossoms in a tangle of dirt and roots, freshly begun to die.

20

THE FIRST TIME MOTHER went to the bathroom after I came in from cleaning up the garden, I took my engagement ring from my pocket and zipped it into the bottom of a compartment in my purse with tissue, pen, lipstick and a roll of Life Savers scrunched together over it. I set to dusting, cleaning the bathroom, washing dishes crusted with old, unidentifiable remains, billing her students' parents, getting groceries into the house. I didn't allow myself to think about Evan. I knew he'd be worried that I hadn't called him, but he'd know enough not to call me. He'd guess something was wrong. I had to stay focused on shoring her up; even thinking about Evan could have been dangerous. I could feel her watching me, listening.

I didn't even put the ring back on my finger until I'd changed trains in New Haven. It was as if my life had split into two: where I had to be, where I wanted to be. I'd spent the first part of the trip trying to figure out how to proceed with Mother. From New Haven to New York, I concentrated on Evan, how to tell him that I hadn't told Mother, and why.

WE WERE IN THE COFFEE shop right outside Grand Central on Forty-second Street, where Evan had met me. "We just have to start all over," I said to him. My hair felt stifling, too heavy on my neck and shoulders and I gathered it in my hands wishing

I could fasten it out of my way. "She couldn't have begun to handle it if it had turned out to be true after your mother's call."

"I guess I can see any woman's mother being a little hurt that the man's parents knew and she didn't, but couldn't you just tell her that you wanted to surprise her with the ring?" He was annoyed or disappointed or both, trying not to show it.

Suddenly I was exhausted. I leaned back in the booth and closed my eyes, too heavy with uncried tears to hold open. "I've told you she's…she's got serious problems, emotional problems. You don't know…how sick she is. You know I have to take care of her. I'm sorry, I'm really sorry, but I've tried and tried to explain to you." Frustration must have been on my face or in my voice, because Evan stood so he could reach across the table to get a hold of my arm, then my hand. He pulled it up onto the table where he could hold it.

"I'm so sorry my mother called. I had no idea she was going to do that. I hadn't mentioned the problems to them, it didn't seem the time. I should have thought of it. I'll take care of it, see that nothing like that happens again." I hated the thought of Evan trying to explain to them. They might have kept on liking me. "Shouldn't we try to get some help for her, a doctor? Not that I think you haven't done that."

I knew exactly how my mother would react to any suggestion something was wrong with her, so I went around the question, circling back to the issue at hand. "The truth is it was probably too soon to tell her anyway. We had an incident of sorts right before I came back to school, after she saw us kissing in the kitchen, when I was on your lap, you know, when she was giving a lesson, and she didn't take it well. I probably wasn't being realistic about telling her this weekend."

I watched the struggle on Evan's face. How bizarre it must seem to him. Neither of us was fourteen, or even sixteen. If we wanted to kiss, whatever we wanted to do, wasn't it our business? What did this have to do with taking care of a sick woman, even a mentally ill one, if I could bring myself to using those words?

"Look, whether I understand all that or not, I trust your

judgment. You're the one who's been living with this all these years. I promised I'd help and I will. You tell me what we need to do."

"Oh, Evan. Oh, sweetheart, thank you. I'm sorry it's like this. I'm so sorry, but thank you. I do love you."

BY THE END OF THE WEEK, I had what I thought was a plan. Thursday night, we had dinner in his apartment. "I'll go home by myself again this weekend. This time I'll mention your name."

His fork stopped midway and went back down. "You didn't even mention me last weekend?"

"Evan, you said…"

"I'm sorry. Okay. What will be stage two, if mentioning my name is stage one?"

"I need to tell you more of what happened." I told him about the zinnias, how close to the edge I'd seen her. I didn't tell him what had happened the last time she'd gone over the edge, because then he'd see me, too: complicit, guilty, dirtied by rage and the infliction of pain. He might see all the way back to blue capsules, a glass of clear water pierced by a straw of evil, not mercy.

I'd put more than enough on his plate already. "It scared me," I finished. "I've seen that look on her before…sometimes she'd disappear for days when Roger and I were kids."

"What?" His eyebrows made diagonal lines of shock, incredulity, anger. I'd told him too much now.

"Oh, we were old enough," I covered. "That's not the point. It's just that she can really lose control of herself."

"Does she lose control of herself when she loses control of you?"

Bingo, I thought, even though I'd not once realized it that clearly myself. Finally I said, "Well, that may be some of it. But it's because she's so frightened of losing me. I'm all she has."

"*Are* you under her control, or do you just try to keep her believing you are?"

Truth. "I used to be. Completely. But have you noticed my new jewelry?" I gestured to the ring on my left hand. "And stage two will be to ask her if you can come with me sometime soon. I'll say you've been calling, and that you mentioned how much you'd like to see the two of us again."

"So it's yes to the second part, that you're going to try to keep her believing you are. I don't know, Ruthie." He shook his head, not in disagreement, but in concern. "Push is going to knock on shove's door sooner or later." He wadded up his napkin and tossed it down.

"I'll handle it," I said, and leaned over the table to kiss him as we stood up to go. Her control of me wasn't an illusion. Not by a long shot. But I spent Thursday night with Evan, sleeping in a T-shirt of his, my underwear washed out and draped around his bathroom to dry. He ran out to the drugstore and bought me a toothbrush and a hairbrush, which I pointedly left there when, a little late, I took off for school the next morning.

I PROCEEDED WITH STAGE one of the plan. Saturday afternoon, after I'd thoroughly cleaned, caught up the laundry and waited for the best mood she was likely to be in, I said, "Oh, I meant to tell you, Evan called."

She tensed, I thought. "What did he want?"

"Oh, he wanted to have dinner. I was too busy, though, getting settled in with classes. He said he'd call back."

"Are you going to go?" I knew that her phrasing it as a question was largely a trap. This was vintage Mother.

"What do you think I should do?"

Was I imagining it or did that answer relieve her? "As long as it's just a dinner, I suppose. Don't stay out late, though. And stick to a public place."

THE NEXT WEEKEND, IT was she who brought it up before I had identified a good moment. "So did you go out to dinner with that…Evan?" Another trap. If I said yes, then I'd have been hiding it, having not told her immediately myself. I was becoming wily, slipping ahead of her like a cat in the jungle, guarding against any misstep.

"Not yet. He called, but I told him next week was better. You know I would have told you."

She thought I didn't see it, but I did: she smiled.

The next Wednesday I called her. "Well, I'm having dinner with Evan tomorrow night."

"That's nice. Remember, stick to public places. Make him send you back to the dorm in a taxi, too."

"Oh, this won't be such a big deal. I think we're just going to a place nearby, and keep it short. I have a lot of studying to do."

"Good. You remember what's important."

Evan was disappointed, a little impatient at this pace of "bringing her around." My days were filled with classes, and I was doing a practicum at the hospital, too. Of course, he worked during the days anyway. The weekends, which we could have spent together, I was in Connecticut, doing repair work. We fell into a pattern of spending at least two nights a week in his apartment. We'd have dinner, sometimes carry-in, sometimes—if my schoolwork wasn't too backed up—we'd cook. More and more of my things ended up at Evan's: a nightgown, extra makeup, a few clean blouses, two sweaters. He gave me a drawer in his dresser, a side of his closet, a shelf in the medicine cabinet.

"It kills me to give up every Saturday and Sunday," he said on Friday morning, when he had to leave for work before I did for school. "I need you, too, you know. We can't go on like this."

I still didn't feel like he was threatening me, though. Not setting an ultimatum. So I just said, "I know. I'm sorry. I'm doing the best I can."

MAYBE IT WAS FEAR OF an ultimatum, though, because the next day I went ahead and tried. "Mother, Evan called again," I said, over the canned chicken chow mein we were having for dinner. "He said he would really like to see the two of us again, and wondered if he could come here to visit sometime."

"What does he want with *me?*" Somehow she got it into her tone, though the words hung like silent ghosts in the air: *I know damn well what he wants with you.*

"I think he just likes you." What a fine, fine liar I was becoming. "Harrumph." A snort.

"Do you think it would be okay? I'm sure he'd fix the bathroom door." A hinge had been broken for quite a while, and though I thought I could fix it, this was better. "He'd probably help with the storm windows, too. You know it's hard on your back to hand them to me."

"Well, if he'll do that, I guess he can come. I don't want him here the whole weekend, though."

"Oh, I'm sure he didn't expect anything like that."

BETWEEN THE FIRST OF October and the middle of November, Evan washed and hung the storm windows, turned the garden over, fixed the bathroom door, changed the oil in Mother's car and replaced one of the back porch steps. He bought and hung a storm door in place of the rickety screen, which was all the Jensens had ever had there. He'd come three times, each time carefully not touching me, each time paying a good deal of attention to Mother. Mother had begun to flirt with him again, just a little, and finally, when he said, "I've got to get going, or I'll miss that train. Ruthie, could you run me to the station?" on the Saturday night of the third visit, she came out.

"Oh, why don't you just stay and go back tomorrow with Ruth?"

"Mrs. Kenley, that's so kind of you. I'd really like to do that, but I didn't bring anything with me, and I don't have a reservation."

"I see. Of course. Well, next time, then?"

"That would be wonderful. Thank you so much for the invitation."

In the car, we hugged, exultant. "It's working! Thank you sweetheart!" I said. His hands looked like he worked in a garage; he'd changed the oil in Mother's car. I licked two fingers and cleaned a smudge from his face before he got out at the station.

"Hey, don't thank me. I don't really mind the work. In the second place, even if I did, you're worth it. It's stupid that you have to manipulate just to have your own life...but...well. It's strange, you know? She can seem so nice. Sometimes you'd never know anything was wrong." Those last words worried me; there was so much not on display. "What train will you be on tomorrow?"

"I'll try to be on the one that gets in at 6:06," I said, knowing it would be a struggle to get away midafternoon as I'd have to.

"Ah, I'd hoped for earlier, but I'll be there."

"You don't have to meet me."

"Don't be slow-witted. How else could I kidnap you and make sure we spend the night together?" he laughed.

"How about we invite your mother to Thanksgiving at my parents' with us? I can certainly get them to play dumb, and maybe we could tell them all at the same time that we want to get married?"

The idea seemed riddled with risks to me. "Oh, sweetheart. We've come so far in working this out. There's so many chances for it to go wrong. Anyone could let something slip. We can't go through this all over."

I'd disappointed him again. "How about over Christmas break? Maybe between now and then, we can tell her ourselves, then have her meet your parents during the break. I won't be so pushed for time, and we can do it in two steps instead of one," I proposed.

Evan agreed, his face relaxing. "All right. As long as we're getting along with it, I guess I can handle a couple extra weeks. Mom and Dad will be disappointed, though. They're wanting to get this in the paper, get a date set, all that. And what I want is to marry you."

"I don't think anyone can want that as much as I do."

"I know. I know. It's okay."

CHRISTMAS WAS RAPIDLY approaching, but Mother became despondent when Roger said he'd met a girl he liked a great deal and had been invited to her family's for Christmas. He intended to go. I couldn't fool myself into thinking she'd respond well. I felt Evan's frustration that Roger had eclipsed our plans. "Roger didn't know," I said, guessing what he wasn't saying.

"Then I wish you'd told him," he said. Still, we split the time by my spending Hanukah with his family, which came before the university's Christmas break so Mother didn't notice, and Evan spending Christmas with Mother and me. He and I had to make whatever there was of cheer; Mother had been unable or unwilling to shake her upset over Roger, and I could feel her making a silent point to me as surely as a jabbing finger.

Weeks passed, in the same pattern as the fall, indistinguishable one from the next except by whether Evan came up to Connecticut. He didn't joke as much. We slept together at his apartment, but every weekend, the diamond would come off my hand until Sunday night on my way back to New York. Though he kept his promise, staying tolerant, even understanding, on the smooth surface of what he showed me, I sensed Evan's growing impatience, his assessment that it really couldn't be such a bad thing to just tell her. "She's going to have to deal with it sometime. And so are we." I knew how critical timing was, that Mother believe it was her idea.

March was pressing up to an early Easter, and I suggested to Evan that maybe he could come with me for the holiday. "We can take her to church and out to dinner, and maybe talk about it then," I said.

"Okay by me. Mom doesn't make a big deal out of Easter, usually. At least we won't have to deal with two families wanting both of us. The thing is, Ruthie, it's not the families, it's that I want to be with you. Do you know that?"

"I do, and that's what I want, too." But the truth was that what *I* wanted was something I hardly thought about anymore. There wasn't space in my mind.

EASTER WAS GRAY AND RAINY, a close sadness in a low-hung sky. We'd been to church and were taking Mother out to dinner at an historic inn she'd read about. We were in the foothills of the Berkshires, what should have been a beautiful route, but the dank weather permeated the landscape in which there were no noticeable signs of spring. On a distant hill, three wooden crosses had been erected, large as highway billboards. I missed it, but apparently Evan made some minute sound. Mother, who was sitting in between us in the front seat, presumably to prevent my body from touching Evan's, said, "What, Evan?"

"What what?" he asked, puzzled.

"I heard you sigh."

"Oh. Really, nothing. I think we're nearly there, if I've got the directions right."

But Mother wouldn't let it go. "It sounded as if you didn't like something." I glanced at her as she spoke and saw her eyes narrowed, her chin slightly upraised: her poised stance.

"Those crosses. I just don't care for people putting up advertising for their religious beliefs where billboards are banned. There was a big debate about it when I was in grad school." He answered evenly, undefensively. I knew he wasn't trying to provoke her just as surely as I knew he would. I tensed up, trying to think of a way to divert her.

"Mother, what magazine did you say had the article about this inn we're going to?" I tried to keep my voice relaxed and casual, but tension had a deathgrip on my body.

She completely ignored me anyway, turning her head toward Evan's profile. He wore a navy suit and a tie I'd bought him, a wide red and blue paisley. Handsome. Solid. A good, good man willing to work with a situation that made Rockland State Hospital look like a sane community. And she was determined to ruin it. "I think this is a little different, don't you? It's not advertising, it's a reminder of Truth," she challenged.

Could he have just said, "I see your point"? Maybe he'd just been pushed too far over the last six months. Maybe I'd used up the last real chance we had.

"Well, certainly, it's what some people accept as truth. I believe that Jesus lived, had a profound impact on people and was crucified. And I believe that in the sense of the impact his life had on history that he is indeed immortal. But, the real point is…" I knew he was going to explain about advertising, which had been his real interest in the subject anyway.

"No. I don't believe you understand the real point of it. The real point is the sacrifice of God's Son to save us."

"Mrs. Kenley, I respect your faith, and I'm not about to argue with you."

"So you don't accept The Truth?" I heard her capitalize the words.

"If you mean, do I personally believe in the propitiatory sacrifice, the answer is no. It's because I believe we are each ultimately responsible for and answerable for what we do here on earth."

"You don't believe Christ gave his life to save yours." It was a statement, and, I knew, a damnation. I glanced sideways at her. She was clutching the cross she wore around her neck.

"What I mean, Mrs. Kenley, is this." For the first time, I heard anger in Evan's voice, and I realized he had guessed more about my childhood than I'd wanted him to. "I don't think murderers, or rapists, *or people who hurt their children* are forgiven and saved because of Jesus. And this has nothing to do with my father's being Jewish or whether Jesus was or was not the true Messiah. This is simply what I, Evan Mairson, believe." The car rang with tension. Mother hung on to her cross and stared straight ahead, her eyes fixed on the road. There was nothing I could say. I knew what I should have said, at least according to my mother, but I just couldn't. I couldn't save any of us anymore.

21

MASTER, FATHER, BROTHER, Son, it is Elizabeth Ruth, come in prayer without ceasing. Flesh of Thy flesh, flesh of my flesh, blood of Thy blood, blood of my blood: Elizabeth Ruth, Ruth Elizabeth, the inversion of my soul, but never its perversion. Never have I fallen since the sacrifices, which were Your will, that I might know sin and overcome. God's chosen are tempted and tempted, but I have overcome, and when I was tempted again, I was cleansed of temptation. I was always cleansed. I am clean in body, mind, spirit, yet I confess I have not cleansed Your Ruth, have not saved her. You know there is no want of Love, as I know Your love, and You love her through me, having given her to my keeping; yet now I see she has accepted sin.

When You brought me to a man, to give my body to Your will, I was afraid, yet I knew You would not give me this task were I not worthy, if you would not restore me. I knew the sign You gave when his head flamed in red and gold like the bush you set ablaze, and he bore the name, John, like he who was sacrificed in your name, and John, my earthly father. He was the third, the John who bore your flaming sign. When his hands were kind on my flesh, it was You, opening me to his seed, and he spoke your word, Love. I knew You were present, and gave me Your child, named for the Ruth who never left, Your gift laid in my hand, to be raised in Truth, saved from sin. This is my charge.

But Ruth is fallen to sin and untruth as her brother fell before her. She has been tested according to Your will. There was no holy sign directing her path, and she was warned as You would have her be, I saw to that. Yet I have harmed the gift, the one true word that came from the tempter, for she is not saved.

I have waited, wrestling with what You require of me. In all ways may I be like You, wrestling with the one who said, "You have harmed the gift, the gift cannot be saved." By night, he comes and says it again. He is evil who says, "Not Father, Son, Nor Holy Spirit, can save Elizabeth or Ruth." The tempter longs that I accept sin, as I long to keep her with me, like the Ruth for whom she is named. Forty days, the appointed time, and then more, I have wrestled, and now I see Your will. We are washed in the blood; in the blood are we cleansed. I shall be cleansed of her brother's turn from grace, I shall be cleansed of harming the gift; I shall be cleansed when Ruth is cleansed and saved. Amen. Amen. Amen.

"RUTH AND EVAN, I require and charge you both to remember that no human ties are more tender, no vows more sacred than those you are about to assume."

Sandy, in the exact blue of her eyes, is to my left and Evan, tall, meticulous, in a black pin-stripe suit, to my right. He's wearing a tie he says is the exact blue of his eyes, his joke because his eyes are hazel. Today he is not joking around, but I see him smiling at me with his hazel eyes. I do not know how to smile with my eyes. My long white dress came off a rack on Seventh Avenue. Sandy and Mrs. Mairson, Elaine I mean, said, Ruthie, it's you. This one is you, which must mean that I am really here right now. Everything on me is white, as Mother always said it should properly be, a symbol, virgin snow about to be melted.

Evan gave me the strand of real pearls around my neck, pearl earrings, too. I've hardly worn earrings since right after I had my ears pierced, when...but the holes are still in my ears and Evan's earrings are there now. I clutch pink roses, baby's breath and trailing ivy—a touch of God's greenery doesn't break the white rule—though the pink does, and I thought it was an ap-

*propriate concession to honesty. My hair is caught up in a halo
of baby's breath, Elaine's idea. Everything is white except my
lips and hair; there wasn't enough rouge manufactured in New
York for Sandy to get color into my cheeks.*

"...and forsaking all others, promise to keep thee only unto
him, until death do you part?"

*Forsaking all others. A separate mind than the one I use to
collect the minister's words is circling tightly as a bird of prey
above my head asking how many times did you promise that
you'd never forsake your mother? I won't forsake her, not even
now. Nor Roger, whatever promises he's broken. He'd said he
would come and stand with me at my wedding if only it were
possible; couldn't we wait until the end of summer when he'd
have a break before his Master's program started?*

*Evan isn't waiting anymore, certainly not for Roger who left
me in this mess. He's not forsaking anyone, either, I see that.
His parents stand not four feet behind us with Doug and Jon.
Mark is grinning and solemn at once next to Evan, a gold
wedding band pressed in his palm. A minister speaks now, but
Evan's father has produced a rabbi to join him. It will be the
rabbi's turn next, reading in Hebrew. I didn't even know that
Evan had gone to Hebrew School, but then, I didn't know his
mother had made him go to Sunday School, either. What else
don't I know?*

*If my voice comes out, I will know it's a sign from God. Surely
He will strike me dumb if the marriage isn't right. Can a
marriage be legal if your mother doesn't know you're being
married? Of course it can. Of course. You're of age, the clerk at
city hall said, it's legal as long as it's what you want, you have
fifteen dollars, a blood test and no other husband. Do you have
those?*

"Yes." *Is it what you want?* "I do."

"I, Evan, take you Ruth, as my lawful, wedded wife, to have
and to hold from this day forward, for better, for worse, for
richer, for poorer, in sickness and in health, to love, honor and
cherish until death do us part."

If the ring fits my finger, I will take it as a sign. Still, I will keep calling Mother. The time will come when she does not hang up. She will send me a key to fit the new locks on the doors to our house. Sandy will call me that there is a letter in my old mailbox at the dorm with Mother's return address on it. My letters will not come back marked Refused in angry ink red as my hair. Red as blood.

"With this ring, I thee wed." *My left hand trembles like a wounded bird in Evan's. The ring slides over my knuckle far more smoothly than it did when I tried it on in the jewelry store.*

"...wear it as a token of my constant faith, abiding love." *My hand does not look like my own   nails polished, and my own wedding ring already in place—as I slide Evan's ring onto his left hand.*

"Those whom God hath joined together, let no one put asunder." *The rabbi steps forward with a stemmed glass wrapped in a cloth, and puts it at Evan's feet. In one strong step, it is done. The chapel rings with the sound of breakage. Amen, Shalom, Amen.*

22

WE HAD A LONG WEEKEND honeymoon, on Fire Island, from Friday night, after our wedding dinner with Evan's family and Sandy, until Monday night. Evan's parents had friends with a cottage there; the use of it was their wedding gift to us. I wished our first married night to be a culmination, but we arrived late, in a champagne drunk and just slept naked, in each other's arms. Saturday, Evan explored me as he hadn't before, with unabashed eyes, hands and mouth. I was dry, guilty-feeling. He was my husband; I was his wife, and still, my body did not answer until his mouth was on my breasts, his hand opening the door he was ready to enter. Then, I felt it again, the need that aches between a woman's legs and wants the empty place to be filled, and filled again. Evan had surprised me by having *You Light Up My Life* sung at our wedding by an old friend of his from school who'd gone to Julliard. It had been exactly right, with its lyrics about hope. I would take all the hope he could give me.

IT WAS AWKWARD, having Evan's big family and his parents' friends sending elaborate gifts to his apartment, ours now. Nightly I wrote thank you notes to people I'd never met. Of course, there were no gifts from any family of mine. Some college friends who lived on Sandy's and my floor chipped in for a party and a blender, but I didn't have a lot of friends of my own. I'd spent my college life going home weekends to attend to my mother. Now, though, she had utterly shut me out. Her previous withdrawals were disappearing acts of her own, or the kind of withdrawal that keeps you totally engaged because it is so enacted in your presence. This was new. I continued to call; she continued to hang up. I continued to write; she continued to refuse the mail. I did not go back, though. It was too painful to knock repeatedly at the door in which my key no longer fit, and glimpse an occasional motion through a crack of drawn drapes. Unless she truly was psychic—which she'd given me reason to believe she was when I was a child—she had no idea I was married. Roger never would have told her, I trusted that much.

Now I had a husband to attend to, and I took refuge in the role if not always the fact of being with Evan. We were determined I would finish school on schedule, but I threw myself into being a wife with the conviction that, being a failed daughter, I had but one chance at salvation.

But I wasn't enjoying it. "Sweetheart, sweetheart," Evan said. "She's all right. You know she's all right, and you know she's playing her trump card. Whether she ever speaks to you again or not, if you let her take away your life—*our* life—she automatically wins. Please, listen to me."

I did. I listened. Of course, Evan was right. It had never occurred to me that she wouldn't win, that it wasn't an immutable law, the natural order of things. "Pork chops or hamburgers tonight?" I asked. "Which do you want?"

"I want *you*," he'd answer. "Just you, but I really want *you*."

"A carry-out picnic in Central Park, then, and a carriage ride, in that case. And don't forget the expensive Chablis," I answered, baiting him because we were trying to save at least a little of his salary.

"A bargain at any price, if you'd like it," he answered, dead serious, and I saw how much I'd been denying him.

By the end of the summer, I was coming around. Maybe I was just getting used to the way things were, but Evan laughed at his own jokes more, to encourage me, and I guess it was working. I'd gotten a rocky start in my summer classes, but by midterm had pulled my averages up enough that I was within shouting distance of getting A's. We needed to keep my financial aid. Almost every weekend we saw Sandy and Mark, who pretended to be mad that we'd eclipsed their long-planned wedding. Sandy kept working on me.

"You did everything you could. Even your brother says so."

"Nothing's come in the mail, I take it? You'd tell me if she called, wouldn't you?"

"Yes, but I can't say I'd be too thrilled about it," she answered, tearing iceberg lettuce into minute shreds in my kitchen. "I love how you've put up those prints. The kitchen needed some color," she said. "This place was always gorgeous when it was just Evan's, but you've added such nice touches. It looks like you, too, now. Mark and I will never be able to afford a brownstone flat. I wish we could."

"I've hardly done anything. Mostly it's Evan's ideas. Sometimes I feel like a visitor, you know? This doesn't feel like it's really mine. I guess I've been too distracted for it all to really sink in, yet."

Sandy sliced carrots, the knife hit the cutting board with unnecessary force. "It's not fair. This should be the happiest time of your life." She'd let her hair grow longer so she could wear it up for their wedding. She'd let it loose tonight, though, which made it easy to spot her head shake of sadness or anger because of the moving shine.

"It is," I said. Was I that transparent?

"If anything had happened to her, you'd be notified, you know," she went on, as if I hadn't spoken. "She's fine and dandy, and pulling your chain. Let it go, I say. She'll come to her senses if she thinks you're not going to beg and grovel."

I sighed. "Sandy, I know you care and I don't know what I would have done without you. But you don't understand. My mother is…she has…"

"I know. I know. She has serious problems, she's suffered a lot and she needs you." Her tone was just faintly mocking as she ticked off three fingers one by one before she went back to slicing vegetables. "You've told me a hundred times. No, a thousand. But you're the one who doesn't understand. Having problems isn't a license for her to drain the blood out of you or keep you from having a life of your own."

I put my hands out, palms up. What did she want? "My own mother doesn't know that I'm married. Is it so strange that that bothers me?"

Sandy put the knife down and turned to face me. "And exactly whose fault is it that she doesn't know? For God's sake, Ruthie, it's not like you haven't tried to talk to her."

"Tell her, Sandy," Evan called in from the living room where he was pouring wine. Sometimes it was more than I could bear, as though I were a skinny tree with whiplike branches encased in ice, weighted with layers of guilt and worry.

"You belong to Evan now, anyway," she said, carrying the salad to the table and getting the last word over her shoulder. Her hair was backlit by the setting sun which came through the living room window, and she looked like an angel. Her voice had its usual ring of authority and kindness at once, as though she always knew something that I didn't, when really, it was the other way around. The knowledge left me lonely.

"Sandy was right, you know," Evan said later that night in bed, his head between my breasts muffling the tease he'd put into his voice. "You're all mine, now. *Surely* you wouldn't suggest that I'm not *more* than enough." He took my hand and pulled it down to feel the size of his swollen sex. I could hear his heart, or mine, or the pulse of the darkness throbbing in my ears while his hands and lips searched out how to melt me into him again.

I LOVED IT WHEN EVAN said, "You're all mine," at the same time it chilled me like a window left open for the arms of a storm to reach in. Two people claimed me wholly, body and soul. And I knew Evan's declaration didn't mean a thing; even if it were a fact, it wasn't true. Even if I wanted her to, my mother wasn't one to quit until she could claim victory. Sooner or later, she would pick the time, the place, the way. Then my punishment would begin—not the passive kind that was going on, but the phase of active suffering.

"It's not going to happen, sweetheart," Evan said, too many times. "We're together now...she'll have to take us both on." Sometimes he'd take off his glasses, the way he did to see better into my eyes, and hold my chin with his hand.

He was wrong as rain traveling from the ground up, I knew, but after the first month, I stopped arguing with him. He wanted me to believe he could protect me; the notion was set in his mind like concrete. I wished I could just do what he wanted and count on him for my life. At the same time, that old primal tie to my mother kept tugging at me. That, and the scent of danger; nothing could be right until I somehow made it right with her and kept my promise.

"Is THIS MRS. MAIRSON?" The voice on the telephone was hoarse, and the connection was poor. It took me back for a moment, wondering why Elaine would be getting a phone call at our apartment.

"No, she doesn...oops. Did you want Elaine Mairson or Ruth?" But the phone clicked repeatedly, as though someone were trying to reestablish the connection, and then the dial tone droned.

"Who was that, honey?" Evan called from the bedroom.

"I don't know, I lost the call. The first time someone asks for Mrs. Mairson, and I think it's for your mother." I laughed. "Sounded like a businessperson, actually, probably it was for you. Did that bank person call for you again?"

"Not yet. I'll try again tomorrow, unless that was him and he calls again today. They've got free checking, and if we can establish ourselves with them, it'll help when we want to go for a mortgage loan."

"Whoa. I thought we were waiting until I'm finished school and you're ready to look for a teaching job."

Evan looked at me strangely. "I'll take care of it," he said.

"I know you will. I'd just like to know what's going on."

"Don't you trust me? You concentrate on school. Taking care of us is my job."

So we were off onto another subject, Evan's favorite these

days—his ability to provide for us—and I never thought about the call until I caught up with Sandy at school on Monday. We often had lunch together at the snack shop; both of us were taking summer classes, hoping to cram in prerequisites before our senior year. "Someone called for you the day before yesterday," she said, and bit into her tuna sandwich. "Damn. This is soggy." She inspected it, peeling off some of the offending bread.

I got the impression she might not be saying all she knew. "My mother? Sandy, you promised you'd let me know right away."

"Hold your horses. I have no idea who it was, but she didn't leave a message anyway. Karen answered our buzzer—because I was in the bathroom and she figured it might be Mark. Whoever was on bells didn't even know you'd moved out of the dorm. Too much trouble to look at the list, I guess."

"What did Karen say?"

"She just gave Evan's number—I mean *your* number—and said you could be reached there. Hey, we've only got twenty more minutes. Are you going to eat or not?"

I wasn't interested in my chicken salad. I leaned in over the booth to try to read her face and shut out the lunchtime commotion in the snack shop. "Sandy, do you think? Karen didn't say I was married or had moved out, did she?"

"No, I don't think so. And as far as I know, Karen just gave the phone number. I didn't quiz her for exact quotes. Did you start your paper yet?"

"Barely. I've looked for sources, that's all. It's just that someone called Saturday and asked for Mrs. Mairson. I thought they wanted Elaine, you know, and while I was stammering around remembering that I was Mrs. Mairson, the phone clicked like someone was jiggling it, and then I got a dial tone."

"And you thought it was your mother?" Her ponytail swung when she shook her head. Her cheerleader look I called it, and today the round-collared white blouse she wore completed the wholesome-girl-on-the-*Seventeen*-magazine image, although after our freshman year she'd started subscribing to *Modern Bride*.

"Not at the time. The voice wasn't like hers, but I thought it was a woman."

"Get a grip on yourself, Ruthie. If it was your mother wanting to talk to you, she would have talked to you. You can't live in fear of her. You look great today, you know? You've gotten really good doing your eyes—thanks to my genius tutoring—and that green shirt mat—" She stopped herself and studied me. That's the kind of friend she was. She could read when I was obsessing, knew when she could distract me and when it was pointless to keep trying. "Ruth, honey. Look at me. Pay attention."

I did. She took a long sip of her soda, to lay down silence between us, to make me focus on waiting. Then she deliberately set it down on the chipped and nicked table between us, and let another five seconds pass.

"You've got a wonderful husband who adores you and whom you adore. Your mother creates her own misery. I'm begging you not to do the same thing, not to waste your own happiness, whether it was your mother calling or not. And secondly, the mystery caller was probably the bursar tracking you down to collect a special fee you owe them for moving out…sounds like this university, doesn't it? Or the librarian calling about your thirteen overdue books."

"I don't have any overdue books."

"See what I mean? Like I said, get a grip. Your sense of humor is nonexistent anymore."

I knew what was wrong with Sandy's argument. It was the same problem with how Evan saw the situation: they thought Mother had a choice about how she thought and what she did, and I was sure she didn't, any more than the patients at Rockland chose their sickness. Isn't that the difference? Isn't evil chosen and sickness not chosen?

I forced a smile. "Okay, okay. You're right. The overdue books are on Evan's card, anyway." Sandy, who'd never returned a library book on time in her life, rewarded me with her familiar warm laughter. "Ah. The true benefits of marriage," she said. "Can't wait."

BUT LESS THAN A WEEK later when I called Mother again, she did not hang up as soon as she heard my voice. Instead there was a long, swollen silence floating above the flowing river whoosh of the long distance line.

"Mother?" I repeated. "Please don't hang up. It's me. Are you all right?"

Again, a long silence while I felt myself go shaky as autumn, with a sourceless, unexpected chill. "Mother?" I tried again. "Please, will you talk to me?" Then the phone clicked down as if putting a period to the end of a smooth deliberation, not in an exclamation point of ragged rage like all the times when I'd not gotten out the second syllable of her name before the connection was broken. But I knew her language. I'd been schooled in the nuances of her silences. She had signaled me that she was ready to begin whatever she'd decided to do with me.

23

I WAS AFRAID TO TELL EVAN. He'd say, "She's playing another stupid game. Don't call again unless you tell her, 'Look, when you want to talk to me, give me a call.' Let her come to you for once. This is ridiculous and destructive and you don't deserve it. *We* don't deserve it." It was that *we* he'd throw in that got me every time.

"She doesn't even know there *is* a *we*." I'd tried to remind him more than once.

"Bullshit. That's what this is all about. Sweetheart, she *needs* to see a psychiatrist, she *needs* treatment."

"Oh, Evan. I can't be torn between the two of you, I can't handle it." The conversations had begun to take on an aura of hopeless familiarity, Evan stuck with his lines and me with mine, like some script we were doomed to read.

"I've not asked you to give up loving your family," I told him one night over another spaghetti dinner. It was already dark by the time we'd sat down to eat, both of us tired from a long day, a long week.

"My family has taken you in and loves you," he retaliated. "They respect us. That's all I want from your mother."

"You're way ahead of the game. Your parents knew about our engagement, they were at our wedding. Can't you see how hard it's going to be to tell her? If things were...*normal,* it would be hard."

He erupted. "But my parents are the kind of people we could tell, for God's sake. She's the one who brought this about, not you, not us. Even your brother says that." He threw his napkin on the table and got up. That was hard-line, tired-of-this-crap Evan speaking. There was gentle, supportive Evan, too, the one I'd married who sometimes still said, "We'll bring her around together. I understand, and I'm here to help you." There was no way to know which one would answer me if I told him about Mother listening to my warm-up pleas before she hung up, and so I did not tell him.

I did the dishes by myself that night, though our habit was for him to wash and me to dry. Evan didn't even make an excuse, just went into the study and read. That night I dreamed her more distinctly than I ever had in my life. It was so real a dream that sometimes I confuse it with memory, even now, when memory must be trustworthy or I will never sort out words like *blame* and *waste* and *inevitability*.

In the dream, I was at home, in the driveway of the Jensen house, after a winter storm. The car was idling, its windows coated with a layer of ice, and I was using a scraper to chip at it. It took a long time to clear even an inch at the top of the passenger side windshield, which is where I'd started, to create an area from which I could pry underneath the thick opacity. As I worked down the glass, my mother's face began to emerge. First there was the deep wave of brown hair, scarcely graying, over her eyebrow, and then the taut skin of her forehead with the two horizontal lines etched across it, the shorter one underneath, as though by a sculptor's chisel. As I uncovered her eyes, she did not look at me, but stared straight ahead. Her eyes were not narrowed, not angry, but without a hint of light, and I was surprised at how small a part of her face they were. And then I was surprised at how pinched her nose appeared, and how thin her lips. I spoke to her through the glass but she did not stir or answer. The rest of her face emerged slowly as I worked on, like some thing wooden, jaw set, clenched and unyielding. The whole while I chipped and scraped to clear the window, she did not stir or respond to my wave or smile, though I knew she saw me.

*Now we see as through a glass darkly, but then…*I woke with the passage in my mind, but I could not interpret the dream. Where was the magical, beautiful woman who'd made collages of found objects, baked gingerbread men, made up games to make us laugh, to whom God whispered His secrets? Hadn't she sung "Amazing Grace" to the radiant ocean and been gilded in answer? But that had been the day we had let the fire go out. Had Roger and I done this to her, or had we made her up? Had she once been the mother we needed and adored, then changed? Deteriorated? Had I imagined the safety of her care, the joy of pleasing her when I was small? If she'd been all right once, couldn't she be again? What was memory and what was desire? What was justification and who could be justified?

It cannot be a surprise that I called her again, the same day the dream awakened me. I cut a class to be home well before Evan, so he would not catch me trying, so he wouldn't hear me subjugate myself in a profusion of apologies and admissions.

"Mother?" Silence, but no click of disconnection. "Mother, it's me. Please talk to me. I'm so sorry you've been hurt. Please forgive me. I think I understand what you've been going through."

She spoke for the first time. "You have no idea what I've been going through." Her tone was dead, without inflection as she spit the words out slowly. Then she hung up.

I recognized the pattern, as I had the last time when she'd only listened a while. She would punish me this way a few more times, to make me long for the real punishment of her rage which would come before any reconciliation. Strange to say, I took encouragement from the familiarity, though there was no map for telling her about my marriage. I had no idea how I would do that, only that I had to put one foot in front of the other to get back home first. The spurt of separate strength I'd called up to marry Evan had dissipated.

I knew to wait a couple of days before I called again, to demonstrate that I'd taken in her pain. Again, I came home early for the certainty of privacy. I sat on Evan's and my bed, the double bed which had been almost the only piece of furniture we'd had to buy, so well had Evan already furnished the apartment. I'd picked out a sea-green spread, and hung a print of a beach that reminded me of Ben Chance's dunes above the bed. A woman in a wide-brimmed straw hat was looking out at the sea, while a small girl knelt, intent on what was perhaps a shell, in a foreground of sand. Something in the picture was wistful and reminiscent, perhaps of the first days we'd spent at the Cape, when Mother had been happy and time seemed to stretch out like a hopeful road. I looked at the picture before I dialed and tried to claim that hope.

"Mother?" I tried. Silence. "Please let me come home to see you." I heard her intake of breath.

"All right."

"Oh, Mother. Thank you so much. I am so sorry for all the pain I've caused you." It was a start. "When may I come?"

"I have things to do. You may come Friday and plan to stay." Her voice was impenetrable. Evan would not be happy, I knew; weekends were important to him, our time together the thin filling between the thick slices of long weekdays, my classes and his job.

"I'll be there. Thank you so much."

"I'll need to know exactly what train you'll be on. I'm going to leave the car at the station for you."

"I don't mind walking, Mother. I certainly don't want you to walk or have to come get me."

"I said the car will be at the station for you, but I want to know exactly what train you'll be on."

"I can check the timetable right now, if you like."

"Do that."

I set the phone down and ran to the kitchen where I'd stuck the current timetable in the drawer with the telephone book. "There's an express that gets in at 7:32 Friday evening," I said, out of breath from rushing so she would not reconsider and hang up again.

"I take it you're planning to attend classes that day?"

I realized she might have been testing whether I put seeing her above all else, but it was too late. "Not if you'd like me to come early Friday."

"That won't be necessary. I expect you'll be on the 7:32, however, and that you will come directly…here. Do you understand?" What I was supposed to understand, I thought, was that she deliberately did not use the word home. That would be a term I'd have to earn, but that was nothing new. I thought it was still possible.

"Of course, Mother. I will be on the 7:32 and come directly... there."

24

ALL DAY FRIDAY I FELT SWEATY and afraid. I'd made an error thinking I could go to classes and retain anything. I avoided lunch with Sandy, claiming I'd not finished some required reading and was going to hide out and get it done instead of eating. The night before, I tried much the same with Evan, telling him I had a mound of homework. What I'd really done was close the door to our bedroom, enduring the faint sounds of the television in the living room, and try to script and rehearse what I would say to Mother.

I hadn't told Evan I'd called Mother again or that I was going to see her. I didn't think I could manage his being angry or entreating me not to go, but it was more than that; I was trying to separate myself from him as much as I could. I had a superstitious notion that if I let him touch me or even talked with him—especially about her—when I arrived, Mother would smell Evan on me, the way a mother bird knows if a hatchling has been handled by a human, and won't accept it back into the nest. I'd hoped to slide into bed before Evan finished his show, and pretend sleep, but Evan hadn't been about to cooperate. He must have heard me getting ready for bed. I was brushing my teeth when suddenly, he was there behind me in the bathroom, sliding his hands around me from behind, taking a breast in each hand like a piece of ripe fruit.

"How's my gorgeous wife? It's not all that late—did you get through the reading quicker than you thought?"

"You scared me!" I said, trying to wriggle from his grasp without it being obvious.

"Ah, I mean not to scare you, merely to seduce and over-whelm you with my irresistible kiss. I shall demonstrate my skill. Perhaps you were not aware that I hold the gold medal from the last Olympics in lovemaking. Modesty has prevented me from mentioning it earlier, but, once I received tens from all the judges in technical merit, the artistic program was a cinch."

"I see. And exactly who, may I ask, were the judges?" We were speaking to each other's image in the bathroom mirror.

"A lovely, lovely little tribe of virgin trolls, wearing chastity belts of course. I was saving myself for you. And I regret to inform you…"

"Yes?"

"I have today received an official telegram informing me that the International Olympic Committee insists I establish my eligibility for the next games this very night. I throw myself on your mercy. You have been chosen sole arbitrator."

"Evan, honey, I have to—"

He turned me around to face him and cut me off with a kiss which was hard and gentle at once. "I love you," he whispered. Then, teasing and tickling me, he got me backing up out of the bathroom, toward the bedroom. "Oh, no, no, you cannot deny me the advancement of my career. It is not for myself I make these pathetic entreaties, but for humanity. Men—yes, and women, too—rely on me to advance scientific knowledge in the field. Everywhere, people demand to know, can passion actually set bodies on fire during the act itself? Can stock be sold for a share of the great one's sperm? What about movie rights?" I gave up, laughing helplessly, and in the moment, wanting him as much as I ever had and more. His hands raised my nightgown over my head and he aped total shock that I wore no underwear.

"Olympic rules. You risk disqualification if I catch you with underwear. Submit to a body check immediately," I screeched, as if I were carefree or merely in love, as if I had a right to be either.

FRIDAY, I FELT GUILTY, faintly nauseous, tired. Evan and I had fallen onto the bed Thursday night, convulsed in laughter, I naked and Evan switching roles and pretending to be horrified that I was removing his clothes. "What has the youth of America come to?" he cried, using the cardboard from a roll of toilet paper as an imaginary microphone. "Ladies and gentlemen of our viewing audience, I present to you a case in point. Before your very eyes, you see a child so corrupt and crazed that she is tearing at the clothing of this reporter, an elderly gentleman and distinguished scholar." Pushing him to a seat on the bed, I stifled him by nuzzling his mouth with my breast as I unbuttoned his shirt. Evan tossed the microphone aside, and grabbed my rear with both hands as he muttered, "Well, perhaps too voluptuous to be called a child. But a very delinquent teen…very delinquent, I mean this is simply terrible. I must devote my life to studying this horrifying phenomenon. Ladies and gentlemen, good night and goodbye."

Why was it then that the constraints of the past weeks fell away again? Evan drove himself into me, but my body opened in welcome and answer. When I climaxed, I clung on, satisfied and unsatisfied at once, needing something I couldn't define.

"Sweetheart, what is it?" Evan tightened his arms around me.

I could only shake my head and feel the hair on his chest with my fingers. "I love you," I whispered. Even to me, my voice sounded distant, like the faint street noises beyond our window. "That was like the first and the last time we make love." I was crying, the combination of first relief and the tension beneath it undoing me.

Evan held me, stroking my hair and kissing the top of my head. "Not the last time. I promise you, not the last time."

The raucous and tender night before had hardened into stone and ashes by the time I cut my last class, and went home to pack an overnight bag, knowing Evan would be at work. I left him a note.

Evan sweetheart; Mother has finally agreed to see me and wants me to come home tonight. Don't worry if I don't call—you know how she is. I have to handle this alone. Don't ever forget how much I love you.
Ruth.

What more could I tell him? In retrospect, though, I can see how it was my fault; I should have written more. I should have assured him I would be back, even if I couldn't absolutely know that myself. I should have guessed what might happen, but I was too busy being weak and distracted, just as I had been the night before.

He caught up with me at Grand Central as I was entering the gateway to track 27. It sounds impossible, or at least improbable, but remember, he well knew my exact route home. "Ruth! Ruth! Wait!" I heard his voice grow louder as his half run brought him closer. "Jesus Christ. I never thought I'd find you, I didn't know when you left." He was panting.

"I'm sorry. I *have* to go, Evan. I'm sorry, I didn't want to upset you."

"I'd have been a lot *less* upset if you'd *told* me what was going on. We have to talk."

"I've got to make this train."

"Take the next one." Then, seeing my face close, "When does it leave?"

I glanced at the enormous central clock. "Twelve minutes…I wanted to get a seat." The last sentence sounded limp, and I was ashamed. "I mean, if I don't get a seat, I can't read my homework on the way."

"Look, you *have* to talk to me."

Evan took my arm and led me toward a seating area in the terminal, as I protested, "I've got to make that train." Mother's *I'll expect you on the 7:32* circled in my head like a cawing gull.

Friday night commuters thronged across the station and sorted themselves into gates. "We've got to get out of the way," Evan said.

"Why aren't you at work?" I asked.

"Counting on that, weren't you?" he said, a sliver of bitterness like an almond between his teeth. "I was going to surprise you. Goddammit, what's going on? Did your mother talk you into leaving me?"

"Oh, God, no, Evan. I didn't even tell her anything about us. All she did was agree to see me. I called…" I trailed off, the wispy fade of a lost plane, realizing I didn't want him to know that I'd planned this for days. Then I followed Evan's eyes to my left hand, resting on the shoulder strap of my purse. I'd taken off my wedding ring. "No, no, Evan, I'm sorry, it's not that. I'm so sorry…I took it off because she doesn't know. I have to tell her, you know that, I can't just walk in there wearing a wedding ring and a name tag that says 'Hello, my name is Ruth Mairson.'" I tried a smile.

"If it's not that, why didn't you tell me?" I had hurt him, another layer of damage done. I glanced at the clock.

"Sweetheart, I'm so sorry. I knew you wouldn't want me to go. I didn't have the strength to fight you. I didn't want to fight. I have to do this, but I don't want to hurt you. Not ever. You've got to know how much I love you."

"But we're married. These are things we face together."

"I know how you feel about how Mother's acted. It wouldn't work…you don't…"

"I don't understand?" he anticipated the word. "I guess not. But I've stuck by you, haven't I? That's more than I can say for you." He was angry with me, for the first time, for the first time, really angry with *me*.

I tried to soften him with my eye, searching his face for a flicker of relent. "Please, I love you. I can't stand this. I didn't mean to hurt you. I've got to go, I can't miss the train."

"So I guess we see what or who comes first." When he said that, how could I turn and leave?

"Evan, you know I love you. I married you, you're my husband. Nothing about that is changed. Please, let me do this. You understood before. Please understand now."

When I convinced myself that there was a slight acceptance on his face, I stood on my toes to kiss him with as much attention as I could and ran for the train. I saw it, still in the underground station, but pulling out toward where the light would take it on.

WHEN I GOT BACK INTO THE chaos of the main terminal, Evan was gone. Panicked, I stood in line at the circular information booth until I was in front of a middle-aged man whose tie was loosened in a tired-looking way.

"When's the next train to New Haven? Is there any way I can make a connection with the 5:14 Hartford line? I have to be on that train."

He rolled his eyes. "Just missed it."

"I know. When's the next? Can I connect?"

"Where's the fire?"

"Pardon me?"

"Where are you going?" He spoke in an exaggerated manner, dragging words like heavy sacks, patiently displaying his meaning as though I were slow.

"Malone, Connecticut."

He studied posted charts, following a line across with his fingers. "Can't do it."

Tears embarrassed me. "What's the best I can do?" I'd have to call Mother.

Tears embarrassed him, too. He became brusque. "Well, little lady, give me a minute here. If you can stand to get in seven minutes later, you can skip the next two locals and wait for the late express. Take it to Meridan, that's two stops past New Haven, but it only makes one stop before that. You can change onto the 5:39—that's an express, too—and backtrack a little, but Malone's the third stop. Get on over to track 19. You've got a wait, but it'll be crowded. Cost you an extra $3.35."

"Thank you so much. Only seven minutes later?"

"Seven minutes, miss."

Seven minutes would be close enough. She'd never need to know I missed the train. Trains run four or five minutes late every now and then. I could have had to search the parking lot for the car; the keys could be buried at the bottom of my purse. Someone could have stopped me to ask for directions. I'd just make sure none of those things did happen, and I'd walk in the door almost exactly when she expected me to get on about the enormity of my task.

I BELIEVE I WAS SO overwhelmed with failure that I fell asleep on the train, in spite of the anxiety churning as though the train wheels were within instead of beneath me. The sun sunk in the sky and shone directly through my window and into my eyes, doing the initial work of closing them. By habit I woke before New Haven, and rode on to change trains as I'd been instructed; the connection was running exactly on time, a good sign I thought, and began to encourage myself.

There was another good sign, a spectacular sunset, the sky streaked with spreading red. "Red sky at night, sailor's delight," Mother used to say. If it was going to be nice, perhaps I could get her to take a walk in the woods tomorrow. Perhaps things would go well enough that I'd even be able to tell her about Evan and me. I glanced at my left hand, which seemed more my own without the rings, but thought *I do love him, I do,* and let the notions cancel each other out as the wheels beneath me hopelessly chased the ones ahead.

IT WAS BY FAR THE LONGEST I'd been away from Malone since Mother and I had driven to Seattle. Everything seemed utterly unchanged—as it had when she and I returned from that trip—yet, as I had then, I felt utterly different, as though I no longer had the smallest place there. Most of the passengers were suited men with briefcases whose wives were waiting for them in idling station wagons, so the parking lot emptied quickly, and I spotted Mother's car readily. Good sign, I thought again, trying to shake the memory of Grandmother that appeared when I'd thought of when I last went so long without seeing Malone. I could make up another minute or so. The keys were already in my hand as I jogged to the car. The town was absorbing the forty or so who had disembarked from the train as though we'd stepped into cotton; the sleepy main street barely blinked as they pulled out of the parking lot one at a time. I'd moved so quickly that I was nowhere near the last. Good, good sign, I heartened myself once more.

It was a short drive to the house. Even so, I sped. I did not want her to even guess that everything was not exactly as I'd said it would be. Although it was not dark, when I pulled into the yard, a few fireflies danced over the garden, which I noticed was grossly untended. I hurried up the steps of the back porch. The one Evan had fixed was holding firm and I would have smiled had I dared. I fixed my face and knocked on the back door.

A moment later, I knocked again. The lights were on, and I heard music inside, but sensed no motion. Another knock. I must have lost another minute and a half of the time I'd gained back against lateness just standing there, certain I was being tested but without a glimmer shining on what I should do. Finally I carefully tried the doorknob. Unlocked. I pushed it open by perhaps an inch and called in. "Mother? Mother? May I come in?"

Organ music swelled into the kitchen which was a shambles, dirty dishes, used napkins, emptied boxes and cans everywhere. I'd come home to messes like this before, and understood the message to be that I was needed there, to manage things, to do the labor that would allow her to keep going. I wondered what state the bank account was in, if she'd been collecting the money for her lessons. If she'd been canceling them again, she might have run out of money. Evan and I had enough in our account that I could write her a check, if I could only tell her about us. I wished I'd thought to bring a supply of cash.

A requiem mass was on the record player in the studio room, the one she used for teaching. It was because of the music that at first I didn't recognize the sound of running water. The bathroom door was closed, and I remember being relieved. She hadn't answered the door because she was taking a bath and hadn't heard me. I waited another minute, looking around the kitchen, gauging how long it had been let go.

"Mother?" I called again. She wouldn't answer. I went to the bathroom door and knocked softly. "Mother? I hope you don't mind. I came in when there was no answer at the back door. I didn't want to startle you."

I have no idea how long I stood at the door. Was she becoming enraged that I wasn't respecting her silence? I paced a little bit, and went into the living room and sat, folding my hands in my lap, determined to wait for instructions. But then I couldn't endure it. I got up and went back to the bathroom door, knocking softly again. "Mother? I don't want to bother you. Would you just let me know you've heard me? Then I'll just wait in the living room." I babbled some nonsense like that a couple of times, letting precious seconds elapse until I heard, or felt or sensed the water seeping around my shoes, and I finally opened the bathroom door.

My mother was lying naked on the floor, her legs together and knees slightly bent, her arms extended horizontally from her body in the odd grace of a resting crucifix. Deep gashes sliced both upturned wrists several times, blood widely pooled beneath them and still spreading. The tub looked to be completely filled with blood. Water ran on at low pressure. It had begun to overflow, and the running water mixed into the tub of blood and the pools of blood, the river of her life flowing above, below, around and from my mother directly at my feet, where it ended.

25

HEAR MY CONFESSION. I, Elizabeth Ruth, have done those things which I ought not to have done, and have not done what I ought to have done. I present myself to be cleansed.

I the fist, I the rope, I the whip and, at the last, the knife. Loneliness, pain, sorrow: these are His scourges, that I might yield praise for His Love, eternal, untouchable by the filthy hand of man. If thy daughter weds herself to unbelief, then cleanse and save her, and she will not doubt again. I am the instrument of your salvation, the weapon of the Lord.

Cleansed, I give the last true measure of devotion. I give my life that another might have life. My blood shall douse the flames of betrayal. When peace comes, you will know that by me, you are given life a second time. So be it, Amen.

26

STRANGE HOW SHOCK AFFECTS THE mind, what it sees, what it retains. I have no memory of calling the ambulance, or approaching sirens and, though I knelt in the blood and water that crept around my mother the whole while, I have no memory of the coroner's arrival after the ambulance workers said they were sorry, sorry, sorry.

The coroner ruled it an accidental death. *Although the deceased initially attempted suicide,* he wrote upon the conclusion of his investigation, *the ratio of blood to water in the tub, with the volume flow of the running water factored in, along with a significant swelling on the back of the dead woman's head justify the conclusion that she changed her mind, and therefore, the ruling of accidental death. After she'd cut her wrists— holding each under water—she lay in the tub as water continued to run for perhaps ten minutes.* How it must have brightened, the water, slowly rising, slowly deepening from faint pink in increments of red, blood being thicker than water any day of the year as she'd often proclaimed. *It was then she apparently changed her mind* (the wind-up clock—which no one but Roger and I know was always on the nightstand beside her bed—is still where she last placed it: on the toilet tank in full view of the head of the tub where she rested her head), *rising and climbing out in the manner of a small child, by supporting herself with both hands on the rim of the tub while securing both feet on the floor. Then she appears to have stood and attempted to walk.* She'd been going to call for help, I'm sure of it; the phone was plugged in and on the kitchen table, the closest to the bathroom it would stretch, not her bedroom where it usually stayed. *Light-headedness would have overtaken her immediately upon becoming upright due to heat and blood loss, and upon fainting, she fell backward, striking her head on the edge of the tub, a conclusion based on the head injury and the position of the body when it was discovered by her daughter. Elizabeth Ruth Kenley laid on the floor for up to ten minutes during some of which she may have been conscious, and bled to death from self-inflicted wounds caused by a razor blade, subsequently recovered from the scene. Her daughter,* who had failed to arrive when instructed, failed again to obey, *discovered the body and called for emergency aid. Additional observations: the daughter of the deceased arrived approximately five minutes after the deceased struck her head, but was not aware anything was amiss as the bathwater was running, a tragedy for which no one is to blame.* This is the blatant error in the official report. I do not know if it is the result of ignorance or a kindly, pointless effort to spare me. *A note found by the dead woman's daughter suggests that the woman was depressed and perhaps suffering from delusions. It has been photographed, entered into the official case document file and returned to the family,* where it remains to complete the work of the Bride of Christ, who knew her daughter had married herself in secret, and to an unbeliever. I know she knew I was married. She buried the fact in her last words.

27

It sounds cruel when I tell it, but I wouldn't let Evan come to me. It seemed disrespectful to Mother; that's how I justified it, but the truth is I didn't know how I felt about my husband, and couldn't bear to have him ask me. My wedding rings stayed wrapped in Kleenex, zipped in a compartment of my purse. I didn't know how I felt about Mother, either, how to understand what she'd done, the note she'd written, but my mother was dead, and the fact alone threw such a stifling black blanket of guilt over my mind that sorting individual strands of anger, manipulation and madness was impossible then. Once again, one of my feet was in a boat and the other on the dock as the engine of the boat shifted into gear.

I confessed to Roger how I'd been late because I'd let Evan stop me at the station. I had to. I couldn't accept his assuring me over and over *"it's not your fault, it's not your fault."*

"Of course it's my fault," I shouted at him, the night he arrived, twenty-three hours after Mother died. I'd been up all night, of course, between the police and the coroner, and I suppose it might have been excusable if that's all I'd shouted. But then when he took me in his arms the way I longed for him to, I was suddenly furious. I shoved him back, hitting his chest and screaming, "And it's your fault, too, every bit as much as mine. You broke every promise you ever made to her, and to me.

532

I told you I couldn't do it alone and you didn't care. You didn't care. You have no idea all that's happened because you didn't care." I'd struck pay dirt; his bloodshot eyes, ringed with the mark of a smudgy thumb, filled involuntarily. We were in the living room, then, in semidarkness because neither of us had noticed enough to turn on the lights.

He sank into the blue sofa, bent double as though I'd punched him in the stomach. "I know. Oh, God, Ruthie, I'm sorry. I'm sorry."

I had no judgment or restraint left. "Yes, you are. A sorry son, and sorry brother. You and Evan, you're both so…goddamn sorry." It was a moment's relief to rage at him, to blame him. All I really wanted was that there be some identifiable fault line—or intersecting lines—where my earth had erupted into so much destruction. I, Roger, Evan, it didn't matter: I just wanted someone or something I could point to and say, *See, there, that's the cause of all this incurable grief, that's why love was never ever enough to save any of us.* "It's like a sick joke, the point-lessness of it. Mother's dying could no more save me than anything I've ever done saved her. But the Bride of Christ took it all on, didn't she? I just don't get why she couldn't have done it for Judas. Guess she just didn't love *you* enough, it was better to be a boy when we were kids, but lookie here, when we grew up, I got lucky, she kept all the really good stuff for me," I railed on. Here we were, deposited beyond the edge of the endurable world, lost. I was beyond making sense.

Roger's face was buried in his hands, his shoulders shaking. As quickly as I'd ignited, the flame died and I was overcome with shame. "Oh, Rog, Rog, I don't mean any of that. Look, look at me, please, Rog, I don't know what I'm saying. It's not your fault. I understand. I do…I got married for God's sake. How could I not understand?" I put my arms around him and buried my face into the space between the back of his neck and his shoulder, my tears running down into his chin and doubtless mixing with his own, a little stream like the running water into which Mother had mixed her blood.

We went on like that, back and forth, recriminating and forgiving, scourging and soothing each other with words and tears. Mother's body was released the next morning, and together, Roger and I decided upon cremation.

"RUTHIE, YOU'VE GOT TO let Evan come for the service."

"How did you get so high on Evan? It's not like you met him at my wedding or anything." I was at Roger again, aggravated that based on two telephone conversations with Evan, he was suddenly my husband's new best friend. We'd flitted around like disoriented birds all day, trying to put together a small memorial service for Mother, trying to decide what to do with her ashes, sorting through the contents of the house. Her clothing and shoes had been boxed for Goodwill, and we'd arranged for them to pick up most of the motley furniture, too.

"I'd like Mother's flute," Roger said. We were cleaning out the refrigerator at the time, throwing out ketchup and mustard that was older than either of us. "Unless you think you would. I think you should keep the car. Why was it *we* didn't get music lessons?"

"What'll I do with a car in New York City?"

"So you plan to go back?"

"Of course. It's where I live. I go to school there, remember?"

"I meant, what about where you'll live? With Evan?" He said it casually, timing the question for when his back was turned, pitching old jelly jars into the trash.

"Leave me alone about it. I just can't see him right now. You don't know the scene that went on between him and mother. She killed herself proving him wrong."

"But if I got your drift, which I admit I may not, she ended up proving him right."

The conversation went in circular spurts like that, with me angry, sarcastic, then remorseful again. Roger was holding up under my onslaughts, but I thought he wanted Evan around to take some of the heat off himself, and that made me angry all over again. We were packing the old mismatched plates and silverware in the kitchen by then, the signs of our chaotic but shared life vanishing as we moved through the house. I'd ducked past the window seats, with the six boxes of Roger's and my heritage. I didn't think I could bear to just pull them out of their hiding place and give them away, not after all that Mother had made of them, but how could I ever look at that chocolate-brown dress with the white fur neckline?

"She sure didn't have much, did she?" I remarked. Really, it was amazing how little it all added up to when it was tightly packed, condensed into airless boxes.

"*We* didn't have much," he corrected. "Except, of course, the immensely helpful knowledge that we were each the result of immaculate conception. Our *heritage,* my ass." He shook his head as he said the last, his voice bitter.

"For a while we had each other," I said, but not with the cutting edge that had been unsheathed since he'd arrived. Rather, it was wistful and nostalgic, which must have been what gave him the courage to answer.

"We could have each other again…and you could have Evan."

"You just don't get it, Rog. I don't even have myself," I said. I didn't say it to wound him, but, of course, I did.

I GUESS I FINALLY TIRED OF inflicting wounds. "The memorial service is tomorrow at noon," I said to Evan on the phone. "If you want to come."

"Of course I want to come. You know I want to come."

"Okay. I checked the timetable and you could come in at 10:33. I can pick you up at the station. We're having it at the funeral home…it just got too crazy trying to think about a church, she went to so many, and you know, the, uh, circumstances make it awkward. This is simpler, because we can greet people there. Rog and I have this place almost emptied out. Just big stuff left. Anyway, it'll be mainly her students and parents, the Jensens and us."

"Mark and Sandy want to be there. Okay? Can they just come with me?"

"Okay. Have Sandy come pick something for me to wear out of the closet, and bring it, will you?"

"I can do that. How are you? I've been so worried."

"I know. I'm sorry. That's all I can say lately, I'm sorry." I was on Mother's pastel blue princess phone, the one with the light-up dial she'd raved about. Using it to talk to Evan made me feel nervous and guilty.

"No need to be. Just let me love you." His voice came through static on the wire, a bit of pleading in it. He must be feeling guilty, too, I thought. Well, that was all right with me.

"Not much left to love, Ev. I've gotta go." I wasn't about to make him feel better. Although I was tired of inflicting wounds, apparently I wasn't tired enough to stop.

THE HEAT BORE DOWN from a sky that glared like the white of a fevered eye, but the air-conditioning inside, like a refrigerated morgue, was the victor. Mother's ashes were in a brass urn on a table at one end, chairs approximating the pews in a chapel arranged facing the table. I'd given the funeral director the only portrait of Mother I had: one from her performing days, before Roger and I were born. She was heavily made up, dramatically looking up as though at a remote secret heaven. Next to the framed picture was a single red rose for Mother, flanked by two white roses, one each for Roger and me. It had been Roger's idea. In front of the arrangement of portrait and roses, her silver flute gleamed in silence.

I got through the service in the pastel-upholstered funeral home by paying no attention. Roger had done most of the work on the service without me, and finally engaged a Universal Life minister whose church she'd intermittently attended, to offici-ate. I had been largely useless, unable to think of a single thing I believed anymore. Evan, next to me in a navy-blue suit and white shirt, wore a muted tie he must have bought for the occasion, his others presumably being too festive. His hair looked darker, and I noticed he kept his glasses on. Doubtless, he didn't want to look at anything too closely today. Who could blame him for that? He wiped sweat from his forehead with a white monogrammed handkerchief his mother had given him last Christmas. I spent my time noticing he'd polished his shoes and that his socks were black instead of the blue he usually wore with that suit. Roger was underdressed in a sports coat and khaki pants, the best clothes he owned, he'd apologized to me, embarrassed, and Evan had said, "I could have brought you a suit if I'd known." He'd given Sandy his credit card and sent her to Bloomingdale's to get the black dress with white lace collar I wore.

"Rog, it doesn't matter. Wear a bathing suit for all I care," I said.

"You're not yourself, Ruthie. Take it easy," Evan said, touching my elbow, but I pulled away—discreetly, I thought.

Amazing grace, how sweet the sound, that saved a wretch like me. Roger had asked Anna DeLue, mother's favorite student, the gifted one, to play the flute. When the first silver notes of the hymn shimmered toward us like Taps, I shot a sharp look at him. He fixed his face into rigid lines and planes, but when he met my eyes, his shoulders began heaving. Of course he remembered. And finally, I began to cry.

"I told her she could play whatever she wanted that was appropriate," he choked out before we had to greet people, after the final Amen. "I should have specified."

As people left, they came to speak to us. "Your mother was a wonderful woman. I'll never forget how far she took Anna. She helped her get into the conservatory, did you know that?" said Mrs. DeLue.

Anna herself was crying. "Thank you for asking me to play," she said. "I could always talk to her. Sometimes she'd give me the last lesson of the day and we'd talk for a long time afterward. She always encouraged…"

"You'll miss her terribly, I know," said another parent. "She must have taught you so much."

"She'll always be with you," another one whispered, "but God must have called her home. I'm sure she's with the angels, playing the flute for them. She had such a good heart, a kind soul."

"Wasn't she funny, too. Such a sense of humor." Then, in a conspiratorial tone, someone I'd never met said, "I guess sometimes we don't know who is suffering. Such a shame no one could help her, when she'd helped so many young people."

I was taken aback. They were talking about the charismatic,

magical woman, the one I'd seen often enough to love without reservation or criticism when I was a child. I'd thought that woman had disappeared, that Roger and I were to blame. It must have taken everything she had to pull herself together for students and their parents. I was proud that she'd been able to do it, at the same time it made me desperately lonely. No one really knew, no one except Roger.

Evan was certain he did, but of course, there was far too much I'd never told him. I wanted to spill it all out to him, to sort it out into columns and say, "Look, this is the tally of what really happened. It's much more than what you witnessed that brought us here." I almost couldn't believe that he thought the little of it he'd seen was an adequate map to the terrible place at which we'd arrived. I'd not shown him what she'd written; it too suffused me with shame in both of us.

EVAN, ROGER AND I ALL got a little drunk that night. Rog had bought a half gallon of red wine when he'd gone out to get us pizza and salads after we'd come back from the service. We took Sandy and Mark to the railroad station but Evan and Roger joined forces on the issue of whether Evan would stay or go. "I could use help getting the rest of the stuff out of the basement, but I'm too shot to do it now," Roger said.

"No problem," Evan replied, both of them bypassing me. I hadn't the inclination to argue anyway. I was in another place, my mind numbly observing the goings-on at the funeral parlor and here, in the home of so many sorrows, as if from a great distance.

We all changed into shorts and T-shirts—the house wasn't air-conditioned—and sat on the floor with the stub of a candle stuck in an empty Coke bottle Roger fished out of the trash. The night sank around us, as we picked at pizza and drank the Chianti out of paper cups. None of us could handle anymore; we talked very little about Mother, but instead Roger and I rehashed our few poor stories about incidents in our lives that didn't directly feature her.

"Remember Mr. VanFrank? He was one great guy," Roger said. "I actually thought about calling him today." He was lying on the floor, propped up on his elbows, while trying to stay in the track of the oscillating fan.

"He came in the diner a couple of times when I was waitressing. It was nice, you know, he'd always order the same thing and stay to talk to me if it wasn't too busy. He told me I should try to be an exchange student."

"You were a waitress?" said Evan.

"Oh, man, you ought to see her sling hash."

"But not as well as you sling bull," I laughed in Roger's direction, lost in the brief mercy of wine.

"No, be serious. What else don't I know about my wife?"

The laughter dried on my lips. "That's what worries me," I answered.

"Oh, come on! That's not what I meant. There's nothing to worry about, I'm just *interested.*"

But I was thinking about the blue sofa, how Mother had braced herself against it when she'd made me beat her, and how once I started, I had enough anger in me to keep going. Had I shouted aloud that day I'd thought it was only in my mind? Had I killed my mother with my hatred as surely as I'd helped her kill hers? Would Evan think his wife capable of murder—direct, indirect, either way, it didn't matter: I could claim credit for one of each. No, he would never really know me. I didn't want him to. I could kill him, too. I seemed to be acquiring a repertoire of techniques as varied as Mother's music.

It was because I'd had too much to drink that I let Evan and Roger take over. Dimly (*through a glass darkly,* I remember how the phrase came back to me like an echo of the minister's voice reading that passage at the service), I heard Roger say, "You and Ruth take the bed, I'll grab one of the couches." I heard a protest rumble from Evan, then Roger said, "Hell, it's the last night. Ruth and I both slept on couches the whole time we lived here. Goodwill said the truck would be here by ten for the furniture. Is there anything in this place that you and Ruth could use? She said no, but I obviously can't drag it to Colorado, so if you see anything, take it." Then, finally, Roger's voice a last time, "Well, none of it's worth anything anyway. Can you look at this stuff about probate? I don't want Ruth to have to mess with it, but I'm not sure how some of it gets filed...it's a good thing Ruth's signature is good on the checking account. She did a lot more than her share with Mother." I heard Evan agree, but his tone had lost its hostility on the subject.

Then I was on Mother's bed, Evan sliding my shorts off and covering me with just the sheet. I wanted to protest, *I don't want to sleep in here, I don't want to...* I thought the words, but nothing came out. Outside the open window, in darkness too dense with heat and moisture for starlight to penetrate, crickets were chanting *Amen, Amen,* as though they had forever and nothing else to say. *Amen.* The urn containing Mother's ashes— her smoldering last note folded into the indentation beneath its base—was on her empty bureau, six feet from my head, while my husband's body weighed the bed down next to me. On that uncomfortable slant between the two of them, I tumbled dizzily toward sleep.

28

WHATEVER ELSE WAS IN THE dream that impelled my eyes suddenly open, I recognized my mother's voice in the last instant. Dawn was raising the dark toward gray, enough that I could tell where I was and see the urn on the bureau. Evan was next to me, in what looked and sounded like a peaceful sleep, the sheet rumpled across his bare chest. What was it Mother had been saying to me? What had awakened me was horror, all my maneuverings shameful in retrospect.

How had I let this happen, that I'd slept with Evan in her bed? I sat up and swung my feet toward the floor, my head setting up a pounding protest. Had I had sex with him? Was it possible that I'd done that, too, like a willful gesture of rejection, with her ashes and letter set by my head? My mouth tasted rotten and stale; I was nauseous.

I walked unsteadily toward the bathroom, picking up my shorts, T-shirt and bra from the floor as I went, each retrieval setting off a new series of overlapping throbs. I was wearing Evan's undershirt, as I sometimes did at our apartment, like an oversize cotton nightshirt. I tiptoed past Roger, fully clothed, dead out on the couch. Once in the bathroom, I pulled on yesterday's clothes, washed my face in cold water and brushed my teeth and fumbled through the medicine cabinet for aspirin. I had to clear my head, figure out what to do. The image that stared back at me in the mirror was of a chalky woman, whose fading freckles looked like gray scars in that weak light. The dawn made me a black and white portrait of myself, the deep circles ringing dull eyes like a study of the living dead. Maybe that was what she'd wanted.

The swinging door between the kitchen and living room squeaked when I eased it shut, but Roger didn't seem to stir. As quietly as I could, I made a pot of coffee and tried to think. When the coffee was ready, I poured a cup and went out onto the back porch. From the back steps, even in the still-muted light, the disarray of the garden accused me.

"RUTHIE, FOR GOD'S SAKE, what are you doing?" It was Roger, slamming the screen door behind him and hurrying down the porch stairs. The sun was high, the sweat running along my body as though my whole being were in tears. "We had no idea where you were." Then he yelled over his shoulder toward the house, "I've got her, she's out here." Evan's face appeared, ghostly behind the screen.

"Quit yelling," I hissed. "The Jensens! Let them sleep." Two large piles of weeds and dead blossoms had grown along the border of the garden. No zinnias this year.

"I can't believe this. You don't need to be doing this. Goodwill is due in fifteen minutes, and then we're out of here. Did you pay that past due rent yet?"

"Yesterday. And the last month of the lease, like you said. I stuck it in their mailbox."

"Okay. Well, we don't owe the Jensens anything. In fact, they're almost a month ahead if they rent this place right away. There's nothing in the lease about keeping up the yard."

"I know."

"Ruthie, here, stand up." He extended his hand, which I ignored. My knees had cramped from too much kneeling, and I had to use both hands on the ground to slowly straighten them and work my way up to standing. "Come inside, please. We need to talk about who's doing what."

"You do what you want and I'll do the rest. Isn't that the way it always is?"

I saw him flinch. "Please. Please, don't let's start this again," he said, and I was ashamed. That was the thing, I bounced from shame to anger to raw pain without the least warning, not to myself, not to Rog or Evan. "You go in and clean up, okay? You're soaked and all dirty. I'll get rid of these weeds. Look, you did a good job, all right? The garden looks good. She would have liked that. I do understand, okay? I do."

In the kitchen, Evan looked awkward. "Hi," he said. "How're you doing this morning, honey?" He was trying so hard.

"I'm okay," I said, making an effort not to be curt, yet I knew it had come out with a definite shortness. "Excuse me. I've got to clean up."

I showered, letting the water run with my oldest tears, the ones left over from being eleven or twelve and not knowing what to do for Mother, terrified of the gulf between where I was and pleasing her. The shower curtain had splotches of gray mildew at the bottom, like the freckles I'd seen on my face that morning. I took Mother's robe off the hook behind the door and wrapped myself in it before heading to her bedroom where my clean clothes were.

But once there, I was suddenly exhausted and sank onto the bed, dazed. In a moment, I got up, lifted the urn and took out the letter to read it again. The indictment was unmistakable.

I HADN'T MOVED AT ALL when Evan knocked. "Ruthie, sweetheart, the Goodwill truck is here. We need to get in to strip the bed and get the rest of the furniture, too." I pulled on some clothes and hurriedly ran a brush through my damp hair, tangled from washing. Strands of wet-darkened red collected in it, and when I pulled it out, I recognized Mother's brown hair now mixed with mine. I stuffed it back into the bristles, and put the brush in my small suitcase.

"I'm coming," I called. "I'm coming."

Loading the truck went almost too quickly, Roger and Evan working along with the driver. I held the door and handed them boxes. Everything went except the personal things like Mother's brush and comb, her jewelry, her flute. (I'd given her library of sheet music to her students, but Roger and I had divided the small but exquisite collection of classical hi-fi records.) Everything except the six boxes of Roger's and my heritage, which I couldn't bring myself to give away, nor open.

Roger wanted no part of them. "They should go to you, if we keep them at all," he said. "You're the one who stayed, you're the one who—" His voice broke and he turned away then. So they were loaded into Mother's car, four crammed into the trunk, two in the backseat. The Goodwill truck backed by inches out of the gravel driveway and disappeared.

"There goes our life," I said. "Seems like it ought to take longer to dismantle." Roger kept his face blank. Evan reached for my hand, but I pretended not to see and he didn't persist. I turned away and went around to the front door, the Jensens's entrance, and knocked to say goodbye and return their keys. Mrs. Jensen's arthritic shuffle—she was using a walker now— required a long time to answer a knock. The old rockers were still there, dirty and mildewed. I wished I'd scrubbed them down and spray painted them—I could have done that if I'd noticed sooner. I could have done a lot of things.

"I will miss your wonderful mother," she said loudly when she got the door open. Mother had counted on the landlords' deafness for years, when there would be commotion in the downstairs we inhabited. "And you, dear, you are such a lovely girl."

"Will you advertise for new tenants?"

"Speak up, dearie."

"Will new people move in downstairs?"

"No. No, sad to say. We think we have to sell now," she said, shaking her head with its disheveled white cloud of hair. "Max isn't doing well. I don't want to, but he says we must. This has been my home for over fifty years, you know." She spoke more slowly than she used to, though Mrs. Jensen had been ancient from the first time I'd met her. I wished again I'd done more to help her, but she and Mother intermittently feuded over petty things, and I hadn't dared.

"Mrs. Jensen, I'm sorry for the times my mother might have upset you. I know she wasn't always easy to get along with. Thank you for renting to us for so long. This place is home to me, too. I never lived anyplace else for as long as here."

"Dearie, dearie. You're a good girl," she said, patting my arm. "You have a good life with your young man."

"Thank you," I said. "May I say goodbye to Mr. Jensen?"

She began the laborious motion of moving her body sideways and backward, to let me in off the porch. I'd been propping the screen door open with my back. "He's in the bedroom, looking out at your garden. He does enjoy that."

"I'm sorry it wasn't kept up this summer," I said, holding my hand out to prevent the screen door from slamming.

"Well, my goodness, when your mother said you'd gotten married, we knew why you weren't here to do it."

"She told you?"

"Oh my, yes. She was in quite a state about it, wasn't she? I don't know why. He's a handsome young man. I saw him out the window. But I told her to tell you that we wished you a long and happy marriage. Did she tell you?"

"She must have forgotten."

"Oh, well, my dear, I'm sorry. I would have sent you a card, you know."

So she did know, and know for sure. I'd comforted myself with the notion that perhaps she didn't. After all, there was no real proof; I could cling to the rambling lack of specificity in what she'd written even though I'd sensed her knowing.

Everything was coming to a close.

ROGER HADN'T WANTED A say in what to do with Mother's ashes. The Goodwill truck was gone, and I'd returned from the Jensens's upstairs. Rog and I stood awkwardly on uncovered worn hardwood in the emptied living room, where I'd set the urn on the window seat that had hidden the six cardboard boxes. A late morning sun glared through the window, revealing dirt and smudges. Dust motes swam toward us. "I just don't think that way, Ruthie. It's not meaningful to me, you know? Unless you don't want to any more than I do, I'd just as soon we do whatever you want with them. Keep them on your mantel or bury them, or whatever people do with ashes."

"It would mean something to her."

"Maybe so."

"I just don't know what she'd want, specifically, I mean, where…"

"Look, whatever you want is fine with me, but we need to do it soon. I've got to get to LaGuardia." He was standing at the kitchen counter stuffing underwear and shirts into his big duffel with uncharacteristic messiness. When he folded his sports coat and crammed it on top, I had an impulse to push him aside and redo it all, the way Mother would have made him do it.

"I told you, I can take you."

"And I appreciate that, but we've got to get going. I want to be there well before the plane time—that airport's a zoo."

"Nothing seems right yet, I don't know what she'd want." I looked at my brother, square-built, high-colored, Mother's hair, and desperately wanted something from him.

"If you want, then, you can just hold on to them, and when you figure out what to do, go ahead and do it."

"That doesn't seem right, you should be there."

"I'd do it for you, if that's what you want, but it's not important to me. I've said goodbye, as best I can. So, if you want to do it now, let's do it." He picked up his duffel as if we might just dump ashes in the driveway on our way to the car.

"Okay. No. I don't know."

He shook his head in exasperation. "Fine. I already said it. Do what you think best, whenever." Then he must have realized how harsh he sounded, and touched my arm lightly. I studied the dark hair on his knuckles. His hand was a completely different shape than Evan's. I could tell them apart in an instant glance. "You're the one with rights here," he said. "I mean it. Anything you want is okay by me."

And that was that. The ashes would stay with me. Now I had Evan to contend with. I let him corner me in Mother's bedroom when I went in to fold my clothes back into my suitcase. I'd laid them out on the bare floor where her bed had been. "Honey," he began, but I interrupted him.

"I can't go back with you," I said abruptly.

"What?" He must have been expecting it, but his eyebrows still shot up over the frame of his glasses, and there was hurt mixed in his shocked tone.

"I just can't. I'm too much of a mess inside. I don't know anything anymore." I didn't know if it was entirely the heat in the house that was making me sweaty, faintly nauseous, or how ashamed I felt then. I lifted my heavy hair off my neck and fastened it to the top of my head with a barrette.

"Ruthie, you know—don't you?—how much I love you. How much we love each other. You don't want to be married to me?"

"I don't know if I mean that." I forced myself to look at him, to remember how good he was, but how anyone's love can get poisoned. How I could be the one holding the vial that could kill us both.

"How can you not know if we love each other?"

"I just don't know if I can make you happy." I folded a shirt on the floor and stayed on my knees.

"Wouldn't that be up to me to decide?"

"I guess." My shorts went into the suitcase. Poor Evan. I could feel his agitation. He squatted down by me to try for eye contact.

"Then it's that you don't know if I can make you happy."

"I have no idea what being happy is. I know you can't understand that. I don't want to let you down anymore. I don't want to mess up any more lives."

"Ruthie!" He was distressed, both his hands out. "You don't mess up my life. I need you, I want you, I love you."

"Just try to understand. Please. I promise I'll call you." I could see how he wrestled with himself, knowing I'd made up my mind yet casting for something, anything he could say that would change it. I couldn't endure hurting him again. I fastened the latches on either side of the suitcase, stood and picked it up by the handle.

He got up, too, and put himself between me and the bedroom

door. "How can I just let you go? I don't know what's going to happen. Can't you let me help you? Where are you going? What are you going to do?" I didn't answer. A minute passed and the one side of Evan pinned the other to the mat. "Here, you'll need money." Then he had his wallet out and open. "I got cash before I left the city because I didn't know what we might need."

"No, Ev, I'm okay."

"This much. Ruthie, I'm asking you this much. Just take this money."

"I do love you, it's not that I don't." But was I saying that because he was insisting on stuffing a wad of folded bills in my skirt pocket and I felt like I had to give something back?

"Then?" I saw light flicker on his features.

"I'll call you when I can. That's all I can promise."

Evan stepped to the side, letting me pass.

So Roger and I and Evan set out in Mother's car, the trunk crammed with our heritage and Mother's ashes. Evan rode with us down to Route 95, and before the route to LaGuardia diverged, we got off the thruway and dropped Evan at the Port Chester railroad station for the short hop into the city. When I kissed Evan goodbye, his eyes filled, but I was numb. Then it was just Rog and me. We talked as I drove, which wasn't as difficult as it might have been if I'd had to look at him.

"I'll keep you posted about probate, if you'll make sure to let me know where you are. I take it I shouldn't call your home…I mean Evan's. Where are you going?"

"I'm not exactly sure. I can't go back to school right now, and I can't go home. Whatever home is, anyway. I just need some time to think." An enormous semi passed me on the right, and I realized I wasn't paying enough attention to traffic. I moved into the slowest lane.

"I'll need an address," Roger said. "There'll be things I need you to sign. You could come stay with me. You know that, I've told you."

"Maybe. Nothing feels right just now. I keep trying to explain that I don't know. I appreciate your taking care of the legal stuff."

"Okay, Ruthie. It's okay. It's just formalities, hoops to jump through. Call me collect, any evening. You've got the number at the department, too, right? Are you all right for money?"

"For a while. Evan insisted I take all his cash, plus I've got a credit card. I don't want to use his money, though. It's not right."

"For God's sake. Use it. You haven't asked me, but I've got to put in one thing. He's a great guy, Ruthie. I really like him." He'd swiveled his body toward me on the seat, emphatic.

"I know." I sounded defensive, a shrug implicit in my voice, not what I meant at all.

"You know he's a great guy or you know I really like him?"

"Both."

I parked the car and waited with Roger for his plane. He'd been right, as usual: there wasn't all that much time to spare. We sat at his gate and drank coffee out of cardboard cups and deliberately talked about nothing of consequence. A uniformed man called for his flight to board; he wrapped me in his arms and put his cheek to mine. "I'm sorry, Ruthie. I'm sorry," he whispered into my hair, and then he was gone.

I THINK I KNEW ALL ALONG where I would go, but I wouldn't let myself name it so there would be no lie involved to Evan, or even Roger. I was going back to Cape Cod. In spite of how it had ended, the first nine days Mother and I spent there were the happiest I remembered her, and the happiest I remembered myself. Of course, the irony wasn't lost on me that I was traveling with my mother's ashes, just as she and I had journeyed with Grandmother's. Yes, of course I wondered whether poison just ran in my veins, like those of the women before me, and whether the same diseases of anger and alienation were an inescapable heredity. I was clinging to the memory of a brief time when it had seemed there might be an endurable world, even a good world, for Mother—though it had turned out not to be so. I didn't know if there could be one for me, but the hope of it had been so shiningly real once; and the Cape was where I located it in the geography of my heart.

It wasn't difficult to be driving Mother's car. I'd used it on a daily basis the summer I worked at the nursing home, and it had come to seem mine as much as hers. It was the only property—paid for—of any value that Mother had owned; Roger had been generous in insisting I keep it. In a lot of ways, it would have made more sense for him to have it, unless I wasn't going back to New York. I rolled the window all the way down and let the wind pull ends of hair from the barrette that held it all back and whip it around my face. That morning had brought the first break in an extended stretch of heat and humidity, and now the air was almost sparkling with dry, crisp light. Though I was tired, the solitude of the drive was a great relief. The back of the afternoon rush hour had been broken while I was at the airport, so traffic wasn't much problem.

The car hummed north, back into Connecticut on the thruway, just inland from the coastal towns. At New London, I stopped for the night. Darkness had overtaken me and the Cape was still several hours away. This was the first time I'd been in a motel since Mother and I had made our cross-country trek to Grandmother, and I'd not anticipated how memory would rise like cream to the surface of consciousness. The motel room was generic, the kind of cheap, Mom-and-Pop operation where you pull in late, pay cash, park a foot from the door of your room and unlock the door to worn-out carpeting, a colorless decor and a bathroom that's clean but hardly "sparkling." You would not want to spend any time barefoot in the place, and the bed springs have likely been long sprung, but it's well-enough lit, cheap, and you'll probably sleep in spite of the highway noise because you're that tired.

And I did sleep, without a person or ghost beside me, even though I'd brought take-out food in with me, just as Mother and I had done so many times on that trip, and though the room was a ringer for any of a half-dozen of the drab variations we'd sampled.

In the morning, I showered and checked out, feeling almost rested. It was just after seven when, with only a cup of coffee, I was back on the thruway, driving into the rising sun. I put on the radio after a while, and when it warmed up, after nine, rolled down the window and stuck my arm out. I do not recall ever feeling so free in my life.

That feeling of freedom, truthfully almost joy, persisted and increased when I crossed the Sagamore Bridge onto the Cape. The landscape felt familiar, more home than I felt in Malone or New York. A brisk out-of-season breeze blew the ocean scent into the car, and I began singing with the radio. In Eastham, I stopped at The Lobster Shack, and treated myself to a lobster roll and Coke. Then, still humming with this strange and welcome lightness, I drove on to Truro.

I KNEW TO LEAVE ROUTE 6 in North Truro and head down 6A; I remembered all the little colonies of efficiency cottages on the bay between there and Provincetown. I could be self-sufficient for a while, get my bearings. Within an hour, though, I was wondering if I'd lost my mind. How could I not have realized that early August would be high season? At each place I stopped, the man or woman at the desk nearly laughed when I asked if they had a cottage I could take for a week or so. And, of course, no one had any suggestions. I went all the way into Provincetown. There, even the old houses with widow's walks on the roofs and "Rooms To Let" signs in front windows lining East and West Commercial Street, and every alley—with their tiny fenced gardens, window boxes spilling geraniums and ivy, and slant-wise views of the harbor—had little signs up that said Sorry, or just a blunt No Vacancy.

The buoyant mood that had carried me from New York deflated like a balloon with a slow leak until I was flat and dejected again. I bought a chocolate ice-cream cone and sat on a bench in front of the town hall, watching throngs of tourists crowding the old, narrow street. Behind the stores on the water side of the street, two huge wharves extended into the harbor, crowded with moored boats. It seemed there was no choice except to turn around, stopping along the way to check for a motel vacancy, an unsatisfying alternative for more than a night.

I'd hoped to walk the ocean beach below the Mack house again and realized that I'd have to do it then, if I was turning back toward the upper Cape. I wondered who was renting or using the house now. Maybe I could just knock at the door and whoever was there wouldn't mind. Better yet, maybe no one would be there, and I could park down the road a bit and use the steps without asking.

I claimed the Rambler from the packed municipal lot and headed toward Truro's ocean side. I wasn't sure I remembered exactly how to get to the Mack house, but nothing had changed, and I found the narrow private road fringed with scrub pines easily.

The house stood exactly as memory had it, solitary and majestic in its setting and size, but unpretentiously welcoming. The paint job had been kept up, I could see, and bright dahlias bloomed in front of the porch. Two big pots of geraniums flanked the front door. A car with Massachusetts plates was parked and the house looked intimidatingly inhabited. Renters, I supposed, and began the laborious process of turning the car around in the area where the paved road dead ended into the dune cliffs covered with spartina. As I tugged the steering wheel, I heard a commotion of dogs and the screen door slapped. Two black Labrador retrievers flew into the rough grass and bounded toward the car exuberantly. The screen door opened again, and a short woman wearing oversize glasses stepped out. I recognized Marilyn, Ben's wife.

"Shadow! Tina! Stay down!" she called, and began walking down the path toward the car. I put the brakes on and waited.

"Are you lost?" she asked, stopping a distance from the car. She looked the same as I remembered her, tiny, with mousy-brown hair tucked behind her ears. She might have been wearing khaki shorts, T-shirt and sandals then, too, but what I remembered was the warmth that seemed to travel out in front of her like a soft breeze.

"Are you Marilyn? Marilyn Chance?"

"Yes, I am. I'm afraid I don't know…"

"Oh, you wouldn't remember me. We met once, years ago. I'm Ruth Kenley. My mother and I stayed here for almost two weeks, let's see, it would have been…six years ago. Ben was painting the house—Lorna let us use it, Mother taught your niece Hannah the flute." I kept supplying little details, watching Marilyn's face for any sign of recollection. "Ben brought me to your house for lunch." I was embarrassed. How much had Ben told her after Mother stormed at him with her accusations?

I saw the memory come. "Yes. Yes! I should have remembered—that gorgeous red hair! Of course. Goodness how you've grown up. Please, please come in. Ben's here, he'd love to say hello."

I put the car in Park and turned off the ignition, but sat a moment longer. "I don't want to bother you. I'd just wanted to ask permission to walk along the beach below you this afternoon."

"Well, of course you can. Good heavens! Is that all? Where are you staying?"

I got out of the car and began walking toward the house with her as we spoke. "Actually I'm not staying. I mean, I couldn't find anything, so I thought I'd head back toward Eastham, or even Hyannis and see if there's something down there."

"Ben! Ben!" Marilyn was calling as I finished my sentence. She turned and said, "You could stay here, except we have sort of a houseful right now. Ben's mother and father are here."

"Goodness, I wouldn't dream of it. Really, I just wanted to go down on your part of the beach for a bit."

"Is your mother with you?"

"No, she's...not."

Ben walked around from the back of the house then. For a split second he looked quizzical, then his face split into a warm grin. "Well hi, Red." He put out his hand to shake and when I gave him mine, he covered it with his other hand and held it an extra few seconds. He looked more weathered, like a good Cape cedar shake house. A few more wrinkles, gray salting his hair, but I'd have known him immediately, anywhere. A pair of glasses was tucked in his shirt pocket.

"Do you remember Ruth...Kenley? Right?" Marilyn said to Ben. I heard her say Kenley, and realized I'd not added Mairson when I introduced myself, but didn't bring it up now. My wedding rings were still zipped in a compartment of my purse as they'd been since I took them off on the train, while Mother was living the last hours of her life. There'd been pain on Evan's face when he noticed my bare left hand, but he'd said nothing about it, and I hadn't, either.

"I don't know if you'd remember, I stayed here with my mother."

"Of course I remember you! How are you? How's your mother?"

I hesitated. Gulls circled, riding the thermals just as I always pictured it. "Mother died last week."

Ben and Marilyn both looked horrified, their "Oh, no, was she sick?" exclamations of shock giving way to the expressions of pity I'd seen on so many faces in the last week and a half.

"No, it was sudden." I tried to put enough closure on the sentence that they'd not ask questions. Marilyn picked up quickly.

"Honey, Ruth just wanted to walk on the beach, but she's not been able to find a place to stay. I was wondering about Bonnie and Susan."

"Possibly." Then, to me, "How long do you need a place for, Ruth?"

"Really, I didn't come to ask you to help me find a place, or anything like that. I just loved this house and beach so much when I was here, well, I just wanted to see it and take a walk. Please, don't do anything on my account."

Marilyn said, "You wanted to stay around Truro, didn't you?"

"Yes, but it's okay. I should have known everything would be taken. I guess I wasn't thinking very clearly."

"That's certainly understandable," Marilyn said softly and touched my shoulder.

Ben cut in. "It's just a possibility, but what Marilyn was thinking of is a cottage that some people we know—they own a cottage colony over on 6A—built. One of their mothers wasn't well, and they built a little one for her just beyond their house, where they could keep an eye on her but she'd be in a separate place. She died in February, and as far as I know, they don't rent it out usually. It's smaller than the family cottages they operate, and Bonnie's mother's furniture is in it, that sort of thing."

"Do you think they'd rent it to me? I'd take really good care of everything." I couldn't resist, though I felt as if I were giving the lie to all I'd said about not having come to ask for help.

"Might. Let me give a call. I know Bonnie from town council. How long do you need a place for?"

"I'm not sure…a few days, maybe longer. I'm sort of at loose ends. I should be at school, but right now, I—"

"Let me see if I can get one of them on the phone," Ben cut

in, checking his watch, and taking the porch steps two at a time, the way I remembered him doing.

"Thank you so much, it's really nice of you."

"Happy to do it," he called back.

"Would you like a glass of iced tea?" Marilyn asked. "Come sit on the porch with me while we see what Ben can do."

"I'm being a bother…" I said, shielding my eyes from the sun with one hand.

"Not at all," she answered. "I wish I could have you here. This must be such a hard time for you." As she spoke, a teenage boy in bathing trunks appeared, slamming the screen door behind him. I barely recognized him. He must have been three feet taller than when I'd last seen him. "This is Matt. Matt, this is Ruth Kenley. She stayed here before we moved from our other house."

"Hi," the boy said indifferently in my direction. "Mom, where's the tube? Gram said to bring it for Jenny when I came back down."

"I think she left it propped by the outdoor shower. You all okay down there? Don't let Gram run herself ragged, please," Marilyn said as the boy went off, down the steps and around the house muttering, "Yeah, okay."

"That's right. We lived over the Provincetown line when you were here. Four years ago, Ben and I finally managed to buy my sisters out. We needed a bigger place, that's for sure, and Ben had been doing the maintenance for a long time."

"I remember how much he did," I said, thinking of the painting and his good-natured grumbling about keeping it up.

"I'll get us some tea," she said. "I could use a break myself. I'm glad you showed up."

I sat in a wicker chair on the porch and looked out at the ocean. A few gulls rose over the beach, which I couldn't see because of how the house was set back from the edge of the dune cliff. The old path still led through the tall grass and beach plums toward the wooden stairs down to the expanse of sand. The separate strands of the grasses were silvered in the intensity of reflected light, and the breeze arched them as though to display the shining.

Marilyn appeared with two tall glasses of iced tea, round,

translucent lemon suns perched on top and sprigs of mint poking from beneath the ice. Even tea looked cared for here. "Thank you. This is beautiful," I said, and she smiled.

"Ben's got Bonnie on the phone," she said. "I heard him telling her about you."

"It's as beautiful as I remembered it," I said, gesturing over the beach grass to the ocean.

"Isn't it?" she agreed. "It almost seems to transcend… anything, I mean, things that hurt us. Oh, really, Ruth, what I'm trying to say is how sorry I am about your mother and that I understand why you'd want to come here. There's a healing about certain places for certain people, you know?"

"Yes. That's it." It was a relief to have someone articulate it for me.

I heard Ben's footsteps approaching through the kitchen. The screen door squeaked slightly on its hinges. I remembered that sound, Mother opening the door in her blue sundress.

"Good news. Susan said to send you on over, and you and they can take a look at each other. They'll consider renting it to you if you're a quiet sort. I had to vouch for you, Red, so no loud parties, unless of course you invite us."

"Ben!" That from Marilyn, to Ben's laugh. She laughed then, too, seeing me smile.

"I'll try to control myself. I guess I should get over there, not take the time to go for a walk now?"

"Ach. I didn't think to tell her you'd be a while. I can call back."

"No. That's fine. If it works out, maybe I could just come another time to walk down there?"

"Of course. You come anytime, whether we're here or not. Walk all you want," Marilyn said, Ben nodding agreement as she spoke.

"You can get over to 6A right?" Ben asked. I nodded. "Okay, just go under 6 and cross 6A. Dutra's Market will be on the right, you know?" he went on. "You'll be heading for the bay. Go up the hill and where the road splits, go left onto Hilltop Road. You'll go over a big hill, and then it winds down toward the water. Watch for a sign for Landings. That's the name of the cottages. You'll see a drive with a big house set off to the left. Actually, there's a little sign that says Office, and points to the house. Just go there. It's Bonnie Madison and Susan James you want. Good people. You'll like them."

"Susan James and Bonnie Madison," I repeated. "Landings. I've got it. Cross 6A and left onto Hilltop. How can I thank you?"

"No need to. Stay in touch, okay?"

"How about coming over for dinner one night?" Marilyn added the tag to Ben's sentence.

"I don't want to put you to any more trouble," I said, hiking my purse strap up my shoulder.

"Will you stop with that trouble stuff? One more place is no trouble. How about tomorrow night? We'll let you get settled."

"I'd love to. Thank you."

THE COTTAGE WAS TINY and simple, but more than I'd hoped when I'd first had the notion of coming. Sided with cedar shakes like the main house, but behind it and away from the rental cottages, it sat by itself, the nearest structure to the bay, tucked between dunes and surrounded by scrubby vegetation. An over-grown sandy path led perhaps twenty-five feet to the beach and a longer paved one back to the main house, laid for Bonnie's elderly mother to get back and forth with easy footing. It had a front stoop facing the water, large enough for the painted wooden rocker on it.

Bonnie, tall, bony, plain-faced with gray strands in her straight, close-cropped brown hair, showed me the cottage herself. "Ben said your mother just died. That's why I was willing to rent to you. I know what that's like. Did he tell you I lost my mother in February?"

I nodded. "I'm sorry," I whispered, my voice an unexpected failure.

"My mother and I had a row to hoe," she said. "She had a lot of trouble accepting it, when Susan and I bought this place together?" It was a statement, but her voice inflected it as a question, and I gathered she was asking whether I understood.

I nodded, though I didn't know to what she might be referring. "Anyway, I don't think she ever really was okay about it, even after she got sick and I moved her here. Susan was so good to her, too." There was a pause, while Bonnie looked out over the water, a suggestion of tears in her eyes which she blinked back. "Mine had a stroke. What did your mother die of?" A blunt, direct question.

"She died of...suicide."

"God." She took it in for a minute. "That must be really tough. I don't know if I could have handled that. I'm really sorry. Look, you can rent the place for as long as you want. I think twenty-five dollars a day would be fair. If you go by the week, we'll call it a hundred fifty. Is that too much? It's a lot less than the cottages go for."

"That's more than fair. I really appreciate it."

"Let me show you the ins and outs of the place," she said, and busied herself pointing out the details of the two rooms. The main room had a kitchen arranged along part of two walls, with a sink, small stove and refrigerator, and equipped cabinets above and below the small white counter space. "Those are Mother's dishes and silver. I've left them here, for now, you know."

"I'll be really careful with them."

"Well, don't worry about the pots and pans, anyway. They're nothing special."

Windows opened on three of the walls in that pine-paneled main room, big ones on both sides of the screen door out onto the porch, and one on each of the adjacent walls. An antique wooden eating table was set up with two straight chairs, not near the appliances, but across the room, by one of the windows, overlooking the water. The only other furniture was a green couch, an end table on either side of it and a small television in the opposite corner. The room was cheerfully flooded with light. Bonnie threw the screened windows open. "Let's get you some air in here. See what great cross-ventilation it has?"

"I love the pictures. Did someone you know paint them?" Beautifully rendered, subtle oil paintings on the wall behind the couch were of scenes that looked so familiar I was certain they had to be of Truro dunes and sea views. Another, smaller one depicted the horseshoe-shaped bay right in front of me, the Provincetown monument visible in the distance of a twilight scene of two white-sailed boats.

"Actually, Susan did. She's an artist. Her work is in the Blue Heron gallery in Wellfleet."

"They're incredible," I said, and Bonnie smiled.

"*She's* incredible," she said.

There was no door into the bedroom, just an opening in the wall where the kitchen part ran out. A four-poster double bed scarcely fit, the room was so small, with barely space for a tall bureau and one nightstand, both antiques. The closet-size bathroom with just a stand-up shower was behind a pine door. Two high, wide windows in the bedroom and another in the bathroom provided light and ventilation. A blue and green cotton print valance was above each, matching the bedspread. A doorless cubbyhole had a bar for hanging clothes. Another deceptively simple, magnificent painting—a sidelong view of the ocean and enormous dunes along the oceanside coast—hung on one of the knotty pine-paneled walls.

"This is wonderful," I said. "It's all that I need and more. I love it. Thank you so much for trusting me. I'll be very careful, I promise."

"Well, what's in here is Mother's. It's all I could keep of her, you know?"

"I do know," I said, thinking of the boxes of our heritage locked in the black airlessness of the trunk, and Mother's ashes there, too, her letter folded and wedged into the base of the urn.

ALL I HAD TO CARRY IN was the one suitcase, plus a duffel bag with some extra things Evan had brought me from our apartment. It wasn't even dark by the time I'd unpacked and driven up to the little market for a chicken sandwich to go from the meat and deli counter, and some coffee, cereal and milk for the next morning. When I'd unpacked those, I pulled on a sweatshirt of Mother's that I'd saved from the Goodwill offerings, and walked down to the beach, where the sun was setting.

The Cape is like a long, bent arm that extends into the water and curls back westward, toward the mainland. On the bay side of the peninsula—if you're above the elbow, near land's end—you can face the water and look into spectacular sunsets over the Provincetown harbor. When I reached the beach, the sky was spread like watercolor in shades of red, magenta, melon, peach and gold melding upward into the gray-blue of evening. The low tidewater and sand took on a pink-gold tinge, so luminous and intense was the color. It seemed like a sign of sorts, and I walked toward it, alone and relieved to be so, until darkness had nearly taken over. Then I turned back, watching for the lights I'd left on to guide me. Locking the door behind me, but without eating the sandwich I'd bought, or so much as washing my face, I shed my clothes, turned the lamps off and dropped into an exhausted, blank sleep.

30

I WOKE EARLY, TO THE SOFT, rhythmic sound of the bay's small waves, and with no memory of going to bed. After pulling on some clean clothes, I made coffee and took it out onto the little porch and drank it while I got my bearings. The tide was half out or half in—I didn't yet have the internal tide clock I'd develop in time—and I watched the water a while, gray, still, in the edgeless light. I went in to eat some cereal, and made a production of washing, drying and replacing the three dishes, and another production of unpacking the suitcase and duffel into the bureau drawers and closet, and arranging toiletries in the bathroom medicine chest. After that, I was at loose ends again. All I didn't want to think about—what to do about school, for example—began to push into my mind, and in an effort to keep moving and keep distracted, I went out onto the beach for a walk. Already the light had strengthened, scattering diamonds onto the surface of the bay, and it kept moving so the facets would glitter, just as I'd moved my hand to show off my engagement ring in another life.

She hadn't been there when I was drinking coffee, or she'd blended with the sand and early light well enough that I simply hadn't seen, but right at the end of my short path onto the beach lay a gull. She lay on her side, utterly still but alive. One of her wings quivered at my approach. Her feathers were variations of tan, brown and white, which was why I deemed her female. Did I remember Ben telling me the brown ones were? Perhaps I just saw something dying and assumed it was female, like Mother, like me.

I had no idea how to help her, but I couldn't go by her, either. I squatted six feet away and spoke gently, hoping to soothe her enough that she would let me pick her up. Maybe I could take her to someone who would know what to do. I couldn't hear footsteps, but a voice was approaching from behind me on the path. It was Bonnie talking to a dog, a golden retriever trotting ahead of her.

"Hi, Ruth. Did you sleep well?" she called when I turned. "Wow, your hair is something—it looks like…like…that burning bush story about who was it? Moses?"

I felt myself blush. My hair *must* look like a bush, I thought; I had only brushed it out and left it thickly loose, to hang below my shoulders. I gathered it into one hand. "I know, it's a mess right now. The wind got it."

"Hey, I meant it as a compliment!" She furrowed her brow. "I'm way too blunt. Susan tells me that all the time."

"No, it's okay, I mean, I'm sorry." I was almost stammering. I rarely knew how to take what someone said to me. "But look, I'm worried about this gull. Do you think she'd let me pick her up? Is there someplace I could take her, a vet maybe, or is there some wildlife place?"

Bonnie put her hand on the dog's collar. "Here, you hold the beast, and I'll take a look. This is Nellie…Nellie, this is Ruth." The dog—a lush-coated, eager beauty—nuzzled my free hand as I held her with the other, and I wished I had a scrap for her. Bonnie squeezed past me on the path lined with dune grass and bent directly over the gull. "No. Just leave her alone."

"But she's not…all right."

Bonnie gave me a strange look. "Sometimes it's just time for something to die," she said. "It's just time. It's natural, you know. I don't see any sign of injury, a fish hook or line, or anything like that. I've got to get on now." She moved away from the gull and then beckoned to Nellie.

"You can let her go now. Get over here, girl." Then, to me, "Nel needs her run and there's lots of work waiting back at the ranch. See you later," she said with a wave and strode on into the early sun, Nellie shining and prancing ahead. Bonnie's legs were not thick, but sturdy and brown, and she had a solid look to her body. She had on khaki shorts and a blue, men's long-sleeved shirt, sleeves rolled up for business, and walked like a woman who knew where she was going and why.

I stayed, sitting nearby in the sand, and talked to the gull. I cried a little and when I felt I couldn't endure watching any longer I still wouldn't let myself leave. The sun had risen a good deal more, and she was still alive, when I went back to the cottage and drove to town to escape, calling myself coward all the while. I couldn't help someone live, and I couldn't help her die, either.

IN PROVINCETOWN, the streets were empty of tourists. Locals and shopkeepers were the only people around, sweeping shop stoops, watering flower boxes and the like. Few places were open yet, even though it was past nine-thirty. I walked each side of the street, up and down Commercial Street, peering into shop windows, studying the hand-crafted jewelry, pottery, displayed paintings. The bakeries' doors were open, aromas of fresh bread and pastry wafting onto the street. The Portuguese bakery had a tiny, fenced-in café area outside, and I thought to buy an elephant ear and coffee and read a newspaper there. As I went through the gate, I heard a man and woman inside, arguing violently.

"How much did you spend last night?" he shouted at the same time she was repeating, "Shut up, I told you, I'm not going to talk to you when you're like this." I sat down at one of the wooden café tables, embarrassed at what I was overhearing. A glass shattered near the door, and I jumped, afraid, and suddenly seeing how the sun glinted on the bay like broken glass. Everything comes down to this, I thought, the giving and receiving of pain, no matter what anyone says he or she intends.

It was quiet, then. A glass case slid open along its track, then shut, and some chairs were pushed into tables rather noisily, but there were no more words. I dreaded going in, what I'd see on their faces. I'd just leave, I decided, but when I stood and glanced in uncertainly, I saw them. The woman stood close to the man, breaking a doughnut. It was round and sugared, and she tore it into two parts like an invited sadness. Like two passions, the equal hope and hopelessness of love, she fed half to her own mouth and half to his. I saw him lick her fingers.

I had absolutely no idea of what to think or to do with myself then. After I read the *New York Times* and *Provincetown Advocate* over too many cups of coffee, I walked the streets, mapping them in my mind, for a long time before I gave up and just returned to the cottage beach. By then, it was after two. At first, I couldn't tell if the gull was still alive, but then I saw a nearly imperceptible flutter on her chest, her heart beating on, however erratically. I'm sure it will sound strange, but I spread out a towel from the cottage and just sat, waiting on the beach as though I were compelled. I was being with my mother.

By late afternoon, I had to go in to shower and get ready to go to dinner at Ben and Marilyn's. Somehow, that felt all right to do, as if I'd given the full measure, and now there was someplace else I was supposed to be. When I came back, well after dark, stars glinted richly in the sky, and quivered on the moving water as though a portion of them had dislodged and fallen into the bay. The gull was there, though now I could not tell if she was dead yet. I sat by her a while, speaking only a soft few words, and then went in to a troubled sleep. In the morning, I carried a child's plastic sand shovel I'd bought at Dutra's to the beach where I dug a hole and buried her body.

"EVAN? HI, IT'S ME, RUTH," I said loudly into the static of the pay phone. It was early evening, the same day I'd buried the gull.

I'd bought a paperback novel and lay on the beach reading most of the day, trying to put something into the vacated shell of my mind. "I promised I'd call."

"Are you all right? Where are you?"

"I'm on Cape Cod in a pay phone."

"Where?"

"In a pay phone on Cape Cod." I raised my voice, and turned my back to the traffic, wincing as I scraped my sunburned shoulder against the phone box. The booth was less than a mile from my cottage, outside a motel farther down the beach on 6A. Landings had phones in the cottages, and therefore no pay phone.

"No, I mean where on Cape Cod?"

I hesitated. What was I holding back?

"In the Provincetown area."

"Where are you staying?"

"I've rented a little cottage on the beach."

"Is there any way I can reach you?"

"No, I haven't got a phone." This was mainly true, except that Bonnie had given me the main number and said they'd run a message down if there was an emergency call. Bonnie had said I could pay to have the phone in my cottage—disconnected after her mother died—hooked back up, but I didn't want it.

"Ruthie, Ruthie, talk to me, please. How are you? What's going on?"

He wasn't asking a single question he didn't have every right to ask, I knew that. It was just that it sounded so…well, stupid, that I didn't know the answers. "I'm just trying to get ahold of myself, Ev. I'm okay."

"Do you need anything? Can I send you some more money? Or, just use the credit card for anything, you can do that, too."

"I know. Don't worry, I'm okay."

"Ruthie, can we talk sometime? I mean really talk, about us? I love you. I'm…going a little nuts, here. I feel like I'm married to a phantom."

I froze, unable to recall my old ability to say what someone needed or wanted to hear. "I'm sorry, Ev. I can't right now. I know it's not fair, and I'm sorry."

He must have heard the change in my voice and forced some lightness into his. "Oy vey, it's all right. Not to worry. But, please, call me. You've got to call me…wait! Is there somewhere I can write you?"

"I don't even know the mailing address. There's not a mailbox outside my cottage or anything. I'll call you."

"Well, remember I'm here, and your home is here waiting. I love you, Ruthie."

"I appreciate that, Ev. I'll talk to you soon." The pain my last words caused vibrated back like a string in me plucked from a distance: still connected to him in spite of all my efforts. I hung up, crossed a parking lot to the beach and began walking along the shoreline. The tide was nearly high and the sand left exposed was dry; each foot sunk in with each step. Behind me, another vivid sunset was beginning. The sun hung just above the Provincetown harbor like an enormous red ball. As it lowered itself, reflected color began to spread across the sky and reflect a path onto the water. I wished I could walk over the low tide shoals, through the pools between sandbars and keep going to where I couldn't ever hurt another human being.

DAYS PASSED, A SAMENESS TO them, a weight on and in me I couldn't shake. I called the chair of the department at school and told her I needed a leave of absence. "I understand, Ruth. I completely understand. Whatever you do, though, be sure you do come back and finish. You're too close, and too talented not to. Will you promise me that much? Next semester? You could finish by the end of next summer then."

I did promise, mainly because I knew she was right about how close I was to my degree, not because I could feel any desire to go back. But I wasn't really feeling anything. I had put myself in Neutral. At the end of the first week, when Bonnie and Susan had said I could stay as long as I liked, I took out a library card as a resident, though I'd paid the rent for only another week, and was without any real plan. I'd begun talking to them—briefly at first, then conversations of increasing length when I passed one or the other in their garden or on their porch as I went to my car. Nellie became my friend; I bought Milk-Bones so I could always have one in my jeans pocket. I could put my arms around her and feel her, alive and loving me back.

Susan was a small woman, plain until I got to know her and recognize the warmth of the particular deep brown of her eyes, matched by her brows and hair. Her heart-shaped face was fair complected, framed with a thick luxury of wavy hair, chin-length and often pulled back in a barrette, especially when she was at a canvas. Like Bonnie, she wore no makeup that I could discern, but she was naturally pretty enough, especially up close and when she smiled, that I didn't notice the lack the way I did on Bonnie. Susan was the easier to talk to, but it was Bonnie who invited me to dinner first. "If you feel like some company," she'd added. "It's okay if you don't." But I did, maybe because Bonnie had alluded to difficulties with her dead mother. I went that night, a bottle of Mateus in hand, and felt fairly at ease within a half hour. Their house wasn't elaborate, but the artful blend of blues, greens and browns in eclectic furniture and original artwork made it stunning. An expanse of windows, clearly added long after the original house was built, opened the airy living room to a panorama of dune grass and sea. Paintings by Susan, mainly seascapes and studies of the Provincetown harbor, were displayed, and pieces of hand-thrown pottery, glazed in earth and water tones, adorned the various tables. A hanging lamp lay a soft circle of amber light over the dining table, where dark blue-gray candles waited for a match.

"This is so beautiful," I said, picking up a graceful cream pitcher, richly glazed in brown-edged blue that sat by a matching sugar bowl on the sideboard.

"Susan made those for me," Bonnie commented.

"It started out as a vase, but just kept insisting on being a pitcher, so I finally gave up and let the clay be what it wanted. Like it has a soul…you know, and you have to feel what it really is meant to be. My teacher used to say that," Susan said. She wore a nutmeg-colored top with a scoop neck, black pants and lipstick tonight. "Then, of course, I had to make its mate." She smiled at Bonnie.

"I love clay," I said, sitting on the couch and smoothing my dark skirt over my knees, glad I'd changed, though Bonnie was in her jeans and an Oxford shirt. "I learned a little when I was an occupational therapy intern in a hospital. Then, I worked last summer in a nursing home, and they let me buy a wheel for the patients. They liked it a lot, you know, even the ones in wheelchairs could do it. I got one with an adjustable height."

"It does something for you," Susan agreed. "There are classes, you know, right up at Castle Hill. You can sign up for a week at a time." She pointed in what must have been the direction of the art studio, and her arm was graceful as a dancer's.

I felt a rush of pleasure at the thought, then quickly shut it off. "What can I do to help with dinner?"

"In a few minutes you can pour the wine," Bonnie answered. "Unless you want to do it now." I did, and got up to busy myself, to keep the conversation from going to the subject of what I was going to do.

After a rich vegetable-garden stew and homemade bread, we sat in rockers on their porch, drinking tea and watching the stars while crickets and frogs tuned legs and throats for their approaching fall symphony. Chill had seeped into the air and Susan brought out a woven, long-fringed shawl and wrapped it around my shoulders.

"How are you getting along?" Bonnie asked me, working her arms into a sweater. "I mean, alone and all. Sometimes we worry about you a little. I don't know how I'd have survived after Mother died if I hadn't had Susan."

Susan laughed. "How on earth can you say that?" Then she turned to me in a mock-confidential aside. "She felt so guilty she'd barely speak to me for days at a time. I didn't think she'd ever pull out of it." She reached over and rubbed Bonnie's shoulder. "But you finally did. Took you long enough, though, right?"

"There you go," laughed Bonnie in response. "Something else to feel guilty about."

It surprised me more than either of them when I said quietly, "I understand better than you'd think. I'm married."

Neither of them spoke for a moment, but Bonnie touched my hand briefly. "Where's your husband?" she asked softly.

I chose to take the question literally. "In New York." Then, abruptly even to me, I changed the subject. The talk turned lighter then, to the attitude of permanent residents toward tourists, and not too long later I went on back to my cottage.

IT WAS THE BEGINNING of my third week. Mother's ashes remained in the trunk of the car with Roger's and my heritage while I read novels and took long walks. Mornings I walked in sneakers on the rocky bay side, in either direction from my cottage. Early afternoons, I read on the beach or went into Provincetown and picked up fresh fish and some fresh vegetables. By midafternoon, I'd driven to the ocean side to park at Ben and Marilyn's where I hiked barefoot, dodging surf as it hammered the sand, paler, and tiny-grained over there, and let the wind blow thought out of my mind. Evenings, I'd take a mug of hot tea and rock on my own little porch and watch the sun flame. Sometimes old, solitary fishermen in rubber boots, with a tackle box and bucket next to them, flung long lines into the water, then set the rod in a sand-anchored holder and sat in a folding chair to wait patient as eternity while they stared across the bay's small ripples.

Slowly, though, as these routines became established, restlessness crept in. There wasn't enough to keep my mind from Mother, the scene I'd found in the bathroom, the endless calculations of by how much or how little time I'd failed to save her.

Susan's comment about Castle Hill popped into my mind two days later when, out in search of a fish market Bonnie had mentioned, I passed a sign that pointed to its location. On impulse I swung the steering wheel to the right. An old converted barn, with several additions sprawling to one side and behind, sat in a secluded area in the Truro hills. Without allowing myself to think it over, I parked and walked around the building in search of a door. By the time I was back to the Rambler, I'd signed to join an ongoing workshop in basic pottery. "Sure, we do that all the time because there are so many temporary residents in the summer," the wild-haired woman who bustled out to greet me wiping paint-stained hands on a rag had said. "That's Marcy's workshop. You'll love her. Basically, for your fee you get studio space, equipment and materials, and an artist who's working on his or her own pieces to give you guidance and answer questions. It's not an actual class, it's a studio situation. There's a one-week minimum, but you can do as many or as few weeks as you want."

"Perfect," I answered, and with only a twinge of guilt, paid in cash for the next week from the stash Evan had pressed on me.

A WEEK LATER, I WALKED down the beach after an early supper to the same pay phone to call Evan again. We had much the same conversation as each time I'd called him, his voice husky around his pleading, and mine distant with involuntary refusals. As I made my way back (slow going because the tide was high and the beach still exposed above the highwater mark was extra soft), an unusual number of fishermen dotted the sand. "Catch anything?" I asked one.

"Yes, ma'am! The blues are running!"

Indeed, I thought, the words seeming clairvoyant even the second moment, when I got it: he was referring to fish.

"Whoa!" he yelled then, reeling hard. "And here's one now! You must be luck." But I looked at his bucket and saw it was nearly full. Just a couple of dozen feet separated him from another fisherman, and so on. Farther up the beach, I saw Bonnie and Susan with a man and woman I recognized as renters in one of their cottages.

"Sorry, but I have to go spread the luck around." I smiled, gesturing that I was going to duck under his line.

"Whoa!" he yelled again. "Don't walk under the line, go behind me. If the fish runs with my line, it may drop hard and tight, slit your neck just as you walk into it." Feeling foolish, not knowing if he was serious, I stopped short and made to go around him. He must have seen my skepticism. "It's a thing can kill you, missy. You never know."

"Thanks." Lately I'd been paying attention to warnings, afraid to ignore anything that might be a sign of impending disaster. Nothing was safe. Nothing.

When I reached Bonnie and Susan, they immediately pulled me in to their circle. "Watch the line," Bonnie cautioned. "Dangerous. Look, my God, they're practically jumping out of the water into the bucket without waiting for the hook. Aren't you ashamed, George? This is way too easy. You're running out of bait. Do you want me to get you more? I've got some up at the house."

"Nah," the middle-aged man replied, patting his paunch. "Got too many as it is. You girls want some?"

"Seriously," his wife added, her red jacket a striking splotch of color that echoed the last sun on the evening-muted beach. "Even if we could get them all cleaned tonight, we'll have to freeze them to get them home."

"Sure. We'll take a few. Ruth will help us clean them, won't you, Ruth?"

"Oh, there's nothing I'd love better," I picked up the banter, "except that I have a formal dinner dance to attend and I've got to do my nails immediately. So sorry."

"Well, cancel your date, honey, because you've now got other plans. George, give us a couple extra, so we can teach this here landlubber to clean fish."

"Take all you can use, girls, all you can use."

"Please," his wife tacked on, and laughed. "For my sake."

The mood was playful and animated on the beach as we walked past my cottage up to Bonnie and Susan's house, each of our six hands dangling a fish by the tail, Nellie bounding ahead and circling back as if we were her charges. In the kitchen, darkness overcame the blue dusk that had followed the lowering of the huge red circle sun, degree by degree below the horizon. Susan switched on lights as Bonnie brought out a collection of special knives and set to work in the kitchen.

"Our actual role here is to keep her company," Susan explained, pulling out two chairs for us. "She's such a damn expert at this, she could never tolerate our shoddy work anyway. Personally, I'm not much for fishing, but she loves it."

"Well, I'll admit a certain relief at that," I said. "Although I would have done it. If you held a loaded gun to my head, that is. And cocked the trigger."

"Don't think I don't have one," Bonnie chuckled. She was at the sink and had the water running already.

Susan made a pot of tea, and brought out a box of cookies. The three of us talked easily, though the focus was pottery. "I took classes with Marcy, too," Susan said, "quite a while ago, before I focused in on painting."

"Before her paintings began to sell," Bonnie added. "Did you know that some have gone to museums?" She'd turned from the counter to tell me this, swiveling from her hips, and waving the knife as if it were merely an extension of her hand.

"Stop it," Susan said. "I've been lucky. There are so many wonderful, gifted artists around."

"She's excessively modest." Bonnie turned again to direct the comment to me while she looked at Susan, pride spreading its own light across her face.

"Anyway, you like working with Marcy? She's been at Castle Hill for years. She says she likes having beginners around, it keeps her fresh."

"Very much, though I look at how she pulls something up out of that lump she starts with and it's magical. Like making a flower bloom in her hands. Very intimidating. And when I ask her what she's going to make half the time she says she doesn't know yet. I can't seem to get decent curves. I stretch it too far or too fast and it collapses," I said. "I was trying to make a bowl with a rim, but the edge got way too thin. When I tried again, and kept it slow, it was so thick the whole thing looked like a bomb that hadn't been detonated yet."

"Maybe the clay doesn't want to be a bowl. Sounds silly, I know, but that's what I was telling you last time, what she told me. Have you noticed how she feels the clay for a long time? It looks like she is just playing with it on the wheel, but she's very quiet and that's when she doesn't want to be interrupted, right?" Susan had a lively, expressive face, and her brows were like moving punctuation marks.

"Yes." I had noticed that.

"She said she feels what it wants to be, lets it speak to her about what beautiful expression of itself the lump is hiding and to let that come out. Very metaphysical, but I'm telling you it's true. If you stay around long enough and she thinks you really care, you watch, she'll explain it to you. The real magic is in feeling out the soul of something and helping it to reveal itself. I find it in my painting, though that's a little different, of course, and if you ask me, it's true of people, too."

"I can see I'm in trouble. Two of you," Bonnie interrupted. "How about some attention to the true artistry going on right here?" She gestured, and I obligingly got up and stepped to the sink to examine what she pointed at with her knife.

Suddenly I was dizzy and overcome with heat and nausea. Pale, watery blood was pooled all over the Formica counter, severed fish heads in a clear glass bowl, their former iridescence utterly gone, dull eyes open in a stare of accusation. The faucet under which Bonnie was rinsing the decapitated bodies was still open, running freely into the filling sink like an open wound, that sound. A roar of blackness began to shutter the lights and I felt myself begin the great fall.

I CAME TO SLOWLY, THE roaring only slightly subsided, fighting toward consciousness and memory as though from far below the surface of water. I was on the couch in Bonnie and Susan's living room, Bonnie sponging my face with a cool washcloth. Her voice barely penetrating. "It's all right, you're all right," she said soothingly. "Don't try to move yet. Just lie still." She threw her voice over her shoulder into the kitchen, then. "No, don't call. She's coming around."

Susan appeared above Bonnie, who was squatting on one knee beside me. "Ruth, are you all right? Ruth...come on, honey. You're here with us, you'll be okay."

Bonnie kept sponging my face. Nellie nosed in and put her chin on my thigh while Susan disappeared and returned with a glass of water. Bonnie propped my head up for a sip, and then I struggled to a sitting position, and reached for the glass. I held its coolness against my cheek and closed my eyes. Mother appeared, lying on the bathroom floor in the flesh and water and blood scene that had seared itself into every cell of my being.

Bonnie sat on the portion of the couch my head had just vacated and gently pulled me back down on the uneven pillow of her lap. A cold sweat beaded my face and neck as I tried to fight down Mother's image. Bonnie lifted my heavy hair—left down that evening in the dry crispness of early Indian summer— off my neck and gathered it up into her hand. Susan fanned me with a magazine. "Better?" she asked. Bonnie stroked the bangs off my forehead.

"I think I understand," she said. "I'm so sorry. It was my fault. I never thought...did she use a knife?" With those words, spoken in a tone gentle and motherly and foreign to my experience, I began to heave and shake in silent, dry sobs until the sobs turned wet as the running water, wet as dissolving rock, before they subsided into a swollen, shuddering exhaustion.

Time passed in the looping, muted shadow of a wall-mounted lamp. Bonnie's heart beat against my ear, rhythmic and benign as the bay washing the sand, taking away what refuse it can from other seasons. Perhaps I slept a moment or two. Perhaps I dreamed. "Let it go," I heard a voice neither male nor female say. *Bonnie* I thought, then another part of my mind argued, *no, it's Evan.* "Let it go, love. You're allowed to save yourself. It's not your dying that lets others live, it's your living. Live now. Live." Mysterious, merciful fingers made themselves into a tender comb, undoing my unruly damp tangle of hair, redoing and holding it, like a fastening in place.

31

I HAVE NO IDEA HOW LONG I lay like that in Bonnie's arms. Susan sat on the floor beside me and held one of my hands in hers. Nellie stopped her anxious checking and splayed out next to Susan. Much later, I felt my head on a bed pillow and a blanket being settled over me. I gave myself over to the comfort and did not try to open my eyes.

The morning light was dreary, thick with impending rain when I woke. Not too long after, I heard Bonnie and Susan speaking to one another in an upstairs room and got up to go to the bathroom. When I came out, Bonnie appeared in on the stairway in a blue nightshirt.

"How're you doing this morning?" she said gently, hardly a question to it at all.

"Better," I said. "I'm so sorry, I—"

"Now you'd better turn that off right now," she interrupted, sounding more like the tough Bonnie I knew best. "No one understands better than I," she said into my ear as she gave me a brisk hug. "Not even Susan. Maybe it's the same with your husband? Susan was *involved,* I mean, in everything." I nodded.

She pulled back and looked at me intently from a distance of inches, one hand on the side of my neck, and caressing the line of my chin with her thumb. She kept her voice low, and I realized she didn't want Susan to hear. "I know what I'm talking about on this one, I've been there. I hope you're listening. I'd put money on this much—you did everything you could and still hold on to your own sanity. There's no good in it to do more. People have to live the lives they're given to live. And that includes you," she said, then stepped back, smiled and raised her voice to a normal level. "How about some coffee? I make a mean omelet, just ask Susan."

"I'd love some coffee. Maybe I should run on home, though, and get out of these clothes."

"Oh, for heaven's sake. Run upstairs and shower if you want. There's plenty of towels right in the bathroom closet up there. Susan's not much bigger than you. She'll give you a clean shirt. Stay here for a while." She wasn't asking, she was almost ordering, and it was easy enough just to do what she said.

I came downstairs, my head wrapped in a towel and in yesterday's clothes, but feeling much better. Susan was downstairs, already dressed in her painting jeans and a black turtleneck, waiting with a heathered sweatshirt for me. "It's a little chilly. Pull this on, why don't you?"

Bonnie was standing at the stove, a metal spatula in her hand. The whole mess from last night had been cleaned up from the counter. When had they done that?

"So when is your studio time?" Susan asked. Without thinking, I glanced at my wrist, then realized my watch was up in the bathroom.

"Ten," I answered. "I have no idea what time it is."

"Barely eight," Bonnie said. "Good, you've got plenty of time to eat."

"She can't stand for anyone to give any of her cooking short shrift," Susan said, pouring a mug of coffee and handing it to me.

"That smells wonderful," I said, and took a sip before I set it on the table. "Before I forget, I'm going to run up to get my watch. I left it on the bathroom sink. And I hate to ask this, but do either of you have a brush I could use? I can wait to brush my teeth, but if my hair dries into knots like this, I'm in trouble."

"Turn to the left at the top of the stairs, first room," Bonnie said. "There's one out on my dresser."

Upstairs, I retrieved my watch, then went past the stairs to the left of them as she'd said, and entered a large bedroom with white curtains framing two windows that looked right over my cottage to a wide oceanview. The floor was polished hardwood largely covered by two oriental area rugs that put me in mind of Evan right away. An unmade four-poster double bed was set against the wall opposite the windows. Above it hung a large painting I was sure was Susan's, so subtly had the nude women been rendered in tones to echo those of the rugs. I stood a moment looking at the painting and at the bed, slowly coming to grasp the choices we're required to make even when no choice can be wholly seen. I picked up Bonnie's brush and used her mirror to fix myself.

"I SURE HOPE YOU MEANT it when you said I could stay on as long as I want," I said to Bonnie a week later. I'd stopped in at their house as I was on the way back to mine after a trip into Provincetown. Through the window behind her, I could see the bay all smooth, relaxed in waning light. "Because I got a job today."

"You're kidding." Her brows went up, but so did the sides of her mouth.

"No kidding. I'm running low on money and I don't feel right about asking Evan for it."

"Look, if you need…I mean, don't worry about the rent."

"Thanks, Bonnie. That's so good of you, but I'm okay. I'm waitressing at Front Street in P-town. All their summer help is gone and I've had a disgusting amount of waitressing experience from my high school days. They had a little sign out, and on impulse I just walked in and applied."

"What about…I mean, does Evan…?"

"I know. This isn't about Evan, though. I just need to stay here now. Besides, did you see that last pot I fired? It might hold water! I'm going to call Evan tonight. I think I'm ready to see him, and I hope that'll mean something to him. You know, that all his patience isn't a waste."

"Good," she said without hesitation. "I'd like to meet him. Susan would, too, I'm sure."

Bonnie and Susan reminded me of Evan. So did Ben and Marilyn. Good people with goodwill to spare, a storehouse of it. Was there enough, though? In them, especially in *him,* in the world…could *any* amount be enough to accept me if they really knew all of it?

"Well, I'd like for him to meet you," I said. "And Ben and Marilyn…and maybe he can come to the studio with me, too. And he can come to the restaurant with me, maybe. They said it's really slow early evenings."

"You want to show him your life, don't you?" she said quietly in that way she had of asking a question that was really a statement.

"I guess I do."

"Are you planning to invite him into it?"

"I don't know yet. But this is the first one I've had of my own, and I can't give it up just now."

"Understood," she said. "Understood."

I WASN'T PREPARED FOR THE well of emotions that threatened to break loose when Evan stepped off the last step of the little plane that had brought him from LaGuardia to the Hyannis airport and engulfed me in his embrace as soon as he was inside the little terminal building. How could I have forgotten how tall he was, the strength of his embrace? When I pulled back to look at him, his eyes were filled with tears. Then mine did, and we hugged again. He took off his glasses, the way he did when he wanted to really see something, up close, and we absorbed each other's faces. His dark blond hair had just been cut, I saw, and his shave was fresh. He must have gone home after working during the morning to shave again before he came. Such care he'd taken to impress me again. I'd forgotten the exact hazel of his eyes, a rare gold color.

I'd worn a low-cut green top, a hand-me-down from Susan

she said would be too beautiful on me for her to wear in good conscience anymore, and a navy and green print skirt I'd gotten for three dollars at Wellfleet's secondhand shop. I'd washed my hair and let it wave down loose, the way Evan loved. Gold earrings. My mother would have said I looked like a tramp.

"Ruthie, Ruthie. My God, I've missed you so much. How are you? You look so good, so beautiful." His hands swallowed mine. "Let's get out of here," he said, shaking his head, and I knew he felt his emotions were on a billboard for strangers to read.

In the parking lot, the Cape's washed air made me expansive and I slid my arm around his waist. "I'm so glad you're here. I have so much to show you. And I want to hear all about Mark and Sandy and your job and your family…just everything." This was what I wanted: to be back at the beginning, without a history—without my history—in the exuberance of discovery. As if that were possible. As if I weren't who I was.

"They're your family, too," he said. "They've been almost as worried about you as I have," he said, snapping me back to reality.

"I didn't want to worry anyone," I said quickly, unlocking the car. Evan looked at the car, almost wary of it, I thought. My mother's car. He'd told her what he believed and what he didn't, like a fair warning, and the great standoff had begun. A standoff she'd won, I guessed, however she'd done it. Still, he got in.

"They know that," he said. "But they love you, and they'd do anything to help."

I had no response. I didn't want to be pulled back into the life Evan had made and brought me into. "Evan, about that…"

"No. I'm sorry. I shouldn't have said it. Not that it isn't true, but I wasn't trying to make you feel bad."

I pulled into a traffic circle. It was Friday afternoon and weekenders were pouring onto the Cape, though once we got down past Wellfleet, it would thin out until Provincetown, which would be hopping all weekend. I thought like a native now, craving the midweek peace. "That's not it. It's just that I have to…I'm finding my own way."

"I'm not sure I get what you mean."

"I know. I'm sorry." I took one hand from the Rambler's steering wheel and put it on top of his as I headed the car for Route 6, toward home.

WE STOPPED IN WELLFLEET to eat, so it was early evening when we arrived at Landings. Although I knew Bonnie and Susan were home, I brought Evan past their house and my cottage to the little path onto the beach. The October sunset, which had begun even before we reached Truro, was peaking, its intensity and range of color across most of the western sky over the harbor and reflected in the bay, a serene gray tonight.

"Oy vey," Evan said quietly. "I see what you mean." His words gave me great satisfaction, and I squeezed his hand.

"You stay here and watch," I said. "I'll be right back."

"I'd rather stay with you," he said.

"No, wait here. I get to see this all the time. I've got something for us." I knew he watched me instead of the sunset as I hurried to the cottage. And he was still watching the path, his back to the sunset when I came back with blankets, a bottle of wine and two glasses.

I spread one of the blankets for us to sit on and we draped the other across our backs and around us. The day had been warm, Indian summer lingering so long that Bonnie was still picking green tomatoes to fry from the garden, but the evenings lately had had some teeth. "Let me help with that," he said, reaching for the wine.

"I've got it," I said, working in the corkscrew and deftly popping the cork out. "It's my specialty at work."

"You don't need to be doing that, waitressing," Evan said.

"Yes. I do."

"But what about finishing your degree? You have an actual career. You can't let that go. Aren't you going to finish?"

"Yes, I am."

"When?"

"When I'm ready." A small sharp edge underlined the words, but I felt myself weaken a little. Evan didn't respond right away.

"Okay. I won't argue with you." He kept his eyes on the sky and suppressed a sigh.

"Good. Thank you. Now look, watch how it's like the whole sky starts melting into the water." That sliver of tension remained in the skin we still shared. Evan wanting something from me I wasn't willing to give again, not recognizing there was something else. The sand was picking up the evening chill on the surface, and I burrowed my feet down and in where the day's warmth was still captive.

Later, though, back in my cottage, what had always been was again. Though my bed was a castle of unsettled air, I swayed over Evan, naked as spartina bending before approaching weather. Such greed for each other's bodies, such a rush of passion, even as I had no idea how much to trust the demand of my body. I tried to remind myself that not everything gives way to love, not everything can be taken up again.

"I need you to need me," he whispered afterward, as I lay spent, with my head on his shoulder and one leg bent across his resting thighs.

"I know. But I can't let that happen again."

"Don't you trust me? I wouldn't hurt you for the world."

"Ev, Ev. It's not that. That's not the point. I can't have you carry me. There's something poisonous about it. Please. If you can't understand, just you try trusting me this time."

"Will you put your rings back on? I need *something,* some indication of which way this is going."

"Oh, Ev. I don't know. Let's just see, okay?" I knew he was fighting with himself not to pressure me.

A long hesitation. "Okay," he sighed.

THE NEXT DAY, SATURDAY, I didn't have studio time, but I knew Marcy would likely be working by herself, so I took Evan to

Castle Hill. Her ancient gray Subaru was there. The day was autumn Cape, all russets and beach plums in shining air. The dunes turned silver as the breeze turned up the undersides of their long grasses, and the bay was almost navy-blue, peaked with little whitecaps all the way to the horizon.

"Marcy? Hi, it's me, Ruth. Can we come in?" I called from the entrance into her studio, a ramshackle wooden structure that might have been a converted outbuilding with a sprawling addition.

"Hi, Ruth. Who's 'we'?"

I took Evan's hand and led him inside where Marcy sat at the wheel, her graying hair pulled back into a hasty barrette, wearing jeans and an old blue smock. "This is my husband, Evan Mairson." Evan looked out of place, too neatly dressed in khakis, polished loafers and open-neck but tailored shirt.

Marcy looked startled, then used the back of a wrist to push her glasses into place and pulled up a polite smile. "Well hi, Evan," she said. "It's nice to meet you. I'd shake hands but…" She held them up to show the wet clay caked on them. "Are you…visiting, or…"

"Visiting," I inserted quickly. I should have told Marcy I was married if I was going to bring Evan here; he was hurt that I hadn't.

"Did you want to show him your work?"

"Oh, well, there's not much to see on that score yet, but at least the studio."

"Don't underestimate yourself," Marcy said. Then, to Evan, "She's getting quite competent."

"Nothing special yet, though."

"It'll come."

"Look, I worked on this for two days." I unwrapped a graceless vase I'd thrown over and over. "Definitely nothing special."

"You've got to wait for the feel of it to come, let it tell you…" Then Marcy stopped, but I knew what she had started to say from what Susan had told me. I smiled to myself. It meant she thought I was serious.

"What else have you made?" Evan asked. I showed him some of the finished work I'd fired and glazed and refired.

"This is amazing," he said quietly. "I had no idea you could do this. I like the colors you use, the way they blend."

"Well, to be honest, this really isn't very good. But I'm getting the hang of it."

He was silent, inspecting each piece, turning it over to where my RK initials were etched into the unglazed bottom.

"Thanks, Marcy. I don't want to interrupt you. I just wanted Evan to see this place, because I love it so much."

"I'm glad you did, Ruth. Nice to meet you, Evan. Come back anytime."

"I'd like that," he answered her, but looked at me as he spoke.

As we drove, I pointed out the library, stores I particularly liked and who owned them, where the best beaches were for walking and swimming. Bonnie and Susan were home when we returned to Landings, so I brought Evan up their porch steps. Susan was at the door before I could knock, which I was going to do even though I'd grown accustomed to just opening the door to poke my head in and call for them.

"Susan, this is Evan." Evan murmured polite greetings, but Susan clasped his outstretched hand with both of hers.

"We're so delighted to meet you," she said. "Bonnie! Come down! Ruth's here with Evan. Come in, come visit for a while. When did you get here?"

Evan's answer was interrupted by Bonnie's appearance. More warmly than was characteristic of her with strangers, she urged him to sit down while she made tea for us. I knew what she was thinking: *go on, Ruth. Do it. You do not need forgiveness for living.*

There's more to it, I thought, as silent as she in the wordless communication. *I don't know what it all is, but there's more to it. It's Mother, but it's something else, too.*

We visited, the four of us talking lightly until I glanced at my watch. "Oops. I'm going to be late for work. I got tomorrow off, Ev, but Saturday night is the biggie. Of course, an off-season 'biggie' would be the slowest imaginable night in August. Do you want to go with me or stay home and read or something?"

"I'll go," he said. "If it gets too busy, I'll come on back and pick you up when you're off."

"It's a plan, then. Bye you two. Thanks so much." I gave each a quick embrace as Evan shook hands with the other in turn.

IT WAS A SLOW SATURDAY. EVAN sat at the bar and, much of the time, I could stand behind it with Sam, the bartender, and the three of us talked. Front Street is casually elegant, dark wood-paneled walls beneath a low, exposed beam ceiling, with stained-glass Tiffany lamps hung over the tables and classical music playing; people come in jeans, people come in suits, ties and cocktail dresses—those more rarely—but inside, it all merges into an eclectic aura of taste and a certain, expensive flair. Original paintings are well hung on the close-in walls; it is not a large restaurant, just a very, very good one with a coterie of "regulars," residents who are devotees of the chef's seafood specialties and the cozy familiarity of a place they've made their own.

"Hey, Red," Sam said each night when I arrived. "Wow, you're looking good!" He flirted shamelessly and harmlessly; we'd become friends. A graduate school dropout, ponytailed and ear-ringed, Sam lived the simplest of desires in his wire-rimmed glasses and goatee: to be what he was, a leather-crafter by day, a bartender by night, and take each day for what it brought him without asking or wanting for anything beyond. "If it doesn't make you happy, why do it? You'd best have an awfully good reason, because things rarely turn out much different in the future than the present. I say, don't count on change." He'd repeated his motto, and I found the notion mysterious and dis-turbing as I tried to decide if it was true. At first, Evan was ill-at-ease, seeing customers hail me, the chef complain to me about the owner, the other two waiters working that night tease me about a regular customer none of us wanted to serve because he regularly "forgot" a tip. As the evening progressed, though, he removed his jacket, loosened his tie and I could see him let go of discomfort and begin to enjoy himself. He sat at the bar, talking with Sam when I was busy, or just comfortably taking in the ambience.

A busty blonde made up like Marilyn Monroe sat her sky-eyed, white-toothed smile on the stool next to Evan. Her nails were bright red elongated ovals, and her earrings might or might not have been diamonds. She leaned over to say something to him and to give him a better look at her chest. Overkill for Front Street to be sure, her short, tight cocktail dress was sequined in a pattern that swirled around her chest. I knew her, so her flirting with Evan was to play with me as much as with him. "Pour them a couple," I whispered to Sam. He shot me a grin.

"You got it, Red." He gave a little salute and pretended to look at me admiringly. "You're bad. You're really bad."

Sam went over to them. "What may I get for you?"

The blonde immediately purred, "A Manhattan would be delish."

"I'm good for now," Evan said, but Sam brought him another beer when he brought the Manhattan.

"The gentleman is running a tab," Sam said to her.

"Thank you, sweetie," said the blonde to Evan.

"Oh, I didn't—" he began to explain.

"I just l-o-v-e a good Man…hattan," she cut him off and strung out the word love and the man syllable of Manhattan. It was all-out flirting of the kind most discomforting and most flattering to any man. She lifted the drink to her lips, pinky out, and looked at Evan suggestively through long, fake eyelashes.

I had an order up, so I couldn't hear if or how Evan managed an explanation. I could see him talking to her as I carried trays. Sam winked at me, and I winked back. Evan was laughing at something Marilyn had said, though he looked a little fidgety. She had a second Manhattan while they sat talking for the better part of an hour, the blonde doing most of it. I didn't go behind the bar again.

At quarter to nine, the blonde checked her tiny gold watch. "God, I've got to get to work," she said.

She took powder and lipstick out of her purse and did a

touch-up right there at the bar before she sprayed herself with cologne. Teasing, she sprayed some cologne around Evan's head and said, "This is to make you think of me," just as I was passing behind the two of them on my way to a table. I heard Evan say, "Oh, I don't think I'll forget," as his neck reddened in one of his rare blushes. He glanced my direction, checking to see if I'd overheard.

"Maybe I'll see you here again, honey," Marilyn said, and swung her hips as she sashayed out on spike heels.

"They all sure like you," Evan said later after we closed and he and I were in the car on the way to the cottage.

"Well, *somebody* sure seemed to like *you*," I said.

"Listen, Ruthie, I'm sorry about that. She parked herself there, and Sam let her think I was buying her drinks...but then after she left, he said 'no charge.' I don't know what that was about, but I don't want you to think I was encouraging her."

"Didn't look like you were exactly holding her off with a gun," I said. "I'm not usually a jealous type, but…"

"Honey, I swear…."

I'm almost ashamed to say how long I tormented him: all the way back to the cottage.

Once we were inside, when he was still stuttering explanations, I started to unbutton his shirt. "Well," I said. "It's okay. I know her, she's a friend of mine. You're not her type."

"What?" he said. He couldn't quite decide between being mildly insulted and relieved that I'd said it was okay.

"You're not her type," I repeated.

"What's her type?" he asked, unbuttoning the simple white blouse the waitstaff at Front Street wore.

"Oh…someone more like me, maybe," I said, sitting on the bed and taking off my black slacks slowly, one suggestive leg at a time.

"Huh?"

"Well, honey, that was Mike you were talking to. He's a cross-dresser from the show at the Pilgrim House."

I watched it register, and when I knew he got it, I broke up laughing. Evan's chuckle grew in his chest until there were mirth-tears on his cheeks. "You'll pay for that one," he said. "Prepare yourself…" he shouted, and the chase began.

"P-town has what we like to call an eclectic population. This town isn't only famous for art. I really like them," I said later, turning serious as I lay in his arms, warmed so well by sex and laughter that we had only the sheet over us. "It's completely different from when I waitressed in high school, not that I'm thinking of spending my life at this. But it does let me see how much I've changed. I was afraid of people, everything, really."

"Hmm. So this capacity for duplicity you demonstrated tonight, setting me up with Miss Mike—it's new, huh?" He twirled a piece of my hair then pulled it playfully.

He was kidding, I knew, but I gave him a serious answer. "There's too much you don't know about me, Ev. No, it's not new."

"I can't imagine why," Evan muttered, an oblique reference to Mother, the first he'd made. "Of course, it looks like she's won after all. You haven't buried her yet, I take it?"

"I know we have to talk about it," I said, ignoring the question. "Just not now, not yet." He didn't answer, but, rather, looked out the bedroom window at the three-quarter moon.

"Have you talked to Roger?" he asked.

"Twice. How much are you paying him to be president of your fan club?"

I felt rather than saw Evan smile in the dim light, but then he said, "Roger's a good man, but he wants things to work to get himself off the meat hook. He knows he didn't do his part, and he knows I know it."

"Harvest moon week after next," I said after a long moment of difficult silence. "Some nights when I come home, I go down onto the beach to look at the moon. When the bay is quiet, sometimes the reflection looks like a path you could walk on all the way to…wherever you want, I guess."

"I'd like to see it with you."

"Would you want to come back that soon?"

"Yes."

"Then come." I surprised myself by saying it, just as I'd surprised myself by holding my own with Evan, who'd always shone so much clearer than I and been so much himself.

32

So TWO WEEKS LATER, Evan was back. I'd begun to acknowledge that there was a decision required of me, though I couldn't seem to confront it head-on. "Face into the wind;" Mother's aphorism. It seemed like good advice, though the memory was tainted with the scene that had followed an expression of it, when I'd given the copper-tooled plaque to Roger. I wondered if he still had it. Had any of what had transpired between us all held a kernel of goodness? A vein of guilt as real as flowing blood connected us, that much I knew for sure, and love had proven to be nowhere close to enough to save us from harming and being harmed. I wondered how Evan could miss it; in spite of my best intentions and efforts, already I'd scarred him, strong as he was. Surely it was only time until he would reciprocate, and the circle would reseed itself.

Yet, the night he returned to Truro, I could feel his need and the need of my own I'd so wanted to refuse. I lit candles in the cottage bedroom and we undressed each other gently, each of us holding back and tentative at first. Unspoken questions were in our fingers, in the air we breathed, their various resolutions elusive as specters in a dance of continuously changing partners above our heads. But then it was as if we were our own beginnings, swimming again in the dark, finding our way flowing over each other like water, loosening secrets, dissolving the hardened places until all that was fearsome dissolved and streamed together, forgiven. I remember thinking that maybe it could be this easy to die, falling like rain into the ocean and lifted as mist in the early haze where there are no edges. But seamlessness never lasts.

Evan slipped into sleep, still pressing me to him. When I felt him relax, I extricated myself and propped my back upright against the pillow, pulling the sheet and blanket over my nipples, returned to softness now, and over Evan's bare chest. I tried to read, but kept losing my place, so often did I check on him, just outside the amber circle of my wakefulness. Keeping watch was what I was doing, thinking of how to protect him from what I knew about the course of human ties, wondering if I could protect him from me. The bay had tired into sighs: sorrow and love, sorrow and love, sorrow and love, sounds washing up and back through the open window.

IN THE MORNING, I FIXED us a brunch of juice, eggs, blueberry muffins from Front Street and coffee; this was still my place, not Evan's, and I wasn't willing to relinquish his guest status yet. We'd slept until nearly eleven, and when we sat at the small table by the window, the sun was high, unimpeded by clouds, glaring off the water to redouble its power. Evan's face was sidelit as he read the newspaper and he did not catch me studying him. When had those tiny lines begun to emanate from the corners of his eyes? He wasn't thirty yet. The newspaper had smeared ink onto his fingers. Smudged, they looked different than I'd seen them before, vulnerable, capable of frailty. He was going to grow old. I wanted to take his hands in mine and tenderly clean them with a moistened towel, as one might clean a child's.

I wondered if Evan had ever studied me in full window light, keeping silence with his observations, as I did then. He looked up, not catching me (I had anticipated the shift of his eyes), only to point out an article about the effort to save the terns. He knew I'd grown to love the little birds that darted after the waves on the beach. I nodded.

"But I think I'm giving up on the notion that anyone can be

saved," I said, not intending the switch from birds to humans, but hearing it as though someone else were speaking.

"I think I'm coming to that, too," he answered. He put the paper on the table and pushed it away from himself in an emphatic motion, making it clear he intended to talk. Leaning in, he said, "But notice, that you really can't *kill* anyone, either, unless they *let* you. Look how you've survived your mother. I'm finally getting to the point where I know I can't save you—that it's as crazy for me to try, in a way, as what your mother did. Who am I to say what's best for you, even if I want it to be me?" He gestured toward me, a palm-up, open hand. "Look at you. You've made a life here, your own. Obviously you can save yourself. It's your privilege, not mine, much as I wanted to claim it. And you've got to quit thinking you can kill me. I won't let that happen." I'd had no idea that Evan knew what I feared.

Something in me broke open like a bursting pod then, and I had to know if the seeds were poisonous. "*Listen* to me. I helped my mother kill my grandmother. She opened sleeping pills, they were blue capsules, and dumped them in her own mother's water. She put a straw in it, and I sat there, I didn't do anything to stop it, I *helped* her." As I got the words out, forced them out, I knew I had to tell him the rest, even though Evan's face told me he was trying to take in what I'd said about Grandmother.

"You were a child," he said. "How can you—"

I interrupted. Now I used the side of my arm to push my coffee mug back, to use the table for support—or a drawing board, I suppose, if I had to draw pictures for him to get it. "It wasn't just when I was a child. I... Oh, God, Evan, you don't know what I'm capable of."

"So tell me," he challenged.

"I'm trying to. When I was in college—after I knew you, after we were in love, after we were engaged, for God's sake—when I went home to tell her... Remember?"

"And my mother had called her and caused..."

"Right. She was waiting for me, in one of her crazy times. She'd seen us kissing, or she'd been flirting with you, or whatever. She must have gotten aroused. Well, don't you know, virgins aren't supposed to get aroused." Even then I heard the bitter almond between my own teeth. "She wanted me to beat her. I refused and she started beating me, with a belt."

His face got angry, the outraged kind of anger. But it was at her.

"No, listen, you don't get it. I *did* beat her. I hated her. Do you hear me? I think I shouted I hated her and that she was going to tell me who my father was and she had no right to keep me from having a life. I don't even *know* what I said. She made me do it, Ev, but once I started she had to beg me to stop. Do you see? I beat her, I told her I hated her, and *she* killed *herself?* No, Ev—*I* killed her."

"Oh, my God," he said, his eyes getting glassy with tears.

I had nothing else to say. When he stood up, I honestly thought he was probably leaving. But he took one step, pulled me up by the arms and drew me against him. "You've been carrying this… I do understand. Now I do."

We stood like that, I folded in his arms. Both of us cried.

"Do you still think we can do it?" I asked, knowing the question vague and unspecific. Evan knew what I was getting at.

"Yes, Ruthie, I think we can be together and not kill ourselves or each other. I want to try, I know that. I really want to try."

"I'm afraid of what we'll do to each other. It seems as though it's such a dangerous thing, loving and destroying all mixed together."

"It does, doesn't it? I know I haven't been through what you have, and maybe you'll think I'm just naive, but I still think that love rises, like cream over milk, you know, that what's rich and good comes out on top and sometimes you *can* separate them if you're careful. But it's *all* part of who we are. And that's okay. I trust the cream in us to rise, Ruthie."

"Like cream over milk," I repeated softly, something in the image familiar, though perhaps it was my imagination. "When I was really little, one place we lived, we had milk delivered. I remember the milkman would leave these glass bottles on the back doorstep in a metal milkbox before we got up, and Mother would shake the bottles really hard before she opened them to mix the milk and cream together. I actually remember that. I'll have to make you a pitcher for just the cream sometime."

"Don't think I expect we'll have only cream. But I'd treasure it, Ruthie."

We left it at that, and somehow managed not to discuss it further. Evan went back to New York, the fragile understanding we'd reached stretching between us like a cord of hope that neither of us were willing to strain by pushing to decide a specific course of action. There was too much I still had to do.

33

ALMOST ALL THE LEAVES were down thanks to a heavy storm on November first. The dune grass had browned, though in certain casts of sunlight it shone as if gilded. The beach plums were a subdued copper; land blended into the dunes in a limited spectrum of color, more subtle than summer's, until it reached the sea and exploded into brilliance. Of course, the air was colder almost daily, except for isolated days, one or two at a time, when Indian summer returned to linger. Then I would go to Ben and Marilyn's to walk the ocean beach after working in the studio all morning. On the colder days, the bay side was the only place I could take my long walks without being buffeted by a wind so intense it stung my eyes and made my ears ache.

I didn't make a conscious decision to go through the boxes of our heritage. They were jammed in the trunk of Mother's car, along with her ashes and, in retrospect, I guess it was fitting that I still carried them all with me everywhere I went. What brought me to take the boxes into the cottage was pragmatic enough: I went out to the car one morning and found it listing heavily onto a flat tire. It didn't surprise me that Bonnie knew how to change a tire; she did most of the repairs on the rental cottages, and the off-season maintenance.

"Well, have you got a spare?" she demanded in her brusque

way when I went to their house to use the phone. "If you've got a spare, I can change it for you."

"I guess so," I answered. Actually, I had no idea.

"Let me get a jacket," she said. We went to the car and, of course, to get into the tire well, the boxes all had to be removed. Bonnie and I carted them to my cottage in three trips. I stuck the urn with Mother's ashes into the backseat. Bonnie didn't comment.

"What's in these, for heaven's sake?"

I hesitated for only a minute. Bonnie had been there. She knew how hard it was. "The last of Mother's things," I told her. "My brother and I gave everything else away. This is the stuff she had kept for years. I haven't…well, you know, I just haven't been able."

"It's probably time," she said. "Do you want help?"

"I don't think so. But thanks."

"Let me know," she said.

Bonnie was right, it *was* time, but for a couple of days the boxes just sat there, obstacles to nearly every move. I considered moving them back to the trunk of the car, but didn't. Then, one afternoon, I'd had enough. I made a pot of tea, put on the space heater against the damp chill and opened the first box.

My mother's perfume, the one she had worn daily, drifted faintly into the air when I unfolded what was on top: the chocolate-brown dress with the white fur collar. (It had been I who had folded and replaced it after the episode when she'd last put it on. We'd only gotten to the fourth box.) That moment it seemed as if she had appeared at the door, so large a rush of memory and sadness seized me. I had an impulse to apologize yet again for being too late to save her, but it passed even as it occurred. For the first time, I said this to myself and believed it: *I did the best I could.*

There was a great silence around and within me. I believe I half expected to hear her condemning voice, but I did not. Nor did I hear anything I could interpret as the voice of God. But in the silence was a release. She had made her decisions, now I would make mine. Like everyone else, in the last analysis I was alone in my own skin.

I set to work, removing everything from the boxes and examining each article. Most I studied, then folded neatly and
replaced. There was one sweater I thought I remembered my
Mother wearing when I was quite small, a Norwegian knit
cardigan in blue and white, with silver buttons. I had an image
of her laughing, the pastel blue almost exactly matching her
eyes, when she was the world and the world was—for however
long it lasted—good, safe, bearable. I kept that one sweater,
and—from another box—a palm-size edition of the New Tes-
tament that was tucked in the pocket of a dress. The handwrit-
ing of the inscription was unfamiliar, which made me grieve
what hadn't been as much as what had. "For Elizabeth, beloved
daughter, with great faith, Mother." Of the first five boxes of my
heritage, that was all I chose to save.

In the last cardboard box, the smallest, a size to hold a pair
of men's winter boots, were a few articles of baby clothing.
Perhaps they'd been mine; certainly the pink smocked, lace-
edged dress wouldn't have been Roger's, although perhaps it had
been one of Mother's Grandmother had saved. How would I ever
know? There was a pair of baby shoes, a report card from my
first and third grade years. A brown teddy bear missing eyes,
matted and sucked-on. Then this: folded in a tiny white knit suit
with a yellowed spit-up stain on the front was a piece of discol-
ored paper. The ink on it had faded, as fountain pen ink does in
time.

Donald Sandburg, 52 West Merritt Street, Seattle, it said. It
was paper-clipped to Roger's hospital record of birth, a scroll-
edged document that was a memento, not a legal paper. I knew
what it meant, then, that saying about hearing blood in your ears.
My heart thudded as if the pounding was from outside rather
than in. I began to empty the box faster, still being careful to
examine each item as I took it out. A lace-edged bonnet, white.
A yellow baby sweater, hand crocheted.

Yes. It was there, too. A homemade christening dress hemmed
in feathery stitches, the lace on it matching the lace on the bonnet,
and a black and white picture of a boy…or a man, the picture trying
to roll itself up as if to keep the image hidden, its creamy border

scalloped. The subject looked young, a hand up to shield his eyes from too much outdoor light. On the back, John Meyer Miller, Oct., 1957. That was all. I studied the picture, though I couldn't tell what the background was. Did I look like him? Maybe. The features were indistinct and there was no way to tell about freckles or red hair or narrow hips or whether his big toe was longer or shorter than the second. But I thought it: this is my father.

Then, on the bottom, more pictures, some very old ones, a few with dates and unfamiliar names. Sarah, one said. Some had dates on the back, most didn't. I had no sense of the passage of time that afternoon. I knelt on the floor by the open box looking at each secret until my legs had cemented themselves in that awkward position and I had to work just to stand.

I had no idea what I'd do. But, for the first time, there would be a new place from which to start. Whenever, whatever I willed to start. I straightened up and turned on a lamp. One day was gone, but I had reason to believe in another.

WHEN I WAS FINISHED, I went to the car and got the urn. I believe I held it with a greater compassion and less fear than previously. In the cottage, I removed Mother's final words to God from where they were still wedged in the base. I did not read the letter again, but removed the top of the urn, laid it on top of the ashes, and there, set it on fire. Not all of it burned, of course, a word here or there escaped, but I crumbled the cooled new ashes and scraps of paper in with Mother's remains.

Then, in the dark, I carried the boxes—all except the little one, where I'd replaced the papers and the pictures—and the urn back to the car. During the rest of the evening, the welcome inner silence remained, as though something were at last over. The next morning I didn't go to the studio, but drove to Hyannis, the closest place where there was a Goodwill collection center according to the phone book. So much of what we'd had had come from them, it seemed right that the last of my Mother's life should go toward saving women who needed what Mother could give: small protection from the elements until they found their own way in the end.

I did not return directly to my cottage, but went to Ben and Marilyn's. They were used to my showing up; sometimes I'd just park and go down to the beach, and other times I would knock at the door and join Marilyn for a cup of tea. This time I parked and carried the urn directly to the beach where I'd seen such joy on Mother's face. On sun-warmed sand below Ben's house, I removed the top. The afternoon was soft, unseasonably mild, another unexpected gift. When Mother had disposed of Grand-mother's ashes, a gray, substantive cloud had risen from the canyon as though to rebuke and choke us both. I thought of it and almost stopped. I put my hand into the grayish dust and felt the pebbly fragments of remaining bone.

I tried to think of something to say, but all that came was "Mother…Mother." In the end, I hummed "Amazing Grace," in memory of what was not to be saved and what was, as I lifted my mother's remains by handfuls and released them downwind to the sand, the sea and the air. A quiet breeze carried them away from me. I did not breathe her again.

THE NEXT DAY, I RESUMED my morning studio work. Lately the pots I'd been throwing were more graceful, narrowing above a wide base then widening out again at the top. "Slow down," Marcy kept saying. "Just feel it this time. Wait. It's like your life, you know? Let the clay tell you what it most is, the shape that will be right. It's a matter of trust." I tried to listen, but until the day after I'd let Mother go, I couldn't hear clearly enough. Marcy said, "You can always make something ordinary by imposing on the clay. The extraordinary piece comes, the *art* comes, when you trust the spirit instead of reciting a creed." Then she laughed at herself, and said, "Oh, good grief, listen to me. But see, it's the closest I come to religion." When she said that, I understood. I had to take a chance. I had to trust what came to me through my own hands and eyes and ears.

And that day, I finally made a piece to fire and glaze for Evan. It had a handle, sturdy and nearly S shaped for his large hand, the open hand I'd loved from the beginning. I heard the clay saying it wanted to be a pitcher, and I knew Evan and I would set cream out on the table in the home we would make together.

For her fiftieth birthday party,
Ellie Frost will pretend that everything is fine.

That she's celebrating, not mourning. That she and Curt are
still in love, not mentally signing divorce papers. For one
night, thrown closer together than they've been for months,
Ellie and Curt confront the betrayals and guilt that have
eaten away at their life together. But with love as the
foundation, their "home on Hope Street" still stands—they
just need the courage to cross the threshold again.

HOPE STREET
From acclaimed author
Judith Arnold

Don't miss this wonderful novel, available in stores now.

Free bonus book in this volume!

The Marriage Bed, where there is no room for
secrets between the sheets.

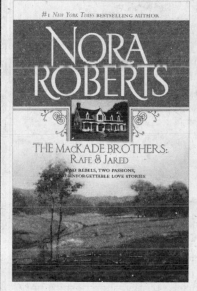
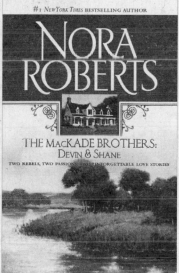

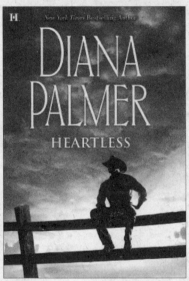